★ NO TIME ★

Master Sergeant Biltz had two nicknames in the regiment. One, Blitzen, as in Santa's reindeer, was used to get his goat. The other, though, Blitz—*Lightning*—was altogether more serious and an indicator that everyone had faith in his ability to think and act like lightning when under pressure.

He was already rolling—*no time*—toward the nearest Vampire gunner—*to clear the backblast area*—when the nearest Venezuelan Scorpion—*no time*—was about fifty meter away—*to even him.*

Biltz—Blitz—snatched the Vampire from its gunner's hands and stood upright, slinging the thing to one shoulder as he did. Automatically, his right leg stepped back as he lined the muzzle up approximately with the center of the light tank.

Now it was a Venezuelan soldier's eyes that grew wide at the apparition of an enemy growing straight up from the ground with what looked like a murderous weapon aimed at him.

Caught between trying to give commands to his crew and trying to swing his own machine gun around, the tan... either before Blitz...

COUNTDOWN
★ M DAY ★

★ ★ ★

TOM KRATMAN

COUNTDOWN: M DAY

This is a work of fiction. All the characters and events portrayed in this book are fictional, and any resemblance to real people or incidents is purely coincidental.

Copyright © 2011 by Tom Kratman

A Baen Books Original

Baen Publishing Enterprises

www.baen.com

ISBN 13: 978-1-4391-3464-1

Cover art by Kurt Miller

First printing, September 2011

Distributed by Simon & Schuster
1230 Avenue of the Americas
New York, NY 10020

Library of Congress Cataloging-in-Publication Data: t/k

Printed in the United States of America

10 9 8 7 6 5 4 3 2 1

★★★
For Nezi
★★★

COUNTDOWN

★ M DAY ★

★PROLOGUE★

The fate of the world economy is now totally
dependent on the growth of the U.S. economy,
which is dependent on the stock market, whose growth is
dependent upon about 50 stocks, half of which
have never reported any earnings.
—Paul Volcker

Miraflores Palace, Caracas, Venezuela

In a boomerang-shaped green park west of the palace,
bounded by it, by *Avenida Sucre*, and by *Avenida Urdaneta*,
Ernesto "Che" Morales and Michael Antoniewicz, sometimes called "Eeyore," stood wearing red shirts amidst a sea
of red shirts. Between them stood a very tiny, very pretty,
and very young-seeming milk-skinned girl. She, Lada, was
by background a spy, of sorts, though she often described
her job in more pungent terms: "I'm an organizational
whore." Morales and Eeyore were former U.S. Navy SEALs.
All three now worked for M Day, Inc., or, as its members
and friends called it, "The Regiment." Lada was a veteran of
some years service with Russia's FSB.

1

On the other side of *Avenida Sucre*, where the park continued and transformed into a baseball diamond, were still more people and still more red shirts. *Lots* of red shirts. It was a political rally. The sound of that rally was deafening and the smell defied precise description, being composed of a mix of flowers, exhaust fumes, garbage, the sea undulating some miles to the north, sweet-smelling, dark and beautiful girls wearing perfume and as little else as minimal modesty permitted, all overlaid with the greater aroma of a human sea, much of which hadn't seen water for bathing in a while.

"I don't know about you, Morales," said Eeyore, who was an aficionado of science fiction, "but these red shirts give me the creeps." He plucked at the material for emphasis.

Morales shook his head. "You and your science fiction bullshit. There's nothing magic or fated about red shirts."

The two men were much of a type, being short, stocky, immensely strong, and swarthy. If Eeyore looked more eastern European than Latin, and he did, Morales was so typically Puerto Rican in appearance that any given up-to-date encyclopedia might have had a two-by-three color glossy of his face next to the entry for Puerto Rico. For all that, neither looked especially out of place in the cosmopolitan capital of Venezuela, a city of such mixed genetic heritage that it could produce both a string of Miss Worlds, Miss Universes, and Miss Internationals, *and* the—as the regiment's Chief of Staff and Executive Officer, Boxer, had phrased it—"short, fat, neckless, baboon-faced, wannabe Stalin-dancing-a-Joropo" who currently occupied the palace on the other side of the street.

For that matter, the Russian girl with them, Lada, wasn't entirely out of the mainstream, looks-wise, and she was chalk-white, raven-haired, and looked about fourteen years old.

"It's still creepy," Eeyore responded, speaking literally over the girl's head.

"Shut up, Eeyore," Morales said, his face scowling. "Listen to the crowd. The bastard's about to speak."

The forty thousand people crammed into the park across the street and the Plaza to the south represented less than one percent of the metropolitan area's population. Still, as they chanted, "Hugo! Hugo! Hugo! Hugo!" they sounded like all of it, together. They were, in fact, so loud that they filled the palace itself with sound, making the windows rattle and contributing mightily to Hugo Chavez's already crushing headache.

I suppose I have to speak to the rabble, thought Chavez, seated at his desk, elbows upon it, rubbing his temples for whatever relief that might bring. To his credit, thinking the word "rabble" made him immediately ashamed. He put the unkind thought down to the headache.

What is it? The third time today? Or maybe the fourth, if we count that midnight rally. And don't count the TV time. Fuck. Like I don't have enough troubles.

And troubles the president of Venezuela had in plenty. Some were of his own making. Others had come from events far outside of his control. Of these, the worst, the most insuperable, was the state of the world's economy and the absolutely crappy price for oil. Oil built Venezuela. It funded it. It had funded Chavez's military buildup, such as it was. It had bought him allies on several continents and any number of islands.

And I'm lucky when I can get twenty freaking United States dollars a barrel when I need a hundred. Oh, sure, it might cost the never sufficiently to be damned gringos and Euros twelve or fifteen dollars a gallon for gasoline, the few of them that can afford it and a car, but that's all tax, and it goes to their government, not to me. And the more they tax, the less they use. The less they use, the more the price drops. And at some point, and we've reached that, the price drops to where survival kicks in, and the rulers of OPEC countries can't keep production down and the price up, or they'll all end up dangling from lampposts. As I will, in time, if I don't find some way to divert people from the fact that my Bolivarian Revolution is close to bankrupt, that I can't pay for the giveaways anymore. Shit. I don't want to end up like Evo, down in Bolivia, kicking my life away, and shit and piss off my toes, at the end of a length of telephone wire.

And the bloody army? Can't trust the bastards. Bitch, bitch, bitch, all the time. "We've got these shiny new toys, Mr. President, but no money to train with them." "We can't guarantee to stop the gringos for five minutes, Mr. President, if they decide you have to go." Worst of all, "Mr. President, there are some currents among the junior officers that are worrisome, at best. They've lost faith in the Revolution."

They try to sound sincere when they say that, their voices all full of concern, the hypocritical swine. But they mean it as a threat. Crap!

The chanting outside reached a crescendo again, causing Chavez to wince with the pain in his head.

Oh, well, time to meet my "public." Again. Maybe I can find some way to distract them, preferably before *they try to make me a date with the hangman.*

Taking a deep breath to steady his nerves, the president of the Bolivarian Republic of Venezuela waited for the liveried guard to open the glass doors before emerging to speak to the crowd.

★ CHAPTER ONE ★

I can picture in my mind a world without war,
a world without hate. And I can picture us attacking
that world, because they'd never expect it.
—Jack Handey, *Deep Thoughts*

Ring Road, Camp Robert B. Fulton, Guyana

From somewhere in the distance a macaw shrieked with indignation at having its repose interrupted by gargantuan, smelly, noisy creatures that had, so far as it was concerned, no business whatsoever in *its* jungle.

Indifferent to the bird and its complaining, Wes Stauer tapped his foot against the floor of his Land Rover impatiently. He was a big man, Stauer, six-two, unbent, still with a full head of hair, though now gone completely gray. Pale blue eyes were framed by deep crow's feet. If he'd once been considered a son of a bitch, and he had, that had mostly abated since he'd been able to stop dealing with the politicians, and politicians in uniform, who had been, so he thought, as much the enemy as anyone who ever popped a cap in his direction.

7

The Rover carried standard Guyanan license plates, but the bumper was painted with, "M Day, Inc." and the regiment's logo, a diving raptor. It sat, engine humming, on a two lane, black asphalt road, just shy of a broad, whitish, concrete pad set into that same road. Stauer, like his driver, wore pixilated tiger-striped jungle fatigues, with little in the way of insignia. On both their heads were perched broad-brimmed jungle hats of the same material.

Fucking Reilly, Stauer fumed silently. *Had to take his battalion out—all of it, naturally—and had to do it at precisely the time I need to get back to base.*

Antennae whipping, a camouflage-painted tank—looking low, mean, and predatory—ground its way across the white concrete pad on the road and down into the jungle-lined dirt tank trail to the west. The concrete shuddered as it passed, little bits of gravel bouncing with the vibration. Not for first the first time, Stauer thought that the tank looked less like the T-55 that had provided its basic body, and more like an American M-1 that had somehow suffered fetal alcohol syndrome.

As if on cue, a turretless Eland armored car, with loud-speakers mounted to the sides, nosed up onto the road. Standing in the open-topped back of it, broad grin written across his face, rocking with the motion, Seamus Reilly gave a mock-serious salute and then waved happily at Stauer's scowl. The grin and the wave made the middle-aged Reilly appear much younger than he was.

As the Eland followed the tank to disappear into the perpetual twilight of the Guyanan jungle, Reilly turned his face back to the front. Stauer was pretty sure he was singing one of those awful Irish or German songs he inflicted on his command.

As that armored car disappeared, it was immediately replaced by another vehicle, this one a turreted Eland, its 90mm gun pointing generally in Stauer's direction. Stauer couldn't be sure, what with the helmet and boom mike half covering the Eland commander's dark face, but he thought it was one of Reilly special pets, Sergeant Towns, commanding the thing. And singing.

Stauer sighed. *Twenty tanks—assuming they're all working and he's pulled none from the operational float— twelve turreted Elands, twelve antitank Ferrets, nine scout Ferrets, fifty-two turretless Elands, carrying infantry and mortars, mostly, and about sixty-five wheels . . . at twenty- five kilometers an hour . . . I've got quite a wait.*

"I can take a chance going in between them, sir," Stauer's Guyanan driver, Corporal Hosein, offered, sensing his colonel's impatience. Hosein was a tall, dark, frankly skinny, Bihari-descended corporal handpicked for unflap- pability by the corporation's, which is to say the regiment's, Sergeant Major, RSM Joshua. "Or get out and stop traffic, Sir."

Stauer shook his head. "Nah, Hosein. Fuckers would like as not just run you or us over and then where would we be?"

"Pretty flat and low to the ground, sir," the corporal agreed, white teeth flashing in an ashy, dark face. "Still, sir, it's going to be a wait."

"Yeah," the colonel agreed as the muzzle of another tank began to jut out from the trees. "But let the bloody harp have his fun."

Suddenly, the muzzle stopped its advance and began to swing up and down. The mechanical roar coming from the right of the road likewise dropped in volume. A few moments later a uniformed man wearing a tanker's helmet appeared on the side of the road and began waving the Land Rover to pass. The free end of a detached communications cable ran from the helmet down past the signaling tanker's waist.

"Colonel Reilly must have radioed to let us through," Hosein observed as he put his vehicle into gear and began to roll forward.

"You never really know with Reilly," Stauer said softly as the Land Rover rolled forward. He glanced to the right at the tank vibrating half-hidden in the murk, adding, "It could be a trap."

"Headquarters, atten . . . shun!" shouted Joshua from his office several doors back from the front entrance. There'd be hell to pay for someone, later on, that he was the first one to see the colonel enter the building.

"At ease," Stauer called out. *I was hoping nobody would notice I'd come back. Should have known better. Now the RSM is going to ream somebody's ass for it.*

He stuck his head inside Joshua's door. The RSM said, without being asked, "Your interview is waiting in your office, sir."

"Thanks, Top. Has he been waiting long?"

Joshua shook his gray-haired head, a smile briefly lighting his deeply seamed black face. "Nah. As soon as I heard the plane and realized Reilly would be tying up the roads, I told the duty driver to take his time about getting back. Colonel Von Ahlenfeld's been here maybe five minutes."

"Great. I'd tell you 'good thinking,' but you already know that."

Stauer turned away and walked past the adjutant, seated now at his desk in the open area surrounded by the offices of the rest of the regiment's primary staff. The adjutant, DeWitt, just nodded greetings as he went back to his paperwork, muttering dark imprecations at—to Stauer's complete lack of surprise—Reilly and the First Battalion.

Stauer shook his head, thinking, *Anybody who can piss off the adjutant daily can't be all bad.*

At his own office door, Stauer stopped, spent a second composing himself, and then bellowed inward, "And no, Lee, you can't have a company. Company commanders I've got coming out the wazoo. What I need is a *battalion* commander."

"I just *knew* you were going to be difficult about that," von Ahlenfeld said softly, as Stauer entered the office. Taller, at six-three, than even Stauer himself, blond where he wasn't gray, and mustached, the newcomer stood in front of a map of the newly built up areas, studying it.

"Forget the map," Stauer said. "I'll give you the guided tour in a little bit." He stuck out one hand, which von Ahlenfeld took warmly. "How have you been, Lava, you old bastard?" Stauer asked.

"Bored," Lee A. von Ahlenfeld answered, frowning. "Bored out of my frigging mind." He sighed, adding, "Which is rather why I'd have preferred the excitement of a company."

"You're too old," Stauer replied, "too capable, and—as

mentioned—I've got company commanders coming out my ass. I need somebody for my Second *Battalion*.

"If it's any consolation, that's only about the size of a big company. Sorta. Kinda."

"Sorta? Kinda? Care to explain?" von Ahlenfeld asked.

"Second Batt's got five companies," Stauer replied. "In theory, A through C are lane walker and instructor companies for the jungle training we provide here, while D Company handles our internal training, from basic to leadership to special combat skills. The last one's the headquarters. Strength is two hundred and thirty Euros and gringos and seventy-nine locals."

"Big company," von Ahlenfeld said skeptically.

"Yeah . . . well. In a sense, it's bigger than that," Stauer admitted. "The three predominantly local battalions, Third and Fourth Light Infantry and Fifth Combat Support, each have their own command and staff at battalion level, but the cadre of each of the four companies of those are also what amounts to A teams, detached from or affiliated with—depending on how you want to look at it—one of Second Battalion's companies. So while your line companies might look like big platoons, with fifty-one men each, three A detachments and a fifteen man headquarters, in fact they *can* have seven teams and a headquarters, if we stripped every spec ops man out of the Guyanan battalions. Course, the Guyanan battalions would be useless then, so we never do that.

"And, no, before you ask, that's *not* racist. We've got them—some of them—up to being fairly good squad and team leaders. But we haven't been at it long enough to make good senior noncoms. And officers have to be made by society long before the military gets its hands on them."

"Why set it up that way?" von Ahlenfeld asked.

Stauer shrugged. "Few reasons. I don't want the SF types going altogether native, so I have them stay affiliated, regimentalized, if you will. And it gives us some fair flexibility in assignments. Plus . . . well . . . one of the problems with SF types is we forget we're part of the army—not that *we're* part of *the* Army anymore, mind you—and forget how to do our primary mission, which is to train locals to fight as regulars and lead them in so doing. That half of Second Battalion's operatives are detached . . . or attached . . . or whatever . . . they are doing just that means they won't forget. And it's awful damned convenient that the company doing lane walking for the jungle school has a close, intimate relationship with the leadership of the battalion playing guerilla for our rotational unit. Cuts way down on problems in the field.

"And, yeah," he admitted, "it is kind of a personnel management pain in the ass for Second Battalion's commander, since he ends up assigning people to the Guyanan battalions and quasi-managing them."

"My ODAs?" von Ahlenfeld asked. "They're up to strength?"

"Strength, yes. But we've got shortages in MOS's"— Military Occupational Specialties; jobs—"and ranks that are persistent and difficult to overcome. We barely manage to have one Delta"—18D; Special Forces medic—"or corpsman per team. The alternate's usually a weapons guy that we put through a course here and at one or another of the local hospitals. They're good; but they're not Deltas. We did give Second Battalion all the navy corpsmen but two. Engineers and communications aren't quite as badly off. We've got a surplus of weapons guys, though some of them are just regular infantry, albeit tabbed. Most of your teams are led by noncoms, not officers. They are not a bit less capable for that lack."

I can probably live with that, von Ahlenfeld thought, then asked, "How are your Guyanan battalions?"

Stauer made a so-so gesture, shaking his wide-spread fingers, palm down, and hand held low. "Technically and tactically, they're pretty fair," he explained. "Morally? For battle? Not so great. Not awful. Not great, either. But they're getting better. Cazz's Third, in particular, shows promise.

"See, there's not a lot of military tradition here. Sure, they did what they could for the old Empire, but that was very damned little. When we had that little dust-up with Suriname, maybe a quarter of them deserted. Naturally, we didn't let the deserters back afterwards. We'd probably have lost another quarter if the Surinamese hadn't folded as quick as they did. To be fair, they were newer then."

"What happened with Suriname, anyway?" von Ahlenfeld asked. "I mean the whole thing. I read about it in the papers, but those were long on condemnation and short on facts."

Stauer pointed to a different map on his wall than the one von Ahlenfeld had been studying previously. This map showed the entire top and northeast corner of South America.

"This place," he said, "is in the possibly unique position of having almost its entire territory claimed by its neighbors. It's Poland, but without the tradition of *nationhood*."

Stauer's finger shifted left. "To the west of the Essequibo River, Venezuela claims better than half the country. Bad as the fucking Palestinians with Israel, Venezuelan maps in school kids' textbooks show the place as part of Venezuela. Hell, back about 2006, Venezuela even added another star to their flag to represent Guyana, or the portion of it they claim, and that's *always* a bad sign."

The finger flicked to the right. "To the east, Suriname claims a good deal of what's left. And it's been arbitrated— repeatedly arbitrated—and all parties have agreed on the current borders. And those agreements are simply discarded almost as soon as the ink is dry on them and the claims get raised again.

"There was a Canadian energy company that tried to do some exploratory drilling in one of the disputed zones, out to sea. The Surinamese navy showed up and carted off their drilling platform. That was the second time that had happened, so the Guyanan government asked us for help. I said we were willing, but we extracted some serious concessions out of them for it. Like our own legal system and laws, recognized and accepted by them, right to use their defense establishment, such as it is, to recruit locally, to order arms and equipment, that sort of thing, plus an official status.

"One of the side effects of recruiting locally is that we've essentially wrecked Guyana's own Defense Force, by the way. All the best recruits come to us and even some of their leadership has defected over to us because we train better, live better, and can pay a *lot* better. You will find a number of former Guyanan captains wearing sergeant's and corporal's stripes here.

"So we sank Suriname's navy, then landed Second Battalion at their major base and killed or captured most of what was left, people-wise. Then we crossed over the border with Reilly and his band of cutthroats, wrecking the Surinamese land force, too. About the time we were halfway from the border to Paramaribo, the Surinamese government decided that, since the Dutch Marines wouldn't get here in time to help, maybe the old border and offshore drilling were just fine, after all. However, given the history and nature of boundary disputes here, the Canadians pay us a retainer to keep ready, because there will be a next time."

I'm counting on it, von Ahlenfeld thought. *If not, I wouldn't even be here.*

"God knows," Stauer continued, "the locals couldn't afford to pay us for their defense. They're dirt poor and they'll stay dirt poor, too, because almost no one is willing to invest here lest the country be partitioned and they lose their investment. The Canadians are almost unique, and either very cagey or very stupid, for putting new money into the place.

"So, anyway . . . that's a few of the Second Battalion's missions: to provide training support to—well, to be honest, to *be*—the jungle school here, to manage personnel to provide company command for the three Guyanan battalions, and to provide initial entry and more advanced training. There's one other."

"Yes?"

Stauer smiled. "Yes. Typically we only need one of your three line companies for lane walking squads and platoons for the jungle school at any given time. One of the others trains itself. The last mission, for whichever company isn't doing one of those two, is to be ready to conduct and to conduct special operations, on order, on our own behalf, or, more typically, on behalf of someone who has contracted for our services.

"Now, do you want to look the place over before you make a decision? We can grab lunch at the O Club on the way."

"Sounds good," Lee agreed. "By the way, were those tanks I saw from the air as I came in? And if so, where did they come from? I didn't recognize the model."

Stauer nodded. "Yeah, those were tanks. Half of them we captured in Africa, the other half we bought from Israel through the good offices of the government of Guyana, of which we've been an official reserve since about five hours before we landed near Paramaribo. They're Ti-67s2 tanks; that's what the Israeli company that did the mods calls them, anyway. The mods themselves were from China and Textron, who call the model the Jaguar.' We just call them 'tanks.' Basically they're modified T-55's with a new American turret configuration, a thermal-sleeved 105mm gun, Israeli fire control, explosive reactive armor, and a host of other improvements. They're a good buy for the money, and when you capture half of what you need . . . "

"Should I ask?"

Stauer shook his head. "Nah. I could tell you, but . . . 'On the other hand, I *can* tell you that, outside of your battalion's, most of our arms are Russian."

Von Ahlenfeld didn't sneer, as some might have.

"We mostly went *high end* Russian, mind you," Stauer continued. "No Kalashnikovs, for example. We bought Abakans. No PKM's, we've got Pechenegs. Grenade launchers are GM-94's. Heavy machine guns are KORD's. Our light machine guns are RPK-74's, though.

"We stayed away from RPG-7's. Instead we've got RPG-16's. For medium anti-armor work we've got Vampires. Chile sold us a couple of dozen Israeli-built 60mm High Velocity guns on old QF Six Pounder carriages, plus spare barrels and a shitload of ammunition. We've got a very limited number of SPG-9's. We didn't bother with antitank guided missiles, other than a couple of launchers in your battalion, and Reilly's antitank platoon, because the terrain just doesn't generally suit them.

"For artillery we went French, because they were available. Mortars are Israeli. Sniper rifles are Barretts, in .338, from home.

"And then, every light battalion has a platoon of Eland 90's as armored gun systems . . ."

"If you don't mind my asking," von Ahlenfeld queried, "meaning that I'll survive the answer, where did you get all that shit?"

Stauer scratched lightly at his nose, hesitated a moment, then answered, "Mostly . . . ummm . . . Victor."

"Victor? No shit?" Von Ahlenfeld looked and sounded incredulous. "We were all sure he was dead."

"He would be," Stauer replied. "He would be right quick like, if he ever tried to settle down somewhere without at least a regiment to keep him alive."

Stauer had released Hosein to the RSM and was driving

himself. He hated riding in the back of a vehicle, didn't much like making someone else do so, and wanted to talk to von Ahlenfeld one on one.

"How the *fuck* do you pay for all this?" von Ahlenfeld asked as Stauer's Land Rover passed a row of substantial, white stucco-covered barracks before turning north from the last outlying camp, Camp Python, to head back to Camp Fulton. A housing area lined the eastern side of the road as they progressed. A sign announced that the name of the place was "Glen Livet." It, too, was white stucco, though unlike the barracks, built mostly to single floor plans.

"I mentioned that Canadian energy company," Stauer answered. "We have funding, some of it regular, some of it spotty, from eight other sources.

"Our jungle school makes a profit—pretty good profit, as a matter of fact—from selling training to the Army and Marines. We can handle up to a regiment or brigade at a time. And, once a year, we give the Guyanan's own infantry battalion a free rotation. I write that off as a goodwill measure. We go pretty easy on them, actually, which is only fair since, as mentioned, we've wrecked them.

"You will, by the way, see a lot of oddities in our table of organization because, officially, we primarily support a jungle school. For example, we've got mules and small submarines, hovercraft, unmarked civvie cars, and even bicycles because you can reasonably expect an irregular force to use any or all of those to move people and supplies. And landing craft because a regular force can expect to be moved by those, sometimes, anyway."

Stauer paused, then added, "Anyway, we wrecked the

Guyanans. Except for their Second Infantry Battalion—
'Two Battalion,' they call it. It's a reserve formation and
it's better than you would expect because a number of
the people who take their discharge from us, and take on
civilian employment, opt to keep their hand in with the
GDF reserve. We don't have a reserve of our own, though
we've considered it. Each of our two light infantry
battalions have adopted two of those four GDF companies,
unofficially. Our Third Battalion took on 'Big Brother'
duties for their 242 and 244 companies, while our Fourth,
FitzMarcach's crew, helps out their 243 and 245 companies.

"Doesn't cost us much, really. And they're happy to get
whatever help we can give them.

Von Ahlenfeld coughed in such a way as to mean, *And,
again, you* pay *for this how?*

"Oh, right," Stauer said. "At any given time, some of
Third and Fourth Infantry battalions, along with Fifth
Combat Support and Eighth Service Support, are away
under a personal security contract. Right now it's ninety-four
gringos and Euros and five hundred and ninety-one
Guyanans deployed. Those battalions are all overstrength,
anyway. We make a pretty fair amount of money out of
those, more than enough to pay the expenses of those four
battalions. But then you'd know all about *that*."

Von Ahlenfeld just smiled. Post retirement from the
Army, he'd been CEO of a major security provider for
quite a few years before he'd gotten tired of the thing.

"And, yes," Stauer said, "I knew you were sick of it, so
I didn't even think about offering you that job.

"We also get the occasional paid mission for one of
Second Battalion's line companies, or a portion thereof.

We charge through the nose for those, though. You may recall those eight ships running Israel's blockade of Gaza that sank in the Med?"

"What did the Israelis pay you for that one?"

Stauer smiled broadly. "The *Israelis* didn't. They could have done it themselves for cheaps, if they still had the balls for that kind for thing. A pro-Israel group in the United States did. It was just good luck that a storm picked up when the limpets started going off." His broad smile became a laugh. "Just think of it; seven hundred and nineteen 'peace activists'—unusually well-armed 'peace activists,' at that—drowned overnight. Except for the fifty or so who blew to atoms when the mine set off the what we think were a hundred and fifty-odd tons of rockets, shells, and explosives they had hidden under the concrete and food."

Stauer sighed contentedly. "Sometimes, you know, the satisfaction of just knowing you're doing the Lord's work is more important than what you're paid. One of our ex-SEAL types is Jewish. He took special pleasure in mining the *Saint Rachel of Ihop*."

Von Ahlenfeld thought, *Oh, yes, I am going to enjoy this job.*

"Are you the folks who fed Julian Assange and his eight pals feet first into a wood chipper and then posted the video on Wikileaks?" he asked.

Stauer shook his head, "Nah. We'd have done it, happily—happily killed the fuckers, anyway—but someone beat us to it. Not sure who, maybe it was Mossad." For the briefest of moments, his face looked mildly piqued, as if he wished it had been his people who had done the killing. The look faded.

"We run a shipping company with a freighter we originally leased but later decided to buy, plus a sister model we outright bought, and another eleven we lease. Two of the crews and all of the captains and XOs are our people, but we never move anything for ourselves, or anything under the table, except with a ship fully crewed by our folks. Sometimes we exchange crews completely so we can do that with ships we're surer nobody's watching.

"Mostly all I expect out of the freighter business is that it pay for itself, while letting us move people and things around. It does. Barely. Long term, if the economy turns around, we should make a good profit.

"Sometimes, but not often, we use the freighters to run arms. We make a lot more money on those jobs but they're tricky."

Stauer pulled into the parking lot by headquarters, parked, tossed the keys to a waiting Hosein, then led von Ahlenfeld back to his office.

Without missing a beat, he continued there, "Then there's what we make off of local resources."

Von Ahlenfeld looked at him from under a furled brow. "Huh?"

Stauer rocked his head back and forth a few times before answering, "We bought this area"—Stauer stood and walked to a map and began to trace with his finger— "bounded by the Mazaruni River, the Kaburi River, and the Issano Road, plus some small outlying parcels. It's just over four hundred thousand acres' worth, for . . . well, for shit, basically. And the Guyanan government was happy to get such a good price. Besides timber, it's got rubber, gold, bauxite, gems . . . Trust me, we make a fair profit on the deal and they get fifteen percent of our net. Plus we own a chunk down in Brazil that we don't use for anything but profit."

"How big a chunk?" von Ahlenfeld asked.

"Think Rhode Island. Big chunk. We can't use it ourselves because the Brazilians are highly suspicious of us, in general. They don't know what we did, but they know we did something there that they wouldn't like if they knew about it."

Stauer looked Heavenward, almost as if he expected the skies to open and lighting to strike him down. "And then . . . well . . . we made a lot of money on our first operation, in Africa. A lot more than we were supposed to make, shall we say? That's been invested and gives a pretty good return." When no lightning came down he visibly relaxed and turned his eyes back to his guest. "And, since the world's economy is already about as down as it can be, those investments are pretty safe, too."

"I'm almost sold," von Ahlenfeld said. "And the money you're offering is . . . enough, if on the low side of what outfits like yours pay. But what I really want to know is, how much independence of command do I get?"

"Oh, c'mon, Lee," Stauer admonished. "You know me. I don't care *how* you get the job done so long as you get it done. Christ, I put up with *Reilly*, don't I?"

Von Ahlenfeld sighed contentedly. "Good point. If you can stand him, you can stand me. Okay, pending any shocking revelations, I'm in."

"What? You don't even want to see the house that goes with the job?"

"Is it in 'Glen Livet'?"

"Ummm . . . no. The Second Battalion's housing area's called 'Glen Fiddich'. And, yes, it's sort of an inside joke."

"What? No Glen Morangie?" von Ahlenfeld asked.

"That's Reilly's battalion's housing area," Stauer replied, straight-faced.

"And the housing area for Headquarters is?"

"Woodford Reserve," Stauer answered, then added, "Yeah, I fucked up and let Reilly and the sergeant major lay out the camps and name them. So sue me."

★CHAPTER TWO★

No one starts a war—or rather, no one in his
senses ought to do so—without first being clear in his
mind what he intends to achieve by that war and
how he intends to conduct it.
—Karl von Clausewitz, *On War*

Joaquin Crespo Room, Miraflores Palace, Caracas, Venezuela

The only thing that really bothered the president was that
he'd come to the decision so easily. That said, it was an
obvious decision. When one has a domestic problem
one cannot overcome, very often the best—at least, the
quickest—way to solve it was to create a foreign problem
to take people's minds off their petty domestic concerns.
Some would have called it cynical; to Chavez, it was
simply realistic.

He'd given the military arms thirty days to prepare a
plan. Today, their thirty days were up and he would
demand some answers.

And the filth better have some, he thought, as he sat
centered among sundry civil, political, and military advisors.

Red shirts interspersed with occasional green, tan, white, or blue uniforms lined one side and both ends of the long conference table. It was a closed meeting, so that behind that seated line there were no other shirts and no other uniforms. Before the president, standing by a map on one wall with his pointer resting on the map, stood a general staff officer in tans. The beribboned general removed the end of his pointer from the map from which he'd been briefing, letting the end fall to rest on the marble-tiled floor.

"And so you see, Mr. President," said General Quintero, "we need to keep First through Third Infantry Divisions facing Colombia, along with Fourth Armored and the most of the Novena Division." *Even though, since your friends at Metalurgica Van Dam refitted the French tanks, the turrets won't even turn and a machine gun can penetrate the sides. At least they* look *threatening.*

"Thus, all that is available for the liberation of our Province of Guyana is Fifth Infantry Division, the Parachute Brigade, reinforced by a certain portion of our commando strength—whatever can be spared from the confrontation with Colombia—every helicopter we can muster, and the Marine Corps, and a small portion of Novena. We can probably muster and move two companies of Scorpion 90 light tanks, and another of AMX-13's. And of the Marines, the most we can expect to be able to lift, given the age and condition of our LST's, is perhaps one brigade, in three to four lifts. Even for that, we'll have to find some auxiliary shipping, and get a certain portion of the Navy in proper condition for active service to escort the amphibious ships."

An admiral of the grandiosely titled "Bolivarian Armada," seated down at one end of the conference table, exhaled loudly. "We're in no condition now," he said. "There were *reasons* why Russia was never really a naval power, despite putting on a good show during the Cold War with the gringos." *So, of course, we had to buy Russian ships, didn't we? Well . . . to be fair, the LST's, at least, are Korean. No thanks to you, since the slant eyes built them for us back in the 1980s.*

The general turned his attention to the admiral, asking, "How long to get the fleet in shape?" *Hopefully never, or this neckless and reckless maniac will have us at war.*

Shrugging, the sailor answered, "Three months, bare minimum. *If* the money is made available *now*." *Which, with luck, it won't be.*

Turning back to the president, the general said, "That's pretty close to how long we believe it will take to get Fifth Division and the paras ready for combat, too. They're only at about fifty percent strength. The commandos are, of course, already ready since they've had a priority on personnel, training funds and ammunition. But most of them are needed elsewhere." *And because you've been so dead set on aiding those murdering bastards from FARC.*

"And about the same for the Marines . . . for *half* the Marines," the admiral agreed. "It would take longer if we couldn't use half of them to get the other half ready." *Please, please, Chavez, you pig of a peasant, come up with some good reason why we can't use half of them to prepare the other half.*

Chavez was no fool. No one who rises to the level he had could be an outright fool. *I know perfectly well what you overbred oppressors of the masses are thinking. And I'm afraid you're doomed to be disappointed.*

He turned his large square head to his left, toward a woman, right on the cusp between mildly attractive and rather un-. "Blanca," he asked, "how long to whip up some patriotic fervor to reclaim our stolen province?"

"We never really stopped," the woman answered, nostrils widening in a somewhat piggish nose. "Even under previous regimes. But if you want something more serious?"

"As serious as can be," Chavez said.

"Well . . . if I can borrow some of the Army to arrange a couple of border incidents, that would be a help. Do we have any antisocial elements locked up in Yare"—this was a prison southeast of Caracas—"that could be used to provide a few bodies?"

Seeing that the president's face showed no objection to sacrificing a few enemies of the people on the people's behalf, she finished, "The ninety days the general and admiral have claimed should be sufficient."

A man, looking for all the world like a close cousin of the late Saddam Hussein, right down to the mustache and slicked-back hair, harrumphed from Chavez's right.

"You have an objection, Nicholas?" Chavez asked of his foreign minister.

The minister spoke with calm and reserve, belying his youthful days as a radical. He was one of a very few in a good enough political position, as well as a position of trust, to be able to speak freely to the president. "Not an objection, so much, Hugo," he said, "as a series of concerns. You do realize that the Colombian army is seven or eight times bigger than ours? That it has thirty combat brigades it manages to keep at full strength? That FARC can't tie down more than a small portion of it? That our present fifth column in Guyana is only a few hundred, and those committed more to the stipend we pay them than to the revolution? That the English may not take the occupation of their old colony lying down? That the gringos, despite having a regime at the moment in sympathy with us, tend to support the English? Ask Argentina what that means." *In short, when's the last time someone got away with what you're planning?*

The general raised his pointer again, tapping it onto a section of the map in the western portion of Guyana. "There's another factor, too, Mr. President. There are a number, a fairly large number, of gringo mercenaries with local auxiliaries here. It's the same group that trounced Suriname. The United States might not take well to their nationals being killed."

"Fuck the United States!" Chavez shouted, his demeanor changing from calm and serious to frothing and furious in an instant. He slammed a fist to the table, knocking over several cups of coffee with the force of his blow. "Fuck those little boy buggerers! And fuck their mercenaries who are illegally in *our* province."

Chavez forced himself to a calm he didn't feel. *God, I fucking hate gringos.*

"General?" Chavez looked directly at the Army's senior officer.

The general at the map gulped and went pale. "Yes, Mr. President?" he asked meekly.

"When we retake our stolen province, I want every

gringo in it *dead*, as an object lesson to interlopers." Chavez gave a little mirthless chuckle. "Think of it," he added, "as disposing of the garbage."

The admiral's face remained blank even as he thought, *Isn't that a fascinating thought; getting rid of the garbage. I'll have to think on that one.*

Castillo san Filipe, Puerto Cabello, Venezuela

The air was filled with the smell of the sea and the sound of a port. Ship's engines *thrummed;* horns blared; cranes and gantries squealed and squeaked. Overhead and at the shoreline, white and gray birds' cries arose as they hovered and hunted for bits of floating and beached garbage.

"What would you say, old man," asked the white-uniformed admiral. Fernandez, of the bronze, bow-tied bust of Francisco de Miranda, *el Precursor,* "what would you say today if you saw what our country has become? Not that it was your country, of course . . . merely your dream."

"His dream," said the general, Quintero, standing ahead of the admiral on a ramp that led from the courtyard of the fortress up to the crumbling battlements. "His dream," he repeated, sneering. "Our nightmare."

"Maybe not," Fernandez countered, somewhat cryptically. "Or maybe it's a way to wake up from the nightmare."

Quintero made a "give forth" gesture.

"Well," the admiral began, "I was against this whole scheme at first. But the more I think upon it the more I like it. After all, what's the worst that can happen?"

Quintero guffawed. "We piss off the gringos and they decide to visit us to teach us a sharp lesson." He turned to walk up the ramp.

"Right," said the admiral, following behind. "You survive that. I survive that. But who doesn't survive that?"

"My troops? Your sailors?"

"And so?" Fernandez shrugged.

"Good point," the general conceded.

"And who else is unlikely to survive the experience?"

That brought a smile to the general's face. "Better point," he said. "Much better."

"And what's the best thing that can happen?" the admiral asked.

The general considered this while continuing to walk. He reached the crenellations and stood there for a moment, watching a midsized freighter pass into the harbor through its narrow mouth. "If his mad scheme works, we actually take Guyana."

"Right again," said Fernandez, also watching the passing ship. "And for that best to happen, what must also happen?"

"Money."

"Indeed. Money for my ships. Money for your tanks and infantry and artillery. Money to become combat effective again. And why don't we have and haven't we had any money?"

"Because the bastard doesn't trust us." The general's head rocked from side to side several times. "As he has good reason not to," he admitted.

"Exactly. And if we have the money, and you—especially you—become combat effective again?"

"We toss the peasant piece of shit into Yare prison and throw away the key?"

"Better to just shoot him," said the admiral, with a sneer.

The general considered that. "Firing squad, all formal, or just a bullet the back of the head, do you think?"

"We'll have to consider that later," said Fernandez. "There are advantages to both methods. And leaving aside the best and the worst, what's the middle case?"

The general thought upon that for several moments, quietly. A slight smile creased his face. "We don't get the money; we fail and . . . "

"And his attempt to turn the people's minds away from their own and the nation's problems backfires. In that case, I think we should go formal, really formal."

"What? A silk rope?"

"Silk?" The admiral shrugged. "Whatever seems best to you. Personally, I think good old fashioned hemp would do. I'd be glad to provide it from the Navy's own stores."

"Something else also seems best to me," Quintero said.

"What's that?"

"The Fifth Division is possibly the *least* combat effective formation we have, though at least they're spared the humiliation of tank turrets that won't turn. I think it might be a good thing if we ask Chavez to fill it and the paras up with volunteers from his youngest and most fanatical Bolivarian supporters."

The admiral thought on that for a moment or two, then said, "He'd like that. Then he can claim more of a personal victory."

"Exactly," said the general. "And, if we lose, then we're

rid of them. Of course, we'll have to be truly serious about at least getting them *to* Guyana to have any good effect. To say nothing of not being carted off to Yare ourselves."

The admiral sighed, then smiled broadly. "Who says soldiers are stupid?"

Miraflores Palace, Caracas, Venezuela

Stupid fucking generals and admirals, Chavez thought, sipping a cool fruit juice at a patio table, in the shade of a palm tree growing from the palace's central courtyard. Though he indulged in occasional tobacco, always in private, Chavez never drank alcohol, hated the stuff, indeed hated the very fact of the existence of the stuff.

He refused to make money available for the import of whiskey. He taxed the hell out of both alcohol and tobacco. He'd forbidden sales directly from beer trucks in neighborhoods. He'd even forbidden the sale of alcoholic beverages during Holy Week.

Of course, he also nagged the nation to avoid hot sauce, to drive within speed limits, to not buy Barbie dolls for their daughters, to avoid breast augmentation, and to not eat high cholesterol foods.

In a different universe and a different time, and provided they didn't know of his addiction to women, Cotton Mather and any given surgeon general of the United States would have loved the man. For the matter, the current surgeon general did love him, but on ideological rather than health grounds.

"They're stupid, you know, Martinez," Chavez said to

an aide, standing by with a pack of cigarettes and lighter to hand. The president's finger pointed at an open folder on the table in front of him.

"Mr. President?"

"The generals, the admirals, the Army, the Navy, and the Air Force. They're all box of rocks *stupid*. You couldn't find an appreciation for the defense needs of the nation among them. Or any other needs, for that matter. Their thinking on the subject is so wrongheaded, so completely out of tune with the facts, that even chance wouldn't, couldn't produce an intelligent opinion if you queried them all. Under torture."

"I'm afraid I don't know anything about the military, Mr. President," the aide answered. "Or torture."

"Just as well," Chavez said, stubbing out his cigarette and holding out his hand for another. He was something of a binge smoker, too. Martinez passed over the cigarette and lighter, rather than stooping to light the thing himself. The president, even in private, was too much a man of the people to permit such slavish decadence. His self image would never permit it.

Chavez took a deep drag, both enjoying the sensation and hating the fact that he did enjoy it. "Martinez, go home to your wife or something. If you stick around, I'll smoke the whole damned pack. Anyway, leave me alone; I need to think."

"Yes, Mr. President."

As the aide walked off, Chavez, left alone, turned his thoughts to his and his country's problems. In his mind, these often blurred. Then again, of whom in his position would this not have been true? He turned his attention back to the folder, and especially the operations matrix it contained.

The basic plan is reasonable, I suppose, Chavez thought, *no matter what I told Martinez. It begins with a propaganda campaign both inside Guyana and here. Here, our people are reminded of their historic rights and their obligations to the future. There, our revolutionary fifth column demonstrates for liberation. Our money— while it lasts—swells the ranks of those demonstrating even as it ensures a fair amount of press coverage in favor of re-annexation. Then there'll be a riot or two. A border incident in which some people in Guyanan uniforms are killed on our soil, as will be a dozen or so—however many enemies of the people Yare may have to spare at the time— 'innocent civilians.' Maybe. Fake civilians might be over- doing it. Blanca always was too dramatic.*

Chavez felt a minor twinge of conscience, brushing it aside with thoughts of omelets, eggs, and the price demanded by the future.

Meanwhile, the forces required expand and train: Marines, Fifth Infantry Division, the Parachute Brigade, a couple of companies of commandos, one battalion's worth of light tanks and an extra of artillery, the Navy, and the Air Force.

Marines . . . one battalion's worth . . . hey, I like that. Who would have thought they'd be so clever? The rest, via ship, leave Puerto la Cruz, Puerto Cabello and land directly at Georgetown, then push south toward the air- port, clearing the road so we can resupply by sea. The LST's ferry in the remainder of that brigade. The paras jump into and take control over Cheddi Jagan airport from Ciudad Bolivar. *A forward refueling point goes in well beforehand, just off of Highway Ten, near Tumeremo, for the helicopters that don't have the range to make the round trip between Guyana and Ciudad Bolivar. Fifth Division stages out of Ciudad Bolivar and Tumeremo, moving on helicopters, mostly, since the smaller Guyanan fields can't take either the Boeings or the Airbus.*

The Air Force, of course, pastes the Guyana armed forces, such as they are, in their barracks, before the first helicopter or plane touches down. Assuming that the ass-fuckers can find their targets, of course. This is not something I can guarantee.

Unfortunately, we can't have them paste the gringo mercenaries. Or at least we can't count on having them do it. There's usually a regular battalion or two of gringos training there. Too risky to take a chance bombing them, even if the current regime in Washington is in sympathy with us.

Note to self: work really hard on getting the United States to not send anybody to train there during the time we'll be operating. The planned riots should help there, a bit. If so, we can bomb the mercenaries.

Chavez exhaled in what was almost a sigh. *It's a simple enough plan, really, despite having a lot a moving parts to it. I wouldn't trust any of them to do anything too very complex. Not that the generals and admirals aren't devious; they are. But they're politically devious without being, at the same time, militarily all that clever.*

Politically, they're thinking that with the expansion of the ground forces, they can get rid of me. Too clever by half. Little do they suspect that that expansion is going to come entirely from my most fanatical young supporters. Let them try a coup when their force is my force. Assholes. Idiots.

★CHAPTER THREE★

> Many intelligence reports in war are contradictory;
> even more are false, and most are uncertain.
> —Karl von Clausewitz, *On War*

SCIF, Camp Fulton, Guyana

There was a framed poster on the wall of Boxer's officer. The picture was a copy of the very famous painting by Leutze, "Washington Crossing the Delaware." The caption underneath said, "Americans. We will cross an icy river to kill you in your sleep. On Christmas."

"Sir, however much they might like to occupy this place—and, based on what we saw on the streets, Chavez has some serious domestic political and economic problems he'd probably like to take people's minds off of—I just don't see the assholes being capable of doing much of anything," Eeyore Antoniewicz told the regimental Chief of Staff, Boxer. Both Morales and the Russian woman, Lada, emphatically nodded their heads in agreement, Lada more so than Morales. All three of the operatives were in the regiment's field uniform, as was Boxer, himself. On Lada, pixilated tiger stripes actually looked cute.

Boxer was a few years older than Stauer, grayer, and of about the same height though not in such good shape. He'd been an Air Force two-star working intelligence for the Joint Chiefs of Staff when he'd finally balked over the sending of one too many overly optimistic, in fact doctored, intelligence summaries to the White House. He'd been with the regiment from within a few hours of its being proposed. His rank in the regiment was colonel, and he was, inarguably, the second ranking man in the organization.

The building in which Boxer made his main office, and in which he was being briefed on the team's findings from their trip to Venezuela, was officially called "the SCIF," the Special Compartmentalized Information Facility. This was a matter of sheer habit. In fact, it never had seen and in all probability never would see anything officially classified as "Special Compartmentalized Information," since the regiment and corporation didn't use the designation. On the other hand, the building was thick concrete, half buried under ground and covered with jungle growth. It was impervious to electronic penetration. It was surrounded by barbed wire. It was permanently guarded with both an interior and an exterior guard. And not just anybody was allowed into it. Thus, "SCIF" was accurate enough.

Besides, it held all the regiment's and corporation's secrets. All of them. This accounted for its two-less formal names, one of which was "the Warren."

"Details," Boxer ordered.

"Yes, sir," answered Eeyore. "We spent a bit over two weeks in Venezuela, based mostly out of Caracas. We checked all of the major naval bases—Puerto Cabello, Punto Fijo, and la Guaira. There we saw four LST's, six frigates, two corvettes, one larger supply ship, two LCU's, and three submarines, one of them one of the newly built Kilos.

"Sir, they never moved. None of them. They didn't look like they even *could* move. It's hard to explain . . . but when a ship's seaworthy, it *looks*, it *feels* seaworthy. At least to the trained eye it does. Their fleet looks like compressed rust held together by paint."

Morales gave Eeyore a dirty look, and shook his head, saying, "Sir, that's an exaggeration. The most we can fairly say is that their ships don't look well maintained."

"Could they sail?" Boxer asked.

Morales shook his head slowly. "Not without some work, I don't think, sir. Well . . . maybe the Kilo could. Probably the Kilo could. At least there were crew that went to the Kilo every day. Couldn't say that about the frigates or the corvettes, the amphibs or the other subs."

"Just to confirm I was seeing what I thought I was seeing," Morales continued, "I went down by the port until I found a sailors' bar. We're talking a seriously demoralized crew there, sir."

"The Air Force vas chust as bat," Lada said. "Vile Peddy Ovizer Morales vas scouting out ze whore barz—"

"It wasn't a whore bar," Morales interjected. "It was a sailors' bar."

"What's the difference?" Boxer asked, grinning. "Oh, never mind. Continue, Lada."

"Anyvay," she said, "I pud on an Aerovlot stewardess's univorm and vent to ze airport. If anyvun asked, I hat my

Russian pazzport. I vaited for one of zeir air vorce pilots to pick me up, which took approximately fife minutes. Including small talk. Two zirds of zeir aircravt vill not vly. Zis includes eqvipmend newly purchazed vrom Russia."

Something about that last datum brought a look of utter disgust to the Russian woman's face.

"While they were doing that," Eeyore said, "I went to look over the harbor; the main naval one, I mean, Puerto Cabello.

"It's a really nice harbor, sir. Except that it has one entrance, narrow, and easily mined. The only defense there was a fortress I make to be late eighteenth or early nineteenth century, with no armaments except for some antique ones on display, and no defenders except a bronze bust of a seriously pissed off looking dude with a bow tie. Mine that, sir, and their fleet, for all practical purposes, is locked up, even if it could sail, which it can't. The *Namu* would be overtaxed but the *Naughtius* could do a decent job of mining it."

The *Namu* was the regiment's first submarine, lost during and then recovered just after the operation in Africa. It had lost its long ago killer whale paint scheme, trading that in for naval gray. Still, the name stuck. The *Naughtius*, larger and more capable, was an indirect purchase from Montenegro, through the good offices of the government of Guyana. The regiment had actually had to purchase both of the midget subs Montenegro had had for sale, along with Croatia's *Velebit*, to make one decent one, and then pay for major refit for that one. It was even arguable which submarine the *Naughtius* really was. The hull had been *Velebit's* but slightly more than half of the interior components had come from the other two. They'd attached the name *Naughtius*, as a sop to Croatia, which didn't want to be blamed for the possible misuse of its former submarine. It had been a difficult project. On the other hand, since nobody else wanted the things, Montenegro and Croatia had been quite reasonable on the price.

The regiment still had two hulls, though one of those was up on blocks, on land, at their small base of Wineperu.

"You know we don't own any real naval mines, right?" Boxer asked. "Just the concrete dummies we use to support the jungle school."

"Yes, sir," Antoniewicz answered. "Maybe Victor should fix that."

Boxer considered that for a moment. "Round up the rest of your team, please, along with Captain Kosciusko. I want to meet after lunch." Then he punched a button on the intercom on his desk and said, "Lox, come on in, would you?"

Not everything secret was informational. Some of it was process. Other portions were personal. Since he was a person wanted for arms trafficking on every continent except, possibly, Antarctica, and since he had the process down pat for producing illegal arms pretty much wherever and whenever asked for, Victor Inning was, so to speak, a secret in himself.

Down the carpeted hall from Boxer's office, there was a sign or, rather, there were three of them. One, with an arrow pointing straight ahead, said, "Contracting," aka

Lawyers. That was Matt Bridges' purview, though he double-hatted as the regiment's S-2, or intelligence officer. On the next one down, with an arrow pointing to the left, it said, "Procurement," aka Guns. The third, headed toward the comptroller, Meredith's, office, said, "Comptroller and Investments," aka Money. This accounted for the other unofficial name for the facility: "Lawyers, Guns, and Money."

Around the corner to the left from where the SEALs and the Russian woman briefed the regimental Chief of Staff, behind a door with the innocent label "PROCUREMENT," Victor Inning conversed with his former subordinate, Major Konstantin.

"Ever since the old man passed on," Victor said, "life has sucked. Dull, dull, dull. I'm telling you, Konstantin, Hell is not a hot place, it's a dull one."

The old man of whom Victor spoke was his late father-in-law, a very high ranker in the FSB, which was the successor to the old KGB.

"So leave." The major shrugged. "Nothing holds you here."

Inning sighed. He shook his head, saying, "It's not that easy anymore. This is the only place I can hide now. Here, just up the road from the middle of nowhere. The old man's enemies back in the Lubyanka want me dead. Most of the governments in the world want me dead. The world economy is so shitty hardly anybody can afford decent arms anymore."

"Oh, c'mon, Victor," Konstantin chided. "It isn't that bad. Stauer still gives you the odd mission, here and there."

"Oh, *sure* he does," Victor agreed. "Provided that the recipients meet *his* ideological standards. Arms for Christians in the Sudan? Fine. Arms for the anti-Taliban resistance in Afghanistan, since the Americans gave up on most of that horrible place? Fine. Rifles for the IRA? Not. Antivehicular land mines for FARC or the ELN? Not.

"Bah! The things he lets me do aren't even a challenge."

"Well, if you want more excitement," Konstantin said, "there's an opening in Second—"

The knock on the door stopped whatever it was the major was about to offer. Without waiting for a welcoming answer, Peter Lox, Bridges' senior assistant, turned the knob and walked in.

"Major," greeted Lox to Konstantin. "Glad I caught you here."

"Peter Petrovich," the major answered, with a head nod.

"Boxer wants the three of us, plus Captain Kosciusko, Bridges, the SEALs and Lada, Waggoner from Operations, plus Meredith and Gordon, to meet in his conference room after lunch."

Harry Gordon, nicknamed "Gordo," was fat. He was not jolly. He wasn't even happy. Then again, logisticians are rarely very happy. Tankers who are not allowed to play with tanks are less happy still. And Reilly refused to let him command the First Battalion's tank company, since he already had somebody there he was happy with, while Stauer refused to let him leave the Four Shop, since he had no adequate replacement.

He wasn't made any happier by Inning's news: "I've got

some limpets, still, but that's it. I don't have any serious naval mines in stockpile, not anywhere, and, frankly, I don't know where to get any. Could we make some?"

Every set of eyes turned to look at Victor with disdain.

"Um . . . I guess not," he admitted.

Richard "Biggus Dickus" Thornton, supplied, "I don't know about you fuckers, but neither myself nor any of my people are going to carry, set up, or have one fucking blessed thing to do with any homemade, jury-rigged contraption that goes boom in the water. Not happening. No how. No way." That Thornton was physically huge, a cross between a human being and a gorilla on steroids, gave his words considerable emphasis.

"Frankly," said Gordo, "I don't understand the problem." He turned to Boxer, saying, "You've told us—or the trained pinnipeds have—that there is essentially no way for Venezuela to get to us as they are now. So why worry about mining their harbors?"

"SEALs," said Biggus Dickus, bristling, "*not* 'trained pinnipeds.'"

"Close enough," Gordo replied, with a lack of a smile that reminded Thornton, *Never fuck with the supply people. They can get even.*

Boxer leaned back in his chair, rested his elbows on the arms, put his hands together and let his chin rest on them. He sat that way, silently, for half a minute before he began to speak.

"Ed," he asked of Captain Kosciusko, "if the way the SEALs and Lada described their ships is accurate, how long would it take you to get their fleet seaworthy again?"

"Minimum six weeks; maximum twelve months,"

Kosciusko answered. He rubbed his hand across a bald pate and added, "Assuming someone shat them the money, of course. And assuming that everything they might need, to include expertise, is on hand or can be bought."

"Between six weeks and twelve months is a lot of variance," Boxer said.

"Ships are the most complex machines ever made by man," Kosciusko replied. "You never really know until you start digging into them. Six weeks is based on the fact that the individual ships are fairly small. Twelve months on the fact that their flotilla is fairly large and, as reported, in poor shape."

Boxer turned his attention to the operations officer, Waggoner. "Ken, also assuming that what they've reported on the Venezuelan air force and army is accurate, how long to make them combat worthy?"

"To fight who?" Waggoner asked. "All the really important parts of training are in the society outside of the military. And 'you are what you were back when.' They're not a culture that produces any really large number of first class soldiers. Some? Sure. Everybody produces some. But to fight, say, the United States, they'd have to have started about five hundred years ago, when the Spanish took over the area. To fight Guyana, minus us . . . three months, probably. If they're serious about preparing and if the money is there. But why?"

With his chin still resting on his hands, Boxer answered. "Because Venezuela's economy is tanking along with the world's, only a bit faster. Because Chavez needs a foreign crisis and can't play the gringo card anymore;

DC—rather the current regime there—is his moral ally. Because of the three places he could create that crisis, two—Brazil and Colombia—would kick his ass. Which leaves us, here."

"I don't think they could do it even here," Gordo said, "not even if they were the best soldiers since Caesar's legions. There's just no good way to get here. Not a single road connection and only a couple of really shitty cattle trails between the two countries. No rail lines between them."

"Which leaves the sea and the air," Boxer said, "which is why I'm going to Stauer to recommend we prepare for that, given that we probably *are* on Chavez's to-do list. Which is why I'm giving you people the heads up to prepare to block those avenues. Because everything you folks are telling me is that no matter how long Chavez's lead time may be, ours is longer still."

CH801 Number Six, over the Mazaruni River, Guyana

A lone harpy eagle, light against the jungle's green background, floated on the breeze, scanning for its next meal. Below the eagle, the river appeared as more a series of narrow islands with watery borders than a river, pure and true. South, to the left, one could catch faint, misty glimpses of white-stuccoed camps set along and among the flatter spots of the Ebini Hills. To the west of that, bright flashes and the occasional glimpse of an armored vehicle creeping or charging, as circumstances warranted, told that Reilly's battalion was once again assaulting the impact area north of Hill 780.

"Those two sets of falls," a pointing Stauer told von Ahlenfeld from the airplane as it banked right to give a better view—he had to shout to be heard over the roar of engine and wind—"are Koirimap and Mora. We don't own but do lease a chunk of the north side, about three miles in radius. You can't see it from up here, but there's a small base camp there we use as a final objective—one of five different ones we've set up here and there—for the jungle school."

Von Ahlenfeld looked at the two sets of falls, then had his attention drawn by four large muzzle flashes. "What guns are those?" he asked, also shouting.

"We've got a dozen French LG1's we bought—well, Victor bought—surplus from Singapore," Stauer answered. "We had them reconditioned and improved with the Canadian package, minus the muzzle brake. And that's just a question of ordering replacement barrels from Depro GVB in Canada when we need to.

"Nice guns, very light, good range. Only downside is that they're a little unstable in action and the barrels wear out about annually. They get maybe a fifth of the barrel life the French claimed for them. Fortunately, Victor also bought fifty extra barrels from the Singaporeans, so we're good for several years."

Von Ahlenfeld nodded deeply—the gesture the typical exaggeration when hearing is difficult—as the light plane moved on. As it wound over a broad, placid spot in the river, he asked, "Is the river fordable?"

"Depends on the season and the spot," Stauer answered, still shouting. "A lot of places that are unfordable during the wet season are anywhere from possible to pretty easy during the dry. If you're that curious about fords you can ask the S-2 shop. Or Reilly, who has a more practical appreciation for the problems and possibilities. Of course, the sneaky bastard creates fords he won't tell any of the other battalions about until after he's snuck a company up their rectal cavities.

"Son of a bitch has been pestering me for months, too, to buy him eighty or so Polish Opal-I's, so he can cross even where there's no ford. It's just not in the budget, though."

"With all the rapids and falls, how the hell do you operate landing craft in the river?" von Ahlenfeld asked.

Stauer shook his head. "For most of it, we don't. We own a small facility of about twenty acres at Wineperu, on the Essequibo River. That's where we keep the landing craft, patrol boats, one old one and a newer Israeli-built Super Dvora Mark Three"—Stauer shuddered in remembrance of the cost of that one—"which we call, unoriginally enough, 'Dvora,' a 'fishing' boat, and the midget subs. The Essequibo's navigable from there to the sea. We've also got some leased covered space by the docks at Georgetown. Comes in handy, from time to time."

Tapping the pilot, Stauer ordered him, "Doc, skirt the river to Honey Camp, then follow the road east . . . "

"What's 'Honey Camp'?" von Ahlenfeld shouted. "You've told me about Camp Jaguar, Camp Puma, Camp Mule, Camp Python, and Camp Tecumseh. And I've been to Camp Fulton. But Honey Camp?"

"Well . . . it's not really a camp. And the name predates us. I don't know what it started as, but now it's more or less

the regimental party town. See, there were these
Romanian girls . . . "

Honey Camp, Guyana

"I like to think of this place," said Stauer, "as the chaos on
the other side of the orderly whirlpool after you flush the
toilet."

Von Ahlenfeld, standing like Stauer atop a road
seemingly composed entirely of discarded, mostly sunken
liquor bottles, said, "Reminds me of pictures I've seen of
Colon, Panama, when they were first building the Canal."

Stauer nodded, slowly and seriously. "That thought has
occurred. Anyway, you wanted to see it, so come on."

The glass-surfaced road led into a town of sorts, laid
out irregularly to either side, with the occasional alley
winding drunkenly off between the buildings to end who
knew where. The buildings ranged from the presentable
to the ramshackle, with signs out front advertising in
words and silhouettes the goods and services to be
obtained within. Some of the goods, scantily clad goods at
that, advertised themselves and their wares from porches
and balconies fronting the street.

As squalid as the place was, there were signs, here and
there, of better construction ongoing, particularly as the
two progressed up the street toward the river.

Undistracted by the building, Von Ahlenfeld stepped
carefully over a plainly comatose body, lying across some
of the bottles, a bottle clutched in each hand. He asked,
"Why do you—"

"The regiment doesn't own this," Stauer cut him off. "Two hundred meters thataway"—he jerked his thumb backwards toward the dirt strip where McCaverty waited with the CH801—"we own. This we don't. And if we did own it, and made it different and decent"—Stauer pointed south—"two hundred meters *that* way, its twin would spring up as if by magic. The most we can do—and we do—is to medically inspect and license the whores to service the regiment. And even if we don't own it, we provide electricity. Free. If we charged, Tatiana and the rest of the girls would just raise their prices to cover the difference. And that would just lead to a demand for a pay hike. So . . . "

Von Ahlenfeld stopped for a moment and listened. "You know, I haven't heard a generator since I got here."

"And you won't," Stauer said. "Up until about two years ago you would have; we had a battery of generators. Fuel supplies, though, have gotten a little iffy—and even when not, getting enough diesel up here via LCM is a bitch—so about two years ago we bought a power module, nuclear, from Hyperion up in New Mexico. That's one of the reasons we provide free electricity; the thing produces five times more energy than we can hope to use."

A feral dog ran yelping past, chased by half a dozen laughing and shouting children bearing sticks. The kids wore things that were way past the point of being called "rags."

"Whose—"

"Nobody really knows," Stauer answered, shaking his head. "Not for most of them. The chaplain makes sure they don't starve, and brings them to the clinic on Camp Fulton if they need it. And Tatiana—"

"She's the Romanian hooker you mentioned?" von Ahlenfeld asked.

"Yeah. There were thirteen of them on their way to a slave auction—we think—when Biggus Dickus and his pirates rescued them. She's . . . well, you'll see. She was kind of scrawny when we . . . umm . . . acquired her. She's grown."

The road turned to the right, edging closer to the river. It led between two rows of well-trimmed hedges. Just past the hedges the scene changed radically, from an open human sewer to a manicured lawn and extensive flowerbeds surrounding a very large, white-painted, single-floor bungalow raised up on columns. A new Lexus, also white, was parked out front, with a dark man, in shorts only, painstakingly waxing the thing. On the porch, relaxed in a wooden chair by a table, an iced drink beside her, a very young woman, wearing sunglasses, a white hat and a dress that was mostly red silk but patterned with flowers of blue, white, and purple, fanned herself. She rose to her feet and pulled off the sunglasses with a graceful gesture. Then she smiled in a way—brilliant white and darker than sin, all at the same time—that seemed to rob the surrounded jungle of all its oxygen.

"Tatiana's house. And"—Stauer sighed—"Tatiana."

★CHAPTER FOUR★

From the moment that [Clearchus] led them to victory,
the elements which went to make his soldiers efficient
were numerous enough. There was the feeling of
confidence in facing the foe, which never left them, and
there was the dread of punishment at his hands to keep
them orderly. In this way and to this extent he knew how
to rule; but to play a subordinate part himself he had no
great taste; so, at any rate, it was said. At the time of his
death he must have been about fifty years of age.
—Xenophon, *Anabasis*

Karl Marx Impact Area, Guyana

In another place, with a different organization and organizational ethos, the area might have been named for some
geographic feature, or some widely revered hero. Here it
was a case of, as Reilly said, "the sheer joy of being able to
shoot the son of a bitch on a daily basis."

Reilly's battalion was the regimental mechanized force.
It consisted of two infantry companies, a tank company,
and a headquarters and headquarters company.

The infantry companies consisted each of three rifle platoons in turretless Elands, plus a weapons platoon with two 120mm mortars that were carried by more Elands and had to be dismounted to fire, nine forward observers, and an antitank section with three gunned and turreted Elands and two antitank guns, plus a small headquarters. The infantry companies were almost pure American and European, with only thirteen to fifteen hand-picked locals, each. Generally speaking, the Guyanans were there to learn, before being sent back to one of the other battalions to become junior noncoms.

The infantry companies were commanded by Hilfer, in Alpha, and Snyder, in Bravo.

In the tank company was a weapons platoon indistinguishable from those of the rifle companies, except that there were only four forward observers, rather than nine. There were also three platoons of six each heavily modified T-55's or Type-59 tanks, with another two tanks in the headquarters. Green commanded the tank company. Only the weapons platoon and company headquarters had Guyanans on strength, since there wasn't a lot of point to teaching them to become tankers, only to send them back to become infantry team leaders.

Reilly had developed, rather he had borrowed, four standard methods of task organizing the battalion, dubbed, "companies pure," "armor Alpha," "armor Bravo," and "companies balanced." All he had to do was give one of those phrases, preceded by the command "reconfigure," and the battalion would shift its setup with a minimum of fuss. Even on the move.

The former, pure, required no cross attaching; each

company kept its own organic forces. For the second and third, Green sent either his first platoon to A Company and picked up A Company's first platoon in return, or his second to B Company, picking up B's second platoon.

For the last, "balanced," the tank company gave up both its first and second platoons, picking up A Company's first and B Company's second.

The last company in the battalion, Headquarters and Headquarters Company, was commanded by Reilly's South African-born, Israeli-national wife, Lana Mendes-Reilly. She had, it was generally acknowledged, the toughest command in the battalion, with twenty-seven different job skill sets—"MOS's," the mother Army would have called them—and more than a hundred if one counted different skills being required for different ranks within the same MOS, organized in twelve different platoons and sections: Command, the four staffs, S-1 through -4, Maintenance, Medical, Supply and Transport, Signal, General Support Mortars, Scouts, and her own company headquarters. The complexity of the job was perhaps part of the reason she'd never acquired a nickname.

HHC had two hundred and seventy-five men (and one woman) on strength, the bulk of them being Guyanans. That was another reason the bloody job was so hard; the unit was twice as big as any other, bigger, in fact, than some of the regiment's battalions and squadrons. At the end of any given day, Lana's right hand was cramped and sore from the sheer frequency she had to scrawl her name across some document or other.

She was also responsible for the twenty-two cooks the battalion picked up from the regimental mess company, still slaving under Master Sergeant Island, whenever the battalion was in the field. Which was often.

Still . . .

★ ★ ★

I love *my job*, Lana thought, stroking her elegantly rebuilt nose lightly as she observed some of the mechanics struggling with, and finally conquering, a recalcitrant camouflage net that caught on every little projection and corner of the truck they were trying to screen. The men worked diligently, and with only the minimum necessary cursing for a job that every soldier who'd ever had to do it simply hated.

The nose Lana stroked was perfect, as it ought to have been since the regiment had paid for a new one, or the old one in a new and improved shape, after she'd smashed it to pulp in combat in Africa. The rest of her wasn't bad, either. She was tall, slender—with "cute but not large tits"—and olive-toned, shading to dark under the Guyanan sun. Lana's face was high-cheekboned, with large, liquid-brown eyes, full lips, and a delicate chin. The thing everybody remembered about her, at least when they'd seen her in mufti, was her hair. It was said of many women that their hair "cascaded." In Lana's case, it was true; she had—when she let her hair down—an auburn waterfall that simply flooded her shoulders and upper back.

In the present case, of course, being in uniform, and in the field, that waterfall was dammed up into a tight bun at the back of her head, just below where the helmet band kept her helmet firmly fixed in place.

I love my job, she thought again, *but* God *it's hot. I'd* love to take my helmet off and just let my hair down, but Seamus is death on taking your helmet off in the field, no matter how fucking hot and miserable it is. And, being his wife, while I could get away with it, it would hurt him if I presumed, and that would hurt me.

And my "cute but not large tits" are getting larger and they're miserable too, but I can hardly go braless out here. Note to self: Maternity bras, padded against external irritation, to mail order, soonest. Unless I can find a couple in Georgetown. Further note to self: Long talk with Seamus about whether I continue to command or turn the company over to someone else when I hit about the five months' point.

And, speaking . . . errr, thinking . . . of things that come in twos, I'd better go see if Danni Viljoen and Dumisani have C15 up and running yet. Since I'm not going to get First Sergeant Abdan out of my hair until he leaves with the tank.

Ioney Camp, Guyana

In their own closet Tatiana still maintained the uniforms and field gear she'd been issued back when she was still a member in good standing—*or kneeling, or lying down, or on all fours*—of the regiment. She'd be loath to admit it to anyone, but those uniforms and that gear were stored lovingly, and regularly taken out and cared for. Just because the regiment hadn't been what she'd set her heart on in life didn't mean she wasn't fond of it, or proud of her service as a medic in it.

And I was a damned good field medic, too, she thought

Tatiana sighed, thinking, *I miss it sometimes, too. I* *was the only decent family I ever knew. And the only system that ever treated me fairly. But I had my goals and I had my needs . . . still . . . if they ever really needed me . . .*

And I see that I have guests.

"Jesus!" von Ahlenfeld breathed as Tatiana smiled in his general direction.

"Closer than you may think." Stauer chuckled. "By all reports, a night with Tatiana is as near to Heaven as a man may come on this Earth. Not that I'd know. And, as with any drug dealer, the first taste is always free . . . for field grades and top three noncoms, anyway. And just like with the drug dealer's free samples, I *strongly* advise against accepting.

"C'mon, I'll introduce you."

When von Ahlenfeld didn't move, but just stood there staring, Stauer plucked as his elbow. "C'mon, before you embarrass us."

The woman met them at the head of the stairs. "My dear Colonel Stauer," she said, offering her cheek to be kissed. "You never come around. I'd almost think you don't like me."

"It's not that at all, Tati," Stauer answered. "But I'm only mortal and Phillie would make me very dead if I came around too often."

"Nonsense," the hooker replied, her smile, if possible, even more brilliant. "I know Phillie very well and she'd never . . . oh . . . cut your balls off, say, and feed them to you while you slept." Tati's head tilted. She reconsidered her previous statement and amended, "Um . . . yes, she would. Now be a gentleman and introduce me to your friend."

"Easy enough," Stauer said. "Lee von Ahlenfeld; Tatiana Manduleanu. Lee's taking over Second Battalion, Tati."

Tatiana asked, "*Really?* I suppose you already advised him against the free sample?"

"He's my friend, Tati, and I'd hate to see him impoverish himself through instantaneous addiction. That, or have a heart attack."

"Tsk," the woman said. "He wouldn't have a heart attack; a man is only as old as the woman he feels. And you know I have a very busy schedule and can't afford to spend enough time on any one man to outright impoverish him. Though there is one . . . oh, never mind."

Stauer smiled, wickedly, saying, "The sergeant major sends greetings, too, Tati."

The woman shook her head, plainly perplexed. "For him *all* the samples would be free. And my schedule would always be open. But does he take me up on it? No. I seriously wonder, Colonel Stauer, if you do not have a madman as your regimental sergeant major."

Stauer, too, shook his head. "He's not insane, Tati, just very, very proper. If you would treat it as a professional liaison, he'd be glad to spend some time and some money on you. But since you refuse to take any money from him, he feels that it would be both improper and unprofessional."

"Fool man," the Romanian clucked. "Still," she conceded, "it's an admirable foolishness. Part of the reason why I love him so, too, I suppose."

Tatiana clapped her hands for one of the half dozen servants she kept on staff. When one arrived, white-liveried, dark-skinned, and earnest-looking, she commanded, "See to my guests, Arun, while I change into something that will either send Colonel—it is 'colonel,' isn't it, Lee?—von Ahlenfeld into cardiac arrest or increase my client base by one."

"Yes, Madam," the Indo-Guyanan said, with a half bow.

"She was one of *yours*?" von Ahlenfeld asked, incredulously.

"A corporal, there, when she left," Stauer acknowledged, nodding. "Good one, too, for being all of just turned eighteen. See—we, which is to say Biggus Dickus Thornton's boys . . . errr . . . liberated some Romanian girls on their way to a slave auction. The thirteen of them were locked up in a shipping container. We couldn't let them go at the time and they figured they owed us and wanted to help. So we made them medics. Tati was one, and the only one who didn't necessarily object to the fate that would have been in store for her. Still, she did her duty for as long as it was her duty. Then she took her walking papers and set up in business here.

"Her . . . earnings don't seem to stay just in her account. She had this house built on her own ticket. And," Stauer pointed through a gap in the trees to where a white spire was slowly rising, "she's having a chapel built over there, with a school for the little rabble you saw chasing that dog. I'm told she's hunting for a Romanian Orthodox priest, though whether a priest can accept being supported by a whore, I don't know. Supposedly, she's contracted for someone to put in a sewer system, though in this part of this country I'll believe it when it happens.

"To the extent anyone is, she's sort of the mayor of this . . . place."

"And Joshua?" von Ahlenfeld asked.

"Well . . . I was being tactful. He likes her a lot, but can't fuck her for free or a presumption of affection, affection that would also presumably run both ways, would arise. As the RSM, his position doesn't permit him to have what amounts to a girlfriend who damned near everyone else of any rank in the regiment is fucking or has fucked. Simple, brutal fact of life."

Von Ahlenfeld caught a glimpse of an extremely feminine figure through the gauze of the curtains on the windows. He drew breath in a rush.

"You say the first sample is always free, is it?"

"For field grades and senior noncoms only. And to get anywhere near her you have to produce a clean blood test from within the last *week*."

"So how do you . . . ?"

"Just ask her to put you on the schedule. For today, however, *we* have a schedule to keep."

"By the way," von Ahlenfeld asked, "why do you call the pilot 'Doc'?"

Stauer laughed. "Because Doc McCaverty's a neurosurgeon that we can only keep on strength—for what we can afford to pay—if we let him fly, generally, and fly combat, in particular."

"A *neurosurgeon?* You, Wes, have a very odd crew here."

"You don't know the half of it."

Karl Marx Impact Area, Guyana

"And that's the other reason," Lana said, in Reilly's tent, a few dozen meters from the battalion command post. "I'm . . . I'm . . . "

"'Um, um,'" Reilly gently mocked. He was over fifty, compared to his wife's mere thirty-one, and tended to tease her for her youth, among other things.

"Gonna have a baby," Lana finished. "In about six months."

Reilly had been sipping at a folding tin cup of coffee when Lana had come into his tent. *Sua sponte*, his hand opened up, letting the cup fall to the tent's dirt floor.

"No shit?" he asked, unintelligently.

"No," she answered sardonically, "shit comes out of one side. *Babies* come out the other side."

He was on his feet in the next instant, physically picking her up and setting her protesting form—"I am pregnant; I am *not* fragile!"—down on his field chair. Then, legs gone weak, he sat straight down onto the dirt. "No shit," Reilly muttered.

"I take it, then," Lana said, "that you do not object to the idea?"

Speechless for the nonce, he just shook his silly-smiling head in negation.

I've made you happy, she thought, also smiling. *That, alone, is worth what I'm going to go through.*

Still smiling, she said, "Good. But we still have the

problem of the company. Doc Joseph isn't an obstetrician—
we don't *have* an American or Euro-trained obstetrician—
but he made a call to a friend of his in the States who is,
and the two of them decided I'll be fine up to about the
end of the fifth month. At that point, it would be better—
safer, anyway—for me and the baby, both, if I stay out of
the excessive heat and generally take it easy. That's not
consistent with being a company commander."

"We'll worry about the company later," Reilly
answered, finally finding some meaningful words. "We
have time. What's more important is that the regiment's
hospital doesn't have an obstetrician on staff."

"That's not true," Lana said. "There is one, though all
of his patients tend to be local, like himself."

"Where did he go to medical school?" Reilly asked. "If
it wasn't top notch from America, Israel, or Europe . . . "

Lana held up a shushing hand. "He delivered both of
Phillie Stauer's without a hitch."

Reilly took her small hand and wrapped it in his own.
"I'm not in love with or married to Phillie Stauer," he said.
"I am with you. So I don't care what was good enough for
her and hers. I care about what's good enough for you and
ours, and a local isn't likely to cut it."

"Doc Joseph checked on that, too, and there is a first
rate OB-GYN in Georgetown, a graduate of the All India
Institute of Medical Sciences, in Delhi. That, Joseph says,
is the best in India, as good as any in the world and better
than most."

"All right," Reilly conceded, though not necessarily
with any good grace. "You can go to see this Doctor . . .
what did you say his name was?"

Lana sighed. "You really *are* getting old, short term memory loss and everything. I *didn't* say. But it's Singh, and Joseph already made me an appointment for next week. The hospital's paying Singh enough for him to come here rather than me going there, too."

"Good," Reilly said, "because neither of my babies is getting on a plane any time soon. And forget about going by what passes for roads here.

"Singh, eh? Good. Probably means he's a Sikh. I approve of Sikhs."

★ CHAPTER FIVE ★

There never was a new prince who has disarmed
his subjects; rather when he has found them disarmed he
has always armed them, because, by arming them, those
arms become yours, those men who were distrusted
become faithful, and those who were faithful are kept so,
and your subjects become your adherents.
—Machiavelli, *The Prince*

Caracas, Venezuela

It was easy to understand how someone like Chavez could
end up as effective dictator of the country. What was hard
was to understand what had taken so long. Most countries
in Latin America had vast inequalities of wealth and little
in the way of a social safety net. For most of the previous
century, Venezuela's oil had made these inequalities even
vaster than the Latin norm. Worse, nowhere was the
difference between the have-everythings and the have-
nothings quite so glaring, and quite so galling, as they
were here.

In most places, the rich were out of sight and away

from the view of the poor. Here, the poor huddled in unsanitary and unsafe—mudslides might without warning kill thirty-thousand and render a million more homeless overnight—barrios up on the hills surrounded the city, with the sight of gleaming skyscrapers and the mansions of the rich an ever-present and continuously insulting reality. Safe behind their guarded gates, what did the rich know or care of the city's murder rate, five times greater than that of New Orleans at its pre-Katrina worst? And the middle class had begun to emulate the rich, with their own walls and private guards.

Of the rest, the great masses of unwashed and miserably poor, more than half saw some member of the family the victim of a crime every few months.

And the police? Of Caracas' respectably proportioned, indeed bloated, police force of thirteen thousand, most— as much as eighty percent in some areas—were in administrative jobs rather than walking a beat. That meant a mere six or seven percent of the police forces available were at any given time actually doing something active and visible to combat crime. Outnumbered, often outgunned, and demoralized, of those who were walking a beat, that tiny, tiny percent, most simply didn't care anymore . . . if they ever had.

The sun was beginning to set behind the hills and shanties to the west. Moving from bright, tropical light to darkened shadows, cutting across broken sidewalks and potholed street, walked Carlos Villareal, aged nineteen. Carlos wore a red T-shirt and a rifle slung from one shoulder. Walking past the gutted ruins of the la Dolorita police station on his way to the meeting, he spared the ruin barely a glance. So much had it become a mere and accepted part of the landscape. He'd been little more than a boy the first time the residents of the barrio had attacked the thing with sledgehammers, axes, and home-made Molotov cocktails. It had been wrecked at least twice over again since that day. Now, windowless and with the scorching of gasoline-fed flames marking the walls over the holes that had been windows, it was abandoned and ignored by residents and police alike.

Most places in what passed for the civilized world, mobs attacked police stations in protest over police brutality, often enough with racial undertones. Here, the station had been ruined not over brutality, but over sheer indifference and incompetence. Nor had it made the slightest negative difference. Once the police gave up and moved away, the citizens of la Dolorita had taken matters into their own hands. They'd also taken into their own hands the rifles passed out with free abandon by the Chavez government in aid of developing a force of citizen militia. These arms had been given notionally to deter or combat a gringo invasion. In intent they were to raise the threat of civil war should the right ever return to power. In practice they had served, at least here in la Dolorita, to arm the death squads that sprang up to preserve security when civilization began to fail.

Not that Carlos thought of himself as belonging to a death squad. Militia, yes. Vigilante, yes. Death squad? No.

And, hell, thought Carlos, not without some satisfaction, *we haven't had to actually kill anybody in . . . oh, must be over a year now; those three boys who beat up and raped*

*the Vargas girl, Lily. For that matter, we didn't do that.
We just rounded the filth up and presented them, bound
and gagged, to Lily Vargas, along with a rifle. She actually
pulled the trigger on the filth . . . then signed up with us.*

*Like the group leader says, "Justice is a result, not a
process."*

The Revolution had taken over more than a few
businesses. Sometimes the businesses concerned survived
the experience; sometimes they did not. In this particular
case, a former supermarket that had ultimately proved
gringo-owned, hence eminently seizable, the business had
not survived but the building still provided a place for the
weekly party meetings and the smaller, nightly gathering
of the barrio's vigilantes.

Early, as she usually was, Lily—short, dark, pretty, and
hourglassy—stood off to one side of the gathering. She
chain smoked, something she hadn't done before being
assaulted. And, sure, the Leader didn't officially approve
of tobacco, but, under the circumstances, nobody was
going to yell at Lily over it.

Carlos, standing in the door, looked around the crowded
room of standing, red-shirted vigilantes for the telltale
column of smoke. His eyes passed quickly over the group
leader, Rojas, and the uniformed man standing beside
him on the slightly raised dais at one end of the large
room.

Ah, there she is. He threaded his way carefully through
the crowd, making sure the magazine on his Kalashnikov
didn't poke anyone, to stand at her side.

Lily gave him a quick and furtive smile, albeit without

even the tiniest flash of white. Politeness demanded as much. Still though, she couldn't help remembering that it was a simple smile that had led . . .

She tossed her cigarette to the floor and stamped on it. The group leader was about to speak.

Normally, the group leader, a balding light-skinned man of medium height and weight, began the meetings with a review of the previous day's events. This time he didn't bother. He cleared his throat, but only to catch the attention of the hubbubbing mass below where he stood on the short dais.

"Your patrolling assignments are on the map on the wall behind me," he said, once they'd quieted down a bit. "Read them when I've finished. You know what to do from there. We've got a more serious matter."

That shut everybody up, where a simple throat clearing hadn't, quite.

"Hugo," the group leader said, "needs volunteers . . . for the Army. About twenty-five thousand of them. We're supposed to come up with twenty, from all six shifts. I can take more." Rojas' head inclined slightly, indicating the uniformed man standing beside him, an army officer, the attendees guessed, from the quality and cut of his uniform. The officer looked stout, fairly young, and quite fit. He wore a red beret, which didn't necessarily imply any revolutionary leanings. "Captain Larralde, here, is from the Army. Fifth Division, was it, Captain?"

Miguel Larralde shook his head, answering, "Parachute Brigade, only attached to Fifth Division, and that only since about last week. I'm here on behalf of both, though I can only take a relative few of the most fit and capable, from this group and about nine others, into the Parachute Brigade. I've got room for both men and women, though I need more of the former.

"The pay's not bad," Larralde continued, "a lot better than the stipend you get for what you're doing now. But if you volunteer, you can forget all this revolutionary, egalitarian bullshit. The Army's a hierarchy and that is not going to change. It's harsh, and it's hard, and that's not going to change, either.

"That said, you'll eat pretty well. Moreover, you'll live clean except when in the field, and you'll stay as clean as possible even there.

"And you'll work like mules . . . no, that's not right. A mule or a horse will give up and die when a good man or woman is still trying. You'll work harder than *slaves*.

"If you're willing, I'll be here still when you finish your nightly patrols. Come see me."

Walking the broken pavement, under a set of streetlights of which perhaps one in seven worked, Lily was even more subdued than usual.

"You're thinking about it, aren't you?" Carlos asked. "Joining, I mean."

"Yes," she replied. "Aren't you?"

He hadn't been. Even so, he answered, "Yes, of course." *Never do to be behind a woman in defense of the country,* he thought, *particularly one so cute.*

"My question, though," Carlos continued, "is, 'why now?' What's different that Hugo wants to bring the Army up to strength again after cutting it by fifty percent? I read the papers, Lily, and we are in trouble as a country. And we're going to stay in trouble until and unless the world economy turns around and the price of oil goes up again. So why start spending money on the military?"

· "Maybe Hugo thinks the gringos will attack us while we're weak and their own need for oil is low," she replied.

That made him shrug. "It's possible," he agreed. "But I've got a cousin in the gringo Marine Corps, and he tells his mother that they're in bad shape, too. Nothing like when they knocked over some of the Arabs. No money, either, and old equipment, too."

"You mean you don't think they could pull off an invasion?" she asked, stopping for the moment.

"Way above my skill set," he said, though he continued his walk. She joined him after he'd gone no more than a few paces.

"But I'd suppose they could. If they were going to, though, they'd be bringing their own armed forces up to par. And that, they're not doing."

"If not the gringos, maybe Hugo's worried about Colombia or Brazil," she offered, not unreasonably. "Or, more likely, about the residue of the oligarchs right here at home."

"That's all possible," Carlos conceded. Contemplatively, he added, "The Colombians are our brothers in everything but name; I'd rather not fight them if I didn't have to. The Brazilians? Eh," he shrugged, "why not? As for the oligarchs; I'd pay for my own ammunition, if I could afford it."

"I feel about the same way," Lily agreed. "But if we sign up, I somehow doubt we'll get much choice."

"*We*," Carlos wondered. *I didn't realize we were a*

package deal. Still, she is *awfully cute and . . . so . . . maybe . . . "we."*

"Then we'll talk to Captain Larralde when we finish our patrol?"

Miraflores Palace, Caracas, Venezuela

In a continuously guarded private office, small and cramped, one which few advisors—and those only the closest—were allowed into, Chavez studied the antique map on his wall. In a way, the map was the reason none but his closest followers were allowed into the office and cameras *never*, and most especially not the cameras of the media, left or right. For them, there were other rooms, other offices.

The internationalist left always sees what it wants to see, Hugo thought disparagingly, looking at the map's grand scheme. *And refuses to see what doesn't fit what it wants to see. I take control of some industry, nationalize a few assets owned by foreigners, clamp down a bit on the press, mouth the words of socialism, shunt a very little support to various left-wing guerilla movements, and even follow through on a couple of socialism's tenets, and they see in me another Fidel, only with more money to spread the Revolution. Admittedly, I do my not inconsiderable best to foster all that, be it playing baseball with Fidel back in '99, slipping him a little oil, or providing a safe haven for FARC.*

Still, you would think that the absence of show trials, gulags, reeducation camps and mass graves would tip them off. But nooo . . .

The president shook his head with wonder, saying aloud, "They always miss that, while Bolivar is my hero, and his dreams are my dreams, *his* dreams—and mine— are not *theirs*."

Chavez mentally sneered. *Like that idiotic Englishman who wrote that book. Couldn't bring himself to realize the truth of the matter here. Had to write "socialistic nationalism," instead of facing the truth. As if switching a couple of words around changes reality on the ground. And how the morons missed the parallels between my "failed" coup in '92 and certain events in Munich, sixty-nine years before that . . .*

The sneer reached the president's face, briefly.

I am a firm believer that, while history may not repeat itself, it does rhyme and should rhyme, and only a fool fails to catch the meter of the piece.

Never mind; first things first. And first I've got to ride out the currently crappy economy. Only then can I advance Bolivar's dream, and my own. And to ride out the crappy economy, I still need to distract the people for a while.

He sighed, and again speaking aloud, said, "And to that end, let's see what the military has come up with . . ."

Chavez unsealed and opened a brown folder—leather; only the best for the president, after all—and began to shuffle through the papers therein. These he sorted into stacks on his desk, mentally and physically classifying them: Operations Order—labeled "Renania," Logistical Annex, Recruiting and Training, Air Movement Annex, Air Support Annex, Sea Movement Annex, all three of those last with their appendices, Naval Maintenance

Upgrades and Aviation Maintenance Upgrades, plus the Intelligence Annex.

It was to some extent a matter of personal taste, but Chavez, being a methodical sort, began with the Intelligence Annex. Only with that clear in his mind would operations or logistics make sense to him, or anyone, even as neither the air nor the sea scheme would make the slightest sense without logistic requirements being understood.

Stacks of paper all properly ordered, he pulled out a writing pad and pen. Then he twisted his chair to place one arm close to the desk and cross the opposite leg over the thigh nearest the desk. With the Intelligence Annex in one hand, and pen in the other, he began jotting down notes and questions: *"Enemy force, definite: One regular infantry battalion, poorly trained. Four reserve infantry companies, probably even less well trained. One artillery battery, which has not fired its guns in years. An engineer company. No real air force. No navy, to speak of. Probable: One brigade of mixed gringos and Guyanans, and a few others, elderly, well trained and equipped, with some air and some naval capability, but see terrain analysis. Possible: normally one regular gringo battalion, Army or Marines, undergoing jungle training.*

Hmmm, Chavez thought, *let's see whether our supporters and allies in Washington can be induced to not have that battalion in Guyana on the pertinent dates.*

He read some more, then wrote: *United States: unlikely to interfere. Brazil: Unlikely to be concerned. Colombia . . .* Chavez stopped writing a moment just to think.

How do I take Colombia out of the equation for at least

long enough? They're also Latin and so unlikely to care too much about an English-speaking colony. But they know I'm an enemy and might use this as an excuse. Bribe FARC to do something really major to tie their army down? Bribe the Colombian government directly? If so, how? Money? I've hardly have enough to spare. Maybe an agreement to provide oil that I do have and that they can already barely afford, even at depressed prices. Clamp down on FARC, here? Take away their safe haven and arrest or disband the battalion they keep on our soil? Crack down on FARC's "revolutionary" drug trade, on which some of them live very well indeed? Or maybe the better answer is to appear *to do all those things, while doing none of them.*

Consider this carefully. We cannot face an attack by Colombia while we are engaged in Guyana.

But then again, can they even think about paying for a war? Maybe not. Maybe I'm worrying over nothing. Best have a chat with Nicholas.

After reading the Intelligence Annex, and filling four pages with hand-scrawled notes, Chavez turned to Operations. There he found nothing unexceptionable, except perhaps for a certain overoptimism. Certainly the plan for preparation of the target was good. *Of course, the fucking generals had nothing much to do with that.* And, *The seizure of the airfields at Kaieteur and Cheddi Jagan International to serve as bases for expansion . . . no choice there; there's no other way to supply our troops initially, while landing the Marines at Georgetown, even while little penny packets of second stringers take helicopters and light planes in to the . . . um . . . one . . . two . . . fifteen . . . call it "thirty" odd little airstrips west of the Essequibo.*

Okay, as those are occupied a little further in with each lift, it looks more and more to the ignorant press like an inexorable advance in overwhelming force. And, of course, we'll play to their incarnate, insuperable ignorance and brief it exactly that way.

And I'll look so very reasonable to the international community when I give Georgetown and the area east of the Essequibo back again, since that's not part of our legitimate claim.

Hugo mentally shrugged. *On the other hand, maybe I shouldn't give it back. If Guyana isn't extinguished, there's always the possibility—small, to be sure—of revenge.*

Reading on, Chavez came to the section on amphibious movement. *Idiots. Just idiots. Why, oh why, do we stage the Marines out of the northern coast when we can move at least some of them by land to a port closer and cut the time to fully deploy them in half?* He scrawled furiously, the anger expressing itself in letters rough and crude on the pad of paper.

Hugo finished up with operations, put that section aside, then picked up the Logistics annex. He was about halfway through this, and on page twenty-seven of his note-taking, when he realized, *Those fucking assholes. They've got this plan done in a vacuum. Where the hell is their plan for secrecy? Why haven't the silly shits made a plan for securing the embassies—especially the gringo embassy—in Georgetown?*

They'll have plans—and they'd better be good—three days from now or I'll have new commanding generals . . . and an admiral . . . for all three services, plus a new minister of defense.

Chavez looked up from his papers to the antique map of *Gran Colombia* on his private office wall. *Because Bolivar and I share a dream.*

★ CHAPTER SIX ★

If everything were to be discountenanced in
peace by which an accident might possibly occur,
soldiers would be greatly sinned against, since they
would be enfeebled and rendered inept for war, the
chances of losses being doubled at the same time.
—Field Marshal Colmar Freiherr von der Goltz,
The Nation in Arms

Camp Fulton, Guyana

Trees, close together this close to the open, asphalted strip
and the free ambient sunlight, passed by in a rattling blur.
Although the road was less than four years old and had
been well-built to begin with, the jungle, aided by heavy
vehicle traffic—heavy in both senses—took a severe and
continuing toll.

"Day after tomorrow is assumption of command?" von
Ahlenfeld asked.

"Zero nine hundred," Stauer answered as he twisted
the Land Rover's steering wheel to guide it around a
sharp, jungle-shrouded curve. "Don't be fucking late."

Past the curve, on the straightaway, the Rover passed a small and abandoned trailer park, with about a third of the lots still filled with empty mobile homes. A dark skinned man in a white suit argued with another, white and so probably American, or at least Euro, in pixilated tiger stripes. The white's hands remained clasped behind his back, while the brown's moved frantically. Von Ahlenfeld searched his memory for where he had seen the white suit.

"Tatiana's majordomo," Stauer answered, after being asked. "Arun . . . mmm . . . shit; what the fuck was the rest of his name? No matter. The other one was Gary Trim, our regimental and facilities engineer and commander of the combat engineer company. He's a Brit.

"We had to start out with mobile homes and tents," Stauer explained. "But we got the last family into decent permanent housing about a year and a half ago. Little by little we've been selling off the mobile homes, usually at about fifteen or twenty cents on the dollar. If Arun is there, odds are Tati's trying to buy one . . . or more."

"Why would she do that?" von Ahlenfeld asked.

Stauer shook his head. "With her, you never really know."

"You really don't, boss," piped in a voice from the back seat. The third passenger in the Rover was the sergeant major for the Second Battalion, Rob "Rattus" Hampson. His voice was full of humor as he spoke.

"Rattus" was still very much an unknown quantity to von Ahlenfeld. He knew the sergeant major was a medical type, a "Delta," in Special Forces parlance. This was something he found rather suspect, even from Special

Forces where medicos were nearly as much trigger pullers as was anyone else in a green beanie.

Still, even with SF, their attitude is often just a little off. But Stauer says he's a good man . . . so we'll give it a chance.

The Land Rover passed a group of mostly Guyanan troops, singing while marching in the general direction of the impact area to the west.

"They look decent," von Ahlenfeld commented.

"Yeah . . . kinda," Stauer half agreed. "We've got an internal problem though."

"What's that?"

"Pay disparity," Stauer answered, briefly turning his head to see von Ahlenfeld's reaction. The latter has a single quizzical eyebrow raised. "Unavoidable, really, though we've done what we can to mitigate it.

"See, we have to pay our Euros and Americans a certain amount, just to keep them. Most of them are retired, so with retired pay, equivalent regular pay, and a not insubstantial cost of living allowance based on the States, they're happy enough and they provide the leadership to make the whole regiment fairly effective. Oh, sure, there are some of those who would pay for the privilege, but in the main? No. It's as much a prestige thing as anything.

"The Guyanans, on the other hand—and it makes not a whit of difference whether they're brown, black, yellow, white, or red—can be had for beans.

"It's a poor country. Real income here is about one thirtieth that of the States. Purchasing power parity is better, about a tenth. So in a purely rational world, we'd pay, say, a Guyanan private with the regiment maybe forty dollars a month and found, or at most a hundred and twenty-five or so. A Guyanan staff sergeant—of which we've raised a few, so far—might be worth a hundred and sixty or, again at most, five hundred.

"That's great money, here, but not so good when they look at Americans, Euros, Israelis, Brits, South Africans, etc., making ten or twenty times more . . .

"We couldn't afford to pay them the same and still keep Americans and such on hand, and without them, there'd be no regiment and, hence, no place for the Guyanans at all."

Von Ahlenfeld had seen the same problem, repeatedly, in his prior position. There, the company had simply dumped using any group that demanded pay parity, and gone with cheaper, elsewhere.

"How'd you handle it?" he asked Stauer.

"Few different approaches," Stauer replied. "In the first place, we took what total non-Guyanan pay would be, then split non-Guyanan pay into two increments, basic pay—which is rather less than American standard—and a *much* larger than standard United States-based cost of living allowance. We did the same with Guyanan pay, except we split it into basic pay and local cost of living allowance, of which there isn't any for troops living in the barracks or in regimental family housing. Though the latter get separate rations.

"Also, the original members of the regiment—which, by the way, includes a helluva lot of non-Americans; we've got South Africans, Israelis, Brits, Germans, Russians, Mexicans, and Chinese—each own one or more shares in the corporation. Holding those requires membership in the regiment at or above a certain rank. Those almost always pay a good dividend.

"Then we indexed Guyanan pay to non-Guyanan pay, but with a multiplier of between one and point one. Sergeants major, of which we have no Guyanans and won't for about twenty years, get an index, a multiplier, of one. Privates, of which we have many, get an index of point one, for recruits, or point two-one for trained privates. Staff sergeants, of which we have some, and to take a median figure, get a multiplier of point six-six, which, minus the U.S. cost of living portion, works out to just under twelve hundred a month. Locally, that's princely.

"It's not perfect, but we can at least hold out to the Guyanans the chance to have what looks like equal pay, eventually. Sort of, because there'll still be a big chunk that's cost of living indexed and, for them, indexed to here. And they still need to be platoon sergeant or above before they can buy a share of stock.

"They still resent it, but on the other hand, since they can lord what they do get over their mostly unemployed peers, and get well fed, clothed, and housed, their resentment isn't so bad.

"We also have a uniform combat or danger pay kicker that, while fairly trivial from an American or European perspective, about doubles the pay of a trained Guyanan private. They spend about one year in four overseas doing personnel security, so that's a big factor.

"If you need a more detailed explanation, see She-whose-smile-lights-up-the-jungle."

"Huh?"

"Warrant Officer Lahela Corrigan, sir," Rattus Hampson

supplied. "She runs the finance section in the comptroller's office. If you're in the jungle at midnight, and it suddenly lights up but you can't see a chemlight, much less the moon or stars? That's Lahela, smiling. You won't see *her*, of course, because she's about five foot, even."

"She's good folks," Stauer added. "A pro."

"My battalion has how many locals?" von Ahlenfeld asked, considering the political and morale problem Stauer had probably mostly elided over.

"Forty-three in headquarters, sir," Rattus answered, "and forty-five in Delta Company, which handles internal training for the regiment. The latter are almost entirely promising young NCOs. Every one's a graduate of the Jaeger Course—"

"Jaeger Course?" von Ahlenfeld interrupted.

"Ranger School," Stauer answered, shrugging slightly. "Hey, we needed a name. And if you've got a Ranger tab, you have the option of wearing either one. Your Delta Company runs our own, twice a year, plus a primary noncom's course, twice, and an advanced noncom's course, once. Wash-out rate's pretty high for Jaeger."

"No OCS?"

"You figure out for yourself whether we need one and should have one," Stauer said. "For various reasons, the regimental council is against it. This, despite the fact that, without one, there's no good way for me to commission Tatiana's cousin, Elena, who *ought* to be an officer."

"What *is* the rationale?"

"Same reason we wouldn't accept any first generation Guyanan-Americans, of any race, even if they've got serious military backgrounds; it complicates the pay scheme and is likely to lead to what is really political trouble. Sucky, I agree, but I didn't make the world; I just have to live in it."

Regimental Hospital, Camp Fulton, Guyana

Things only begin to need names when there are two of them. Things may also acquire names if someone is to be memorialized. Since the regiment only had one hospital— a sixty bed, but quite up-to-date, facility—and had not yet lost a medical trooper in action, it was known, both inside the medical company and to the regiment at large, simply as "the hospital."

Although respectable, neither the hospital itself nor its staff could be considered large. Indeed, oversized for the work it had to do, normally and routinely, it proved necessary to send the medicos out to treat the locals, on a *pro bono* basis, just to keep their skills up. Nurses, of course, were always too few and too overtasked, for their numbers, even with the regimental hospital's routine case-load, and even counting that half of the dozen Romanian girls remaining had their RNs. Still, surgeons did much of their cutting and pasting in one or another of Georgetown's main hospitals; Georgetown Public, West Demerara, or Saint Joseph's. Medics spent about one week in nine attached to one or another of Georgetown's or Bartica's ambulance services. The aeromedical evacuation section had sometimes been volunteered to fly as far as Amaruri to keep their hand in.

And yet there were days . . .

Karl Marx Impact Area, Guyana

The dirt road wound ahead, between two ridges that had been largely cleared by fire of their lesser natural vegetation. Some of that fire over the last three years had been of the burning variety. Some, however, had been of the explosive sort. The latter had often driven the former as the former had burned off all but the stoutest trees along the ridges.

Overhead, a steady stream of freight-train rumbles shook the sky, almost but not quite drowning out the muzzle blasts of the 105mm guns driving those forty pound freight trains from ten miles to the east. Ahead, the ground shook as a round came in nearly every second to one side of the road or the other. Nearest the road, the four guns firing had set their fuses for delay, thus letting the shells drive themselves into the ground before detonating and sending great plumes of earth and rock skyward. Farther out, another four guns had set their fuses to explode on contact, further slashing what vegetation remained and adding to the exercise the *piquancy* of an occasional shell splinter coming just that little bit too close.

The bombardment had only begun four minutes earlier, at a time when Reilly could say with a straight face that the point of the battalion was within antitank missile range. After those four minutes, there were still monkeys leaping through the trees as they shat themselves, while loudly and indignantly crying macaws winged over the treetops.

Reilly had some decidedly odd views on training. One of these was that, if the training didn't contain a moral component, it was hardly worth doing, most of the time.

But I'm half full of shit, he thought, riding forward in the back of his own Eland toward the wall of explosions wracking the two sides of the narrow pass to his front. *Sure, the moral component is critical. But if there were a way to condition men chemically against the dangers and stress of war, I'd still do it this way. Why? Because I need the danger and the excitement. And the boys do, too.*

He thought of them as "boys," or, more commonly, "my boys." In fact, while the average age had dropped substantially since the African operation, it was still considerably north of thirty. No matter; they were still his "boys," to include his sixty-two year old sergeant major, George, and all of his roughly equivalent-aged first sergeants.

For no other reason than to exercise the system, Reilly keyed the microphone by flicking a switch on his combat vehicle crewman's helmet and ordered, "Battalion, this is Black Six. Reconfigure, companies balanced, now."

C Company, the tank company, which had been leading with two platoons of tanks and one of infantry, slowed their pace slightly. Rather, the Third Platoon did. Those tankers slowed their speed not by taking their feet off the gas but by zigzagging. Meanwhile, Second Platoon, also tanks, peeled off to the right and, likewise zigzagging, moved rearward, though in no particular hurry. The infantry platoon, Alpha Company's First, attached to Charlie, on the other hand, picked up the pace to close the gap filled by Second Platoon's leaving of the column.

Somewhere in the rear, Bravo Company's Second Platoon of mechanized infantry began to race forward to their new posting with C Company.

I love my job, Reilly thought, ducking down behind the armor to avoid being splashed as the wheels of Bravo's Second churned through the mud at a breakneck pace, toward the still growing and thickening wall of smoke, dust, and fire ahead.

First Sergeant Pete Schetrompf—who was also Command Sergeant Major (Retired) Pete Schetrompf—tended to be of a somewhat philosophical bent. In his thirty-five years with the United States Army, he'd been to two major wars, where "major" is defined as "half a million troops committed . . . on our side," along with any (mostly classified) number of (classified) in (classified), (classified), and, of course, (classified). Oh, and (*really* classified). That sort of experience tended to give one a certain perspective, a degree of detachment, so to speak.

For example, a less experienced soldier would have been hard pressed to determine anything from the three steady sounds coming from the artillery. For that less experienced soldier, it would likely have proven impossible to consciously figure out the meaning of any given oddity in the mild and repetitive *thumping* coming from the distant firing position, the passage of the overhead freight trains, and the explosions coming from fairly close up ahead. In his own detached way, Schetrompf's mind kept track of all three.

On the other hand, it's kind of hard to maintain detachment when that lunatic . . .

Suddenly, Schetrompf rolled his eyes in his Marty Feldmanesque face and began to dive into the safety of the Eland's compartment. He'd sensed something wrong, an off key note in the artillery symphony. Later on he would figure out that it had probably been the absence of one freight train that had keyed him.

"DUCK, MOTHERFUCKERS!" Schetrompf shouted loud enough to be heard over all three artillery sounds, over the roar of tank and Eland engines, through the muzzle blasts of C Company's tanks, firing at targets as they broke past the two ridges, and even through the ear-encompassing crewmen's helmets and the enveloping armor. Even two or three vehicles away.

Staff Sergeant Dan Kemp barely fit inside the Eland. He was just too big, a huge bear of a man. He was also fairly new in the regiment and corporation, having only taken his retirement and punched out of a billet with Third Battalion, Five-O-Second Infantry about fifteen months prior. He'd arrived here several months after that, having found civilian life degrading to the point of disgusting. Sadly, from his point of view, he'd missed the Suriname dustup. Fortunately, however, next month he'd have completed his years' probation, at which point they'd jump him up to Sergeant First Class and let him buy a share in the regiment's owning corporation, M Day, Inc. Then, he'd truly belong.

About armored vehicles he'd known little at the time, beyond avoiding the bastards, though he'd since learned quite a bit. The mindset had come tougher, learning to think while moving not at two and a half miles an hour, but t anything up to forty or, on a good road, about sixty-five.

This, of course, was barely a road at all, so speed was ot a lot over ten miles an hour. Kemp appreciated that, s it gave him the chance to review the mission and make ome educated guesses at the follow-ons Reilly would toss he battalion's way once they passed the ridges.

Behind and ahead of Kemp's vehicle, the machine unners were letting loose with their pintle-mounted uns, Russian-made KORDs in 12.7mm. These were not nly considerably lighter than the American M-2, they ired at a much higher rate. Even with that higher rate, hough, they weren't really expecting to hit anything, ut—just as in combat—fast flying lead, especially if it ad an audible *crack* to announce its passage, was just the hing to keep an RPG gunner's head down until you were ast his defense and eating his, and his unit's, vitals.

Kemp thought he saw some targets, or perhaps just a adly camouflaged or artillery-uncamouflaged fighting osition, up on the left side ridge's military crest. He eached out to tap the machine gunner, Wilkes, to grab his ttention and direct his fire when the world went bang. nd *bang*. And *Bang*. And *BANG*.

"Oh, shit!" First Sergeant Schetrompf exclaimed from is perch behind the assault line. He'd heard the first all- o-near explosion, then the second nearer one, and finally he one that seemed right next door. The concussion was ke a club laid up alongside the head. Nonetheless, what- ver mental computer had told Schetrompf to duck also ld him it was all clear. He got his head up above the rim f the Eland's passenger compartment in time to see one

of his company vehicles spinning like a top on its left rea
corner, flinging antennae, scraps of tires, weapons, plu
troopers and parts of troopers, in all directions.

Schetrompf lunged for the radio. "Dustoff! Dustof
Dustoff! NOW!"

Air Strip, Regimental Hospital, Camp Fulton, Guyana

Eyes shut tight, Kemp had no idea where he was an
only the vaguest idea of how he'd gotten there. Image
jumbled in a confused, disoriented, frankly shocked sill
mind, all jockeying for place. He recalled clearly only
few things; the top of his driver Wilkes' head coming of
the front end of the Eland lifting while the thing began t
spin, and then himself flying through the air and seein
the armored car spin in a view framed by his flailing leg.

His head hurt and he wanted to puke. Maybe wors
was the pain in his back. He felt pressure lift from h
back, but that did nothing for the pain. Between th
concussion—he was pretty sure he was concussed—an
what felt like a fast descent, he couldn't hold his gorge an
longer. Turning his head to one side, he opened his mout
and spewed forth. That made it a little better until th
aroma reached his nose when it caused his stomach t
lurch.

He felt the landing—it was a hard one, with muc
bouncing—and screamed from the refreshed agony of h
back. He barely noticed the change in pitch from th
motor—*an airplane motor . . . they must have dusted m
off*—as the pilot reversed thrust. That hurt, too.

For a moment, Kemp lost consciousness. When he came to, someone was already pushing the stretcher and backboard on which he lay outward toward the rear of—*a plane . . . they carried me from the range in a small plane*—the aerial ambulance.

As Kemp began to drift off, he caught a glimpse of a pretty face, framed by blond hair. He didn't think he'd seen that face before.

"Are you an angel?" he asked, weakly. "And am I dead?"

The face smiled, angelically enough. "Yes, I am and no, you're not. I'm Elena Constantinescu, one of the hospital nurses. We're going to take good care of you"—Kemp didn't see as she took a quick glance at his evacuation tag—"Sergeant Kemp. And with any luck at all, you'll be fine." Very calmly and confidently, she added, "You've had a bad day, but it's going to get better."

★ CHAPTER SEVEN ★

> "It's a rough war, son, and your own people will steal
> your best men if you don't watch 'em."
> —Robert A. Heinlein, *Starship Troopers*

Surgeons' Lounge, Regimental Hospital, Camp Fulton, Guyana

Though the sign on the door said, "Surgeons' Lounge," in fact the room was open to anyone who owned a share in the corporation, along with the few local doctors and nurses employed by the hospital. Richly paneled from local lumber, it had very much of a "dark wood and dead animals" ambience to it, quite despite there not being a single stuffed trophy on the walls. Indeed, what animal products there were came in the form of leather chairs and sofas that, but for the continuously running air conditioning, would probably have rotted away in short order. Even with the air conditioning, the furniture gave off a sweet smell that suggested that some microorganism or other was trying to eat the leather anyway. It was also, quite possibly, the only American-run hospital in the world where the surgeons' lounge was a smoking area.

"For all his other failings, mental and moral," said McCaverty, through a dense cloud of cigar smoke, "thank God Reilly's an asshole about making the troops wear their helmets." He looked quizzically at the growing ash on the end of his cigar and, deciding enough was enough, flicked it into a cigar ashtray stationed by his usual chair.

"He's an asshole, all right," agreed Phillie Stauer, nee Potter, who still bore a grudge against Reilly over some humiliation he had once dished out to her. The tall, blond, jade-eyed chief of nursing could still turn heads, and regularly did. Considering she'd borne two children, neither of them small, in the last four years since the regiment formed, her waist was remarkably narrow and her hips exceptionally well defined.

Scott Joseph, Regimental Medical Officer, Chief of the Hospital and, for the last day, the back-up surgeon, just nodded, exhausted. He was the spitting image of Ghostbusters' Egon, except considerably more tired looking at the moment.

"We'd have had at least three more dead if he weren't," McCaverty added. "Or maybe four."

"Not four," Joseph said. "Helmet had nothing to do with Patricks. Thing I can't figure is that with all that mayhem and blood, bodies and parts of bodies everywhere, he gets up and walks away with hardly a scratch. I mean, it's not like he didn't get thrown."

"Not so odd," Elena Constantinescu said, her Romanian accent nearly gone by now, after four years with the regiment. "I asked him when I was stitching up the one little cut he had. He said that he'd been standing up asleep and so was completely relaxed when he hit.

Didn't even know a shell had landed nearby unt
someone told him so."

"Still freaky," Joseph insisted. "How the hell doe
someone *sleep* with that shit going on?" he aske
rhetorically.

"I asked that, too," Elena replied. "He says unless the
bullets are really flying with hostile intent, he tends to find
life boring in general."

Joseph shook his head. There were some things about
the people in the regiment he found incomprehensible,
even now.

"What do you want to do with Kemp?" McCaverty
asked, changing the subject. "They immobilized him well
at the scene, and I've got a regimen of methylpred-
nisolone going. But do we try to treat him here or send
him Stateside?"

Joseph considered that. "I've got a pretty good in at
Baylor, which is a great place for physical and occupational
therapy. Surgery, too, for that matter. We could send him
there."

"Budget cover it?"

Joseph shrugged. "It's not a budgetary issue; Kemp's
covered by Tricare. I'm sure Stauer will supplement any
difference; line of duty and all."

"How badly off is he?" Elena asked.

McCaverty took a deep, lung-destroying puff of his
cigar. "Hard to say," he answered. "His injuries were his
back and one knee, plus a concussion. I'd stake thirty
years of neuro experience that he's fine in the head, but
backs and knees are tough. They rarely really heal perfectly,
even in a young man. And Kemp's not that young."

★ ★ ★

"You're getting too old for this, you know, Sergeant Kemp," said Reilly, visiting his wounded in their hospital rooms. He'd showered and put on a clean uniform, not for his own sake, but because Doc Joseph and the medical staff would have met him at the door with rifles if he'd tried to bring any unnecessary dirt into *their* pride and joy.

Kemp shook his head *no* but verbally agreed. "No shit, sir." His leg was in a cast. Reilly was pleased to see that he wasn't in any kind of traction.

"They won't tell me anything here—afraid to upset me, I guess—but who did we lose?"

"Well . . . Milo Wilkes is dead. Do you remember that much?"

"Yes, sir," Kemp replied. "Better now than at first. You're not likely to live when half your brain goes up in the air while the rest of it stays behind your face."

"No, not likely," Reilly agreed. "Anyway, we lost him and Simowitz, dead . . . "

"What happened to Sim?" Kemp asked.

"Hit a tree head first. Broke his neck."

"Shit."

"Shit," Reilly agreed. "Thing is, we were actually lucky. If your Eland had been moving half a kilometer an hour faster, the thing probably would have hit it. Then nobody would have survived."

"What are we doing with the bodies?"

"Milo's folks wanted him sent home. His corpse goes out tonight with an escort. Simo's don't seem to care much; he's going into the regimental cemetery tomorrow afternoon. We, at least, care."

That seemed reasonable to Kemp. He asked, "Do we know what happened?"

Reilly nodded his head, then explained, "We froze the battery in place and checked all data. It was fine. Then we grilled the crews. They swear there was no change to the settings after the freeze order. Right now we think—we're pretty sure—that it was a bad lot of one-o-five. Going through that lot, we've found defective charges in about an eighth of the boxes we've looked at so far. Stauer's ordered the entire lot sequestered and destroyed, about a million bucks' worth. We're not going to have much 105mm firing in support for about four months; that's how long it will be before an order for more will be filled. I think there are only about twelve hundred rounds left in the inventory after the bad lot's taken out. And Stauer says we can't use any of it until our full load is replaced."

Kemp nodded his head, but only once before a wave of nausea overtook him. After several long moments of heavy breathing, he asked, "The others?"

"All hurt, except for one, but they'll be fine."

"The Eland?" Kemp asked.

"Seriously fucked up. We going to part it out and take a new, rather a rebuilt, one from the float park."

Kemp nodded, then winced. That made sense. Hesitating, in the way a man will when he doesn't neces-sarily want to hear the answer, he asked, "Me?"

Reilly sighed. "You're a problem," he admitted. "Right now you're doped up. Doubt you can even feel much of what's wrong with you. But your injuries make it extremely unlikely you'll be fit for a squad, let alone a platoon, any-time this side of the sun running out of hydrogen."

Doped up or not, for Kemp that was a jolt of pure fear for the future. "So now what? Am I out on the street, sir?"

Reilly shook his head. "The regiment doesn't play that way. You've got some choices. You can take a lump sum disability—and it isn't especially ungenerous—and go home to therapy. Doc Joseph's working on setting something up in Houston for that. Or you can go as a supernumerary to either the regimental three or four shop. For that, we can hire a local physical therapist and you'll take time off from your normal duties for therapy. Or, you can go to Texas for therapy, still draw regular pay, and then go to either regimental three or four."

The three shop, for "S-3," under the American, which is to say the French, system, handled operations and training. The four was logistics.

"Can I think about that?" Kemp asked.

"Sure. Take your time. And speaking of time,"—Reilly glanced at his watch—"I've got to get my ass out to the parade field for the assumption of command of the new Second Battalion commander. You could see it from your window, but if you get out of bed before the medicos say you can I'll send Sergeant Major George over to break your other leg."

Kemp chuckled. That caused him to wince, too. *Not that I don't think for a minute you wouldn't have the sergeant major do just that.*

As Reilly turned to leave, Kemp asked, "Are you in any shit over this, sir?"

Reilly shrugged. "Other than how it feels inside to lose two of my boys, no. Oh, Stauer's not happy with me, but then he rarely is."

Building 26, Camp Fulton, Guyana
(Second Battalion Headquarters)

Von Ahlenfeld hadn't been this happy in, *Oh, a very long time.*

My own battalion of Special Forces, and without a single fucking politician to report to; how great is that?

Sitting behind a wooden desk that was perhaps a trifle too small to comfortably fit his large frame, von Ahlenfeld looked from face to face of the commanders, staff and senior noncoms that made up the leadership of his battalion. These included the Russian executive office, Konstantin—balding, graying where not balding, solid like a bear and with clear blue eyes, Welch—commanding A Company, not as solid through the body as Konstantin but perhaps even more muscular and certainly taller, Hilton— a little bit of a runt—commanding Bravo, Charlie, under White, the oldest of the crew of commanders, though for all that he was old, he fidgeted with the energy of a much younger man, Gene Maldon—in charge of D Company and therefore of the battalion's initial training, specialist training—most of it, and leadership training programs, and, lastly of the commanders, a rather somber Headquarters Company commander, Wahab, an African who was hiding out from the vengeance of his chief for permitting the regiment to get away with a really outrageous sum of cash, and to screw said chief out of a vast estate in Brazil.

Also present was the sergeant major, Rob "Rattus"

Hampson. Of the entire crew, von Ahlenfeld had only had the chance to get to know Rattus to any degree. So far, his opinion confirmed Stauer's: "Good man, for all he's a medic."

At a long conference table that stretched forth from von Ahlenfeld's large but still undersized desk, the others sat in order: Welch, Hilton, White, Konstantin—at the very end, with the staff in a line behind him, Maldon, Wahab, and—"seated at the right hand of the father"— the sergeant major.

"Sir," began Konstantin, in an accent in which the Russian was virtually lost. He'd been well trained in American English at some time in the past. "Your commanders and staff are formed and present."

"Very good, XO," the new commander said. "Now, gentlemen, by companies and then staff sections, tell me about this battalion."

"So you're telling me that our number one priority has to be to convince the regimental commander to break this attachment, or detachment, or habitual relationship, with the Third, Fourth, and Fifth Battalions?"

"Yes, sir," Hilton confirmed. "It *sounded* like a good idea when we started, but it hasn't ever quite worked out. The leadership of those companies never knows which way to look, us here or the battalions' own command and staff. Some of them aren't above playing us off against each other, either."

The adjutant added, "Sir, and that's not even counting the administrative nightmare of the D Companies . . . "

"D Companies?"

"Deployed companies, sir," the adjutant answered. "Though, in fact, they are the Delta Companies, reinforced, of the Third and Fourth Battalions, and the Fourth Platoons of Fifth Battalion's companies and the battery."

"I concur with Major Hilton, sir," Rattus offered. "Sure, there are a couple of advantages, coordination-wise, to doing it this way. But those guys are generally pros. They'll work well with us even if we don't have that constant flow between the two."

"Also, sir," offered the battalion's adjutant, "we're short as shit on medics. If we can transfer some of them out of Third, Fourth, and Fifth we could be one hundred percent here, even if most of them wouldn't be Delta"—Special Forces Medic—"qualified."

"Sir," said Rattus, "get me control of them back again and I'll *make* them into Deltas. Personally."

"All right," von Ahlenfeld agreed. "You think it's that important; I'll go to the wall with Stauer over this."

"Won't be much going to the wall required, sir," Rattus replied. "He hides it, but he's been ambivalent about the arrangement for . . . well, for a good long time. Guaranteed; he'll only need a nudge.

"And, sir? I guarantee you you'll make friends for life out of those battalion commanders, especially Cazz, in Third. As much of a pain in the ass this has been for us, for them it's been worse."

"There is a downside, sir," the adjutant offered. "Reilly, in first battalion, is a thief. Of people. That habitual relationship—or whatever you want to call it—has protected the cadres of the mostly Guyanan companies. Take it away, and he'll be looting them for personnel in no time."

Building 16, Camp Fulton, Guyana

"Sir," announced Sergeant Major George, big, red-headed, and beefy, "there's a captain here, from Third Battalion, who would like a brief word with you."

"Ah," Reilly smiled to match his senior noncom, "that would be Captain Coleman. By all means, send him in, Top."

"I took the liberty of calling Coleman's operations-*cum*-first sergeant, sir," George said before turning away. "He comes highly recommended."

"Who's the first shirt over there, Top?"

"Harrelson. He's good troops."

Reilly nodded. If George said that X recommended Y and X was good troops, that was good enough for him. "What about Webster?" he asked.

George shook his head. "Nah. I figured you still might not want Coleman, even with your wife in the family way, and if I ask Webster he'll tell Cazz and then Coleman's life will be made living hell for his 'disloyalty.' "

Reilly waved a finger. "See? I *knew* there were reasons I kept you on."

"Besides that, without me, you couldn't pour piss from a boot with the instructions written on the heel?" George joked.

"Right," Reilly agreed, smiling, "besides that. Send Coleman in."

"Well, that settles that," said Reilly, as he and George

watched a deliriously happy Captain Coleman walk—no, float—above the asphalt between the headquarters and his car.

George asked, "Does he know what a fucking hard job it is and how bloody difficult it's going to be to fill Lana's shoes?"

"I told him," Reilly replied. "I'm not sure he really understands, but I told him."

"What are you going to do with Lana?" the sergeant major asked.

"First things first," Reilly said. "And first I've got to do a little finessing and some horse trading to a) find a slot for Lana she won't find insulting and b) bribe Cazz to let Coleman go. Unless, of course, Coleman succeeds in what I told him to do and gets Cazz to accept the political benefits of having someone from his battalion in a good position to get support from this battalion. I mean, hell, we've got more trucks than the rest combined. That alone would make it worth it."

"Well . . . it's true enough," George said. "There are a lot of potential benefits to Third Batt if First owes them a favor."

"You know that," Reilly answered. "I know that. But Cazz is a jarhead . . . "

"Hey, hey, sir!" George mock-warned. "I served in the Corps, too, for four long years."

"Sure. But I try not to hold that one black mark against you."

★ CHAPTER EIGHT ★

I offer hunger, thirst, forced marches,
battles and death. Let him who loves his country in his
heart and not with his lips only, follow me.
—Giuseppe Garibaldi

Highway 15, Easter Valley, Venezuela

Under thick, weeping skies, amidst the roar of a tropical
deluge pounding roof, trees, and ground, the Venezuelan
Army bus crept slowly along the potted asphalt road. The
wipers tried to keep the windshield clear, but just weren't
up to the task at any speed beyond a crawl. For that matter,
the roof of the bus was subpar for keeping the water out;
a steady drip-drip-drip splashed driver and passengers
alike. Near the front, just behind the driver, the uniformed
sergeant escorting the volunteers rocked, more or less
asleep, with the movement of the bus.

Staring out a left side window, Lily Vargas' sleeping
head resting on his right shoulder, Carlos Villareal saw
only intermittently, when the lightning flashed, say, or
another vehicle passed the bus in either direction.

Though passing this bus, he thought, *on a night like this, is more foolhardy than anything Lily and I signed up for. At least, I* hope *it is.*

With a sigh, Carlos reached up—careful not to disturb the sleeping Lily—to wipe away some of the water that had collected in his hair and was beginning to run down his forehead.

Oh, well. At least it isn't cold.

Yet, he amended. He understood that it could get quite chilly in the mountains, or when you were wet and the wind picked up. Oh, maybe not cold as a gringo might define it, but cold enough for someone used to Venezuela's usual oppressive and moisture-laden heat.

The pair, plus the other eighteen volunteers from his neighborhood security group, had turned in their rifles and been issued small vouchers for meals and considerably larger—two million Bolivars, about a thousand gringo dollars—enlistment bonuses.

On the hunch that the money might soon depreciate radically, Carlos had cashed his check and given the money to his mother with the firm instructions, "Buy necessities, Mama. Things that might get tight if we end up in a war. Or something." He could only hope that his mother, never the most responsible of women, would follow his guidance.

Lily, on the other hand, had put hers in the bank. Only time would tell which approach had been the right one if, indeed, it would make any difference.

Maybe we should have each bought land. But how can you be sure the government wouldn't take it? And how could we be sure that they wouldn't seize some rich bastards' estates and give them away . . . as long as you didn't already own some of your own.

Headquarters, Fifth Division, *Ciudad* Bolivar, Venezuela

It was the squealing of the brakes as the bus slowed to pull through the gates of 5th Division's main cantonment that awakened Carlos. Lily still slept until he nudged her.

"Wazzafugama?" she murmured, blinking sleep from her eyes.

"We're here, Lily," Carlos answered.

Lily sat straight up then, rubbed at her eyes, and leaned over to stare out the bus window.

"Crap," she said, looking at the ruins of what had once been a rather neat and tidy military base. "And I thought la Dolorita was a dump."

Carlos didn't have time to comment before the bus driver jumped to attention. Waving the driver back to his seat, Captain Larralde stepped up onto the main deck of the bus.

"Relax," Larralde said. "This is not where you're going. Though compared to where you *are* going, you may think this place is not so bad."

"Where's that, sir?" Lily asked, as she thought, *Worse than this? Oh, hell.*

"A tent city we've set up near the clothing and equipment issue warehouse," he replied, not so much to Lily as to the new recruits present, generally. "We'll be there about two days; that's how long it will take to get you fitted and get all your inoculations . . . of which there are many. There are several thousand of you, so it could take longer, maybe four days at the outside. When you're not standing in line, for equipment issue or shots, my sergeants will be giving you the rudiments of military drill. That, and physical training." He shrugged. "It's not the best thing for you to be doing, but it's about all we can do, here and now.

"From here," he continued, "we'll be heading, about a hundred of you people and fifty of mine, to another tent city, out in the . . . well . . . it's not the exact middle of nowhere, but you can see it from there on a clear day. Which won't happen very often. That's where you'll do most of your training in the time we have."

Larralde forced himself not to shake his head with despair and disgust. Whatever its other flaws, and he knew they were many, the Venezuelan army had never before in his experience stinted on time to train new troops.

We used to take nearly a year, the captain thought, *to turn a civilian into a soldier. And I suspect we needed every day of it. Cowardly culture? No. But military culture? Also no. I've got my doubts we can do it in a mere ten or eleven weeks. Maybe the gringos can, but they're different, a different culture. And unless procurement does a better job than they usually do, we'll be lucky even to put the veneer of competence on this rabble in the time we have.*

And, of course, politics dictates we train the women and the men together . . . and at that we have no experience whatsoever.

Larralde sighed again, expecting that it would become a major feature of his routine respiration. "You won't be seeing a lot of me in the near future. So let me introduce you to . . ."

★ ★ ★

Sergento-Mayor de Segunda, or Second Sergeant Major, Arrivillaga was a *very* unhappy man. Bad enough that the captain had dumped this one on him; at least he wasn't unique in that regard. But the rules he was told to operate under:

"No, Sergeant Major, you may not beat the new recruits with sticks. No, you may not run them until they suffer cardiac arrest. No, you may not chop off their food with no notice for a week at a time. No, you may not keep them from sleeping for more than twenty-four hours at a time. Oh, all right; thirty-six hours. But no, you may not shout at them—especially not the girls—until they cry. You must use *positive* motivators."

Oh, Captain, Arrivillaga thought, *have you any idea at all what you're asking of me? Of us? What positive motivators? I let the top performing boys fuck the girls? Let top performing girls at the captain? Bah.*

Even so, Arrivillaga knew the captain had his best interests at heart. These were all *revolutionary* boys and girls, which is to say each and every one of them had a hotline to someone who had a hotline to Chavez. And, if abused, or if they thought they were being abused, Arrivillaga might well find himself counting monkeys in Amazonas State, a fate devoutly to be avoided. *Though, on the other hand, I've got a hotline to Chavez, too. Still, rather not use it if I don't have to.*

Arrivillaga, five foot eight, stocky, and mestizo, with hair gone steel-gray, was something of a rarity in Venezuelan military circles, as was his captain. Both could speak English, though that was not that unusual. Far more rare, almost unique, in fact, both were graduates of the United States Army's Ranger School, based out of Fort Benning, Georgia. This had been in the past when United States-Venezuelan relations had been both good and noncontroversial. They were fairly good again, of course, officially. The difference was that, in the past, the again growing Republican Party hadn't wanted Venezuela's leader strung up.

It was that, the experience of Ranger School, that had led Larralde to caution Arrivillaga, personally and especially.

Sighing, as had his captain before him, Arrivillaga stepped onto the bus at Larralde's beckoning signal. The captain had then taken off for the next bus in line.

Arrivillaga couldn't keep a frown of distaste from his face, or scorn from his voice, as he said, "Boys and girls, I am Second Sergeant Major Mao Stalin Arrivillaga. No, I am not a communist; neither was my father. No, I am not an internationalist; neither was my father. No, I am neither Russian nor Chinese nor Georgian, in whole or in part.

"My father simply admired Russian and Chinese military achievements. Hence my name.

"I am a nationalist, a Bolivarian to the extent that I care about *this* country. I care about no other.

"For you . . . creatures, it doesn't matter anyway. For you, I am Sergeant Major Arrivillaga . . . or sir.

"Now, when I turn my back on you rabble, and step off the bus, I will begin to count. By the time I reach three—not four, not two, and five's right out—you will be off this bus and standing in two lines . . ."

★ ★ ★

Lily groaned as she lay back on her stiff folding cot. Every muscle and joint hurt, and she was pretty sure it was not from the light physical training she'd done, so much as a reaction to the twenty-one distinct inoculations she'd received, ranging from hepatitis to typhoid, tetanus to yellow fever.

On the other side of the tent, likewise behind the thin cloth partition—nothing more than a couple of white sheets—someone had strung up to separate the boys from the girls, Eva Gollarza tsked, sympathetically. Her sympathy was somewhat strained, however, since she'd had exactly the same shots and felt approximately as miserable as Lily.

Even so, Eva dragged herself out of her own cot and staggered over to feel Lily's forehead.

"You know," Eva said, "I'd say you don't have a fever except that I'm sure I *do* and if you feel normal to me . . ."

"What I want to know, sir," Arrivillaga said, "is where the fucking inoculations came from. Half my new people are sick, and the rest are sicker."

Larralde found himself sighing again. "Cuba, Mao, they came from Cuba."

"Let me guess; Fidel had an excess of old, contaminated, and condemned stocks that nobody would buy and so he donated them to the cause?"

"Good a guess as any," the captain conceded. "We should have known better to listen to that fat, gringo propagandist.

"Now what's this going to do to our schedule?" Larralde asked. "Every platoon is in the same boat."

"Not much good," Arrivillaga replied, with a headshake.

"Not here anyway. I can make them draw equipment while they puke. Besides that, we weren't doing anything *here* all that important. And who cares about square bashing? But if they don't get better soon . . ."

"Yeah, I know. By the way, did anybody *not* get sick?"

Arrivillaga inflated his cheeks, then let the air escape with a raspberry sound. "Villareal got over it in about a day, which would be normal even with *safe* inoculations. I figure the boy has a strong constitution. Seems like a good kid. Shame we're not going to be allowed to turn him into a real soldier."

Carlos had been the only one able to go to the mess tent under his own power. As such, Arrivillaga had told him to wash his hands carefully and get a container—the sergeant major actually said "Mermite can," whatever that was—and pick up breakfast for the rest.

The cooks had been happy enough having someone to deliver the meal. They were already overtasked trying to feed groups where *nobody* was fit to walk.

"Make sure you bring this back as soon as possible," the beefy mess sergeant had insisted, tapping the can. "We just don't have enough and unless this is back and cleaned before lunch *nobody's* going to be eating at midday."

Breakfast had been simple: *Perico*—a national dish mainly consisting of scrambled eggs, with an admixture of onions, olives, and peppers—as well as several loaves of round bread. The cooks had bundled the bread, along with some paper plates and plastic spoons, plus twenty small cardboard juice boxes and a plastic garbage bag, into a napkin. The *perico* they'd packed into the greenish, thick-walled can which Carlos then had to struggle with all the way back to the tent. It wouldn't have been such a pain in the ass except that the napkin was large enough to drag on the ground if he used both hands, as he had to, to transport the container.

He cursed the can and the napkin the entire way.

There was no sense in asking the people to line up to be fed. This much Carlos understood immediately. And if he hadn't, the smell of vomit and shit would have told him so. Instead, he opened the can and laid out the napkin in the center of the tent. The *perico* had smelled pretty good back in the mess tent. Here? It just couldn't compete.

First, he delivered the boxes of fruit juice on the twin theory that a) people who couldn't eat could still drink and b) they'd damned well better. *Besides,* he thought, *if they'll drink a little something maybe they'll have the strength to eat.*

As he delivered the fruit juice, he checked each of his fellow volunteers for excessive fever, the simple way, as his mother had checked him in his boyish years, hand to forehead. *Nothing seems outright life-threatening.*

Drinks delivered, he had a better idea of who would and would not eat. Most were willing to try, though Lily just shook her head before leaning over the edge of her cot to retch into a washpan.

By twos, Carlos filled paper plates with the mixture and added a slab of bread to each. He didn't have a knife, so that was a matter of breaking it with his hands. Then, again by twos, he carried the full plates to his comrades. In some cases the plates sat there untouched on quivering stomachs. Still, most tried to choke down a bite or two.

"You'll have to feed Lily, Carlos," Eva said weakly after Villareal placed her plate on her belly. Eva's hand waved in the direction of Lily's cot. "She just can't eat on her own."

"Feed . . . . ? I suppose you're right." *But, God, she stinks. Still . . . sure.*

Carefully averting his nose as he pushed the filthy washpan away, Carlos knelt beside Lily, placed the plate on her, lifted her head with one hand and began to scoop with a spoon held in the other.

She only threw up three more times in the course of the meal.

"The medicos figured out what's wrong," Larralde told Arrivillaga. "The fucking Hepatitis A was contaminated with salmonella."

"What are they going to do about it?" the sergeant major asked.

"Nothing much they can do. We're advised to give the troops plenty of rest, plenty of liquids, soft and bland foods. The mess section's going to get some real yoghurt, which will supposedly help. I'm not sure how. We can draw electrolyte mixes from the hospital . . . that and something for the diarrhea. There's no way they can handle all the cases individually so starting this evening the doctors will issue something they call 'cipromax' which was *not* donated by Cuba."

"How long to recovery?"

"As much as three weeks, though we can hope for less."

"Fuck!"

★CHAPTER NINE★

One might have thought the world would stop ascribing
moral equivalence between acts of terrorism and acts of
punishing terrorism. It has not happened that way.
—Theadore Bikel

SCIF, Camp Fulton, Guyana

The signs confused him. Based on the message he'd
received, von Ahlenfeld didn't know if he should head for
"lawyers," "guns," or "money." He'd have been standing
there, still confused, if Peter Lox hadn't come on the
scene and showed him the way to the facility conference
room.

"It doesn't have a nickname, sir," Lox informed him.
"We're still working on that."

Boxer was there when von Ahlenfeld arrived, as was
Waggoner, the operations officer, Stauer, Kosciusko, the
chief of the naval squadron, Cruz from aviation, plus
"Gordo" Gordan and Victor Inning from logistics and
procurement, respectively. All were seated around a large

wooden conference table that von Ahlenfeld suspected strongly was local mahogany. Oddly enough, one of the Second Battalion commander's company chiefs, Welch, face covered in camouflage paint, was already there and waiting.

"They tapped me when I was out in the training area, giving the final after action review to First of the Fifth Marines, sir," Welch explained. Von Ahlenfeld noticed that both of the men to Welch's side had edged their chairs away as far as possible.

"We've got a contract for a heavily reinforced company for up to three months," Stauer began, without preamble. "But we're not sure we want to take it."

"We *don't* want to take it, Wes," Boxer objected. "And not because of any other ramifications but because of what's going on west of here."

"We'll talk about that later," Stauer commanded. "For now, let's handle one problem at a time. Brief him, please, Ralph. Have a seat, Lee."

Shaking his head, Boxer stood up and walked to a podium at one end of the conference table. A map of the Philippines flashed on a wall display, a plasma screen, behind Boxer. He picked up a thumb sized remote control and pressed a small button on it.

"Three days ago," the Chief of Staff began, as an explosive symbol appeared on the map, over Manila, "the second richest man in the Philippines, Lucio Ayala, was kidnapped by what we believe to be a splinter organization off of Abu Sayyaf, known as 'al Harrikat,' the Movement. The split appears to have been based more on financial than ideological or religious reasons, though those may well be present, too. It is also possible that the kidnapping was arranged by one or more of Ayala's children, impatient at the old man's refusal to die and leave them his fortune."

"We don't know that," Waggoner objected.

Boxer shook his head. "No, we don't. But at least one of my contacts in the Philippines thinks it more than merely possible. As does Ayala's wife, who actually arranged for us to be contacted, on my contact's advice."

"Who's your contact?" Stauer asked, then amended, "You don't have to give me a name, of course."

Boxer shrugged. "In her case she's a pretty well-known name, at least locally. Aida Farallon, Police Inspector. Joined the Manila police at age thirty-seven, seeking revenge for a policeman husband who'd been killed. Hurt al Qaeda *badly*, all on her own, and probably saved the pope's life. The old pope, I mean." Boxer looked around the room at gray heads and weathered faces and smiled. "You know, now that I think about it, Aida would fit in here to a T."

"She might at that," Stauer said. "I've no objection to you making an offer, if you think we could use her."

Boxer went silent, thinking about that for a moment. "Maybe," he finally half agreed. "For her family's sake, she might, if you were willing to take a package deal."

"We've done these sorts of things before, three times," Stauer explained for the newcomer's benefit. "And we've established something of an SOP for dealing with kidnapping cases where we can't find the victim for a rescue, but can identify the kidnappers and, more importantly, their families."

"You take counterhostages?" von Ahlenfeld asked.

"Yes. Precisely. But for a couple of reasons, that's not

likely to work here." Stauer indicated with a chin point that Boxer was to continue.

"Al Harrikat," Boxer said, "doesn't appear to *have* families, or at least none that can be identified. They're a splinter group, so it is believed, because the rest of Abu Sayyaf got so disgusted with them they were cast out. If you know anything about the Abus, you know the al Harrikats must be singularly vile.

"We can pin Ayala down, or at least we think we can, to Mindanao"—the map flashed to the Philippine Republic's large, southern island—"which is too big to help much. That said, by now, he may have been moved to Basilan, which is smaller, but even more densely populated and more of an al Harrikat stronghold than Mindanao is."

Having a sudden thought, Boxer looked at Lox. "Don't you speak Tagalog, Peter?" he asked.

"I do," Lox agreed, "but it wouldn't necessarily be all that much help. Down Mindanao-way most people speak Cebuano. There are some points of congruency but they're not all that many or close. They're not mutually intelligible, anyway."

"May still be useful," Stauer said. "Keep going, Ralph."

Boxer nodded. "Roger. The Harrikats have demanded one hundred and twenty-five million United States dollars for the old man's return. That represents about a fifteenth of his total net worth, but probably everything the family could come up with on short notice without a distress sale.

"They've forced the old man to produce a video ordering his family to pay. The children are hiding behind Philippine law, which is one reason my contacts there think one or more of them is in on it, and refusing. The Harrikats have threatened to send them one of Ayala's fingers as a gesture of sincerity."

"Nasty fuckers," von Ahlenfeld said, without emotion. After all, it wasn't as if sending dismembered body parts wasn't a fairly normal procedure for this sort of thing. "How do we do this?"

"We don't," Boxer insisted. "If we did hire ourselves out to the family, the one or more of them behind the kidnapping would let al Harrikat know we're coming. And how we're coming. Exercise in futility and we have more important things to worry about."

"Maybe we don't but maybe we do," Stauer replied. "Certainly, we don't let ourselves get hired by the whole family to mount a rescue. Is there anyone in the family we can trust?"

"There is," Boxer conceded. "Philippine Intelligence says the matriarch of the clan, Paloma Ayala, is extremely unlikely to be part of any plot on the part of any of her children to do away with her husband."

"Would she be willing to let *us* keep a bit over half the ransom, provided we get her husband back for her?" Stauer asked.

"What do you mean?" Waggoner asked.

"Well, what did they offer us to get the old man back? Thirty-five million, right? So we make it a double or nothing deal; we get him back and keep seventy, returning the rest, or we fail to get him back and get nothing."

"In that case," asked Boxer, "why should they make a deal with us. They can get him back . . . ohhh . . . right, forget what I just said."

"Exactly," said Stauer. "If they pay the ransom they'll never get him back. And, to tell the truth, I would undertake this—assuming it can be done—on our own ticket just to keep the fucking lunatics from having that much money to hand."

"You're fucking up, Wes," Boxer growled. "We have a growing problem to the west of us. I can *feel* it in my bones. And this is a losing proposition."

"It's a losing proposition to let al Harrikat get their hands on that much money, too," Stauer countered. He pushed his chair away from the table and stood up. Then he began to pace.

"Gentleman," Stauer asked, "*why* does this regiment and corporation exist?"

Boxer snorted. "We exist because a whole bunch of us hated civilian life and didn't want to just fade away, or to go gently into that good night. That, and that the money's decent."

Stauer shook his head. "No, Ralph, that's why we came to exist. It isn't why we still do exist. Nor even the money. Or, at least, it isn't all of it."

Sighing, Stauer said, "We exist because civilization is on the ropes. The consensus for it, among those who ought most to be defending it, is breaking down. It wasn't perfect, so the elites have lost interest in it. Gangs rule. Borders are either superfluous or are fast becoming so. Citizenship means less and less with each passing day, and with each passing day and each further breakdown in civilization, people look out for what matters, their families. Power is devolving to an unelected and unutterably corrupt elite who wrap themselves in some pretty damned thin shrouds of cosmopolitan holiness but who *really* watch out for their own gene pools.

"This used to be true only in the Third World. Increasingly, it's everywhere."

Victor Inning and Ralph Boxer exchanged glances. Victor's late father-in-law had once said something very similar to that, in a café not far from the Lubyanka.

"States can no longer summon the will to do what must be done to preserve civilization," Stauer continued. "Simple as that. And the very transnational progressives who are undermining the rule of states stand with gaping jaws because groups like ours have arisen to fill the gap.

"Well, who else is to do it?" Stauer scoffed. "The UN, competent only in corruption? The International Committee of the Red Cross and Red Crescent? Puhleeze! OXFAM? MerciCorps? Amnesty International? No, they're too busy making sure states crumble, and keeping wars going by making sure all combatants on all sides are fed, to do much about maintaining civilization.

"What would it mean if a group like al Harrikat got its hands on a hundred and twenty million dollars?"

"Two nuclear weapons," Victor Inning muttered. "Maybe three."

"What was that?" Stauer asked. "Loud enough for everyone to hear, please."

"I said," Victor repeated, louder, "that that much money could buy two nuclear weapons, or maybe three." He looked shamefaced as he added, "Look, I sold guns. Retail death, and not always for a bad purpose or to a bad result. But I *know*—I'm *not* guessing—that any of the ninety-seven nuclear weapons still unaccounted for from old Soviet stockpiles are for sale for between thirty and fifty million dollars apiece."

"Ninety-seven?" Boxer asked. "I thought it was one hundred and four."

Inning sighed. "Al Qaeda has seven of them already. But they bought cheap and so haven't been able to get one to work."

Boxer had good reason to believe that Victor's sources were, or at least had been, impeccable. "Fuck."

"Indeed," Victor agreed.

"Fine," Boxer conceded to Stauer. "Maybe we do have an obligation to take care of this. But that doesn't mean we can."

"No. No, it doesn't. Who or what should we send to give us the best possible chance?"

Welch, who appeared to have been doodling, looked over at his new battalion commander. Von Ahlenfeld gave an *I am too new to have any freaking idea* shrug. Terry piped up, "My company plus one infantry company from Third or Fourth Battalion, three HIPs, both the MI-28 gunships, three CH-750's, three or four RPV's, whatever can be spared, one of the two assault transport capable freighters, one patrol boat and two LCM's—that's all we've got covered space for in Georgetown, anyway, right?—and proportional combat and service support packages from all the above." Welch cast a wary glance at the naval commander, asking, "Sir, any chance I could get one of the midget subs?"

Kosciusko answered, "I can let you have *Namu* and a two-man crew. *Naughtius*, as usual, needs some servicing."

"That'll work, sir." Terry tallied some numbers,

announcing, "I make it just about three hundred and eighty personnel, pending some finessing."

Boxer, however, stood firm. "No, Terry, you can't have the *Namu*. We can shit you a couple of SeaBobs, but the sub's going to be needed elsewhere. And we're likely to need the helicopters. And you can't have a whole infantry company."

Stauer considered this and, ultimately, agreed with Boxer about the sub. "No minisub, Terry. No Hips. You can have both of the MI-28's, since they wouldn't survive long against serious fighter cover. You can also have one LCM, and no patrol boats." He considered that request for an infantry company. "Delta Company, Third Battalion, is coming off contract within the next three weeks. You can take Charlie, Third Battalion, and Delta will fall back in on Cazz to replace Charlie."

"Not replacing them on the contract mission?" von Ahlenfeld asked.

"We don't *have* that mission anymore," Boxer said. He gave Lava a dirty look. "We were underbid."

"Not my doing," von Ahlenfeld insisted.

Stauer looked at Lava and considered, *Send Cazz to be in charge on the ground or let Terry spread his wings? Terry's good, but young. Not Cazz, since most of Cazz's troops stay here . . . and . . . mmm . . . Waggoner to be in overall charge? No, I need him here. Hate to send von Ahlenfeld out, given that he's still getting his feet on the ground. But I think it will have to be him. On the other hand, I can give Lee a month or five weeks here, then he can fly to meet the ship somewhere. Maybe even in the Philippines.*

Stauer turned to Kosciusko. "How long to get them there?"

"Be a week to switch around the crews and have an assault capable ship at Georgetown. Another four days to load, surreptitiously. Assuming we want to avoid going through the Panama Canal—"

"We do," Stauer said.

"—then thirty-six to thirty-eight days sailing. On site in about seven weeks from when you say 'go.' I could cut that by five days or so but only at the cost of a prodigious amount of fuel."

"We'll discuss time on target later," Stauer replied. "At this point, it's too early to say. Lee, you'll be going as OIC, though you don't have to leave when the ship sails. Terry, that schedule work for you?"

"Not exactly," Welch said. "As soon as the boat departs, I'll leave by air with a small party, one team and half the headquarters plus . . . if you don't mind, sir,"—that last was directed as Boxer—"Mr. Lox. He may not speak Cebuano, but he knows the Philippines."

"Since the boss is not going to listen to me about the big thing," Boxer said, with poor grace, "I've no objection to the trivia. Except you should not match your departure to the ship. Leave soon, as soon as possible."

"Be smarter," said Lox, "if you send me first, with Terry, as in tomorrow or the day after, to contact and coordinate with Mrs. Ayala and Philippine Intel."

Stauer thought about that for all of two seconds before saying, "Agreed. Except . . . ."

"How do we buy time," Lox interrupted, "while we're

waiting for the ship to get there? A lot can happen in seven weeks."

Boxer shook his head. "As much as I don't like this idea, in general, Filipino kidnappers rarely have any issues with hanging on to their captives for years at a time. Worse than FARC that way. God save us from patient terrorists."

"Advise the family," Stauer told Lox, "rather, advise the matriarch to buy time with token payments, a few hundred thousand here and there. If there's a chance, use that time to get as much information on the Harrikats as possible."

"What if we can grab a few?" Welch asked. "Grab them in some way that doesn't point to a rescue."

"Break out the pincers, the charcoal, the pliers, and the field telephones," Stauer answered soberly. "These people have no rights. Moreover, they must not get and keep that money, because there is no difference in practice between the money and what it can buy."

"Now go."

"Okay," Stauer told Boxer, once the meeting had broken up in haste on his utterance, "Go." "What did you need to talk about? I know you've got a bee in your bonnet over Venezuela. What I don't fully understand is *why*."

In four short sentences, Boxer explained why. "Venezuela's economy is crumbling. Chavez needs a foreign adventure to distract the people. Colombia and Brazil are too tough. That leaves us, here."

Stauer considered that. It was a persuasive case, for all that it was a brief one. "So what do you think we should do about it? I'm not going to start a war with a sovereign country—especially one that much bigger than us—preemptively."

"No, not that," Boxer said, shaking his head. "But warning could be critical, as could a fast reaction. I want to rent an apartment—or, minimally, a hotel room—in Puerto Cabello and move a couple of our people in, maybe Morales and Lada, to keep an eye on their navy. At least I want them to stay until I can make contact with Colombian Intelligence and get them to watch the things for us.

"I want to recon the Lake Maracaibo area. And I want to insert some ground recon to keep an eye on their military establishment in the area nearest to us, Bolivar State. Also, I want to do some overflights of some of the eastern parts of their Bolivar State. Lastly, since we can't take out their navy preemptively, I want to make sure it's not capable of doing a second sortie against us, once they launch the first. Also to cripple them economically."

"How?"

"Mine their major harbors and the entrance to Lake Maracaibo. There are only three ports and a river that need to be blocked to effectively shut off their imports and exports. Two ports to cripple their navy, which go along with two of the other three . . . more or less. And, really, we can skip el Palito.

"Also we need to be able to mine Georgetown, here. And we need a good way to shut down the airports."

"They'll clear the mines," Stauer said, "even if we had the mines and the means to emplace them, which we don't."

"No, 'they' won't," Boxer countered. "Venezuela owns

not a single minesweeper. Fairly typically, for a Third World force, they've bought the flashy and showy, and neglected the less flashy but critical.

"They could get some from Cuba, I imagine, but I doubt it would be quick. For that matter, it's not clear how much, if any, of Cuba's once impressive minesweeping force even floats anymore. And we can get mines, says Victor, though we might have to steal them."

"The United States' reaction?"

Boxer shook his head. "Not much, I think. Oil's a glut on the market and America's stockages are more than adequate for the first time in maybe forty years, since with a nine dollar a gallon tax on gas for anything except public conveyances nobody, hardly, can afford to run a car much. They might condemn, but I doubt they'd do anything about it."

Stauer consider that. "Still . . . be damned uncomfortable having a battalion or two here, on *our* base, if we defended ourselves . . . mmm . . . actively and they got the order to prevent us from doing so."

Boxer sighed. "Yeah, I know. I wonder if they'd obey those orders though."

"I wouldn't count on them *not* obeying. I wouldn't bet the farm on it. Would you?"

"Maybe not. We *still* need to dig into Venezuela's shit and find out what they're up to."

"Will you be happy if I order the recons?" Stauer asked.

"No, but I'll be *happier*."

★CHAPTER TEN★

"Memories, light the corners of my mind . . . "
—Alan and Marilyn Bergman, "The Way We Were"

Camp Fulton, Guyana

By night, the hospital was quiet, with only the chirping of the insects and the occasional howls of the monkeys lurking in the trees of the camp to interrupt the steady hum of medical machinery. One of those humming machines—the "pain machine," they perversely called it—fed a steady if not quite frequent enough dollop of some opiate or other. Kemp didn't know the name except that it wasn't Demerol.

Opiate or not, Kemp would have been a lot happier if only he could have figured out what to do. Those choices were broken down: *Houston and severance pay, Houston and return here, stay here and get back to work, as soon as I'm able, risking worse damage . . . Assuming, of course . . .*

Some of the differences were subtle and personal. Going to Baylor, in Houston, didn't frighten him, exactly. What did frighten him was the prospect of being alone, with not a fellow soldier for miles, and no friends at hand. Maybe worse was the prospect of unutterable boredom.

I suppose I could catch up on my reading. Bah. I'd rather be doing than reading.

On the other hand, would it be just as bad here, being surrounded by the best regiment I've ever been in, and me restricted to pushing papers? And if I stay here, what are the odds I get first class therapy? Best available in country? No doubt. But how good is that going to be on the ass end of nowhere?

Goddamn bad luck, that shell. On the other hand . . .

The thought was interrupted by the entrance of a pretty nurse, a young blond girl. Kemp wasn't quite sure where he'd seen her before, though he was certain he had.

"Weren't you . . . ?" he began.

"I helped unload you from the dustoff bird," she answered, in an accent he couldn't quite place. She made a little mock bow, not deep enough to expose any cleavage in the prim nurse's uniform. It wasn't a terribly feminine gesture, though she was plainly female enough, prim clothing or not. "Elena Constantinescu, at your service."

"Ohhh . . . you're the angel," he said, in dawning, if fuzzy, recognition.

"And you're neither dead nor in Heaven," she replied. "You were very lucky."

"Interesting subject, luck," he answered noncommittally. Then, changing the subject, he asked, "Where are you from? I can't quite place your accent."

The nurse's eyes flashed. "My English is as good as yours," she said huffily. "As good as anyone's. And I am from the regiment. No place else is home."

Kemp, suddenly realizing, if not quite why, that the question of origins was a touchy one with the girl, apologized hastily. "Your English is probably better than mine, Elena. I think your accent is really nice, lovely even. I was just making talk."

"Okay," she replied, relenting. She turned her attention from him then, as she puttered about, checking the readings on several machines and making notes on a chart. Satisfied for the moment, she added, "I was born in Romania. The regiment saved me from . . . well . . . from something really bad. Now *it* is home."

"*Legio Patria Nostra,*" Kemp muttered.

The words sounded very familiar to the nurse. "What was that?" she asked. "What language?"

"Latin, I think," Kemp answered. "It means . . ."

"It means, 'The Legion is our fatherland,'" she supplied. Romanian was yet another of Latin's many daughters. "Exactly so. The regiment is my home . . . now . . . forever . . . as long as it and I exist."

"Well . . . *that* I can understand." Kemp's face fell, where it had brightened considerably upon her arrival, at once again facing the prospect of being homeless and rootless.

"Are you in pain?" she asked, her face suddenly full of concern. She hustled over to check the "pain machine."

"No," he answered, waving her away. "It's just that I don't know what to do or where I should go."

"Ohhh," she said. "You should go to Baylor, in Houston. No question about it. At least for long enough to be sure that there's nothing wrong with you that we haven't caught and to get a start on your therapy."

"But I thought this place was . . ."

"We're a good hospital of our type," she interrupted. "But we have our limits. Our doctors are good, very good even. But we don't have a specialist in spinal injuries. Baylor," she finished.

"Baylor?"

"Baylor." She was quite definite on the point. "For a while, at least. It's your best chance for having a normal life."

Kemp blew air between rattling lips. "Okay," he agreed, "you've sold me."

Elena smiled then. "Of *course* I did. That's why Doc Joseph told me to come see you. Full disclosure: There's something in it for me, too."

Officers' Club, Camp Fulton, Guyana

From the main bar came the sound of a mix of American, British, German, Russian, and Chinese voices singing "Always look on the bright side of life . . ." The singing was not precisely *good*, though perhaps the alcohol had something to do with that. Reilly and Doc Joseph both winced at one particularly off-key singer, who, sadly, was also one of the louder ones.

Reilly had many flaws, a point with which he would readily have agreed. Among these, however, was not lack of consideration for his troops. He might kill them in training them, to be sure, but if they didn't outright die, he'd take care of them.

"I *don't* want my man to be alone up there, Doc," Reilly said.

"He won't be," the Egon-of-Ghostbusters-fame look-alike assured him. "I'm killing two birds with one stone."

"Eh?"

"I've got some nurses we sent to school in the States for their degrees—"

"The Romanian girls?" Reilly interrupted. "I knew about them."

"Them, plus two of the girls we liberated in Africa, both of whom have now married into the regiment and can't be sent elsewhere. Anyway, we only had time to send them to a two-year RN program and none of them are specialized yet. I want to send one of them—Elena—to a specialist course for physical and occupational therapy—"

"Why her?"

Sighing with exasperation, Joseph said, "Would you *please* stop interrupting?"

"Sorry," Reilly answered, looking down. "I have many flaws—"

"Among which is impatience. Fine. Anyway, both of those require a certain hardness, not exactly lack of sympathy with pain but ruthlessness when dealing with it. They also require something highly analogous to combat leadership. I think she has all of that. My opinion, of course, is questionable, but Coffee agrees and his is *not*. So she goes to Baylor with Kemp, becomes an assistant under a certification and training program in their rehabilitation section, with Kemp as her training dummy, and, at the end of some months, you get back a trooper who is as fit as he's going to be, while I get back a therapist."

"Clever," Reilly said, admiringly.

"Isn't it just?"

Reilly swirled his drink in his glass, contemplatively, making ice cubes tinkle. "I wish everything had that clever a solution."

"Eh?" queried Joseph.

"My wife. She's having to give up her company—sooner or later . . . and the sooner, the better, as far as I'm concerned—because she just can't stay in the field with us while carrying a baby. Or, even if she could, past some point—"

"About five months."

"Now who's interrupting?"

"Sorry."

Reilly shrugged it off. "Anyway, it might be unhealthy for her. And I don't have a place to send her. And, knowing her, sitting around doing make-work would drive her insane. And the baby's going to make her insane enough. But there's no really good slot for her."

Joseph shook his head. "You're a dumb ass, you know that?"

"Huh?"

"If a slot doesn't exist, *make* one. Jeez . . ."

"I'm kind of skidding on thin ice with Stauer as is," Reilly said, putting his hand out, palm down and fingers spread, wriggling it.

Joseph smiled. "I'm not. How's this sound? Right now, I'm 'commander' of the medical company. I don't know how to be a commander. To quote a certain fictional character: 'I'm a doctor, Jim, not a miracle worker.' Master Sergeant Coffee, who *is* a miracle worker, has his hands full playing first sergeant, and I'm not a lot of help to him.

So we create a new slot for Lana, and make her the medical company commander."

"I dunno," Reilly said, doubtfully. "She despises REMFs, in general, though she'll make personal exceptions." *The unambiguously gay duo, for example.* "If you knew the trouble I had getting her to take over Headquarters Company, rather than the tank company she wanted . . ."

"Coffee's no REMF," Joseph insisted.

Reilly snorted. "No. Oh, no, he's not. We went to Ranger School together, you know."

The doctor's eyebrows raised of their own accord. "I didn't. Isn't that a hoot?"

"Yeah. Also served a few years in the same infantry battalion. He's pretty stout. And I don't mean fat." Reilly laughed, for no obvious reason. "Someday, remind me to tell you the story of when he was my platoon sergeant for a while. That was back in Panama . . ."

As if at mention of the name "Panama," the clouds above poured forth a deluge onto the camp. This was no gentle pitter-patter, but loud enough hitting the roof to make hearing difficult.

Joseph signaled the barmaid for a couple more drinks. "You're not going anywhere in this shit. Tell me now," he insisted, his voice raised over the pounding rain.

The afternoon rain had come and gone, leaving behind it a simmering stew of oppressive heat and cloying moisture. With a curse—"Motherfucker!"—a very young Lieutenant Reilly used his folding shovel to lever a rock out from the floor of the fighting position he, along with his radio telephone operator, were digging. Bending over and picking the thing up, he tossed it outside.

"Save that one for the burster layer," he told the RTO, who was prone with his rifle pointed down range toward where the rest of Headquarters company was setting up targets for the coming live fire exercise.

Muttering, "Son of a bitch had probably been down there since they dug out the Gaillard Cut," he went back to his digging. Sweat pouring off of him, he continued until he was standing about waist deep.

"Your turn, Ramirez," he said, exiting the rectangular excavation.

"Roger, sir. You need a break?"

"Not that so much. I need to troop the line."

Ramirez snorted as he jumped into the hole, saying, "Lotsa luck, sir." The RTO was the only man from Reilly's usual platoon. For the rest, he'd been stuck with an odd collection of cooks, medics, truck drivers, wire layers, mechanics, and clerks.

Pulling on his load-carrying equipment and taking rifle in hand, Reilly walked the line of troops busily digging fighting position. That is, they were all busily digging, until he came to the shallow scraping of one Private Gilbert, a cook. Gilbert himself was asleep, though he'd propped his face on his rifle in an attempt to look alert.

Reilly's mud-encrusted boot connected with the private's midsection, hard enough to sting if not to raise a bruise.

"Wake up, asshole!"

"I wasn't sleeping, sir," Gilbert lied.

"Bullshit," Reilly said, squatting down. Grabbing both sides of Gilbert's helmet, he forced the private's eyes generally forward and asked, "Do you see that copse of trees over there, Gilbert?"

"Yes, sir."

"That's the OP. Get your ass out there and relieve the man on duty. Do you know what you do on an OP, Private?"

"Yes, sir."

"Good. Go. Now."

Reilly saw the cook off then, shaking his head, turned to walk the rest of the line. Things were basically okay further on, and the medics manning the fifty-caliber machine gun were doing a fine job. That, he attributed to his platoon sergeant for the exercise, Sergeant First Class Coffee, now down in a hole, covered with mud, while slinging spoil out of the hole onto a poncho laying next to it.

"Oh, Ranger Buddy!" Reilly said.

Coffee picked up the litany without batting an eyelash or taking his attention from his work. "Please, please forgive me. I did not mean to run away and leave you all alone. I still love you, Ranger Buddy."

"How's it going, sir?" Coffee asked, more seriously. Looking up, he let the shovel rest for the moment.

Smiling benignly, the lieutenant answered, "My ticks are well fed and fattening up nicely, thank you. The chiggers are dug in to standard, with overhead cover. My ringworm garden overfloweth. My athlete's foot is coming along, though I think I need to wrap my feet in plastic bags for a while to get a really world class case. And then there's some kind of rot on my crotch that I can't quite *identify but which definitely shows promise, character development-wise . . . Oh, you mean besides those?"*

Coffee kept his face serious, for all he thought the litany funny. "Yes, sir; besides those."

Reilly sighed, then squatted down. "Well . . . I haven't shot Gilbert yet. That's got to be a good thing, no?"

"Caught him sleeping, too, huh?"

"Yeah."

"What did you do with him? Ass chewings just don't work. And I need a good excuse for my methods."

"Sent him out to the OP. I figure, if we forget about him, he can be down range when we open fire."

Coffee did a double take. He didn't think Reilly would actually leave Gilbert out there, but you never really knew.

"Oh, stop worrying. I'll get him before we shoot the miserable son of a bitch."

Coffee breathed a little easier. Sure, Gilbert would be no great loss, but Reilly actually showed considerable promise and it would be a shame for the Army to lose such a fine officer. Indeed, most of the senior noncoms in the battalion felt the same way and informally took turns watching out for the boy.

"Speaking of which," Reilly said, looking up, "the fucker is dead asleep again. Goddamn, miserable, useless . . . ."

Reilly strode off, in the direction of the private.

The next kick was not gentle. "Get up, shitbird!"

Gilbert writhed from the blow. "I can't, sir; I'm sick."

Reilly's voice grew very gentle then. He squatted beside the private and, voice full of seeming sympathy and concern, said, "Oh, you're sick, are you? Well then, we'll just have to take care of you."

Standing once again, Reilly shouted out. "Sergeant Coffee!"

Back at the machine gun position, Coffee stood to attention. "Sir!"

"Private Gilbert here says he's sick. See to him, would you?"

Coffee's voice was full of anticipation as he answered, "Sirrr!"

Grabbing two big medics, his aid bag, and a poncho, Coffee and party began to trot for the "sick" private. About the time they were halfway there, Gilbert suddenly remembered the Sergeant Coffee Method of dealing with malingerers.

"Sir, um, I'm feeling better."

"Nonsense, Private. You're ill. SERGEANT COFFEE!"

"SIRRR!"

"Hurry, Sergeant. I think Gilbert's delirious."

"Sirrr . . ."

"I'm not sick!" the private insisted. "I'm not sick!"

And then Coffee and his two assistants were there. The medics picked Gilbert up bodily, one hand on each of his wrists and ankles. Meanwhile, Coffee flapped the poncho out onto the ground. The medics slammed the cook down. Hard.

Then they sat on him while Coffee withdrew from his aid bag an intravenous needle so big and so crude that rumor was he'd been bequeathed a special supply of the things by his great-grandfather, presumably a medic in the First World War.

He made sure Gilbert could see the needle.

"I'M NOT SICK! Please . . . oh, please, I'm not sick,"
the private begged.

"Damn, this is serious, Sergeant Coffee," the lieutenant
said. "Better hurry."

"Sirrr . . ."

To Gilbert, Coffee whispered, "This is really going to
hurt you a lot more than me."

Then he stuck him. The private shrieked. "Oh, God, no
. . . please . . . I'm not SICK!"

"Dammit, sir, I missed," said Coffee.

Reilly smiled broadly. "Dammit, Sergeant Coffee, you
missed. Well . . . train to standard, not to time. Stick the
malingering son of a bitch again."

"YeeaARRRGHGH! I'm not sick!"

"Dammit, sir, I missed again."

"Train to standard . . ."

" . . . not to time."

"Aiaiaiaiai!"

Fourteen stickings later, with blood flowing across the
poncho's plastic surface and gathering in the low spots, a
weeping, quivering private begging to be allowed to go
back to duty, Coffee looked up at Reilly as much as to ask,
"You think he's had enough?"

Reilly nodded, then squatted yet again. "Are you sure,
Private, that you're not so sick you can't do your duty?"

Between sobs, Gilbert answered, "I'm"—sniff—
"sure"—sniff—"sir . . . ." sniff . . . "Please . . . Puhleeze
don't stick me anymore."

Reilly lifted his chin at the sergeant, who gave one last—
this time properly done—jab, raising a final howl of pain.

★ ★ ★

Joseph had tears rolling down his face. "'Dammit, Sergeant Coffee, you missed. Well . . . train to standard, not to time. Stick the malingering son of a bitch again.' Oh, *God*, that's funny."

"Absolutely true, Scott, every bit of it."

"And neither you nor Coffee got court-martialled?"

"Scott, with the ignorant or the stupid you can get away with anything you act like you can get away with. Since we acted like we could, Gilbert just assumed."

"Shit . . . you *were* a bastard."

"Eh?" Reilly shrugged. "I'm a lot more even tempered than I used to be, but I'm *still* a bastard."

★ CHAPTER ELEVEN ★

Tell me not, Sweet, I am unkind
That from the nunnery
Of thy chaste breast and quiet mind
To war and arms I fly.
—Richard Lovelace,
"To Lucasta, On Going to the Wars"

Quarters 212, Glen Fiddich Housing Area, Guyana

"Ayanna, honey, I'm home," Terry Welch called from the front door to the one story bungalow.

From the kitchen, carrying a mixing spoon and voicing a delighted squeal, pattered a very tall, very slender, very dark woman with amazingly large and liquid brown eyes. Ayanna hadn't seen her husband in the three weeks he'd been in the jungle with 1/5 Marines. This, she considered, was all too long a separation. And the occasional flights she served on the regiment's "executive" aircraft didn't do much to relieve the boredom.

She didn't mind the stink. And the greasepaint on his

face didn't deter her for a moment in covering it with kisses as she melted against him. If Terry wasn't her god, he had been—in a very real sense—her savior. What was a little stink compared to that? Less still some faded camouflage paint.

"I missed you," she said, once the formalities were completed. Her English had gotten markedly better in the last four years since the regiment, in the person of Welch, had liberated her from slavery.

"Honey, you have no idea," he replied, then pressed her to himself in case she misunderstood. She took his breath away. Indeed, rather than becoming less in his eyes, she'd grown with the years.

"You bathe first," she insisted. "I love you, nasty stink and all, but . . . better you bathe. Then eat; you too skinny. *Then* make love. Or anything you want."

"I won't argue with those orders," Welch answered. "But I'll be leaving in two days and . . ."

That changed priorities. "Screw stink," she said, definitively, taking his hand to lead him off. "I turn off stove. We make love *now*. I wash sheets later."

When the regiment had been in the process of building the camps and their accompanying dependent housing, they'd had an advantage more long established armed forces could never have had. It was a highly temporary advantage, to be sure, since people would move and would die. Still, in the process of building housing, they'd allowed the slated occupants to pay for any of a number of custom features at their own expense.

Given the—to say the least—*rigorous* life the regiment

offered, especially considering that the bulk of them were quite getting on in years, the very most popular custom modification to civil housing had been large, one-or-two-person whirlpool baths.

In one of those—a two-person job with padded footrests; white acrylic, and steaming—with the sound of the washing machine droning distantly on the other side of the wall, Welch lounged while the water jets massaged away not only an impressive degree of funk but also the little—and not so little—aches and pains that accompanied any military service that was worth having or doing.

Unlike most of the regiment's cadre, aged and crotchety types that they were, Terry was young enough not to actually need the tub. Normally. Still, it had advantages.

Sighing contentedly and closing his eyes, Terry never noticed, over the sound of washer and water jet, when his woman padded in on quiet, bare feet. She bore a light dinner—Horn of Africa finger foods, really—on a tray. Rather, he didn't notice until he smelled the food. Then it was: "Ahhh . . . *tibs*. Yummy."

Ayanna didn't pass Terry the food immediately. Instead, she set it down on a small folding towel bench just out of his reach. Then she turned her back away from him and, undoing a couple of buttons, let her dress slide off her shoulders to gather in a swirl at the floor. Only then did she pick up the tray and, still careful to keep her back away from him, step nimbly into the tub.

"After make love," she said, "I stink, too. I join you."

She keeps her back from me because the pattern of thin scars from the beatings she's received embarrass her. I wish she could identify what village she got them in, before she was sold off to the village I liberated her from. I'd destroy it and every free man in it to punish the bastard who did that.

If Ayanna couldn't read his mind, she did a damned good imitation of being able to. "I not embarrassed. Just not want remind you, or me, about past life and time. Forget. Nothing to be done now. Besides, bastard-motherfucker-piece-of-shit not know any better."

"It's still on my to-do list, love," Welch answered. "I just don't know if I'll ever be able to get to it."

She shook her head. "Just forget. Help me forget."

He sighed. "All right; I'll try." *No, I won't. I just don't know when I'll be able to get to it. But I'll feel a whole lot better when the men who hurt and abused you are six feet under . . . and preferably still alive while we fill in the holes.*

Wineperu, Guyana

There was a ferry that connected the west bank of the Essequibo River with Rockstone. For any number of reasons, the regiment was loath to use it. Instead, Terry, one team, a portion of his company headquarters, and three Eland drivers from Cazz's battalion would take LCMs from the naval squadron's small base at Wineperu, down the Essequibo to the sea, then east to Georgetown. From there, some would fly to other major airports in the region, while others would take the long drive down Brazil 401 and Brazil 174 to Manaus, thence to spread out to another half dozen airports, while still others would be taking a regimental Pilatus P-6, marked "AirVenture," to Port of Spain, in Trinidad. All but the Eland crew would spread out in twos and threes from there before taking flights, eventually, to Manila. They were going unarmed, although their principal had promised to have a package of suitable small arms and other ancillary equipment to them within a couple of days of arrival in the Philippines. Field uniforms and equipment would come on the ship, currently the other freighter suitable for assault landings, the MV *Richard Bland*.

In all, if the flight schedules worked out, they'd be assembled in Manila within roughly ninety-six hours.

The LCM's couldn't be disguised, though their cargoes could. They were crowded, despite the small load of personnel, with two Eland armored cars, in one case, and one plus a Land Rover, in the other. The top of the Land Rover was there to be seen—for anybody with either night vision equipment or the eyesight of a wolf—but all three Elands had been covered with tarps, with boxes and bits of lumber between vehicles and canvas to hide the shape of the things. Terry's men and their limited personal baggage were loosely piled in, on, and around those.

"We're loaded, Skipper," the senior of the two chiefs of the boats said.

Terry nodded. "Take us out."

Here on the river the sweet smell of the jungle, half flowers and half decay, was strong enough to be noticed even by men who spent most of their time in the jungle. This was especially true as the landing craft kept as far in toward the banks, and under the protective umbrella of the trees there, as prudence permitted. Once, at least, the boats passed under some red howler monkeys, whose caterwauling announced the boats' presence, even as the monkeys pelted the crews and passengers with feces.

At a mere seven knots, rather less than top speed due to the light available, the towns—Hipaia, Monkey Jump, Saint Mary's—passed by slowly to port and starboard, often with no more to mark them than a dim candlelight shining through an unscreened window. Only Bartica looked civilized as they passed it, showing streetlights and the occasional auto. The men slept or stared into the jungle or the water as the mood took them. Most slept.

Terry did not sleep; there'd be altogether too much time for that on his flight to Manila.

For all his nonchalance in the meeting, and his apparent enthusiasm for the mission, Terry had his doubts.

Sure, if I can find the guy, the force we're bringing is enough to free him, given the quality of the opposition. But finding him? That's going to be a bitch, a pure bitch, despite Stauer's permission to use any means of persuasion that might be useful.

Assuming I have the stomach for that, of course, which I'm not sure I do. He thought briefly of Ayanna's former owners and amended, *At least, I'm not sure I do for this. I could make exceptions.*

He'd only been separated from his woman for a few hours, and already he missed her. That feeling would only grow, he knew, as the days passed and the miles lengthened.

Never had anybody really devoted to me before. I like

it. No, that's not honest. I need it, and her. Wish I could be sure it's really love on her part, rather than just gratitude for her liberation. Then again, if it isn't love, she puts on a hell of a simulation.

For just a moment Terry laughed at himself. If someone had told me ten or fifteen years ago that I'd be in thrall to a tall, skinny, more or less black girl from the Third World, I'd have laughed in their faces.

Then again, ten or fifteen years ago who would have believed that the world would be in the shape it's in? Who would have believed that the only forces available— employable, anyway—to defend civilization would be private? Who would have believed . . .

Georgetown, Guyana

Meh believe to hear de sound of landin' craf', strainin' again' de tide, thought Mr. Drake.

Probably the best way to characterize the customs inspector, Drake, was as a friend and retainer of the regiment. The "friend" part had been a little iffy. Then Drake's daughter, Elizabeth, had married the senior noncom of the engineer company of the Fifth Combat Support Battalion, Victor Babcock-Moore, a Jamaican émigré to the United Kingdom, thence a sapper with the Royal Army, and thence to the regiment with his captain, Gary Trim. Following the wedding, though, and eager to make his sole child's life a happy one, Drake had become a true friend.

Dat de regimen' punish dem arrogant mutherfuckers

from Suriname no hurt any, either. Drake considered some rumors floating around the capital as well. *And, all t'ings considered, it be good dey here if t'ings blow up again. We ain't nevah quite got rid dem red muthafuckers used to run dis place.*

The "retainer" part was, *and, well, my retiremen' fund done pretty damned good from helping dese boys out. Used to do some better, of course, before they became all legal and such. Still, every little bit help.*

Drake was of indeterminate race, which is to say of pretty much every ethnic group in Guyana. If he'd bothered to trace it, he'd have found among his ancestry green-eyed Irish and blond Scots, black slaves and brown indentured servants, round eyed folk and others with yellow folds narrowing their eyes, and more than a couple of reds . . . of both varieties. His own skin was brown and weathered, though that was as much a function of his job as his genetics.

He was up rather earlier than usual, and had only managed to catch a little cat nap between seeing that the patrol boat that had come down a bit earlier was stashed under cover and heading out again to meet the landing craft.

The regiment had given Drake a set of night vision goggles long since. He'd asked for a rifle, too, once, and they'd given him that. The rifle he kept hidden in the small house he shared with nobody anymore, unless Elizabeth brought the children down. For the goggles, even when he had to work at night, he usually didn't wear them. He found the things beastly uncomfortable in Guyana's muggy clime.

He had the goggles around his neck now, though, hanging by their head straps. Keeping one hand on the wheelhouse for steadiness, he used the other to pull the goggles to his eyes. Scanning left and right, he caught first one ramp, standing almost upright above the tide, and then the other. He rapped knuckles on the wooden wheelhouse and ordered his pilot to set a course and speed to intercept the boats.

Wish meh be a younger man, thought Drake. *Wouldn't mind being able to go where dese folks go and doin' what dey do. Nothin' much excitin' evah happen here. Course, lot o' dem, dey older'n me. But different, somehow.*

Drake normally thought in the local patois but, between his daughter's nagging, his son-in-law's example, and frequent close contact with the regiment, generally, over the last four years he'd learned to slough off the local lingo at need and speak something fairly close to the Queen's English.

His cell phone rang in his pocket. *De "far recognition signal," dey calls dat.*

"Drake here."

"Mark yourself."

Drake bent an infrared light stick—he had a crate of them, also provided by the regiment—breaking a small glass vial inside. He shook the stick, waited a moment for the thing to mix properly and begin to react, then waved it overhead, from side to side, slowly.

"I see one waving infrared lightstick."

"Dat be me."

"We're coming along. Lead us to the covered docks."

★ ★ ★

Under the covered space reaching over the water—well lit inside, since it was shielded from outside view—were both a short dock and a ramp, as well as more than a dozen containers, several of them already open on one end, that formed the back wall. Some of those who had come on the patrol boat busied themselves with setting up something like a field mess inside. Still others assembled cots that they placed around the edges of a few of the containers.

The patrol boat, temporarily under one of the Chinese members of the regiment, Chief Petty Officer Chong, was already tied up and its crew lolling about, waiting for a job to do. They weren't going on this trip, but, being faster, had been used to get the early-required support down for those who were. One of the LCM's nosed up to the shore beside the dock, holding itself in place by a very minor effort of the engines. Terry's people formed a line that extended up the ramp and began passing over the baggage. This began to form a neat pile at the end of the line.

The other LCM—the one carrying the Land Rover—pulled up to the concrete ramp and dropped its own steel ramp down. After starting with a muted cough, the Land Rover pulled forward, its wheels initially spinning and whining on the dampened deck before catching and moving forward with a lurch. It bounded up, bouncing over the steel cleats of the deck, before settling down, once on dry land.

While that was going on, the three Eland drivers stripped off the tarp, lumber, and boxes covering their combat cars. This took a bit longer than unloading the Land Rover had. Terry fumed impatiently until, at last, the first Eland, too, roared to life and began to move over the cleated steel deck under the positive control of one of the drivers, walking a few meters ahead.

The ground-guiding driver led that Eland forward to one of the open containers. He made the thing back up and re-aim itself several times before, satisfied, he got out of the way and let the driver ease it inside. Buckling and bracing the thing for movement could wait—after all the freighter wouldn't be here for a couple of days yet. The driver emerged from his compartment, then crawled over the hull and around the turret. Then he and the ground guide left the container and went to join the other driver, even now stripping off the coverings from one of the other two Elands.

Terry Welch looked around the area, muttering, "So far, so good."

★CHAPTER TWELVE★

Agitate the enemy and ascertain the pattern of his
movement. Determine his dispositions and so ascertain
the field of battle. Probe him and learn where his
strength is abundant and where deficient.
—Sun Tzu, *The Art of War*

"Lawyers, Guns, and Money" (SCIF), Camp Fulton, Guyana

Boxer had permission to launch reconnaissance into
Venezuela. He intended to do a lot more of it than Stauer
had perhaps had in mind. Moreover, he, Victor, and Gordo
intended to make a few, or a few thousand purchases.
That, however, required a little coordination with the
comptroller, now seated in Boxer's office.

"We really don't have time to finish the operations plan
before we start buying things," Victor said to Boxer and
Meredith, the comptroller. "Some of what's needed we
probably can't even get unless we steal it."

"Fair enough," Boxer agreed. "Let's consider what we
do need." He stood and walked to a map of Venezuela and
Guyana on one wall.

"We want to be able to hurt them economically. That means fucking with imports, especially of food, and exports, especially of oil. Even if the price is depressed, that's still Chavez's biggest source of income. We probably also want to attack their transportation net and power grid."

His finger tapped the map near a large body of water by the western edge of the country. "Most of the oil flows out of Maracaibo and Punto Fijo, to the northeast. That can be considered one target and it's a toughie. We either block Punto Fijo and both channels into Lake Maracaibo, or we try to block the entrance into the sea. Three targets or one, but the one is *wide*. Even if I had a way to get into it, it would take too many."

"Maybe not," Victor said. "That channel to the north is what, sixty or sixty-five kilometers?"

"About that."

"How many mines can we introduce there?"

"Depends on what kind you can get and how much they weigh," Boxer replied. "I'm thinking forty or fifty."

"That would be barely enough for the two channels into the lake and the one port to the northeast," Victor said, shaking his head. "For something that wide—sixty or more kilometers—that's nothing."

Gordo scratched at his nose for a moment, then said, "Real mines are probably beyond us, or at least sophisticated ones are. The fusing is just way out of our league. But we could make a very large number of dummies here. Would that help?"

Boxer shook his head. "Not so much as you think. If we could get dummies planted we could get real ones planted, assuming about the same size and weight. But we're limited on getting *anything* laid."

"Why assume the same size and weight?" Gordo asked. "A twelve-to eighteen-inch-in-diameter steel plate, maybe an eighth of an inch thick, will probably give the same sonar reading as a mine, and only weigh . . . ummm . . . call it . . . eight or nine pounds. That's a lot of dummies for the weight of a single mine."

"That's a fair point," Boxer conceded. "I suppose you can task the welding shop to start cutting up plates.

"Use some of our freighters to lay them?" Victor suggested.

"S-3 thought of that. The problem is we've got four— rather, five—major targets: the Maracaibo area, the big naval port at Puerto Cabello, two other ports along the northern coast, and the River Orinoco.

"Between Chavez's air defense group and the new Sukhois he's got based to the east of there, we *can't* use aircraft on Puerto Cabello or the northern coast between there and Trinidad. That means we'll have to use a ship on one or both. The more ships we try to introduce, the greater the chance one of them is discovered and the greater the chance we lose surprise and so lose them all. So one freighter and one only, and that *has* to go to Puerto Cabello. It may also be able to drop mine barrages outside the northern coastal ports. Waggoner and Kosciusko seem to think it can. I think that's risky and iffy.

"So the aircraft will have to take care of Maracaibo. And they're only going to get one bite at the apple unless Colombia joins the war on our side. But that's a distant hope, which is not a plan. All we can plan on is one sortie

from each of two Antonovs, before they land themselves—
probably in Colombia—for internment.

"We've also got the *Naughtius,* once it comes out of
routine servicing, that we can use to either make a mine
barrage somewhere—probably damned slowly—or to
reseed anything they clear. The problem with the
Naughtius is it has to be based out of somewhere. It's slow
and short ranged. We can't count on using any settled
part of Guyana. Columbia would, for the same reasons as
the aircraft, be touchy; the Dutch hate our guts over
Suriname, so Aruba and the Netherlands Antilles are right
out. That leaves either Trinidad and Tobago as a base, or
we could use a ship. And using another ship is also touchy,
for much the same reasons. Or we have to set up a base
for *Naughtius* somewhere not too far from the middle of
nowhere.

"That last is probably what we'll have to do."

Meredith said, "I wouldn't be too worried about the
Orinoco River; it's within easy range of even our small
craft. For that matter, we could fly the helicopters in,
nap-of-the-earth, and mine it that way. Hell, we could fly
them into the hinterland where nobody but a few Indians
live and float them downstream on timers."

"Not helicopters," Boxer disagreed. "We're likely to
need them for something else."

Gordo asked, "What's the fifth target? That was only
four."

"We need to be able to shut down sea transportation to
here, too," Boxer answered. "And we need to be able to do
it in a way that doesn't have to be made known to the
Guyanan government because, if they knew, Chavez

would certainly find out, and if he found that out, he'd
start thinking about where else we might mine."

"That's all well and good," Victor said, "but until I know
what you need I can't do much."

Boxer smiled without a trace of mirth. "Yeah. Let's try
this approach; start tracking down anything you can get
your hands on, any way you get your hands on it that
doesn't lead back to us.

"And, in the interim, I'll be sending some folks to try to
figure out what we really do need. The S-3 and I will give
you a better picture when we've figured it out."

*And I need to get an e-mail off to Wicked Lasers to see
if they can fill a need. Or get something for us from
Norinco.*

River Orinoco, Venezuela

There were any number of ways to introduce a reconnaissance team into hostile territory, some sophisticated,
some simple, some safe and some quite dangerous. The
regiment's theory on the matter could be summed up as
"We're old and fragile. Simple and safe will do, wherever
it will do."

"Well enough," muttered *Praporschik* Baluyev, as the
fishing boat turned generally south to enter the river's
mouth. Shortly, they would turn east, toward Curiapo, and
from there probably as far as *Ciudad* Guyana and, if their
luck held, as far as *Ciudad* Bolivar. Sailing a Bertram fishing
boat, albeit at some fifty feet a fairly large and noticeable
one, along the coast from Georgetown and up the river

had the advantages of simplicity and safety. That suited Baluyev just fine.

Other recon teams would be going in other ways. Morales and Lada were flying commercial to Caracas, for example, thence to set up housekeeping in Puerto Cabello to keep an eye on the major part of the Venezuelan Navy. Another team, of twelve, from Second Battalion, was also flying commercial, but to Ernesto Cortissoz airport, near Barranquilla, Colombia.

Nobody was going in by parachute, hang glider, submarine or tunneling, swimming, or overland. Not yet anyway. There was a team preparing to HALO—High Altitude Low Opening—insert by parachute near the major training areas for Venezuela's Fifth Division. Likewise, a few individuals and a couple of groups of two or three from Second Battalion and Biggus Dickus Thornton's platoon of former SEALs would be looking at other targets: Airfields, small ports, bridges, oil platforms, and the like.

That, however, was for the future. They weren't going in—nobody was going in—unless the regiment also had a way to get them out again. And for Baluyev's crew, for now, there was a river to navigate, currents to measure, depths and hazards to confirm, open areas by the banks to scout, and ship traffic to analyze. There were also crocodiles, watching from the banks and from the very surface of the stream, to be avoided.

"Pull in to Curiapo," Baluyev ordered. "Let's see what we can pick up from the rumor mills. And I'm told you can get a good meal at the Hotel Orchidea."

"Got to beat Kravchenko's cooking," observed Timer Musin, sourly.

"What's eating you, Tim?" Baluyev asked.

Puerto Cabello, Venezuela

The COPA flight from Tocumen, east of Panama City, had been reasonably pleasant. The taxi ride from Arturo Michelina International Airport, in Valencia, had been unreasonably not. Still, Morales and Lada had arrived. Eventually.

"Odd," he'd said to her, "that a place this economically depressed still has more cars on the road than, say, San Antonio."

"Not zo ztrange," she'd answered. "Zey haven't yet gotten around to tryink to mandate a particular government design of auto here. And gas is cheaper zan drinking vater."

"I suppose," he'd agreed.

There'd been any number of quite decent, even luxurious hotels in Valencia or to the east, in Maracay. None were close enough to conveniently accomplish the mission.

Puerto Cabello, on the other hand, had nothing in the way of high-rise luxury, inn-wise. Instead, it had a few lower end establishments, suitable perhaps for merchant sailors in port, military or naval types on temporary duty, whores, and mid-level businessmen and party bosses taking their secretaries for a little afternoon dictation.

Lada, bearing a parasol, had taken one look at each of the available establishments and announced to Morales, "Zey're being vatched by local zecurity vorces."

"Damn," he answered, "and the Venezia was in a perfect spot to keep track of the port."

"Zat's *vhy* zey're being vatched by local zecurity vorces," she replied.

Morales nodded. He may have been a highly trained pinniped, but she was an *operator*, quite probably of world class, from an intelligence service justifiably famous for its thoroughness and paranoia. If she said the place was unsuitable, that was good enough for him.

"Plan B?" he asked. "The bed and breakfast with the tower?"

"Let's see how it looks."

The inn, the Posada Santa Margarita, looked pretty good, actually, if a bit garish. The façade was painted blue, with a white, studded double door framed by gold. Lada was fairly indifferent to the aesthetics of the thing, though, aesthetics having no bearing on mission accomplishment. She more or less sniffed and said, "Good. No zecurity here," she said, in English.

"Probably also no internet," Morales countered.

She shrugged, then switched to Spanish, saying, "We didn't expect to be able to use the net locally. Chavez has long since pulled most of his electronic warfare people to internal security work. We *need* to get the room with the tower above it. I don't fancy our chances of getting the SatCom to work unless we have uninterrupted line of sight."

Morales nodded. "Supposedly, we have reservations."

"Indeed," she agreed. "And since our reservations are for a married couple . . ."—She transferred her parasol to her left shoulder, sidestepped over to him and put one arm around his waist—"we had better look the part."

Ernesto Cortissoz Airport, Barranquilla, Colombia

There was really no disguising the dozen men who landed at Barranquilla, despite coming in on three separate flights, taking rental on three separate autos, and intended to rooms in at least two different hotels in a city to the east, Santa Marta. They might have been, indeed were, much older on average than the special operations norm. Yet a lion still looks the part, even in his winter.

"Exactly twelve of them I saw go through here," said the customs agent, a second sergeant, to his boss, the captain.

"Twelve what?"

"Twelve guys, gringos—oh, most of them were about as dark as us but they were gringos all the same. Almost all older, with arms the size of my legs and legs that don't bear thinking about, short hair, stick-up-their butts postures, and an aura that said 'do not fuck with me.' That's what."

Something about the number twelve bothered the captain. "Diplomatic passports?" he asked.

"No, all normal, private documents, with civilian visas."

"Did they say why they came?"

"One group said they wanted to do some scuba diving. Another that they came for the whores. The third I never got the chance to ask anything."

"So what do you think, then?" the captain asked. "Drugs? Personal security for some rich bastard? Training our army? Training FARC or ELN? Wait a minute . . . twelve, you said?"

"*Si*, twelve."

"Ah," the captain said, with sudden understanding, "a U.S. Army special forces team. They're not here to run drugs or help the rebels. What that leaves is . . ." The captain thought furiously for a moment before continuing. "What that leaves is you didn't see a damned thing."

"But—"

"You saw *nothing*, Pedro. Clear?"

Neptune Dive Shop and Resort, Taganga, Colombia

The dogs began barking and wagging their tails joyfully as soon as the team leader, Sergeant Ryan, stepped through the door. The three men who followed him in just increased the dogs' frenzy.

"Sepp! Franz! Quiet!" said Ryan to the pooches. They stopped barking and sat, tongues lolling, as if expecting a treat.

"Buy you both dinner later, boys," Ryan said to the dogs. They seemed content with the promise.

The woman at the desk, shapely if a bit coarse-featured, stood with a delighted squeal, then stepped around her desk and launched herself at Ryan, wrapping well muscled arms around his waist. "Mike, you *bastardo!* You never call. You never write. You never even e-mail! Where the fuck have you been?"

"Been busy, Kati," he answered, picking her up and giving her a couple of spins for old time's sake. He set her down, then asked, "Is Max in?"

"No," she answered. "He's out with a group of students.

Don't expect him back for maybe two . . . three more hours." Just then Kati, the secretary, noticed the three other men with Ryan.

He noticed that she noticed. "Oh, sorry, Kati. These are my . . . friends. I told them about this place and they insisted on coming here for some diving."

Ryan pointed in turn at them, announcing a name with each. His finger first went to a tiny little guy, seemingly as broad in the shoulders as he was tall. "This one goes by 'Bronto,' on account of his being so big." The finger moved to a more normally sized sort, slightly olive-tinged, with something of an intellectual look about him. "This is Bob Fail. He gets touchy if we call him 'Failure' so we call him 'Loser,' instead." Again the finger shifted, this time to an older man, with a narrow hatchet of a nose. "The last is Ted Rohrer. He doesn't have a nickname, yet. We're working on it." The finger dropped. "Guys, meet Kati, the woman responsible for keeping the establishment in business."

"Don't you say that to Max," she warned. "He's touchy, you know. Typical Boer."

"Kati," Ryan said, "Max is the only Boer you've ever met."

She cocked her head as if puzzled. "Which makes him completely typical in my experience then, doesn't it?"

Ryan sighed. There was no arguing with logic like that.

"You should get some lunch," Kati advised. "Los Baguettes is always good."

"You get a kickback or something, Kati?" Ryan asked.

She shook her head. "No, but Max says to always recommend Los Baguettes de Maria. He says his home boy, Arthur, is the only one he can speak Afrikaans with, so he needs to watch out for him."

Ryan shook his head. He'd met Arthur, a black South African, married to a white Colombian, and found it immensely funny that half Arthur's business referrals came from a Boer. *But then, maybe culture and country trump race, the more so as you're surrounded by people different in all three.*

"You need a place to stay?" Katia asked.

"Nah. We booked rooms at the White House."

"Beats the Blue Whale," she admitted, her nose curling into a sneer, "but you should have stayed here. Or at Maria's."

"I've got eight more friends coming, Katia. Can you make arrangements . . . ?"

"For how long?" she asked.

"Here? Just a few days," Ryan answered. "In the medium term, we're better finding an apartment or two to rent."

"Consider it done," she answered. "Half here, half to Maria's. Now go get lunch while you wait for Max. I'll send him over when he gets here."

"And my stuff?" Ryan asked.

"Max has it; still locked up for you. What is all that stuff anyway?" Katia asked.

"Oh, just some specialized diving gear. No big deal."

★CHAPTER THIRTEEN★

If the general remains silent while the statesman
commits a nation to war with insufficient means, he
shares culpability for the results.
—LTC Paul Yingling

Bolivar State, Venezuela

"Mao, would you *please* knock it off?" Larralde asked.

"Knock what off, sir?" the second sergeant major queried
as his legs pumped, keeping himself running in place.

Larralde sighed from where he sat, releasing the foot
he'd been inspecting to point at his subordinate's thumping
feet. "Knock *that* off; there's no reason to show off."

"But I'm not . . . oh, all right, sir." Arrivillaga stopped
his running and went to sit next to his captain. From
where they sat both could see the long line of the new
privates, to where it straggled off in the distance. The
sergeant major looked, shook his head, then let his chin
sink to his chest.

"We're so fucked," he muttered. "There's no chance

we'll ever get these people jump qualified in time. Zero, zip, zilch, none, *nada*. This wasn't even that long a road march and look at them. Just *look* at them.

"This is stupid, you know," Arrivillaga continued. "Brigade set us to do this march not because they're going to have to march much, but because they can't prioritize. Dumb asses."

Sighing again, Larralde agreed, "Even if we could— and I agree that we can't, not with all the time lost to the inoculations—I shudder to think what would be left of them after the training and the qualification jumps. We'd be pushing people down the ramp in wheelchairs. Half of them would be hopping to the doors on one leg with a pair of crutches strapped to the other."

"Do we *have* to jump, sir? Really? Surely there's a better way, one that might give us half a chance to use the extra three weeks to make soldiers of them."

Larralde stayed silent for a few moments, as he pulled a sticky sock back on, then reseated and laced up a boot. As he began unlacing the other, he said, "I've been thinking about that. I'm not convinced that the general staff wants us to jump in for any better reason than that it just looks ever so cool. We really don't have to. We could airland. Hell, we could maybe even airland in the regularly scheduled civilian flight."

Arrivillaga thought about that for all of thirty second before saying, "So why don't you bring that idea to Hugo?"

Larralde scoffed. "Me? Go direct to Chavez? I'd find myself assigned as an assistant division vector control officer, counting flies on flypaper, before I got two feet inside the palace. I don't know anyone—"

"I do," the sergeant major interrupted.

The captain looked incredulous. "*You* do?"

"Yeah," Arrivillaga insisted. "*I* do. Hugo fucks my cousin Marielena sometimes. And I'm *her* favorite cousin. I could get you an appointment. Or . . . she could."

Larralde's eyes squinched shut as his mouth half opened. His head tilted and shook, slightly. "And *why* is this the first I'm hearing about this?"

It was the sergeant major's turn to shrug. "It's not like it's something to brag about, sir."

"Well . . . put that way . . . I suppose not," Larralde agreed. "Even so, I'm just a lousy captain and—"

Again, the sergeant major interrupted. "In the first place, no, you're not a 'lousy' captain. I'll deny it if you ever say I said this, but you're one of the better ones. Besides, Hugo *likes* junior officers. He's really one, at heart, himself. It's generals he can't stand. Or our generals, anyway."

"Shit, I don't know, Mao."

"I'm not saying it's a sure thing. You'll have to have your ducks in order. But if you go to Hugo with a better plan than the one the *Estado Mayor* came up with—and how hard is that likely to be?—Hugo will give you a fair hearing.

"It's *gotta* beat jumping with crutches and pushing people in wheelchairs down the ramp of an Antonov, sir. So shall I give my cousin a call?"

Again, Larralde went silent, as he and Arrivillaga watched the still mostly civilian-at-heart rabble they were supposed to transform into soldiers stagger past in little driblets of twos and threes.

Larralde chewed his lower lip, thinking, *Hell, most of*

these kids ought to be on bedrest still. And still *they're at least trying. I owe them more than to let them be sacrificed to a shitty plan that's doomed to failure already. What was it the gringo lieutenants used to say in Ranger School? Oh, yeah: "Bet your bar time." Wonderful phrase. Sooo . . .*

"Sergeant Major Arrivillaga"—sigh—"call your cousin"—sigh—"set it up"—sigh—"and I'll do the best I can."

"See?" Arrivillaga said. "I *told* you that you were one of the better ones. Though I'll still deny in public that I ever said anything remotely like that."

"No doubt," Larralde agreed, as he laced up his boot. "And now, since you have so much energy, let's run in place while we wait for the rest of the company to catch up."

"Dirty bastards," a still pale Lily Vargas muttered under her breath as she strained forward and upward under the weight of a heavy pack.

"What's that, Lily?" Carlos Villareal asked, his head slumped down facing the dirt of the road they both trod.

"Up there, on the hill," she answered, pointing with her chin. "That son of a bitch, Larralde, and that asshole, Arrivillaga, are mocking us. Don't they know how damned sick and weak we still are?"

Miraflores Palace, Caracas, Venezuela

It was a week before Larralde thought he had "his ducks in order" enough to risk trying to persuade Chavez. He'd taken a short pass and flown to Caracas from *Ciudad Bolivar*, just in time to shower up, change into dress uniform, and catch a taxi to the palace. He was met there by a tall woman, who bore no visible relationship to his second sergeant major.

"*You're* Mao Arrivillaga's cousin?" Larralde asked, wide-eyed and incredulous. "But . . ."

"He took after one of our grandfathers," answered Marielena Arrivillaga—tall, shapely, and very, very pretty, with large eyes, high cheekbones, and an essentially perfect nose. She shrugged and added, "I took after one of our grandmothers. Why, what were you expecting?"

Larralde shook his head, dumbly, while thinking, *I was not expecting a potential contender for Miss Venezuela. Then again, I suppose Hugo is the president and is entitled to first pick.*

"I am *not,* by the way, despite whatever my cousin may think or may have told you, Hugo's mistress. I'm his secretary and that's *all* I am."

"But . . ." Larralde objected, "but you're so . . ."

The woman shook her head. "Hugo doesn't really like them all that good looking." She shook her head again, as if puzzled. "I'm not sure why. But really; his ideal woman is a peasant girl, a little thick through the middle, and with, at most, a mildly pretty mestiza face. Sometimes I think the reason I got this job is because he knew I was too good looking—that's not vanity; facts are facts—above all too Euro looking, to interest him, so he could be sure I'd work for him rather than use him for a sinecure."

"How very . . ."

"Odd?" she asked. "You don't know the half of it,

Captain." She turned away, at the same time asking over her shoulder, "And now, if you'll follow me?"

As Larralde watched the gently swaying form precede him, he thought, *I'm glad you said 'follow me,' because I couldn't 'walk this' . . . err . . . that 'way' if my life depended on it.*

"*Señor Presidente*," Marielena announced, after cracking the thick wooden door, "Captain Larralde is here to see you. He has an appointment."

"Show the captain in," Chavez said. Marielena opened the door just enough for easy passage, waited for Larralde to pass, then closed it again behind him.

Once inside, Larralde saw his president, half hidden behind the papers piled on his desk. He stood to attention and saluted, stiffly, which salute Chavez returned just as formally. Once Larralde had dropped his and returned to the position of attention, Chavez stood, walked around, thrust out his hand, and said, "Welcome. My secretary told me you had something important to say and she thought I should see you. What is it? A coup?"

Larralde shook the president's hand, answering, "No, sir, not a coup. At least, not as far as I know. It's about the upcoming, um, operation." Larralde looked around furtively, as if seeking eavesdroppers or even listening devices.

"You can speak freely here, Captain," Chavez insisted. "If my office is bugged and I don't know about it, we're screwed anyway." Chavez pointed to a couple of seats separated by a low end table. "Sit. Speak," he said.

"Yes, sir," Larralde answered. He sat, placed his

briefing on his lap, and waited for Chavez to likewise sit. That didn't happen. Instead the president parked his posterior on the edge of his desk, folded his arms, and looked down at the captain, repeating, "Speak."

Larralde gulped. He hadn't realized it until just then, but he'd been counting on the formality of his briefing to act as a sort of shield. And he wasn't going to get to use it as a shield.

"Speak," Chavez repeated.

It all came out in a rush. "Mr. President, I don't know every aspect of the upcoming operation. I only know my unit's part of it. And we're screwed. I mean without grease and without being kissed afterwards. There is no chance, Mr. President, not even a tiny one, of us being able to take a bunch of city boys and girls, train them to soldier, train them to jump, and then actually *jump* on even an unsuspecting and unresisting objective. Not in the time we have. No chance, sir. We'll defeat ourselves and won't need an enemy for the process. It'll be a catastrophe. The whole country will be a laughingstock. And anyone who's been telling you otherwise is either a liar or an ignoramus. Sir, it'sjustnotpossible!"

It was that "liar or ignoramus" line that caused Chavez to even consider the rest of what Larralde had to say, since those sentiments meshed with his own opinions of the general staff to a T. He sneered and, for a moment, Larralde thought the sneer was directed at him.

"You have a better plan, I take it?" Chavez asked.

"I have a plan that has a chance, sir."

"Okay, you have my ear, Captain. What's this great plan of yours?"

Larralde opened the folder on his lap and pulled out a map and a sketch. The rest of the folder he closed and placed on the table next to him. Then he slid forward to place one knee on the floor and began to spread the map out. Beside it he put the sketch.

Curiosity piqued, Chavez unfolded his arms, lifted his rear end from the desk, and took the couple of steps needed to place him standing over the map.

Larralde looked up and said, "The key points, Mr. President, are that a) we can't jump and b) we really don't have to."

"Do you have any idea of how much trouble you're in for jumping your chain of command?" the president asked.

"Yes, sir," the captain admitted, "I've got some little idea of that. I figure I'm going to end up as assistant division vector control officer. Or worse."

"So what made you do it?"

"Couple of reasons, sir. For one, I hate to lose. I really hate to lose. For another . . . well, the kids I'm supposed to command deserve better than to be wrecked before they even fight. It's not their fault they'll still half-civilian."

Chavez sat down on the floor next to the map and asked, "You don't happen to have a cigarette, do you, Captain?"

Larralde reached into a pocket and pulled out a pack of Belmonts. These he handed over before reaching for his lighter.

"I try to cut down by usually not having any around," Chavez explained, puffing the thing to life. "But I'm still addicted to the motherfuckers. Okay, now explain to me again, everything from your proposed training program to boarding at *Ciudad* Bolivar to securing Cheddi-Jagan to vectoring in the follow-on flights . . ."

The pack of Belmonts had just about run dry before Chavez leaned back, away from the map. "Okay, Major," he said, "you've sold me. But we've still got the problem of you and that slot as vector control officer that has your name written all over it. So here's what I propose:

"You're going back to your battalion, tonight. In three days, I'm going to show up for an unannounced inspection. I will insist on an operational and training briefing. Your battalion will fail, badly. I will then relieve your battalion commander and most of his staff. Maybe brigade, too. I will look around the room carefully and my eye will alight on you. You must look confident when I do. I will then assign you to command the battalion. And—"

"—Did you say 'Major,' sir?" Larralde interrupted.

"Shut up and listen," Chavez answered. "And I will promote you to major on the spot. I will then give you back pretty much exactly the plan you've just given me. You will express your doubts but end with, 'I'll try, Mr. President.' I shall, of course, say, 'You'll do better than try, Larralde; you'll succeed.'

"Now, is there anyone in that battalion you absolutely want to get rid of or keep?"

As he found himself doing more and more of late, Larralde sighed. "The battalion commander doesn't deserve relief, Mr. President. And the staff's basically decent."

"Then why didn't one of *them* come to me?"

"Mr. President," Larralde answered, "if my second sergeant major hadn't had a connection to you, *I* wouldn't have come to you either."

"A connection?"

Larralde made a torso-waist-hip wavy motion with one hand.

"Ohhh . . . Marielena. When you get back, would you please tell Mao that I am *not* fucking his cousin. For one thing, she's just the wrong . . . type for me. I'd feel self conscious."

"Yes, sir," Larralde agreed, "I'll do that." *And I'm not about to ask how you know my second sergeant major.* "In any case, sir, *Coronel* Sanchez doesn't deserve relief. Neither does his staff."

"So what do you propose then?"

Larralde went silent for a moment, thinking hard. At length he answered, "Taking the airfield is really only a job for one company. Sure, it needs to be a bigger company than mine is but, still, just a company. If you really want me to lead this, detach me and the company from the battalion and give me first picks on drafting in some fillers. I'd need some anyway, if only for the airfield control party and engineers. You don't even need to promote me for that. And I can fall back in on the battalion after it finishes forming at the airport."

"You turning the promotion down?" Chavez asked.

"I'm saying it can wait, Mr. President. Anyway, you do everything up to relieving anyone. Chew ass as much as you're comfortable with. Then you order me detached and direct that I get priority on anything I need. With that, I can get you that airfield."

Chavez smiled. "And so all this remains our little secret, then?"

"God, I hope so, Mr. President."

★CHAPTER FOURTEEN★

Time spent on reconnaissance
is seldom wasted.
—British Army *Field Service Regulations,* 1912

Riohacha, Colombia

The city of about one hundred thousand had an interesting history, having been founded, improbably enough, by a German *conquistador*, Nickolaus Federmann; repetitively sacked by pirates, to include Sir Francis Drake; been a prime revolutionary recruiting ground for sailors to fight against Spain; and lately, a port in the drug trade between Colombia, North America, and Europe. About the city's history neither Ryan nor Bronto cared a whit. All that mattered to them was that it was big enough to procure several safe houses, cosmopolitan enough for a team selected mostly based on swarthiness to blend in, and close enough to—in fact, on—a beach to facilitate above- and underwater operations. Though it wasn't a particularly touristy place, the beach on which the city fronted was still half-crowded with people, fully half of them women. They were very ostentatiously women, as a matter of fact.

"Sergeant Ryan," said Bronto, tightening his harness, "I don't see the point. We can't swim to Puerto Fijo or Maracaibo from here. The SeaBobs won't range nearly that far, not a quarter that far, even with the extra battery packs. And even if we could or they would, we don't have anything—not so much as a firecracker—to do anything on the far side, anyway."

"Have a little faith, Bronto," Ryan answered, as he likewise donned his scuba gear. "What we need will be provided."

"'The check's in the mail,'" the diminutive diver recited, his eyes rolling. "'I'll meet you halfway. It's already laid on . . .'"

"'And I won't come in your mouth,'" Ryan finished, as he tugged at his Henderson *Titanium* tropical wetsuit. "Even so, the *Namu,* which Terry and von Ahlenfeld probably could use for the contract mission, isn't going to them. And *Namu* can range. Our job, for now, is just recon, in part to see if we can effectively base *Namu* out of here, since good recon also includes the approach and the assembly area. So stop bitching and stand up where I can check your gear. You're too fucking short for me to bend that far without risking a back injury."

Bronto stood up. *Not that it makes all that much difference,* Ryan thought, as he bent at the waist to visually inspect.

"And another thing," the short ex-Green Beret said, flicking his chin in the direction of the sun, "I don't like doing this in the daytime."

"So you think we should do this at night?" Ryan asked. "When we'd be the only ones on the beach? And obvious as tits on a bull? When we're going to have to do it more than once?"

"Well, since you put it that way . . . um . . . no."

"And look at the bright side," the team leader added. "In the daytime you can see the *girls* strutting their stuff."

"There is that," Bronto conceded, his wandering eye taking in a trio of brown-skinned beauties in butt floss and bikini tops that were very nearly not there.

"Funny there aren't any topless beaches here," Bronto said.

"Pretty Catholic place, Colombia," Ryan replied. "Or, at least, they tend to follow the forms. And get your eyes off of *those* girls; they're too young for you."

Bronto looked highly skeptical. "You sure? What's the age of consent?"

"Here? Fourteen, and they're *still* too young for you."

Bronto did a double take of the girls. "Less than *fourteen*? No fucking way."

"Less than fourteen," Ryan confirmed. "And you do *not* want to spend time in a Colombian prison. Though at least you would be safe there from me, because if you compromise the mission by getting arrested for fucking a child, I *will* shoot you.

Holding his hands up defensively, Bronto said, "No problem, Sarge. I like women, not children." Bronto shook his head, then picked up his SeaBob and fins and began walking across the hot sand to the water.

"But, Jesus; under *fourteen*? That's just wrong on so many levels."

Puerto Cabello, Venezuela

Sunglasses added five or ten years to Lada's apparent age.

Morales and Lada stepped out through the Posada Santa Margarita's gold-framed, studded, white double door and turned east, toward that part of the port devoted to maintenance. Morales walked on the right, next to some little projections rising from the curb that reminded him of nothing so much as hitching posts for Shetland Ponies. *Small Shetland Ponies.*

The former SEAL wore local dress, which was nothing too very different from his native Puerto Rico . . . or Florida, for that matter. Likewise, Lada wore conservative local dress for respectable women—which was a lot more concealing than the Floridian norm, and without any jewelry that might tempt a thief. Her hair was naturally dark and she wore brown contacts to color her bright blue eyes in case she had to doff the sunglasses. Normally milk-white, her skin was artificially well tanned; hopefully it was well tanned enough not to excite or invite comment from the locals. She'd put on a much oversized bra, and stuffed it well, on the theory that most men would never raise their eyes from her chest long enough to make a good identification of her face or to notice that her tan was a chemically acquired tone. Along with sunglasses to add to her age, she wore a broad woven hat.

Her parasol, of course, was collapsed and partially dis-assembled, sitting on the bottom of her suitcase. It just wouldn't do to be carrying around their only satellite-capable antenna.

"Those are mostly Russian workers around the ships," Lada said, as she and Morales sat on a bench and watched some fairly large crews working diligently at two frigates marked "F-23" and "F-24." They'd already identified the other four frigates, as well as the three "PORVEEs" already purchased from Spain, as still tied up to the military quay to the west.

"How do you know?" Morales asked, hastily adding, "Not that I don't believe you."

"It's how we walk," she answered. "Rather, it's how we carry ourselves when we walk . . . as if we still had the burden of Mongols, Tsars, Bolsheviks, Nazis, and—now—organized crime perched on our shoulders. Nobody else has quite that burden of historic misery, though perhaps no one but ourselves can see it. They're Russians, all right."

Morales nodded, "Like I said, Lada, I believe you. Right now I'm trying to figure out how I know that that ship is about two hundred percent more ready for war than it was the last time we were here."

The Russian woman shrugged. "Can't help you. Not my specialty."

"It *is* mine, or a part of mine. Last time Boxer accepted our judgment because it's easier to accept decay and rot than it is to accept 'Bristol fashion.' This time, he's going to want more to go on."

"Well . . . I don't know how you can tell any better, Ernesto," she replied. Lada rarely, if ever, used his team name. "It's not like you can get inside to do an inspection of the electronics."

"That *is* one thing I can tell him," Morales said. He gave a subtle little flick of his finger in the direction of the dry dock. Among other things present were half a dozen absolutely huge rolls of electronic wiring. "All that cable out there isn't there for no reason. And the rolls are about a quarter empty, so they *are* putting it into the ships."

"Okay," Lada said, dropping into something like coaching mode, "what else?"

Morales thought back a bit. "Hmmm. Last time we were here they were putting a fresh coat of paint on the things." He shrugged, then added, "That's kind of a never-ending thing in the Navy. Anybody's navy, really.

"Now, though, there are some biggish patches where there's . . . ahhh."

"Yes?" she prodded.

"I understand it now. Before, they were painting over rust. People do that when they really either don't or can't give a shit. Now they've chipped off the paint and removed the rust. They're a *lot* more serious than they were."

"I could see that," the woman agreed. "The odd thing, though, is that if they are planning on annexing Guyana, these ships are nearly useless. Guyana—to include our regiment—has nothing to stand up to them. And the United States—if the current regime were to object . . . unlikely, I agree—is so powerful at sea that these ships would be scrap in minutes."

Morales nodded, seriously, then said, "They *do* have five inch—okay, *okay*—127mm guns. Useful to support a landing." His eyes darted around then turned west to where a ship with the designator "T-62" was turning around the headland that jutted north into the harbor. "And there is one of the landing craft now, *Essequibo*, if I remember correctly."

"We'd best get back to our room and report," Lada decided.

"That," Morales agreed, "and rehearse our bug out plan."

Orinoco River,
Fifteen Kilometers West of *Ciudad* Guayana, Venezuela

Baluyev's Bertram sport fisher passed almost quietly between the distant riverbanks. Other boats and ships, some commercial and some sport, passed to either side. On rare occasion, the otherwise invisible highway to the south showed up in the form of large trucks moving east or west.

The boat stayed away from the busy central lanes, the ones where the freighters and tankers plied their trade, bringing food, manufactures and iron ore out of *Ciudades* Bolivar and Guayana, and other goods in. Those shipping lanes, and their depth, were a matter of great interest to the team, of course. It was not, however, necessary to oversail them to map them.

There were two depthfinders *cum* fishfinders aboard the Bertram sport fisher. One of these, by far the less sophisticated of the two, was mounted next to the wheel at which Baluyev sat. The other, which was an order of magnitude better (and orders of magnitude higher in price, too; a civilian model side-imaging sonar unit with all the bells and whistles) remained below.

While *Praporschik* Baluyev steered, slowly, Litvinov provided camouflage by fishing off the stern. Below decks Kravchenko prepared his latest culinary crime against the people. Forward of and below that, Timer Musin monitored the sonar.

That was arguably the best place for Musin, since he'd been irritable almost to the point of fisticuffs for weeks. On the other hand, since the side imager recorded everything on its own, and only needed him in case there was a power outage, equally arguably it was the worst place to put him, since it gave him limitless opportunities to brood.

I might as well admit it, Tim thought, *if only to myself. I've got it bad for the girl, quite despite what she's done—what I've seen her do—and what she does.*

He sighed helplessly and hopelessly. *Love isn't just blind; it's deaf and dumb and stupid, to boot.*

But she's up north with someone else, sharing a hotel room and pretending to be married . . . Tim felt a sudden agony, a wrenching in his gut at the unwelcome arrival of an altogether too graphic image of Lada and Morales, wiling away the hours at Puerto Cabello. The pain was etched on his face, though none could see it. He tried to push the image from his mind. That just made it stand out in sharper focus.

And I'm an idiot; she's never made me any promise, never treated me as anything but an older brother.

But I can't help being an idiot. Can anyone?

★ ★ ★

Baluyev looked through the glass shield above the wheel with keen interest. *Orinoquia Bridge coming up*, he thought. *Love to drop it, if we could . . . if we should or must. But . . . way above my skill set. Hmmm . . . Krav's been to the course.*

The *praporschik* shouted down to the galley, "Kravchenko, you black-hearted enemy of the masses, get up here and give me your professional opinion. No, do not worry about burning that capitalist plot you call 'food.' Burning could only improve it."

"Yes, Chief?" Kravchenko asked when he arrived topside, wiping his hands on a semi-clean cloth.

"How would you drop that bridge?" Baluyev asked. It wasn't necessary to point; the bridge was both huge and solitary.

Kravchenko looked at the massive structure, stretching four kilometers from bank to bank, supported by cables held up by four massive, H-shaped pylons, and whistled. He cocked his head at an angle, calculating even while taking it the sheer extent of the problem.

"Be a bitch to drop one of the pylons, Chief. Probably more explosive than we could carry in this thing. The best bet would probably be to use a big—and I do mean *big*—shaped charge to cut one of the cables, either at the anchor points on the ends or at the top of one of the pylons. Might have to cut two of them, even. And . . . might have to cut them on top because there were too many to cut at the bridge level. That said, it's a close question that would depend on a lot of nondemolition factors." Kravchenko looked more carefully and said, "On second thought, I don't think those cables join on top, so we'd have to cut them at the base."

"Why a shaped charge?" Baluyev asked.

Kravchenko wrinkled his nose, answering, "However tightly wrapped a cable might be, there's always some air in there between strands that prevents the shock from being passed on properly. The plasma jet from a shaped charge just cuts through pretty much evenly."

"How big a charge, then? Or charges, if we would have to cut them at the bridge level."

Shaking his head, Kravchenko answered, "I'd have to crack the books for that one. Those I had to leave behind. And I'd need a pretty precise measure of the diameter of the cables, the material, and the method they used to weave the things together."

"Fair enough," the warrant answered. He adjusted the throttle slightly, and said, "I'm going to drop anchor a little ways up the river. As soon as the sun drops, I want you and Litvinov to start getting ready to recon the thing. Assuming we survive your cooking of course. And tomorrow I'll want you to look over the structures supporting those power lines."

"Don't sweat the electric tower, Chief," Kravchenko said. "I can tell you from here what I'd need to drop that. Easy. And I didn't *ask* to become the cook for this mission," he finished.

"It was you or Litvinov," Baluyev replied, "and as bad as your cooking is, it is usually survivable. The same cannot be said of his."

Seated after, fishing pole in hand, Litvinov smiled to the city receding sternward. *Pays to think ahead. Pays to really fuck it up sometimes when someone tasks you with something you would rather not do.*

★ CHAPTER FIFTEEN ★

Theory has, therefore, to consider
the nature of means and ends.
—Clausewitz, *On War*

Camp Fulton, Guyana

Victor Inning, ethnically a Great Russian who had, once
upon a happier time, 'served the Soviet Union,' lay abed
next to his gently snoring and equally Russian wife.

Damn, but I miss the old man, he thought, meaning by
that that he missed his wife's late father, an old cold warrior,
a *very* high ranking officer of first the KGB, and then the
FSB. The old man had died, in harness, in the Lubyanka,
as he'd have wanted to go. Even so, *Damn, but I miss him.
Not only was he a voice of sanity in a world that should be
institutionalized, if we could just find an asylum big
enough, but I could have gone to him for the fucking mines
Boxer and Stauer want.*

So Boxer and Waggoner figured out roughly what we
need and where I can't go to get them. *"No place in Latin*

America," they said. "Some places love Chavez and some hate his guts; but they're all potentially infiltrated, including Brazil. No place in North America. None of the core EU states. Not North Korea. Not Vietnam. Not China. Not Russia."

Most of that I could have come up with on my own.

Where, where, can I get them and in the quantity needed? They didn't have to forbid me from going to the EU; no member of the core of the EU will sell. I can't ask Russia even if I didn't think they'd pass it on. Even my old comrades in the FSB are pissed at me—some of them to the shoot on sight level—for joining the regiment.

"Though I still wouldn't have," he whispered to the darkness. "I still wouldn't have if the old man hadn't told me to take his daughter and get out while we still could. And this was the only place that would take me and not arrest me."

The United States is . . . well . . . right out. Besides, while they've got mines, they seem to prefer modifying aerial bombs to turn them into "destructors." Or sometimes purpose building mines to be dropped from aircraft. And I don't have any contacts there anyway, not to speak of, not that I could use. And even if I did, we don't have any aircraft for which the purchase of even the bombs, let alone the destructor kits, would make sense.

Canada? Well, emotionally they might as well be part of the EU.

Guyana could get them for us, openly, and from nearly anybody that has or makes them. But what Guyana buys for us, Guyana knows about. And what they know about, Chavez will know about quickly. So says Boxer, anyway, and I've learned to trust him on these things.

I'd go to Iran or Iraq, but not only are they back at de facto war with each other, they've both got civil wars going on. What they make, they use on each other and themselves. Kind of pointlessly, too, since oil's a glut on the market and nobody cares all that much if they export any or not.

Singapore makes a good series. So does Taiwan. But Taiwan is busy mining the approaches from China and will have few to spare, while Singapore is just plain touchy about selling arms under the table. Not that they hesitated about selling us five thousand rounds of new 105mm, mind, once I put them the offer. But that was above board.

South Africa has a shitpot of old ones, dating back to the Great Patriotic War. But that's really old. I wouldn't trust them to do the job. Maybe they could recondition them. Wouldn't hurt to ask ARMSCOR, I suppose. Or maybe even skip them and go straight to Pretoria Metal Pressings-Denel.

Damned pity it is that that bad lot of 105 is just too low in explosive filler to make a good mine for anything but . . .

Hmmm. Now isn't that an interesting thought. Partial solution? Maybe.

"Lawyers, Guns, and Money" (SCIF), Camp Fulton, Guyana

The SCIF, which served a lot more functions than merely being a facility to hold and discuss highly sensitive intelligence, was, as usual, silent. Oh, there were possibly as many as a hundred people working there, but the nature of the work suggested librarylike levels of quiet.

"You want *what?*" Gordo asked incredulously.

Victor smiled. "I want about five or six hundred of those four thousand and change artillery shells, the ones condemned for having the questionable propellant. Oh, and money. We'll need some money."

"What for? For both, I mean."

"The shells to become naval mines," Inning answered. "The money to buy fuses and have a factory somewhere else mill out connectors to screw regular influence fuses—we'd need a mix of them, pressure, magnetic, and acoustic—to turn them into mines. We can drop them over the side of frigging *canoes*, if that's all we have left."

"To use where?" Gordo asked.

"Here in Guyana. If a 105 had more explosive, we could maybe use them somewhere else. As is, I don't see a lot of value in using them anywhere but to mine Georgetown and the Demerara River, and *maybe* the mouth of Puerto Cabello. Even so, that's one or two of five targets taken care of."

"They're not 'taken care of,'" Gordo corrected, "until they're armed and laid."

"Not my problem," Victor answered, then primly countered, "Moreover, 'an action passed on is an action completed.'"

"You've spent way too much time around Americans, Victor," Gordo observed.

"Pshaw. It was the same in Russia and the Soviet Union. It's the same everywhere."

Gordo considered that, then decided, "Yeah, it probably is. Sad, ain't it."

"So can I have the money and the shells?" Victor asked.

Nodding, Gordo replied, "Yes, you can have the shells, certainly, and I'll hold the comptroller upside down by his heels and shake until the money falls out. But what about the rest of the job? And where are you going to get the fuses in the first place?"

"Working on it," Victor answered as he turned to leave.

"Working on it," Victor repeated to himself, as his footsteps echoed down the tile-floored and concrete-walled corridor, heading for his office.

"It's times like these," Victor muttered, once seated behind his desk, "that I wish the Czech Republic had access to the sea. They may be part of the EU, but the Bohemians will still sell anything they make. Unfortunately, they don't make anything that isn't useful to *them*. And they've got no use for naval mines. Pity.

"Still, the idea of using shells for mines isn't a bad one, even if I do say so myself. So I wonder what they've got for shells."

Victor twirled his chair around to face a bookcase. From that he selected a large blue-bound volume, fingering it out of the tightly packed shelf. Kicking his chair back to face his desk, he opened the reference. Then he laid a legal pad next to the book, set a pen next to that, and began thumbing pages.

Hmmm, he thought, *that's interesting. Though the fuse wells are different sizes, what we can do with 105mm*

*shells we can do with 240mm shells. Those, the Czechs
have. Let's see about . . . aha . . . roughly forty kilograms
equivalent high explosive in a 240mm shell. That ought to
be good for medium depths—say, sixty meters or less—for
other than first class warships. Death to a medium merchie
or landing craft, probably for a tanker, too. Still, to get
those shells without the mortars that fire them would be
suspicious. The Czechs only have . . .* Victor thumbed
some more pages. *Ah . . . they've a grand total of four
tubes. They won't sell. So . . . have to add . . . ummm . . .
two, I think . . . yes, two M-240's . . . that's the minimum
for testing, all from Russia. No, let's make it four. And
might as well have Guyana order the shells from there,
too. That should allay any suspicions in that regards. Hey,
Boxer said we couldn't go to Russia for mines; he said
nothing about going to them for shells or guns. And they
won't go to waste; the line battalions can use the mortars
to present a better opposing force for the U.S. armed
forces that come here. Also, they're fairly cheap since the
Russian Army has gone to the self-propelled version and
put the towed ones in depots. The comptroller shouldn't
bitch much.*

"Okay, so how many would we need?" Victor picked up
the pen and began to tap it against his cheek. "No, that's
not the right question. The right question, is how many can
we deliver." He started some calculations on the yellow
pad, while thinking, *Let's see. Maracaibo Area? Mission
for the Antonovs, and two Antonovs can carry, say, fifteen
tons between them. Each shell is a pubic hair over one
seventh of a ton, so we need . . . call it . . . one hundred and
. . . five. No, that's not right. We'll want to drop ten or*

twenty flat steel fakes for every real mine. And at least a few serious, purpose-made mines; if I can find any. Sooo . . . drop the number deliverable to a maximum of an even hundred and probably more like eighty. That's totally inadequate, of course, to actually block the Gulf of Venezuela, but it's probably enough to frighten anyone out of using it. At least if we can supplement them with some- thing better.

Then there's the Orinoco River. Call it . . . oh . . . thirty shells for that.

Outside the mouth of Puerto Cabello? Maybe another fifty. And to mine the waters north of each port east of there . . . two hundred more? Make it three hundred.

And, for here? Seventy ought to do for Georgetown and to help block the Demerara.

All righty, then. Let's factor in P for "plenty." Four mortars and a thousand big shells takes care of a lot of the problem. Well, with the 105's and assuming I can get the influence fuses and have fuse well adapters made, it does. I wonder if Pretoria Metal Pressings can handle that many. Hmmm . . . maybe not. Shit, I hate making things more complex than necessary. Shit. And where do I get the fuses? Israel? Would they sell the fuses?

The thought of fuses sparked another thought. *How do I throw my old comrades off the scent? How indeed? I could order some Smelchek fuses. Then they'd be sure I wanted the shells for mortars, rather than mines. Okay . . . kind of a waste but we'll do that. Now let's see about Israel and destructors.*

Victor reached for a different, blue-bound volume, nearly indistinguishable from the first. *Ah, yes. They make destructor kits now. They've found a need to use them off the coast of Gaza. Would they do the adapters? Surely they could. Less certain they could hide the destructor kit sales, though, and they'd insist on hiding them. And the two together raise too many questions, anyway.*

Notes to self: send my Hassidic outfit to the cleaners, today. Start work to get Guyanan Defense to order the mortars and shells, tomorrow. Travel arrangements to South Africa and Israel, soonest.

And . . . um—his finger came to rest on a different passage of the first book—*side trip to Montenegro. They like me well enough. As well they should, since I was the instrument of them unloading the* Naughtius *on the regiment.*

Victor felt a sudden shiver of anticipation. It had been a while since he'd really had the chance to practice his true calling, which was clandestine arms smuggling, not mere procurement. It was a good feeling to get back into the saddle again.

★CHAPTER SIXTEEN★

He was the most theatrical of men, busy at all times
not merely being a general but doing it in the most
dramatic way possible, the Great MacArthur, who played
in nothing less than the theater of history—as if life were
always a stage and the world his audience.
—David Halberstam,
The Coldest Winter: America and the Korean War

Bolivar State, Venezuela

It had been a bright afternoon when Chavez finished his
inspection of the parachute brigade and ordered the
brigade commander to summon all his officers to a huge
mess tent set up under some trees and a net. The sun was
long down and the mosquitoes having a feast and he was
still talking.

I know he likes to talk, thought Larralde, like the rest
of the commanders and staff of the battalion, standing at
attention as Hugo Chavez went into his third hour of
continuous tongue lashing with no sign of flagging. *He*

*likes to talk, but this is getting fucking ridiculous. Get to
the point, Mr. President; an hour spent listening to you
would be better spent training my people. Sure, they're all
. . . we're all . . . lacking in true Bolivarian revolutionary
spirit. So fucking what? Maybe I should never have . . .*

"And in conclusion," Chavez said, glaring out over the
heads of the officers assembled, "I am sorely tempted to
fire the lot of you for your lack of military ability, lack of
initiative, and lack of the spirit of Bolivar.

"So now I'll tell you what we're going to do." Chavez
pointed at Larralde and demanded, "Who are you,
Captain?"

Larralde braced to a stiffer attention and answered,
"Captain Larralde, Miguel, Mr. President. Commanding
Company B, Second Battalion."

Chavez nodded, causing his jowls to shake. "While I've
been talking and the rest of these pussies have been
quaking in their all too shiny boots, you've at least *looked*
like a man. Here's what I want from you. I want you to take
your B Company and just forget the idea of parachuting.
It was a silly idea in the first place and there's no way you'll
be ready to do it." The president's eyes swept around the
crowded tent. "That goes for the rest of the brigade, too.
Prepare, instead, for an air landing."

Turning back to Larralde, but speaking to the crowd,
he asked, "Now what do you need besides your company?"

Larralde parroted the force list he'd given Chavez at
Miraflores Palace. Chavez nodded, turned to the brigade
commander, and said, "Get it to him. No later than
tomorrow." Chavez went silent for a moment, then said,
quite despite what Larralde had requested, "A captain is

too junior to command a force that size. Consider yourself a major, effective right now. And tell your second sergeant major that he is now a first sergeant major. Brigade commander?"

"Mr. President?" that colonel asked nervously.

"Shuffle your officers around as much as necessary to build up Larralde's unit to full commissioned strength. *And* get him the attachments he needs."

It was late and all of the other officers and noncoms had left the mess tent. Larralde and his new—and unwitting—first sergeant major sat across a table from each other, with a bottle of cola and another of rum with the number 1796 printed boldly on the label. There wasn't any ice but one couldn't expect everything.

"Where did you get this shit, sir?" Arrivillaga asked, sipping his cup straight.

"Hugo insisted I take a couple of bottles back with me. I've been saving them."

"Ordinarily, I prefer bourbon," Arrivillaga said, sipping again. "But this"—he twirled the glass contemplatively— "this isn't bad."

"Figured you could use the moral fortification before I lay out what we have to do."

Arrivillaga drained the metal cup, slapped it to the table, then announced, "Okay, sir, I'm ready."

Larralde then proceeded to tell his senior sergeant about both his own and the sergeant major's promotion, the new troops they'd be getting, and the change to the plan. He neglected to mention that Chavez's orders were, mostly, his own idea. Mao already knew that, anyway.

"The promotion is nice, of course," said the newly promoted First Sergeant Major Arrivillaga, totally unfazed by the news, "but you realize, right, sir, that you've made us a perilous amount of work."

"Win a little, lose a little, Mao," Larralde shrugged. "At least this way we have a chance."

"So how are we going to do it? To prepare, I mean; you've already told me how we're going to take the airfield."

"We're going to prepare for it by preparing for it," the new major answered.

Arrivillaga scowled. "You're not a general yet, you know, to be coming up with that kind of mindless, self-serving bullshit."

Larralde laughed and bent his head to scratch behind an ear. "I'm actually serious. We don't have the time to prepare everyone for general combat. But they don't need to know how to do a deliberate attack, or a movement to contact, or an ambush. They don't need to march forty kilometers at a whack. They need to know how to use their weapons and the basic soldier skills. And they need toughening. But they've got to be able to board and debark from a particular airplane, specifically, to move fast once they debark, to clear certain *specific* buildings at the airfield, and how to do a hasty defense. And, whenever we can scrape a few minutes or hours from teaching the basic soldiering they need, we're going to be rehearsing the actual operation. They'll learn the collective things they need to do based on what they *really* need to do."

The sergeant major looked dubious. He held up one hand, the middle and ring fingers pointed at Larralde, the index finger raised and the little finger lolling a bit. The hand moved just enough to give an element of warning to the shaking of the index finger.

"I can see that working, sir, as long as everything goes well. But if we're not training them for the general problems they *might* face, and then they must face them, we'll be in trouble."

"Yeah, Mao," Larralde agreed. "I know. But it's an either-or proposition. You, yourself, were the one who pointed out that spending a bunch of time road marching was simply bad prioritization."

"Well, sure," the sergeant major said. "That's my job, to point out silly shit so you can tell me to fix it. But spending a lot of time that we don't have, learning to put one foot in front of the other, is one thing. Skipping core missions . . . color me skeptical."

"Skeptical? That's a color formed by mixing Bolivarian red and shit brown, isn't it?" Larralde joked. "With just a hint of shiny?"

"As long as the shiny is thin and flakes off easily," Arrivillaga replied, with a tight smile.

There was a rustle of canvas by the tent door. Mao looked up, then quietly announced, "Your other officers are here, sir. And they look a little scared. I'd better go get some more cups."

Ah. Time to meet my 'public.' Again.

As Arrivillaga stood and walked in the direction of the kitchen, Larralde smiled and turned halfway around in his folding metal chair. "Gentlemen," he said, beckoning with one hand, "Come. Sit. We have much to discuss. Because we're going to have much great fun together."

★ ★ ★

"'Fun,' the son of a bitch called it," muttered Lily, sprawling under some wide shade trees at the back end of the rifle range, facing away. Behind her came the steady *poppoppop* of Kalishnikovs peppering—or at least lightly sprinkling; they weren't the most accurate of rifles—paper targets downrange.

Lily, Villareal, and the rest of the platoon were covered with mud, scratched, and sweaty from the individual movement techniques they'd been put through by Sergeant Major Arrivillaga every spare moment they'd not actually been engaged in marksmanship training. Likewise muddy, but disassembled for cleaning, were their rifles, spread out on plasticized ponchos on the grass before each man and woman.

Carlos Villareal, using a toothbrush to pick caked-on carbon from his rifle's bolt, said nothing and carefully kept his face blank. There was no sense in offending Lily, after all. But, to him, it *had* been fun, possibly the most fun he'd ever had with his clothes on. What was a little mud and sweat for that?

On the other hand, he thought, *to the girls this has not been fun at all. What was that old gringo song? Oh, yes: "I don't like spiders and snakes." And they don't. Different . . .*

Carlos's thoughts were interrupted by someone calling out, "Attention!" He dropped the toothbrush and bolt onto the poncho, getting to his feet and snapping to attention along with the rest of the platoon.

I hate *Kalashnikovs,* thought Mao, bitterly, as he sauntered up to the gaggle of rifle cleaners. *Oh, sure, they're simple and easy to train on . . . to train people to miss, that is. I want my goddamned FNC back. I want these ever-so-far-from-soldierly rabble to have FNCs. I want to dump these fucking stamped pieces of shit in the nearest river. I want . . . ahhh, fuckit.*

The FNC, for which Mao pined, was a Belgian design, in the NATO standard caliber of 5.56x45. It impressed nearly everyone who used it. Moreover, Venezuela had many FNC's in its depots, better than fifty thousand of them. The Kalashnikov, specifically the folding stock AK-104's that the troops had been issued, had its virtues. Fine accuracy was not among them.

The reason Larralde's command, indeed none of the invasion force, had FNC's was . . .

Mere fucking appearances, fumed Arrivillaga. *The fucking communists—freedom fighters, one and all, of course—use them so we have to use them, too. To look the same. Bah.*

Mao glared around at the stiffly braced recruits and shouted, "Go back to what you were doing, you crawling shits. Your rifle is more important than I am."

Still silently cursing, Arrivillaga went to find the company commander.

Larralde sat comfortably, or as comfortably as the open top allowed under the glaring sun, in his command vehicle, a Venezuelan-made Tiuna. Behind him, on the seat, rested a charcoal-colored plastic case, about four feet long and a foot or so wide.

Larralde patted his command vehicle. The Tiuna, at least, had worked out reasonably well.

Better than that fucking abortion of a tank rebuild Hugo's cronies foisted on us, thought the major. *On the other hand, it's even more expensive than the gringo Hummer, and probably not as good. Oh, well.*

Larralde sensed his first sergeant major's arrival before he saw him. He looked over at the scowling noncom, smiled, and said, "I can read you like a book, you know."

"Bullshit, sir."

"Well . . ." the major half-conceded, "I can read you at the moment. You came to bitch—for the umpteenth time—about the Kalashnikovs, didn't you?"

"So?" Arrivillaga answered. "Is there a decent soldier in the army who knows any better that wouldn't bitch about them? No mind reading required."

Mao scowled. "You know, sir, it wouldn't be quite so infuriating if the assholes-that-be hadn't also left us with our Belgian-made light machine guns. I could see the logic, maybe, if we had ammunition commonality. But we don't. We've got rifles in 7.62 short, light machine guns in 5.56, and machine guns in NATO 7.62. Makes no fucking sense at all."

"Going to get worse, too," Larralde said, "at least it will if we don't make a few adjustments. He nodded his head backwards in the direction of the charcoal gray case behind him.

Arrivillaga shrugged his shoulders and muttered something unmentionable, then took the couple of steps needed to stand next to the Tiuna. He leaned over, unsnapped the latches to the case, and flipped it open.

"Ooo . . . shiny," the first sergeant major whispered as

he pulled a long, almost spindly rifle out. "Dragunov. Me like."

Then Mao's shoulders slumped again. "But *another* fucking caliber. What the hell are they thinking?"

"Not exactly," Larralde corrected. "In the first place, that's in 7.62 NATO, so it will match our MAG's." The MAG was another Belgian machine gun, a general purpose gun, in that caliber. "And, in the second place, I called Hugo's office to make a date with your cousin and had her put me through to him. We're dumping the other Belgian guns and getting RPK light machine guns to match our rifles."

"That makes a little more sense." Mao's scowl deepened, as he said, "You better not even *think* about screwing my cousin, sir."

Larralde shook his head in puzzlement. "You didn't seem to mind when you thought Hugo was fucking her."

"You're not Hugo," the sergeant major answered, turning abruptly to walk back to the firing line.

★CHAPTER SEVENTEEN★

Mines are equal opportunity weapons.
—*Murphy's Laws of Combat Operations*

Russian Embassy, 3 Public Road, Kitty, Georgetown, Guyana

It was ten in the morning and already beastly hot. And with the Atlantic just the other side of the seawall, and that just the other side of the road, it was drippingly muggy, to boot.

Major Sergei Pakhamov, military attaché for the Embassy of the Russian Federation to Guyana, loosened the collar of his shirt and cursed. The air conditioning was down again, and the town's thick heat oppressed him greatly. Sweat crawled down his back, itching and tickling on its way. He cursed that, too.

And cursing the one will have just as much effect as cursing the other. Oh, well, let's see what business there is—damned little, I'm sure—to amuse me in this otherwise make-work-while-the-world-forgets-you-exist little spot of limbo.

"Anything interesting, Katya?" Pakhamov called out through the open door to his office.

"Request to purchase arms for testing, in your otherwise empty inbox," "Katya" replied.

The woman, over fifty and turning plump, was actually named Catherine Persons. While dark of hair, skin, and eye, she was ethnically indeterminate, as with many Guyanese, being a thorough mix of at least six groups, from Arawak to Hindu, Iberian to Irish. She'd been a sufficiently dedicated communist that she'd been affiliated with, if not officially an employee of, the embassy back when it had been the legation of the Soviet Union. The permanent job had come shortly after that empire's collapse. How she felt about the whole dictatorship of the proletariat now she kept to herself. From her reaction to some of his ribbing, Pakhamov was reasonably sure she remained a communist and, like most such, a very disappointed and frustrated one.

"What arms?"

"Local forces want to buy four heavy mortars for testing, along with a package of ammunition and laser guidance packages," she replied. "Along with two laser designators. It's bullshit, by the way. I have it from my cousin in Defense that our people don't want the things; they're for the Americans up river. Officially a 'reserve of the Guyanan Defense Force.' Which is also bullshit."

"Can you think of any reason not to recommend approval, Katya?" Pakhamov asked.

"Other than general distaste, no," she admitted.

"Neither can I. And it would be nice to have something to do. Take a letter, Katya," Pakhamov said, rising from his sweaty seat and moving out of his own stuffy office into his secretary's only marginally better one.

Tivat Arsenal, Gulf of Kotor, Montenegro

Victor Inning could, in theory, have flown in. The town of Tivat had, after all, its own airport, with a fair number of convenient connections to other spots of Europe. Moreover, he was good with disguises and had any number of false passports to see him through customs. The one he was currently using was American, under the name of "Victor Turpin."

He'd decided against flying directly in, going instead via Athens, Greece—"If it's good enough for half the terrorists in the world; it's good enough for me"—and renting a car there, then driving across the border to Montenegro. Once at the marina—for the old naval arsenal had been mostly converted to the uses of the very wealthy—*who somehow,* thought Victor, *never seemed to suffer from, nor to alter their extravagant lifestyles merely because of the fact that the world's economy is in the tank*—he'd checked into a small hotel and waited for his best contact in the old Yugoslav, later the Montenegrin, Navy to arrive.

Feels like old times, Victor silently exulted, as he nursed a scotch in the hotel's tiny bar, waiting for his contact to arrive. *Even if it's a lot safer for me, here and now, than it sometimes was in other places, at other times.*

Victor was on the verge of consulting his watch when he heard and felt the stool next to his being pulled back.

He looked toward it and said, in English, "You've put on weight, Lazar, since last I saw you."

The Montenegrin, Lazar Toldorovic, late captain of the Yugoslav, then the Montenegrin Navy, nodded a half-bald head, answering in the same language, "So my wife tells me. Every fucking day. I don't need to hear it from you, too, Victor. Finish up your drink. I'll wait."

"Yes, I have mines," Toldorovic said slowly, as his car wound through the darkness and the sharp turns and steep hills above the town. "Not many. Definitely not new. But I have some. M-70 acoustic-induction jobs."

"Define 'not new,' please," Victor requested. He already had the basic statistics on the weapons: twenty-one inches across, one hundred and eleven inches long, a ton in weight, exclusive of dunnage, of which seventy percent was explosive.

Toldorovic nodded. "'Not new' is pretty *old*, Victor. Decades old. Worse, not maintained. Sitting in a bunker at the old naval arsenal for a long time before I picked them up, along with anything else that wasn't nailed down. I've sold off most of the rest. Frankly, I'd like to get rid of the M-70's—assuming, of course, that your offer is fair— and just retire from this little sidelight. The reason why I'm fat is that I eat too much. Oh, and drink, of course. The reason I do that is *stress* because my *house* is sitting on twenty fucking tons of high explosive. There have been nuclear weapons that didn't pack so much punch."

Victor tsked commiseratingly, then asked, "How many have you got?"

"Thirty-two, plus a testing kit for the fuses and wiring.

The mines are mostly still in their dunnage. I doubt they were much maintained even before the old federation fell apart."

"How much, Free On Board, at Tivat, for the lot?"

And so began the haggling.

Rosoboronexport, 21 Gogolevsky Blvd, Moscow, Russian Federation

There had been a time, a period of over a decade, when Russian arms exportation had been an exercise in chaos, if not outright anarchy. Factories had sold directly to customers. Military branches and even fairly small organizations—motorized rifle divisions, say—had sold direct. The air arms had sold adventure tourism using the latest in Russian fighter technology. Private individuals had also gotten in on the game. This was, indeed, how Victor Inning had begun. There'd been no control, no direction. Worse, with all those independents operating against each other, profits on the trade had been abysmal.

No more. By Decree 1834 of 4 November, 2000, the president of the Russian Federation had set up Rosoboronexport as a monopoly, the sole official intermediary in arms trading. Others still traded on the margins, of course, but the advantages of having the backing of the resurgent Russian state were immense. Better than ninety percent of Russian arms that were exported went through the state monopoly. Moreover, they tended to be relatively quick with their deliveries.

At the desk in charge of Latin American and Caribbean

sales, a weary-looking, suited bureaucrat heard an artificial cough from his open office door. He looked up to see a junior assistant standing with head half bowed and a folder in hand.

"We have a small problem, boss," the junior said.

"Which is?" the senior asked.

"That small order, from Guyana, for four M-240 mortars, a thousand standard shells for them, and eighty Smelchek fuses. The military attaché there recommended approval. Maybe out of boredom." The junior shrugged.

"So what's the problem?"

Again the junior shrugged. "It should have been routine. It's *quite* a small order, after all. But when I brought it by the Ministry of Foreign Affairs they wanted to think about it and get approval. No explanation; they just said to wait."

Boeing 777, Emirates Flight EK763 (Dubai to Johannesburg)

I still think the bastard screwed me, Victor fumed. *Three hundred thousand Euros for some things we don't even know work? Well, to be fair, the test set did indicate that at least three of the five I tested were functional. And the others might be repairable. Maybe. I suppose that, if sixty percent of them work, about twenty thousand USD for a large naval mine isn't entirely outrageous. Assuming, of course, that the test set itself wasn't screwed up. Then again, if it were screwed up it probably wouldn't have said some were good while others were bad.*

But why did I ever agree to that price? He needed the

money more than he knew I needed mines. Oh, Victor, I fear you're getting soft in your old age.

Then one of Emirates' almost invariably lovely and always young and healthy stewardesses swayed by in her stylish uniform and minimal-concession-to-Islam, quasi-veiled cap.

Victor watched the slowing receding rump for a quarter of a minute, just long enough to know, *Okay, maybe not entirely soft in my old age. Yet.*

Victor rode business class, which was at least as good on Emirates as any other airline. The same could not be said for economy, in which the airline crammed people in, ten across on a 777, even more than the industry's miserably uncomfortable standard called for. They claimed their seats were more comfortable.

Yeah? Bullshit. I could swear I heard the crack of a whip, somebody pounding drums, and an overseer shouting, "Row, you infidel swine. Row!"

Pretoria, South Africa

The place hasn't improved any since the last time I was here, thought Victor, on the short drive from Tambo Airport to the headquarters of Pretoria Metal Pressings-Denel. PMP-D had sent a car, driver, and armed guard to meet him at the airport. That had become mere common sense, if the company hoped to do any business at all. Few places in the world had made the jump from civilization to barbarization quite so far as South Africa had, though most were racing to catch up.

What Victor was looking for, two sizes of threaded metal adapters to allow naval mine fuses to be screwed into artillery and mortar shells, plus explosive inserts to carry the explosion from fuse to shell, was really too small a job to garner him any more attention than a car, driver, and armed guard from PMP-D. That suited him just fine. Attention was not something he craved, especially this trip.

Thus. he was somewhat surprised to be led by his guard directly into the large, red brick headquarters and to the chief of marketing, a large rustic, moderately elderly, and not too intelligent looking Boer who introduced himself as "Dirk Cilliers, Mr. Turpin. Welcome to Pretoria. Please; please have a seat."

Victor sat as directed, then laid a folder on his lap, opened it, and pulled out a specifications sheet. "We need several hundred of two kinds of adapters, Mr. Cilliers. For mining work." He handed the sheet over.

The veneer of stupidity on Cilliers' face fell away, as he looked over the sheet. "I can't tell what you want to adapt to them, but why do you want adapters for NATO and Russian artillery shells?" the Boer asked.

Before Victor could answer, Cilliers looked up and said, "I only *look* stupid, Mr . . . Turpin. And only when I want to."

Victor sighed. *Too clever. I was being too clever. Time for a little honesty? Yes, but not too much.*

"Mines," he answered. "The people I represent want to turn a number of artillery shells, which they have, into mines, which they need."

"Congo?" Cilliers mused. "Uganda? Rwanda again?

Colombia, perhaps? Peru? Never mind, I really don't need to know."

"You're not worried about this being a sting?" Victor asked.

The Boer snorted. "Here? In South Africa? When the people who run the country are so desperate for safe-haven cash they'll do or permit anything so long as they get their cut? No, Mr. Turpin, I'm not worried about a sting.

"I am, however, a little concerned that you possibly haven't thought your problem quite through."

"How's that?"

Cilliers laid the paper on his desk and tapped it with his finger. "The interior dimensions for the adapters you want are wrong. We make a number of booster charges, for mining, generally, and those correspond to certain well known uses. None of them will fit your adapters. It is not, however, an unsolvable problem."

Head cocked, Cilliers asked, "You *did* want to buy boosters for your adapters, too, didn't you, Mr. Turpin? For 'mining' purposes?"

"Ummm. Yes."

"Very good. We can handle this. It would help immeasurably, however, if you could tell us the metrics on the fuses that these adaptors are to connect."

"It'll be about a week for that," Victor replied. "Maybe a few days less."

"That will be fine. You can expect the adapters about three weeks after you get us that information. Boosters, too. That's three weeks to being ready, here, ready to move to whatever port or airport you would like."

God, I wish I could ask him about getting some of

*South Africa's stock of old naval mines reconditioned and
sold to us. But that would probably be a bit too much.
Besides, I'm not sure we could deliver any more heavy
mines than I've contracted for.*

"You don't foresee a problem, then, delivering this . . .
mining equipment to port and getting it loaded?"

Cilliers laughed, and the last vestige of apparent stupidity
disappeared as he did so. "Mr. Turpin, I spent twenty
years of my life busting embargoes on my country. And
that was when the whole world was officially interested in
consigning us to the grave. They succeeded, of course;
they buried us. But it wasn't because we couldn't get
around their silly laws. And this is much easier—less than
a single container—than most of the things we used to do.
So, no, no problem. And if you want them FedExed, we
can do that, too. It's only a couple of tons, after all. Of
'mining equipment.' And supplies."

Ministry of Foreign Affairs, 32 Smolenskaya-Sennaya Square, Moscow, Russian Federation

The best one could say about Russian architecture that
dated back to Stalinist times was that it was not *quite* as
bad as had been the Nazis' plans for Berlin. The building
housing the main offices of the Russian Federation's
Ministry of Foreign Affairs was not a positive exception to
this rule. Overengineered, because the Soviet Union of
the late forties and early fifties had lacked the knowledge
and skill for economy, the neo-gothic ministry had set back
construction of desperately needed housing by a significant

degree, all on its own. And it hadn't been the only major, and gaudy, similar project decreed by Stalin.

In an intimate conference room in one of the rear wings of this Stalinist monstrosity, high enough and far enough back to keep at bay the sounds of the dense traffic below, a couple of midlevel bureaucrats pondered what should on the face of it have been a non-problem: Deliver the arms or don't, and, whichever, so what?

"Except that refusal to sell is, in this case, as bad as selling," said one of the two.

"I don't understand," said the other. "What difference does it make?"

"The attaché in Caracas says that Chavez is planning on occupying that part of Guyana Venezuela has claimed for the past couple of centuries. It should be easy, he thinks."

"And?"

"Well, if we send arms to Guyana, Chavez will be pissed off. And he is not only one of our two or three best customers, but he's a serious annoyance to the United States. Or at least he tries to be, has been, and will become so again as soon as the current American president is turned out of office."

"So refuse to allow the arms to be sent."

The first bureaucrat shook his head. "Not that simple. Refusal to sell, when we have no particularly good reason not to sell, might put Guyana on notice that they're on Venezuela's shopping list. This would be as bad for Chavez, or worse, than if we'd delivered the mortars."

"Ah."

"'Ah.'"

"I think I have a solution. What did you say that request consisted of?"

Boeing 767, El Al Flight LY 054 (Johannesburg to Tel Aviv)

The food on Emirates was better, Victor thought, staring down at a barely touched tray of kosher something-or-other. *The stewardesses were better looking too, even if they weren't authentic the way these girls are authentic Israelis. Oh, well, can't win 'em all.*

None of the stewardesses would look him in the eye, and most of them avoided him like the plague. *I suppose it's the Hassidic outfit. Some of those people are worse than Arabs for their disgust for women. Silly sots.*

Menachem Begin Road, Tel Aviv, Israel

Victor and his best Israeli contact, Dov, were seated, as usual on the rare occasions they met, at a table pushed flush against the railing surrounding the outdoor café portion of an eatery that fronted on the main thoroughfare. Between traffic, pedestrian talk, and the hubbub from the other patrons, no one was likely to hear anything said between the two men. Even so, they stuck to Russian as being somewhat less likely to be understood, and considerably more likely to be misunderstood, than the English they also shared.

"That's just too expensive, Dov," Victor insisted, shaking his head and causing his false curls to swirl about his face. "There's no way . . ."

"Can it, Victor," the Israeli responded, holding up one hand, palm towards the Russian. "The . . . items you want are not simple, nor cheap, nor easy to make. Neither are they particularly easy to disappear—which is what my company will have to arrange for, with another company, no less—if we're to get them for you.

"These things are made to be dropped from aircraft, high *speed* aircraft, Victor, then survive that drop, finish arming themselves, and have all their delicate little electronic components working perfectly. That kind of reliability, under those kinds of circumstances, doesn't come cheap."

Victor lowered his head to his hands, thinking furiously. *At the price he's quoting, the redundant 105mm shells are just not enough bang for the buck. So what's that leave me? Thirty-two purpose built, ex-Yugoslav M-70's, and a thousand heavy mortar shells. And maybe we can get some explosive, some barrels, and gin up a better mine, if I have the fuse packages. Maybe. Hell, the fuses and sensors have always been the problem with these things.*

"Six hundred," Victor said, raising his head. "At that price that's all I can afford." *Which is bullshit, but he won't know that.*

"That's bullshit, Victor," Dov replied. "It may be all you have of bombs—you want them for bombs, yes?—but you and your organization can afford damned near anything, if you want to."

"It's all we can use then," Victor conceded, neglecting to mention that, no, they didn't actually have any bombs. "And one other thing. I need the exact specifications for the threading on your destructor kits."

"That's easy. You realize, right," Dov asked, "that at that number the unit price goes up?"

"Yes, I realize that, Dov. Now, what can you come up with to turn a 105mm shell into a landmine? And don't try to screw me on the price."

Rosoboronexport, 21 Gogolevsky Blvd, Moscow, Russian Federation

"So we can transfer the arms to Guyana, but we have to screw them on the deal?"

The assistant nodded, stopped, then explained, "No, we *must* transfer the arms to Guyana *and* screw them on the deal. Partially transfer them, that is. We're supposed to send the shells and the guidance packages, but hold off on the actual mortars. 'People pay little attention to ammunition,' said the foreign ministry, 'and much to real arms.' I suppose there's some truth to that."

The senior of the two went silent, thinking. At length he said, "All right. Make the arrangements for the ammunition. Tell the military attaché in Guyana to tell the customer that the mortars need to be thoroughly rebuilt at the depot before we can forward them. 'Sorry, sir, but we don't have a firm date yet.' But assure them the delivery will be made as soon as possible. After all, we have our reputation as arms makers and dealers to think about."

"Where do we send the shells?"

"Trieste."

★CHAPTER EIGHTEEN★

Elements within the British establishment were notoriously sympathetic to Hitler. Today the Islamists enjoy similar support. In the 1930's it was Edward VIII, aristocrats and the *Daily Mail*; this time it is left-wing activists, *The Guardian* and sections of the BBC. They may not want a global theocracy, but they are like the West's apologists for the Soviet Union—useful idiots.
—Anthony Browne, *The Times,* 1 August, 2005

Turkeyen Campus, University of Guyana, Georgetown, Guyana

In the green parkland west of the main campus, red flags the approximate color of blood waved above a sea—or at least a decent sized lake—of humanity. In that swaying, shimmering crowd, surrounded by the hundred and twenty-two people she had paid a thousand Guyanan dollars—about five United States dollars, or a bit less—each to attend, Catherine Persons waved such a flag, herself. She'd actually paid a hundred and fifty people, but a few of those had taken the money and then quietly disappeared. For the rest:

Except for the students, Catherine thought, *they have no revolutionary fervor whatsoever.* She laughed at herself. *Fervor? They don't even have any interest. But it doesn't matter. Interest will be provided.*

It was, perhaps, not entirely without significance that the university had been founded under the auspices of the People's Progressive Party, initially a hard left, but nationalist, group, which much later morphed into something recognizably social democratic. The PPP had been in power through most of the period 1966 to 1992, and continuously from 1992 to the present day. Nor was it insignificant that among those who had had been contacted for input into the recruitment for the initial faculty of the university was one Paul A. Baran, a Russian Empire-born, naturalized American citizen. Baran had the distinction of being the first neo-Marxist, indeed Marxist of any degree of antiquity, to claim that poverty in the Third World was not a natural condition, but had been introduced and deliberately fostered by capitalism. Marx and Engels would have been surprised by this revelation, of course. Even Lenin, who thought that the exploitation of the Third World was a mere artifact of the attempt to postpone the immiseration of workers in the industrialized world, might have been a little nonplussed. Indeed, any number of starving Indians, prior to the British Raj, might have been surprised to discover that they weren't really poor and wouldn't be until the introduction of capitalism in the West.

In any case, the university remained what it had been designed to be, a center for fairly hard left indoctrination, with a few high points where people actually tried to learn something useful to their own lives and to their country and people. In this, it was not notably different from most any American institute of higher education.

"Power to the people!" finished the final speaker for the morning's festivities. His clenched fist shot up over his head, a sort of physical exclamation point.

With that, the red flags, carried by such as Catherine Persons, began moving to the south, where Dennis Street bordered that edge of the campus. The followers, both paid but unmotivated citizens and unpaid but motivated students, trooped along, generally in close company with the banner bearers. Mixed in were a number of better paid thugs, but their job wouldn't come until a bit later. The initial echoes of "Power to the people" were rather badly out of synch. This improved, however, as the marchers caught their rhythm.

And, thought Catherine, her band clustered around her, *the chants are better than a song, since almost none of these know the right songs. "Rise up ye victims of privation . . ."*

Intersection, Sheriff Street-Dennis Street, Georgetown, Guyana

Neither riots nor demonstrations were particularly uncommon here in Georgetown. Nor were the police ill-equipped or ill-trained for dealing with either. They did lack for certain items of major equipment—mobile water cannons were hard to come by, for example, and sundry high tech items that were just being fielded in Europe and the United States were just a dream at this point. Still they were individually well equipped, and pretty well drilled, enough to deal with either demonstration or riot. Best of all, they had tear gas.

The trick, though, thought police Sergeant James Cumberbatch, standing behind his thin line of riot-equipped constables, *is preventing the one from turning into the other.*

Cumberbatch—like most of his men, tall and dark and rather thin—watched the approaching mass and tried to guess their numbers by the number of revolutionary flags they carried.

Too many, too thick, to count. Not good. Not at all good. Still, they're orderly enough so far.

As the mass neared, and their chanting grew louder, both of Cumberbatch's immediate subordinates, Corporal Singh and Lance Corporal Corbin, turned to glance his way, looking for a sign of confidence. The sergeant didn't disappoint; his return smile said, "Routine, boys, just routine."

Cumberbatch had set his line back about twenty meters from the intersection, just about where Dennis Street changed name to Lamaha Street. This was far enough back to provide a little reaction time, should the mob get unruly, but not so far back that the thin line of riot troops would fail to intimidate.

The sergeant breathed a deep sigh of relief when the point of the column turned south, along Sheriff, toward the Botanical Gardens. This was precisely where the marchers had said they were going—*for more pointless speeches, no doubt, right at Revolution Square*—and also precisely where the government wanted them to go. He relaxed still further when many among the mob waved or called out friendly greetings as they passed.

Moving at less than two miles per hour, the long and ragged column continued to pass. It slowed at one point; Sergeant Cumberbatch assumed because the point had reached Revolution Square, causing a backup. Still, his experienced ear didn't pick up any of the changes in tone that would indicate a crowd's mood growing ugly. Better still, the volume of the crowd's chants dropped as the tail of the mass neared Cumberbatch's station. Not that the chanting was any less enthusiastic; it was only that there were fewer mouths pointed in the sergeant's direction.

Even better, the forest of flags had thinned to where Cumberbatch could actually see through their staffs to clear sky beyond. He turned around to address the men.

"Relax, boys," the sergeant announced. "It's almost ove—"

The sergeant's words were cut off by a very large, very fast moving rock that struck him on the back of his helmet, stunning him and knocking him to his hands and knees.

Square of the Revolution, Georgetown, Guyana

The square was doubly misnamed. It was not, in the first place, a square, but more of a spot, with a hideous monument to the failed 1763 slave rebellion, topped by a grotesque statute of its leader, "Cuffy," stuck in the curve of Vlissengen Road, at the western end of a long park.

Secondly, Guyana had never really had a revolution, being just one of those places that formerly imperial powers had decided weren't even worth their time and sweat, let alone their blood, to keep direct control over.

Whether those decisions—perhaps better said, refusals to *make* decisions—had been correct was an arguable point. Indeed, the nascent nationalism Harold MacMillan had sensed across the Empire, though especially in colonized Africa, and which had given rise to his "Wind of Change" speech before South Africa's parliament, in 1960, had proven ephemeral. If there had been any real Wind of Change it was not in the colonies, but in the hearts and minds of those in the West who no longer had the will to keep them. "Wind of Change" would have been better and more honestly phrased as "Vacuum of Will."

If there had been little or no true nationalism, antiimperialism there had been, of course. Still, once the imperialists had departed so went all the meat of it, barring only pointless rhetoric, as old colonies reverted to rule by tribes and clans, and the faux-Marxist ethnic dictators who depended on those.

Guyana, at least, had so far been spared the worst of *that*.

Catherine Persons positioned herself and the flag she carried to place the latter between herself and the sun, about halfway down its arc, to the west. Others did likewise. She, like the other banner bearers, remained standing while the mass took seats on the grass around the square. Here and there local news types, and at least one team from one of the international agencies, stood under hastily erected canopies, with cameras on tripods.

A thin line of riot-equipped police arced around the square, on the far side of Vlissengen Road. They seemed relaxed enough, if no more comfortable than Catherine was, standing mostly in the sun.

The speakers from the university portion of the demonstration were going to be recycled to speak again, here, by Cuffy's statue. It wouldn't do to have them speak to only half a crowd, however. While the tail closed up and found seats, entertainment was being provided by one of Georgetown's local bands. Catherine was a little amused to see the riot police tapping feet and swaying in time to the band's music.

If she'd been amused, she was very surprised when the swaying and tapping stopped, and the police stiffened to attention and dressed their ranks. She was more surprised still when they began a cadenced advance, clear riot shields in front of them and batons poking past those. A few men behind the skirmish line held canisters in their hands she assumed were tear gas.

"This is bullshit," Catherine said aloud. "We're *peaceful*, not a riot."

She cursed herself for a fool. *Why didn't I bring my goddamned gas mask?*

Inspector Isaacson stood relaxed, leaning against a patrol car parked on the north side of Brickdam Street, listening to the radio reports. It was all wonderfully and relaxingly routine until he heard:

"This is Corporal Singh . . ." In the background were

screams punctuated by several shots, probably pistol
shots. "Sergeant Cumberbatch and Lance Corbin are
down . . . we're under attack by the mob. They attacked
out of nowhere . . . no reason . . . none at all. For God's
sake; help us!"

A few moments later came a call from a patrol car, giving its location as, "Vlissengen and Lamaha. The mob is
armed and heading north. We are under fire."

North? thought Isaacson. *Defense Force Headquarters.
And arms. Shit.*

From the west came the sounds of police sirens.
Isaacson followed those by ear until he was sure enough
that they, too, recognized the threat and were going to
secure the GDF headquarters. *But the major threat—the
major potential threat, anyway—is here, where the mass is.*

*We need to move them away from the center of town. If
they want to run riot at the university, that's their problem.
But if I let the shops on Regent Street and Stabroek
Market be looted, it's mine.*

With a rueful shake of his head, the inspector left the
patrol car behind him, walking east to where he could give
orders to the riot police to move the demonstrators out.

"Lawyers, Guns, and Money" (SCIF), Camp Fulton, Guyana

"How interesting," Boxer said aloud, though he was the
only one in the conference room watching the plasma
screen on one wall. The screen showed scenes from
Georgetown, to the north. Those scenes—riot and blood
and arson—were live.

"What's interesting?" Stauer asked, walking into the conference room and taking a seat.

Boxer didn't turn his eyes from the screen, but just nodded in that direction. "Riot isn't so unusual here. Riot on *that* scale *is*. And we didn't have any warning. Apparently nobody in the government expected this."

"It's a pretty poor place," Stauer answered. "Lots of discrepancy between the haves and the have-nots."

"Yeah, sure," Boxer agreed. "And that accounts for the demonstration and even some of the rioting. But as near as I can piece together, this is a different order of magnitude. Those people have guns, some of them, modern rifles. Where did those come from? In the numbers the police are seeing, anyway?"

"Got me. Where do you think?"

Boxer shook his head. "If I knew, we'd have tipped off the government. And they could have been bought locally, of course, but, if so, where did the money come from? No, I don't know the answer to that, either. Bridges and his people are working the question. Still, the timing is suspicious, given everything else happening hereabouts."

Stauer smiled. "You're suspicious of everything."

"It's part of my job . . . or at least my training."

"Fair enough," Stauer conceded. "So what's the purpose?"

Miraflores Palace, Caracas, Venezuela.

Hugo Chavez smiled at the screen. His was considerably larger and more expensive than the one in the Camp Fulton SCIF conference room.

Beautiful, he thought, at the images of fire and destruction, *just beautiful. Now the gringos will cancel the visit of their own battalion to that mercenary group on our soil. That eliminates the chance of killing official gringos when we liberate the place. Better still, as long as we can keep the violence up, and there's no reason we can't, when we invade we can claim to the world that we're there to restore peace. Definitely good public relations there. Best of all, we might even be able to get the idiots in their government to invite us in. Wouldn't that be just lovely?*

Chavez watched the screen with satisfaction for a few more minutes. Finally certain that that part of the plan was coming together nicely, he pressed a button on his intercom and said, "Marielena, there's no real hurry on this, but fence some time in my schedule to visit the troops around *Ciudad* Bolivar and make the travel and security arrangements once you do. Don't tell anybody anything they don't need to know. No, not even your cousin, Mao."

Time for a little follow up, I think.

★CHAPTER NINETEEN★

To sit back hoping that someday, some way, someone
will make things right is to go on feeding the crocodile,
hoping he will eat you last—but eat you he will.
—Ronald Reagan

Room 227, Hotel Venezia, Puerto Cabello, Venezuela

The advantages, Lada thought, *of playing a whore rather
than just a horny girlfriend are immense. For one thing,
the whore comes in contact with a great many more men,
and thus information. More importantly, though, men
will talk to a whore—and the fools always need to talk to
someone—more openly because whores don't matter.*

Dressed again, and freshly showered, she bent over the
slumbering form on the bed, gave it a chaste kiss, and then
stood, turned, and left the room, silently. Her "customer"
hadn't paid for, nor expected, an all night event, in any
case.

Taking the stairs down, she passed through a fire door
and turned toward the main entrance. Nobody seemed to
spare her a second thought.

Over the clicking of her heels on the sidewalk, Lada sensed someone trailing her as she turned right on *Calle 13 Miranda* for the walk back to the hotel she shared with Morales. She had a small roll of medium denomination bills tucked between her breasts, her payment from the Russian shipfitter desperate for a little taste of home. Next to the cash was a small, thin, but very sharp switchblade. Well, a working girl—even a fake one—had to watch out for herself, didn't she?

At an intersection, she carefully looked left and right before crossing. She looked especially carefully to the left, making sure that there was, in fact, someone following her and, more importantly, making sure he didn't notice that she did.

As her feet carried her quickly across the street, she wondered, *Criminal or cop? And does it make any difference? He looked fit, from what I could see. I doubt I can outrun him. And, even if I could, if he's a cop he can call in backup. I dare not lead him to my hotel; then Morales and I will both be up for a slow interrogation and a quick bullet.*

Lada's eyes glanced left and right as she walked, looking for some suitable ambush position or, at least, some kind of refuge.

Okay, so worst case; it's a cop. What turned him on to me? I'm hardly the only Russian selling her ass in Venezuela. Was the room bugged? Did they hear— hmmm, what was that shipfitter's name? Ah, yes, Dmitri. Did they hear Dmitri telling me when the job would be finished? Seems too likely.

Again, she stopped to check for traffic before crossing

an intersection. Again she saw that her tail was still there. She also saw a narrow alley, to her left front.

That's where it will have to be.

Lada crossed the street at a normal pace, then began to run just as she reached the far side. She ran only so far as the alley she had seen. Bending, she took off her high heeled shoes and threw them as far as she could up the street. Then she ducked into the alley, her nose wrinkling at the stink of long uncollected garbage. She placed two fingers into the cleft of her breasts and pulled out her knife. Holding one palm to the device as she pressed the button, Lada then moved that palm and the gripping hand apart slowly enough to muffle both of the switchblade's characteristic clicks.

Finally she pressed her back to the alley wall nearest the direction from which she'd come and waited, listening carefully to the rising sound of footsteps.

Lada's heart began to beat rapidly as the footsteps neared. She ruthlessly suppressed it; forcing herself to an unnatural calm. She bent her knees, ready to spring, and waited those last few tension-filled seconds for her pursuer to appear.

And then he was there, walking swiftly with his head and eyes turned up the street. Her face a mask of pure defensive rage, on bare feet Lada pattered behind him. He seemed for a moment to hesitate, as if he sensed that he were now the quarry. If he did sense it, it was too late as Lada's left arm snaked around his neck and the right hand drove her knife deep, deep into his abdominal cavity. She twisted the thing, searching out the kidney and ensuring her victim's pain would be too great even for him to cry out.

His body spasmed in unimaginable agony. Still with the searching knife stuck in his back she pulled with her left arm, then pushed slightly forward, easing him down to the ground. As he sank she withdrew her blade, then stuck it into his throat, sawing her way forward until rewarded with a splash of blood, gushing away.

Posada Santa Margarita, Puerto Cabello, Venezuela

Morales' eyes were fixed on scenes of rioting back near to what he'd come to think of as home. He was alone in the room, since Lada was out doing what she did best, trading her looks, and sometimes her body, for information.

He heard the lock being worked quickly. Immediately he reached one hand down into the cushion and wrapped it around the knife he'd secreted there. He hadn't had the local "ins" to safely buy a decent firearm and, so, knives for himself and Lada had had to do. About the time his fingers began to curl the door opened and Lada stepped in.

"I was followed," she said, as calmly as she might have observed that it was going to rain.

"How do you know it wasn't just a rapist stalking a hot blonde?" Morales asked, not quite so calmly. After all, there *were* some substantial red spots on her clothing.

She huffed, "Because when I killed him and searched him he had an ID that said '*Dirección de los Servicios de Inteligencia y Prevención,*' that's how. I pulled the body into an alley fairly overrun with garbage. It shouldn't be found before morning, if then."

"Works for me," Morales agreed. *We can discuss the need to kill him later.* "Time to bug out."

Lada reached into her handbag and pulled out a pistol, a Glock, in a shoulder holster with the straps wrapped around it. This she tossed to Morales. "Figured we could use this. I kept the wallet and ID, too."

"Good girl," Morales answered. "But get moving."

"Do we have enough information?" she asked.

"Of what we were sent to get, yes," he replied. "Precise early warning that the invasion is en route . . . someone else will have to provide."

"Good enough," she said, tearing off a blond wig and racing across the suite to pull out her "run like hell" clothes. If Morales' presence caused any reluctance on her part to strip down to panties, it was tolerably hard to see.

Gulf of Venezuela, Colombian side (barely)

By the strobe-like light of Lake Maracaibo's distant, natural lighthouse, the *Relámpago del Catatumbo,* Ryan and Rohrer helped Bronto ease himself over the side of their small, gently rocking rental craft. His Cayago SeaBob already floated in the water nearby. Just past that a neutrally buoyant lump of metal and air mattress, about the size of a small naval mine, was attached by a rope to a D-ring clipped to a belt at Bronto's waist.

Though the frequent flashes, even at this distance, could, in theory, make the boat more visible, as a practical matter Ryan was sure that it would do more to ruin night vision than to aid normal vision.

"This is box-o-rocks stupid, you know," Bronto said, still hanging on to the boat's gunwale. His night vision equipped mask was perched back on his forehead. "We've already determined that there is no fucking way in hell for us to get from Colombia to Puerto Fijo to mine any of the ships there. Not without a sub, we can't."

"Yeah," Ryan agreed, "but I want to see how far you can get on one of those things on half a charge to see if we can't reseed the mines—assuming anybody comes up with some—that a passing merchant ship might blow. So go out as far as you can on half a charge, surface, get a GPS reading, then come back. It's simple. And stop bitching about it."

"Yeah," chimed in Rohrer. "Don't you know how much people pay for the privilege of driving one of those expensive toys?"

"Then *you* do it," Bronto answered.

"Nah. I mass too much. Bad test."

"Now go," Ryan ordered. "And conserve power."

"Fuck," Bronto muttered, before emplacing his mouthpiece, lowering his mask, rotating the eyepiece, and swimming the few short strokes to the SeaBob.

"So what are we going to do, Chief?" Rohrer asked. "Since we can't—no how, no way—do what we came to try to figure out a way to do?"

"Maybe we can do half of it," Ryan said. "Maybe we can hump SCUBA gear over sixty miles of mountain, river, swamp and jungle to get to the lake to plant limpets on a few ships at Maracaibo. Maybe. As for the rest . . ." He looked off generally to the east, in the direction of

Venezuela's Puerto Fijo. He shook his head and admitted, "I don't know. Maybe we get a small stockpile of mines in Colombia, so we can reseed the bay. Maybe. But the more I think about it, the more I think we're pissing up a rope with that one, too."

"Why?"

"Because once the initial mines are laid, any one of them might get set off at any time. What if one of them goes off while one of us is within a klick of it?"

"World class case of the bends?"

Half seen in the flash of the *Relámpago del Catatumbo*, Ryan smiled mirthlessly. "We'd get bent, in any case.

"I mean, it would be different if we could base over on that side. But we're really obvious in a sea of Latins."

"So what then?"

"I'm thinking a one-time direct action. Cross from Colombia. We can get Zodiacs, I think. So we cross on those, low, slow, and quiet. We land. We attack. And we basically smash the shit out of the oil storage facilities, refineries, and maybe the pipeline. Then we get the hell out of dodge and maybe get ourselves interned in Colombia."

"Arms and explosives?" Rohrer asked.

The team chief shrugged. "Buy 'em off FARC? Bribe someone in the Colombian Army to shit us some? Get one of the teams from the U.S. Army working in Colombia to get them for us, on the sly? Have them landed by night by a passing ship? Not really my problem. Yet."

"You know," Rohrer said, "if we did that there's no saying that a couple of us couldn't SCUBA to Puerto Fijo and put limpets on a couple of random ships. While the main attack was going on, I mean."

"Even if we didn't do it but said we would, that would have one distinct advantage," Ryan replied.

"What's that?"

"The asshole—whoever it was—that came up with the idea of using limpets to supplement the real mines wouldn't be embarrassed, so would be less likely to fight us over it."

"I could see that."

The rope leading to the mine simulator tugged at his waist.

I can't see shit *in this muck*, thought Bronto as he moved forward under the power of his Cayago SeaBob. He was perhaps a fathom below the surface. *Even* with *the frigging night vision device in front of my eye I* still *can't see* shit. *Well . . . that's not entirely true. I can see the control panel. But only because the SOB is illuminated and right in front of my face. And I can see the surface. But only because of the lightning flash reflecting from the clouds.*

Slow, the man said. Bronto's left thumb pushed a red button, causing the SeaBob to slow to a comparative crawl. The tug of the towrope immediately lessened.

A combined compass and GPS was strapped to the SeaBob, just below the control panel. The GPS was useless enough down here, but the compass was critical. Bronto paid attention to that to keep himself on a due east bearing.

In the Gulf of Venezuela, one of the larger specimens of *Crocodylus acutus,* the American crocodile, rarely worried about his bearings. Where food was, that was a good direction to head in; where food wasn't, wasn't. Since he couldn't see any better than Bronto could, and in the absence of any particular notice of food, one direction was pretty much as good as another.

This particular crocodile—his mother had never bothered to name him, of course, though he usually thought of himself as "Buz," from the sounds made by the flock of winged minions who followed him adoringly whenever he was on land—was moving generally westward in a slow, sinuous, almost snakelike, swim. Buz was a particularly handsome specimen of his sex and race. All the girl crocodiles said so. At least they would have said so, Buz was sure, if they could have said anything.

Of course, in crocodile terms, handsome was somewhat relative and largely driven by the concept of BIG. And Buz, at nearly seven meters, and just at a metric ton, was quite large indeed.

Buz was also quite hungry.

While Bronto couldn't see much beyond his control panel, he couldn't help but notice both the shadow passing above and the turbulence that shadow created. Still keeping his hands on the control levers, he lifted his head as far back as he could without risking the current tugging off his mask.

And Bronto saw . . . and he saw some more . . . and he saw . . .

And then his mind screamed, *DINOSAUR!*

Buz was somewhat distantly aware of the strange creature passing a tail or so below him. It didn't sound like food. It didn't smell or taste like food. And, since it didn't run, like nearly any sensible food creature would have, Buz assumed, not unreasonably, that it probably wasn't food.

He intended to ignore it. But then it took off like a . . . *Well . . . Buz dunno. But run like food; must be food.*

Buz was not only big for his species, but also a veritable genius. That's how he'd gotten to be so big. He pointed his snout down and made a twisting lunge for what seemed to be the tail of his prey.

Bronto's right thumb frantically worked the green button to get to top speed as fast as possible. Sadly, a SeaBob hauling a man and a dummy mine is not necessarily faster than a dinosaur that didn't know it was supposed to be extinct. Before the machine could get up to speed, Bronto was literally pulled off of it by the rope around his waist. Worse, he felt himself being tugged backwards in sharp, skin-ripping jolts.

Desperately, on autopilot, his right hand sought the knife he kept strapped to his leg. It had to be done on autopilot, since his mind was screaming, *Oh, my God, oh, my God, oh, my God, it's gonna eat me!*

Terror lent speed. While the dimly seen reptile in front of him worried at the dummy mine, Bronto's knife cut, cut—*cut, you bastard!*—through the tow rope. Once free, he began swimming—*Oh, my God, oh, my God, oh, my God, it's gonna eat me!*—away as fast as he could stroke and paddle.

Fortunately for Bronto, the SeaBob was designed for human error as well. As soon as he'd been pulled off of it, and his hands from the controls, it had automatically stopped dead in the water. He almost swam past it, mesmerized, looking backwards at the gigantic twisting shadow in the water, so great was his fear. Fortunately, the control panel was still lit, and seeing that from the corner of one eye, he lunged for the sled.

Hands sought the controls. *Oh, my God, oh, my God, oh, my God, it's gonna eat me!* Right thumb pounded the green "Go" button, and the thing took off at its top submerged speed of just under ten miles an hour.

Sadly, a crocodile can swim faster, at least in the short term.

Whereas Buz had been hungry, therefore a little grumpy, before, now he was positively angry. The damned unfairness of the thing. It acted like food; he struck; he caught; and then the damned thing refused to taste like food. All that was bad enough, but he'd broken a tooth—possibly two of them—in the process, and it or they *hurt.*

Somebody's gonna pay!

And I know who.

Bronto's teeth were so tightly clenched on his mouthpiece, and his hands on the control sticks, that both hands and his jaw would have looked white had it been possible to see them.

Of course, he wasn't looking even at his hands. Instead, his head was turned around almost one hundred and eighty degrees where, with the combined aid of lightning flashes from the distant mouth of the Catatumbo and his mask's integral night vision monocular, he could *just* make out the dinosaur—*Gotta be a dinosaur*—pursuing him.

Rather, he could just make out a head that seemed longer than he was and twin serrated rows of teeth.

Oh, my God, oh, my God, oh, my God, it's gonna eat me! was way too complex a thought at that point. Instead, his mind yammered, *fuckfuckfuckfuckfuckfuckfuck!*

A sudden slush of turbulence and a sudden heavy pull on his right foot told him that the beast's maw had closed. Since he didn't faint from pain, and since his foot, once encased in rubber, now felt water rushing over it, he assumed the creature had just missed the foot, tearing off, instead, one of his flippers.

Fuckfuckfuckfuckfuckfuckfuck!

He pulled up a bit, bending his body to lauch the SeaBob for the surface. *Aiaiaiaiai! Make better time on the surface. Fuckfuckfuckfuckfuckfuckfuck!*

He broached like a small whale. Immediately he spat out his mouth piece, screaming, "Rrryyyaaannn! Rrrooohhhrrreeerrr! Helllppp meee!"

Then he splashed back into the water, the crocodile in hot pursuit.

"Did you hear something, Ryan?" Rohrer asked.

"Something like what?" the team chief responded.

"Dunno. Odd sound. Like a . . . long, drawn out shriek of terror. But not from anything necessarily human."

Ryan shook his head. "Your hearing's better than mine. Too many loud booms over the years, doncha know?

"You *sure* you heard something?"

"Pretty sure," Rohrer replied. He went silent for a moment, listening carefully. "There it goes again. Maybe we oughta go look."

★ CHAPTER TWENTY ★

> But good horses with competent riders will
> manage to escape even from hopeless situations.
> —Xenophon, *On Horsemanship*

Posada Santa Margarita, Puerto Cabello, Venezuela

Lada carried her own large handbag, into which she'd stuffed their GPS unit.

"You drive," Morales said, tossing Lada the keys to their rental car. She snatched them from midair and started for the door. Morales then took their bags, not because the contents were particularly valuable in themselves as that anyone leaving bags behind in a hotel, not too very far from where a secret policeman was killed, was likely to come under suspicion. And they needed at least some time to put some distance between themselves and the probable investigation, and possibly as much as twelve hours to get closer to one of the prearranged extraction points.

Leaving openly but in a hurry is suspicious, too, Morales thought. *But not as badly.*

They walked with remarkable calm down to the front desk, chatted for a few moments with the matron at the desk, mentioned a death in the family, and then paid their bill. Calmly, they strolled out the garish door and round back to the parked rental. The bags were quickly stuffed into the trunk.

"Which direction?" Lada asked, as she slid in behind the wheel.

Morales whipped out a cell phone and began to type a message. "Just get us out of town while I see who's available. It'll be either Ryan's team or the Spetz on the boat."

Port of Spain, Trinidad

"Message from Lada," Kravchenko announced. Musin was standing over his shoulder in an instant. He read off the screen quickly, it was a simple coded message: "What's for dinner? I'm famished."

"They need an extraction," Musin said to Baluyev, as the latter descended into the lower, darkened cabin. "Quick as possible."

"Who's closer?" Baluyev asked. "Us or the team at the Gulf of Venezuela?"

"Them," Kravcheko said, "but it doesn't really matter. Lada and Che have a car, or they're supposed to. So they can move to meet either of us. And we know we've got the message. The Americans haven't answered yet."

Baluyev considered that. *The whole crew is aboard. We're not terribly suspicious, ourselves, not as suspicious as some more obvious special operations types in a small boat*

would be. So . . . how long to get to one of the linkup points?
Figure at least eighty kilometers an hour for Lada and
Morales, twenty for us. Sooo . . . Ideal linkup would be at
Carupano. He looked at the map mounted on the bulkhead
and said, "Send back, 'Borscht, at Chez Colombo.'"

Puerto Cabello, Venezuela

"Head toward Valencia," Morales said, after seeing the
message pop up on the screen of his cell. "When we get
close, start looking for the highway east."

Lada nodded. "Where's the pickup?"

"Carupano. It's about two hundred and fifty miles east
of here on the coast."

"Sea or air?" she asked. She knew there was an airstrip
at the town.

"Sea."

"Damn!"

"Why's that?" Morales asked.

"Tim Musin," she replied. "And I don't know what to
do about him."

Gulf of Venezuela

Rohrer was steering from the small outboard motor at the
stern. Ryan, kneeling forward, had placed a set of night
vision goggles over his face. He pulled them away from his
eyes for a moment, blinking and not quite believing what
the eyes and goggles told him.

"Holy shit!"

"Gedidawayfrommeee!" Bronto screamed, still punching the green "Go" button for all he was worth.

"What is it, Chief?" Rohrer asked.

There was disbelief in Ryan's voice when he answered, "Biggest fucking alligator—or maybe crocodile—you ever saw. Bigger than this boat. Too big to fuck with."

"Man," Rohrer said, "we can't just let it eat him."

"No . . . no." The team leader pushed the goggles back on his head, then turned and began rifling through a small kit box, mounted amidships, that came with the rental. He emerged holding a 26.5mm flare gun in one hand, and three flares gripped in the spaces between his fingers.

"Gemmeoutaherrre!"

Snivel, snivel, snivel, Ryan thought as he used a thumb to break open the pistol at the breech. He slid one of the flares in, then bounced the barrel off of his left forearm to lock it back in place. The same forearm then served as a brace to push the goggles back over his eyes.

"Aiaiaiai!"

Shit, Ryan thought. *I've never actually fired one of these things before. The Army only used the self-contained jobbies. Shit.*

Using both hands, he attempted to aim the thing at the grainy crocodilian head showing in his goggles. No good, *the things focus far or near, but not both. Crap. Have to rely on instinct. I hate that.*

Keeping his vision on the croc, Ryan, kneeling again, aimed the pistol as best he could guess at it, and squeezed the trigger. The recoil was something immense, compared to the .45 caliber and 9mm pistols he was used to. It rocked him back off his knees and onto his back, the sharp corner of the emergency kit digging into his flesh. *Gah, that hurts.* He scrambled back in time to determine that he'd missed the thing completely. The remnants of the flare were burning on the surface of the water, far past his man and the croc.

"JesusChristRyanyouasshole! Youalmosthitmeee!"

Blow the mission or lose one of my men? Screw it; the mission's impossible anyway. Turning backwards, Ryan shouted, "Stand by to put us near alongside the croc, then to make a run for Bronto."

Ryan flipped the goggles off his head and let them fall into the bilge. *Screw them, too.* Again he broke open the flare gun and inserted a round. He pointed the thing up and pulled the trigger. This time he was ready enough and balanced enough not to be knocked over.

The flare flew reasonably straight and true before blossoming into a bright red sun. While it was flying, Ryan reloaded and waited. As soon as the flare lit off, he shouted "Hard left" to Rohrer, and "ahead, slow."

As the boat turned, then steadied on a course roughly parallel to Bronto and the croc, the team chief took aim again. He delayed for a few seconds, judging the rocking of the boat. Just as the light overhead began to die out, he pulled the trigger.

"Now sprint it for Bronto!"

Buz might have been a genius among crocodiles. This still made him a fairly dumb creature. When he felt the impact of the flare in the water, and saw the bright red flame, he snapped at it.

What he thought, when his jaws closed on the solid fire, was impossible to translate into English, and unprintable if it could have been.

"Left . . . left . . . right . . . left . . . straight." Ryan perched himself just back from the bow, and waited as the boat drew near the bucking SeaBob. The croc was writhing in a pretty good simulation of agony as they passed it. Ryan thought he saw red light gleaming from between the creature's rows of teeth.

"Match speed!" Ryan shouted, then reached out and grabbed Bronto by the regulator of his tank. He pulled the man off the device, which dutifully stopped. Then, bending low, he pulled Bronto to the side of the hull. "Get in, godammit," he commanded, as he helped haul the man over the side. *Screw the SeaBob.*

"Now get the fuck out of here! To shore! Fast!"

Now Buz was *really* annoyed. He saw the boat screaming away to the west. *I'm tired and it's moving too fast*, he thought. The frustration was really more than a crocodile ought to have to bear. Then he saw the SeaBob, sitting there on the surface unmoving. *Hah, it must be more tired than I am. Well, I'll sure show it a thing or two.*

Savoring the prelude to his revenge, the croc swam in a leisurely fashion. As he neared, he opened his massive jaws wide to encompass the sea sled. At precisely the right moment, he slammed them together, smashing the SeaBob and incidentally letting water at the batteries.

Boom.

★ ★ ★

"What the fuck was that?" Rohrer asked, as the explosion a hundred meters behind the boat roiled the water.

"Dunno," Ryan answered. "And who cares? Just get us to shore."

"Who . . . cares?" Bronto echoed, breathlessly. The poor bastard was still shaking. "And . . . I . . . am . . . never . . . getting . . . into . . . the water . . . near here . . . again. Not. Ever."

Can't say I blame you, Ryan thought. *But we'll be back, even so. So I suppose I'd better leave two men at the apartment and pay a few months' rent in advance.*

Highway 9, Venezuela

Lada kept her speed down to just above the posted limit. There was no sense in attracting attention from the police, which both obeying the limit and flagrantly ignoring it might have invited. Caracas and its lighted skyline were well behind them now. The highway, beginning to need repair, rumbled below them.

"What's Tim's problem?" Morales asked. "Does he blame you for what you do for the regiment?"

"He would if he let himself think about it, maybe," Lada answered. "But if he'd let himself think about it, he'd realize I'm poison in *any* dose. So he doesn't let himself think about it."

Morales grinned. "Well . . . none of us do. Men, I mean. Frankly, we can't stand being in the same room, maybe even on the same planet, as someone who's had the woman we love. We are not entirely—which is to say, not at all—rational about matters of love and sex."

"I know," Lada said. She shook her head, despairingly. "But Tim . . . ah, hell; he's such a nice guy, so sweet. He deserves a lot better than me."

"He is a good guy," Che agreed. "Good soldier, too." He laughed.

"What's funny?" Lada asked, her hackles rising.

Morales laughed again. "I spent a good chunk of my life training to kill people like him. I thought of them as good troops, but never as good guys. Strange what being in the same outfit will do to one's perspectives."

"At least if I accepted his courting me, he wouldn't have to worry about my screwing someone *in* the regiment."

"That would be a plus," Morales agreed. He hesitated, then asked, "If you don't mind a personal question . . . ?"

She didn't wait for it. "I do it because I love the sense of power it gives me. For the sex, who cares? I usually feel nothing . . . well . . . nothing but weight. But when I can use it to control a man, and with the added benefit of doing my job? *That's* better than a blinding orgasm. For one thing, the satisfaction lasts."

"Fair point," Morales conceded. "Though it doesn't help you with your Tim problem."

She nodded, dimly visible by the instrument lights glowing on the panel in front of her. "I know. I don't know if there is, or even can be, any help there."

"Have you tried talking to him?" Before she could reply, Morales changed the question to "Let me rephrase that; do you care enough about him to talk to him about it?"

"I care about him too much to talk to him about it."

"Well . . . maybe even more so in that case; I think you should."

"Maybe," Lada half-admitted. "Maybe I should. Ummm . . . Che, we spent quite some time in a hotel room together, both this trip and the previous one with Eeyore. Why didn't you ever : . ."

"Come on to you?" Again, he chuckled. "I can't say about Antoniewicz, but for me, while most men are hard wired to youth, you just look *too* young. Sorry, Lada, but everything about you screams 'jailbait.' Yeah, I know you're not fourteen. But you still *look* fourteen, fifteen at the outside, and I just . . . couldn't."

The light from the dash was too little to see her faint smile. She thought, *You're a good man, too, Che.*

Carupano, Venezuela

A fifteen-foot Zodiac undulated in the waves next to the Bertram sport fisher, the latter being anchored perhaps six hundred meters from the beach. The inflatable rubber boat itself was a veteran of the first operation in Punt, some years prior. In shade, the boat was as black as a pawnbroker's soul. A small electric motor was mounted to the stern. A midnight-clad Kravchenko sat in the Zodiac, ready to move on command. Musin and Litvinov, likewise in black, stood on the Bertram's deck, scanning, waiting with Baluyev for the recognition signal from the shore. In both Musin's and Litvinov's hands were grasped pistols with suppressors, retrieved for the occasion from a very difficult to find hide that appeared to be part of the fuel tanks. You just never knew what might be waiting on shore. All three, Baluyev, Musin, and Litvinov, wore civilian model night vision goggles hanging by the straps around their necks.

Lada twisted the wheel, then slammed on the brakes at a parking lot parallel to and very near the shore. The sea was visible for a good distance out.

Almost as soon as the car stopped, Morales dug the GPS out of Lada's handbag, flicked it on, and waited for it to give a valid position. Time was more important than secrecy, this close to pickup. As soon as he had the grid coordinates he messaged it to Baluyev's Spetz. An acknowledging message was returned almost instantly. Somewhere not too far out to sea, a marine engine growled to life.

"Far signal," he told Lada. Immediately, she flicked the car's beams to high three times.

He was about to get out of the car to retrieve the bags, when Lada put a restraining hand on his arm. "Kiss me," she commanded.

"Wha'?

"Just do it. Cop." She leaned over to him.

With a resigned sigh, Morales went along. *Maybe the cop will do the decent thing and disappear. And . . . it's not . . . exactly . . . ummm . . . unpleasant.*

"Go," Baluyev ordered, as soon as he saw the lights ashore flash three times. As Litvinov untied the rope, Musin fairly sprang over the gunwale and into the Zodiac, causing it to shudder violently. Kravchenko started the near-silent electric outboard, holding the craft against the Bertram while Litvinov boarded. Once everyone was seated, he reversed throttle and backed away, then returned to forward thrust, guiding the rubber boat around its mother and heading it to shore.

Morales backed off just enough to leave space for the Holy Spirit. "Cop still there?"

"Yes," Lada whispered, moving her head as if still in full buss. "I think we need to get rid of him."

"How? I don't want to kill him; he's just a regular guy."

"Yeah," she admitted, then commanded, "Lean back in your seat."

"What?"

"Just do it."

Morales did as commanded. He wasn't quite sure what Lada intended until she bent her head over his lap. Once she had, he was sure what she intended, but, *I don't know whether to be pleased or disappointed.*

He was wrong. She went through the motions, the simulated belt unbuckling, the head bobbing, but that was it. As her head bobbed, quite to no direct purpose, she whispered, "He either does the decent thing and goes away or he comes over here to arrest us where you can kill him."

And I still don't know whether to be pleased or disappointed.

Morales looked at the cop, standing a bare thirty feet away. One hand placed itself more easily to reach the pistol Lada had acquired. The cop looked back, sternly, then laughed, shook his head, and turned away to continue his stroll down the beach.

"Lada," Che said, "you can come up now."

"I'll kill the son of a bitch," Tim said, as the rubber boat scrunched its way up the sand. He drew his pistol, adding, "He's dead."

"What are you talking about?" Litvinov asked.

Musin launched himself for the shore, saying, "That fucking American. With Lada." His feet churned sand as he raced for the car.

"You're being a fool, Tim," Litvinov muttered, following at a brisk trot.

Outside the rental car, Morales scanned around for the cop that had been there. There was no sign of him. Satisfied they were safe from arrest, he went to the trunk, opened it, and began unloading their couple of bags to carry down to the shore. Lada emerged on the other side, her head twisting back and forth, searching for both cop and rescue party. She walked back to join Morales at the rear of the car.

Lada managed to get out, "I see them," only a split second before Tim was upon them, and the fist bearing the pistol had lunged out, striking Morales to the asphalt below.

"You son of a bitch; I'll kill you," Musin said, taking aim.

"What the fuck?" Lada threw herself across Morales' prostrate form and, over her shoulder said, "Tim, stop it. What do you think you're doing?"

"I . . ." The muzzle wavered a bit.

"Tim," she said, sadness in her voice, "stop being an idiot. You and I need to have a long talk. A very long talk. But none of that is about him, because he and I did nothing. Understand? Nothing.

"Now put away that pistol and get the bags." Musin hesitated, though his pistol's muzzle moved away from Lada and Morales. "Now!"

★CHAPTER TWENTY-ONE★

Victory, speedy and complete, awaits the side
that employs airpower as it should be employed.
—Sir Arthur "Bomber" Harris

Bolivar State, Venezuela

It's amazing, thought Larralde, *what the words "Hugo wants" will do to move things along. "Hugo wants," and I get an open area as big as Cheddi Jagan airport. "Hugo wants," and I get nine maintenance tents. "Hugo wants," and I get engineer support like I never dreamed of to build us a pretty good mockup of the airport. "Hugo wants," and I get chairs and lumber and damned well anything else I want, and right fucking now, too.*

A series of Quonset-hut-shaped maintenance tents sat on elevated berms the engineers had thrown up. The tents were set up in groups of three, end to end. As such, they mimicked very closely the interior dimensions of the three transport aircraft—all American-built C-130's—Larralde was going to use to move his reinforced company. Venezuela owned four of them but Larralde's plan assumed that at least one would go down between now and M Day.

The flight crews for the actual aircraft—all four of them—were currently sleeping. They had to be, since they'd spent the previous several nights practicing near-to-the-earth formation flying and rapid sequential landing.

"Behind" each of the aircraft mockups were well-constructed wooden platforms with cleats, also put together by the engineers to simulate the loading ramps. Inside each of two of the mockups were an AMX-13C tank—a French-built light job with a 90mm gun—while along each side of the hull, in chairs set up to simulate troop seats, an additional forty-four armed and equipped soldiers sat. The other mockup contained no tank, but one Tiuna utility vehicle, and ninety-two sardine-packed soldiers. That last mockup was on the left of the three.

For operational security's sake, Larralde had a number of vehicles parked around the area. It did, in fact, look a lot more like a maintenance facility than like three aircraft mockups set up for a rehearsal.

Larralde stood in that central mockup, though in practice he would be belted in along with the troops. Beside him stood a member of the Bolivarian Air Force, a Captain Monegas—large and beefy and surprisingly Irish looking—with a hand-held loudspeaker.

"Tell 'em," Larralde said.

"All right," said Monegas. He lifted the loudspeaker to his mouth and announced, "Though you'll all have had anti-airsickness pills, we'll be flying low and rough. So this is what the inside of the aircraft is going to look and smell like."

Monegas pointed at the deck with one hand. He waved the hand slowly, from one side of the mockup to the other, as if following some unseen tide.

"There's going to be a sea of vomit there, about an inch thick if it were even. But it won't be even. Every time the plane banks right, that sea is going to turn into a tide that washes left before receding. When we bank left; it's going to roll right. All over your boots and maybe up to your ankles."

The air force officer began swaying from side to side. "You might think you have a strong stomach. You don't; not for that. No one does. Yeah, yeah, you'll have air sickness bags. They won't help all that much. And for those of you with really strong stomachs, no matter. That first heady whiff of puke is going to have you shooting the contents of your guts all the way to the other side of the plane."

Monegas laughed, jerked a thumb forward, and added, "Which, by the way, is why the hatch to the cockpit is going to be sealed. Trust me; you don't want your flight crew barfing, too.

"Now some of you might have the bright idea of using your gas masks to seal off the stench. And it *is* a bright idea. How-the-fuck-ever, if you get a whiff of the puke in there with you, you will fill up those masks with vomit before you can get them off. And, even if you don't, ninety percent of you are going to hurl just from air sickness. The masks, if anything, will make that worse."

The flier looked around at the twin rows of faces and was quite pleased to see how many of them had gone pale already. Indeed, a couple of them looked ready to throw up at the thought alone. And one girl, perhaps with more imagination than most of the troops, seemed to be following with her head and eyes an imaginary wave, rolling back and forth across the deck.

"We'll give you a signal," Monegas continued, pointing at a wall mounted light, "a red light, when we're five minutes out. That's not normal procedure, no. We're modifying procedure for you folks.

"If you think that the ride was rough before that, you won't have seen anything yet. It's gonna get worse, boys and girls. A lot worse.

"And then we'll give you another signal, a green light, when we start to descend. That descent is going to be fast and rough, too. The next thing you know, you'll be bouncing down the strip, puke flying up in big globules. Then your pilot will have reversed engines to try to stop as quickly as possible. Expect that the puke will fly and roll forward.

"At that point, it is not improbable that one or two of you will have shat yourselves . . ."

Lily Vargas, balancing on her lap a rucksack that was almost bigger than she was, with her chin resting of the pack's frame, looked seriously queasy. Her eyes fixed on the Air Force officer recounting the horror-story-to-be, watching with terrified fascination as the flier bounced and swayed and made projectile vomiting motions.

"Never flown before?" Carlos Villareal asked in a whisper.

She gulped, shaking her head "no."

"Neither have I," he admitted, patting her thigh for

comfort's sake. "But how bad can it be, really? People do it all the time."

"Not usually like he's describing," she answered.

"It'll be fine," Carlos insisted. "Don't worry so much."

Lily forced a smile, glancing at her squad mate, sitting calm and confident or, at least, unworried. After a moment, and for a change, the smile reached her eyes.

Mao Arrivillaga tried to hide his smirk as the air force lecturer on his mockup, Number Two, to the right of center, did his best to terrify the new personnel. He was saved by a beep from his belt mounted radio and the words, "XO, Sergeant Major, Larralde here."

Mao pulled the radio to his mouth, covering the smirk, and announced he was monitoring. The XO likewise answered.

"Yeah," Larralde said, "we're about finished here with the Air Force's terror session. You guys?"

Mao replied, "I think they rehearsed it. From what I can hear, what your guy is saying there my guy is within a few seconds of."

"Same here," agreed the XO.

"Good . . . standby . . . all right . . . he's talking . . . he's describing bouncing down the strip . . . and the 'plane' has stopped. Out, here."

"We're down!" Larralde announced. Maybe the air force guy needed the loudspeaker but he, by God, was a soldier and could do without the gizmos. "Tank team and unbuckling team; *Go!* The ramp is coming down."

Immediately the three man crew of the AMX-13 raced

to their vehicle. The engine cranked, stalled, and then growled to life. While that was happening, four others, two from each side, all of them medics or supply personnel, ran to the vehicle and began loosening the buckles to the straps that held it down. Those were attached to only a rough simulation of the actual deck arrangements, but they would do. A seventh trooper, bearing a radio in his rucksack, went to stand next to his commander.

All the others, thirty-five of them, stood, recovered their rucksacks, and put those on.

"Infantry sections, *Go!*"

The remaining troops faced aft and began filing out at the double. Larralde watched them break into teams and disappear around the sides.

As soon as all four of the unbuckling team were standing, Larralde and his radio bearer jumped onto the back of the AMX-13. They helped the others load up, pulling the men and women onto the vehicle by main strength. Larralde then said to the driver, "*Go!* The terminal."

As soon as the tank bumped its way down the cleated mock loading ramp to the ground, Larralde's eyes began searching the area. The other "planes" were already unloading, first Mao's, then the XO's. The other teams from his were hoofing it—maybe a little uncertainly—for their initial objectives. *So far, so good . . . so far, so—shit.*

Mao was the first dismounted soldier off of his plane, right behind the churning tracks of the AMX-13. He stopped once his feet hit the ground and began encouraging the troops onward. Like his commander, Mao's eyes, too, scanned the developing deployment.

"That bitch," Mao said aloud, as soon as he saw the presidential limousine. "Next time Larralde takes my cousin on a date, he has my express permission to fuck her . . . in the ass . . . without grease. Imagine the cunt not telling me Hugo was going to be here." The sergeant major shook his head with disgust. "What the hell has happened to family *loyalty* in this country, anyway?"

Mao still had the radio in one hand, a rifle in the other. He moved the radio to his lips and said, "You go report to him, boss. The XO and I can handle this well enough." *Rather, we can handle watching it turn into a disaster as well without you as with you.*

Despite Mao's and the XO's best efforts, the thing unfolding on the field looked disastrous, just a ruin of a plan. Troops milled about aimlessly. Two sets of two had taken to fisticuffs on the field. Chavez, though more politician than soldier, noticed. He couldn't help but notice. And he had to ask.

"What do you expect, Mr. President?" Larralde answered. "It's their first full-speed-run through so of *course* they fucked it up. We'll be doing this fifty more times before we're done."

Chavez nodded, saying, "I believe you." He was really kind of pleased that Larralde had actually thought through what looked like a competent rehearsal plan. It wasn't something one could count on, with the army in the state he'd driven it to.

"Bottom line, Larralde; are they going to be ready?"

"That's . . . a qualified 'yes,' Mr. President. By M Day, they'll be able to board the aircraft, fly, unload in a hurry, overcome light resistance, if there is any, and secure the airport. The specialist teams will be able to do their part, running the control tower and refueling from the stocks there in Guyana. That's the most I can promise. I think it's enough for your purposes."

"Do they know what their mission's going to be?"

The major shook his head in negation. "Mao does; my XO, too. Nobody else beyond very broad lines we've tried really hard to blur."

"When are you planning on telling them?"

"Not more than forty-eight hours out, sir. And they'll be in isolation by the time we do. I can't vouch for operational security from any other group. Mine . . . we'll have it."

Chavez gave off a snort. "I can't vouch for operational security, either," he said. "I can tell you that we don't have any reason to suspect we're compromised. Yet. And I can tell you that all the other components are going into isolation, too, three days before we jump off."

"Oh, and I can tell you one other thing. The gringos won't have any troops in country at that mercenary *cum* training base."

Larralde thought about that for a moment. If he were inclined to be honest with his president he'd have said he really didn't want to fight the gringos. Instead, he simply asked, "How did you manage that, sir?"

"Two ways. One is that we're behind—far behind, but behind—the riots that have been sweeping Guyana of late. That gave the gringos the excuse not to send any troops for a while. The other way is that someone in the White House is our ally."

"Their president?" Larralde asked. He didn't believe it.

"No," Hugo replied. "Oh, he's sympathetic, but it isn't him. One of their president's mentors has pushed to cancel that deployment, even before we got the riots started. The riots helped. The riots also got us a few other things we can use, but you don't need to know about those.

"And now, if you don't mind, Major, get your people back on those mockups and show me a dry run that *doesn't* end in disaster. However many it takes; I've got all day."

The sun was long down. Monkey and other jungle dwellers were out, the monkeys, in particular, raising a hellacious racket.

Lily Vargas—who normally did not much care for spiders and snakes—groaned as she lay down atop her poncho. Sore and tired, even putting up a mosquito net was beyond her strength. At least she'd found the strength to douse herself liberally with insect repellent.

Carlos Villareal, standing over her, said, "Mao sees you sleeping without your mosquito bar, he'll stake you out over an ant hill. He said he would. I believe him."

"I'm just so *tired* Carlos," she replied. "We did that pointless shit all day. In the sun. With hardly a break. *And my fucking rucksack and rifle together weigh more than I do!*"

"Yeah . . . yeah," he said, "I understand." Without another word he took one knee beside her rucksack and began to rifle through it. Eventually, he touched upon the unmistakable stiff mesh of a fairly new mosquito net. This he took out and began to erect over her supine form, using a couple of trees that framed her at head and feet.

The alignment wasn't perfect so, since trees were not going to be moved, Carlos walked around to the other side of the girl and dragged her by the poncho to a better position. Then he spent a few minutes arranging the net so it would have a fair chance of not coming in contact with her skin. He'd already learned the hard way just how many of the little winged bastards could gather for a feast on any flesh that touched the net. He was *still* scratching from that one.

"Thanks, honey," Lily said when he was done. She thought about it for just a moment—*Carlos always does things like that, whether it's helping me over an obstacle or feeding me when I'm sick or just generally being nice. A girl could do worse*—before adding, "Would you like to join me in here? I stink, but . . ."

"I didn't do it for that," Carlos replied, turning away, embarrassed.

"I know," she agreed. "If you had, I wouldn't have invited you."

★ CHAPTER TWENTY-TWO ★

When an army is overthrown and its leader slain,
the cause will surely be found among the five dangerous
faults. Let them be a subject of meditation.
—Sun Tzu, *The Art of War*

"Lawyers, Guns, and Money" (SCIF), Camp Fulton, Guyana

Tucked away at one end of the SCIF was a small auditorium,
a multifunction screen against one wall and a dozen tiers
of fabric-covered theater seats rising toward the back. The
room contained enough seats for the regimental command
and staff section, the battalions' commanders and their
staffs, the company commanders and first sergeants,
plus a few to spare. There were some openings in Second
Battalion's section, due to the departure of the bulk of
Welch's company for the Philippines. Ordinarily, Second
Battalion would have even more open spots. The United
States having cancelled the next several rotations to the
regiment-run jungle warfare course had left that battalion's
companies out of the jungle for a change.

Other battalions, likewise, had a couple of vacant seats

each for their deployed companies doing contract work around the globe. Still, the rows of seats were mostly filling up, old men complaining at the pain in the knees from walking the steeply descending central aisle.

Unusually enough, in the back, next to Raffick Hosein, Stauer's driver, sat a stunning, slightly olive skinned, rather young woman in a brightly flowered silk dress. Tatiana had never before been invited to one of these, not even when she was still in the regiment. In this case, though, Stauer—on Joshua's advice—had thought she should be, if only because she was the de facto leader of what amounted to the regiment's recreational specialists. Hosein had driven her to the assembly.

Besides, Stauer thought, *Tati is loyal to the regiment, maybe even more loyal than she knows.*

Tatiana stared intently at the tall, ramrod-straight, black regimental sergeant major standing to the left—her right—of the screen. Joshua was patently trying to ignore her presence, so much so that it became obvious he was *extremely* aware of her.

That's all right, the courtesan thought. *If you did anything else, you wouldn't be you, and then I would not love you so.*

In the front row, flanking the regimental staff, sat Lada, Morales—sporting a not unimpressive shiner, Baluyev, Ryan, and the leaders of two of the ground recon teams that had crossed the border—rather, *tried* to cross the border—on foot. They hadn't gotten far before some surprisingly aggressive Venezuelan patrolling had forced them to abort. That was quite significant, in itself. The front row was distinguished from most of the rest by actually having a slight majority of people in it who were not gray-headed and pushing—or past—sixty.

Well past sixty was the RSM. His lips were curled in a habitual sneer. He glared at the "snivelers."

"Shut the fuck up and take your seats," Sergeant Major Joshua ordered. "Christ, you would think you people were twenty-somethings, the way you whine, whine, whine. 'Oh, my pussy hurts!'"

I'm twenty-something, Tatiana thought, *and you can hurt any part of me you like, any time you want to. Foolish man.*

At the opposite side, leaning slightly on a podium, Stauer suppressed a rueful smile. *My fucking back and knees hurt, too, Top,* he thought. *And so do yours; you just refuse to admit it, even to yourself.*

Joshua's curt ass-chewing was sufficient to quiet the hubbub and get people scampering to their seats rather nimbly, ancient and arthritic knees notwithstanding. As soon as the last man was seated, the RSM gave the nod to Stauer. He didn't need it, of course, but the procedure was traditional, an informal equivalent of an exchange of salutes at a formation. In effect, it said, "Okay, *now* they're yours."

"Chilluns, we got problems," Stauer said. He shared a look with his young wife, Phillie, that said, *I couldn't tell you anything before.* The look she returned was, *You are so going to pay for that.*

Stauer shrugged. *Cost of doing business.*

"The short version of that is that we think—no, we're pretty damned sure—that Guyana is about to get heavily 'liberated' by Venezuela." Stauer pointed at the front row, sweeping his hand back and forth. "Over the last month, plus, we've had teams reconning our Bolivarian neighbor. They'll give you what they found—or, in the case of some of the ground teams, what they were blocked from finding—later. For now, we've got some decisions to make.

"Our choices are basically to hit Chavez first, to wait for him to hit us, then defend and counterattack, to run like hell for another base in some other country, or to convince Venezuela—which is to say, Chavez—that we'll hurt him too badly to be worth this place." Stauer let a sneer flash across his face. "Oh . . . or we could try to cut a deal. For reasons I won't bore you with, it's the staff's consensus that no deal that leaves us to continue to practice our trade is possible. I concur in that consensus.

"Also, the first option is right out. Ladies, gents; we're mercenaries. The whole fucking world hates our guts on general principle. We hit a sovereign country—however fucked up, however much an international pain in the ass it may be—we're going to find ourselves at the bottom of a funnel with more military force than we can handle being poured in.

"Some of that force just might come from the United States."

Stauer shook his head. "I'm not going to fight the United States. Just isn't happening. That oath I took, same as most of you? It didn't have an expiration date on it."

"Option Three—pack up and move out—has some problems." Stauer looked up toward Tatiana and said, "Corporal Hosein, please stand." *That's right, son, there are reasons I wanted you here that had nothing to do with chauffeuring everyone's favorite hooker and sometime field medic.*

"Raffick," Stauer asked, "suppose we left? Would the Guyanan troops want to come with us or would they stay to defend their country?"

Hosein shrugged, "I can't speak for everyone, sir, but all the good ones, I think, would prefer to stay and fight."

"Sergeant Major?"

Joshua nodded. "The boy's right. Most of the dirtbags got driven out after we fought Suriname. The ones who are left . . . mostly . . . would stay and defend their country. I'm not sure we'd want the ones who wouldn't."

Neither am I, Stauer silently agreed.

"So we've got a moral problem, folks. We *wrecked* these people's own army to build our regiment. When we did that, we inherited the obligation to defend them. Worse, when we took all these Guyanans under our wing— all thirty-five hundred of them—we also acquired, even if we didn't know it at the time, an obligation to them, the same as we'd have to any troops, not to abandon them.

"Leaders don't run out on the led."

Looking back up into the seats, Stauer ordered, "Sit down, Corporal Hosein."

"That leaves us options two and four. The problem with four is that, while we can beat Venezuela here, and hurt them *really* badly there, we can only do it if they're not expecting it. We tell them how we'd do it, they'd be perfectly able to guard against it, and then we'd have lost our chance. The short version of that is that deterrence, to work, has to be something both obvious and which cannot be guarded against. We fail on both counts.

"Sad, ain't it?"

Seated next to Reilly, Sergeant Major George raised his hand.

"Yes, Sergeant Major?" Stauer asked.

George stood and said, "I'm not interested in running out, either, sir, but we're not the only ones at issue. A good chunk of our men, U.S., Euro, and local, have wives and families. How fair and moral is it to expose them to a real war with a not entirely insignificant regional power?"

Stauer nodded. "Yeah, that's come up in planning. We're thinking of evacuating the families—maybe mostly to Brazil—and using them to give the impression that we've all bugged out. Not sure on that one yet." Looking up for a moment, Stauer waited for the next comment or question. *Will it be Phillie or Lana Reilly?*

"Colonel Stauer?"

Ah, Lana. No matter, they'd both say about the same thing.

"Yes, Lana."

She, as had George, stood, her belly standing out just enough to be noticed, even through her loose-fitting battle dress. Lana's normally cascading hair was done up in a bun at the back of her neck. "Some families are also with the regiment, as soldiers." She looked down, adding, "Or passengers. "

Lana hesitated for a moment, glancing at her husband first, then back to Stauer. She then said, "Like Corporal Hosein, I can't speak for everyone, only for me and *my* passenger. I'm not leaving. *We're* not leaving." She sat down.

Love it when a plan comes together, Stauer thought.

Now none of the men can bug out, even if they were so inclined. Even old men hate being shown up by a girl. Heh. Good girl, Lana!

Stauer couldn't resist a searching look at Reilly, Senior, who seemed torn between pride and utter horror. *Serves you right, you bastard.*

"All right then. Is there anyone present who disagrees with the following: The regiment, also known as 'M Day, Inc.,' stands and fights? If there are, just go to the rear." *And let a nice Jewish girl show you all up as pussies.*

Seeing that there were no takers, Stauer looked up at the Second Battalion's section and said to von Ahlenfeld, "Lava, change to your plans; Welch in the Philippines is on his own. You're staying here." Then he turned his attention down at the rough center of the front row. "Order of brief is Chief of Staff, S-2, S-3, S-4, S-1. Boxer, your show. Take it away."

The big screen at the front of the auditorium projected a map of the northeast corner of South America and its nearby waters and islands. To the lower right, the map showed part of Suriname. To the upper left was the Colombian-Venezuelan border area. Parts of Brazil were shown, as was all of Guyana and Venezuela. Various arrows and other symbols, all in red, illustrated Boxer's best guesstimate of the presumptive enemy's plans.

"The really bad part," Boxer said, after laying out what he did know, or thought he could guess at, especially as concerned how a Venezuelan invasion might come, "is that I have no human intelligence on a time line for this. None of my contacts at State, NRO, NSA, or the Agency are looking at Venezuela, and the ones who will still talk to me tell me they wouldn't tell me even if they did know something. Apparently, Hugo has become Washington's fair haired boy. That is unlikely to change until Chavez says something good about the United States, which is to say, never."

He shrugged, with resignation, then sighed, "As you may imagine, I consider this a bad sign.

"Colombian Intelligence, on the other hand, does keep close track of Venezuela. How-the-fuck-ever, they've got limited capabilities. They mostly keep track of their common border area, which doesn't interest most of us much, their air force, and the coast. The Colombians have agreed—very willingly agreed—to keep me posted on the activities and positions of Venezuela's not inconsiderable amphibious fleet and the combat aircraft, which is all Colombia really cares about, air force-wise. They *might* be willing to tell us what they can of the activities of certain . . . personages."

Boxer pointed at Lada and Morales. "We already know from those two that Venezuela's five amphibs are very nearly ready for sea, after months—even years—of neglect. I should know when they begin loading. That will be our key to when to begin to disperse and to move the families out of here.

"We have to be careful about provoking Colombia by violating their neutrality. Doesn't mean we won't do it, just that we have to be careful."

The S-3, or Operations Officer, Lieutenant Colonel Waggoner, took over from Boxer. Waggoner was grayed blond, where he wasn't balding, and chubby, almost to the point of cherubic, but amazingly strong in every particular.

Waggoner looked out over the rising tide of faces, scanning left to right, bottom to top, trying to gauge the regiment's leadership's emotional reaction to the news. Some seemed grayed or paled, or at least deeply concerned. Still others, most especially Reilly and his sergeant major, George, seemed almost thrilled, broad smiles shining, eyes glowing. At the top of the tiers of seats, seated next to the colonel's driver, Tatiana's lower lip had almost disappeared into her chewing teeth. She seemed as if uncertain of her future, as they almost all were, and still more uncertain as to what she should do.

"Change slides," he said. Almost instantly, the map on the screen updated with various other symbols and arrows, these ones blue in contrast to Boxer's red.

"As Colonel Stauer told us," Waggoner said, "we cannot deter Venezuela; we can only beat them by giving them no warning of what is coming or what is awaiting them. Therefore, we must delay any obvious moves on our part until they're committed on theirs.

"That doesn't mean, however, that we can't do some less than obvious things." Waggoner picked up a wooden pointer—millennia old technology, to be sure, but he was one of the not uncommon men among the regiment who really detested modern technology. Taking a couple of backward steps and turning, his pointer moved to rest on a spot marked "Bow Falls." He announced the name aloud. The pointer shifted slightly down and to the left, as Waggoner said, "Tiboku Falls." Finally, it moved far to the left and up, accompanied by the words, "Apaiwa Falls."

"If none of these existed, our job would be a lot easier. Then again, if all the falls in Guyana weren't there, this place would be rich beyond its people's dreams of avarice.

"B Company, 5th Battalion, Combat engineers?" Waggoner asked.

"Here, sir," Trim announced.

"Starting tomorrow," Waggoner said, "your company gets control of two of the regiment's four cargo hovercraft. You are to move your company to these falls, and, in sequence, build ramps for hovercraft to get around the falls in both directions. Use whichever banks are best, makes no difference to the mission." The pointer moved and tapped a circle where the Mazaruni River bent south to Paeima Falls. "As soon as you have done that, return to base except for one platoon that will serve as guards for a log dump and assembly area, here. That platoon—your Second Platoon, I presume—will support Cazz's battalion. Clear?"

"Clear, sir."

"You may not use explosives. You are on radio listening silence. Any medevac will be by hovercraft or ground, not airplane or helicopter. Still clear?"

Trim nodded. "I don't like it, sir, but, yes, it's clear enough."

"Good." Waggoner shifted attention. "Cazz, you will, not later than three days from now, take your Third Battalion, minus its heavy vehicles, across the Mazaruni River at Kartauri and Turesi Falls. You will have a train of mules from Eighth Service Support Battalion attached to you, as well as your usual support from the Air Defense battery, minus the guns. You'll also have a SATCOM team and a medical team. You may take light vehicles as far as they'll get you, which is unlikely to be all the way to your assembly area. You will move to that assembly area, roughly paralleling the Mazaruni. Under no circumstances are you to get your main body within five miles of that river. If you have a dustoff requirement, get the man or men back by ground, or to the river by ground, and wait for a hovercraft. Yeah, it sucks. Tough."

"Gordo?"

"Yeah, I know," answered the tubby S-4, "my part of this job is to get supply sufficient for Cazz's battalion to operate for at least a month to his assembly area, plus put in a week's worth of consumables at the northwest corner of Hill 890, and another five days worth northeast of Hill 590."

Waggoner nodded, then turned back to Cazz. "Third Battalion will move to its assembly area, then wait on radio listening silence for the word that the attack has begun. Once that has begun, you are to secure the airstrip above Sakaika Falls, then attack across the border, generally to the northeast, ruining the log and aviation base we expect Chavez to set up in the vicinity of Tumeremo. From there, you march onward to *Ciudad* Guyana. It would be a good idea to capture trucks, where possible.

"You are to capture and hold the core of *Ciudad* Guyana, until relieved or ordered to move. I'll cover it in more detail later, but Baluyev's Spetz are tasked to take out the Second Orinoco Crossing, the bridge near *Ciudad* Guyana. They'll escape and evade to you following your seizure of the town."

Cazz shook his head. "You are shitting me, right? That's no town; it's a fucking city, a *big* fucking city."

"No, he isn't," Stauer said, which cut off debate right there.

"Fuck," Cazz muttered, darkly. "Well . . . I'll try. I'll need priority on the tire house and all three of the mock villages for the next few days. Plus tell the ammo people to fuck off over forecasts, I'll need what I'll demand. Fast."

"Agreed," Stauer replied.

"Fourth Battalion," Waggoner announced, again shifting his gaze, "your assembly area, which you are to occupy as soon as possible, is to be approximately six miles south of Crab, Maripa, and Tarpe Falls, south-southwest of Bartica, straddling the cattle trail . . ."

"You mean I have to just sit here and take the first punch?" Reilly asked. "That's absurd!"

"Shut up, Reilly," Stauer said. "You and the bulk of the aviation have to sit here because you're the most noticeable. If Chavez overflies us, and he might—indeed, he may already have—your presence tells him we're expecting nothing. And don't give me any of your bullshit about, 'Tell me what you want done, not how to do it,' because, in this case, what I want done is for you to present a certain kind of bait, in a particular way."

"Yessir," Reilly answered, with suspicious good grace. *I'll just do that, but don't be surprised if I thin the line enough to protect my core assets.*

"Gentlemen and ladies," Gordo finished, "that concludes my logistics brief. Colonel?"

Stauer stood and announced, "you're all dismissed except for Second Battalion, Sixth Naval, and Seventh Aviation commanders, plus Gordo, Boxer, and Waggoner. You people meet me in the small conference room."

★ CHAPTER TWENTY-THREE ★

It is through being wounded that power grows
and can, in the end, become tremendous.
—Friedrich Nietzsche

Airfield, Camp Fulton, Guyana

The morning rain had come and gone, a sudden ferocious downpour that departed as quickly as it had come. Now the sun was busy, turning the rain into a steam that rose in streams around the people waiting for departure and the aircraft waiting to take them.

"I feel like a deserter," Kemp said to Elena Constantinescu, pushing his wheelchair from behind. A line of four more wheelchairs followed behind Elena, each pushed by a medico in battle dress. She, like Kemp, like everyone wheelchair-bound, wore mufti. Other lines of ten or twelve also snaked across the airfield, though in any given line, not more than nine were civilian-clad. Most of the others, including four medical personnel carrying litters, were in battle dress.

"Nonsense," she answered, confidently. "The way you

are, you would be useless to the regiment. This way, you can come back and be useful. And I can come back and be more useful.

"Don't worry, Dan," she added, "the regiment will win without either of us."

"Not the point," he insisted, "and I still feel like a deserter."

A stout, eyeglass, wearing, camouflage-uniformed aviator walked up to meet the party. Kemp thought his bearing had "jarhead" written all over it. Then he saw the nametag, "Cruz," and recognized the head of the regiment's aviation squadron.

"Sergeant Kemp?" the former Marine asked.

"Here, sir," Kemp answered. Since Elena was a nurse, hence out of the chain of command by the regiment's rules, he was actually the senior man in the party.

"If y'all would follow me"—"y'all," from Cruz, was pure affectation; he came from Pennsylvania—"you're on Flight One, the Pilatus PC-12, here to Tocumen Airport, Panama."

The regiment owned a number of aircraft. There were two MI-28 helicopter gunships. These had been a sort of gift from Victor Inning's father-in-law. There were also eight MI-17 cargo helicopters, of which six were usually fit to fly at any given time. These had all been purchased on the open market. There were a half dozen each CH-750 and CH-801 light STOL birds, useful for everything from guided tours to command and control to medevac to light resupply. Both models were, in fact, little more than scaled down and upgraded Fieseler Storchs, built from kits assembled in the Czech Republic. They owned two

Antonov AN-32 cargo aircraft, which were not quite as capable as American C-130's, but had come a lot cheaper. Then there were three Pilatus PC-6's, generally useful planes, and a single PC-12, the executive model. In addition to that, the MI company ran a variable number—variable because they tended to crash the things—of Israeli-made remote piloted vehicles. It was, all in all, a respectable fleet for a private concern.

The more or less military aircraft, the helicopters and most of the CH-750's and -801's, plus the RPV's, were all in camouflage and the regiment's colors. The Antonovs and the PCs, however, along with two CH-801's, were owned by a fairly notional subsidiary, AirVenture, Inc., a corporation set up by Matt Bridges (the "lawyer" desk of Lawyers, Guns, and Money) under the laws of the Cooperative Republic of Guyana. Their paint scheme reflected that, being white and blue, with brightly colored birds, sunshine, and flowers on the tails. That legal distinction, however, was spurious; there was no practical dividing line between Seventh Squadron (Aviation), M Day, Inc., and AirVenture, just as there was no real distinction between Mike Cruz, CEO of AirVenture, and Colonel Cruz, commanding Seventh Squadron. Their staffs were the same, barring only three of the regimental wives, one of whose job was to answer the telephone, in as sweet a voice as she could muster, "AirVenture, Incorporated," and another two who alternated serving from time to time as a stewardess on the PC12. As a matter of fact, the pay for both CEO Cruz, his pilots, and the ground crews came to a whole Guyanan dollar a year, each. On the other hand, they drew full pay and allowances from the regiment.

"How long to Panama, sir?" Kemp asked.

"Fourteen hundred and seventy miles, as the crow flies," Cruz answered. "Be closer to sixteen hundred for you, though, since the pilot's going to skirt around Venezuela. Call it, maybe, five hours in the air, or a tad more." Cruz pulled at one ear and added, somewhat ruefully, "Your pilot's Dr. McCaverty, which has its good points and its bad."

Thinking of his back, Kemp thought, *Oh, this is so going to suck.*

Man, this is the life, Kemp thought, leaning back in the plush leather seat at the rear of the aircraft, while the dark and slender Mrs. Major Welch poured him a scotch over ice. *Beautiful woman. No tits to speak of, but still beautiful. Reminds me of that model, the one married to the ambiguously sexual Brit singer. What was her name?* He looked over at Elena, seated to his right. *I'm surrounded by them. Wish I knew how to surrender.*

Elena glanced back, flashing him a brilliant smile. *Good boy,* she thought. *Never even sniveled as we levered him into the seat. And having to stop at the stairs, turn around and sit, lever his ass all the way up, then crawl to the back? Yes, a good boy, a tough boy.*

The plane suddenly hit an unexpected air pocket and bounced. Kemp flinched with the pain transmitted through his back. Still, he managed to get a smile out. More importantly, he kept the scotch from spilling.

Yes, a good boy. It will be rewarding working with him to get him back to duty.

★ ★ ★

The passengers were mostly asleep, or at least doing a good simulation of it. In any case, none of them seemed to need her at the moment. The pilot called Ayanna forward and said, "Time to do your stuff, Honey. The island and the airstrip are coming up."

She nodded, then turned and retrieved a digital camera from her purse. With that in hand, she walked to one of the windows and looked out. The plane began a gentle descent, then banked left before straightening. *There it is.*

Ayanna wasn't quite sure why she had to take pictures of the airfield at the southern end of the tadpole-shaped island while McCaverty circled, low and slow. She just knew that Colonel Cruz had asked her to, while someone from Regimental Intelligence had drilled her in working the camera. That, for her husband's tribe, was reason good enough.

Tocumen Airport, Panama

Though the Republic of Panama was not without its natural resources, nor entirely unindustrialized, its economy was primarily trade and service-based, and built around its location and its shape, in roughly equal measure. Its location, midway between North and South America, and Europe, Africa, and Asia, ensured it was a nexus for trade and travel between those five continents. Its shape, the narrow isthmus between the Oceans Atlantic and Pacific, in conjunction with the Canal, gave it a favored position for taking a cut of trade across the world. For that matter, even without the Canal, Panama would still have been a prime spot for trade, as it was in the days when convoys of slaves, mules, and burros ported the looted gold and silver of the Americas across the central mountains, on their backs.

Thus, it had been no real problem for the regiment to arrange transportation and helpers to get its wounded off of the PC-12, onto their wheelchairs, through customs, and to a not particularly ostentatious hotel near the airport, while they awaited their next flight.

"You've been to Panama before?" Elena asked, sitting in a chair in Kemp's room. She had a small color brochure on her lap. Her room was next door, with the other four members of the group scattered about close by.

Kemp lay on the bed. Even the best seats on an airplane eventually grew uncomfortable. And the drive over potholed streets had been sheer agony.

"Not the way you mean it," Kemp replied. "I've been to the country, over at the old Jungle Training Operations Center, before we pulled out. I was a young troopie then. But I never got to Panama City." *In fact, the furthest into Panama I ever got was to the brothels of Colon, but you're a nice girl and don't need to know anything about that.* He smiled. *Fun times, though, that they were.* "This place is the dark side of the moon to me."

Elena looked at him suspiciously. "I suspect I know what you're smiling about." She smiled, as well, adding, "I have heard from First Sergeant Coffee that this country was a dream for a young soldier, a wet dream."

Kemp tried to shrug. The effort was painful.

Elena held up the brochure she'd had on her lap. "This

says there is more to see to this place than brothels and bars. I have called for a taxi. Would you like to see the ruins of old Panama? It's not large; I think I can push you enough for that."

"As much as my ass hurts," he answered, "I'd rather lie down. But, still, a little fresh air would be better than staying here."

The four-storied cathedral tower had stood through the centuries. It had been a ruin even since before the fateful day, in 1671, when Welsh pirate Henry Morgan had attacked and sacked the town. The town had been burned in the attack, though not necessarily at Morgan's order or even by his men. Still, through earthquake, Indian attack, pirate attack, fire, and any number of other disasters, the bare stones of the cathedral tower remained standing.

Standing inside the roofless walls of the cathedral, abutting the tower, Elena pointed at a bare stone altar. "Your Colonel Reilly, says First Sergeant Coffee, once fucked a girl on that. What sacrilege!"

"The colonel wasn't always as he is now," Kemp answered, apologetically. "I understand he mellowed with the years."

Elena sneered. "Phillie Stauer says he's an asshole, too, and still."

"With that I can't argue," Kemp replied. "But, if so, he's *our* asshole, and he's good at it."

"He must be good at something, since Colonel Stauer puts up with him."

"Let's just say that he takes some getting used to," Kemp replied. "And if the process of getting used to him doesn't kill or cripple you, then he's a good man to work for."

"He crippled *you*," Elena observed.

"He set up a problem that I was crippled in," Kemp countered. "I was at that problem of my own free will, as I came to the regiment of my own free will. I came to the regiment *precisely* because it was the kind of place where my life and health would be risked, because those would make me feel like, and become, the man I aspire to be."

A degree or two of heat crept into Kemp's voice. "I had a choice, you know. I could have gone to one of the other battalions, at a higher rank, too. I went with First because it was the kind of organization I wanted to be in, because Reilly made it that way. So, if you don't mind, you can please stop shitting on my colonel who isn't here to defend himself."

Elena snorted in derision. Then her face grew slightly contrite, corners of her lips turning down and her nose more or less imitating a rabbit's. "You're right," she admitted, "it's bad manners. I am sorry."

"Fair enough. Let's see the rest of this place."

"May they rest in Hell!" Elena cursed at a ruined building. She then spat at the juncture of bare stone wall and grassy ground for emphasis.

Kemp read the bronze plaque on the wall, such as he could of it. It was in Spanish, so that wasn't much. "The Grillos?" He pronounced it wrong, too, like Brillo, rather than "Griyo."

Romanian and Spanish, however, were close enough. "Slavers." The nurse spat again. "Filthy swine."

"Oh . . . well . . . sure. But?"

"I was a slave once," Elena admitted. Her face was impassive but her eyes burned with hate. "Not for long, but for too long. I was on my way to being auctioned off—thirteen of us there were—when the regiment saved us."

"Ah. I understand." *No, I don't, but it's not my business to pry, either.*

"No you don't," she said. "There were fifty men on that ship. We were all raped at least a half dozen times a day. I was sixteen. Three of us were only fifteen."

Elena turned him from the building. "Come on," she said. "I don't want to see any more."

★CHAPTER TWENTY-FOUR★

WHEN the Waters were dried an' the Earth did appear,
("It's all one," says the Sapper),
The Lord He created the Engineer,
Her Majesty's Royal Engineer,
With the rank and pay of a Sapper!
—Kipling, "Sappers"

Tiboku Falls, Guyana

This, thought Trim, *is going to be a lot harder than it looked on the map. I wish we hadn't had to give up Sergeant Collins to the naval arm; he's one of the best builders we have.*

Middling short, clean cut, slender and generally fit, Trim held the rank of major. This was not because that was the regiment's preferred rank for a company commander. Neither was it because it was the normal rank in his previous army, the British. Rather, the Brit was a major because he held a dual hat as both CO of engineers and regimental engineer. The other engineer, from the early days, Nagy, also a major, currently held the position of Combat Support Battalion Executive Officer.

"Brilliant," announced Trim's first sergeant, Victor Babcock-Moore, a Jamaican émigré to Her Majesty's realm, and later to the Royal Engineers. "Brilliant" was one of those words whose meaning could change entirely with intonation. Looking down at the impossibly steep slope of the Tiboku Range, north of the falls, Moore said it in a way that meant, more or less, "What the hell were they smoking when they told us to build a ramp to get around the falls?" That he also managed to put into his pronunciation a studied accent considerably more respectable than the one Trim grew up with alternatingly amused and irritated the Brit officer. At the moment, he was so irritated at the difficulty, and perhaps impossibility, of the mission that the accent was amusing.

"What's the maximum slope the hovercraft can take?" Trim asked.

Babcock-Moore shook his head, replying, "Empty, maybe seven degrees . . . about sixteen or seventeen percent. Fully loaded, sir, not more than four and possibly as little as three degrees. We cannot dig that far down. Not this decade anyway."

"So we're just fucked, as the Yanks would say?"

The noncom shook his head. "Not necessarily, sir. They told us we could go to either side. There's a small river on the other side that feeds into the Mazaruni just below the falls. Let's go see if it's wide enough to fit the hovercraft."

His commander in tow, Moore began a painful limp—he'd taken a very bad hit in the leg, in Punt, some years before—downhill toward their waiting air cushion vehicle.

★ ★ ★

"Maybe," said Trim, loud enough to be heard over the hovercraft's whine. In the distance, perhaps a mile away, could be heard the muted roar of the falls. "Maybe," he repeated, "if we can clear away the rocks and widen the banks in two spots."

"Three spots, sir," answered Moore. "That place where the river turns appears wide enough for the width, but will not handle the length."

"Fine," the officer agreed, "three spots, then. Can we do it?"

"Not without explosive," the noncom replied. "Some of those boulders are huge and *very* well entrenched."

"No explosives. Orders."

"Forgiveness is often more easily obtained than permission. Besides, I brought the explosives anyway."

Trim gave Moore a dirty look. "The bloody Americans have *contaminated* you."

Babcock-Moore looked remarkably unrepentant as he responded, "I can't deny the charge, sir."

South of Hill 890, Guyana

In their own terms, they'd been well paid, the Indians who had paddled and poled Gordo and his three guards to Oranapai, a little spot of not very much on the Mazaruni, south of Hill 890. If they thought it strange that the men wearing too much clothing were also bearing frightful firepower, the Indians said nothing. *Not our business*, the chief had said, and who were they, humble fisherfolk, slash and burn agriculturalists, and hunter-gatherers, to question their chief. Besides, people wearing the same kind of odd—and altogether too extensive—clothing had come to the village from time to time to treat the sick.

"Stauer is out of his ever-loving mind," Gordo said, as he and his guards trekked afoot along the cattle trail leading from the river to the hill. His entire face curled into a sneer. "Well . . . maybe not . . . if I hire every healthy bloody man in Oranapai, and add in everyone living at The Sands, maybe then I can move seven days of food—ten tons, a couple of days of high quality grain ration for the mules—maybe two tons, two days of water, fourteen thousand liters—sixteen tons, to Hill 890. Shit, twenty-eight tons with about one hundred and thirty men, uphill, fifteen or sixteen miles as the trail winds. Um . . . three tons, call it, every other day; these Indians look pretty scrawny. Eighteen days? Not a lot of time, but maybe.

"But what the hell do I store fourteen thousand liters of water in?"

"Get the engineers to dig a big hole and line it with plastic, sir?" suggested the chief of his guard, Corporal Cuddy, an Afro-Guyanese of imposing dimensions . . . which was why he'd been picked to guard.

"Decent idea, Corp," Gordo agreed, "except they're already overtasked. I think, if any holes are to be dug, we're going to have to do it."

Me and my big fucking mouth, Cuddy cursed. "Or maybe we could have the Indians port up some large water bladders," the corporal suggested, in a last ditch effort to avoid excavating fourteen cubic meters.

"No," Gordo said. "Oh, I've got some, but we need those for several other projects. No, I think your first suggestion is well taken, Corporal Cuddy. A BFH it is. Consider yourself commended."

Ah, fuck me to tears.

Tatiana's Residence, Honey Camp, Guyana

Under a broad sun hat, behind her Dolce & Gabbana shades, Tati's face was blank, a complete mask to her inner feelings. She sat on the porch of her not insubstantial home, staring off at the trees that shielded it from the more wretched areas of the town.

"Something troubling you, ma'am?" the white-jacketed Arun asked.

Still, she said nothing, just shook her head slowly.

"Well," the Bihari continued, "if you need me for anything, I'll be at the silver." He turned to go.

"Wait," Tati said. The majordomo paused and cocked his head expectantly.

Tati chewed her lower lip for a moment, then said, "Please cancel all my appointments for today, and put tomorrow's clients on notice that I might not be available tomorrow."

"Not feeling well, ma'am?" he asked with concern.

"That's not it, exactly," she replied. "I just need to think."

"Very good," he agreed. "Shall I have one of the girls bring you a drink—a nice gin and tonic, perhaps—and instruct the staff to leave you alone after that?"

"You're a treasure, Arun," she replied. "Yes, a drink

would be most welcome." She stood and announced, "I'll be in my own quarters."

Tati's house was, frankly, a five-bedroom, not counting staff quarters, one-woman bordello. Three of those rooms were for short time appointments only. A fourth, somewhat larger and more ornate than the first three, was for use when someone hired her for an entire evening. The last, however, largest and best of all, she never used for business. That room was hers.

And Joshua's, she thought, as she entered it, *if the silly man would ever come to me.*

Before sitting, Tatiana went and opened both sides of a louvered closet. She sighed, then went to sit in a chair facing that closet. On the left side, the regimental patch's diving raptor facing outward from the left sleeve, were her dress whites. Just to the right of that were two pair of khakis, without shoulder insignia, cut generously in the chest to match her bosom. To the right of those were five pair of camouflaged, jungle-cut battle dress. Past that were a like number of hospital whites. Below, on the floor, were her sensible shoes, running shoes, boots, and a fully packed rucksack. In between, on a shelf, lay her load-carrying harness, helmet, beret, broad-brimmed jungle hat, and a very old fashioned brown leather shoulder holster containing a .45 that the regiment had snuck away from her and inscribed, then presented back to her at her discharge party.

At all of these she stared, sometimes focusing on one item, sometimes on the history implied by the entire group. Sometimes the memories raised brought a smile; at other times, tears.

So tightly did Tati concentrate that she didn't hear the knock at first. Arun had to knock again, louder, and then cough.

"Your drink, ma'am," he said, when she finally looked up.

"Do me a favor, Arun."

"Yes, ma'am?"

"Bring me the whole bottle, three of tonic, and a bucket of ice."

Tiboku Falls Bypass (under construction), Guyana

The boulder only stuck up above the streaming water by perhaps three feet. Sadly, this was also a couple of feet too much. Upstream and down, at three places, sections worked with pick and shovel to widen the river at its banks. Trim could hear the steady *plink-plink-plink* of the picks at work, even through the roar of the falls.

"Vic," Trim said, "we are so fucked if we get caught doing this."

Babcock-Moore kept his attention on the shaped charge he was carefully aligning on that particularly recalcitrant boulder. The shaped charge, weighing fifteen pounds, was composed of three-fifths RDX, slightly under two-fifths TNT, and a half a percent of calcium silicate, plus a small two-ounce booster charge to get things going.

"Never interrupt a master at his work, sir," Moore intoned, placing a twig under the thin metal frame supporting the charge, thus making an infinitesimal adjustment to the angle. "Besides, the regiment's thirty miles away; they'll never hear a thing."

"It's that bastard Reilly who's contaminated you, isn't it, Vic?"

"Colonel Reilly? Oh, no, sir, he doesn't even like me. See, he can accept someone who was born a Brit and simply stayed that way, like you. But a self-made Brit like me? He's friendly enough, but I'm an insult to his universe and he doesn't know quite how to deal with it. His sergeant major, on the other hand . . ." After fiddling with the twig, again infinitesimally, Babcock-Moore clucked approval.

Finally satisfied, Vic began to back up, limping, to a thick tree, reeling demolition wire behind him. "Would you care to join me, sir?" he asked, politely. "Regiment won't hear a thing but I expect the charge will ring *your* chimes rather badly."

"Well, *that* was just delightful," said Trim, his ears still ringing from the fifteen pound blast that had gone off less than thirty meters away.

"Wasn't it *just,* sir?" Vic agreed happily. "And now we get the top off this little beauty . . . Sir, would you be so kind as to fetch the demo charges while I clear the hole?"

"Wait a moment, would you, Vic?" Trim asked as the former prepared to hook his blasting machine up to the wires leading to the soon to be defunct boulder.

"What for, sir?"

Trim pointed in the direction of the hovercraft, almost invisible a quarter of a mile away. "You know," he said, "I'm not entirely uncontaminated by the Yanks, either.

And I say that if there is any possible chance of the top of that boulder hitting the hovercraft, it will. I think we ought to move it another quarter mile away."

"Oh, suit yourself, sir."

"And that's why we occasionally need officers," Babcock-Moore muttered, staring at the still smoking top of the boulder, which was sitting *precisely* where the hovercraft had been a mere ten minutes before.

Trim tried very hard to restrain himself from saying it, but, "I told you so."

Oranapai, Guyana

The other hovercraft, which could now make it around Tiboku Falls, showed up every day carrying between them twelve tons of supply. Every other day, the party of hired Indians returned from the dump being established at Hill 890 and picked up three tons of that. There was an additional pile built up by now, sitting on pallets but under tarps, just outside the village.

"The water can go later," Harry Gordon told Corporal Cuddy, both sporting rather badly blistered hands from digging the water hole. "Just make sure it stays full, if you and the boys have to hoof down to the river yourselves. Once Third Battalion arrives, they can take what they want to carry. You and your men get down to the river, put on civvies, and wait for a hovercraft to thumb a ride home."

"Yes, sir," said Cuddy. *And if you will please get your*

*overweight, altogether too white ass out of here so I and
the boys can* rest?

Kartauri Falls, Guyana

In Guyana, what the map often showed as a clearly
defined river, perhaps broken by rapids or falls, often
turned out to be a series of more or less deep streamlets,
interspersed with fairly flat islands, with rapids or falls being
forced into existence by the constraint of those islands.
Cazz had been with the regiment since the beginning, and
in Guyana as long as anyone. He already knew the form of
the Mazaruni River at the place he'd been ordered to
cross over to the west.

Cazz stood, his orderly beside him, in knee-deep, fast
flowing, muddy water. The sun was still too low in the east
to do much more than slightly illuminate the jungle-clad
gloom.

"Shit!" he muttered, looking at the falls to his left, the
island to his front, and more placid stream to his right, or
north. "It's all shit. One fucking piece of shit stream after
another. Fuck." He turned to a half dozen runners tagging
along close by. "Pass the word," he said. "Move out."

Those runners, in teams of two, trotted off parallel to
the river to give the word. Cazz waited, glancing first
upstream, then down, and then up again. The first sign of
the runners having reached their objectives came from
upstream. Cazz held out one hand to his orderly.

"Glasses," he ordered. The orderly, a Guyanese Bihari
by the name of Agal Singh, passed them over. Singh had

already roughly focused them for the distance to the head of the waterfall to the south.

Cazz placed the glasses to his eyes, did a minor focus of his own—*hate admitting it, but the eyes aren't what they used to be*—and scanned across the waterfall's head. Three quarters of the way across, the glasses showed the dim shadows of the upper torsos of the point of Company C, one squad laden like pack mules, stepping across gingerly. The squad crossed while shifting hands over a guide and safety rope that had been strung by the Scout Platoon the day prior. Another took its place, then another.

Looking then north Cazz could see rather more, though the men were still little more than outlines. Satisfied, Cazz himself, at the forefront of his Company B and Headquarters and Support Company, and with most of the battalion's staff trailing along, lifted one hand over his head and made a knifelike jab to the west.

Headquarters and Support went first, piling the half dozen boats they'd dragged to the river with heavier equipment and outsized packages of supply, then pushing the boats out into the stream. A few men waded out and jumped in, as coxswains started engines and backed water. The men would help unload on the far side, then stay there to help unload future ferries, which, having fewer men, would bear more in the way of supply.

A series of rafts, already loaded, waited for the boats to be freed up to tow them across.

Cazz heard the sound of a bell and, turning, saw one of the two bell mares from his attached mule train leading her charges to the water's edge and on. The mule driver—Guyanese Sergeant Henry Daly, from Service Support Battalion—rode the mare, which was otherwise unburdened. The mules in the section, while fully loaded, also had flotation devices to help them stay afloat.

Being a "Marine no longer subject to reveille," even if he was still so subject, if not as a Marine, Cazz had understood the critical importance of first in, last out, logistics-wise. Indeed, he'd lashed his staff mercilessly until he was satisfied with the load and crossing plans. In this respect, a river crossing was not so different from an amphibious landing on an undefended shore. That is to say:

"Jesus, it's going to be a bitch unfucking all this shit on the other side. And this is the *easy* part."

★CHAPTER TWENTY-FIVE★

Il nous faut de l'audace, et encore de l'audace,
et toujours de l'audace.
—Georges Jacques Danton

Quarters One, Glen Morangie Housing Area, Guyana
(Teahouse of the August Nooner)

(Which was approximately what the hiragana-written sign said, over the small spa's double door: てつだいかな)

Constructed of Guyanan Greenheart—a wood so strong that standard tools dulled, boring insects gave up in disgust, and Amundsen and Shackleton had sheathed their exploratory boats in it to defy the ice—the spa had been built by local labor to a vaguely Balinese design created by a Canadian company. Reilly had personally selected the trees from which the wood had come from some forest that had needed clearing to create the Karl Marx Impact Area. The greener tinted wood had gone into the floors, while the walls were more tanned. All sections of the highly polished wood displayed a fine grain to them.

Reilly had been up and mostly on his feet for days, supervising both the presentation of a full regiment from his own small fraction of one, dispersal of key equipment, and nighttime digging of carefully camouflaged fortifications and bomb shelters; to say nothing of overseeing the installation of air raid sirens where none had ever been thought to be needed. He hadn't seen his wife, Lana, except in passing, for all that time.

And I am getting too old for this shit, he thought, stepping from the back porch to the walkway that led to the teahouse. *God, everything hurts, my back, my legs, my feet . . . and my hair's gotten so thin my scalp is frigging sunburned.*

Reilly wore sandals and a bathrobe. He had a towel slung over one shoulder. Gingerly—*my feet* hurt!—he walked the fifty yards to the teahouse, not even stopping to admire either the sculptures that graced the walk at odd intervals, the tiny arch of the wooden bridge over the small creek behind the main house, or even the graceful form of the teahouse itself. All he really cared about at the moment was getting his aching body in hot, jetting water and—hope against hope—that Lana might make it home in time, before he had to get back to duty.

Half asleep, letting the water soothe away the aches, Reilly was alerted by the sound of a heavy auto scrunching across gravel, followed by very faint footsteps, and the sound of something mostly soft being dropped to the ground outside.

By the time Sergeant Major George knocked on the inner screen door, closed to bar the entry of mosquitoes, he was fully awake. He'd recognized his sergeant major's footsteps easily enough.

"Sorry to bug you, boss," George said, once invited in, "but I've had a sort of problem presented to me and I don't know what to do about it."

Reilly sensed there was someone else, waiting outside. Lifting a quizzical eyebrow, he asked, "A personnel problem?"

"Yup," George agreed, bobbing his head vigorously. "Just that; a personnel problem."

"Bring it in, Sergeant Major," Reilly said, his voice tinged with resignation.

"As you wish, sir," George said, drily, followed by, "Corporal Manduleanu; post!"

Manduleanu? Reilly wondered. *We don't have anyone in the battalion named . . .*

"You son of a bitch, George!" he shouted, lunging for the towel as a uniformed Tatiana marched in, stomped to attention, locked her eyes on a spot on the far wall, saluted, and reported:

"Sir, Medical Corporal Manduleanu, Tatiana, Regimental Number 00607, requests permission to rejoin the regiment for the duration of the emergency!"

Hill 890, Guyana

It was an unending drum roll overhead. Rain poured down like a reenactment of the Great Flood, sans only

Noah and the Ark. The thickly intertwined branches and their leaves didn't stop the rain, they simply slowed it down on its way to the ground and the men who walked it. Between the rain and the churning feet, every path Third Battalion trod had become a morass. Every step was three times harder than a normal step, on a normal path, because of the energy it took to pull boots sunk up to the ankle from the slimy, grasping, sucking mud.

The men were beat. Moreover, the rain and muck had slowed them enough that they'd eaten their last food and drunk their last canteened water the day before. Since then it had been snatch a cupful, here and there, as they waded the stream. Of forage there'd been essentially none. They were hungry, somewhat thirsty, and very, very tired.

Still, they were nearly at their first rest stop. And the mules had been eating well.

Ah, shit! Cazz mentally cursed as his feet began sliding back down the muddy trail leading up the east face of the hill. Automatically, his hand lunged out for nearest tree that might support him. Sadly, that tree was— "Godfuckingdammit!"—a respectable member of the palm family, specifically, an Astrocaryum, and Cazz's hand had closed on a row of closely set organic black spikes.

At the loss of a handgrip, Cazz's legs slid out from under him. Falling to one side, he began a swift and muddy descent to the bottom of the hill. As he neared and then began to pass Singh, a few meters behind, the latter squatted down, quite despite his heartbreakingly heavy rucksack, and snatched his colonel by where his shoulder straps went over his shoulder. Cazz came to an abrupt stop.

"Thanks, Singh," Cazz said and he rolled over to hands and knees. The Bihari made the struggle to his feet a bit easier by hauling upward on the old man's rucksack.

Once on his feet and steady Cazz wiped his muddy hands on his battle dress trousers, then used the hands to wipe the rain from his face. It was an automatic gesture and one that, under the circumstances, did no real, lasting good.

"Excelsior, motherfuckers," he whispered as his feet began to churn him forward and upward through the mud, to his rest awaiting on the other side of the hill.

Cazz's uninjured hand absently plucked at the dozen or two vegetable spikes embedded in it. If it hurt like the devil pulling them out, his face never showed it. They'd leave their residue behind, he knew, but there was nothing to be done about that. And better the points than the whole damned things being driven farther in.

Hill 590, Guyana

About forty-five miles to Cazz's northwest, on the western slope of Hill 590, Gordo fumed at the weather. *I did so not special order this shit.*

He looked up at the distant clouds ruefully, then admitted, *But it's not without its advantages. Nobody can see us in this crap. And the stream that leads down to the Mazaruni is swollen enough that I can move the supplies to within two miles of this place. That's a big help when only twenty-two Indians agreed to come this far west to port for pay.*

Pity I couldn't keep more than a platoon of Trim's engineers. But they're needed elsewhere. Still, while I have them, let them work.

Hill 890, Guyana

Cazz sat under a stretched out poncho, atop his rucksack, boots off, inspecting his water-logged and wrinkled feet. Water ran off all four sides of the rubber sheet, pattering to the mud below and then running off in streams in the general direction of the supply dump. There, lines of men moved forward to claim their rations while Sergeant Daly supervised the loading of the mules while the latter munched sodden grain from soggy feedbags.

There were some blisters on his feet, painful but not agonizing. Cazz was pretty sure there were few men in his battalion who didn't have any. At least the medics were very busy with lancing, disinfecting, and wrapping feet, pretty much everywhere within and on the perimeter. It was just one of those things to be expected and endured; march in the mud, soften the callus, and expect to blister.

Everyone in the battalion changed into dry socks. It was more a moral thing than a practical one; the socks would be soaked soon enough.

On the other hand, at least the for-the-time-being-dry socks are clean, Cazz thought. *It won't do a lot for the blistering but will help head off infection.*

And who the hell does Gordo think he is, ordering our entire supply of inclement weather now, when we plainly don't need it, and so soon before the dry season is supposed to be upon us? What will we use to make the troops miserable with if tomorrow's rain's used up today? Fucking thoughtless doggie!

Seven Miles Northeast of Peaima Falls, Guyana

Victor Babcock-Moore shuddered and said, "Oh, shit," when he saw RSM Joshua—bigger than he was, blacker than he was, and twice as mean—step off the newly arrived hovercraft at the tree-covered landing spot. "I *so* do not need this distraction."

Moore had a pack frame with a shelf on his back. The eighty pounds—two 120mm mortar shells, in their packaging, plus a case of rations—he'd previously lugged on it had been dumped off at the center of the camp. He was returning, now, at a pronounced limp, to the landing spot for more.

Joshua took one look and said, "While I admire your leading by example, Moore, you have better things to be doing. Drop that pack and show me around."

"Yes, Sergeant Major," Vic said, sliding the pack frame from his shoulders and tossing in upon a squared-off pile of tarp-covered crates.

More genially, Joshua added, "I made sure to stop off to check on Elizabeth and your daughter before hitching a ride here, Vic. They're fine and ready to move out at a moment's notice."

Vic nodded appreciatively.

Joshua's voice grew hard, then, "And while I appreciate your initiative in ignoring your orders and using demolitions to clear the ramps around the falls, Moore, you still violated orders and *I* am not one of those from whom it is easier to obtain forgiveness than permission. There will be repercussions."

Moore hung his head. "Yes, Sergeant Major. Um . . . Sergeant Major, how did you know?"

"I have eyes to see with, don't I?"

"Yes, Sergeant Major. This way, Sergeant Major."

"You neglected to clear away and hide the spoil," Joshua said, genial again, aware of the couple of odd samples he'd found that he carried in his pockets. "No reason for rock fragments to be scattered in a circle in this shit. They should have washed away years ago. Unless the demo was quite recent." For illustration, he held his hand out to catch the rain in his palm. "*Don't* do it again . . . until you learn how to do it without being caught. By me."

"Yes, Sergeant Major."

Although the smile never reached his face—one rarely did—Joshua actually quite liked the self-made Brit. That wasn't especially because they were both from the Caribbean, nor even that they'd both remade themselves to be soldiers for the polity they chose to join. Rather, it was that Joshua saw in Babcock-Moore a somewhat younger version of himself.

If I can just knock the geniality out of him, and make him as hard as I am.

The assembly area *cum* log base—for this one was a real base, rather than a rest and resupply stop—was crouched in a sort of uneven bowl, mostly defined by the Werushima Mountains. A full stream ran through the western quadrant of the bowl, a steady source of water and also a highway for the hovercraft, who were able to use it to get within three quarters of a mile of the base. That, in practice, meant that each of the hundred plus engineers of Trim's company here could move about a quarter of a ton a day, on his own back, from hovercraft landing to inside the perimeter. Of course, for the far side of that perimeter, much less could be toted.

Laying out camps was an engineer specialty in any army. This one was no exception. Ninety small general purpose—in the parlance, "GP, Small"—tents, suitable, if cramped, for nine hundred men had been hauled in and set up in a serrated triangle on the perimeter and a cluster at the center. Along with those, the center held a half dozen larger ones. Over each was stretched a camouflage screen, not only useful for foiling visual identification but also containing many small metal rings that played havoc with ground or aerial radar. Other nets stretched inward from the edges, these intended to cover the men as they did their routine movements for food—which would usually be cold, no stoves were provided and only enough hexamine for a lukewarm meal per man per day—or to the latrines.

With the tents came the other impedimenta it was hoped would see Cazz's Third Battalion through the coming campaign. There would be sixty tons of packaged food, seventeen tons of ammunition, several tons of medical supplies, approximately a ton of batteries for the radios, night vision devices, field telephones, and GPS receivers, roughly five tons of miscellany, and several more of the battalion's heavy weapons. There was little liquid fuel—

just some cans for the lanterns—but ten tons of high quality fodder for the mules that were coming.

At this range from the regiment's home base, at and around Camp Fulton, each hovercraft could make, at best, one round trip, carrying four tons, every other day. Between the tents, the camouflage screens, the food, the heavy weapons, and everything else, it would take a full two weeks to complete preparations, what with the engineers not being able to devote every man-day to portage.

"It will do," Joshua said, once he'd seen the whole thing.

"If the hovercraft hold up it will," Vic corrected.

"You have reason to worry about them?"

"Just that we're using them *hard*, Sergeant Major."

Joshua nodded. "When I get back, I'll check with maintenance and see."

Puerto la Cruz, Venezuela

M Day was not the only group that had ever been capable of moving a secret military force around, by sea, via clandestine freighter. For one thing, the Germans had done it, in 1940, in Weserübung, their seizure of Denmark and Norway. For another, American writer Tom Clancy had done it, literarily, for his novel, *Red Storm Rising*.

And we're going to do it, too, thought Venezuelan Second Marine Battalion commander, Lieutenant Colonel Francisco Conde, as he watched a forty foot container hoisted aboard the container ship, *Manuel de Cespedes*, leased from Carimar, in Old Havana. The container, he knew, contained a fully equipped platoon of his battalion. Like the rest of Conde's battalion, that container had been loaded near a tent city much further inland before being trucked here. The tent city remained, but the troops?

Almost fully loaded. Along with that television team from VTV that had to give their families as hostage to come with us. Cretinous rats.

Conde wasn't sure if his battalion had been chosen to lead the way because of his and its intrinsic quality, or because he was a second cousin to the commander of the Corps. He rather hoped it was the former but, all things considered, and this being Venezuela, he had to admit to the possibility of the latter.

No matter; if they picked me because of my relations . . . well . . . then I'll just have to do both the country and the family proud.

Farther to Conde's west, near Puerto Cabello and the port of la Guaira, the rest of the Corps' two infantry brigades were encamped, taking turns loading their transports in the sort of desultory way that the unquestioned and unquestionable presence of Colombian spies would be sure to see and report as, "Situation normal."

What the Colombians—and anyone else who was interested—might not see, or at least might not note, was that for every twenty vehicles that were loaded on the landing craft, only eighteen ever left. Within a day or two—*or, this being Venezuela, maybe three or possibly even four; it isn't, after all, like Hugo gave us any money to train until a few months ago*—the time consuming work of heavy loading would be complete, leaving only the relatively quick job of forming the men of the lift and marching them aboard.

The container settled down with a clang. Conde listened carefully for any human sounds that might have come from it. *Nothing. Good. Well . . . I have good boys, and a few girls, after all.* While the captain of the *de Cespedes* knew perfectly well what he'd been chartered for, as did his first officer, the swabbies of the crew did not, nor did Conde see any good reason to let them know until the ship was at sea.

And soon enough, we sail. 'Course, we'll have to make the briefest of brief stops at Port of Spain, just to eliminate reference to here. But we won't do more than anchor, take on some water from a lighter, and leave again.

Conde—a Bolivarian, yes, but also a devout Catholic; this was not necessarily a contradiction in Venezuela— crossed himself, thinking the silent prayer, *Lord of Hosts, Defender and Savior of the People, be with us.*

But I think we have a good trick going, Lord, and I would be happy if You just saw fit not to fuck with us.

★CHAPTER TWENTY-SIX★

All warfare is based on deception.
Hence, when able to attack, we must seem unable;
when using our forces, we must seem inactive;
when we are near, we must make the enemy
believe we are far away; when far away,
we must make him believe we are near.
—Sun Tzu, *The Art of War*

MV *Maria Walewska,* Point Fortin, Trinidad

One of the sergeants, an engineer named Collins, supervised a five man crew of sailors, down in a cavity created by piling up containers around a flat space. The cavity had a broad tarp stretched over it, with just enough space to let in a little air. It had the effect of changing the enclosed area from a metal frying pan to a convection oven. The sweat-dripping crew was busily assembling what appeared to be mostly lumber, plus a small power winch, into an odd framework. There was a steel I-beam there, too, but this would not be assembled today as it was too long to fit under the tarp.

The "lumber"—which, essentially, it was—came out of a container marked, appropriately enough, "lumber." It had come trimmed, but uncut, until Collins had turned some plans into reality.

Some of the lumber went into assembling a turntable mounted atop one of the bottom containers. Most of the wooden chunks were smaller, now, than when they'd begun. The same container had also held the winch, some chain, lots of heavy-duty nuts and bolts, *very* heavy-duty springs, some very large ball bearings, steel trunnions and braces, steel cable, and a sort of steel net. Oh, and a hook; that was important.

They'd been practicing, off and on, for weeks. They could almost do the assembly in the dark.

The *really* tricky part has been setting things up—in good part by underbidding other carriers—so that most of the cargo was both legitimate and legitimately headed for Puerto Cabello, Venezuela. Somewhat like AirVenture, Inc., the regiment's naval arm, minus the obviously military stuff like the landing craft, minisubs, and patrol boats, was held under civilian corporate ownership, and—as was normal in merchant marine circles—through so many cutouts, dummy corporations, leases and leasebacks, that no one could really say who owned what. Also, like AirVenture, though to a much greater extent, not every-one who served those ships was in the regiment. Indeed, it was only a small minority of the officers and crews that were M Day personnel.

This ship, however, was fully regiment-crewed while looking essentially Chinese crewed.

★ ★ ★

Though the continent to the south was under a deluge, the port of Point Fortin was dry for the nonce. *Muggy, but dry,* thought Ed Kosciusko, standing the bridge of the MV *Maria Walewska* (Antigua and Barbuda registry). For this mission, Kosciusko was a commodore, leaving the ship's normal captain, the former PLAN noncom, Liu, as nominal commander. Liu, however, answered to Kosciusko.

The ship, *Countess Marie*, or *the Countess*, as her crew thought of her, was not nearly beautiful enough to live up to her namesake. For one thing, she needed a paint job. Even given that, though, she just wasn't a very pretty ship. One hundred and thirteen meters long, nineteen in beam, with a low freeboard; *the Countess* was of sixty-six hundred and sixty gross registered tons, and carried up to four hundred and thirty-six TEU. She had two thirty-five ton cranes mounted slightly to port. Both of those were currently engaged in transferring a number of containers from another of the regiment's ships to *the Countess*. That other ship had recently finished a very circuitous voyage from Trieste to Kotor, Montenegro to Tel Aviv and then Capetown via the Suez Canal. Its next stop would be Georgetown.

For *the Countess*, however, the next stop would be Puerto Cabello, Venezuela. *Where we shall promptly develop engine difficulties, get towed to the southeast corner, and begin to pile up demurrage, no doubt much to the joy of Venezuelan port authorities. While that joy lasts.*

For Kosciusko knew, as the port authorities at Point Fortin did not, that the cargo containers coming aboard, marked with such innocent labels as "Ocean Buoys,"

"Consumer Electronics," "Acoustical Sensors," and— unintentionally, because all too suggestively—"Deep Mining Adapters" was, in fact, a mix of purpose built, heavy duty, naval mines, heavy mortar shells, naval mine sensors and detonators, explosive-filled barrels, and adapters.

Which is why I am burying them as deep in the hold as I can get them.

Watching the loading, Kosciusko frowned and pressed a button on the intercom.

"Mrs. Liu, here, Skippah," came the accented answer.

"Little rough on that one, Mrs. Liu."

"Felt like cargo shift inside, Skippah. Dumbasfuckinglockscunts who packed it not know what they cocksucking doing, me think."

"All right, but watch it next time."

"No next time, Skippah. Last one being hauled aboard by Number Two clane now. But think bettah check that container I did. Maybe damage, you know?"

"I know. We will." *Any real damage and we'd likely have wrecked half the port.*

"I start bulying new containahs undah o'd," Mrs. Liu said.

"Fine, Mrs. Liu," Kosciusko answered. "Just make sure the 'lumber' stays near the top."

The legal and open captain, though effectively Kosciusko's first officer, was Mrs. Liu's husband. He clucked disapproval. "She not ta'k rike that in Chinese," said Captain Liu. "We mally fo'ty fuckin' years ago and she nevah ta'k rike that. You fuckin' Amelicans contaminate nice gir'."

Mrs. Liu was over sixty, perhaps four foot eleven in height, fairly rotund, gray, and—except in the eyes of her doting husband—not nearly a "girl."

"Yeah," Kosciusko agreed. "But, you know, it's not like she doesn't have a natural talent for vernacular."

"Mebe so," Liu conceded.

"Did you get the package from Victor?" the captain asked.

"By boat, via Fedex, twenty minutes ago. Boat come arong po't side. Give me. I open and rook. Got instluctions for mines, adapters, bombs. Evelything. Must study awhire, though."

"Should have a few days."

San Francique, Trinidad

This time the Bertram Sport Fisher, still under Baluyev's command, came loaded for bear. This time, too, Lada came with them. She was still pretending to being a whore—*not that it's much of a pretense*, she thought—but had agreed with Timur that it would be only a show. No, she wasn't his girl, she was . . . *We'll talk more, and get to know each other, and think about it. But we* will *talk. I promise.*

Baluyev had, of course, a somewhat different take on things. *Mosin, the best of my men, is happy. Better still, none of us have to eat Kravchenko's personal campaign of culinary sabotage directed against the masses. Lada, along with whatever vices and virtues she may have, can cook.*

Still, I wish Konstantin were here. Then it would really be like old times.

Airfield, Camp Fulton, Guyana

There was a single, unarmed observer plane, a CH-801, almost hovering overhead in the updrafts. Two men manned it, an observer and the pilot, Warrant Officer Harley. It wouldn't do anything to interfere with an attack, but might provide a minimum of warning.

Konstantin paid no attention to either the early warning plane above, or to the nearby ground as four heavy transporters pulled up to the strip, behind the two hangar-parked Antonovs, painted in bright, civilian colors. Each heavy truck bore on its back a twenty foot container. Even as the Russian drove in the direction of the half dozen MI-17 helicopters being refueled on the other side of the strip, an engineer crane was lifting one of the containers from the back of the truck that bore it, while a backhoe waited to drag the thing into the shelter of the corrugated metal hangar.

The MI-17s waited in a widely spaced and staggered line—technically it was called, "Staggered Trail Left"—as two fuel trucks leapfrogged around the formation, filling the tanks. Crew chiefs and maintenance personnel crawled over the helicopters, under the supervision of the Chief of Aviation Maintenance, Luis Acosta, walked from one bird to the next, sometimes asking a question or two, sometimes peering in.

Acosta held the rank of chief warrant officer in the regiment (and, incidentally, Chief of Maintenance of AirVenture, Inc.). A former illegal immigrant to the

United States, he'd been enticed into serving as part of what he'd thought at the time was a drug running scheme. Nearer to forty than thirty now, he was short, stout, and brown. Stiff hair, black in the main but shot with gray, jutted straight up from his hairline before rolling back over his head. When he'd decided to stay on, he'd convinced the other sixteen Mexicans who had worked for him to stick it out as well.

Manuel, Acosta's number two man, much taller and much lighter skinned than his chief, was deep in conference with the squadron commander, Mike Cruz, when Acosta reached them at the front of the helicopter formation. Manuel's collar sported the silver bars, each with a single black square, of a much more junior warrant. Behind Cruz stood another man, a master sergeant, with the deep set lines of worry that said "loggie" written across his face.

"I was just telling the colonel," Manuel said, turning to Acosta, "that I don't think number five's going to make two trips; not without we break out the engine and figure out what's causing it to run rough."

"Have we got a replacement engine?" Cruz asked Acosta.

Luis nodded and said, "Yessir. But we'd have to do the switch out here. Be a lot faster and better than trying to do it where we're going."

Cruz's head turned to ask the master sergeant, "What have we got on number five, this lift, and what are we planning on carrying next?"

"Mostly fuel pods, this time, sir," the sergeant answered. "Armament packages and troops next lift. Gonna seriously fuck with the plan unless we have the fuel at the holding area to lift forward to Aguaro-Guariquito national park. Especially since we're losing a lift to bring Colonel Boxer and an escort to Georgetown."

And, thought Cruz, *despite Boxer's protestations to the contrary, we're really not sure how much time we have.*

Cruz knifed a hand toward Acosta. "Chief, get everything set up here to do a quick switch on the engine. She flies this lift, *then* we'll break her down on the return."

Patrol Boat Number One, *The Drunken Bastard*, North of Tobago.

The guns were stowed away below, while a purely nominal superstructure had been built up out of cheap lumber and styrofoam. Even the bow had been camouflaged, in an attempt to disguise the rakish lines that would have told any knowledgeable observer that this was no innocent fishing boat. In order to preserve the illusion, the old, eighty foot and change, ex-Finnish torpedo boat kept her speed down to a sedate twelve knots. A couple of fishing chairs and a railing completed the mask. None of that would take five minutes to undo.

Cramped down below were Ryan and his entire team, minus the two left to guard the equipment at the safe house in Colombia. Also hidden below was a truly outrageous stockpile of arms, explosives, and other equipment. The real crew, mostly Chinese under Captain Chin, with Chong reverting to Chief of Boat, was also mostly hidden. The short and swarthy enough to be genetically indeterminate Bronto, and a few others, remained above.

Chin consulted his GPS and then took a quick glance at the chart laid out before him. "Set course for two-eight-five," he told the helmsman.

"Aye, aye, sir," Bronto replied, "Our course is two-eight-five. He spun the wheel, cutting it hard left. Like a ballet dancer—a Margot Fonteyn in her later, but still graceful, years—the old girl twisted practically on her tail, heading away from the rising sun.

"Not so nimbly, Mister," the Chinese skipper counseled. "We are a sporting boat, not a warship."

"Yes, sir. Sorry, sir. Won't happen again."

"See that it does not."

Wineperu, Guyana, on the Essequibo River

Stauer, possibly the only man in the regiment busier than Reilly and Gordo, stood in the early morning shade and wondered. Looking up, he thought, *No, nothing to see from above. All is as innocent as a newborn baby. Never mind the mines—and mine fixin's—we unloaded last night.* His eyes dropped down to ground level as his head and body turned to scan the entire area. *Nothing to see on land but those half dozen metal sheds, a few workshops, the chain link fence surrounding and a couple of watch towers. But those are normal and manned, as normal.*

Walking forward, toward the river and the rushing sound coming from Head Falls, to the south of the settlement and base, Stauer came to the boat line, holding a number of the LCM-6's that had brought the mines from Urisirima the previous night. There was a gap in that line, courtesy of the one boat heading to the Philippines. In the gap sheltered *Namu,* the killer minisub. Next to those, toward the falls, was the single Dvora Class patrol boat, which was altogether the wrong shape and size for a quick camouflage job to hold for very long. Boat crews puttered about with the landing craft and the *Dvora,* as usual for a warm but not yet hot morning. On the *Dvora,* the engine cowling was fully open with a pair of legs sticking up nearly vertically. *That would be Kehre. Let's hope he's right about that engine.*

They'll scatter on warning. A sudden chill went up Stauer's spine. *If we have warning. I wish Morales and Lada hadn't been compromised.*

North, in the opposite direction from the falls, past the line of landing craft, and farthest from the settlement, more shed space jutted out over the water.

Under the shed sat the ex-Yugoslav, ex-Montenegrin commando sub, *Naughtius,* on the surface of the stream. She could be seen from the land, if not the sky. Still, a landsman's view wouldn't have shown much. For, much like the *Bastard,* the *Naughtius* had received a face-lift. They'd shortly—as soon as *Naughtius* and its disguise moved off— be moving one of the unserviceable hulls they'd gotten as part of the *Naughtius* deal into its place and putting in it a few fuel cans and twenty pounds of explosive.

Around the upper portion of the hull, concealing it and the sub's small sail, was built up a simulacrum of a cabin cruiser, prepared a couple of weeks prior and thrown up last night. It was, like the *Bastard's,* a light construction, though unlike the patrol boat's camouflage job, this one used merely lumber and painted canvas. It wouldn't hold up in a storm, of course, but it wasn't expected to, either. For that matter, the disguise was unlikely to hold up under close inspection. Still, all it had to do was survive the gentle voyage downstream, the coastal trip to the mouth of the Waini River and then about twenty-five miles up that course, to where Biggus Dickus Thornton and his former SEALs were building a hide for the submarine.

Concealed on deck but within the canvas were half a dozen purpose-built seabed mines, and three times that in 240mm mortar shells. Four more mines and a half dozen shells were stowed below, along with the adapters, sensors, and detonators for all twenty-four shells.

Won't close the Orinoco indefinitely, but then again, we couldn't win a long war.

Airfield, Camp Fulton, Guyana

The Antonovs lumbered down the strip, one at a time, then lifted and pulled to the west. They'd cross Brazil and then Colombia, staying as far the hell as possible away from Venezuela. Each of the planes carried a precisely equal load in their cargo bays. This consisted of four ex-Yugoslav M-70 naval mines, eight thirty-gallon barrel mines, and eleven 240mm mortar shells, plus the detonators, sensors, and adapters for the barrels and shells, and a hundred and twelve flat steel plates. Everything was strapped down tightly, and nothing was armed yet. Indeed, the barrels and mortar shells wouldn't even have their suites put in until the planes eventually took off from their interim destination.

"So where the fuck are we actually going, sir?" the co-pilot of Number One in the flight asked.

"Well, since we've taken off, I can tell you," the pilot replied. "We're heading for the *Isla del Rey,* in the Bay of Panama. There's a—"

"There's an old abandoned airfield there, big enough for us. But, Chief, I've looked at that. There is *nothing* there but the airfield, a couple of tiny villages, and some rich gringo vacation housing. No control tower. No refuel facilities—and we're going to need that to get off again. *Nada.*"

"Fuel will be provided," the pilot assured his second.

"By what? By whom?"

"Guy named Leo Ross. One of ours, First Battalion, from way back. Got invalided out of the regiment, took his rehab in Panama, and settled down with one of the local girls. He'll deliver about ten tons' worth, on call, by boat. After that, we wait."

"And where do we *live,* in the interim? If I'd wanted to sleep in the jungle I'd have joined the Army."

The pilot jerked his head back. "We live back there. If that's all right with *you*, I mean."

State House, Georgetown, Guyana

The State House, which was the name given to the official residence of the president of Guyana, was more a collection of additions than a cohesive structure on its own.

Still, not exactly a hovel, thought Boxer, descending down the left side door of the MI-17 that had brought him to the grounds of the presidential palace. Behind him, eight mufti-clad men of one of von Ahlenfeld's teams slept, or read, or stared at the opposite side of the helicopter, as the mood took them. They had no rifles or other, heavier, arms, though each man carried one pistol under his light dress jacket.

Boxer was pleased to see that the captain who met him by the edge of the helipad was in battle dress, rather than the comparatively garish and useless white jacket and green trousers of the Guyanan Defense Force dress uniform. Boxer was reasonably certain that the battle dress was because of the still ongoing rioting, sniping, arson, and not infrequent simple crime that was still consuming the capital.

Turning his attention back to the State House, he thought, *In fact, the white walls and green tile roof are really quite attractive.*

"The president will see you immediately," said the captain, holding on to his soft jungle hat lest it be blown away by rotor wash. Boxer had his own, not dissimilar, headgear clenched in one hand.

"Interesting that you should say that," said Guyana's current chief of state, Mansour Bharrat Paul, resting his chin on interlaced fingers. "Yesterday, the Venezuelan Ambassador's secretary called mine, requesting an appointment 'at my earliest convenience.' I begged off until next Tuesday. Was that a mistake, do you think, Colonel Boxer? Was he trying to warn me?"

A coup d'etat in the offing he'll believe, Boxer thought, *and look to us to save him from. If I'd told him of an invasion from Venezuela, the corrupt, soulless son of a bitch would be legging it trippingly for the Venezuelan embassy, trying to bargain for a good price for his ownership interest in the country.*

Boxer shook his head. "I don't know, Mr. President. It could have been innocent enough. Or he could have more solid information than I do. In any case, that's another reason why I'd . . . or why the regiment would . . . like to supplement your security forces with some of our people. Nothing too ostentatious, just a dozen or so . . . mmm . . . security specialists, plus a cook. Enough to give you a modicum of protection against any form of military coup. After all, our mutual association has been quite fruitful, ever since your election."

Which is bullshit; it's been fruitful ever since you discovered you needed us to keep you from having to learn to speak Dutch. But that's all right, I bullshat you about the possibility of a domestic military coup; why balk at a little politeness?

"Where are your people, your 'security specialists'?" Paul asked.

"Eight of them came with me, Mr. President," Boxer replied. "They're in the helicopter, waiting for word to dismount. The other four—actually five, counting a cook— are coming by surface road, and should be here sometime this evening. The eight are civilian clad. Their uniforms and equipment will be coming in the Land Rovers that are currently on the road. Do you have quarters for them?"

The president's dark brow wrinkled. "No place that wouldn't be inconveniently mixed with my own guard force. Could they, perhaps, squeeze into an apartment?"

"A thousand square feet and at least one bathroom and kitchen with refrigerator would suffice, sir."

"Ah. Well, they can have the former First Lady's quarters. They're almost twice that size and they've been open since I evicted the useless, self-absorbed bitch."

Baylor Rehab Center, Houston, Texas, United States

One of the better features of using a woman, especially an attractive one, to perform physical therapy on a badly injured man was, *I'll be damned if I show how much this hurts. I'll be doubly damned if I quit, or even ask for a break, in front of her.* Especially *since she's been pretty curt with me ever since Panama. Hell, it's not my fault she got enticed into a slave coffle, even if I am a man.*

The first thing they'd done with Kemp's spine, after arrival, was subject him to enough noninvasive scanning, X-raying, etc., to make him glow in the dark. At least he thought so. This was followed by a long session where the surgeon, an Indian chap from Mumbai, explained the options and gave his recommendation: "We'd be best off by going in and fusing the vertebrae. No, it's not without risks but it's the best chance, in your case, for an approximately normal and active life."

Kemp had answered, "I laugh at risk," but then spent a very lonely night worrying about the prospect of permanent, and below the injury, total, paralysis. Finally, he decided, *What the hell; if it doesn't work I can always eat my gun.*

Fortunately, the surgery worked, with no more side

effects than quite a lot of pain, since Kemp insisted on keeping the painkillers to the bare, tolerable minimum. But following the surgery . . .

That's when the real pain began.

I don't know what kind of connections Dr. Joseph had here, Elena thought, *to set this up for me, but they must have been simply awesome. That, or the regiment is stroking one amazingly large check to Baylor to get them to give me all this personal attention.*

Not that it isn't hard, too.

Hard barely began to describe it. Afternoons, she studied and practiced here, for her morning supervised sessions with Kemp or, less often, one of the other patients. Weekends, she drove to Fort Hood to take classes there. Nights, she took more classes here.

Tiring, yes, but I'll get my degree in under two years. Joseph said he'll go to the wall, after that, to get the regiment to commission me. I believe he will, if I do my part.

The proof of which will not be just the degree in physical therapy, but Sergeant Kemp back on duty.

Today's date with the Grand Inquisitor involved the use of two canes. This wasn't for his back, though it wouldn't hurt that, but to keep his legs from atrophying. It was a struggle maintaining such an artificial balance while moving.

And it's a bitch, thought Kemp. *I never thought I'd be using even one cane, ever. To have to use two, and badly, at my age . . . a bitch. A goddamned fucking . . . oh, oh . . .*

★ ★ ★

"Shit!" exclaimed Elena, as she shot from one side of the small therapy suite to the center to catch Kemp before he fell over completely. She deftly dodged the one wildly waving cane on her side before tucking herself up under Kemp's shoulder. She grunted at the strain of holding up a man who probably weighed two and a half times what she did.

"Thank you," Kemp whispered, in lieu of what he really wanted to say. He used the girl's temporary brace to get the cane set firmly on the theoretically nonskid floor. When he was confident he wouldn't fall over immediately, he told her so.

"Okay," she agreed. "Enough for one day, anyway. You wait and *don't* move while I get your chair set up behind you."

HQ, *Departamento Administrativo de Seguridad* (DAS), Bogot·, Colombia

The DAS had odd responsibilities, ranging from foreign intelligence to immigration control. Though it had a number of branch offices, the main office, the headquarters, sat in Bogotá, not far from the intersection of *Carrera* 27 and *Avenida Calle* 19.

The building itself was some twelve stories high, exclusive of basements, and composed of largely undecorated, pale concrete and banks of glass windows. The building had once been subjected to a drug cartel ordered bombing attack—over a half ton of high explosives, hidden in a bus—which attack had killed or injured more than six hundred people. Security around the place remained tight, even decades later.

In the bowels of the place, behind secure gates and armed guards, in a small, cramped, and overstuffed office, a military officer, one Lieutenant Colonel Baretto Gomez, went over a partial intelligence summary from the day prior. The folder containing the summary was labelled "FARC."

It's always a day late, fumed Barreto, *a day late getting here and a day late getting disseminated. I've told them I need more space. I've told them I need a larger staff, but "nooo, the budget won't support it."*

Resigned to what could not be helped, Barreto closed the folder he'd been working on and opened another, labelled "ELN." Three folders beneath that one lay another. That one was marked "Venezuela."

★ CHAPTER TWENTY-SEVEN ★

Let your plans be dark and as impenetrable as night,
and when you move, fall like a thunderbolt.
—Sun Tzu, *The Art of War*

La Linea, Venezuela

There were fifteen unarmed men in the party, along with
twice that many armed ones, plus one. Among the
unarmed men, twelve were black and wore the field
uniforms of the Guyanan Defense Force. The other three
were brown and wore Venezuelan camouflage. Half the
armed men, significantly, carried an extra weapon.

The hands of the armed men were free. The unarmed
were bound, hands behind them. Frightened, with reason,
they'd been hauled from cells in Yare Prison two days
before, brought by boat to the coast, then disembarked
by night. The next morning, unfed but dressed in odd
uniforms, their guards had marched them through the
jungle, along narrow trails, to the little town of La Linea.
Only one man had tried to break away. When the guard

had run him down and dragged him back they'd beaten the man unconscious, then draped his body over the shoulders of the largest and the strongest of the prisoners.

From La Linea the group had moved south three or four miles, carefully skirting the Guyanan frontier. The leader checked a GPS to make sure that the incident would take place on their side of the border.

At the final stop—which would prove very final for fifteen men—they'd split up, two guards and one prisoner to a team, while that extra man, the leader of the group, positioned them exactly as he wanted them. Each prisoner was forced to his knees once that position was reached. The still unconscious prisoner was laid on the ground.

"Back off a little," said the leader, to two of the guards. He waited until they were far enough away to be sure that there would be no powder residue on the prisoner's GDF uniform. When he was satisfied, the leader said, "Good, now kill him. Aim for the stomach first, then the heart."

"Please," the prisoner begged. "No." The guard, chosen, like the rest, for that special mix of Bolivarian fanaticism and sociopathy, ignored the plea. He raised his rifle and fired, bending the prisoner over with the first shot, then stretching him out on the ground with the second.

With the jungle reverberating with the sounds of sustained fire, the monkeys set to howling even as brightly colored birds flocked into the air, and helpless men fell dead.

"But why?" asked the last of the prisoners.

"So Hugo can make a speech, turning some of you into aggressors and others into martyrs, to support his plans," answered the leader of the party. "Now kill him."

"Lawyers, Guns, and Money" (SCIF), Camp Fulton, Guyana

The night was growing old, even the monkeys were tired of howling. Boxer entered the SCIF, got himself passed through by the guards, and headed for Bridges' office. Then again, normal working hours were pretty much in abeyance for the time being. Boxer's boots click-click-clicked past offices, most of them full. Halfway, he met Warrant Officer Corrigan. And, *Sure as hell, her smile does light the world.*

And, speaking of lighting up the world, my new toy from China is here. Give it to the air defense folks? Nah, there's only the one for now, not even enough time to test it and have a couple of dozen more built. And for what the chinks demanded for that one-off job . . . scary. Well, the price will go way down if we order fifty or sixty, as I'd like to.

There being no immediate contracting or legal problems to deal with, Bridges was wearing his S-2 hat this evening. Truth be told, that had been his most pressing duty for a couple of months now. For the moment he was worrying about an odd discrepancy in the reports from Colombia.

Though I'm going to have to consider suing the United States for cancelling the rotation that's supposed to be here about now. Close call; never really considered the possibility of an unpredictable riot amounting almost to an insurrection being sufficient cause to cancel. And the contract is ambiguous. Hurricane, flood, or earthquake? Good cause. Is a riot a natural disaster? Force majeure?

In a place like this it just might be. But if they cancelled because they know we might be hit . . .

"Any new word from Colombia on when we might get hit?" asked Boxer, walking unannounced into Bridges' office.

Bridges suppressed a mild annoyance. Boxer's abruptness was just something one just had to get used to. He shook his head no, then added, "But I've found something odd, a chronological mismatch. Took me a while to catch it," he added, a bit embarrassed.

"What's that?"

"Well . . . Colombian Intel told you we would have any pertinent information 'as soon as available,' right?"

"Yes."

"Did they define 'as soon as available'? Because I think they're defining it as 'as soon as we get it and massage it for a while.' At least, I can't understand the discrepancies between when they're reporting a couple of things and when they actually happened."

Boxer raised an eyebrow. "Such as?"

"Remember when Ryan's team was attacked by a big croc in the Gulf of Venezuela?"

Boxer chuckled in an 'All's well that ends well' way. "Sure."

"Well, we know that there was an explosion, and that there had been a number of distress flares fired, right? The Columbian border folks duly reported that to higher. But it didn't get disseminated for a full forty-eight hours. I didn't catch it because it was old history by the time you got their agreement. But, you know, paranoia is all in the job description so I started digging back.

"Then, once I found that, I looked at a couple of other

things. Morales reported a test sailing of one of their frigates. Colombia noted that . . . two days later. Some jets, Canadair-built F-5's, moved from their normal base to *Ciudad* Bolivar. I found that one online, in a chat room. Colombia Intelligence reported the move, again, about forty-eight hours later than it happened."

Boxer swallowed, nervously. "You mean they might . . ."

"Yes," Bridges confirmed. "It's entirely possible that the Venezuelans have a forty-eight-hour head start on what we think we know of them."

Tomas de Heres Airport, *Ciudad* Bolivar

There were military police thick on the ground, Larralde was pleased to see, all around the loading area. The C-130's were parked in a line but at an angle. Under the lights of the airfield, something over a dozen F-5's were being prepared and loaded with ordnance. For a wonder, all four of the Bolivarian National Air Force's C-130's were working and waiting, with engines running, while the buses pulled up with Larralde's troops. Behind the buses came the tank transporters, hauling the two AMX-13/90 light tanks going with them. The tanks' crews rode the buses.

Shit, thought Larralde, stepping out of his Tiuna and looking upward to read the numbers, "4951," just in front of the tail, *I never expected so much good fortune or I'd had asked for another tank and more engineers.*

"You know, sir," said Mao Arrivillaga, "if you had planned on this, we could have maybe brought another couple of tanks, or some more engineers."

"Well, who would have expected . . ." Larralde began, then stifled the thought. Instead, he said, "No matter, Sergeant Major, the plan calls for bringing in several additional pallets of supply, mostly wire and ammunition, and another Tiuna, if there were to be an extra bird." *Hah, gotcha.*

Carlos Villareal stood and pulled his own pack over his shoulders, then lifted Lily's off her lap, reversed it, and held it out for her while she stood. She smiled, gratefully, then turned around herself to slip her arms through the straps. She couldn't help but grunt with the strain as Carlos released the thing to rest on her shoulders. He gave an affectionate laugh and then patted her on the rump, a move that earned him a dirty look.

"Come on, *querida*," he said, turning toward the front where a gap had appeared as those nearest the door moved out in a sort of reverse spring. "Mao will skin us and roast us if we slow down the load."

One after the other, they filed down the bus's narrow central aisle, then faced right at the stairs to dismount. Laden like mules, as they were, the walk down the few steps to the ground was more of an awkward stagger. The load had formed up outside, even as part of another bus load filled in from the left. And air force sergeant was waiting in the darkness with a lit light wand—a flashlight with a translucent conical projection attached—held in each hand.

And then Sergeant Major Arrivillaga was there, shouting, "You faggots! Get your asses into two—count 'em, *two*, lines, in *exactly* the order you're supposed to load in. That's right, just the way we rehearsed."

El Libertador Air Base (AKA Palo Negro Airport), Maracay, Venezuela

By the direct airbase lighting, as well as the more diffuse light coming from the city of Maracay, less than a kilometer to the north, many more than a dozen SU-30's—"Flankers," in NATO parlance—waited in lines while being serviced and armed at this, Venezuela's largest and most important aerial base. Fuel trucks passed the line of jets, one by one. As each was filled it moved off to the ammunition area to be loaded with anything up to eight tons.

The first four jets to be fully prepared moved via the taxiway to one end of the thirty-one-hundred-and-seventy-meter concrete strip. There, to save fuel and wear and tear, they shut down engines. They would restart in time to launch and launch to time their arrival over central Guyana with that of the F-5's and with the touchdown of the C-130's at Cheddi Jagan airport. The Flankers had a particular mission, though, in contrast to the general support the F-5's were to give to the Army and Marines. They were, so the wing commander had told his pilots, to "smash the clandestine imperialist outpost one hundred and forty kilometers southwest of Georgetown, the place the gringos called, 'Camp Fulton.'"

Tumeremo Airport, Tumeremo, Venezuela

The town had never been large enough to justify the

roughly three-kilometer-long airstrip that had been laid out, and partially constructed, roughly three miles south of the town center. Nor was there anything inside Venezuela within any reasonable range to have justified that kind of expense. The place could only have been intended as an advanced base for an invasion or occupation. And, had Chavez not felt pushed by events, the invasion probably would have waited until the completion of the strip.

No matter, what there was, finished, would do. So, at least, thought the commander of the air force's single squadron of Brazilian-built Embraer 312 Tucanos. *Since, at max load, we need only three hundred and eighty-one meters to take off, and less to land, this will* more *than do.*

And the army's helicopters, he thought, looking north to where two—*hmmph, should have been three*—MI-26's and thirty-two MI-17's had already begun loading troops from the 5th Infantry Division. The MI-17's, except for markings, were indistinguishable from those owned by M Day, Inc. The MI-26, though getting to be an old design, had begun life as, and *still* was, the most capable heavy lift production helicopter in the world. Only one helicopter, also Russian, had ever beaten it and that one had never made it into production. Each of the 26's was loading not one, but *two*, Cadillac-Gage armored cars.

Those helicopters were in two groups of an MI-26, sixteen MI-17's, and two pairs each of late model Hind gunships. These last were updated with the latest in western avionics, and were fully night fighting capable.

The squadron commander consulted his watch. *H minus three. Another two hours and fifty-four minutes. I hate waiting.*

Tomas de Heres Airport, *Ciudad* Bolivar, Guyana

Strapped in to a starboard side bench seat, swaying as the heavy bird lumbered down the strip with its engines straining for its takeoff run, Larralde took his eyes from his watch and did some quick calculations. *H minus two hours and seventeen minutes. That meets the standard.*

The plane gathered speed quickly. In a few brief moments he found himself pressed down into the bench, his heart beating fast, not with fear but with the adventure. Then they were airborne, and on the way.

MV *Manuel de Cespides,* Demerara River mouth, by Georgetown, Guyana

In the east, there was not yet the first glimpse of dawn.

The ship was docked about three hundred meter north of Stabroek Market, by a very large open-sided metal structure, full of the kind of equipment—forklifts, carts, small tractors, one would expect to find somewhere near docking facilities. Conde's mission, and that of his Marines, included securing that structure and the equipment. He didn't need it for himself or his people—they were all lightly equipped. But follow on echelons *would* need it.

Those follow on echelons, Conde knew, would be about a day's sail behind. He didn't much like the idea of being out here, on his own, for an entire twenty-four hours.

On the other hand, I like the idea of a contested landing even less. Everything is a tradeoff, I suppose.

Lieutenant Colonel Conde was standing on the bridge, in sailor's clothes, when the customs man from the port came alongside and aboard. This was not unexpected. Nor had Conde failed to prepare; two of his beefier noncoms, with hidden pistols, were waiting with him.

Drake barely got two words out before Conde ordered, "Take him. Don't hurt him if you can avoid it." Turning back to Mr. Drake, he said, "There is no reason to be hurt, *señor*. My men will take you below until you can safely be released.

"And *viva* the Bolivarian Revolution, *señor*, which, after long centuries, has come to liberate her lost sons!"

Looking at the barrel of a pistol stuck in his face, and hearing Spanish spoken authoritatively, Drake's first thought was, *O, dis be de bad t'ing*, quickly followed by, *Elizabeth, meh gyal! Her people; they got be warned!*

Even as Drake had the thought, the masses of Marines previously hidden in the hold and in containers began emerging and descending the gangways. Under the street-lamps he saw them begin to split up into squads, platoons, and in one case, a full company. That last, arms at high port, began to trot in the direction of Camp Ayanganna, on the northern quadrant of the city, their sergeants calling out the cadence punctuated by their booted feet.

Miraflores Palace, Caracas, Venezuela

In a more ideal world, Chavez would have set up his

personal command post on some military base, possibly at El Libertador, or maybe all the way forward in Tumeremo. But . . .

I don't live in an ideal world. I live in a world where the senior command of my own forces hate my guts. So, thanks, but no thanks. I'll stay here, with my own guards, and these assholes can keep me briefed.

Chavez snuffed out a cigarette in an already overfull ashtray and looked at his man, Martinez, for another. Martinez shrugged, *Ain't got any more, Mr. President*, causing Chavez to scowl.

A steady stream of runners moved between Chavez's conference room *cum* command post and the radio room down the corridor. Each, as he—or she—entered, made some announcement. "Task Force Larralde, in the air," or "Force Alpha Four, Checkpoint Three," before going to the map and presenting a written update to be posted. There was a particular flurry around H Minus Forty-five.

At H plus Ten, one wag, a young lieutenant wearing a broad smile, stood to attention at the door and shouted, "The Marines have landed and have the situation well in hand." Chavez, who was a lot better read than his enemies would have given him credit for, recognized the reference, and laughed. After the lieutenant turned from the situation board the president made a "come hither" gesture.

"Son, do you happen to smoke?"

The lieutenant hung his head in shame—everyone knew Chavez disapproved—but admitted, "Yes, sir."

"Good. Gimme. And go take up a collection from your buddies. Tell 'em it's for the good of the country."

Assembly Area "Mule," Guyana

Cazz lit a new cigarette from a dying one, then ground the embers into the muck below. *Good thing about Gordo*, he thought, *he understands that men will have their vices and includes those in his log planning.* To punctuate, Cazz sipped a concoction of about three quarters reconstituted fruit juice and a quarter rum from his half full canteen cup.

From a spot just below Peaima Falls a cattle trail ran west-northwest to the airstrip next to the six-hundred-and-twenty-nine-foot drop of Sakaika Falls. From that airstrip ran another cattle trail, first generally north, towards the Cuyuni River, then west to the cross-border ferry at Venezuela's San Martin de Turumban. The ferry crossed the Cuyuni River below the Eteringbang Falls.

Above those falls were an additional two airstrips, one north and one south of the river.

From San Martin an all-weather, hard-surfaced road led northwest to Venezuela's Highway 10, at the juncture of Casa Blanca. About fourteen miles northeast of Casa Blanca, by Tumeremo, was what was believed would be a major logistics and aviation support base.

Cazz and his staff—to include the special staff, his engineer platoon leader, and his battalion's scout platoon leader, USMC Master Sergeant (retired) Austin—huddled over a map in the command tent. The S-2 held a red-filtered flashlight focused on the map. In the gloom, Austin's shiny black skin was harder to see than his silver-gray hair.

"I need to know the following four things, Top," Cazz said. As he spoke, he drifted a twig over the map to indicate the precise location he meant. Austin scribbled notes in a waterproof notebook, and occasionally made a mark on his own acetate-covered map.

"First, I need a team to scout out the trail to Sakaika Falls' airstrip. They need to find me a covered and concealed assault position for at least one company. Got it?"

"Clear, sir," Austin replied. "That'll be Sergeant Ahern. He's local, but a good'un." Austin had a hard time keeping his voice calm. *This is going to be so much* fun.

"Second, one team is to scout out the ferry at San Martin and to find us a possible crossing point . . . I should probably say, 'a crossing point, *if possible*,' for the whole battalion, somewhere between the ferry and a point on the river about eight miles east of that."

Austin nodded, thinking, *You can cross anything on a poncho raft, at least until the raft fills with water, sinks, and you drown.*

"Third, one team is to escort the heavy mortar platoon leader as far as they can get him, while he scouts a good mortar position, nine klicks north of Sakaika Falls."

Austin looked dubious. "North, sir?"

Cazz nodded. "If we hit—if we *can* hit—the airstrip at the falls and the ferry at the same time, the ferry's the only place the Venezuelans can mount a counterattack. But they're not going to be able to do it quickly. It'll be at least two hours, maybe three, possibly even four, before they can assemble and move a mobile force from Tumeremo to the ferry. I want the mortars in position to support at San Martin before that happens. If they're firing from near the cattle trail, north of Sakaika, they can break the guns down and haul ass to get in range of the ferry."

Austin's obsidian head rocked from side to side for a few moments before he pronounced, "Makes sense. And my last team?"

"They're going to break the rules," Cazz said. "I want them to cross the river, east of the ferry, and find me a good antiarmor ambush position somewhere on the Casa Blanca-San Martin road, within six miles of San Martin. Then I want them to move generally north to Tumeremo and find me where the Venezuelans have the log base we believe they've put up. Those frigging helicopters—at least I think they were just helicopters—we've been hearing for days are coming from somewhere in that area."

Again, Austin looked pretty dubious. "The doggies couldn't get through, sir."

"Yeah, but the Venezuelans who had that screening mission don't need to worry about OPSEC once the invasion gets close; everyone in the world will know they've invaded Guyana. Since that can't be too far away, they've probably been pulled back. And besides . . ."

"Yes, sir?"

"Besides, we're not doggies. We're Guyanan jungle runners led by the finest group of retirees Uncle Sam's Misguided Children ever shat out."

A red-tinged smile flashed in the old noncom's face. "Yeah . . . yeah, sir, I guess we are. And . . . mmm . . . since you put it that way, sir, I'll be going with that last group then."

"That's what I thought," Cazz said. "Go, brother." He turned to his engineer platoon leader, Master Sergeant

Rutledge. "Rutt, I want you to follow that first scout team to here"—his twig touched on a spot where two streams converged to form one, before the one emptied into the Mazaruni. "There I want you to put up a couple of three-rope bridges for the foot troops, and find or make me a crossing site for the mules and mortars."

"Clear, sir," Rutledge replied.

"Signal?"

"Here, sir."

"That ridge to our east? Did you get the half-rhombic antenna up, pointed directly at Camp Fulton? Did you finish running wire down to here?"

"Yessir."

"Good. I hate being cut off from commo. In a couple of days, I'm going to want to know the main regiment's status."

"Clear, sir."

"Supply and Transport Platoon—and you, too, Sergeant Daly—we're going to have to figure out what we can carry on mule back, then displace what we can't as far forward as possible without getting caught at it."

"Can't carry more than eight tons, sir," Daly said, "between my mules and your own, not with having to haul the mortars and with a few of my critters being lame or otherwise indisposed."

"I know. But every ton we can move a mile forward now is a ton that's easier to retrieve when we must . . ."

Cazz stopped speaking to listen for a moment. There was a sound, arising in the west. He waited very briefly until the sound became distinctive enough for him to tell the radio operator, "Screw listening silence. Call base. Tell them they've got vampires inbound! Shitloads of 'em."

★EXCURSUS★

From Legio Patria Nostra:
The Continuing Rise of the Mercenary Profession,
Baen Historical Press, Copyright ©, 2027

It is a truth not without its amusingly ironic aspect that those who most decry the proliferation of not merely military contractors, but of genuine mercenary organizations around the globe, are also those most responsible for that rise.

There are other factors and influences involved, too, of course. The continuing depression, coupled with military drawdowns everywhere the troops were paid more than a pittance, fed more than scraps, and armed with anything better than worn out and rusty rifles, provided the manpower and the motivation. Yet motivated manpower could have starved just as well within those mercenary organizations as outside of them, had there been no employment for those regiments.

Employment, however, there generally has been, whether by Pavlov's Guards (see Chapter XIX), paid by the Russian state to keep a large portion of the southern glacis of the reborn Russian Empire from becoming a route into the <u>Rodina</u>, the NORINCO-owned and run Black Flag Brigade, busily hunting down Moslems for pay in China's Xinjiang and Gansu provinces (see Chapter XXI), the German-speaking GvB AG, based in the Congo (see Chapter XX), or the Guyana-based M Day, Inc. (see Chapter XXIV), whose funding is more mysterious but appeared at last reckoning to have made a great deal from training regular American forces and a great deal more from other investments and payoffs.

This, however, is to beg the question of precisely *why* there has been such steady employment for these mercenary corporations.

The answer is simplicity itself: the mercenaries are hired because national forces, in most cases, have become useless.

This is not, for the greater part, because those forces have dwindled to insignificance. Indeed, most of the traditional military powers maintain substantial forces, generally well equipped and well trained. Rather, it is that those regular forces now find themselves constrained by an ever-tightening mesh of treaties and limitations, which put their officer corps at risk of prosecution for doing the military and politically necessary but aesthetically distasteful, and even subject national civilian leaders to the threat of prosecution by politically motivated courts and prosecutors, egged on by an often rabid press, an always politicized international judiciary, and an invariably corrupt transnational bureaucracy.

Sadly for those who thought to expand civilization by placing legal limits on uncivilized conduct, only those who were civilized—some have said, "too civilized"—feel any constraint from that web of treaties or any obligations to what is called "international law."

The mercenaries feel no such constraints. Sometimes sheltering behind figurehead sovereign states, sometimes serving as fronts for sovereign states, sometimes totally independent but locally quite powerful, they will do, for pay or principle, the distasteful things no one else is permitted to, and will laugh in the face of judge or prosecutor bold enough to try to bring them to heel. Indeed, sometimes they will do more than laugh in their faces.

Thus, the net effect of trying to exercise excess control of force through law has led to a substantial segment of force providers over which law has no control whatsoever.

★ CHAPTER TWENTY-EIGHT ★

Mass, Objective, Security, SURPRISE,
Maneuver, Offensive, Unity of Command,
Simplicity, Economy of Force
—*The Principles of War, FM 3-0*

Quarters One, Glen Morangie Housing Area, Camp Fulton, Guyana

Lana was moaning softly as Reilly moved carefully inside her. She had been surprised to discover that pregnancy made her unbearably horny most of the time. Worse, the horniness increased as the pregnancy progressed.

That soft sound of love and desire was soon overwhelmed in an unusual sort of "did the earth move for you, too" moment.

The screaming of the sirens didn't beat the first bombs by all that much. The difference was enough, if barely, to get a cursing—"*dirtynogoodrottenpuritanicalantisexmotherfuckers!*"—Reilly out of Lana and into his battle dress trousers. His feet went into his boots without bothering to lace them. On his way out of the house he grabbed a razor, his hat, his pistol, and his jacket. Everything else was already in his Land Rover.

He shouted over one shoulder, "Just follow the plan, Lana!" as he burst out the front door. In fact, the only delay he suffered was getting his left arm out of the screen, as he'd punched entirely through it in the rush.

Lousy fucking timing, Lana thought, in a mix of anger and sheer frustration, as she struggled to don her own uniform. She wasn't as quick as her husband, despite being quite a bit younger, as she had to battle to get her let-out-by-the-post-tailor battle dress over her distended belly. She was buttoning the jacket by the time the first bomb struck, shattering the glass in every window in the house, rocking it on its foundation, and knocking her to her rear end.

"Never actually been on the receiving end of this shit before," Reilly muttered, strapping himself in automatically, then tossing the Land Rover into reverse and backing quickly out of the driveway. "Should have combat parked, you asshole, Reilly! You're getting old; you're getting old. Lana remembered to."

Cutting the wheel, he threw the shift into forward and began weaving his Land Rover up the asphalt of the road leading to his own battalion's headquarters. "And I *don't* like it." Though the sun was not yet up, he'd kept the presence of mind, barely, not to turn on the Rover's headlights. This didn't make the driving any easier.

Something—a jet, he supposed—screeched overhead, close enough to shake the vehicle. This was followed by a not terribly well aimed bomb, behind him and not all that far away. The flash lit up the housing area, even as the concussive wave shook the Land Rover. It skidded momentarily, making him jerk the wheel to regain control.

The last house in Glen Morangie passed quickly behind him. Then the jungle began on his left. A flat, grassy open area sometimes used as a parade field and other times as a pickup zone for helicopter operations opened up on his right. On either side of the asphalt, a deep concrete-revetted drainage ditch paralleled the road. The lights of the post illuminated a row of white buildings—barracks—on the far side of the field. A single rocket lanced upward, following that jet in a revenge shot. If it hit, Reilly couldn't see it for the immense fireball that suddenly arose over the horizon in the direction of the airfield.

Reilly felt a momentary surge of despair. *Let's hope that was just the surface filling station tanks, not the buried ones.*

Another jet streaked overhead. Its first bomb landed in the field, the second halfway to the buildings, while the third struck one of them either directly or close enough to directly to crumple it like a cast-off *origami*. There was a fourth bomb, farther on, but Reilly didn't know where that one landed.

Then a rocket, one of a salvo of seven, coming from behind him somewhere, streaked by. It missed the Land Rover, itself, but landed close enough to the left front wheel to shred that, to shatter the glass of the windshield, and to send the auto careening to the left, into the drainage ditch.

Reilly never noticed the propeller driven Tucano that passed by, overhead, following the road.

State House, Main Street, Georgetown, Guyana

The security team Boxer had placed on President Paul was something of an interior guard. They left security of the perimeter of the State House grounds to local forces, concentrating on securing the president's person. This meant four men, operating two hours on, four off, at night, and four and eight in the day, fully armed, wearing the best body armor available on the open market, with night vision goggles either ready or worn. Their arms they'd drawn from Second Battalion's special weapons armory. These were silenced Sterling submachine guns, with aiming lasers fitted. Each man also carried a pistol and wore a short range radio, with earpiece and boom mike. Other, heavier arms remained with their vehicles.

The team leader, Jose "Little Joe" Venegas, had two men on the president's door. Another one walked the second floor porches and balconies. When it was his shift, Venegas roved, sniffing for trouble. Right now he was on the first floor, in the main hall.

The first notice of trouble came not from his nose or his eyes, but from the earpiece stuck in his left ear. "Little Joe, I got people in formation moving through the streets, a shit pot of them."

"Changing of the guard? Or the GDF people on riot control and support to the cops?" Venegas asked.

"I don't think so since—"

Venegas heard the shots fired toward the east, but close, as if just on the other side of the fence. His pulse jumped.

"Everybody!" Venegas ordered, over his radio. "Move out, now. Prez team; get the big guy off of his latest bimbo. Who's awake in the hooch?"

"Baker, chief," came the answer.

"Everybody up. Get the cars ready. Order of march as rehearsed, His Sticky-fingeredness in Number Two. Go."

The two men at Paul's door looked at each other and grinned. The horny bastard had been pumping away steadily for freaking *hours*, with some whore who couldn't have been over fourteen. New one every goddamned night, too. And when *they* couldn't have any? Oh, yes; *great* fun.

As one man they turned around, bent their legs up, and kicked in the presidential door. It came completely off its hinges, loudly clattering to the floor. The girl screamed. The president screamed. And then the troops were on him, one to each side, dragging him out of the for-the-nonce quadrupedal hooker, and then backwards out the door, down the stairs, through the hall, and out to the thrumming Land Rovers.

Venegas, already behind the machine gun mounted atop the first Land Rover shouted, "You fuckers couldn't have left him his pants?"

One of the guards pulled a set of heavy torso armor over the president then tossed him head first into the vehicle. The other one then stepped right on top of his almost naked, flabby form to man the gun on the roof. The gunner shouted back, "But you said 'now,' chief! No pleasing you, is there."

"Ah, fuckit. Move out; take a left and head north, toward Lamaha Street."

As the first Rover inched out into the narrow private alley that divided the block into east and west, a burst of fire, two of them tracers, passed in front. Venegas yanked the gun around and returned fire in long, steady, but not terribly effective bursts. He thought he heard someone on the receiving end cry out something in Spanish, but couldn't be sure. He ceased fire when Number Two, carrying Paul, blocked his line of sight. That gun picked up the fire as Venegas swiveled his own around to the front.

"This wasn't supposed to happen yet," he fumed.

Camp Ayanganna, Guyana

The camp was basically quadrangular, bounded by Vlissengen Road on the east, Thomas Road along the south, Wireless Road to the west, and Carifesta Ave to the north. West of Wireless was Thomas Lands National Park, while past Carifesta, at a distance of anywhere between about thirty meters and two hundred, was open area. Beyond that was the sea.

The post contained perhaps three score buildings, greater or lesser. Some were single story; others were higher. There wasn't a single useful defensive position to the entire roughly forty-five acres of the installation.

The Venezuelan Marine company commander had posted one of his platoons along Thomas, with a brace of machine guns oriented up Vlissingen. Those machine guns had fired a long burst east up the road, just to remind anyone inside the camp that, no, they weren't allowed to leave in that direction. The remaining two platoons were massed to the west, in Thomas Lands, with their mortar section behind them, between the YMCA and the Burrowee School of Art.

Those hundred and fifty-odd nervous Marines waited for their attached loudspeaker team to do its business. Maybe they wouldn't have to fight after all. Still, there had been scattered firing from behind them, coming from throughout the city.

The Chief of Staff of the Guyanan Defense Force waited with his staff for what he fully expected to be the end. It was so sudden, so totally unexpected, that they were, every man and woman, in a state of shock. Relatively few of them were in a full state of dress.

A brace of F-5's skimmed over the tops of the barracks, rattling buildings and their windows, but more importantly rattling the nerves of those inside. The fighters screamed into a turn and began to climb, even as a second pair repeated the intimidating maneuver of the first.

A loudspeaker from somewhere outside the camp's walls and fences began to blare in heavily accented, but understandable, English. The message contained a great many protestations of international amity and brotherhood, three references to liberation, one to "future comrades in arms," and more than a few to Simon Bolivar. None of those, in themselves, made much impression on the men and women of the Guyana Defence Force. What did make an impression was the understated, but jet fighter-punctuated command, "Surrender now or be destroyed."

While that message was being sent with a jet-powered exclamation point, at a greater but still audible distance, other aircraft were busy turning Guyana's GDFS *Essequibo*, which had been built as an armed minesweeper, along with the other vessels of the Guyanan Coast Guard, into scrap. Those sounds had a particular . . . resonance.

"What do we do?" asked the Chief of Staff, of nobody in particular.

"*Jesu Cristo*, sir, where the hell do we put them all?" the commander of the Marine company surrounding the GDF's main base asked of Conde. His voice was a mix of wonder, and shock, with overtones of disbelief. "There must be . . . hell, I dunno. Ten times as many as I have? Fifteen?"

"Fifteen times, I think, Captain," Conde answered. "And the first thing is to treat them with dignity. They're our new fellow citizens, even if few of them can speak Spanish yet." He scanned the weary and demoralized faces of the half-dressed men and women pouring in a steady stream into Thomas Lands. "I didn't expect them to give up this easily. It's a good sign. Put one platoon to guarding them just to the west of here. Send your men in to search the buildings for weapons . . . take the officers with you for that. Once you've collected up anything dangerous, move them back in and set a guard around the perimeter."

Conde, accompanied by the captain, crossed over into Ayanganna. He looked around with a certain satisfaction and added, "And don't *damage* anything! This is a nice little camp and it may just be that *we'll* end up stationed here more or less permanently."

Though, unless we can arrest the president of this pseudo-republic, I, at least will not *be stationed here, but in Yare Prison. Well, at least, we got the prime minister and his family. Maybe I'll get a nice cell. With a view.*

Holding Base Snake (SF and MI-17's), Twenty-two miles south of Jonestown, Guyana

The five working Hips sat in an old slash and burn area, not far from the banks of the Barama River. The helicopters were snug in against the jungle's edge, more or less in a circle around the open area. Camouflage screens, tied fast to those perimeter trees, sloped out and covered them all the way down to the charred stubble with green shoots peeking through.

All their shiny parts, windows, especially, had been covered with dull green canvas. Farther into the jungle were the men of what hadn't been otherwise committed of von Ahlenfeld's Second Battalion. That, less Welch's company in or en route to the Philippines and most of D Company, reinforced by the Hip crews, air and ground, both, amounted to under two hundred soldiers. They had small tents, more nets, and a bare minimum of support.

Overhead, coming from and heading to both directions, were the sounds of steady streams of hostile aircraft.

"Meanwhile, back at the ranch," said Sergeant Major Hampson, aka "Rattus," looking up at the sheltering jungle canopy.

Hilton, commander for B Company piped in, "Grandma was beatin' off the Indians."

"And they still kept coming," finished von Ahlenfeld.

"Well," said Rattus, "at least they haven't figured out we're here. We know this because, in fact, we're *still* here, rather than, say, trying to explain to Saint Peter that we really didn't know she was only fifteen."

"True," agreed the battalion commander. "But I really didn't. I swear."

Ten minutes out from Cheddi Jagan International Airport, Timehri, Guyana

Well, the flyboys didn't lie about that, thought Larralde, as a wave of vomit washed over his boots. *I've got thirty-one jumps in my log, and I've never experienced a flight quite like this one. I wish to hell—*

The thought was cut off by the urgent need to add a little more of the remaining contents of his own stomach to the general pool. Larralde bent over and hurled onto the deck at his feet. It didn't relieve his misery in the slightest.

I could have dealt with the four hour rollercoaster. It's the stench that gets me . . . and most of us, I think.

Eyes swimming from the fumes, Larralde looked across the dimly lit cargo compartment. Half the people there were bent over. The rest seemed to be getting ready to hurl or just recovering from a spasm. The only exception was: *that bastard Villareal. He must have the stomach of a buzzard.*

Carlos really didn't understand. Sure, the place stank. And he'd never imagined that the fumes from the gastric juices would be enough to make his eyes water. But was it worse than the uncollected garbage back in the barrio? He didn't think so. In any case, while he'd had to gulp down his rising bile a couple of times, that hadn't been all that hard to do. And natural tearing took good enough care of the eyes.

Ah, but poor Lily, he thought, rubbing the bent-over girl's back for whatever little comfort that might provide her.

Capitano Sebastian, in control of the lead C-130, looked left. Yes, there was Number Two, so tight onto his own plane's wing that the two would appear as one, as indeed the three had appeared as one, when he'd been queried by the control tower at Cheddi Jagan, an hour previously.

"CAL Flight 483, Miami to Georgetown," he'd replied, in good but accented English. Not that an Hispanic accent in a flight originating in Miami was likely to draw notice.

"You're early, 483," the control tower had answered.

"Grace of God," Sebastian had told them, which seemed as good an explanation as any.

Now, however, the illusion had to end. Not only were the jets due to strike Camp Stephenson, housing the whole Guyanan—Sebastian struggled not to laugh—Air

Force, but also their much more serious artillery park and command, but the flight of three had to split up simply to allow one to land.

He gave the word, received confirmation, then glanced again to his left to ensure Number Two was veering off. Then he began a rocky descent to the airfield.

"If the control tower calls," he said, "ignore them. Unless they turn off the lights. In that case, tell them to turn them on again, quick, or we'll hang them with their own guts."

If the trip down had been sickening, the sudden lurch and violent right turn, followed by a way-too-hard impact on the airstrip, was positively terrifying. Larralde didn't cry out, though more than a few of his troops did. Some of that was pain from restraining belts cutting into laps and legs as the plane bounced. As much was fear of the wild swaying of the light tank strapped down near the loading ramp. More was simply: *ohmyGodwe'regonnacrash;we'reDOOMED!*

Just as the bouncing reduced to something tolerable, the plane's four stout engines kicked into reverse. The rear duly rose. Now the AMX-13 *really* strained at its leash. Larralde looked and, as far as he could see, almost no portion of the tread was resting on the deck. *Fuckfuckfuck.*

Of course, the sudden rapid slowing of the plane had forced his torso forward, so naturally the big chunk of metal was foremost in his field of view. *Fuckfuckfuck.*

And then the plane was actually and noticeably slowing . . . slowing . . . slowing . . . and gently turning.

The plane rumbled along to the east, then virtually

stopped as it swung its ass far around. The engines picked up again, moving it forward. It stopped again, swung right, and then came to a complete stop. The rear of the plane began to whine. A growing sliver of artificial light began to creep in over the loading ramp.

Larralde, never so grateful for a flight to be over in his life, unbuckled himself and stood. "On your feet! Unleash the cargo!" He felt a sudden pride swelling in his chest. *By God, we're really going to* do *this!*

Unsteadily, slipping in puke, the men and woman of Task Force Larralde stood. Some staggered to the tank, others to the Tiuna. A couple slipped and fell into the thin but chunky yellow sea.

At the vehicles muscle memory took over. The vehicles were undone almost as soon as the crews had mounted. The AMX-13's engine cranked . . . coughed . . . cranked and then started, adding diesel to the already noxious fumes of puke and airplane fuel. The commander of the AMX-13 looked around to make sure all the unbucklers were clear, then squatted low in his turret, with only the top of his head and his eyes showing. The was, after all, no sense in having one's torso nipped off by the top of the cargo door. He flicked a switch on his hastily donned helmet and gave a command. Then, slowly, the tank lurched forward and began to descend the loading ramp.

As the tank treaded off, it shook the plane. The plane shook still more as the first concussive waves from the aerial attack on the adjacent Camp Stephenson reached it.

Beginning to recover now, with approximately fresh air washing the interior space clear of the smell of vomit, or at least diluting it, the men and women of the port side trundled forward, peeling off to the left at they reached the edge of the ramp. Their mission was to secure the control tower. Fortunately, that was less than five hundred feet away, northeast across the grassy strip between it and the taxiway.

Wineperu, Guyana

Several things were acting in concert to trash the regiment's small naval base outside this nothing much town on the Essequibo. First, the place hadn't had its warning sirens installed yet. It was a case of "on the to-do list." Second, with Chin running *The Drunken Bastard*, and Kosciusko with *Maria Walewska*, along with any number of the Sixth Naval Squadron's more senior people, there had been no one here to push for a higher priority. Third, the senior naval officer left present on the base, a recent former Federal German Navy acquisition by the name of Thorsten von der Kehre (nickname, "Thor"), hadn't had either the political clout nor the inside contacts and insights to get the base moved up to a higher priority. Fourth, the charge of quarters had been making the rounds, a matter of some twenty minutes' effort, while, fifth, his runner had a sudden overwhelming urge to visit the latrine, all at about the time the staff duty officer at Camp Fulton remembered them. This, sadly, also happened about the time the first two Venezuelan F-5's showed up, a couple of miles up the river, screaming into a northward-aimed turn.

The one thing that the regiment owned that could have

given them more warning was a radar. Sadly, this was on the *Dvora,* and quite masked by buildings, river banks, and trees.

Under glaring lights set up on deck, Kehre, stripped to the waist and with grease up to his armpits, emerged from the *Dvora*'s engine compartment with a look of immense satisfaction. His glasses were streaked with grease, likewise his sun-lightened hair. Broad shouldered, tall, at over six feet, and fairly beefy at one hundred and ninety pounds, squeezing out of the compartment was as tight a maneuver as squeezing in had been.

Three days the bitch's engine's been down. Three unbefuckingglaublich *days!* He'd made a pretty fair estimate of how long it would take to fix her, and had the ammunition and stores brought aboard the previous night. The landing craft were likewise loaded and armed, awaiting the order to scatter to their preplanned hide positions.

Kehre made a thumbs up-finger pointing motion at the helmsman standing by the wheel. The seamen nodded and turned away. A few seconds later, the engine coughed to ragged life before settling down to a steady *thrummm.*

That steady *thrummm* would have been considerably more satisfying had it not been drowned out by the screech of the approaching aircraft. Kehre heard them, gave a single look, and lunged across the deck and up a short ladder for the only siren Wineperu Base had available, the *Dvora*'s own.

Ahwooogaaa! Ahwooogaaa! Ahwooogaaa!

Scheisse. Fight or flight? No question: Flight. Wait for

the crew or run now? We've got many men, but only one Dvora. *We run.*

"Take her out!" Kehre screamed over the wail of the alarm, to the helmsman next to him. Then: *The forward mounted 30mm? No use. Good for surface, not so much for air. At least I've not seen it tried for air defense. The twenty, then.*

Back down the ladder Kehre went, then took at a run the thirty odd feet to the rear mounted, already loaded Oerlikon 20mm, tossing his shoulders into the semi-circular shoulder supports. Several more cylindrical magazines for the gun were secured to the deck at his feet.

With a grunt and a curse, Kehre pulled the bolt back until the sear engaged it. Then, with the boat gaining speed under him, he stepped around the deck and twisted the gun to the south.

It is worth noting that, from 1942 to 1944, roughly a third of all Japanese aircraft downed by the United States Navy fell to the Oerlikon Twenty. Notwithstanding this admirable history, with the boat pulling away from the dock, the plane coming in at about over hundred knots, the cross angle, and the fact that the target was just too close to track well, Kehre's magazine of sixty rounds was emptied, in seven and a half seconds, without a hit. If the fire streaking by the pilot's nose had done any good, it was tolerably hard to see; two of his wing-carried rockets slammed into the first LCM on the boat line, shattering it and sending the just-mounting crew into the river and onto the bank, some of them in pieces. Another one pierced the shed which lay over *Naughtius'* defunct twin.

Wherever it actually hit, the empty hull went up in a flash and a bang, pieces of its steel flying into the air.

Namu, sheltered behind the LCM, was not obviously damaged. The rest of the rockets in the salvo mostly went into the river or onto the fast emptying base. The other attacking plane aimed its ordnance at the workshops and huts of the base. Some of these went up in fireballs; others were left unscathed.

Kehre saw that the remaining LCM's were beginning to make headway. He let go of the gun and went back to the helm. Pointing at the falls to the south, he shouted to the helmsman, "Get us close up under the falls, bring her parallel, and set the ship to hold position. Then get on the weapon station for the forward gun. Might not help, but can't hurt. I want to be able to cover the landing craft until they can scatter to their hides. Shoot at what I shoot at."

There wasn't long to wait. Within a few minutes, two propeller-driven craft—Tucanos, Kehre thought—swarmed over the falls. They immediately aimed themselves for the struggling LCM's, ahead and below. Kehre opened up, once they were well past, firing ahead of the foremost and letting it fly into his fire. The Oerlikon pumped shells out at its usual slow rate, yet the Tucano was itself a slow flyer. The 30mm joined it, but wasn't particularly on target. In any case, one, at least, of the 20mm shells hit *something* explosive. Before the plane could fire a rocket or drop a bomb, it exploded in a very satisfying fireball. The other one, in a fair simulation of panic, flew off, wings wagging, and with its ordnance unspent.

"Motherfuckers! Try to sink *my* boats, eh?"

★CHAPTER TWENTY-NINE★

Long years ago when men were men
    and fancied May of Long
Or lovely Becky Cooper or Maggie's Mary Wong
One woman put them all to shame,
    only one was worthy of the name
And the name of that dame was . . .
    —Traditional, "Dicey Reilly"

Camp Fulton, Guyana

Tatiana almost missed the Land Rover, three quarters overturned in the ditch. In the jungle shrouded, still early daylight gloom of the road, all of that further cloaked by smoke from the explosions and the many fires they'd started around the camp, and with the bulk of the vehicle down out of sight in the ditch, it would have been an easy enough thing to miss.

She wasn't slow to report but, in the absence of orders to move onto post once she'd reenlisted, she'd stayed in her own home.

"I'd have you move in, Tati," a towel-clad Reilly had

said, after administering her oath of enlistment in the
Teahouse of the August Nooner, "but I haven't a single
space in the barracks to put an enlisted *woman*. Certainly
not one who looks like you. Maybe when we can work out
something to get you back to the medical company . . ."

It was the shrieking of the attacking jets, followed by
the concussions emanating from the direction of the camp
that had woken her up and gotten her moving. As was, in
its own way, proper, she hadn't really dressed before
jumping into her Benz and roaring off to the camp. In
practice, this meant that her trousers were on, up, and
half buttoned, her boots on but unlaced, her jacket on
but open, and—since sleeping naked was not only more
comfortable, but also sound business practice—her
breasts quite unconstrained by a bra.

"What the hell," she'd muttered, tooling down Honey
Camp Road at a speed that had more than a little contempt
for death to it, "there's one in my pack. And maybe I'm 'an
absentminded beggar' . . . but my regiment won't need to
send to find me."

She smiled, remembering the tall, black sergeant major
she'd learned that particular line from. The remembrance
brought a sudden tear of love unrequited. The tear caused
her to shake her head, to toss it off. That caused her to
notice the upturned Land Rover. She slammed her foot to
the Benz's brakes, burning up a considerable amount of
rubber as, automotive ass wagging, she skidded down the
road.

The smell of leaked diesel was strong in the air as Tati
scurried down the concrete embankment of the ditch.

Blood dripped steadily from a cut somewhere on Reilly's scalp. Since he was hanging upside down, held in place by seat and shoulder belts, that meant that it collected in a not unimpressive pool on the Land Rover's hardshell roof. That wasn't the only spot from which blood came, as a thin rivulet flowed down his neck, to his chin, and across one cheek. Yet another trailed from his right arm, hanging, like the left, loose and draped on the roof.

"Head wounds bleed freely," she said, softly, once she'd seen. "It's not necessarily all that bad a sign."

"It's not a particularly good one, either," Reilly whispered, then flinched, as if the sound of his own voice were painful.

"Thank God you're alive!" she exclaimed.

"Marginally." He opened one eye, glanced at the girl, and said, "Since I am obviously concussed, hence not entirely responsible for what I say, I say, 'gorgeous tits, and I didn't even have to pay to see them.'"

She flushed, something she almost never did. Then she smiled, saying, "Dirty old man; you'll live."

"I hope so. Now get me the fuck out of this. My right arm seems broken, but I think my spinal column is okay. Middling bad headache."

Tati hesitated. "We really should have a team of us here and get you into a back brace," she said, doubtfully.

"If there were time, I'd agree. There isn't."

"Yes, sir." She pulled a small utility knife from her belt and began sawing at his restraints. "We'll have you to the hospital and splinted and bandaged up in no time, sir."

"Screw the hospital. Get me to the SCIF. That's where headquarters will fall in on, because that's the only place with two-meter-thick concrete walls and roof. You can call a doc from there. . . . Did I ever tell you that you have an excruciatingly sexy voice? It matches the tits."

She smiled. "You never came by for your free sample. Dirty old man."

"Lawyers, Guns, Money" (SCIF), Camp Fulton, Guyana

"Hospital took a bad hit, sir," Joshua said somberly. "I passed it on the way in."

"How many did we lose?" Stauer asked. His voice held a mix of cold fury and pain at the damage a half hour's worth of attack had done to his regiment and his home.

At least I know Phillie wasn't on duty. What if she had been? Don't think about that. Don't let yourself think about that.

Joshua shook his head. "Too much of a mess to say. Only a wall and a couple of corners standing at one end. Dr. Joseph is trying to assemble a list. He told me we'd lost at least fifty, between patients and staff. And maybe close to seventy. He's in a pretty bad way, the doc is, sir. I think you ought talk with him. Earliest convenience."

Stauer nodded. *Yes, of course. As soon as possible.*

"Unit status?" Stauer asked.

"The XO of first battalion is trying to get them assembled at least into company teams in the woods," Waggoner replied, wearily. Half that weariness was shock and fear. He'd been only a minute's walk from Regimental Headquarters when it had gone up in blast, fire, and smoke. "George says he hasn't seen hide nor hair of Reilly, though Lana Reilly says her husband left their quarters moments before she did."

"Losses in First Batt?"

"Under fifty men, dead and wounded combined. Three tanks. Five Eland APC's. A dozen trucks and other thin skinned vehicles. First is combat capable, anyway. Viljoen and Dumisani say they can get all but one tank and two APCs up if they're given some time."

"Time?" Stauer sneered. "We don't have any time . . ."

"Yes we do," Boxer said.

"Bullshit, they'll . . ."

"Yes we do," he repeated. "Let me explain." A broad smile, inexplicable in the circumstances, lit Boxer's face.

"Go ahead," Stauer grumpily agreed. Just having Boxer disagreeing was, in its way, calming.

"This," Boxer said, twirling a finger to indicate the entire base area, "is an epically lousy spot for a parachute jump. Only the DZ we cleared to the east would be worth a shit, and we know they didn't jump there. We also know to a considerable degree of certainty the maximum helicopter lift Venezuela can generate. It's enough for two battalions, give or take. If they had come in with two battalions, right on the heels of the air raid, they could have taken us.

"So why didn't they? Simple: They think there's a lot more than one battalion here to face them. They think we're *all* here, a full regiment, something that, even hard on the heels of the air strikes, would kick their asses as they struggled to dump their chutes and get organized. So they didn't even try."

Stauer thought about that. He looked again at the still

smiling face of his Chief of Staff. Suddenly, a brilliant sunrise of a smile lit his own features. "So they haven't a clue . . ."

Boxer shook his head. "That we're planning on invading *them?* Not clue one."

Stauer's face took on a vicious cast. "Oh, those fuckers are *so* gonna pay. But we need Reilly, even if I hate to admit it. What the hell happened to him? Where the hell is he?"

"Here, sir," came from the door to the conference room. Everyone looked for a moment, before shifting their gaze—like a mob of meerkats watching a car go by— to the gloriously open shirt of the medic supporting him.

Sometimes, Stauer thought, forcing his eyes away, *your problems will cancel each other out.* "Somebody tell Joseph to drop what he's doing and get a medical team here. Now!"

Sergeant Major Joshua was momentarily nonplussed by the image. *Oh, the things I've given up to maintain a professional appearance.* His confusion didn't last long.

"Corporal Manduleanu," he said, "well done." His voice rose incrementally. "Now put down your patient, and get in *uniform*, woman!"

"Yes, Sergeant Major," Tatiana answered, as she walked Reilly forward to ease him into a chair vacated by one of the others. Setting him down, she turned around to button her battle dress jacket. Looking over her shoulder at Joshua, her face said, *See? I* told *you what you've been missing.*

Outside, a couple of the regiment's four twin-barreled

23mm towed anti-aircraft guns began a steady pounding, presumably skyward. They were also, presumably, missing, since yet another series of much larger explosions rocked the camp.

Georgetown, Guyana

"Hah! Motherfuckers missed me again!" Venegas exulted aloud as he cut down a half a squad of guards posted at the key Mandela-East Bank intersection. The enemy seemed not to have been expecting it. They got off only a few wild shots before the machine guns mounted atop the three Land Rovers made an end of them.

"Can I *please* get up now?" asked President Paul, still lying across the seat, naked, to the boots of the gunner standing atop him.

"Not until the chief says so, Mr. President," replied Sergeant Coursus, the submachine gun bearing man to the driver's right.

"But I'm *naked!* This is so undignified. I am politically *doomed* if word ever gets out!"

"You're better where you are," said Coursus. "But, um, Rogers, you're about the president's size. Dig in your pack and find him some trousers he can wear when we can let him up."

The small convoy stopped at the east side of the Demerara Harbor Bridge, one of the world's longest floating bridges, covered by buildings on both sides. Venegas was thinking fast and furious. *Just bull our way over? No sign of the enemy in the last several blocks but they might have a heavy gun aimed to cover the bridge. Too big a risk, since we* must *get the President safely to Camp Fulton. Do they have our descriptions? Yeah, probably, but that description's going to be three vehicles, green, military looking, with machine guns, not one, green, without. Yeah, that's the ticket.*

Venegas keyed his microphone. "Okay, cut the chatter. Everybody, pull in your guns and hide them. Coursus, you go first, then me, then Number Three. We reassemble on the other side. Got it?"

"Sure, Chief . . . Roger, Little Joe."

It took a couple of minutes to pull in the machine gun, have the gunner sit on President Paul, and doff all helmets, armor, and battle dress jackets. When he turned around and visually confirmed that all was as ready and civilian looking as possible, Coursus ordered his driver around Venegas' Land Rover and onto the bridge. The driver moved tentatively, at first, until the vehicle commander said, "No, you idjit! We move like this, we *look* like people expecting to be shot at. Innocent, got it? Just drive."

The driver stepped on the gas, expecting every minute to find a newly grown hole in his head. He was *very* pleased to reach the far side with all his expectations having been disappointed.

Once Venegas saw that the president was over to the other side and safe, or as safe as one could hope for, under the circumstances, he likewise ordered his driver to make the crossing. Whoever was supposed to be on the west bank collecting tolls had apparently deserted his post sometime in the night. This was all to the good, as actually busting through the barrier was likely to attract unwanted attention.

Breathing a heavy sigh of relief once they'd made it over, Venegas ordered the driver to pull in next to the Land Rover carrying the president. The President, Venegas saw through the windows, was hurriedly dressing in a uniform someone had provided him.

Probably Rogers, Venegas thought. *They're about the same size.*

You know, thought Venezuelan Marine Corps Corporal Serafimo Lopez, *one vehicle going by, green, of a particular size, wouldn't be suspicious. Two? That's suspicious. And when we're told to watch out for a group of three?*

Lopez sat on the ground, at the riverbank in the Houston area of Georgetown. Beside him was a MAG machine gun mounted on a tripod and aimed generally south, toward the big bridge. He slapped the gunner and said, "Emilio, you see another big, boxy, green, station wagon sized vehicle trying to cross that bridge, you fire it up. But don't, repeat don't, hit the pontoons the bridge floats on, got it?"

"*Si, Cabo,*" answered the gunner, hunching himself down to make doubly sure his sights were set to engage anything on the bridge.

Venegas, helmeted and again in his body armor, had just finished getting the machine gun back on its pintle when he heard the sound of firing from across the river. He jumped up on the Land Rover's hardshell roof and stepped to the rear, peering around a sheltering corner. From there he had a good view of the very top of the bridge, as the vehicle on it began to fly to pieces under a relentless hammering coming from the other side. Apparently driverless, the targeted Land Rover veered left, then crashed through the barrier on the bridge, spinning end over end, spilling limp bodies and parts of bodies into the drink.

Venegas's first impulse—there was too much rage in it to call it a "thought"—was to get back in his gunning position, have his driver back up, and *Kill the son of a bitch who just killed five of my men!*

That, however, just wouldn't do. *I've got a mission, goddammit.* He dropped back inside and ordered, "Roll north, then west, following the river and the coast."

Mouth of the Orinoco River, Venezuela

The Bertram moved slowly, with Kravchenko on the fishing chair to the rear, trolling, and Lada on the foredeck, sunbathing sans bikini top. The scene was as unremarkably innocent as the several tons of arms and explosives below were not.

Rocking gently with the sport fisher's gentle speed, Baluyev scanned ahead with a pair of binoculars. What he saw was not remotely to his liking; a Venezuelan coastal patrol vessel had a civilian yacht hove to, while uniformed men searched the vessel. They looked, in his eye pieces, quite thorough and very intent. Worse, and the thing that made him absolutely decide not to proceed, was that that was no random search; three more civilian boats swayed in a ragged line, apparently waiting for their turn to be searched.

"Turn around and set course to the north," he ordered Litvinov. "Skip the river."

"But I thought . . ." the former Spetnaz operative began.

"Yes, well circumstances have changed. Sonsabitches hit us early. We were supposed to already be on station before that happened. Now? We are not getting into the river to get anywhere near that bridge. Head to Trinidad. We'll think of something there. Dammit."

As the little yacht turned, Baluyev continued his scanning, this time to the north. He counted aloud what he saw, "One . . . two . . . three . . . call it five amphibious craft, two freighters, and five frigates, a couple of smaller ships with helicopters on deck, all heading to Georgetown."

He let the field glasses drop from his eyes. Averting those eyes—after all, Musin could be touchy—he said, "Lada, do up your top and go below. Prep a coded message to regiment on what's coming. Tell them we had to abort. Remember to leave it in the draft folder so it doesn't pass through anyone's server as having been sent."

Waini River, Guyana

There were several rather neat features to the regiment's coding system. One was its fairly unsuspicious format.

Another was that messages were never actually sent, nor even posted on a bulletin board, but rather left in the draft folder of unique e-mail accounts for each subunit. The third was the key, which were PDF files of various books, one per subunit, from which page numbers, line numbers, and word order in that line, were extracted. A program within a few select laptops, plus those desk tops at base, selected the words from the key, encoded them, and placed them in the message, eliminating them from possible future use in the code. When decoded at the receiving station, those words were likewise automatically removed from possible future selection. Use of them a second time sent up a serious red flag. The books themselves, easily replaceable from on-line sources if lost, were generally lengthy.

At the little ad hoc base for the *Naughtius*, some distance upstream from the mouth of the Waini River, under a camouflaged tent, beneath declining light, a satellite dish connected a laptop with an e-mail account held by a server in the states. From the screen of that laptop, Richard "Biggus Dickus" Thornton read the situation and his orders. In fact, he read them aloud to the sailors gathered around him.

"'We have been attacked, earlier than expected. Losses were bad, but not crippling. Georgetown is under enemy control. We believe the main airport is, as well. The enemy is moving by leaps, in two main efforts, via helicopter, to occupy the western portion of the country. We do not have the chief of state safe and in our control. We have him, not the other side, but getting him to base will be difficult. Do not, repeat, do not begin your operation until we do. If you do not hear from us, but do hear on television, that he has authorized your mission, proceed. You should aid the cause in any other way possible that does not risk your command or its future mission. End of message.'"

"Why's that, Chief?" asked Eeyore, once he'd heard.

Biggus Dickus didn't answer immediately. When he did, it was to say, "I think it's probably a law of war issue. Us mining Venezuelan waters, on our own ticket, is illegal and just possibly piracy. For us to mine those waters, however, as the activated reserve of the Guyanan Defense Force, would be a legitimate act of war. I think." He shrugged. "Not my specialty, after all."

Thornton went silent again for a moment, then told Antoniewicz, "The regiment didn't say, but I've got a hunch that we no longer have the capability of mining Georgetown or the mouth of the Demerara."

"If we can't mine the Orinoco or be considered pirates, Chief," Eeyore asked, "can we maybe use some of the mortar shell-mines to mine Georgetown?"

"Now isn't that a thought? Eeyore, I want you to figure out a way to turn one or more of those mortar shells into a limpet mine. They're heavy, so it won't be all that easy. We're not so far from Georgetown that we couldn't maybe get a freighter at dock or in the harbor. Or maybe even knock off a coast guard boat at the mouth of the Orinoco, if we can find one there."

MV Maria Walewska, *Puerto Cabello,* Venezuela

The ship rode higher at anchor than it had coming into the

harbor. Most of the cargo had been unloaded, leaving the mines considerably less deeply hidden, but much easier to get to.

"Just hear on terevision," Liu told Ed Kosciusko, who was generally hiding below as the more inherently suspicious of the two to Venezuelan internal security. "War begin. Stupid pseudo-commie bastard dictator say 'to bling peace to our neighbor . . . to avenge death of sordiers on border . . . to lecraim rost plovince.' Is burrshit."

"You've been understudying your wife," Kosciusko accused.

"Is not clime," Liu answered, lifting his chin with great, righteous dignity.

"Do we have any orders?" Ed asked. Liu handed over a decoded message, from a source similar to the one *Naughtius's* crew had used, containing similar thoughts, but with emphasis on losses at Wineperu. Kosciusko read it and handed it back for destruction.

"So we develop engine trouble now, rather than later," he said.

"I go see to sabotage engines," Liu answered. "Nothing we no can fix quick."

The Drunken Bastard, off Riohacha, Colombia

They'd waited until it was not only dark, but darker than "three feet up a well digger's ass at midnight," to pull into a position a mile or so from shore and drop anchor. Five rubber boats were tied up along the starboard side of the

Bastard, the side away from shore. Into those Ryan and the other nine members of his team, present, afloat, assisted by Chin's crew, piled and secured a mix of food, arms, ammunition, explosives, the few limpet mines Victor had had remaining in his stockpile, radios, uniforms, civilian clothes, detonators, fuse, fuse igniters, scuba gear, money, and pretty much anything else they thought they might need, consistent with not sinking the boats. The two men Ryan had left behind in Colombia were waiting ashore with a couple of rental trucks.

Ryan and Chin had much the same messages as Thornton and Kosciusko, at core: "Wait. Hide. Do no harm."

"Good luck, Sergeant," Chin said, thrusting out a hand.

Ryan took it, shook, and said, "You, too, sir," before easing himself over the side to start the journey in through the surf. Just before casting off, Ryan asked, "Where are you going to hole up?"

Chin smiled, unseen in the darkness. "That would be *telling*," he replied. *We're heading near to el Porvenir, in Panama. Big enough to get food at, unknown and remote enough that we can hide the boat from the casual glance. Until we get the call.*

★CHAPTER THIRTY★

Breathe deep the gathering gloom.
—The Moody Blues, "Nights in White Satin"

Camp Fulton, Guyana

It had been two and a half days since the attack began. Not much to affect the regiment had happened since, though the steady airstream suggested that Venezuela was building up around Georgetown.

The Venezuelan Air Force still came over intermittently. With better than half the barracks charred cinders and chewed walls, and the troops scattered about in various hides, they didn't stay long or do much while they visited. The dependents, and a limited number of vehicles, were already legging it for Lethem, on the Brazilian border. They were mostly afoot, though, hence slow. The point of the column had as of yet barely reached past the intersection of the Issaro and Bartica Roads.

The staggering line of refugees the Venezuelans had overflown a couple of times, just enough to make sure. They didn't attack it, perhaps because it was so obviously civilian. Even the trucks had had their normal green canvas tarps covered with white sheets to make the point. And the Venezuelan Air Force was not made up of barbarians. The dependents were safe enough, with the surreptitious arms of Second Battalion's Delta Company to guard them from bandits. Most of the whores and parentless children from Honey Camp, following Tatiana's man, Arun, followed at the tail end of the column, their limited baggage stowed in one of the four ramshackle trucks the place had boasted.

With the sun going down now on the third day of the war, Stauer waited by a single CH-750A. Doc McCaverty was pilot.

The light aircraft sat tucked in to the edge of the jungle, its motor still. Farther away, on and around the airfield itself, stood grim, still smoking proof of the efficacy of the Venezuelan attack. There was a ruined MI-17 helicopter, its engine compartment open and empty, as if awaiting a replacement. Here was a Pilatus P-12, split in two, with a hundred yards between the sundered sections. There, two CH's, an 801 and a 750, had burned in their hangar. Here were two more Hips, sagging under the weight of a hangar roof that had collapsed upon them. Over there another Pilatus, a P-6, sat at an angle to the runway, one wing off and the other hanging. And over there . . . over there teams of stretcher bearers were still collecting bodies and parts of bodies for hasty burial until more formal arrangements could be made.

"They fucked us hard," Stauer said quietly.

"No grease," McCaverty agreed. "And not kissed afterwards. But they're still afraid to look us in the face in the morning." Despite the brave words, the doctor-pilot's voice sounded highly demoralized.

Stauer shrugged. "Boxer's pretty much sold me; they think we're all still here or nearby. So no, instead they're trying to box us in so we can't get away.

"But cheer up, Doc, we've got 'em surrounded and the bastards can't get away now."

"How far have their helicopter leaps gotten them?" the doctor asked. The joke, if joke it had been, had fallen flat.

"In the north, they've occupied as far as the airstrip at Charity, we think. But it's got to be a thin occupation. In the south, even thinner, though I expect them to occupy in strength between the Watamung and Iwokrama Mountains. To cut off our escape, you know?"

McCaverty, who, though of an air force background had picked up a lot about ground pounding in his time with the regiment, nodded, then said, "But they don't know about Reilly. How's he doing, by the way?"

"Splinted and pissed about it. Can't shoot. Can't man the machine gun on his command vehicle. Really pissed about that. He and his battalion, with some reinforcements, start exfiltrating out tonight, following the path of our dependents, then hiding before day. Odds are fair no one will even notice."

McCaverty grinned, finally, but then said, "Let's hope nobody notices *me*, either, on my little mission of mercy."

"Yeah," Stauer agreed. "What's your route?"

"From here, east to the Essequibo. From there I'll follow that, skimming the waves and ducking the falls . . .

"Stay away from the Essequibo north of Wineperu," Stauer advised. "Thor got one two days ago, with the

Dvora, that we know of, and might be trying to improve his score. *And* he's escorting one of the remaining LCMs to try to pick up Little Joe and his remaining boys."

"Good to know. Okay, I'll cut a little east after Bribaru Falls, then north to Urisirima. Little Joe's supposed to have the cargo there and a suitable landing strip marked out with IR chem lights. Fair amount of open farm and field, that area, so it shouldn't be a problem. There's already an airstrip nearby, but why take the risk of it being occupied?"

"Return route?"

McCaverty shook his head. "I don't want to take the same route both ways. I'm planning on coming back up the Mazaruni. It's got it downsides but . . . safer, overall, I think."

Wineperu, Guyana

Simmons and Morales sat by the dock of the base, legs hanging over, staring down at the *Namu*. Rather, they stared down dumbly at the muddy, darkening water which overlay it. The minisub itself, despite having not one apparent scratch, had somehow sprung a leak from the earlier attack. One minute, a few hours after the attack, Simmons had turned and walked away to bring back some distilled water for the batteries. A few minutes later, when he'd returned, water was pouring into the open hatch as the thing began to settle to the bottom.

"What are we gonna do?" Simmons asked of Morales, hopelessly. "We're fucked as far as the sub goes."

"I dunno," Morales answered with disgust. "Let me think on it."

Karapu Mountain, Guyana

Sergeant Ahern, born and bred in New Amsterdam, Guyana, was one of those city boys who had a natural feel for living and scouting in the field. They were rare, in anyone's army, but, when found, often brought the best of both worlds, the creativeness in mind and action that comes from solving the everyday problems of city life, plus a country boy's ability to go anywhere, blend in with anything, and find whatever he was looking for.

He'd always wanted to be a soldier, Ahern had, from his earliest days. Though black, he'd never had the political connections to find a spot in the largely black-dominated Guyana Defense Force. When the regiment had shown up, he'd jumped on it with both feet. Doing well in his training, and also in the *Jaeger* course he'd taken a year after that, hadn't hurt any. He was on the fast track to being able to buy into the regiment. Ahern liked that idea just fine. He also wanted to earn it . . . and to speed it up, if possible. He had his eye on a girl and she wouldn't keep forever.

Having made good time from the camp very nearly to Sakaika Falls, Ahern had been rather surprised to find the airfield empty, with not so much as a civilian caretaker on duty.

So if dey ain' be here, where dey be? he'd asked himself. *Colonel Cazz, he gon' wanna know dat.*

Taking his life, to say nothing of his future plans for a career, in hand, Ahern had pushed on, and on, past Karapu's mountain peak to the military crest on the far side. There he'd almost seen what was going on. He *had* seen a piece of the puzzle, and that would help.

What Ahern had seen, far off in the distance, but brought much closer by his 20x50 Bushnells, was an irregular stream of helicopters, to his west-southwest, moving generally northwest to southeast. He watched for a long time through those glasses, judging the dip and the rise and choppers headed hither and yon. He also looked north, since he was already up there. That was harder to make out in detail. Still, he saw helicopters, moving generally east and west. Interestingly, too, there were light and even some medium planes landing at or taking off from the airstrip—or just possibly airstrips, to his northwest, around the ferry near San Martin de Turumban.

A check of his GPS and map told him, *somewhere about San Miguel de Betania, maybe even la Rosa, dats where dey be basin' from. Mak' sense. Got a good road. Same t'ing to de nort'. Bochinche, there meh t'ink. An' dere's a road to de ferry. Buuut . . .* —Ahern checked his map—*dat be two bases. Dey not gonna split support. So la Rosa . . . or Bochinche . . . dey be PZ only. Base at Tumeremo, like Colonel Cazz, he figure.*

By sunset, Ahern had seen enough. He told his team, two plantation boys, an Indian, and a river rat, "Come on, boyos. We go back an' see de colonel now."

With weary grunts, Ahern's team shouldered packs, gripped their rifles, and began the trek back, the declining sun at their receding backs.

Camp Fulton, Guyana

Stauer had left, saying he had to see to the president's reception. In his absence, Doc McCaverty's eyes had followed the lengthening shadows until the shadows had been swallowed down by the darkness.

"About time, *señor*," said Luis Acosta. Acosta was standing by to assist if required. It was about all he could do to avenge his men who'd been caught on the airfield when the Venezuelans attacked. Certainly, he had few aircraft left; one P-6 and a couple of CH's.

McCaverty nodded, turned, and climbed into his airplane. Once seated and buckled, he swung the bubbled out Plexiglas door down behind him, then locked it in place. He was nervous. It was no small thing to be taking an unarmed scout plane up in the air when the enemy had complete air supremacy.

"Manuel," Acosta said, as the CH-750's engine sputtered to life, "go out to the middle of the field and see if there are any enemy aircraft hanging around."

"Move out and draw fire?" Manuel asked.

"Something like that."

Manuel pulled a flashlight from a pocket. "I'll give you three flashes if it's clear," he shouted, over the droning engine of the light plane. Both Acosta and McCaverty nodded.

Manuel stopped at a point in the middle of the airfield complex, just listening for a while. He heard a plane, propeller-driven, somewhere off in the distance. Certain beyond a reasonable doubt that it couldn't be one of theirs—the wreckage of those was everywhere, while the few remaining serviceable ones were being hoarded—he waited until the prop faded. Then, holding his light wand overhead, he flicked it on once . . . twice . . . the third time.

A couple of hundred feet away, a light engine surged. He couldn't see the plane for beans in the dark, but scooted generally out of the line anyway.

McCaverty crossed himself as soon as he saw Manuel's three flashes. Though he wasn't normally all that religious, the habits of a lifetime were hard to break, even if he'd wanted to. *Which, for that matter, I don't.*

After adjusting his night vision goggles to his face, he played with the throttle, gave her the gas, and began rolling forward, picking up speed with every foot. The grassy strip between the actual airfield and the taxiway was slightly humped, as an aid to drainage and a combat to vector-borne disease. Thus, McCaverty was rolling slightly uphill. Between the ridiculously short takeoff run required for a barely laden CH-750A, and the slight upward incline, McCaverty's wheel lifted off the ground well before reaching the summit of the hump. His rear end pressed down into the seat as the plane's wings got the bite of the air.

Don't, repeat don't, *wanna get too high.* McCaverty leveled out, reducing throttle. A quick glance around, again more force of habit that something required under the circumstances, and he moved the centrally mounted, Y-shaped yoke, to move the ailerons, while pushing the right pedal to swing the rudder. The CH-750, as nimble as a hummingbird, responded beautifully. In short seconds it was heading due east for the Essequibo, though to be sure of that McCaverty had to flip up his NVGs to check his bearings. He flipped them down again and picked a familiar constellation. It wasn't a fixed one but for such a short hop it didn't need to be.

Then he settled down to just barely missing the tree-tops, while using every spare second to hunt through the sky for the night-equipped fighter that would end his life, if it could.

Five Miles Southeast of Urisirima, Guyana

A stream flowed generally northeast, about a hundred meters from where Venegas and his team waited for the presidential flight. The two remaining Land Rovers sat off to one side, in some high grass bordering the farmer's field he'd selected as a landing spot. It hadn't taken more than four hours for the remnants of the team to get here from the Demerara Harbour Bridge, and that was with having to duck a Venezuelan Tucano whose pilot had had an altogether too well-developed sense of curiosity. Nor another hour to determine that, yes, here was a place one of the regiment's light, STOL craft could use. Oh, no, what had kept them here was that all of their long-range, secure commo gear had—by one of those flukes of war that one can never really foresee, in precisely the way it's fated to happen—gone into the river with Land Rover Number Three and its crew.

The two and a half days since had been spent scrounging up enough wire to make a decent half rhombic antenna, so that their request for pickup could be sent to regiment, secure from interception and with range enough to reach. That, in turn, had been made worse by having to hump the equipment ten miles to the south, because, had they sent a message from where their current spot was, its back message would have gone straight to occupied Georgetown, in the clear and with full power.

But life's fair, thought Venegas, bitterly. It still rankled to have lost a third of his team without the chance to strike back. *Someday, motherfuckers . . . someday. And payback is gonna be a bitch.*

Fair, too, that he, the stinking child molester, gets out by plane while we, the weasel's saviors, have to wait for a boat. But Boxer was clear; we are not going to get on a plane because they don't have them to spare and we are going to get on an LCM because they need our vehicles back.

Helluva sense of priorities.

Sergeant Coursus, laying on the ground with the president between Venegas and himself announced, "Chief, plane coming. It sounds like one of ours."

Venegas nodded, slapped absently at a mosquito, and, using the very short ranged radios they all still carried—no real chance of interception on those—ordered, "Far recognition signal. Mark the field."

Two men on each side and one each at bottom and top began crushing, bending, and tossing infrared chemical lights along a predetermined path. The team couldn't see it, except those who had NVGs. But it should be clear as a bell to a pilot who had them.

Tucano Number 0040, Venezuelan Air Force, north of Bartica, Guyana

Venezuela had bought a total of thirty-one Embraer 312 Tucanos, back when they were new. Of those, a number had been shot down in a coup attempt back in 1992. Several more had been lost to crashes. Until a couple of days ago, there had been nineteen still operational. They'd lost two, the first day of the liberation. One of those was believed to have crashed all on its own, while the other, piloted by Lieutenant Oropeza, with Lieutenant Lorenzo as copilot, was known to have been shot down from behind, over the Essequibo, while on their first combat mission. Neither lieutenant had survived.

It had been a matter of some debate, back in the *Estado Mayor,* which combat aircraft should be the first to be shifted forward to Cheddi Jagan, once it was secure. The deciding factor had been that the Tucanos could make do with one of the airport's taxiways, thus leaving the runways free for the landing of reinforcements and supplies by heavier cargo aircraft. The army, of course, had put in to have its Russian-built gunships take priority. Sadly, they couldn't really refute that, in a time when every ounce of supply, every increment of service support moved would be critical, a helicopter required more in the way of spare parts than a simply prop-driven craft did. Thus, the MI-35's, along with the other choppers, remained based at Tumeremo.

Of Lieutenant Colonel Perez's seventeen remaining

operational aircraft, four had developed maintenance problems. That was to be expected; they just weren't *new* anymore. He'd waited until half the remainder—six, minus his own—had shifted forward to Cheddi Jagan, then taken the next slot for himself. Naturally, since he was going somewhere where ordnance was limited, he carried what he could on his own, two five-hundred-pound bombs, a rocket pod, and a single .50 caliber machine gun pod. He wanted to get closer to the action because, *I am still pissed about Oropeza and Lorenzo. And somebody's going to pay for killing my boys.* Doctrine had required that he wait until the bulk, if just that, of his squadron was forward.

"Hey, sir?" asked Captain Pedro Radjeskas, a Lithuanian-descended citizen of Venezuela. The captain was copilot for the flight and also his operations officer. He wore NVGs and acted as more an observer than copilot.

"Yes, Captain?"

"No straight lines in nature, right?"

"Meaning?"

"Meaning what looks like a pretty small rectangle just lit up on our starboard side, and there was no mention of us having any troops in this area yet when we left. It only shows up in the goggles, by the way, sir."

"Hang on!" shouted Perez, putting his Tucano into a ninety-degree right hand turn.

McCaverty bounced to a bone-jolting stop. *That was a bad'un,* he thought, still panting from fear. He looked behind and to his right. There, three men, two of them more or less hauling the third, raced out onto the field.

They reached the plane, and, while one lifted the bubble door, the other more or less threw the third in bodily, just before the Plexiglas slammed down shut again.

"Strap in, Mr. President!" McCaverty shouted. Then he noticed an engine sound, just slightly louder than his own. His head snapped forward in time to see bright flames blossoming in the sky. He thought he saw those flames outlining a very predatory shape.

"Oh, shit."

★CHAPTER THIRTY-ONE★

And on each end of the rifle,
we're the same.
—John McCutcheon, "Christmas in the Trenches"

Five miles southeast of Urisirima, Guyana

It took three things, working in concert, to save McCaverty's and President Paul's bacon. One was that light moves faster than a rocket. Two was that his engine was still running. The third, much aided by the first, was that he had, as both doctor and pilot, a remarkable set of reflexes. As soon as he saw the flash from above, he was gunning the engine, rolling down the ad hoc runway, and lifting off.

One rocket hit just behind where the plane had been sitting when Paul was tossed aboard.

Venegas didn't have to give the command. It was a well-drilled response, when under air attack, to simply throw shit up in front of the plane and let it fly through the storm, in the hope of either frightening it off, wrecking its aim, or at least causing it some damage that would have to be repaired when it returned home. Actually shooting one down with small arms was, of course, the stuff of miracles.

Seven rockets in total landed close together and in a more or less ragged line. Venegas hadn't seen them land, exactly, though the flashing explosions had certainly announced their arrival even while totally screwing up his NVGs. For a few seconds, the blasts silenced his eardrums, when that cleared, at least a little, he heard a high pitched scream coming from the field.

Venegas ripped the NVGs off and tossed them to the ground. *Fuck it, survey my ass for them.* He ran toward the scream. He didn't quite get there, though, before stumbling face first to the dirt. *And I was sure the field had been smooth.* Shifting around while still prone, he felt the ground for the obstruction. He found it. He found it in two pieces . . . two *wet* pieces.

But that wasn't the screaming, which was growing louder. Getting up first to all fours and then to his feet, he moved on. He didn't trip over anything this time; the heart-rending shrieks told him when he should stop.

It was Coursus. "Joe . . . Joe . . . help me . . . God, it hurts, Joe . . . please . . . Joe."

"Medic!"

The president was screaming and wailing like a lost little girl.

Doc McCaverty twisted the plane to port as soon as he

was airborne. His left wing almost plowed the field. It *did* manage to stroke the tops of a couple of tree as he gained altitude.

No more than I need to get over—"Shut the fuck up, asshole!"—*the trees.*

Then, still skimming trees, McCaverty gave it full throttle and raced for the nearest potential cover, the Essequibo River.

No way I can make it to the Mazaruni if that bastard's following me.

"Did we get him?" Perez asked heatedly.

Unseen in the back seat, Radjeskas answered, "No, sir. Close, maybe, but I think he got away."

"*Chingada*! Keep looking. I'm turning around for another pass."

"I think maybe we're a little too fast for him."

God, I wish this bitch would go faster. There was no more juice to give it, though; McCaverty made the best speed he could for Sloth Island, a little lump of nothing much in the Essequibo. If he could make it, he could stay close to it, close enough to be very damned hard to see, at least from half the possible angles. *If . . .*

A bright stream of tracers passed by to the starboard side. A minor nudge suggested to the pilot that at least one round had found at least one wing. That meant a possible fuel leak.

"I suppose self sealing-tanks would have been just too hard. Shit."

★ ★ ★

"Goddammit, I missed!'

"Goddammit, sir, you missed," echoed the Three.

"Well, train to standard, not to time. I'm going after the son of a bitch again."

Dvora, Essequibo River, Guyana

Thor had found his crew on the LCM's that had escaped the first attack. Now, besides the black gang and signal rats down below, he had the helmsman, someone on radar, a lookout with NVG's, both fifties manned, a two man crew on the rear Oerlikon, and was watching over the operator's shoulder the screen for the forward thirty's weapon station himself. Everyone was wearing a set of headphones that went to and through the boat's intercom.

While waiting, hidden in a small inlet from the Essequibo, he'd done some thinking, done some pencil drilling, and run a large number of simulations. He thought that maybe, just maybe, he might have a chance with the thirty against an aircraft.

The *Dvora* paralleled the left bank of the river. To the right, on the opposite side, was an LCM that had likewise survived by hiding. Their speed was limited to that of the LCM, about nine knots, or a bit less, what with the potential for obstacles at the banks.

"Captain," radar announced, "I've got an . . . no, I've got *two* aircraft heading this way. Straight up the river they're coming. Right down nearly skimming the water."

"IFF?" von der Kehre asked.

"Neither respond. Our code's probably out of date already."

"All right . . . 'all stop. Hold station. Advise the LCM to snuggle into the bank." *Dvora*'s engines went very quiet, more felt through the deck now than actually heard.

"First or second one, Skipper?" the 30mm weapon station operator asked.

"First one," Thor answered.

"Roger." The 30mm operator picked a spot over the middle of the river, just above the water, and set his stabilized gun to fix on that. Similarly, the Oerlikon swung around to fire in the same general direction. The starboard side .50 took its cue from those.

"Now wait, everybody, until I give the command. I want to throw up a wall of lead in front of him and let him fly right through it. Wait . . . wait . . . it'll be the first one . . . wait."

Perez had dropped his speed down as low as he dared, especially this close to the water. If he hit it, at any real speed, it might as well have been concrete.

Problem is, he thought, *that not only was this thing never designed to be an air-to-air platform, but my freaking gun is all the way out on one wing and my sight's all wrong for an aerial target.*

Even so, you're mine, you bitch, for my lost lieutenants.

He squeezed the trigger, again, and was rewarded with a lot of vibration, a certain amount of torque, but no obvious kill.

"Second plane!" Thor shouted. *It wouldn't have fired if*

the first one were friendly to him. That makes it neutral or friendly to us.

"Wait . . . wait . . . FIRE!"

The muddy waters of the Essequibo were lit by flashes at the rate of several thousand per minute.

"Oh, shit!" Perez said, when he saw the water become a strobe and caught a glimpse of the source. "Ambush!"

He pulled back on his stick, as far as it would go. Still, he was too close, moving too fast even at this reduced speed. He flew through the deadly hail.

Behind him, he heard Radjeskas scream in pain and terror.

"Pedro, are you all right?" Perez asked. He rarely used first names with his subordinates but this was a special occasion.

The captain's answering voice was weak and strained. "Hit . . . pretty bad, sir."

"Right. Fuck this shit; we're heading for Cheddi Jagan and the doctors. You hang on, son. You'll be fine."

McCaverty, in his own later words, "like to shit myself," at the fire that erupted barely behind him. He immediately cut half right, rising over the town of Hippaia. Then he set course straight for Camp Fulton.

"Goddammit, Skipper, we missed," said the helm.

Thor smiled. "*Ja* . . . but we sure scared the *Scheisse* out of him, boys. Tell the LCM to proceed. We'll continue cover."

Airfield, Camp Fulton, Guyana

Stauer was standing by as the plane touched down roughly. Manuel used his flashlight to lead it to the jungle-shrouded hide position from whence it had taken off.

With the regimental commander were two beefy guards, both heavily armed and armored, plus Sergeant Major Joshua. As soon as the engine cut off, he led the guards to the copilot's side of the aircraft. Stauer unlatched the door and lifted it straight up. He smelled puke and, just possibly, shit. He didn't think it came from McCaverty.

With a grimace, he said, "Mr. President, these men will take you to a secure facility where you will meet with my Chief of Staff. I believe you two know each other. There you will be cleaned up, put in a fresh but unmarked uniform, and be given an opportunity to speak to the world. Don't worry about a script; we've already taken care of that in both English and Creole. Sergeant Major, take him away."

"Sir!"

While Paul, still in an obvious state of shock, was marched off, Stauer went around the rear of the aircraft and came up upon McCaverty, who was just dismounting.

"How did it go?" he asked.

McCaverty sat down, bonelessly, to the ground. Staring off into space, he answered, "Oh, routine . . . just routine . . . fug. I am *so* too old for this shit."

Cheddi Jagan Airport, Guyana

Perez had radioed ahead to have an ambulance standing by. It was; he could see it, sitting by the control tower with lights flashing, as he taxied off the main field and went into the zigzag turn to get a near as possible to it. As soon as he'd stopped, the ambulance started up, reaching a point just in front of his aircraft in seconds. Perez immediately popped open his canopy, turned around to glance at his Three, then jumped to get out of the way of the medics.

The first of the medics, having remarkable indifference to the health of the airframe, and much concern with the human being inside, leapt onto the wing. While the others pulled out a gurney, he checked for vital signs. Just about the time the gurney made it to a point under and behind the wing, the medic turned away and made a "no need to hurry" sign with his hand.

"Hey, Colonel," he said to Perez. "I'm really sorry, sir, but your man's dead."

Perez, who had been anxiously looking upward at the medic, put one arm against the side of the Tucano, then rested his head against it. There was no sense in letting them see him cry.

Shit; what am I going to say to his wife?

Three Miles South of Urisirima, Guyana

With three of his remaining men guarding what passed for

a perimeter, or a half of one, and two more sitting behind the wheels of the remaining Land Rovers, Venegas met and guided in the LCM himself. He could barely sense the presence of the *Dvora*, sitting farther out, like a mother hen guarding her chicks.

"I'll take care of guiding them in," the chief of the boat told the warrant, once the ramp had dropped onto the not very steep portion of the bank Venegas had selected. "Just relax. For a change."

One by one, the Land Rovers rolled down, then across the ramp into the spacious cargo area. At least it was spacious when carrying only a couple of Land Rovers. More of the boat's crew lashed the vehicles down.

When that was done, the sailor told Venegas, "Chief, you can call in your men now." The ramp was already whining upwards.

Venegas did. One by one, each turned to take a last chance at sighting a possible threat, then leapt to the top of the ramp and climbed down.

"What's with those two in the back?"

Venegas looked at the still forms, resting upright, in the last of the Rover's back seat. It was hard, very hard, to keep his voice from breaking as he answered, "Them? A couple of good men." Then his voice did break; these had been his men *and* his friends. "They're dead."

★ CHAPTER THIRTY-TWO ★

Be polite; write diplomatically; even in a declaration of
war one observes the rules of politeness.
—Otto von Bismark

"Lawyers, Guns, and Money" (SCIF), Camp Fulton, Guyana

Though Sergeant Major Joshua looked Guyanan enough,
he was not, of course. Corporal Hosein looked just what
he was, a Bihari-descended Indian, but he was Guyanan.
Origin, however, didn't really matter. The two—uniformed
and armed—flanked the similarly uniformed president,
just behind him and just in front of a Guyanan flag, hung
on the wall, for local color. Similarly, Lahela Corrigan, she
whose smile lights up the jungle, sat just to one side.
Corrigan wasn't Guyanan or Guyanan-looking, in any
sense. She was, however, quite tiny and very, very cute.
Boxer expected her to help trip the "save the women and
children" reflex, around the world, with both categories in
one person.

Joshua rolled his eyes—*this being a stage prop gets old,*

quick—when Boxer ordered, "One more time, please, Mr. President, and this time, put a little anger into it; a little righteous anger, if you can muster it."

"I *can't*," President Paul insisted. His voice taking on a note of hysteria, he added, "I'm just too exhausted and I have been through too much. You people have put me through too much."

Us people, huh? Joshua thought. *And there I could have sworn it was Venezuela.* The RSM bent down and whispered something in Paul's ear that apparently shocked him enough to make him turn pale and gulp, nervously. As the tall, black RSM straightened up again and faced the camera, the President of Guyana said, "I think I can go on. But could I have a drink for the nerves?"

Boxer nodded and said to Hosein, "There's a bottle of scotch and a couple of glasses in my desk. Could you bring them, please, Corporal?"

Scotch, apparently, had amazing medicinal virtues. Two drinks, just enough to calm him, not enough to translate to a glazed look on his face, had done wonders for Paul's composure, and no little bit to grease his tongue.

". . . and, so," President Paul summed up, "I call on every loyal and true Guyanan, our resident foreign friends and neighbors, our corporations, our brothers overseas, our friends in America, Asia, Africa, and Europe, to resist this vicious, illegal, trumped up, imperialist, and cowardly land grab, with every means at their and our disposal, until the invader is driven from our dear country with his tail between his legs.

"I instruct our embassies overseas to issue letters of

marque to any legitimate, commercial shipping firm that applies, authorizing them to attack Venezuelan commerce. I further declare a blockade of Guyana's and Venezuela's ports. Neutral shipping has seventy-two hours to vacate, after which those ports may be considered blockaded.

"I order the regular and reserve forces of the Cooperative Republic of Guyana to make the invader's life here a living hell. Deny them the use of our roads. Deny them the use of our ports. Deny them the use of our airports.

"I command our people to give the enemy no aid, no comfort, no sanctuary.

"And, finally, I call upon our mother country, the United Kingdom, and the Queen to whom we pay joint homage, to relieve us in this, our hour of distress."

Not bad delivery, thought Boxer.

"What did you say to him, Sergeant Major?" Boxer asked, later, after the president had finally been allowed to go to a dark office and sleep on a couch.

Joshua chuckled. "I told him fuck what he thinks he's been through. I told him that I've lost friends, and that he would either do what you said, and make it good, or I would build a large wooden cross and nail him to it, then wait for him to die."

"Jesus!" the Chief of Staff exclaimed, not without a certain admiration. "Stauer was right, way back in Brazil. You *are* descended from some Roman centurion."

The sergeant major nodded seriously. "On both sides, I suspect. God knows, my mother was even more of a hard ass than my father. Damned if I know how any of my ancestors ended up as slaves in what became the U.S. Virgin Islands."

"Just lucky, I guess, like old Buckwheat Fulton."

Joshua smiled, though there was tinge of sadness to it. "Ah, Buckwheat. Now there was a fine soldier."

"Yes," Boxer agreed, equally sadly, "yes, he was. On which note, the weasel left us some scotch. Sergeant Major, Corporal Hosein, Mrs. Corrigan, let us have a drink—maybe two or three—to the memory of a good man and a helluva soldier."

Miraflores Palace, Caracas, Venezuela

Chavez knew he had a tendency to engage his mouth before his brain was fully in gear. He knew, and tried to combat it . . . sometimes, anyway. Now? Now he just wasn't sure enough of the *whys* of the thing to comment.

"How many internet sites are hosting this thing? And how many news networks are covering it?"

"Even FOX, in the United States, isn't bothering to cover this, Mr. President," Hugo's flack-in-chief, said. "Too much of a *fait accompli*, really, for them to bother. Guyana ranks somewhere below the Marshall Islands in importance, as far as the gringos are concerned. As for Web sites, fifty to sixty sites, Mr. President, from Afreeca to Zoopy."

Chavez asked, "Can we shut down those sites?"

The flack shrugged. "Some of them, Mr. President, we could. Youtube, in particular, has a reputation for bending over under pressure. However, not all will. And I'd recommend against shutting down any. It would just be free advertising for the video. As is, it matters little. Advertised? Well, it wouldn't be to our betterment."

Hugo nodded. *Okay, I think I can see that. I may not like it, but I can see it.*

"Besides which, Mr. President, your personal popularity is up over eighty-seven percent over your actions in Guyana. And that was from an *honest* poll."

Which is why, Chavez thought, smiling broadly, *I launched this thing.*

"What about this letter of marque bullshit?"

Chavez's legal advisor stood and began a tedious and lengthy lecture on the legality of letters of marque, the nature of sovereignty, the possibly dubious nature of a declaration of war issued by the chief of a democratic state without legislative approval, the probable legitimacy of said president acting in defense of his country's sovereignty, even without that legislative approval, the law of the sea as concerned privateering and piracy and . . .

"Shut the fuck up," Hugo said, waving his right hand, palm out, the heel resting on the table. The gesture meant the same thing. Once the lawyer had, he said, "Just tell me what it might mean."

"Private vessels can attack our shipping. And the one power that really matters, the United States, still allows letters of marque and reprisal. In theory, anyway."

"What do you mean, the gringos are the only ones that matter?"

Admiral Fernandez took that question. "He means, sir, that the United States Navy, alone, can take on all the rest of the world's navies, together, and probably win. And that's without recourse to nuclear weapons, too, or even recalling any of their mothballed ships or reservists. At sea, they're *that* powerful. The British Empire, in its glory days, never presumed to be able to fight more than the second and third naval powers at once. America, however, considers that to be unacceptable passivity and overconfidence. They insist of being able to take on the whole world at sea."

Chavez scowled. *Fucking gringos.*

"Okay, so they could attack our shipping. But we don't really have much shipping of our own," the president objected.

"They could, in theory, still blockade our ports. That . . . man said neutral shipping has seventy-two hours to vacate our ports."

Chavez turned his attention back to Admiral Fernandez. "Can anyone do that, as a practical matter? Any civilian, I mean."

Fernandez shook his head. "Can't see how, Mr. President. Pure bluster. We've got quite a nice little surface and submarine fleet again. No civilian ship is going to want to take it on. Besides, blockades to be binding must be effective." Fernandez snorted. "They couldn't mount an effective boycott, let alone a blockade."

The admiral's enthusiasm, and he did *sound* enthusiastic, was somewhat feigned. *After succeeding in this, Chavez, you baboon, we'll never get rid of you, will we? I suppose I'd best get used to it.*

Naughtius Base, Waini River, Guyana

The sun beat down mercilessly on the trees overhead.

That it didn't quite reach the hidden shelters had the effect of turning a frying pan into an oven. From the chicken's point of view, of course, that wasn't much of an improvement.

Biggus Dickus Thornton wiped sweat from his brow. No matter, it was instantly replaced. *Getting old for this shit*, he thought.

The decoded message sat on a field table next to a chart of the local waters, all the way to the mouth of the Orinoco Rover. Biggus Dickus had studied the chart so long and so closely that he thought he could probably draw it from memory.

The river's got hundreds of mouths but only seven really matter, and of those seven, we could block them all by mining just two small stretches further in. Course, I'm not exactly enthused about trying to get that far inland in the Naughtius. So . . . I'm thinking four M-70s and six 240mm shells in the Rio Grande *stretch, east of Curiapo. Then maybe two and three southeast of the San Francisco de Guaya Mission. Then one and three northeast of Jotajana. And another one, plus three 240mm, southeast of La Esperanza.*

That leaves us two M-70's and nine shells. Maybe we use them to reseed the Orinoco—though going blind into a river we've mined is . . . fuck that; ain't happening. The ones we put out work or they don't. We're not going back up that river. So, no, after we finish the Orinoco, we'll use what's left further out. He glanced down at the situation summary then began his orders.

And our orders are to begin laying them in—Thornton checked his watch—*thirty-seven hours, and set the timers to arm forty-eight hours after laying. Best to put*

*the boys to sleep now, minus a lookout, so they'll be fresh
tomorrow night.*

MV *Maria Walewska*, Puerto Cabello, Guyana

With the excuse of her purely spurious engine problems,
the captain had had the *Countess* towed to the maintenance facilities down by the southeast arm of the port.
This was not a disadvantage; when you really want to close
a port down, it's not a bad thing to mine it from one side
to the other. And for the transverse arms, of which there
were arguably four, they had another trick.

"Are we cleared to leave, Captain Chin?" Kosciusko asked.

The Chinese seaman nodded. "I terr Po't Autholity
boys we got engine fixed up good enough and want get out
before brockade happen."

"What did they say about that?"

"They laugh. Terr me I wolly about nothin'. Hah! They
in for big fuckin' supliz, heheh. You want get tlebuchet
put together now?"

"Not just yet, Skipper. Have your wife move the 'lumber' container to where we can get at it, yes, and put up
the cavity around where we want to build it. And she can
start moving the mines. But let's wait for dark to actually
rebuild the trebuchet."

Coco Point Airfield, *Isla del Rey*, Panama

The airfield ran east-northeast to west-southwest. Jutting

out from it, and nearer to the sea, was a sort of a D-shaped taxiway, flattened at one end. The cops who'd eventually showed up insisted on the two planes being moved there.

"We need to keep the runway clear, *señor*," the senior cop had said, over beer. "Besides," he added with a wink, "it's a lot easier loading from there, no?"

The senior pilot of the four had winked back. "Of course. Yes. Thank you." *And if he thinks we're running drugs, and has no problem with that, who am I to correct him?*

There, at the curved part of the taxiway, so close to the sea that one could almost jump from a wingtip into it, the two crews had gotten in a little fishing, a little snorkeling, and a whole lot bored.

The loadmaster, a Sergeant Lindell, stuck his head into the cockpit. "I put in the call to Leo," he said to the captain and pilot. The latter was going over charts, doing some pencil drilling, and punching flight data and locations into his navigation set.

The pilot, looking up from his charts, asked, "Any problems?

"Nah. As long as we've got the money his brother-in-law will deliver. But *he's* coming along to make sure."

"Tell him to bring some fucking iced beer, too. Preferably XX, since the local stuff is mostly piss."

"Already thought of that, sir," the loadmaster answered, with a chuckle. "Leo says, 'no sweat.' And gratis, no less. We go back to First Battalion, we do, before I got just too damned old for it and shipped over. Good troops, he is."

The chief seemed to be pondering something for a

brief moment. "You want we should start assembling the mines . . . oh, and testing the real mines."

The pilot thought about that. *Why not? The local police came by and left, much happier and not a little richer, without caring a damned thing for what we were carrying except that we had beer.*

Finally, he nodded. "Yeah, start getting them ready. Inside the aircraft. Do *not* start the timers. Wait on setting the counting devices until we assemble them in the order we're planning to drop them. And you may as well get the roll-out platform assembled on the deck."

"Wilco, sir."

The chief turned to go but stopped when the pilot called out, "Hey, can Leo bring us some food? I am sick to death of packaged rations."

"He thought of that, too. His wife's making up a special batch of *empañadas* for us. Oh, and some fried chicken and such."

"Good man."

The far recognition signal was a call on a cell phone. The near one wasn't really needed, since the approaching boat was blaring out Leon Russell at volume.

"Hey, Leo, dude, ain't seen you in fuckin' years! And how'd you get the eight track fixed?"

"Tim! Bubba!" Ross shouted, jumping into the surf from the puttering boat, holding itself against the seashore by engine power. Behind him, he dragged a rope. This he tied off on a nearby tree before running to meet Lindell. Then came a small orgy of hand shaking, back slapping, and "hey whatever happened to?" reunionizing.

Ross turned away, shouting something in Spanish to the captain of the boat. The engine cut out almost immediately.

"Be right back," Leo said to Lindell, then turned and waded out about two thirds of the way to the boat. There the captain, and presumably his brother-in-law, met him, passing over one end of a length of garden hose.

"I got three hundred feet of this crap," Leo shouted over the sounds of the surf. "Think it'll be enough?"

"It will," Lindell replied. "At least while high tide lasts it will. I paced it off."

Leo turned around, saying over one shoulder, "Great. Now how about you run this to your tank, then give me a shout so I can tell my brother-in-law to start pumping?"

"Wilco, bubba . . . Hey, what about the food and beer."

"That's what I'm going back for, dummy!"

Wineperu, Guyana

For whatever reasons—and Boxer thought it was that the Venezuelans were having some serious maintenance backlog back at base—Corporal Hosein wasn't molested on his drive from Camp Fulton to the wrecked naval base. The fact that he'd driven entirely at night probably helped, even if it hadn't guaranteed it.

And I'm not too sure that driving without headlights is necessarily any safer than with headlights and risking being bombed. 'Course, I'm not sure it isn't, either, and safety wasn't the point, anyway.

Hosein arrived just before sunup, and the rosy-fingered bitch, "the child of morning," was just about to peek over the horizon. He'd learned, since joining the regiment, that this was called "BMNT."

He called out for Morales and Simmons. When that didn't work immediately he explained, "It's just me, guys. The colonel sent me to get you but he had to stay behind."

"Oh," said Simmons. "In that case, here I am. Hey, Che, get your lazy ass up."

Hosein had to really peer closely in the direction of the voice before he could just barely make out a human silhouette. "How'd you do that?" he asked.

"Training," Simmons answered, as if that explained everything.

Well . . . maybe it does, thought Hosein.

"The colonel sent me to get you and bring you back to camp. No, I don't know why. Something about a 'special mission,' that's all I know."

"Maaannn," Morales began a gripe. "It's not our fault the sub sank. And we've almost got it recovered." He flicked his head toward the river. "C'mon, take a look."

Shrugging, Hosein followed along. It was getting lighter by the minute. By the time they reached the water's edge, he could see well enough to make out a single tripod, built of logs, sticking up out of the water. A taut cable ran from a shackle near the top of the tripod into the stream. He thought, but couldn't be sure, that he could make out a faintly bulletlike object outlined just below the surface.

"I'm impressed," Hosein agreed. "Makes not a shit of

difference, though; the colonel sent me to get you. And the RSM said something about 'dead or alive.'"

"Ah," Morales replied. "In that case, give us five minutes to pack."

★CHAPTER THIRTY-THREE★

My logisticians are a humorless lot . . . they know
if my campaign fails, they are the first ones I will slay.
—Alexander the Great (attributed)

Cheddi Jagan Airport, Guyana

A single plane, an Airbus-319, empty but for a trivial
number of casualties, most of those the result of accidents,
lumbered down the runway. Even nearly empty, there
wasn't a lot of asphalt left before its wheels lifted off.

That was, of course, Chavez's private plane, having
come to deliver the great man for a tour of "the front," and
with room enough for a minimal entourage and, most
importantly, a news team with video equipment. The fuel
spent getting there was enough to allow it to leave again
with those mostly walking wounded.

Larralde looked down at the medal on his chest, just
pinned there that afternoon.

Sergeant Major Arrivillaga sneered, then looked at his
own new medal and sneered again. "That, and about

twenty Bolivars might get us each a cup of decent coffee," he said.

"You sound bitter, Mao," Larralde observed, carefully keeping his own bitterness out of his voice.

"Bitter? Me? Bitter? Oh, *I'm* not bitter . . . I'm . . ." Mao went into a furious tirade. "Our armed forces have a grand total of forty-three transport aircraft, some of them quite light. I can list them for you, since I've jumped most of them, at one time or another: Four C-130's, one of them supporting the troops at Kaieteur Falls, two Shorts, ten Beechcraft, five of them Army, eight Israeli Aravas, a dozen Polish Skytrucks, three Boeings, two of them only good for fuel, two Dessaults, one Fairchild and . . . and *that!*" He pointed in the Airbus' direction. "And *that* represents better than ten percent of the practical airlift we have. But is it bringing in more troops? No. Food and ammunition? No. Fuel? Spare parts? Medical supplies? No. No. No. How about some vehicles, so we can support ourselves when we finally get off our asses and move off this fucking airstrip? Again, no."

"Ah, cheer up, Mao. You always were too pessimistic. We've got better than half the brigade here now."

"Yes, we *do*," Arrivillaga agreed, nodding deeply. "Finally. After about a week. And you know what, sir? With the air force showing up, giving number one priority to *their* overfed 'needs,' that's all we're likely to have, too. And we're going to sit here for lack of vehicles and lack of fuel to move them if we had them."

Larralde blew air. "I know. Our job was to get us here and get the airport. We did that, pretty much bloodlessly. Well . . . bloodlessly for us, anyway. Our vehicles were supposed to come by air but almost all our supply was supposed to come by sea. As is, until the navy gets the ports unfucked, supply has to come by air, and there's no room for the vehicles."

"There might be," Arrivillaga cursed, "if Hugo would forego his flying bordello."

"Oh, c'mon. You were on that plane, too, getting decorated. There wasn't a whore in sight, just that older . . ."

"Like I told you, sir, Hugo doesn't like them too pretty."

Larralde did a double take. "*You* told *me*?"

Mao ignored that as too inconvenient to deal with. Instead he continued with his general theme. "Or maybe the general staff would get off its collective ass and charter some planes."

Arrivillaga stopped speaking. He'd caught sight of two of the troops, wandering off together and trying to look nonchalant about it. "Ah, fuggit." He stood up, abruptly. "Out of my pay grade anyway. But young Vargas and Villareal, though they don't know it yet, have just volunteered for shit burning detail. Seeing to *that* will make me feel a lot better . . . and it's *within* my pay grade."

Georgetown, Guyana

If "mass" could be defined as a couple of thousand, then there was a "mass rally" by the statue of Cuffy, at Square of the Revolution. Besides banners saying things like, "*Viva la Revolucion*," and "Socialism or Death," there were a fair number of Venezuelan flags being waved in among the crowd.

As there should be, Conde thought, *since we passed them out. But I shouldn't be here, making a stupid speech in a language not my own. Can these creole babblers even understand English? Or am I just wasting my time here?*

Yes, I am, he decided. *I shouldn't be here, wasting my time. I should be down at the docks trying to unfuck the mess we were left when all the workers failed to show up after their president's little pseudo declaration of war.*

Note to self: Next time we invade a country, we need to cut it off from the Internet, too.

Conde mentally spat. *And the army's bitching up a storm that none of their shit's been offloaded. Well, screw 'em. The navy supports us; the air force supports them. That's the deal.*

Looking over the crowd, he wondered, *Can I get some use out of these rabble, unloading the ships? Nah, if they'd had jobs they'd be at them. These are the career unemployables, most of them, who provide the illusion of mass to the revolution.*

Well, at least docking space isn't a problem, thought the XO of the First Marine Brigade, Colonel de Castro, standing on the roof of a building not far from Stabroek Market and overlooking the river. The XO was in charge, for the nonce. This would stay that way until the next increment of troops showed up, along with the brigade commander.

De Castro grimaced with annoyance. *No, docking space isn't an issue. Unfortunately, longshoremen are.*

Up to a point, things had gone well. Certainly the town

had been seized easily. Then the ramped amphibs had come in, on the north side where the slope of the shore was suitable, and let loose their cargo.

But that was almost all vehicles, some wheeled transport, yes, but more combat. We've got all the AMTRAKS, all the Engesas, all the Land Rovers, Tiunas, and M-151's we can use.

And a grand total of thirteen trucks, for almost two thousand of our people. And we need all of those, and twice as many trucks over, if we're even going to live here, while the two thousand barely suffice for keeping order in the place and securing—lightly, be it noted—the town.

Oh, sure, in a week or eight days the amphibs will come back, this time with lots more trucks and another thousand troops. And the brigade commander. Which will add to, rather than reduce, my problems.

De Castro looked down at two thin and ragged lines, staggering down one of the gangways of one of the ships, and up the other. The former column then massed up in a gaggle as they tried to jam close enough to two standing trucks to get rid of their burdens.

Of course, it's not as bad as all that. I have managed to pull out a couple of hundred of our people, to unload the ships by hand. And they're managing to get to the dock a grand total of about a hundred and fifty tons a day. At that rate, the last of the ships we currently have in harbor will be unloaded, oh, in about three months.

He scowled. *A hundred and fifty tons a day. Which is more than enough to live on, true, since we only use up about twelve to fifteen tons. But it is not enough—not without a lot more trucks—to actually get anywhere. New*

Amsterdam and Linden? I've got a platoon in each, just enough to guard the flags we raised over the public buildings.

God help us if the air bridge doesn't hold up and we have to use what little transport we have to support the fucking army.

God help us, too, if we can't get the food flowing to the civilians again. They're about out of held stocks and when that runs out we're going to need to bring into port a thousand tons a day for them alone. On the plus side, when we tell them "unload or starve," we'll probably get the dock workers back.

But I shudder to think of the problems when I have to start into the food wholesale business. And, now that I think of it, what are their merchants going to do for money, since the Guyanan dollar has become worthless? Wish we had thought of that.

Note to self: call the brigade commander and ask him to get us sent about half a billion Bolivars and an accountant team to do currency exchanges.

Kaieteur International Airport, Guyana

It was international because of both regularly scheduled, plus frequent charter, flights from Venezuela and Brazil, and sometimes Montreal, Quebec. For something in the middle of the jungle, the airfield was not unimpressive, at ninety-six hundred feet and fully asphalted. More impressive still was the reason for its being there, the seven-hundred and forty-seven foot falls to the southeast. Nor was the

Kaieteur Falls a mere trickle; it dumped over twenty-three thousand cubic feet of water down to the Potaro River *every second*. One could hear the roar even at the airport, six kilometers away. When the wind was right, one could hear it even through the walls of the austere guest house the commander of the brigade, Colonel Camejo, had commandeered for his headquarters.

"You know what bugs me, Sergeant Major?" the rather tall and eager-looking Camejo asked.

Straight-faced, Zamora, the brigade's senior noncom answered, "If it isn't that while the goody-two-shoes Marines and Hugo's pets, the paratroopers, got priority on everything, with us getting whatever was left over, or that while they got plussed up to strength while we're sitting at under sixty percent, or that we get one lousy C-130 lift every other day, which brings barely enough to eat, or that the helicopters got so overworked the last week that instead of eighty percent of them being up, eighty percent are back at Tumeremo and *down*, for maintenance, or that those fat bureaucrats in Caracas *still* haven't finished cutting contracts for air charters . . . other than those things, sir, no, I can't imagine what's bugging you."

"Nobody likes a cynic, Sergeant Major," Camejo intoned, waving a disapproving finger.

At Zamora's raised eyebrow, Camejo added, "I understand the first charter is due in here today. From Rutaca Airlines. Don't know what kind of plane it will be."

"I'll believe it when I see it, sir. And it will probably be a biplane they dug out of a museum."

Camejo chose to ignore that. Instead, he said, "What

bugs me is that we have absolutely no contact with the enemy." He waved to the northeast, in the direction of Ebini Hills and the presumptively gringo base there. "There are five thousand of the bastards down there; so intelligence says, anyway, and we have not clue one what they're doing."

Zamora shrugged. *Well, of* course *we don't. Finding out would take some troops moving, and that would require lift we just don't have. No sense in saying that though, the colonel already knows it.*

Instead, Zamora said, "On that note, we've got a bevy . . . well, more of a horde, really . . . of civilians coming up the road to Lethem, on the Brazilian border."

"How many?"

"The air force's best guess is maybe eight thousand."

"Shit. We can't feed them."

It was not insignificant that neither Zamora nor his chief even thought of the possibility of taking the civilians hostage, to force the surrender of the troops at the camp. They were civilized men and even, in their own eyes at least, vanguards of civilization.

"Oh, hell, no, sir," Zamora agreed. "Thing is, we don't seem to have to. *Somebody* laid out stockpiles for them, about every three days' march. They've been living on those. I put a guard on the one that's right under Mahdiana Eagle Mountain, to keep our own people from pilfering it."

"Good thought," Camejo commended. His face grew momentarily troubled. "Odd, isn't it, Sergeant Major that someone—"

Whatever he was about to say, the colonel was

interrupted by the sound of a heavy jet, passing low overhead and straining its engines in a turn. The two rushed outside and looked up, just as a big, lumbering Boeing 737 was making its final run onto the airfield. The jet had "RUTACA," in big blue letters, painted on the side.

"So shoot me; I was wrong," said Zamora sullenly.

Cheddi Jagan Airport, Guyana

The smell of burning feces—worse than either the human waste or the mixed in diesel, alone, would have been—was everywhere. At least it was everywhere Carlos and Lily could get to, between his having to drag the half-full, odiferous barrels to the burn area, while she had to tote twenty-liter cans of fuel, mix it in, torch it off, and stir the mixture as it burned.

"Well, there's one thing, one good thing," Lily admitted, as Carlos let go the latest overfull barrel of waste, jumping out of the way, backwards and fast, to avoid the splash.

"What's that, hon?"

She had tears running down her face, not from the work but from the smell and the fumes. She wiped those away, leaving a series of dirty streaks on her skin. "There's nothing like burning shit to take away a case of the hornies."

"Where *you're* concerned, lover," Carlos answered, with a leer, "even *that* isn't enough."

★ CHAPTER THIRTY-FOUR ★

"Fetchez la vache!"
—*Monty Python and The Holy Grail*

MV *Maria Walewska,* Puerto Cabello, Venezuela

The port pilot's own launch had been released on Liu's promise that he'd have the pilot brought back to port in his own boat. That wasn't going to happen.

"I'm afraid you'll be coming with us," Kosciusko told the port pilot, Carver, standing in temporary command on the bridge. Carver was an American, a former merchant skipper—a former naval officer, too—who'd elected to settle down with one of the local girls. They knew of each other, but only by reputation.

With Kosciusko were two armed guards. Liu, standing beside the pilot, reached over and flicked off the radio as soon as the leader of the regiment's naval squadron made his appearance. Besides the guard, there was a uniformed sapper, Sergeant Collins of the Engineer Company. To him, Kosciusko said, "You may man your engine, Sergeant. Commence fire at my command."

"Yessir," Collins replied, giving a hasty salute and racing off the bridge to the reassembled trebuchet that sat in the reformed cavity made of the containers.

"Captain Liu, have the flag of Guyana run up, then take us out."

"You sure you no want Jorry Logah?"

The Countess already had her dispensable cargo laid out. At the stern were two ex-Yugoslav M-70, four 240mm shells, and seven thirty-gallon barrels, all fused, all programmed, and all set to be armed. These rested on two broad beams the crew had turned into a roll-off system, of sorts, that they'd salvaged from scrap in the "lumber" container. A stack of half meter by three millimeter steel dummies sat off to one side.

To port and starboard, each side, were another four shells and six barrels. These sat right on the edge of the gunwale, waiting to be heaved over. These, too, had their dummies standing by.

In the center was the turntable mounted trebuchet, aimed for now to port. Six shells and six barrels waited in a line, off to one side.

The shells weighed nearly three-hundred pounds, with adaptors and destructor kits. And the explosive-filled thirty-gallon drums they'd thrown together for more blast effect, deeper, were four-hundred and thirty. Even for a trebuchet, this was a lot, and didn't give all that much range.

Fortunately, it didn't have to give much. The objective was mainly to scatter them, so that no precise line could be calculated from finding two of them and matching it to the ship's course.

"Stern?" Kosciusko asked, over a small, handheld, short-ranged radio.

"Here, Skippah," came the answer.

Hmmm. What's Mrs. Liu doing back there? Oh, well, if she can load precisely, she can unload as well.

"You may commence unloading in the sequence as given."

"Aye, aye, Skippah! We fucking staht now."

"Port side, starboard side; begin sequence now."

"Aye, sir . . . aye, aye, Commodore."

"Sergeant Collins?"

"Here, sir."

"Your target one and target two are coming up on the port. Fire as she bears."

"Yessir."

It wasn't a classical trebuchet, since it lacked a counter-weight. Neither was it an onager, which relied on the power of torsion in the form of twisted skeins. Instead, the motive power came from a battery of six helical springs, attached to a welded-on crosspiece at the bottom of the lever, above, and to the frame, below. These were already at full extension, and practically humming with the urge to release.

At the other end of the lever was a hook. From the hook hung a steel eyebolt, from which a cable ran. Just below it, from another eyebolt, this one affixed to the beam, ran another section of cable. Still below that was another cable, this one hung on a hook and running through a shackle to a power winch. A rope led off from the hook to one of the Chinese-born sailors, Yee.

Both of those upper cables led to a net of steel mesh, laid out under the crosspiece of the lever. Inside the net, laid transversely, was a single 240mm shell with an odd extension screwed into the fuse well.

Collins had already set the arming delay and the counter, electronically, using a kit supplied by Victor and his Israeli pals.

"We're ready," Collins said to himself, with no small amount of pride.

"Yee?" he asked.

"Yes, Sa'gin?"

"At my command."

"Yes, Sa'gin."

The ship was picking up speed, if only slightly. Collins ran to an eight-foot ladder, previously placed against and tied off to one of the surrounding containers, and scaled it. The ladder was set off well to one side, because, *You never really know, do you?*

Above the ladder's top, on the container, Collins had also put down two cans of food, still filled, that he'd earlier scrounged from the galley and emplaced to define a line parallel to the swing of the trebuchet's beam. Next to those was a single night vision scope.

He flicked it on. The navy never got the best of such things, of course, since they didn't need them. This one was old, Gen One, technology. It whined, most annoyingly.

Sighting that along the cans, Collins saw the grainy

green image of the opening of one of the port's sub-harbors, his "target one."

"Fire," he said.

Yee pulled the rope, which twisted the hook off its restraining eyebolt. Now freed, the lever swung up, dragging the net and the shell with it. The netted shell, accelerated by the swing, arced out and then up. The top hook kept the net in control until it was just past apogee. Then the net's eyebolt let go of the hook, releasing the mine to sail forward and onward. The springs groaned and whined with their torture as the upright lever hit its padded stop, making the entire contraption shudder.

Collins just caught the spash, about two hundred meters away, and perhaps fifty inward, past the mouth of the sub-port.

"Reload," he shouted, as one of the sailors rolled a plastic barrel up to a convenient load point, and Yee scrambled up the framework to reattach his hook. The long steel lever began to descend as the winch turned. As the beam reached the reload point, Collins was sure he heard a splash from the port side of the ship.

The RSM is absolutely right, thought Collins, with satisfaction. *It's been all downhill since Varus lost his legions and his eagles.*

Two Venezuelan sailors, wearing brassards indicating a certain police authority, walked the dock by which three of Venezuela's five frigates were tied. The frigates had come back, after escorting the amphibious ships back to harbor. From here they would return to Georgetown, after the transports picked up a largish chunk of First Marine Brigade's wheels. The lack of those trucks was seriously hampering the effort to spread out over settled Guyana from Georgetown.

"Did you hear something?" one of the sailors asked of the other.

The other shook his head. "Something like what?"

"I dunno . . . a kind of an odd clang. Can't recall ever hearing anything like it before."

The second sailor again shook his head. "No, not really. Probably some construction going on further into town. You know how the harbor distorts and carries sound."

"Yeah, but this was really odd. Like . . . oh . . . maybe a chunk of metal hitting wood at really high speed, with a sort of aerial *buzz* tossed in there somewhere, too.

"Aha, there it is again," the first sailor insisted, "coming from that freighter just pulling out of port."

"Maybe," the second one half-agreed. "But ships are always making odd sounds."

"And I think I heard a splash. A big one."

"Now *there* you're imagining things. A splash in port? Oh, my, that's ever so unusual."

The second sailor, who was actually the senior of the pair, consulted his watch and said, "C'mon, let's get back to the guard shack for our relief."

"Bring us around north for two miles and then head east, Captain," Kosciusko commanded, as the ship eased out of the harbor. "We've got a lot more mischief to do before we turn ourselves in."

Carver, the American-born pilot, still on the bridge and

watching events with keen interest, asked, "Um . . . what happens to me?"

"You'll be freed as soon as we turn ourselves in for internment at Trinidad." Kosciusko shrugged. "Assuming they believe us when we tell them you're a captive rather than one of us."

"Yeah, but what are the odds?"

Naughtius, Waini River, Guyana

The sub had doffed her thin disguise, back at what passed for a base. Now, just a couple of meters below the surface, with only her periscope showing, she cruised a very sedate three knots. Inside her, along with her four-man crew, sailed Biggus Dickus Thornton, Eeyore Antoniewicz, two M-70 mines, two thirty-gallon barrel mines, and two 240mm shells, all fused and almost armed.

I really don't like this poor, worn out excuse for a commando sub, Biggus Dickus mentally bitched. He had to keep his complaints unvoiced; there was no sense in worrying the men.

The problems with *Naughtius* were multifold. She was old. She'd been rode hard for years. She'd been put away wet. And she hadn't really been cared for in years, before the regiment took her. Even in her best days, she'd been, to quote the film *Dragnet,* "The cutting edge of Serbo-Croatian technology."

So, of course, someone had to start telling Yugo jokes, suitably modified. Of course that somebody was the sub's crew.

"Hey," asked the helmsman from his perch, over one shoulder, "what do you call a Yugo Class on the surface of the ocean?"

"Dunno," said the sub's commander, though he clearly did.

"A miracle."

"What's the problem with diving a Yugo?"

"Yugo down, but you can't stop."

The seaman who normally manned the diver lock out chamber asked, "What's Yugo?"

Helm replied, "What doesn't happen when we give 'er the gas or blow ballast."

Then the captain of the boat started to sing, a parody of a parody:

"As the engine dies . . .

"In a used sub lot at Kotor town

"Gordo the loggie and Victor the clown . . ."

"BUY A YUGO!"

I fucking hate submarine crews, Thornton thought. *Bunch of morbid bastards. Though I gotta confess, buying this thing was maybe not one of Victor's smoothest moves.*

Coco Point Airstrip, *Isla del Rey,* Panama

Leo Ross waved to the Antonovs as the second to launch joined the circling first, before they both veered to the northeast. It was pointless, of course; there were no useful windows facing in the right direction. Even so, it seemed the thing to do.

He stood there, on the beach, by the charred residue

of the fire pit they'd cooked over for the last few days, until the planes were lost in the darkness. A part of him yearned to have gone, or to be with his old battalion, despite the really shitty position they were in, by all reports.

He shook his head. *But I can't now, not anymore. Settled down. Have responsibilities. Kid on the way . . . even at my age. No need to let the baby grow up an orphan just so daddy can have fun.*

Still, it was nice to be a part of it all again, to feel a little younger, if only for a few days.

"Come on, *cuñado*," he said, finally. "Let's get back to Chitre."

After leaving Panamanian airspace, the Antonovs skirted Colombia's northern coast for hundreds of miles, staying low and just out of territorial waters as long as possible. Veering sharply just past the town of Manaure, Columbia, both planes, close together, popped over Colombia's eastern *cordillera* before diving low parallel to the slope of the far side. They weren't quite skimming the treetops, but they weren't all that far above them, either. Hearts were beating fast, breath coming in forced gulps, as the pilots leveled off just before reaching the Gulf of Venezuela.

There they split up, number two striking for Puerto Fijo to the northeast, while number one aimed itself for the narrow passageway east of San Carlos that was Lake Maracaibo's access to the sea.

"Ready on the barrels, Tim," the pilot warned as he used his dash controls to lower the rear cargo ramp. Wet, tropical air rushed into the cargo compartment, bringing with it smells of jungle and shore, and the fumes from the engines.

"Got it, boss," Lindell answered. He signaled with his head for his assistant to stand by on the other side of the mine shell. Those would go first, in this first pass, as fast as they could be rolled to ramp.

"Stand by the first four," the pilot announced. "Five . . . four . . . three . . . two . . . roll, roll, roll, roll."

Out the open space that had been filled by the ramp, Lindell could just see the spit of land that held the small town of San Carlos. As the last of the M-240 shells disappeared over the ramp's edge, to tumble to the sea, he thought that the plane was doing under eighty knots, and flying so close to the surface that it was actually getting some surface effect.

"Good drop," the pilot announced. "Next gap, three shell mines, stand by to roll in ninety seconds . . . Five . . . four . . . three . . . two . . . roll, roll, roll."

That time he was sure he saw a splash rise up, almost as high as the plane. *Oh, yeah, this is how even the cargo Air Force gets its moments of excitement.*

"Stand by for course change," was sounded just in time for Tim to expect to be thrown to his butt. He managed to get to his feet in time to hear, "Two shells in two minutes . . . Five . . . four . . . three . . . two . . . roll . . . roll. Three shells in two minutes . . . roll . . . roll . . . roll."

That time Tim was certain he saw a splash.

"Okay," the pilot said. "Next we're going to drop dummies, as many as you can shove out the ramp. Course change in one minute."

Lindell swayed over to the ramp and a stack of three-millimeter-thick, half-meter-in-diameter steel plates. His assistant did the same on the far side, both men waiting until the turn was complete, hanging on for dear life while it was underway, before undoing the straps that held the dummy plates in position.

"Ready . . . start tossing the dummies . . . continuous until ordered otherwise."

Two more passes and all eight barrel-mines had been unloaded. Another added yet more dummies. Now came the really back-breaking part, getting the one-ton ex-Yugoslav M-70 mines out the door. The pilot swung out over Lake Maracaibo, then assumed a north-northeastern heading, aiming for the major outlet to the sea by San Carlos. As best he could, he aimed his aircraft along the most common track for ships leaving the lake for the Gulf.

"Roll . . . roll. Last two in four minutes . . . Roll . . . roll.

"And, boys and girls, as your captain for this journey I hope you had an enjoyable time flying with AirVenture, your guaranteed mine delivery service. Now let's go to Colombia and turn ourselves in."

"Um, Captain," Lindell asked, "I realize that I'm just lowly loadmaster and all, but why the fuck are we turning ourselves in?"

"Because, O ye of little vision, we've been ordered to. Now if you want my personal guess, I think headquarters wants the Colombians to give us sanctuary, which will piss off the Venezuelans, so that they do something that will piss off Colombia."

★ CHAPTER THIRTY-FIVE ★

Blockades, in order to be binding, must be effective,
that is to say, maintained by a force sufficient really to
prevent access to the coast of the enemy.
—Treaty of Paris (1856)

MV *Manuel de Cespedes*, Puerto Cabello, Guyana

She was still under charter, and her captain under orders
from Raul Castro's government to give all possible support
to Hugo Chavez. Thus, having dropped off Conde's
Marines, the *de Cespedes* had gone to Puerto Cabello, this
time to pick up a mixed load of a couple of hundred
Marines and a slightly larger number of dock workers
who—on promise of a substantial bonus for helping out in
Georgetown—had volunteered for the enterprise. All of
these were camped out, catch as catch can, anyplace
horizontal that was at least two square meters. She also
carried about four thousand tons of miscellaneous
supplies, some of them explosive, but mostly inert.

De Cespedes backed up from the dock under her own

power, although under the guidance of a port pilot called in at the last minute to replace the unaccountably disappeared scheduled pilot. A tug shoved her around to aim generally to the east. Then, under her own, but minimal, power, she began to make slow way out of the complex port.

The mine had no name, but only a number. Indeed, the number wasn't even really *of* the 240mm shell that made up the bulk of it, but of the modified destructor kit that had converted it into a mine. Neither the shell nor the kit was capable of caring a whit, one way or the other.

In any case, the mine was armed and counting. It sensed the passage overhead of a fairly large body of ferrous material, making the requisite noises. Had the mine been capable of caring, it would have thought something like: *Aha, a target.*

Happily for the *de Cespedes*, however, this mine was set to go off on "three." Since the ship was "one," it did not quite meet parameters. The mine stood down. *Better luck next time. Two more to go.* Not that it cared.

Quite unwitting, *de Cespedes* increased speed slightly as its bow came to point directly at the harbor mouth. It passed over another 240mm mine, a barrel, another barrel, and then an M-70. All of those were set to count and for none of them was "one" the number.

Fully laden, *de Cespedes* passed out the narrow channel, and then veered right to assume a northerly heading. This was also, approximately, the route followed not so long before by *The Countess*.

★ ★ ★

The M-70, a ton in weight, seventy percent of that weight explosive, waited at the bottom of the sea with as much indifferent patience as had its brethren inside the port. In many ways, being considerably older in its design than the Israeli-supplied destructor kits on the other, ad hoc mines, it was less sophisticated than they were. Still, it met the broad parameters.

Inside the M-70, a sensor detected the sounds of an approaching vessel. This was enough for it to power up its other sensors. These normally remained dormant until powered up, to save life on the battery. Mines, after all, had to last for a while.

The second sensor, now brought to life, felt around itself for the proper magnetic field. There was one, but it was a little too distant for the nonce to justify suicide. Still, that field came closer . . . and closer . . . and closer. Soon, between it and the noise, the relatively primitive computer inside the mine could have said with a fair degree of confidence that it was a ship, that the ship was coming close enough to justify detonation, that the ship was probably big enough to justify detonation, and that—here, a less digital form of intelligence might have exulted, *Oh, boy, oh, boy, oh, boy! This is going to be so much* fun!—the pressure wave from the ship's passage was also going to be large enough, and close enough, to justify detonation.

Happily, if not for the mine, still less the ship, then at least for the organization at whose behest it had been laid, the M-70's counter was set to "one."

And then the magnetic field decreased ever so slightly. The sensors all reported what they had to the central processing unit. It decided that things were about as good as they were going to get. It sent the message, in the form of a straight, uncoded jolt to the detonator.

Boom.

Nearly three-quarters of a ton of high explosive is not small change. When it detonates, as this one just had, it creates a large bubble of hot gas in the water. Pressure then collapses that bubble, as this one collapsed. Internal pressure will recreate it. That cycle lasts until the bubble breaks free to the surface.

The pressure, however, is not even. It comes mostly from the bottom, where pressure is greater. This acts to drive the bubble upward, much—very much—faster than a normal bubble rises. Pure factors of natural physics will guide this bubble, without any human intervention, in the direction of a hull that it is not too far off from directly above. Between that, and the pressure, and the power of the initial explosion, if that bubble hits a ship's hull it forms a water jet that is, in its effects, not all that different from the hot gas jet of a hollow-charge antiarmor warhead. Except much, much bigger.

Standing right at the broad glass forward-facing windows of the bridge, the captain never felt a thing and barely had time to notice the rising bubble of water on one side of his ship. The water jet cut through the hull, tore its way through the cargo—some of that cargo human, none of whom felt a thing, either—through the deck of the bridge and then through the captain. It was large enough to take out the bridge crew, as well, barring, oddly enough, the captain's dog, which was off in one corner, asleep, and thus out of the path of the jet.

This alone would have been enough to sink *de Cespedes*. It was not, however, the lone effect. Additionally, there was a shock wave that loosened most of her seams. This, too, would have eventually sunk her. Worse still, the bubble that arose, initially on one side, before the jet pierced her, had the effect of also raising the ship's center, straining her keel. As the jet was passing through her, and before the bubble entirely collapsed, there was a brief moment when nothing supported the ship except the water at bow and stern. The center, keel already strained to the breaking point, collapsed into the remnants of the bubble. At that point the keel was broken, though sections of the hull still held together.

And then the water returned as the bubble escaped upwards. It slammed into the ship with unimaginable force, breaking her back entirely. She split in two.

Of the two sections, the forward one capsized almost immediately. A couple of people who had been on deck were thrown overboard. They died quickly as the ship turned over on them. The rest were caught below decks. Most drowned, civilians and Marines both, in a panic-stricken cacophony of screams and pleas to the Maker. The drowning was not quick, but rather quite a slow and disgusting process.

The rear section, to which the bridge was mostly still attached, bobbed like a cork for a few moments. Then water rushed in, filling her from forward to rear. She slid beneath the waves in a long, drawn out *gurgle*. There was just enough time for some few of the people caught in the stern section to escape and hurl themselves into the water.

Most never had the chance before the stern, too, slid beneath the waves.

Happily, the dog, sensible critter, waited until the water was almost flush with the bridge, jumped off, and paddled to shore.

Lake Maracaibo, Venezuela

Half a million barrels of heavy crude can make for quite a maritime bonfire.

Of the ship that had been carrying that half million barrels, there was not a sign. One minute it had been there. The next it was gone with a roaring fire in its place. Worse, the fire was growing and spreading out as more oil arose from below to feed it.

The fireboats, some from Maracaibo itself, others from Puerto Fijo and other spots, were totally outclassed. A tanker rupture they could have dealt with. The sudden dumping of that much oil? Not a chance. Instead of beating the fire back, it was beating them back, and threatening them with being fatally outflanked wherever they tried to make a stand.

Indeed, one of those fireboats had disappeared. And nobody quite knew how or why; it was just gone.

Outside the lake, toward the northern end of the Gulf of Venezuela, a thin picket line of Coast Guard patrol boats was being established. The crews of those boats were distinctly nervous. They had a pretty good idea of the problem—ships, particularly big oil tankers—don't just disintegrate on their own as a general rule.

★ ★ ★

Buz, the crocodile, had had about enough. Home just wasn't home anymore. First there had been that dammittohell baited trap that had caused him to lose a large number of his teeth, to say nothing of searing his taste buds so badly that he hadn't even been able to relish the savory deliciousness of mostly rotten meat ever since.

Then had come that nasty thump running through the water that almost caused him to choke up his last meal. If he'd been any closer, he was pretty sure he wouldn't have made it.

Last, and worst, was the glowing stuff out on the water. Sure, Buz knew that fire was a bad thing; he'd had to run to the water more than once in his life to escape it. But when the fire was on the water, too? And it stank? And made the air stink?

Nope, I've had about enough. When the going gets tough, the smart move on.

Without another word—without *any* word, for that matter; Buz was a crocodile, after all—he turned his snout to the north and his tail to the south and began paddling off.

Orinoco River Mouth—*la Boca Grande, Venezuela*

With jungle on either side, at a distance of several miles, the propeller of the steamer churned water to a muddy froth behind it.

The cargo was mixed; clothing from India, electronics from Japan, medicines picked up in Vancouver, and food from the United States' west coast. Venezuela produced little or none of any of that, except for food. Even so, it was still, since not long after the reorientation of the country's economy away from agriculture and toward oil, not self-sufficient in food.

The Orinoco was deep here, especially with runoff from the recently ended rainy season. Thus, while the mine was a barrel, and contained the equivalent of about six hundred pounds of TNT, the shock, the jet, and the bubble were not sufficient to rend it in two . . . or even to kill anybody. They just sprung a few of the seams in minor ways, while the jet pierced the engine compartment, shutting down both speed and power.

The ship sank gently. The crew, barring only one unfortunate killed in the engine room, was able to get off in good order, some directly to the boats, others to the water in which they swam for the boats.

Buz would have been very surprised to learn that he had a distant—as in about a million years' removed—cousin, living on the banks of the Orinoco. The cousin, quite a bit smaller than Buz and not as bright, made his living, such as it was, off the fish of the river and the occasional unwary quadruped. When not hunting for food, that croc's major interest was watching the ships go by. Sometimes, even, when hunting was poor, it went out to investigate in the hope of getting a handout from the ships' garbage.

Hunting had sucked for the last week. It decided it was time for a little panhandling. It hesitated for a moment as it felt an uncomfortable rippling *thud* in the water. That passed and it noticed the ship had stopped moving. *Oh, boy, free eats!* The crocodile speeded up as he noticed the ship getting lower. Behind it, forty-odd more of its closer cousins likewise dove into the water.

Number One Lime Street, London, United Kingdom

"No, sir," said the broker, "I am sorry, but your ship was lost to an act of war, while sailing into a declared war zone, and you did not have a war risks policy . . . No sir, I am afraid that it is far too late for reinsurance . . . Yes, sir, I am aware your company is going to be sued for those poor sailors eaten by crocodiles . . . No, sir, so far as I am aware, nobody intends to underwrite war risk policies for ships sailing to and from Venezuela, and certainly not after so many losses in such a short time . . . Yes, sir, I am sure you do have hulls currently stuck in Venezuelan ports . . . Well, sir, I suppose you will just have to leave them there, and pay the demurrage, or have them sail out, and risk the greater loss . . . You do have my sympathies, sir . . ."

Miraflores Palace, Caracas, Venezuela

Hugo was livid. He stormed around his conference room *cum* command center, swearing, throwing things, kicking over chairs, verbally abusing the staff.

His didn't stop with mere verbal abuse. Throwing a book at Admiral Fernandez, he cursed, "You fat little bung boy; it was your job to stop this. I am a laughing stock and it is *all* your fault. Piece of shit!"

Hitting Fernandez in the head with a book wasn't quite satisfying enough. Chavez stormed to the admiral's chair, lifted him bodily from it, and began slapping his face. "Why"—slap—"didn't"—slap—"your overpriced"—slap—"fucking navy"—slap—"stop this before it happened?" Slap, slap, slap. Chavez let go of the material of the sailor's uniform, letting him fall back, stunned and humiliated, to his chair.

"What the fuck *happened,* anyway? How did someone put mines in *our* waters?"

The intelligence chief, an air force general, raised a hand timidly. "I think I know, Mr. President . . . some of it, at least."

"So spill your guts, you incompetent faggot!"

The general went down the list of what he did know, two aircraft that had done some complicated maneuvers over Lake Maracaibo and the Gulf, a gringo-born boat pilot who had materialized in Trinidad and phoned in an appalling story.

"But I don't know what mined the Orinoco, Mr. President. The Coast Guard has been watching that and they report nothing."

"The coast guard reports nothing," Chavez parroted, with a sneer. "And that tells us precisely *what*? They used a submarine. But you air force pussies told me both of the submarines in Guyana were destroyed, didn't you?"

"The pilot said it went up in a blast, sir," the intel chief insisted. "Maybe the gringos . . ."

"Bullshit!"

Chavez turned his attention back to the pale and trembling admiral. "And what about the ship that mined us?"

"Interned in Trinidad, Mr. President. Out of our reach."

"And the airplanes?"

The intel chief gulped. "Interned in Colombia."

"I want those fuckers! I'll personally give the commands to the firing squads that shoot them."

Nicholas—the pre-hanging Saddam Hussein lookalike—coughed and spoke up. He wasn't shy about it; after all the fiasco with the ports was none of *his* doing.

"I checked with the legal department, Hugo. Both Trinidad and Colombia are perfectly correct in not turning over those people to us."

"I don't give a shit about the law," Chavez snarled. "I just want those pirates dead."

Nicholas shook his head. *Not going to happen. Not without another war we can't handle.*

Chavez nodded, forcing himself back to a degree of calm he really didn't feel. "How," he asked of Fernandez, "are you going to get the ports cleared?"

"I don't have a single minesweeper, sir," the admiral answered, gulping. For the moment, fear of being stood against a wall and shot overcame rage at the treatment Chavez had meted out to him. "And divers are not good risks for this. We have considered just filling a hull with wood and driving it back and forth to clear lanes. The problem is that we think—really, we're sure—that these mines are on counters. Just because a ship goes over a stretch of sea and there's no explosion doesn't mean there isn't a mine still there, waiting."

"Who does have minesweepers?"

Again, Fernandez gulped. "Cuba, and they've promised

to send us whatever they have . . . in a month or two when they can get one, maybe two, ready for sea."

"We'll start to starve before then, Hugo," Nicholas said. "We'll start to starve *long* before then. Oh, Hugo, we're sitting on more oil than we could ever use ourselves, and we refine enough gasoline to export three or four hundred thousand barrels a day . . . but we can't *eat* it."

Chavez sneered. "Fuck your doom-mongering, Nicholas. "Now here's what I want. General?" Chavez looked at his Army chief, Quintero.

"Sir?"

"I want you to move substantial forces to the Colombian border. Everything that's not in Guyana or scheduled to go. Heavy on the tanks. And I want them to *look* threatening, but I don't want them to cross."

General Quintero shook his head, not understanding.

"What I want them to do, General, is provide cover for the FARC freedom fighters on our side of the border. But to them, once the troops are all in position, I am going to say, 'Go fuck with the Colombian army, or these tanks will destroy you.'

"See how the bastard Colombians like it when we *punish* them for sheltering those pirates."

★CHAPTER THIRTY-SIX★

The human factor will decide the fate of war,
of all wars. Not the Mirage, nor any other plane,
and not the screwdriver, or the wrench or radar
or missiles or all the newest technology and electronic
innovations. Men—and not just men of action,
but men of thought. Men for whom the expression
'By ruses shall ye make war' is a philosophy of life,
not just the object of lip service.
—Ezer Weizman, *On Eagles' Wings*

Lawyers, Guns, and Money (SCIF), Camp Fulton, Guyana

"You're late," Stauer said.

Morales nodded, without any appearance of remorse.
"We had to duck some of those nimble little fucking attack
aircraft they use, about a half a dozen times between here
and Wineperu."

"Fair enough," the colonel agreed, then explained why
he'd wanted them to risk coming, what he wanted them to
do, and with what.

"What's the wind pattern like at the airport?" Che Morales asked of Stauer. With them were Boxer and, because of his legal background, Bridges. Between Morales and Simmons, and the three regimental officers, on a table sat something that looked like a cross between a tripoded, short-barreled heavy machine gun and a refugee from a science fiction movie set. The something was a Chinese-made ZM-87, a laser blinder.

"Easterly," Boxer replied. "You two are going to have to work your way around to the east, to catch the transports as they come in." His mouth twisted up on one side. "You *may* have to work your way back around to the west, again, once they decide to screw ease of landing and come in from a direction where they don't know there's a laser waiting. For that matter, the shorter cross strip may require some attention. You're going to have to give the impression of being four or five laser projector teams, rather than one diligent one."

"I dunno," Simmons muttered. "Seems . . . dirty to me."

"It would be illegal," Bridges said, nodding, "if you were to use it to try permanently blind someone. But, since you're going to use it at a range that will only *temporarily* blind them, so that they crash and become permanently *dead*, I think it's fine."

To Morales, no less than Simmons, the whole idea of attacking a man's eyes made him literally queasy; this, from two men who had no real objection to taking human life for a good purpose. But *eyes?* The idea of being blinded was so much more objectionable than the thought of being killed to them that that objection extended even to the enemy.

"You can't just give us some missiles to backpack?"

Stauer shook his head. "We could, but you couldn't carry enough to matter and no shoulder-launched missile has the range this does, or is as hard to spot the launch of as this thing is. The Venezuelans aren't going to see much, if anything."

Morales' lip curled with distaste. "Where did you come up with it?"

Boxer replied, "There were, supposedly, twenty-two of these made by NORINCO, back in the Nineties. So far as I know, that was, in fact, how many were made. But they made more parts than that before shutting down production.

"I went to Wicked Lasers—those are the guys who make the really *dangerous* laser 'pointers,' some of them by disassembling laser projectors—and asked them to get hold of enough of those parts to build us anywhere up to fifty of the things. They got one thrown together, tested, and sent to us, along with some extra power packs, before the invasion started."

"They'll start wearing shades," Morales objected.

Boxer shook his head *no*. "This thing fires pulses on two different frequencies. A set of glasses that protect the eyes from both . . . you couldn't see through them anyway."

"Oh." *No salvation there, I suppose.* "What about civilian chartered flights?"

"It's a war zone," said Bridges, "and a blockade has been declared. If they fly, they die, and it's all on them."

Stauer harrumphed. "Your objections are noted, Che. If you have no more questions . . . ?"

"No, sir."

"Fine. You and Simmons are to take this thing, along with your usual gear and anything else you deem necessary and can port. You will be transported by surface to the Essequibo River, west of Mount Arisaru. Your transportation will have a rubber boat to take you across to the east bank. If you think it might be useful, we've got a couple of bicycles you can have. From there you will hump or cycle—avoiding all contact with anyone, friend or foe, and moving only by night, until you link up with a Captain—you guys might know him as Sergeant—Byng, at Dalgin on the Demerara River. From there, Byng will lead you to a point approximately four miles east of Cheddi Jagan Airport. There, you are take whatever actions are required to shut down the airport to all cargo traffic, displacing as appropriate. Byng does not know what you will be carrying and is not to be allowed to find out before you have used it.

"Good luck and Godspeed."

Simmons, still disgusted, answered, "God's not gonna smile on us for doing *this*."

Intersection Issaro Road and Bartica-Potaro Road, Guyana

Because Reilly's location was as secret as they could make it, they really couldn't broadcast via radio. For the troops, this meant landline communications from regiment, to battalion, and then on down to company, platoon and squad. To Reilly, it was highly suboptimal from a command and control point of view, but . . .

"It beats the shit out of the Venezuelan Air Force pounding the shit out of us night and day. And we're physically close enough to intervene if they ever do try an airmobile assault on what's left of base."

Reilly's First Battalion had been reinforced with Cazz's battalion's armored car section, two platoons of engineers plus the engineer company's headquarters and bridging troops, the entire twelve-gun artillery battery, a platoon of air defense troops with a mix of missiles, towed light ADA guns, and all four of the self propelled guns, plus their normal attachments from the service support battalion, and a remotely piloted vehicle section flown by the intelligence types. Those last were attached to Reilly, but not co-located. Rather, they were back at a bunker by the Camp Fulton airfield.

For that matter, most of his trains, plus the headquarters and support troops, were back at Camp Fulton and its environs, doing their damndest to look like an entire combat regiment for the Venezuelan Air Force. The VAF still evidenced an interest, daily, in what was going on there. They also took a certain interest in killing whatever could be seen amidst the ruins. The job of being bait had never been an easy one.

The RPV's provided much less of a clear picture than one would have hoped for. Initially, they'd been just fine, providing real time intelligence on the build up at Kaieteur Airport and the area around the falls. But after losing two—and the supply was quite limited—to no discernable reason, the MI commander had suggested that the Venezuelans were interfering with electronic controls. It might or might not have been true, but since the supply was so limited, they'd adopted a different approach. Now, instead of flying the things around, they sent them out preprogrammed to fly a particular route and record what they saw, then return to base. At base, control for the landings was resumed, but with very low power settings on the control stations. This meant more or less lengthy delays.

Not a problem though, Reilly thought, studying his maps and comparing them to the images brought back by the RPV's and hand carried to him by one of the intelligence rats. *Not a problem because nothing moves really fast in the jungle. We know there are two understrength battalions, plus support, at the Falls, and another one strung out in little penny packets all the way back to Venezuela. I can't get at them; no frigging roads and the terrain and vegetation are impossible for my vehicles. And they don't have the transportation to support any more than a company near the road to Lethem.*

"I'll start to worry when I see one of those planes unload a few hundred mules," he muttered.

"What was that, sir?" Sergeant Major George asked.

"Huh? Was I thinking out loud?"

George smiled. "You might say that. But what was it you *said*?"

"Oh, I was just thinking that they can't support any force big enough to worry about at any distance from Kaieteur Falls unless they get animal transportation."

"That's not exactly true," George disagreed.

"How's that?" Reilly asked.

"Well . . . Brazil's taking a pretty neutral, hands-off approach, no?"

Reilly shrugged. "Sure. So?"

"What's to prevent Venezuela from renting every private Brazilian truck that's for rent within five hundred miles of Lethem, then taking them across the border, full of food and Class IV?" Class IV was milspeak for construction and barrier materials.

"Now there's a scary thought," Reilly said. "But I haven't read anything in the intelligence summaries to suggest it's happening."

George shook his head. "Neither have I. And it may not be—operative word—*yet*. But eventually?"

"Yeah. Crap. What do we do about it?"

"Not a lot *we* can do," George said. "But were I you, I'd go see Stauer and have him try to get a team from Second Battalion somewhere along that road, with a shitpot of mines. That, or enough explosive to drop the Lethem Bridge. Or, better, both."

"Mines, maybe," Reilly replied. "If things work out, *we'll* need the Lethem bridge."

He shook his head over a lost opportunity. "You know, if we'd thought of it in time, we could have had Gordo stockpile that shit somewhere convenient, just like he stockpiled food for the dependents. Ah, well, can't think of everything." Reilly shuffled through his stack of maps until he found a large scale one of the Lethem area. "Tell me again why you decided to stay in the NCO ranks?"

"Couldn't deal with being numbered among the idjits, sir," George replied, straight faced. "Besides, even the *Marine* officer corps didn't want me, as my parents were married . . . to each other."

"A terrible handicap," Reilly agreed, trying very hard to

keep a straight face as he did. "You really do have to be born a bastard to make a first class officer."

"Exactly, sir," George agreed, mock solemnly.

Reilly grunted, rather than formulating a reply. *I don't really know what I'd do without this guy to keep me entertained. And humble.*

Growing serious again, Reilly said, "Okay, fun's fun, but tell me about the patrols to Mahdia Eagle Mountain and Twasinki Mountain."

"Left this morning, sir, uniformed, armed, and on bicycles. Michaels' recon team is going to Mahdia; Martinez's to Twasinki. Their vehicles are unmanned now. I was going to suggest turning them over to the Gay Avengers . . ."

"Nah," Reilly cut off his sergeant major. "We've got plenty of light recon from having most of Third Battalion's gun section. Viljoen and Dumisani are a lot more important keeping the vehicles up than pulling recon, even if they'd be good at it."

Chaguaramas, Trinidad

The base had been constructed by the United States, back in 1940, under the Destroyers for Bases Agreement with Great Britain. This was the same agreement that had seen to the construction of the airfield at Timehri, now called "Cheddi Jagan." America had abandoned most of these in 1949, though Chaguaramas had lasted longer. With the dissolution of the British Empire, the bases had, for the most part, been taken over by local defense forces.

Kosciusko, Liu, Collins, and crew had nothing really to

complain of about their treatment at the hands of the Trinidad and Tobago Defence Force. After turning themselves in at Port of Spain, and informing the authorities of what they'd done to Venezuela's northern ports, they'd been duly put under guard and incarcerated in one of the unused buildings of the base. Captain and Mrs. Liu, naturally, had their own suite.

But when the guard, mused Kosciusko, *the sergeant of the guard, their commanding officer, and* his *commanding officer all insist on shaking your hands when they arrest you, you know life isn't going to be bad. That their Chief of Defense Staff showed up to make sure we were being well cared for, and brought us a case of—gotta admit it— some of the finest rum I've ever had, well, life is good. And why shouldn't they like us? It's not like these people aren't a lot closer culturally, linguistically, and historically, to Guyana than they ever could be to Venezuela. Or that any sympathy they have isn't for their brothers across the waters.*

Seated under an awning, with Liu and his wife, the latter waving a fan to keep off the flies, Kosciusko sipped at a little of the rum—straight up, it was too good to ruin with Coke—when one of the guards came up and saluted.

"Sir," said Corporal McLean, "there's someone who wishes to speak with you. He says you'll know him, sir, a Mister Baluyev."

Kosciusko sputtered out a little of the rum. *Baluyev? Here? He was supposed to have . . . Well, apparently he didn't or couldn't. Therefore, hell, yes, I want to see him.*

"Please, Corporal, if you could pass him through the gate."

"Surely, sir," said McLean, like most of his people, very polite and, frankly, *veddy* British. "Shall I send one of the cook lads over with some more ice?"

"If you would be so kind, Corporal."

"I'll leave you a little privacy, sir," McLean said, saluting and stomping off to resume his guard post.

Baluyev watched the stout black corporal stride away, then said, "I don't get it."

"They *like* us, Mr. Baluyev," Kosciusko explained. "Now, why are you here, and why is the bridge at *Ciudad* Guyana still standing?"

"It's still standing because we're here, sir," Baluyev replied, "and we're here because we couldn't get the boat up the river. They were searching everything. So I came, once we heard you had all been"—Baluyev looked around at the very decent surroundings—"put into durance vile. And I must say, sir, it sure seems vile to me. Ahem."

"Sir, you know the big plan, whatever's left of it. I only knew the little one. Sir, I need orders. Or guidance, anyway."

"Regiment isn't communicating via the e-mail drop?"

"No . . . I mean, yes, they are. But they've got no orders except 'hang loose.' What kind of orders are those, sir?"

Kosciusko, who was much more in-briefed than Baluyev, thought about the sea between the Netherlands Antilles and Venezuela, and said, "Well . . . why don't you and your people just hang loose. Get in a little fishing, maybe. Something useful for you to do will come up; I'm certain of it."

Ferry, San Martin de Turumban
(on some maps marked as "Anton"), Venezuela

Cazz's boys had grown thin, no doubt about it. Oh, rations hadn't been all that short, not yet—though they'd had to stretch them out a bit toward the end—but a man lost weight in the jungle, no matter what. A lot of that came from serving as a grazing ground for swarms of mosquitoes. Some of it was water loss. Some of it was burning off fat as they worked like the mules that supported them. Indeed, they'd worked harder; men weren't really built to carry the kind of loads they did, not the way mules were. And a mule would quit, eventually. A man?

Cazz grinned. *Mules wouldn't put up with it. Men will hump until they die.*

Since leaving their temporary log base inside the Werushima Mountains, they'd moved at night and slept in the day, if "sleep" it could be called. Two men from A Company and half a dozen mules had drowned crossing the Cuyuni River, northeast of the Maugaru Mountains. All Cazz could hope for was that, if the bodies were found, they were found someplace where there was no phone or radio to report it.

At least, Cazz thought, looking up at the light beginning to filter through the interwoven trees, *at least for the next ten minutes.*

Last night the troops had moved painstakingly to their final positions before the attack. Two days prior Cazz had sent two companies across the Cuyuni, one to set up an ambush position on the road between Carrizal and San Martin, one to wait in an assault position to the west of the ferry. He hardly needed that level of force for the short platoon the Venezuelans had posted there. What he needed it for was to take the ferry quickly, once he committed to the attack, to set up a defense on the far side, should the ambush fail. And he needed the ferry taken intact, so that he could get his bloody mules and mortars across without losing any more. If they could strike so hard and so fast that they managed to grab a couple of the trucks waiting with the Venezuelan troops, so much the better.

They wouldn't even have the ferry manned, if they weren't using the two airfields as supplementary positions to resupply forward. Me, I wouldn't have bothered with the airstrips.

More trucks he expected to grab from the ambush, a couple anyway. Still more were waiting at the Venezuelan forward base at Tumeremo. Austin and one scout team had made it that far and reported it as a potential paradise—pandemonium, anyway—of destruction and loot. There were trucks by the score, fuel by the bladder, food in mountains, ammunition by the crate, and—best of all—about two thirds of Venezuela's helicopter fleet being serviced at any given time. To say nothing of a small fleet of light, fixed-wing aircraft. For defense, the scouts had seen one company of light armor, maybe a company of fairly lackadaisical infantry and—based on the number of tents and latrines the scouts had counted—"about eight hundred REMFs."

"And, sir," Austin had said, via a directional antenna, "them light strike craft the Venezuelans use. I saw the last of 'em fly out heading east a couple of days ago and they never came back. Figure they're in Guyana, sir."

Which makes sense to me, Cazz thought.

"I can't fly the choppers," Cazz muttered, in the gloom south of the river, "but I can sure as shit burn them so no one else can either . . . them, and any fixed-wing birds we find on the field. Gonna be fun."

For the battalion's main force it had been radio listening silence all the way, with only a few exceptions permitted, and those only after midnight, this morning. In very short bursts of electromagnetic traffic the mortars had reported up and ready to fire. A Company, Captain Lott, commanding, had said they were occupying the ambush position. B Company, Captain Newman, commanding, reported that it was ready to assault the ferry from the east and D Company, Captain Jarrett, commanding, confirmed that it was ready to charge the southern end. The engineers hadn't had to report; they were with Cazz. The bulk of the scout platoon—Master Sergeant Austin and one team still keeping their eyes on Tumeremo and its airfield—was overlooking the airfield on the friendly side and radioed, "Ready to attack." Assault wasn't really their job, of course, but, *Needs must when the devil drives*.

Cazz made a *gimme* gesture to Singh, carrying the battalion radio for the festivities. Singh passed over the microphone.

With his heart beginning to race, not with fear but with excitement and anticipation, Cazz pushed the microphone's button and ordered, "All companies, this is Six, actual. Attack."

★ CHAPTER THIRTY-SEVEN ★

"Strike—till the last armed foe expires;
  Strike—for your altars and your spires;
  Strike—for the green graves of your sires;
  God—and your native land!"

—Fitz-Greene Halleck, "Marco Bozzaris"

Airfield, Eteringbang Falls

The scouts opened up first, by a matter of seconds. Each of the three teams present carried one Pecheneg machine gun. These had been grouped under Sergeant Ahern, with his other three scouts in support.

The Pecheneg was, at core, simply a PKM. The PKM was generally a decent gun, at least until it came time to change the barrel. It had, arguably, the worst barrel change mechanism in machine gun history, requiring that the gunner lift the feed tray cover, and use a block of wood—sometimes a block of wood and a *hammer*—to pound a sliding piece of half-moon-indented metal out to one side. Only then could the old, overheated barrel be removed.

The Pecheneg, conversely, had taken a step forward by taking a step back. Inspired, quite likely, by the Great War's Lewis Gun, it had a shroud, or jacket, around the barrel with oval windows or slots cut toward the rear. Blast at the muzzle drew air in through those windows, which air cooled the barrel enough that, as a practical matter, barrel changes weren't needed. Indeed, changing the barrel was a depot-level job; gunner, keep your grubby fingers off.

Ahern had spent a good part of the time between about two AM and sunrise sighting the guns in via image intensifying scopes to cover the field properly. One gun he'd had aimed in at the sole tent, a medium job capable of holding no more than a dozen men comfortably. The other two he'd directed onto the one known guard post, in one case, and to fire straight up the short field, south-southwest to north-northeast, in the other. There were no aircraft at this field, though one had landed on the field on the opposite side, during the night. Once this one was clear, the scouts would have to cross the river on foot to clear out the larger strip.

In any case, whether an ambush or, as this was, a raid, one opened fire with the greatest casualty producing weapons available. That was Ahern and his trio of machine guns.

His radio attuned to the battalion sequence for frequency hopping, Ahern heard the order, "Attack," and immediately gave the command. The Pecheneg nearest to him, the one sighted at the tent, opened up. In the gloom, its muzzle seemed like a strobe light.

What was inside the tent none could tell. Still, it was the dry season now, and the tent itself was dry. One or more of the green tracers passing through caught it alight. A small horde of screaming and cursing men tumbled out, pulling on equipment even as they tripped over each other. The machine gunner shifted fire imperceptibly, cutting them to pieces. Most went down with looks more of disbelieving shock than fear.

Each blast from the muzzle was like a blow to Ahern, but it was the kind of blow he'd learned to take and not, in any case, nearly as bad as those falling upon the Venezuelans.

Bare milliseconds after that first gun opened fire, the other two joined in. Green tracers danced up the airfield lengthwise, while others cut across it, slaughtering the lone guard post on the eastern side. After a minute's worth of that, the platoon sergeant ordered the gun firing up the field to cease fire and accompany him. He, with the Pecheneg gunner and the remaining eight scouts, assaulted up the field, following it to the north-northeast. At that point Ahern ordered his other two guns "out of action," and, with his own squad, followed in the footsteps of the platoon sergeant.

He met them at the riverbank, where the scouts were busily shooting up a few Venezuelans, attempting to swim for safety, in the back.

"Teach de muthafuckahs a lesson," was Ahern's comment.

"Cross, you bastards," the platoon sergeant shouted. "KP for the last man to make it to the other side."

San Martin de Turumban Ferry, Guyana side

The Venezuelan cooks had apparently delivered chow via the ferry to their troops on the south bank. At least, that was the only good reason any of the men in Delta Company could think of for the enemy to just line up like that, with only a minimal guard.

The river, past where D Company lined up, a hundred and fifty meters south and east, was brown and about two hundred meters wide. The town, past the river, was within easy small arms range of the south bank. Most of the ground in between the far bank and the town was open and low, and probably flooded regularly. Past the open ground, hidden in a moderately sized stretch of woods, east of the town, was Company B.

"Nothing fancy," Cazz had told Jarrett, the D Company commander. "Speed matters more; I want a straight up, on line, marching fire attack. Fast!"

What he'd asked for, he got. Delta's commander had stretched his troops, with about two meters between men in the three forward platoons, in a long, mostly straight line. His RPG gunners were going to be worthless for this, so Cazz had stripped them off, days ago, along with Delta's weapons platoon sergeant, and given them over as a complete section of six launchers and fourteen men to Alpha.

At the company commander's order, Delta had stood

up, opened fire, and begun trotting forward, their steps preceded by a wall of copper-jacketed lead.

They didn't hit much; Cazz hadn't expected them to. What that wall of fire did—he later estimated they'd put out about ten thousand rounds in the single minute it took to close to the friendly bank—was scare the unsuspecting Venezuelan troops waiting for breakfast, shitless causing them to drop their weapons and scurry for the river and a hoped-for safety.

At the river, Delta's commander ordered his men into a hasty defense, even while shouting, "And kill the bastards; don't let a one get away!"

The men took him at his word; little spurts began erupting from the water as they took aim at the swimming, fleeing backs. One by one the fleeing troops gave off cries of pain as the bullets found them. Body by body they began to float, face down and dead, downstream.

Then, from the south bank, Company D began a slow, desultory fire toward the town.

"Master Sergeant Austin, sir," Singh announced, handing Cazz the microphone.

"Six, here. Whatcha got?"

"The tank company, sir. I count a dozen . . . nooo . . . make it thirteen Scorpions, and half a dozen trucks loading up with infantry. They'll be moving out soon."

"Good," Cazz said. "Break . . . Alpha, you copy?"

"Roger," answered the A Company commander. "Ready."

"Bravo, remember to hold your boys in check. I want the garrison of the town to be screaming bloody murder for help against an attack that those tanks could defeat. You hit them too soon, and the bait will be gone."

"Roger, sir," Bravo agreed. "We know the plan." There was a tone in the words that suggested, *Teach your grandmother to suck eggs, sir.*

Cazz kept his answering voice neutral but firm. "Good. Stick to it."

"They're leaving now," Austin advised. "Heading south. They're moving fast, too, tanks and trucks intermixed. No real order; they look like they're in a hurry to save their buddies."

"We're ready," A Company said.

Southeast of Carrizal, Venezuela

Nine miles north of San Martin, the road to Tumeremo took a sharp, ultimately approximately ninety-degree bend, southeast of the town of Carrizal. That was where A Company's commander had aimed for, and that, thanks to GPS, was where he'd put his reinforced company into an ambush position.

He'd gone for a simple "V" shape based on the lay of the road, with one platoon reinforced by two of Delta's RPG's right at the bend, and the other two flanking that, parallel to the road as it ran before them. The rightmost, or westernmost, platoon had further kicked a team of riflemen even more to the west by about half a mile, to provide early warning.

All three platoons, plus the reinforcements, were to the east or north of the strip of dirt, with their fires oriented such that nobody should be firing on any friendlies. In total, the ambush position stretched over roughly seven hundred meters. Second Platoon, on A Company's left, had wanted to lay a half-dozen antitank mines across the road during the night. Rather, they'd wanted to lay more than that, but one of the blasted mules that had drowned crossing the Cuyuni had been carrying the other half of the load.

Cazz had nixed that, anyway. "No. We need the road clear for us to move up it quickly after we capture some vehicles, and I don't want to have to waste time waiting for the mines to be cleared."

The mines, thus, remained on the back of one very unhappy mule, about nine hundred meters to the rear.

Tumeremo, Venezuela

"Breakfast, sir," said Major Rojas' batman, pushing aside the mosquito net over the opening to the tent and entering to lay a paper plate on the major's field desk. From the operations tent next door came a dull chatter and the occasional static of an unimportant radio message.

Major Rojas, Fifth Venezuelan Infantry Division, hadn't been left behind for incompetence. He hadn't been left behind because he was lazy, or because he was a bad leader, or for any other negative reason. He'd been left behind because he was in charge of the tanks and there was no good way to get Fifth Division's light tanks to Guyana yet, or to support them once they were there.

And, thus, Rojas fumed, for the third time since

awakening and approximately the twenty-five *thousandth* time since arrival at Tumeremo, *whatever the objective truth of the matter, I feel like a lazy, incompetent, shitty, useless* insult *to the memory of Bolivar.*

I so want to be down there, where the action is, and I so don't *want to be here, nursemaiding a bunch of aviation and logistics pussies, my own tanks, a marginal company of infantry, and an even more questionable company of MP's. How will I hold my head up in the club after this? What will I say to my grandson—assuming my daughter produces one—when he asks me,* "Abuelo, *what did you do in the liberation of Guyana?"*

I'll have to tell him something like that gringo general supposedly said, "Grandson, I shoveled mierde in Tumeremo."

Shit. I . . .

"What the hell was that? On the radio?" Rojas asked.

A runner from the Ops tent pattered up the grassless strip in front of Rojas's tent. He managed to tangle himself up in the mosquito netting strung across the door. Eventually, he gave up on the stuff and simply passed over his message. "Major, sir, the troops down at the ferry are under attack."

There is *a God,* Rojas exulted, leaping up and leaving his breakfast behind and the runner still tangled in the netting.

As Rojas reached the flap to the Operations tent he heard the message, heartbreaking and infuriating, both, "They're . . . they're shooting my men in the back as they flee over the river."

"Two things," Rojas said to the officer on duty, "in this

order: Assemble the tanks and the infantry, with enough trucks to carry them, then tell higher what's going on. But not until we've left here, understand?"

An adrenaline rush coursing through his veins, Rojas looked skyward and said, aloud, "Thank You."

San Martin de Turumban, Venezuela

Insignificant, Cazz sneered as the return fire chipped bark from trees and dropped the occasional twig from overhead. With a grin he said, aloud, "These fuckers are never going to know what hit them. At least they won't if Lott in A Company does his job."

Cazz had an additional cause for satisfaction. This was the ferry, to all appearances undamaged, though draped with bodies. Indeed, the ferry's engine was still idling, putting a thin stream of diesel smoke into the air.

When I kick in Bravo company to stomp the enemy flat, we're gonna get the rest across this river in style.

Even light tanks can make a considerable racket. Thus, Lott heard their approach long before the outpost on his far right started reporting their order of march.

Lying in a bush, peering out toward the road, some sixty meters away, Lott, like his men, wore greasepaint to hide the features and the shine of his sweaty face. He held the firing devices—"clackers," in the parlance—for two directional mines, one in each hand. They'd be mostly useless against armor, of course, *though I might get lucky and cap a tank commander or two,* but they were the best things available to indicate to his entire company that the enemy column was exactly where he wanted it and that they should open fire. This was a partial exception to the rule on initiating an ambush with the greatest casualty-producing weapon available. When dealing with both an ambushing force and an enemy of these sizes, positioning of the target—and making sure it was all in the kill zone—was more important than getting a few more kills with the first blow.

From where he lay, Lott could see all the way to the leftmost end of the ambush position nearly four hundred meters away. That would be his key to fire, when their point reached it. To his right, also, Lott could see far up the road. Indeed, his heart leapt as he saw the lead enemy tank, barrel-assing down the road and churning up enough dust that, *Ah, shit, I'm not going to be able to see their point when they reach my left flank. Damn the things you never really think of.*

Lott's heart, which had begun pounding at his first glimpse of the enemy, started to beat so strongly that it almost felt as if he were being tossed a few inches into the air with each stroke.

Four RPG's, and not just any old RPG's, but RPG-29 Vampires, were a lot of firepower.

At his level, Master Sergeant John Biltz, the platoon leader for Second Platoon, didn't have to worry about signaling; he was the one being signaled to. Thus, he had all four of the Vampires near him, on line, and aimed up the road. Two he had set on the same point; that lead tank *must* die, to block the road. The other two, farther to his left, were aimed at points beyond where he intended to kill that first tank.

The Vampire was a bit of an odd duck in the great RPG clan. Much heavier than most, at twenty-seven pounds unloaded, it was really a crew-served weapon in a way that, say, the old RPG-7 had not been. It actually had more in common, and not just in its weight class, with the U.S. Army's old M-67 recoilless rifle. As a heavy piece, it was best, when used in an ambush, to set it for a target and wait for the target to line itself up. Moreover, like the old M-67, it had a monopod for stability. Indeed, since the rocket burned itself out completely before ever leaving the tube, it was, in practice, more of a smoothbore recoilless than it was a rocket launcher.

It didn't have quite the accuracy of the M-67, despite being a much newer design. But what it lacked in accuracy, it more than made up for in punch. The Vampire could defeat explosive reactive armor and *still* burn through thirty inches of steel.

The Scorpions Biltz could see rolling in his direction had, at best, about three percent of that, and aluminum, not steel.

Wide eyed, wide eyed enough, in fact, that the Venezuelans probably could have seen his whites if they'd been looking, Biltz watched the Scorpions roll closer and closer. They were soon well past the point where the commander should have fired his claymores, initiating the ambush.

"What the fuck . . ."

One of the Vampire gunners, his target gone past his scope's line of sight, shot Biltz a questioning, even fearful, glance.

★CHAPTER THIRTY-EIGHT★

If the sky that we look upon
Should tumble and fall
And the mountains should crumble to the sea
I won't cry, I won't cry, no I won't shed a tear
Just as long as you stand, stand by me
—Ben King, "Stand by Me"

Nine Miles North of San Martin de Turumban, Venezuela

Master Sergeant Biltz had two nicknames in the regiment. One, Blitzen, as in Santa's reindeer, was used to get his goat. The other, though, Blitz—*Lightning*—was altogether more serious and an indicator that everyone had faith in his ability to think and act like lightning when under pressure.

He was already rolling—*no time*—toward the nearest Vampire gunner—*to clear the backblast area*—when the nearest Venezuelan Scorpion—*no time*—was about fifty meters away—*to even aim.*

Biltz—Blitz—snatched the Vampire from its gunner's hands and stood upright, slinging the thing to one shoulder as he did. Automatically, his right leg stepped back as he lined the muzzle up approximately with the center of the light tank.

Now it was a Venezuelan soldier's eyes that grew wide at the apparition of an enemy growing straight up from the ground with what looked like a murderous weapon aimed at *him*. Caught between trying to give commands to his crew and trying to swing his own machine gun around, the tank commander succeeded in neither before Biltz fired.

Three things combined to knock Biltz silly. One was that in his unavoidable haste to get the gun into action, he'd neither noticed, nor been able to do anything about it if he had noticed, that there was a rather large tree behind him at the moment he pulled the trigger. The backblast from the rocket hit that tree, bounced off, and effectively slapped him from behind with a vaporous two by four. The second was that, a mere fraction of a second later, the warhead hit the tank, exploding and hitting Biltz from in front with a another figurative two by four. He'd likely have stayed there, swaying in indecision between falling on his face and falling on his ass, except that that jet from the warhead managed to burrow its way into the Scorpion's ready ammo rack, setting it off, blowing the turret and the by now very dead tank commander into the sky, and knocking Biltz flat on his butt.

Lott caught a glimpse of the enemy tank turret rising through the trees, leaving a trail of thick smoke behind it. *Thank God!* His fingers clenched down on the firing devices, setting off the claymores farther forward. One of them hit nothing, so far as Lott could tell. But one was at least in the right position to sweep the rear half of a truck overloaded with infantry. A dozen men or more went down, screaming and shrieking in a spray of blood and gore, while the remainder added a chorus of horror experienced too near at being covered with bits and drops of their comrades.

Lott heard only a couple of the distinctive blasts from his Vampires; they, quite properly, were waiting for a target to come to them. The machine guns, however, along with the rifles, began a continuous volley that sounded like nothing so much as cloth being ripped. That continuous volley, then, was punctuated by more Vampires, and still more as ones that were fired were reloaded and began a more active hunt for targets.

Rojas couldn't feel his legs and was reluctant to look down to see if they were still there. His left arm, he knew— he couldn't help but know—*wasn't* there anymore. Rojas thought that maybe it might be on the ground, on the other side of the tank. His right hand still gripped the machine gun, pintle-mounted atop the turret, but he didn't have the strength to move it. Though he could feel, even more than hear, the firing of heavy weapons, no more rockets were coming his way now. He was distantly aware of that, just as he was distantly aware of the probable reason—the flames arising from the driver's hatch. He wasn't in any pain. If he'd had any doubts about whether or not he was dying, that fact would have dispelled them.

Too eager . . . I was too eager. Damn.

Slowly, reluctantly, Rojas' fingers relaxed their grip on the machine gun. His head nodded forward slowly, finally coming to rest on the edge of his own hatch. *Too . . . eager.*

San Martin de Turumban, Venezuela

Even nine miles away, and even before Lott called to confirm, Cazz knew, because he heard, that the ambush had been sprung. It was time.

"B Company, commence your attack."

From the woods to the right, on the other side of the river, a banshee howl arose, interspersed with heavy machine gun fire and an unmistakable barrage of Vampires, firing thermobaric warheads.

"And don't fuck with my soon-to-be trucks!"

There were a dozen of them, including the three trucks Lott had managed to salvage and send back. The trucks were mostly much the worse for wear, and Lott's haul still dripped blood, but Cazz expected they'd last the sixty-odd miles by road to Tumeremo. Delta and Bravo Companies, with two squads of engineers—the other was running the ferry—plus the bulk of the scout platoon and some of the heavy mortar platoon, was loading them, rather *over*loading them, even now.

To the west, a pillar of smoke arose from the large airfield, where the scouts had managed to catch that one plane on the ground before finishing off the defenders and moving to rejoin the battalion.

Down at the river, the ferry was moving supplies across as the mule train staggered up to the load point. At about thirty laden animals a trip, it was slow going. There weren't any bodies on the ferry anymore; the troops had unceremoniously pitched those over the side, to float downstream.

A half dozen of the trucks had a 120mm mortar attached to their towing pintles. Some of the spillover among the troops hung onto two overloaded Tiunas they'd captured. A line of mortar maggots were even further overloading those, and the trucks, with ammunition they pulled from the backs of the much-relieved mules, as those came across by ferry. A third Tiuna Cazz had grabbed for himself, with Singh at the wheel. The battalion supply sergeant was working on getting a fourth up and running. The S-4 himself sat in the back of Cazz's commandeered vehicle.

Also down by the ferry, a bevy of about fifty Venezuelan POWs sat in the shade under guard. Cazz had ordered that only walking wounded be used for that. He had some few of those. He also had some dead: one scout, two men from Delta, one from Bravo, and eight from Alpha. The Venezuelan tanks had not died easy, nor without a fight, despite being caught in such a shitty position.

Time matters more than ammunition, men, or—in this case—even organization, Cazz thought. *And enough of it's been wasted.*

He strode to the Tiuna and stepped up onto the hood, via the bumper. "Five minutes!" he bellowed, loudly enough to be heard even over the uneven coughing of the trucks' diesel engines.

Tumeremo, Venezuela

Looking through his field glasses at the encampment

around the airfield a few miles south of the town, Master Sergeant Austin grinned. *It's like looking at* Bambi Meets Godzilla, *he thought. The wide eyed innocence . . . the flurry of nervous activity . . . this pervading sense of doom. Hehehe.*

"Hey, sergeant," said Austin's radioman, "de colonel, he wan' you."

The sergeant dropped the binoculars, rolled to his back, and took the microphone from an outstretched hand. "Austin here, sir."

"We're coming, Sergeant. We've got the ferry and we've got some badly overloaded trucks. What's the situation there?"

Unseen, the sergeant nodded. "They seem to be aware of what happened, and are currently somewhere between stout defense and panic mode."

There was a brief delay. Apparently the battalion commander was musing on something. Finally, he asked, "Can you call in the heavy mortars? We didn't have time to load more than maybe fifty rounds, but if you think that might scatter them . . ."

"It might. No promises; I don't read minds. But, yes, I can adjust."

"Stand by."

Highway Ten, South of Tumeremo, Venezuela

Driving at a bone jarring pace, they'd only halted only once and only long enough to enable Delta Company to pick up their AT gunners. The ambush position had been a sickening sight and an even more sickening smell, with the stench of burned bodies, blood, and cordite mixing in the air. With no more ceremony or time given than required to physically haul the Vampires and their crews, plus Delta's weapons platoon sergeant aboard, the column set off again, moving as fast as the dirt road would permit.

At the intersection of the road to San Martin and Highway Ten the column turned right, onto the good asphalt of the latter. The ride immediately smoothed.

"Faster, my brothers!" Cazz had intoned over the radio.

Cazz consulted his map and his GPS, and then mentally reviewed the ground ahead. He looked right and thought, *That will do*. Having reached a decision, he held one hand up beside Singh's face, the hand clenched into a fist. The batman stopped. Behind the Tiuna, the column of trucks likewise came to a halt, amidst a symphony of screaming brakes.

Pointing to a flat spot off to the right, Cazz bellowed, "Mortars, unass the trucks and get your guns. You set up there. Emphasis on getting at least one section laid in, in a hurry. And *don't* forget your fucking ammunition. Mortar platoon leader?"

A lieutenant, though he'd left the Marine Corps as a captain, ran up and saluted.

"You set up there. Master Sergeant Austin has priority of fires. Give me a high sign when you've got everything you need."

"I need about three hundred more rounds, sir."

Cazz snarled, "Don't waste my time. Everything you need of what's available."

"Yessir."

★ ★ ★

"Mount up," Cazz ordered. "Go, Singh."

With the mortars hastily laying in behind him, the column set off again up the highway. Here it was good asphalt and they made good time accordingly. At a point where the road began the second leg of a broad S-turn, about four miles south of the town and a mile and a half from the airfield, Cazz again called a halt and stood up in the Tiuna.

"D Company," he shouted, pointing north in the direction of a ridge that paralleled the highway, "our objective is the airfield on the other side of that ridge. Fix the enemy to the south of the field. Now dismount and *go!* The rest of you, follow me."

"Guns up," Sergeant Austin heard over the radio. "That is to say, one section of three is up and ready to fire. We've got limited ammunition, so use it sparingly."

"Roger," Austin replied. "Adjust fire. Grid."

"Adjust fire, grid, over . . ."

The fire mission was interrupted by Cazz's voice. "Stay the fuck away from the supplies and the trucks, Austin. We need those."

There was a rattling from overhead and forward as B Company dismounted a kilometer north of the end of the S-turn. The rattling ended just before a very loud explosion shook the air.

Newman, the B Company commander, raced up, half out of breath.

"I'm going with you," Cazz said. He pulled open his map and began to point. "We're going to move straight north into those trees, then form on line and face left.

Yeah, yeah, drill's got no place on the battlefield . . . except when it does. This is one of those times." A stubby, stout finger tapped Newman's chest. "Move, Captain."

Turning to his S-4, still in the back of his Tiuna, Cazz said, "*You* stay safe. Here. And, need I repeat, *safe*? We're going to need you and your people to sort the supplies, take what we need, destroy the rest, and get us moving again."

"More fun than herding cats," Austin chuckled, as a heavy round slammed into the ground about a hundred meters from a group of milling about, apparently leaderless MP's. They began to run in the opposite direction.

"Adjust fire, shift," Austin said into the radio. *Hehheheh*.

He called in the shift of target, making sure that he kept it far away from his own people, maneuvering down the north. Then he saw through his glasses a company emerging from some tree-covered low ground, east of the field.

Won't be long, now.

Cazz stood almost precisely where the hard surface of the western portion of the runway gave way to the dirt of the eastern half. On both sides, columns of smoke arose from deliberately burned helicopters. He counted almost three dozen such pyres. There were a few others from fixed wing aircraft caught on the ground. At the bases of several pyres were helicopter gunships, basically upgraded Hinds.

"I was worried about those," he admitted to himself. "I'm still worried about their air force."

Most of the battalion was scattered around the airfield, with their looted trucks. Nearly forty more trucks, from cargo to fuel to long beds with trailers, were lined up in groups of three to five north of the strip. Some of those were the dozen he'd started with. Others were newly acquired. Slowly, too slowly, the trucks were being loaded with loot from the dumps.

We're lucky, too, that the Venezuelans had a mix of ammunition. Most of their people are carrying 7.62 Kalashnikov. Enough of them have 5.45 for us to take two thousand rounds per man, or so. They don't have the mortar ammunition for our 120's. But they did have a couple of thousand rounds of Russian 120mm. We can use that, even if the range is comparative shit and the firing tables on both sides all wrong. We'll figure the right factors for range adjustment, given a little time. For a wonder, we got a few thousand rounds for our light mortars. Fuel, we've got now, in abundance. Food is food and we've captured enough to feed the battalion for about six months. There was even a pile of mines. Damned considerate of Hugo to provide them, and I'll tell him so to his face, if I ever get the chance. God knows why they bothered carrying light antiair missiles here—doctrine, I suppose—but thank God they did. I only had twelve of them before. Now we've got over a hundred.

And, when the two dozen trucks I sent back for Alpha Company and the rest get here, we'll move out. Hope there's . . .

Cazz stopped thinking and started shouting as, from the west, a flight of four Sukhois rolled into an attack.

★CHAPTER THIRTY-NINE★

War was so destructive, argued the false prophets of fake
enlightenment, that only a madman would start one.
—Walter Russell Mead

Miraflores Palace, Caracas, Venezuela

The news of the attack into Venezuelan territory—different
not merely in kind but in principle from the mining of
her harbors—fell not so much like a thunderclap as like
the news of yet another mudslide in Caracas, a thing that
left most silent with horror, and others—those most
affected—dead.

Outside the palace, people gathered by groups and
individuals until there was a mass there as large as that for
any preplanned rally. The crowd was silent for the
moment, but for a confused murmuring.

And that murmuring, thought Chavez, *could as easily
turn into "hang the bastard"—with me being the bastard
in question—if I can't redirect it and salvage the campaign.
Above all, we must get our harbors clear so we can import
food. The few little ports the enemy missed mining just*

aren't enough. He listened again to the forming crowd. *And it's a* bad *sign that they've managed to gather so early in the day.*

Everyone in Chavez's conference room *cum* command post stood respectfully as he entered.

"Seats," he ordered. There was a scraping and shuffling as men, most of them uniformed and most of those overweight, sat down on their well-padded duffs. The atmosphere in the room was far, far past "tense." Truth be told, it was almost all the way up to panic-stricken.

"All right," said the president, "what do we do now? Intel, you first."

A man, uniformed and portly like most of the rest stood. "Mr. President," briefed the chief of Venezuela's intelligence service, "there's not a lot we *can* do." It took everything the man had to keep panic out of his own voice. Indeed, it said something good for Intel that he was able to speak as forcefully and openly as he did.

"Navy says Second Marine Brigade is unfit for combat, having spent most of the last four months getting First Brigade ready. Army tells me that there are no forces between Tumeremo and the Orinoco to throw into the mercenaries' way. They also insist that with the loss of most of their helicopter fleet they can't pull back the 5th Division or the Parachute brigade from Guyana—the parachute brigade that just *closed* on Guyana, actually, and that the soonest the lead elements of the Novena Division can get into the area is three days from now. Even if we hadn't moved them to the Colombian border—"

"There'll be no pullback from Guyana." Chavez's tone was absolute, brooking no question or argument.

"Which movement the Colombians have matched and overmatched, Mr. President," said Hugo's Chief of the Army Staff, Quintero. "Between the cross border raids you"—the general cleared his throat—"*authorized* FARC to undertake, and the fact that we've moved the rest of the army, minus your own guards, to the Maracaibo area, they've gotten frightened. There are usually two Colombian divisions in or close to the border region. Now there are four, there or moving there, and the divisions appear to be receiving an additional brigade each. In terms of raw numbers . . . that's about a hundred and forty thousand soldiers, Mr. President, against which we have under twenty thousand in the area."

Chavez looked considerably paler than usual already. Still more color drained from his face at the news. Some of that was perhaps that he'd been spending so much time indoors. More was fear. He felt his revolution hanging in the balance, even as he felt a purely psychosomatic noose tightening around his neck.

This was not *supposed to happen. It should have been easy. Up until a couple of days ago, it* was *easy. And now the country's laid out like a whore with her legs spread? Where* was *the mistake? The correlation of forces in Guyana favored us totally.*

Hugo looked intently at his intelligence chief. *You never spotted that battalion that was waiting to cross the border, did you? I wonder why? Did you want us to fail? You never spotted that the enemy could lay mines. I wonder why? And then there are those persistent rumors of high ranking officers being unhappy with me and wanting to do something about it.*

Nodding, as if he understood, Chavez looked around for the two personal guards stationed by the door. Pointing at the head of his intelligence service, Hugo's intent look changed to a glare, his face transforming itself into a mask of rage. His pointing finger trembled as the president said, "Arrest this man. Take him to Yare Prison. If he tries to escape, shoot him."

The way that was said, between the tone and the look on Chavez's face, the guards rightly took to mean, simply, "Take him outside and shoot him."

In the time between his former chief of intelligence being hauled off and the flurry of gunshots from just outside the palace, Chavez said nothing. Nor did he permit anyone else to speak. Instead, he glared at the large map mounted on the wall. The glare was replaced by a smile as soon as he heard the gunshots. The smile grew almost broad as the murmuring buzz from outside the palace walls began to diminish as the people, satisfied with the sacrifice, moved off.

After listening for a moment, Chavez said to Army, "Move the Novena Division to *Ciudad* Guayana, as quickly as possible. We'll have to delay the enemy some other way until Novena gets there."

To Nicholas, Chavez said, "Call off FARC and make kissy face with Colombia. Tell them, 'A terrible misunderstanding.' Offer them anything they want, within reason."

"What if FARC won't back off?" Nicholas asked.

"Then we arrest and shoot their high-living leaders."

Turning to the Air Chief of Staff, General Ortiz, Hugo asked, "What can you throw at them?"

With the example of the late chief of Intelligence before him, the Air Chief was understandably nervous. Still, he was by background a fighter pilot. Those are rarely the kind of men who can be frightened off all that easily. He arose to his feet.

"Not as much as we'd like, Mr. President," Ortiz said. Before Chavez could order him shot, as well, he hastened to add, "The problem is multifold. All of the Tucanos, minus the ones we've lost, are already forward in Guyana. Because of the logistic issues there, they've very limited fuel and ordnance. And they're far away. And slow.

"None of our F-16's are serviceable, since the gringos cut off our spares; something I really expected the current regime up there to have corrected by now. They have not, of course.

"Our F-5 fleet is close enough to intervene, but old. And we've been using them hard. Most are down for maintenance. They're not great strike aircraft, in any case."

Chavez let that go. Yes, he knew they were ancient birds, tired and worn.

"Of our forty-six Sukhois," Air continued, "fourteen are in for service. Again, we've been using them hard, Mr. President. Eleven are currently heading to or returning from a mission. Nine are on station, over Guyana. I'll have four ready to intervene at Tumeremo in about an hour, and can launch another four every two hours after that, assuming we launch no more missions into Guyana. I can do that until they simply break down from overuse."

Air, finished, sat down, looking significantly at the Army Chief.

Army said, "If I were that battalion commander,

assuming it *is* a single battalion, I wouldn't want to get over thirty tons of ordnance dropped on my head every two hours for however long it takes."

"Which brings me to my next question," Hugo said. "All this time we've been presupposing that there were three or even four battalions of Guyanans led by gringo mercenaries. That's why we haven't attacked their base yet, yes? If one of them is here, in Venezuela, I wonder how many beyond that one might not be at their base, either."

Army shrugged. "Perhaps the late chief of Intelligence could have told you, sir. I can say with considerable certainty, because our troops have run into them in their patrols, that there are *some* of them, at least, dug in and defending Bartica and points south, along the Essequibo. That, and that their heavy battalion is unlikely to be too far from their base because they can neither hide it, nor support it, very far from there. I can also say, again with considerable certainty, that if you pull our air away from pounding their base area—more importantly, soaring overhead *threatening* to pound anything that moves—we might find that heavy battalion showing up somewhere we don't want them to show up at.

"I can also say—and this time with complete certainty—that our troops at Kaieteur Falls have barely budged from their airstrip there, so we don't know if the enemy heavy battalion is at the base, east of it, or even considerably south of it."

Hugo pounded the conference table hard enough to upset coffee cups. "And *why* are they still sitting on their asses there? Do I need to have another officer shot?"

"It's not unwillingness, sir," Army replied. "There are no roads from Kaieteur and where that brigade is supposed to move to. He can't send more than a fraction of his men very far from there or they'll starve."

Hugo's eyes narrowed. He stood and walked around the conference table to the far wall. There, he peered closely at the map. His finger tapped it. "I see an airport between the Potaro River and Mahdiana Eagle Mountain. If he's supplying by air at Kaieteur, why not there?"

"Dirt field, Mr. President," the Army Chief answered. "Dirt and short. We can use it, with small aircraft, lightly loaded. But not enough to supply more than a battalion." *And a battalion would be tough. Moreover, for every ton we land there we could land almost two someplace else. But you're not going to listen to that, are you?*

"Then move a fucking battalion there!" Chavez nearly screamed, pounding the map with a clenched fist. "And arrange some animal transport to support a second battalion there! Take the fucking initiative away from the enemy! *Jesus*, how did any of you people ever get promoted to general? Is the highest competent officer in the army a fucking major?"

"Yes, Mr. President . . . I mean, no, Mr. Presid . . . I'll give the orders."

Hugo turned to his foreign minister, Nicholas, "Speaking of which, have the Brazilians agreed to let us rent vehicles and buy *food*, at least, to ship across the border?"

"Oddly enough, Mr. President," Nicholas replied, "they were supposed to sign the agreement this afternoon. About the time they should have gotten the word about

Tumeremo, they backed off. I begin to think they doubt our eventual success."

"Portuguese-speaking bastards," Hugo sneered. His face scrunched up in thought for a moment. Then he said, "Get one of my planes, one of the smaller ones, to take me to Kaieteur."

Cheddi Jagan Airport, Guyana

At least some supplies were getting through by vehicle from Georgetown. It was irregular, intermittent, and rarely exactly what was needed, but it portended better things to come.

At least, it did, thought Larralde, returning to his command post after an interminable meeting at brigade.

"You'll be pleased to learn, Sergeant Major," said Larralde to Mao, as he walked through the door, "that we have permission to leave the perimeter."

Arrivillaga sat up at the makeshift desk the troops had thrown together for him. His face immediately grew suspicious. "Why?"

"Because a column of trucks was ambushed two nights ago on the road to Georgetown, and we lost three of them. Three, need I add, that we couldn't afford to lose?"

"The gringos?"

Larralde shook his head no. "Brigade doesn't think so. We didn't find a single white or Hispanic body, and the one prisoner said it was Guyanan reserves, acting on their own. '242 Company,' he said."

Mao scratched his head, trying to remember a long ago

intelligence brief. "Hmmm . . . there were only four of those companies. And that one was based . . . mmm . . . between Georgetown and New Amsterdam, yes?"

"Correct," Larralde agreed.

"What took the brigade so long?" Arrivillaga asked.

"They had to work out how far forward we'd sweep, against how far the Marines would go. We're going as far as the north edge of Friendship, a little town about a day's road march from here, or about three days moving tactically. The Marines are not to go south of three hundred meters north of that."

Mao nodded his head. "When do we move out?"

Larralde gave a chuckle that was totally devoid of mirth. "Two and a half hours ago, according to the order. You see, they didn't give it to me until the meeting was over and . . ."

"Right," the sergeant major agreed. He'd been in the Army a long time; this was nothing new. "I'll start working on finding that time machine. In the interim, will as soon as possible work for you, sir?"

"I think that'll do fine."

"As soon as possible," in Mao's capable hands, turned out to be under an hour.

"Would have been less, sir," he informed Larralde, "except that, since we're in brigade reserve, brigade had them digging a bunker . . . oh, not just any old bunker, no, sir. This one was fully thirty meters by fifteen, with . . . ah, fuggit. We're ready."

Mao had the company lined up in a well-spaced column, northwest of the control tower and pointed toward the

Demerara River. They'd move from there to East Bank Road, appropriately named since it paralleled the Demerara's east bank, then spread out in an echelon right to sweep the road from the riverbank to a line roughly eight hundred meters from it.

Before Larralde could give the order—"move out"—the company heard a big jet coming in from the left, already with its landing gear down. Resupply was always welcome, so, as one, every man and woman in the company turned head and eyes to face it. Larralde and Mao did, as well. Then they, like everyone else in the command, uttered something like, "Oh, shit," or, "ouch," or, in Mao's case, "Motherfucker," before immediately turning away in pain.

Thus they missed, as nearly every soldier on the base missed, the sight of the airplane—it was a chartered Rutaca Boeing 737-230—flipping over to one side and plowing into the ground, before spreading flames, bodies and body parts, and an awful lot of equipment, from the southeast point of the main airfield to past the control tower.

Larralde was seated and had his hands clasped over both his eyes when Mao found his way to him. The sergeant major had water running freely from his own eyes.

"Laser," he said. "Someone hit the flight crew with a laser. I thought those fucking things were illegal."

Larralde, still with his eyes covered, answered, "So's invading a sovereign country, but we did that anyway. And, if I understand it, it's not illegal to temporarily blind someone so they die, only to permanently blind them and leave them alive."

Mao wiped tears from his face and nodded. "Okay, if you say so. But we'd better get off our asses, anyway. Half blind or not, I think aerial resupply here has just become a problem, so we'd better get that road open and clear."

"Still a bunch of dirty bastards, legal or not," Larralde said.

★ CHAPTER FORTY ★

You know, I have one simple request.
And that is to have sharks with frickin' laser beams
attached to their heads!
—Dr. Evil, *Austin Powers: International Man of Mystery*

Four Miles North-northeast of Agricola Village, Guyana

Hosein, the colonel's driver, had met them when they'd left the SCIF, lugging the ZM-87 laser projector. He'd already had a small, uninflated rubber boat, a Zodiac Cadet Fastroller, along with a tiny electric outboard motor, loaded in the back of Stauer's Land Rover. The laser, its mount, and the batteries were placed on top of those.

From Lawyers, Guns, and Money, Hosein had taken them to pick up a pair of bicycles from the S-4, Harry Gordon, then around to various dumps and caches hidden in the small corners of the camp, as well as in the surrounding jungle. There was no trouble with any of this. Apparently the word had already been passed: "Whatever they need, if we've got it, give it to them."

They'd needed a lot. Besides rations, ammunition, and money, they'd needed a small generator to recharge the batteries. For that, Gordo had produced a Bourne BPP-2, a thirty-pound, man-packable hydroelectric device, with a suspension system for anchoring the thing under water and thus drawing power invisibly.

Between the laser, its batteries, the hydro generator, the food, the ammunition, and every other damned thing, the weight had come in at approximately three hundred and twenty-five pounds per man. Yes, they were ex-SEALS. Yes, they were intensely fit, physically. Yes, they were in their thirties, hence much younger than the regimental norm. But still, *three hundred and twenty-five pounds per man?* That was a bit much, hence the bicycles. Of course, loading those in any balanced way was tough, and took a night's trial and error.

Still, eventually they were packed; eventually they were at the bank of the Essequibo; and eventually they were on the other side, struggling with repacking the bicycles to the scheme they'd come up with before leaving. They also had to carry the roughly ninety-seven pound Zodiac inflatable and its motor. They made a total of four miles, pushing all the way, before they'd decided to rest.

The next night, even though fresh, had been worse, as they'd had to push the bicycles *up* the high ground that ran between the Essequibo and Demerara, paralleling those rivers. After that, going downhill, it hadn't gotten any easier, due to the difficulty in controlling the bikes. It had taken two more days to reach the Demerara River, north of Amsterdam and Dalgin.

There they'd met Captain Byng, who spoke remarkably

good and precise standard English, especially for the area. From that point, they'd been in "Injun Country," and they'd had to be very careful, staying off of anything even remotely reminiscent of a trail while they moved. Fortunately, they'd been able to reinflate the boat and take the Mahaica River nearly to Saint Cuthbert's. This had cut several days off the journey, although it had been a risk.

But, "No, they've nobody south of Saint Cuthbert's," Byng had assured them. "Beyond that," the captain had shrugged, "I can't tell you. I've got better commo with the regiment than I do with 242 Company."

They'd followed the edge of the marshy ground the Mahaica fed, staying just west of it, until their GPS had told them they were in the right area. From there, they'd hidden their equipment and found an enormous tree, with a thicker trunk than its neighbors and towering over them by as much as ten meters. They still couldn't see the Cheddi Jagan airstrip, itself, but they could see the space above it. Indeed, they could see planes taking off and landing by night and day.

By night, Che made a hide of woven branches, in among the tree's own. They'd actually uprooted entire plants, wrapped the root balls in plastic and bound those to the main tree. Some kinds of photography could detect the presence of chlorophyll, hence its absence. Dead branches, even if they looked green to the naked eye, could have served as a marker for, "Blast the ever loving crap out of this."

When they were ready, Morales lowered a rope. Then he and Simmons hauled the laser, *sans* tripod, up to it, securing it with bungee cords to the trunk, just loosely enough to aim and track a target that would be following a fairly precise line. One of the batteries, too, was hoisted up. That, however, was tied tightly to the tree and wedged down into a spot where a branch grew off to one side. Finally, Morales put in a rope sling so that he or his comrade could lean back to aim the thing, since it was configured like a heavy machine gun rather than a rifle.

Then they settled down to wait, taking turns in the firing position until just the *right* kind of target showed up: a big, fat, civilian, chartered cargo carrier.

Morales let his binoculars rest by the strap around his neck, calling out, "Simmons, we got one. Big fat blue and white Boeing, with a red belly and tail."

Simmons didn't say anything. Che shrugged, thinking, *Yeah, so it's dirty? So what? Orders are orders.*

Morales powered up the laser emitter, which came to life with a soft whine. Then he slipped into the rope sling and let himself rest back. Pulling a set of goggles from a breast pocket, he slipped those over his eyes. They'd been made expressly to guard against backflash from the frequencies the ZM-87 fired on. Sighting down the barrel of the thing, both hands gripped on the spades, Morales fired.

Rutaca Boeing 737-2S3, YV-216C, Over Cheddi Jagan Airport, Guyana

The pilots were bored.

Which is good, thought Captain Mueller who, quite

despite his name, looked approximately as darkly Venezuelan as Hugo Chavez did. *Nice easy loading, with disciplined troops from the army. None of them sniveling; though their collective sense of humor is a little odd. The stews are happy. And as soon as we refuel, it's back to Caracas where Stefania is, as usual, going to suck me off right here on my own chair before my wife comes to pick me up.*

Mueller flicked a switch, causing the landing gear to whine its way down to locked position. He made a quick glance at his altimeter, then eyeballed the approaching field because, like all good pilots, he really never entirely trusted sophisticated electronics.

Glancing down again at the instruments, then back up, Mueller pulled back on the yoke and . . .

Suddenly, his vision ended, replaced first by a green flash that seemed to come from everywhere and then by utter blackness as his overloaded optic nerves gave out for the nonce. He swore something unintelligible over the agonized scream of his copilot. Then the pain struck, causing him to clasp his hands over his eyes even as his legs spasmed in sympathy against the pedals. Unconstrained, the yoke went off on its own.

It hurt too much, far too much, for Mueller to even note the alarmed shouts of the passengers and his flight crew as the plane heeled over to port. He didn't even sense it heeling over.

Fortunately, it was only a couple of seconds between the blindness and the agony, and the wing digging into the tarmac of the field. It was even less than that before the nose of the plane jackhammered in, killing Mueller and starting the Boeing spinning end over end down the field, before it erupted in a great fireball.

Four Miles North-northeast of Agricola Village, Guyana

Che couldn't see the plane actually impact, though he'd seen the movements that indicated there was no way it wasn't going to crash. He also saw the fireball rise, and then the column of smoke that followed it.

"We'll call that one a kill," he muttered.

"I take it you killed it?" Simmons asked from below.

"Oh, yeah."

"Do we move now, or wait for another one?" Simmons shouted up.

"I don't think we can risk one more shot from here," Morales judged. "We'd better do the bugout boogie."

Morales shook his head, mostly in regret. *No doubt it went down. Poor bastards. And, if we don't have sharks, I suppose SEALs will have to do. And it feels every bit as dirty as Simmons said it would. Shitty way to fight a war.*

Tumeremo Airfield, Venezuela

It wasn't very likely that more than a dozen of his men heard Cazz's warning shout. On the other hand, he wasn't the only one shouting, and for any that missed those, the rising rattle of just about anything the battalion had that would shoot—antitank weapons excepted—generally sufficed to get their attention. For any that might have missed either of those, the impact of ten S-13OF rockets, two pods' worth, fired by the lead Sukhoi and impacting along the field about a half a second apart, was probably enough to catch their interest. And if *that* failed, there was the three-ton truck, spinning as it arose into the air, after one rocket went off directly underneath it.

Cazz had thrown himself to the dirt as soon as he saw the flash from under the attacker's wings. The explosions that followed felt like they were picking him up and slamming him back to earth, repeatedly. Even before those bludgeons ended, he heard chunks of metal buzzing overhead. Someone screamed in agony; one of his Guyanans, he thought.

Soon enough, that first scream was joined by so many that it wasn't possible even to guess at the source. Men cried out for medics. Some of those cries were in Spanish, so at least some of the fragments must have struck among the POWs. Someone—Cazz thought it was his sergeant major, Webster—shouted, "Get a fucking missile on that son of bitch!"

Rolling over to his back and looking up and around, Cazz saw two of the aerial attackers circling overhead, and the one that had just attacked pulling up to join the circle.

That leaves . . . oh, fuck!

The next plane came in at the airfield crossways, and pointed almost directly at the battalion commander. He rolled over and scrambled first to hands and knees, then to his feet as he raced to get out of its path. He fell twice, rolling back to his scrambling feet with an agility that belied his age. The whole time—a seeming eternity—Cazz kept throwing glances over one shoulder.

The plane was low and parallel to the ground when Cazz saw it release two silvery cylinders from the hardpoints under its wings. He had one thought, voiced as soon as it came to his mind:

"NAPAAALLLMMM!"

Cazz ran for his life, parallel to the plane's line of flight. His back suddenly felt intensely hot, even as he felt the hair on the back of his head crisp and curl. He also felt, cutting through his soul, the heartbreaking shrieks of the dozen or so of his troopers caught in a fiery, agonizing death.

The planes had barely departed before the noncoms and junior officers began bringing a little order out of airstrike-induced chaos. It was something one could expect with a good battalion.

And these boys, Cazz thought, *my Americans and my Guyanans, both, are good.*

"Thirty-seven dead, sir," Sergeant Major Webster reported. Normally that would have been the battalion adjutant's job. He, however, was one among a small group of charred corpses, their arms and legs burned into fetal positions, on one side of the airfield. "That we know of. Thirteen more missing. Thirty-two more or less wounded, mostly from Headquarters Company. We don't know how many of the POWs got plastered. Scores, anyway, since they were all grouped together. Our heavy mortar platoon took it particularly bad."

Cazz nodded, saying, "I thought it would be worse."

Webster shrugged, the classically imperturbable *primus pilus*. "Everyone expects that kind of aerial attack to be worse. Still, it was bad enough. The worst thing is it cost us time. And they'll be back, them or their buddies. Soon."

"Yeah," Cazz agreed. "We've got to get the fuck out of here, fast."

"All the trucks, at least, are fueled, sir," the S-4 said. The loggie sounded infinitely weary. His uniform was speckled with drops of blood that had come from someone else. "The ammunition we captured is still enough to do us for a while, but it's mostly not loaded yet."

Cazz rubbed a hand along the back of his head, brushing away the burnt stubble. His other hand fished in a leg-mounted cargo pocket for his map. He unfolded that and measured the distance to his target by eye. "About a hundred and twenty miles," he said. "Two hours, maybe. Maybe less if we really haul ass. If they come back and catch us on the road, we'll get hurt. If we stay here, eventually we'll cease to exist as an organized force."

"Once we're in *Ciudad* Guayana, sir," Webster said, "they'll have a hard time using air on us for *political* reasons. They'll have to dig us out by hand. These are good boys; that won't be easy."

The S-4 added, "Sir, they'll probably leave us alone here once you start rolling north. I've got a better chance of loading the necessary supplies with them concentrating on you than if they're able to concentrate on us, here, as a group. If you move out, I can probably get you enough by this evening, before midnight, anyway, assuming you make sure the road's clear."

"So we say, 'fuck it and drive on'?"

"Boot, don't spatter," Webster replied.

"You've been listening to Reilly," Cazz accused.

"It's not a crime."

Cazz shook his head. "Some places it is. Anyway, Sergeant Major, have the bugler sound the fucking charge. We're going to *Ciudad* Guayana."

"Good," Webster said, then added, "You know, we really need something to take care of the air. The missiles just don't cut it. I'm thinking lasers."

★ CHAPTER FORTY-ONE ★

War, war, is still the cry, "War even to the knife!"
—Byron, *Childe Harold's Pilgrimage*

Mahdiana Eagle Mountain, Guyana

Sergeant Michaels handed a written message to his radio bearer. "Encrypt this and get it to the TOC"—the Tactical Operations Center, basically the First Battalion command post—"immediately." The message contained the locations and composition of every Venezuelan unit Michaels had seen emerge from the jungle to set up housekeeping in and around Mahdia, Guyana, over the last several days. The message would go out compressed and over a half-rhombic antenna, just to be sure. There were, after all, about eight hundred Venezuelan troops within five miles, by Michaels' best estimate, and he really didn't want them to learn they were being watched from above.

At that, Michaels was by no means content with the information he'd been able to gather. He had rough positions—"estimated company digging in across road two kilometers north of Mahdia"—for example. "Heavy mortar platoon, believed 120mm, one thousand meters southwest of Mahdia Airport," for example. "C-12 Huron or Beechcraft King Air, landed Mahdia airport, 0621 hrs, believed unloaded Class IV, to include mines," for example.

It was all good, but it wasn't quite enough.

Lawyers, Guns, and Money (SCIF), Camp Fulton, Guyana

Boxer outranked Reilly, both when they had been a part of the United States' forces and, here and now, in the regiment. If Reilly cared about that, it was tolerably hard to see as the fist from his uncasted arm pounded Boxer's desk and his voice made George Washington and his boat crew, hanging on the concrete walls, shake.

"I"—bang—"don't"—bang—"give"—bang—"a"—bang—"good"—bang—"flying fuck about the welfare of your fucking RPV's!" Bang-bang-bang-bang-bang. "I need two of them over Mahdia!" Bang-bang-bang-bang-bang-bang. "Tomorrow!" BANG!

Boxer smiled. Reilly was basically all right, in his book, but took certain techniques to handle. And you couldn't back down to him, not even once.

He smiled and said, "Calm down, asshole. Or take your theatrics somewhere else."

Reilly shrugged and smiled back. He wasn't even deflated. Instead he said, "Well, it was worth a try. But, no shit, Ralph, I *need* real time intelligence tomorrow morning."

"Yeah," the Chief of Staff agreed, "you do. But you won't get it if our RPV's just go out of our control and crash, will you? Like they started crashing over Kaieteur Falls."

"But this isn't Kaieteur Falls," Reilly insisted. "It's thirty miles to east and we've got no indication that Hugo's set up anything to interfere with radio control."

Boxer agreed, nodding very deeply, and then pointing out, "We didn't see any special radio electronic equipment around the falls, either, but our scout birds still went out of control and crashed."

"Static electricity from the water?" Reilly offered.

Boxer raised one eloquent oh-that's-such-bullshit eyebrow.

"Oh, hell, I don't know," Reilly conceded, "but, look, the MI guys didn't lose control until the things were within twelve miles of the falls, right? Alternatively, they didn't lose control until the things were about fifty miles from the control station. But the control station's rolling with me, and the RPV's won't be more than twenty miles ahead of us, if that."

"Well . . . okay, yes, that's true."

"So take a chance, Ralph. Or, rather, have Bridges take a chance. It could mean life or death for my people."

Boxer's face twisted a bit. He tapped his intercom and said, "Bridges? Come see me in twenty minutes."

After Bridges answered, "Yessir," Boxer turned his attention back to Reilly. Pointing, he said, and his voice was not genial, "You get out of here. Go find your wife and fuck her while you and she can. But . . . if you *ever* think you can come in here and pound on *my* fucking desk again, I'll have you in the same jail where nobody speaks anything you do, the one where you sent those three assholes from Brazil—Kamarang, wasn't it?—so goddamn fast you won't know what hit you.

"And I'll get back to you about the RPV's."

Which means I get them, Reilly thought. *Shame to have to act like a spoiled brat over it, but I didn't make the world, or the human race; I just have to deal with them as I find them.*

Field Hospital, Camp Fulton, Guyana

Ordinarily, the best protection for a field hospital, in time of war, was to be out in the open, and *plainly* marked. It might have been here, too, but, since the Venezuelan Air Force had crumpled the permanent hospital in the initial attack, they couldn't assume it. Thus it was scattered about the jungle, in several score tents, those laying a long arc roughly paralleling the Kaburi River.

It wasn't convenient. It wasn't nearly as sanitary. And people died from both of those factors, in retail fashion. But that was still better than risking wholesale deaths to another airstrike.

Reilly had one of his battalion's Land Rovers, rather than his own. Fortunately, this one had an automatic transmission. For all he knew, and he strongly suspected, his old one was still sitting in the ditch. Reilly drove himself to a parking area, under some netting and with the thick, interwoven jungle canopy above. After stopping at a likely looking spot, he beeped twice, then spun the wheel and began to back up. When he got out he dragged with him a piece of a green tarp, which he draped over the windshield. Rather, he tried to drape it. One arm just wasn't a very effective means to do the job.

He was almost ready to give up when he heard a familiar voice from behind him, "Oh, Ranger buddy."

There is a God.

Reilly turned around, a corner of the tarp still clutched in his left hand. "First Sergeant Coffee," he asked, "could you give me a hand with this motherfucker?"

"I'll do better than that," Coffee said. "I'll drape it on myself. You, on the other hand, can do me a big favor by going to the medical company CP"—Coffee's left hand indicated a direction—"finding my company commander and your lovely albeit somewhat fat for the moment wife, and screwing her silly. Or whatever it takes to get her to stop acting like a loon."

"That bad, huh?"

Coffee rolled his eyes. "You have no . . . okay, well maybe you have *some* idea. Seriously, boss, she's climbing the walls. Maybe it's the hornies; maybe it's the hormones. Maybe— and I think this likely, although frankly inexplicable—she's been worried about you, too."

Coffee took the tarp and began draping it properly. "But do *something*, would you?"

Lana, Reilly thought, holding his wife tightly, albeit one-armed, *crying on my or* anyone's *shoulder? That's just not like her.*

She'd met him at the tent flap door with a gasp, a huge smile, instant tears despite the smile, and a slightly erratic, waddling gait. The waddle wasn't so much from being all that front heavy, as that she was normally so slender even a small offset to center of gravity was enough to throw off her stride. After a few moments of being held, while crying, she pulled away from him for a moment. The sobbing stopped. Then she looked up and said, "You son of a bitch! I've been worried sick about you, about the baby, about *everything*. And do you call? No. Stop by to check on me or the baby? No. Bastard!"

And then she was sobbing again, into his shoulder, as if she'd said nothing of the kind.

All of which goes to show not that I've got something to learn about women, especially pregnant ones, but that I know *nothing about women, especially pregnant ones. But at least I don't think it's the sex she's been missing.*

At which point Lana backed off again, gave him a nasty, dirty look, but took his hand and led him off to her own nearby tent for a little . . . privacy.

Standing not too very far from Lana's tent, Coffee and Doc Joseph smirked while smoking one of Coffee's vile cigarettes. The doctor never, of course, bought cigarettes. This didn't stop him from bumming them from time to time.

"Think it'll help?" Coffee asked, as the tent flap closed behind the couple.

"Can it hurt?" Joseph asked, with a broad grin across his face. "I was ready to try the old sex prescription trick . . . or anything else I could think of that might have settled her down."

Coffee answered, "No, Doc, probably won't hurt any. How about you? You still hurting?"

"Good question," Joseph said, sobering. "And not one I particularly want to answer." He tossed the cigarette to the ground. "And on that note, I need to go make my rounds."

"Cazz's battalion gave us our window," Reilly told his wife, as the two lay together, fitted like spoons, front to back, on an altogether too narrow military folding cot. The cast on the arm he'd thrown over her was something less than comfortable, but better than no arm at all.

"While the Venezuelan air has been concentrating on him, I've been able to shuffle people around, move more freely to give orders, inspect, and buck up the troops, and push out a little more recon."

Lana faced the tent wall, her sweat-soaked back to him. She didn't turn as she said, "But they'll be back as soon as you start to move."

"Not quite as soon," he replied, confidently. "Bridges thinks all the air has been pulled north of the Orinoco River, all the way to Caracas in most cases. They're afraid Cazz is only resting for a day at *Ciudad* Guyana, and will roll on *Ciudad* Bolivar. He's left one bridge over the Caroni River open, after dropping the other two, just to give that impression. It will be anywhere from hours to a half a day before they can get onto us. Maybe more, depending on whether they've succeeded in moving the ground crews and the ordnance from their forward airstrips."

"But Cazz isn't going past *Ciudad* Guyana," she objected. "They'll be back forward."

"They don't know that. In their position, I'd be worried, too." Reilly gave a little laugh.

"What's funny?"

Unseen, he smiled. "Well . . . here I am, with the mechanized force, and there he is, with a light infantry force and some stolen trucks. But—while I'd have to dig in my books, assuming my library survived—"

"It did," she said. "I checked. Though the books are still there waiting for a bomb and the windows are blown out so the bugs can get at them."

His casted arm moved with a shrug. "Nothing to be done about that now. Anyway, while I'd have to check the books, I think Cazz and his—be it noted, *light* infantry battalion—are the current holders of the world historical record for miles of contested advance across the surface of the Earth. It was something like one hundred and ten miles in twenty-four hours, held by one of the SS formations in France in 1940. Third Battalion went well over that, maybe a hundred and sixty miles, in twenty-four hours."

"Then you'll have to beat that, won't you?"

Intersection, Bartica-Potaro Road and Issaro Road, Guyana

Sergeant Michaels had done good work, within his limited capabilities. Now, with two RPV's—for the nonce, at least, still under control—snooping over the Mahdia area, Reilly had a much better idea of what was facing him. Inside his TOC tent, he watched the map being updated as more and more information came in from his attached MI section.

Basically, it looked like he was facing one reinforced battalion.

A single Venezuelan infantry company was dug in along

the Potaro River, opposite Garraway Stream, which wasn't important because of a stream, nor because it was the locus of an unincorporated town, of sorts, but because there was a bridge there.

Even as Reilly watched, one of the TOC-rats began grease-penciling in a thin minefield on the southeastern bank.

"How do we know?" Reilly asked.

"The RPV's picked up the heat signatures of small, round, likely metal objects," answered his S-2, Sadd. "Matching that with Sergeant Michaels' report on mines being unloaded, and I think we're facing a minefield. Probably not dug in, and surely not with antihandling devices yet. But not something we want to charge through, anyway."

"Concur," Reilly said. "Trim, will the bridge take the tanks?"

Trim, the rump of whose company—including the bridge platoon—was attached to First Battalion, answered, "Yes . . . *but*. We're lucky that the old 1930's era suspension bridge went down in the nineties. What they put up to replace it is considerably better. Again, though, *but*. The bridge is not stout enough to stand the passage of seventeen upgraded T-55's, at forty-four tons each, charging across at full pelt. Still, if you take them across at a crawl—and I do mean a crawl, two or three miles an hour—the bridge should survive."

"Right," Reilly said. "We weren't going to charge the bridge anyway. One of your sapper platoons is going to have to go into the river to make sure the thing isn't wired for demolition."

Trim notably paled; that had potential to be a ghastly, bloody exercise. On the other hand, if ordered to do it, his troops would try. Therefore he had no choice but to lead them in it.

Looking back to the map, Reilly noted another infantry company, situated on the reverse slope of some high ground five miles east of Mahdia, right where the cattle trail from Konawaruk crossed the hills. The expected third company was in the town of Mahdia.

"Artillery?" Reilly asked.

"Here, sir."

"Except that I want a thin screen of smoke paralleling the far side of the river to either side of the bridge, your priority of fires are going to be to Bravo Company." He pulled a small laser pointer from a keychain attached to the loop of his trousers and pointed it at the map. The light rested on a spot just north of the Potaro River, and about three miles east-southeast of Garraway Stream. "I want you to support the attack across from here."

The battery commander, Bunn, short, stout, and balding, chewed his lip for a moment, then asked, "That's awfully close to the firing line, isn't it?"

"Yes, but nowhere here do I see any mortars that can range. And I don't think they've moved in anything longer ranged than a 120mm. And from that point I marked, you can support us all the way past Mahdia Airport."

"Sergeant Peters?" Peters led First Battalion's heavy mortar platoon.

A tall noncom—who could have had a direct commission in the regiment if he'd wanted it, but didn't—spat some tobacco juice into a can. "Here, sir."

"Your heavy mortar platoon is OPCON"—under the operational control of—"to the battery."

"Roger."

"Well," Bunn agreed, "the really nice part of firing from there is that the company east of Mahdia is lined up nicely right along the gun-target line. Their reverse slope won't do them a lot of good then. And we can use the shit ammunition."

"Quite. ADA?"

"Here, sir," said that battery commander. His unit, too, had given up attachments to the other battalions. Fully sixty percent of it, though, and all the self-propelled quad 23mm guns, was Reilly's."

"Split your coverage between Garraway Stream and the gunners."

"Wilco, sir."

"Scouts?"

"Here, sir."

"You have your platoon, plus the Elands from Third Battalion that didn't go to the Philippines. You are attached to Bravo Company."

"Roger, sir."

Reilly scanned around for a familiar face. He found one, but not the one he expected. "Maintenance?"

"Sir," said Dumisani, a Zulu who was, improbably enough, partnered with Dani Viljoen, a Boer. Dumisani had one of those South African voices that had made Ladysmith Black Mambazo an international sensation.

"Where's Viljoen?"

"Ass deep in a tank, sir, trying to get the turret not to squeal so much as it traverses."

"Does the turret work?"

"Oh, yes, sir. Well, it did before Dani built two tripods from trees and had it lifted."

"Tell him to drop it back."

"Yes, sir. Anyway, we're good to go, sir. Or will be, as soon as I tell Dani."

"Roger," Reilly said. "Bravo?"

"Here, sir," answered Snyder. He was a tiny sort, stature-wise, but approximately as broad in the shoulders as he was tall.

"You, my friend, are the main effort. While Alpha, Charlie-tank, the ditch diggers, and I make a great show of trying to get across the river at Garraway Stream, you, plus the scouts and Third Batt's Elands, with all the *scunion* the artillery and battalion mortars can bring to bear, are going to wade the river"—again Reilly's laser settled on a spot, this time by the town of Tumatumari—"here, move to Konawaruk, here, then attack to the west along the cattle trail, to seize Mahdia."

Snyder smiled broadly, if not quite as broadly as the span of his shoulders. "Wilco."

Reilly consulted his watch. "Gentlemen, at the tone the time will be . . . zero-one-five-three . . . ready . . . *tone*. We cross the line of departure in three hours and seven minutes, precisely at five AM."

With a truly evil smile, Reilly finished, "Let us make a joyful sound unto the Lord."

★CHAPTER FORTY-TWO★

> Panzergrenadiere,
> Vorwärts, zum Siege voran!
> Panzergrenadiere,
> Vorwärts, wir greifen an!
> —Robert Seeger,
>   "Lied der Panzergrenadiere"

Bartica-Potaro Road, Guyana

For the last two hours ground guides had been leading armored combat vehicles into position to either side of the road. The engines, once the vehicles were in place, were left running. A powerful, heavy, and usually much-abused engine, already running, was much more likely to keep running than one was likely to start again, once shut down.

The troops were used to the sound; they'd long since—decades since in many cases—learned to listen and speak over it. This included the not insubstantial minority who were half or more deaf from it. The Venezuelans, thirty miles or more away, were not going to hear it anyway, not even with all seventeen still functioning tanks, sixty-seven Elands, and twenty-one Ferrets,

Reilly flipped on his night vision goggles, watching a platoon from Charlie Company—five tanks, in this case— grind their way up to his left. The goggles flared suddenly, then went dark, as one and then another of the self-propelled quad 23mm guns opened up on something overhead. They were radar guided and really quite good pieces, although the Russians had newer and allegedly better systems on offer. The ripping-sail sound reached Reilly's ears a moment after the flash blacked out his NVG's. Then a much louder sound struck him, an aerial explosion in the one-ton range.

Most likely a Tucano, he thought, *both for the size of the explosion and that fact it was even around here. All the fast movers are busy fucking with Cazz in* Ciudad Guyana; *Tucanos are all that's in range of us. Come to think of it, I haven't seen many of those, lately, either. Probably Hugo's boys have supply issues at the main airport.*

Every combat vehicle in the column had a frequency-hopping radio. Thus, there was no need of clever call signs.

"Black Six, this is Bravo Six; ready to rock . . . Charlie Six Romeo, the old man says '*Es braust unser Panzer*' . . . Team Alpha, here; what's the hold up?"

Reilly flicked the switch on the side of his combat vehicle commander's helmet, announcing, "Black, this is Black Six. 'We'll come in low out of the rising' . . . oh, wait, wrong movie, wrong soundtrack."

His own vehicle crew literally giggled. Schiebel

thought, *The old man can be goddamned funny when action impends*. More than a few in the other First Battalion tanks and Elands snickered likewise.

One of the crewmen in his vehicle watched Reilly intently. As soon as he gave the signal, the crewman flicked a switch. Out from the loudspeakers mounted on several of the turretless Elands burst a jungle-shredding riff, followed by:

"I AM IRONMAN!"

"Now *that*," Reilly said into his boom mike, "*that* is the right soundtrack." He consulted his watch, waiting for the seconds to tick off. "Black, this is Black Six. Roll, mother-fuckers."

Engines that had been mostly idling roared to life and purpose. Hundreds of barely human voices began rising in an inarticulate scream of hate and rage. Over a hundred horns started to blare, creating a sound wall of pure aggression. They'd been bombed enough, and now it was payback time.

"HAS HE LOST HIS MIND . . ."

Nothing quite like Black Sabbath when you're going to go kick someone's ass.

M-1 Abrams tanks could sneak up on people, more or less. Their engines were quiet enough for it, in any case. No matter; M Day, Inc. owned no M-1's, nor was it likely they'd ever be allowed to buy any. T-55's, on the other hand, which they did have, weren't going to sneak up on anyone not completely deaf. However much updated, they were still powered by conventional diesels. That meant a roar that could be heard miles away. Elands?

They were better, but not by much. And that didn't matter either, because the tanks' roar overrode the lesser cacophony of the wheeled vehicles. As for great heavy trucks hauling cannon? They added a few decibels, but not so much that anyone would notice over the tanks and APC's.

So the wise soldier didn't bother with sneaky things. Instead, he put his efforts into making the most noise possible, creating the greatest terror in the hearts of his opponents that that noise could generate. If he could throw in a little high explosive, too, that was all for the better. If he could be sneaky somewhere else, with something quieter than tanks, that was good, too.

Tumatumari, Guyana

Company B had been in the lead of the column, with battalion's scouts, reinforced with Third Battalion's turreted Elands, in the lead of the company. When the company reached the intersection of Konawaruk Road and Bartica-Potaro Road, Bravo split off to the south, aiming for the ford at Tumatumari. The maps said there was a bridge. That was wrong. What there was, was a marginally navigable strip of boulders, above the cataract, that linked Tumatumari and Tumatumari Landing, south and north of the river, respectively. It also served as the least pleasant leg of the already unpleasant drive along Konawaruk Road.

In other words, it was perfect.

Less than ten minutes after peeling off from the main

column, Snyder was at the riverbank, staring at the white foam frothing the river's surface. He ordered the dismounts of his second platoon—twenty men if at full strength, seventeen now, after the air attacks—into the foam. They waded, rifles at the ready, forward. Most were surprised to see that the water barely rose above waist level unless one slipped on the boulders, as several did. Under their platoon leader, the men pushed on past the river's southern bank. Dogs in the town barked, but no one else paid much attention from the twenty-odd huts and shanties that made up the place.

Listening to his radio, Snyder heard, "Come on across; the water's fine."

Garraway Stream, Guyana

Firing actually started before the tanks reached the river. The Venezuelan commander had done the right thing and pushed at least two observation posts across to the other side. One of these the gunner of Charlie 26, the second platoon leader's tank, found, through his night sight, scampering for the river. He duly engaged the two men, his tracers arcing through the woods and over the water to the far side. The platoon leader, up top, joined in with his KORD 12.7mm almost as soon as he saw the tracers.

I think I probably got one, thought the gunner. *No matter; it isn't like they haven't had a chance to figure out we were coming.*

The tank rolled forward, the turret for the most part remaining within a few degrees of forward. One could use tanks in jungle, assuming it was only jungle and the trees were far apart. But one still had to watch out for getting the gun pointed in one direction, while the driver took his tank around a tree, in another.

Others from that platoon, four of them, rolled around in pairs to either side of the platoon command tank. Forming a rough line—the trees ensured the line would be, at best, rough—the platoon moved forward, firing intermittent bursts from both their coaxial and their top-mounted machine guns.

The platoon leader didn't hear the call sent—naturally enough since the artillery and mortars worked a different sequence of frequency hopping—but he could see white phosphorous shells hitting the far bank on a line as rough as his own. The shells burst with small, muffled explosions that sent glowing white fragments arcing and spinning through the air, trailing thick smoke behind them.

It's very beautiful, the platoon leader thought, *for certain values of beauty.*

Some tracers came in from the other side, harbingers of the half dozen or so bullets that rang off the tank's glacis and the front of the turret. Automatically, the platoon leader's hand reached down to yank the bar that kept his seat so high. The padded chair dropped, carrying him down with it until only his eyes and the top of his CVC helmet showed above the hatch ring. He radioed orders to the rest of the platoon to do likewise.

Not so far back from the front, close enough, in fact, for the odd tracer to reach that far, Reilly took a report from Green, the Charlie Company commander.

"I let 'em see who and what we were, sir," Green said. "I let 'em get a good look before calling in the smoke. We're pelting the bejeezus out of the far bank. Time for the engineers to check the bridge, I think."

"Roger," Reilly replied. "Break, break; Ditchdigger Six"—Trim—"into the water and check out that bridge."

Mahdia, Guyana

Military Intelligence was often, and in more armies than one, called a "self-propelled oxymoron." That wasn't entirely fair. Certainly it was not a case, as many a pacifist, self-righteous antimilitarist, and the occasional outright coward put it, of "soldiers showing their stupidity by their choice of profession." Rather, it was that both sides to a conflict were usually quite bright. Thus, they went to considerable pains to fool each other. The Venezuelan commander who had set up his forward command post at the podunk town of Potaro Landing hadn't known until it was too late how close the gringos were until they lunged south.

Conversely, despite Michaels' reports and the more timely ones from the RPV's, Reilly hadn't known, for example, that his opponent's name was Camejo, that said opponent was not a lieutenant colonel but a full colonel, that he commanded a brigade of which not one but two infantry battalions were present, or that those battalions were accompanied by a battery and a third—eight guns, with more on the way, eventually—of 105mm mountain howitzers.

There had been indicators, of course. One flight that Michaels had not been able to see unloaded had brought in more communications wire than a single battalion could have used in two wars, for example. Two larger planes, landing at Kaieteur Airport, had brought in eighteen Oto-Melara 105's, and enough mules to, interestingly enough, move eight of them. Being mule-ported, they'd stayed off the road until reaching a point about three kilometers south of Potaro Landing. Hence, Michaels had missed them.

Moreover, and this was by no means Michaels' fault alone, since the use of the laser had shut down most air traffic at Cheddi Jagan, and since the cargo planes were still available, they *had* to go somewhere. That somewhere was generally Kaieteur Airport, which had improved the logistic position of the brigade there immeasurably.

The key thing Michaels missed, though, was none of that merely technical detail. What he'd really missed was that one of the planes that had come in to Kaieteur had been an Airbus, carrying none other than Hugo Chavez, who had proceeded to browbeat Camejo into moving to and past Mahdia, even while promising him the means to do so.

On the other hand, there are some things one really can't expect a sergeant, leading a small team, to pick up on. A field marshal would likely have missed it, as well.

Camejo picked up the chattering field phone. "Yes, I'm not deaf," he said. "I can hear it perfectly well. What are you facing? God damn it, Colonel, calm down!"

Angered, Camejo broke communication, slamming the phone back into its cradle. "Sergeant Major!"

"Here, sir," answered that worthy.

"I can't get a stinking clue about what's going on at the bridge from the battalion commander there. Get . . ."

But Sergeant Major Zamora, the commander's second set of eyes and ears, had already slung a portable radio over one shoulder and was already racing for one of the autos the brigade had commandeered on entering the town.

Good man, thought Camejo. "Somebody get me those useless sit-on-their-asses artillerymen on the line!"

Garraway Stream Bridge, Guyana

The bridge hadn't been "wired for sound," something Trim and the one squad of engineers he'd taken with him had figured out very quickly. The rest of the platoon was waiting, belly down behind the tanks, to be called forward if and when needed.

What they hadn't figured out yet, and perhaps never would, was how to get back to the friendly side of the river. Rather, shortly after entering it, they'd been chased all the way across by an enthusiastically pumped Venezuelan machine gun. That gun, or maybe its cousin, still had them pinned on the far, and very *un*friendly, bank. The occasional hand grenade that exploded in the water just past them, along with the steady stream of tracers cracking back and forth overhead, were proof enough of how unwelcome they were there.

"On the other hand," Trim muttered, as the first of a number of artillery shells exploded in the trees on the far side, "maybe we *don't* want to be on that bank."

Konawaruk-Mahdia Cattle Trail, Guyana

Snyder's first notification that he'd perhaps let the point of the company, a scout platoon Ferret, get a little too far was when that Ferret came apart at the seams as a result of three or possibly four hits from largish antitank warheads. The double flashes suggested to Snyder that they were 84mm Carl Gustavs, a system he was familiar with from his time in certain units of the United States Army.

And bad news, at this range.

"Back off! Back off!" Snyder called over the radio. "Redleg, this is Bravo Six, over."

"Redleg, over," came the instant answer. One of the implications of "priority of fires to X" was that the fire direction center would wait very expectantly for any request from X.

"Fire target set Bravo One Zero Four through Bravo One Zero Eight, over." One through Three had been, respectively, Tumatumari Landing, Tumatumari, and Konawaruk. They'd not been needed.

The predawn sky to Snyder's north immediately lit up with what looked like a number of very large strobe lights, as the guns and the heavy mortars began firing to their own south at maximum rate. Snyder guessed that the guns and mortars were firing, between them, about four rounds per second.

"Shot, over."

I can see that. "Shot, out."

"We're giving you a shake and bake," the artillery

announced. "Shake and bake," usually reserved for use on fuel and ammunition dumps and carriers, was mixed high explosive and white phosphorous. Even without that ideally inflammable target, it had some extra moral effect beyond the mere weight of shell. All men fear being badly burned.

"Roger," Snyder acknowledged, "break . . . break, Third Battalion's Eland Section; you're attached to Third Platoon. Third, start working your way around to the *enemy's* left. *Don't* attack until I give the word."

"Roger . . . Roger; at your command."

The obvious reason defenders take up a reverse slope position was to prevent their enemy from seeing them until it's too late for the sight to do them much good. There were other, equally valid, reasons. For one thing, normally the slope itself tends to exaggerate the normal artillery and mortar range-probable-error, such that more shells fall shorter, more longer, and fewer strike around the line of the defense.

Captain Trujillo, commanding a company facing east, just behind the slope, had mostly been concerned with the first advantage and had been only dimly aware of the second. This was, in some ways, just as well as, with the artillery engaging him coming from the north, the second advantage had ceased to operate. Rather worse, from Trujillo's point of view, was that his troops were now *on* the gun-target line. Thus, the normal dispersion of artillery and mortars—usually long and short rather than right or left—meant that even those long- or short-falling shells landed either on his men, or close enough to be dangerous. And the rate of fire, averaging a heavy shell per second on each of his platoon, was quite outside his very limited experience. Perhaps worst of all, the screeching and blasting shells drowned out the sound of the enemy armor. He no longer could tell where they were or what they were doing from the sound alone.

It was no small risk to stick one's head up to see, under the circumstances; every blasting shell was followed by a horde of metal shards, whining omnidirectionally through the air. Indeed, the air seemed full of them. Still, no coward, Trujillo had his responsibilities and high among those was to see, that he might command.

And at least it's getting light enough to have a chance to see something.

Unfortunately, he picked the same moment to lift his head from the shallow scraping that a 105 shell picked to land about fifteen feet in front of him. One particular shard, razor sharp and about nine inches long, buzzed through his face, just under his helmet's rim. It sliced off the top of his head, leaving his cranium and most of his brain still in the helmet, which flew off independently.

The worst thing of all, though, from Trujillo's perspective, and the best, from Snyder's, was that the guns were firing parallel to *Snyder's* line. Thus, he could move forward quite close to the Venezuelan troops, in fair safety.

Leading with his own three gun-armed Eland's, Snyder moved his company up to just past the topographical crest—the very top, in civilian parlance—of the hill that had separated him from the enemy. Smoke from the ruins of the shattered Ferret arose from off to his left. He wasn't too worried about incoming antiarmor fire at this point, as a dozen 105mm guns and half a dozen 120mm mortars were making a living hell out of the reverse military crest along which the Venezuelans had lightly dug themselves in.

Better still, he thought, *with the rising sun at my back most of them can't stand to look in my direction, except at an angle.*

On their own, without command, his own company's three Elands began donating 90mm shells to likely targets, interspersing those with bursts of coaxial machine gun fire. The machine gunners of his turretless Elands, the ones the battalion used as armored personnel carriers, added to the din with the KORD fifties.

Snyder watched calmly for perhaps half a minute, then radioed, "Third, are you in position?"

"Roger, we got delayed and lost a vehicle to an OP"—observation post—"we didn't count on. But we're ready now. Nobody dead, two hurt that we can keep with us. Two more need evacuation. We've called for Medevac. It's on the way. Not moving until you call off the artillery, though."

"Roger," Snyder replied, "break, break, Redleg, lift fire from Target One Zero Four, over."

"Roger," the gunners replied. Give it sixty seconds for the last shells to impact. They'll be four white phosphorous, all together."

"Roger. Third, did you copy."

"Got it, Six. Four Willie Pete and then we go in."

"Affirmative. Do it. Break, break; Redlegs, be prepared to shift onto Target Bravo One Zero Nine, at my command."

"Roger . . . your Willie Peter just left the tubes."

★ CHAPTER FORTY-THREE ★

Since when has the doctor of medicine and
dentistry become such a pantywaist as to require that a
bald responsibility others accept with good grace must
be decked out with certain frills before he will buy it?
—RADM Lamont Pugh, USN,
Surgeon General of the Navy, 1952

First Battalion Aid Station, Bartica-Potaro Road, Guyana

The battalion aid station was set up just north of the road,
flush against the trees that lined it. It wasn't much, just
some tarps pulled out from vehicles and suspended on
poles, then staked down. No more of the equipment had
been unloaded and set up than required for immediate
needs. After all, the battalion had quite a long, running
fight ahead of it, even assuming they could force the
bridge.

Since there wasn't a whole lot of flying to be done,
McCaverty had volunteered his services to Reilly, that
being as close to the action as the good doctor was likely

to get, at least until the Venezuelan Air Force finally went away for good.

The work he was doing now, treating the thin trickle of casualties from Garraway Stream, wasn't the kind of high end surgery for which an absolutely amazing amount of money had been spent training him. Rather, it was cut and paste and stitch and splint, along with the occasional transfusion and more than a little doping against pain, before shunting the wounded back to the field hospital at Camp Fulton.

McCaverty smiled evilly at his next patient, a seated thirty-two year old half-Chinese, half-Hispanic corporal named Chin—no relation to Captain Chin of the naval squadron. A shell splinter had torn across Chin's shoulder, ripping the skin roughly but not doing much damage to the underlying meat. The skin was currently held together by two clamps that reminded the corporal of nothing so much as curved scissors.

Holding up a curved needle from which a black filament dangled, he said to Chin, "This is *really* going to hurt. You sure you don't want that shot?"

"I need to get back to my vehicle and my gun," Chin replied. "Just do it, Doc."

"Okay," McCaverty agreed. "Your funeral. Just so you know, I may have to turn this over to one of the orderlies, midway through, if someone more serious gets carried in." The doctor leaned over and grasped the sides of the wound, causing the corporal to wince slightly. And then the needle went in.

"Oh, fuck!"

"Not too late for the shot," McCaverty said.

"Just . . . do it."

Outside the covered-over area in which McCaverty did his work, someone shouted out for a medevac to retrieve two badly wounded troopers from Bravo Company.

"I'm up next," Corporal Tatiana Manduleanu announced, grabbing her aid bag and beginning the short jog to the Land Rover she'd been assigned. "Come on, Brewer," she shouted to a private who was the entirety of her little command.

In moments Tatiana and her assistant were bouncing merrily down the road, headed for the ford at Tumatumari Landing.

And why, she asked herself, *do I feel so much happier doing this than I ever felt leading off a client for a shitpot of money?*

Garraway Bridge, Guyana

Reilly had had his vehicle driven to within about a hundred and fifty meters of the riverbank. This was behind the tanks, but forward of where he'd let Alpha Company move its own vehicles. From there, he'd dismounted, taking one RTO—radio-telephone operator—with him. There'd been a little fire on the way, but nothing close enough he couldn't classify it as "light and random."

Now, he sheltered behind a tank, low, with his head barely peeking out from around one of the tank's treads. He'd made very sure beforehand to use the telephone mounted to the tank's rear to tell the crew, "Under no circumstances, to include your imminent death, are you people to back up. I'm right behind you." The RTO, standing in the tank's lee, had a microphone to one ear, the tank's phone to the other, and his rifle slung over one shoulder.

Reilly looked, but couldn't see a whole lot. Trim and a few engineers were somewhere in the water; he knew that much. Whether they were still alive, and whether the bridge was clear, he didn't know. Still, he didn't see any odd blocks attached to the span, or otherwise inexplicable wires leading from it, so he assumed the best.

He crawled backwards—no easy maneuver with his arm in a sling—and then stood up. Making a gimme gesture to the RTO, he took the microphone and said, "Bravo, this is Black Six. When are you people going to get off your dead asses?"

"Six, Bravo, moving in now," Snyder's voice replied.

The machine gun fire had stopped zinging the water behind him. Likewise the grenades hadn't come in a while. *It could be the other side is out of grenades,* Trim thought. *It could be they've decided they have bigger problems. It could be they think we're dead. Or it just might be they've forgotten about us.*

The squad with him had only lost one man, so far, and that one about half an hour previous. The sapper, blinded by a grenade that had gone off above water and all too near, had staggered off, shrieking, into the open until a machine gun found him. A dozen small geysers had erupted around him, even as other bullets found their way to and through his head and torso. With a piece of his cranium flying almost straight up, the screaming had abruptly ended as the sapper had been spun around and cast off, broken and ruined. The body, facedown and leaking brains from a huge hole, had floated away downstream, spinning slowly in the current and painting the river pink in a spiral.

One . . . one's not so bad. Could be worse. Could have been all of us. But I wish Reilly would get off his dead ass and clear the river.

Konawaruk-Mahdia Cattle Trail, Guyana

As a large cloud of smoke erupted from his right, Snyder heard from that flank the chattering of fifty calibers interspersed with the deeper booming of the 90mm cannon.

"Redlegs, shift to Target Bravo One Zero Niner."

"Roger. The mortars won't range Mahdia; we're cutting them back to battalion control. Your last shells will be twenty-four rounds of white phosphorous, over."

"Losing the mortars. Understood. Willie Pete, out," Snyder finished. He watched forward intently. There would be a moment of risk when the shells lifted, if the Venezuelans recognized their window of opportunity.

Buuut . . . Snyder saw what he took to be a half dozen uniformed men, no weapons in evidence, running from his right to his left, fleeing the attack of Third Platoon and its attached Elands. A couple were cut down, sprawled in undignified death. *Aha, there they go.*

"Bravo, this is Bravo Six . . . " He waited until he saw huge white flowers blossom across the front. "Into the assault . . . " The machine guns atop the vehicles picked up their fire. Infantry formed up on line, two or three to either side of each APC. "Forward!"

Mahdia, Guyana

Colonel Camejo didn't waste his time radioing Kaieteur for resupply or reinforcement. It was three days travel away by foot and muleback. He'd either win here, with what he had, or lose here, alone.

He looked over his situation map. *Still, it's not looking so bad. Sergeant Major Zamora says the companies at the bridge are holding firm. Says it was iffy until he shot the battalion commander and told the executive officer to take charge. Note to self: that incident will* not *be reported.*

The artillery is finally doing some good. Should I tell them to drop the bridge, or try to? No; we'll need it ourselves, when the order comes to move on the mercenary base.

I wish I knew what was going on to the east. But . . . Trujillo's a good man. His last report said he was holding. He'll not let me down.

"Have we got that medevac flight from Kaieteur, yet?" Camejo asked aloud.

"Inbound, sir," one of the command post rats reported. "Two fixed wing. They'll be here in about five—"

That report wasn't finished, as a rain of fire began to fall onto the town. One nearby shell blew in the windows of the building Camejo had taken over for his command post, though nobody was badly hurt from it.

After that first deluge, the rate of fire slackened to

about a round every five seconds. Still, for a good thirty minutes, Camejo, the one company of infantry in the town, and the bulk of the support troops from both battalions and brigade combined, were shaken, rattled and rolled by a steady stream of high explosive.

"They can keep this up all day, gentlemen," Camejo said. "They can . . ." he chanced to glance out a shattered window as a swarm of troops ran by, emerging from the cattle trail that ran to Konawaruk and Trujillo's company, all the fleeing men heading west " . . . oh, shit."

As if to punctuate the words with an exclamation point, several streams of fifty caliber punched through the air, mostly over the fleeing troops' heads.

"To arms!" the brigade commander shouted. "The gringos are upon us."

What should have been for Snyder a ten-minute drive, in peacetime, took three times that, what with the need to rout the enemy to his front, then collect his own troops and reform them. Pursuit, except by fire, hadn't really been possible.

Besides, thought Snyder, *shooting fleeing men in the back is distasteful, at best.*

The scout platoon, in the lead, reported to him, "We're off the trail and at the outskirts of the town. Recommend lift and shift fires."

Snyder passed that on, along with his control over the battery. Then he said, "Right through the fucking town, gentlemen. Kill 'em all, before they get away."

"Die like a man," Camejo silently quoted. *And what the*

hell? Hugo will have me shot anyway. He made that clear enough when he came to visit us at Kaieteur.

He bent down and took a rifle from a soldier who had more interest in hiding than fighting, then walked out into the street. Facing east, the colonel began walking forward. Hot explosive gasses burst out the shattered windows of a building to his front. He saw a small knot of soldiers begin to enter the building, their point men firing. The soldiers wore strange uniforms but helmets not unlike his own. Raising his commandeered rifle to his shoulder he fired at the last of the soldiers, bringing the man down in the dirt street. Letting the rifle relax to a waist level carry, he moved onward.

From a cloud of red dust, ahead of him, an armored vehicle emerged. It stopped on the road. Camejo saw the machine gun aim low. The gunner called out, in Spanish, *"Arriba los manos!"*

Camejo shook his head and began lifting his rifle back to his shoulder. The last thing he saw was the muzzle flash of the machine gun. He was dead before his body hit the ground.

"Brave bastard," Snyder muttered, leaning back from the gun. "The courage of your enemy honors you."

South of Potaro Landing, Guyana

In the nature of things, when animals, or people, flee a disaster they don't always flee directly away from it. Some will follow low ground, some roads and trails. Some will run off in directions that make no sense to themselves or anyone else. Panic and rout are not exactly intellectual exercises or events.

On the intersection of the roads that led east to the Garraway Stream Bridge and north to Potaro Landing, Sergeant Major Zamora was standing like a rock as the first of what looked to be a small trickle of terrified men reached him.

Zamora took one look at the man's filthy, terrified face, eyes wide in utter panic, and thought, *Oh, shit.*

"Soldier! Halt where you are!"

The man ignored him, but kept running north, glancing behind himself every few seconds at a threat that wasn't there.

"It's not there *yet*, anyway," Zamora muttered. As the soldier reached him the sergeant major straight-armed the boy, knocking him ass down on the dirt. Then the sergeant major crouched down and asked, "What happened?"

The soldier shook his head and started to rise. Zamora palmed the boy's face, knocking him back again.

"I asked you what happened."

"Dead . . . all dead," the panting troop managed to get out.

"Who's dead?"

"My squad leader . . . the brigade commander . . . everybody else. They're behind us . . . with tanks."

Nodding his head, Zamora asked, "And Sergeant Major Zamora? Is he dead, too?"

"Yes! Yes!"

"And Hugo? Did they get Hugo Chavez?"

"They're all dead," the boy insisted.

With his left hand Zamora took a firm grip on the terror-stricken troop's uniform, then stood up, dragging the boy with him. With his other hand, he reached for the pistol at his belt.

"Son," he said, "I'm Zamora. I'm not dead. But unless you calm down, right the fuck now, you will be." He then shook the boy like a rat in a terrier's mouth. By the time he was done, he'd lined the pistol up on the soldier's head. Two eyes crossed, staring straight at the muzzle.

"I . . . I . . . I . . ."

Zamora spoke firmly, in a way that would brook no argument even without the pistol. "Calm down, son. Everybody else panicked, so you did, too. No shame. No crime. Nobody's going to hurt you if you will remember your duty, *now*.

"Now, are you all right?"

The boy drew several shuddering breaths before answering—gasping, really—"I . . . I think so, Sergeant Major."

"Good." Zamora released the lapel. "Now come with me."

The mountain guns were still firing, somewhere off to the southwest, when Zamora led the boy into the battalion command post. To one side of the lightly beaten path a body lay. The body wore lieutenant colonel's insignia.

Zamora announced to the major now in command, "Sir, you're the senior officer I can find at the moment. We are fucked and it is up to *you* to get us unfucked." In as few words as possible, he briefed the major on what he'd been able to glean from the bits and pieces of information the soldier in tow had known.

"I see," answered the major. "And your recommendations, Sergeant Major?"

Having soldiered for better than thirty years, Zamora already had his answer. "We've lost here, sir. Consolidate whatever we can in an arc around Potaro Landing. Pull the troops on the bridge out last. Screw the mountain guns; order the gunners here and save *them*. We'll escape and evade across the river tonight, and then back up the mountain to Kaieteur."

The major nodded, then began barking orders to the staff to set the troops in motion.

Once that was done, the major asked, "How did we lose?"

Zamora gave a bitter smile. "That's easy, sir. We didn't have the vehicles to support one battalion here and one at the other crossing. So we dug in close to the airport, for ease of supply. And, one of our companies did the exact right thing, taking a reverse slope defense, but it turned out to be wrong under the circumstances."

"Shit," said the major."

"Yes, sir," Zamora agreed, "'shit.' Oh, and sir? Get a message to Caracas. Maybe the *Estado Mayor* can get some air down here to take out the bridge. At the very least, our people at Cheddi Jagan need to know the road's open and that they've got company coming."

Garraway Stream Bridge, Guyana

The Venezuelans had pulled out by the time Bravo

Company showed up at the bridge. It still wasn't clear to move across.

Trim heard Vic Babcock-Moore's voice rise above the din, "Pop and drop! Pop and drop!" This was followed by the sounds of footsteps thumping across the span.

Scrambling up the bank, Trim watched two of his engineers, each carrying a satchel slung across from the right shoulder to the opposite side. They ran forward to where Trim guessed the surface laid mines had to be. As a mine was reached, one of the engineers would pull a small charge with a fuse and pull igniter from the satchel. Pulling on the rings of the igniters, they set the fuses to smoldering. The assembly was then dropped on top of or right beside a mine, before each man scurried on to the next one.

"Good old Vic," Trim said, just before remembering that he'd better duck before one of the mines took his head off.

★ CHAPTER FORTY-FOUR ★

All the gods are dead except the god of war.
—Eldridge Cleaver

Mahdia Airport, Guyana

"Look at all the damned *loot!*" Gordo exulted. He was particularly pleased about the several score, mostly pretty healthy mules, as well as the couple of hundred rounds of 105mm.

Look at all the damned bodies, Stauer thought. *Maybe I'm getting too old for this shit after all.*

The loot consisted of the mules, a few light trucks, all classes of supply including ammunition, eight mountain guns, a couple of dozen mortars in 81mm and 120mm. There were also a couple of hundred prisoners, though they were not, properly speaking, "loot." They were also being escorted back toward Camp Fulton by some of the walking wounded. And Venezuela's walking wounded? They just walked, helped by their buddies, where needed.

As for the rest of the Venezuelans, maybe as many as a thousand of them, Reilly had them pinned up against the

Potaro River. He sincerely hoped they'd escape during the night, because he neither wanted to attack them there, nor wanted to leave them behind where they could threaten his future communications with base. Indeed, though he could have closed off the crossing over the Potaro, below Kangaruma, he'd deliberately left it open as an inviting door to safety. Even so, Reilly was having the mortars throw a very limited amount of H and I— harassing and interdicting—fire at them, just to keep them feeling defensive.

The bodies, on the other hand, were twenty-one of the regiment's own. And more were still coming in, in dribs and drabs. They were laid out in nylon body bags, in a neat row, in the shade of a building. The shade wasn't consideration for the dead, but to delay the time until they began to stink. Hopefully, they could be evacuated to the cemetery at Camp Fulton before that happened.

Stauer and Gordo, driven by Hosein, had bullied their way into the order of march, just before the first of the tanks tried to make it across. Since there was some chance that the bridge would collapse under the tanks' weight, they were the very last in order. Even the artillery was already on the south side of the river.

A weary looking sergeant, heavily laden with all the accoutrements of a scout, walked up to the Land Rover and asked Hosein, "Have you seen First Battalion's scout platoon?"

Hosein glanced at the name tape and rank, pointed a finger to the east and said, "I saw some Ferrets that way, Sergeant Michaels."

"Thanks, Corp."

"Sergeant," Stauer asked, "have you seen your battalion commander?"

Michaels shook his head. "No, sir, but I did see Sergeant Major George thataway"—Michaels hooked a thumb in a general southward direction—"and where he is, my colonel's probably in the area."

"Thanks, Sergeant. Good job with the recon, I understand."

Michaels shook his head. "Not so good, sir, missed a lot of shit I should have figured out or seen."

Stauer and Gordo met Reilly, Snyder and George roughly three klicks south of the airport. The latter three were hunched over a spread-out map on the hood of Reilly's Land Rover. Stauer and Gordon stopped a distance away to listen.

"What took you so long?" Reilly demanded of his subordinate. Neither in facial expression nor in tone did he seem to be even remotely happy.

Snyder answered, coolly "There were *two* companies up there, not one. They were understrength, I think, but still there were two of them. We found it out the hard way and had to go smash the second one, too."

Reilly considered this. Finally, relenting, he said, "Fair enough. Well done then. However . . . I need four things from you, Snyder," Reilly said. In tone, the statement was an order. "I need you, the scouts, Third Battalions Elands, and two ADA guns plus four missile teams I'm cutting to your company to move out in thirty minutes. Sooner would be better. Second, grab us the bridge over the Essequibo at Awartun Island. Third, when you get the bridge, secure it; secure it from ground and air attack, both. Yes, that means the quad 23mm guns stay there . . ."

"How long do they stay there, sir?" Snyder asked. "And what can I expect in the way of an enemy there?"

"Bare minimum, expect aerial interdiction to start in about four hours. It will take Hugo that long to call his aerial dogs off of Third Battalion and redirect them against us. I expect that to start with your company. How long do you secure the bridge? Until the sun runs out of hydrogen or Gordo gets the ferry from Rockstone up and running and can supply the battalion that way.

"Sir, I can't be there in four and a half hours," Snyder objected. "Eight would be more like it . . ."

Reilly snarled. "Screw security. Haul ass. Four hours.

"Fourth, I want you to push north past Linden, and preferably all the way to Vryheit, then screen the line Demerara River to St. Cuthberts. We'll be along about three or four hours after you get there, assuming the bridge at Awartun is still standing.

"Assuming you make it to the screen line, and if the paratrooper brigade at Cheddi Jagan comes boiling out, you can fall back as far as a line running from Dalgin eastwards." Reilly traced on the map with a twig. "Now you're going to want to ignore me in that case, and fall back behind this river, north of Linden. I don't want you to do that, I want you to hold—if it comes to that—north of that river. Clear?"

"Clear, sir."

"Good. Go. You now have only four hours and twenty-seven minutes to get to the Awartun Island bridge."

Snyder saluted and walked off, shaking his head. It was

only then that Reilly and George noticed the regimental commander and S-4 standing and listening.

The two walked up to the laid-out map. Stauer didn't bother using a twig as he tapped it by the junction of the Essequibo and Cuyuni Rivers.

"We've still got some landing craft," Stauer said. "Gordo's going to start shunting Fourth Battalion across the Essequibo River, tonight. However, all Fitz's boys can do is parallel the Essequibo north, then cut east along the coast, pinning in Georgetown from that side. I hope, but can't guarantee, that that will force Hugo to pull the paras out of Cheddi Jagan and consolidate on Georgetown."

"I was rather hoping to bait them out of the airport and crush them somewhere between there and Linden," Reilly said.

Stauer nodded. "So we overheard. And, yes, it would be nice if it happened. But I think they're going to fall back to Georgetown."

"Why, sir, if you don't mind my asking?"

A broad smile lit Stauer's face. "Well, you know we didn't, in fact, have anybody set to mine Georgetown harbor. Oh, yes, we intended to, but had never gotten it set up when they caught us with our pants down.

"Interestingly enough"—the smile grew broader still— "Biggus and the *Naughtius* had a couple of mines left over so—"

"They'll figure that out quick," Reilly interrupted. "A couple of mines won't do."

"Ahem . . . if I can finish without being interrupted?"

"Sorry, boss." Reilly really did look chastened.

"There are no mines off of Georgetown, nor in the

Demerara River. And the *Naughtius* had no limpet fuses. But, they did have underwater fuse. So they slipped under an outgoing ship, somehow managed to attach a mortar shell to the hull, and lit the fuse as soon as the ship started to leave harbor, then skedaddled. So it went boom, and Hugo's boys think the harbor is mined, too. I understand Eeyore barely made it into the sub in time for the sub to get out of the effective underwater blast radius."

Reilly looked skeptical. "And we know this because . . ."

"We know what happened because *Naughtius* radioed us and told us. We know what the Venezuelans think happened because Hugo went on the air to condemn our mining and Bridges' signals intercept people picked up a transmission from Georgetown matching Hugo's tirade."

Reilly cast his eyes downward for a moment, thinking. At length, he asked, "So there are probably going to be six battalions in Georgetown? I can't handle that, not even with Fitz's battalion to do the detailed work."

"Don't worry about it," Stauer answered. "Just pin them in the town; starvation will do the rest."

"As it seems to be in Venezuela as a whole," Gordo added. "By the way, you need to go easy on the 105mm. What we still had, plus that eight hundred rounds we got in, and the bit you captured, is it until this campaign is over."

"We didn't use any of that," Reilly said.

"What?"

He shrugged. "We didn't use any of it. Every round we fired crossing the bridge was from condemned stocks. Yes, some shells may have fallen long or short, but the enemy was mostly on the gun-target line. Over was usually still on them. So was short."

Harry Gordon rubbed at his eyes. He was something of a cheapskate, all in the job description, of course, and, "You mean I ordered thousands of shells destroyed and I didn't *have* to?"

"No, no," Reilly counseled. "You did have to destroy them. Eventually. Just luck . . . well, mostly luck, that the unreliable propellant wasn't an issue today. All the good stuff we've saved for the move on Georgetown."

Turning his face back to Stauer, Reilly asked, "Speaking of towns, sir, how's Cazz doing?"

"Holding on," Stauer answered. "Not a lot more than that, though. The Venezuelan Air—"

The regimental commander was interrupted by the blaring of horns, and a large number of men screaming, "Air raiaiaid!"

"Speaking of which, Boss," Reilly said over one shoulder, as he sprinted for his command vehicle, "be seeing you around."

Ciudad Guyana, Venezuela

Leaving the bridge over the Rio Caroni probably bought us two, maybe even three days, thought Cazz. *Fuckers must have shit themselves thinking we'd left it open only to continue our charge and occupy* Ciudad Bolivar.

'Course, the down side of that is that now they're *using it to support the people hemming us in. And nothing we know about them makes sense except that they're a hodge-podge of whatever could be scrapped together in a hurry,*

that they've got some old AMX-30 tanks that the turrets don't seem to traverse well on, and that they outnumber us by . . . well, by a whole lot.

Third Battalion had started out with observation posts, at least, covering all the major roads into town, Highway Ten, *Avenida* Angosturita, *Avenida* Guyana, and *Avenida* Leopoldo Sucre Figerella. The latter two, what with the bridges down, had been mere OP's. The other two, and a few key spots nearby, had been more strongly outposted, a platoon each, with the intent of buying a little time if Hugo made a stronger push, sooner than Cazz really expected.

They'd made the push, though it had come later than expected. It had also come stronger than expected. Now, Cazz's battalion was almost entirely confined to the area he'd picked for his last ditch stand. Basically, that position was the Rio Orinoco at their backs, *Avenida* José Gumilla on their right, Highway Ten on the left, and *Avenida* Guyana to their front. At just under two kilometers, it was a ghastly long front to try to hold in a city, with but a single infantry battalion.

On the other hand, Cazz thought, *They're a lot less willing to destroy the place to get us out than we are to wreck it to keep it. And it's not as if we didn't make them bleed pretty badly driving us back to this.*

From somewhere in the rear, an open space not far from the river, what sounded like a dozen mortar shells thunked outward. Thirty-seven seconds later, Cazz heard the splash of shells somewhere to his south.

Odd, too, that the entire police force, for all practical purposes, elected to surrender to us rather than be let go, as I offered. I suppose they were afraid they'd be used as infantry. They probably would know, if anyone would. Hmmm; should I have driven them out anyway? Nah, they don't eat much and we've got plenty of food. Especially after we looted every state-owned grocery store in the city, near enough. Plus, they've been useful building fortifications. Well, it's not like they're soldiers who can't be put to military work, is it?

The Drunken Bastard, El Porvenir, Panama

If the locals thought the painted Styrofoam boat was a little on the odd side, they didn't say anything about it. Indeed, they seemed pretty happy to have Chin's crew show up for dinner at the local restaurants, or buy their groceries, such as were available, locally. They did a lot of drinking in what passed for the local watering holes.

For his own part, Captain Chin spent his days inspecting his boat and crew, watching CNN, Fox, and the Spanish channels intently, and desperately wishing that regiment would give him a little guidance . . . *some intelligence . . . a word, perhaps, that they still exist. But nooo, they're too busy; they've got more important things—*

"Yeah, what is it," Chin snarled, not happy at having his two minutes of hate interrupted.

"Well, I don't know how important it is, but CNN was in one of their tirades talking about illegal mining of the sea—"

"It's not illegal," the captain said. "They just want it to

be. Trust me; if a non-socialist state were being mined by a socialist one, they'd be all in favor of it."

"But you're a socialist, Captain."

"Yeah, but I'm not a hypocrite. Anyway, what was so fucking important on CNN?"

"Oh, just that in the middle of their editorial, they cut to the international response to this . . . um . . . how'd they phrase it? Ah, yes, high seas terror. It was—"

"The *response,* please?"

"Sorry, Skipper." The crewman hung his head. "Anyway, they showed a film of two minesweepers—one little one, one big one—leaving Santiago de Cuba.

Chin's head shot up. "When," he demanded.

"Um . . . yesterday, I think, Skipper."

"Hah!" In a moment, Chin was at his chart table. "Get your ass to what passes for 'downtown.' Round up the crew, drunk or sober or fucking some of the local oppressed masses or any combination of the above. We're in business!"

Sure, the world was in the middle of a nasty—"oh, please don't call it a"—depression. Sure, hundreds of millions were out of work. But even in a world class depression, business—albeit to a less than ideal degree—continues.

One business that was barely scraping by was a German firm, *Augenblick*. They were in the business of satellite imagery, in real time, for what was actually a fairly modest fee. The resolution was perhaps not everything one might want, though it was entirely suitable for monitoring the advance of glaciers, the increasing snow cover in the northern hemisphere, and sundry matters of agricultural importance. A man in a foxhole? No, that was beyond *Augenblick's* ability.

On the other hand, a ship, a wooden-hulled ship, a forty-eight-point-eight-meter wooden-hulled ship? *That*, the company could handle. And, they kept records, online, which could be downloaded. Of course, going through those could be time consuming. It was dark before the boat was ready to depart.

"There's the bitch, right there," Chin said to his exec, his finger tapping the monitor. The screen showed a presumptive minesweeper, a Sonya Class, leaving Santiago de Cuba. It was moving slow, leaving barely a wake behind.

"Okay, Skipper," the XO agreed, "I can see that. But what's the little one following behind?"

Chin's face scrunched for a moment, thinking far back to certain transfers between the defunct Soviet Union and the moribund hereditary monarchy of Cuba. "That's a Yevgenya class minesweeper. Bet you a week's pay it will be taken under tow by the bigger one, the Sonya Class, within three hundred miles of leaving port, though probably sooner."

Chin faced his first officer, the faces of the pair lit only by the light of the monitor. "I want you to go over the files with a fine tooth comb. Find the speed. Determine if the little one's in tow by now. Determine the speed for that, too."

The exec nodded understanding. "I suppose you'll want a course, too, Skipper."

"Check it, if only for the sake of thoroughness. But I'll bet you another week's pay that the two of them are heading to Maracaibo."

The exec shook his head. "I only look stupid, Captain, and then only when I drink. I won't take either of those bets."

★ CHAPTER FORTY-FIVE ★

Dice are rolling; the knives are out.
Would-be presidents are all around.
I don't say they mean harm,
　　　　but they'd each give an arm
To see us six feet underground.
—Tim Rice and Andrew Lloyd Webber, *Evita*

Miraflores Palace, Caracas, Venezuela

"Stop that column," Chavez demanded, throwing a pen at the map hanging on the wall. "Stop it now! I want every available aircraft dedicated to bombing that armor into scrap!" Hugo was in a fine fury, nor was it made any better by the knowledge that *he* had ordered the brigade at Kaieteur out from its safe fastness to where it could barely be supported and was, in fact, routed.

And, given the example of the late chief of intelligence, thought the Chief of Staff of the Air Force, General Ortiz, *I really don't want to be the one to remind him. Hugo's getting progressively less reasonable.* Ortiz was young looking and fit, with all of his hair, and all of that native black. In his dress blues, gold-trimmed and bemedalled, he was a magnificent sight. Though, if Chavez thought so, he hid that opinion rather well.

Ortiz had a sudden thought. *Funny; the army's treated Chavez with kid gloves ever since the day it realized he might just someday end up as president, which was predictably going to become the office of dictator. I doubt he's ever had someone really disagree with him, much less chew his ass, in thirty years or more.*

Okay, so what are my options? I can bend over, order the useless strikes he wants. Then, when they fail—as they will fail; we aren't worth a flying fuck at bombing moving targets and we don't have the precision guided ordnance to make up for our lack—he'll have my head.

Or, maybe, I can be honest with him and insist we go after the bridge. He'll overrule me; we'll fail; and then he'll have my head.

Or, and this is so risky it makes me shudder, I can throw a screaming shitfit at him, shock him silly, we go after the bridge and take it down, and that stops the column. Of, course, that might cost me my head, too, but it's my best chance and our best chance.

By background Ortiz was a fighter pilot. Neither cowardice nor indecision are notable in the breed, not in any air force worth its salt.

In for a penny, in for a pound.

Ortiz stood so decisively that even Chavez shut up. *Good sign.* He slammed his fist to the huge conference table and said, "No! No, Mr. President, we are not going after the column any more than it takes to slow it down.

We're going after the bridge over the Essequibo that crosses Awartun Island. *That* is our only chance to save this campaign."

For a few moments, Chavez's mouth worked like a fish out of water. *No one has spoken to me like that in . . . I can't remember how long. Do I shoot him for insubordination, or . . .*

"Make your case, General," Chavez said. "But make it quick; there isn't much time."

Ortiz forced away the smile he felt growing on his face. *Huh; so it's going to work.*

"Mr. President," the general said, forcing earnestness and sincerity into his face and his words, "we're already on it. The first flight of Sukhois went after the armored column on the south side of the Potaro. They are still hitting them. They were diverted from a strike on *Ciudad Guyana*, so what they have for weapons is suboptimal. Frankly, we don't have the optimal weapons.

"I've sent the next flight also to intercept the enemy armor. They won't do any more good than the first one did. Everything after that needs to be carrying high explosive and a few antiradiation missiles. And all of that ordnance needs to go onto the bridge until it comes down.

"Our only chance of buying the paratroop brigade at Cheddi Jagan airport enough time to prepare to defend is dropping that bridge."

Ortiz felt his heart sink as Chavez shook his head. As quickly as it sank, it arose still more rapidly when the president said, "Do it. And I hope you know what you're risking."

Ortiz drew himself up with a dignity the mere uniform

couldn't hope to match. "Mr. President," he said, "my youngest son will be leading the first mission to go after the bridge."

I gambled, thought Hugo Chavez, lying in bed next to his latest not-very-pretty hence not-damaging-to-the-ego mistress. *I gambled, and it looks like I'm going to lose. Fucking gringo bastards.*

The sound of the crowd outside the palace hardly ever ended now. More than once Chavez had considered having them dispersed by any means reasonably necessary. Each time he'd refrained. They were *his* people, after all. *They* were the reason he'd taken power in the first place.

My people as long as I'm their leader. How long is that going to last? Imports are cut off, except by truck from Brazil. I can't feed a country by truck; at least I can't feed this *one. No goods in the shops. Plenty for sale on the black market, though, at prices almost nobody can afford. I considered passing out a lot more money, until the economists—even the properly Marxist ones—pointed out that doubling the money supply would just double the price of goods.*

And all the news from the war is bad. A corner of Ciudad Guyana still in enemy hands and the army is helpless to pry them out of it. A whole brigade of the Fifth Division a shattered wreck, trying to escape back to Kaieteur in little penny packets through the jungle.

Can't even tell the people it was a pyrrhic victory for the enemy, either, since that enemy will demonstrate they didn't actually suffer much when they kick our asses at Cheddi Jagan Airport, which I suspect they will.

Can I just declare peace and leave Guyana? Not a chance. "My people" will be dancing under my hanging, tongue-protruding, strangled corpse within the day. And it wouldn't solve the problem, anyway. My ports will still be mined, and the enemy will have no reason to tell us where the mines are, if they even know.

Chavez rolled over, facing the window toward the courtyard and, incidentally, facing away from his paramour. The sound was louder in that posture, causing him to turn the opposite way, facing her.

Maybe the Cubans can clear the mines and save us. This is so not working out the way it was supposed to.

International Waters, Three Hundred and Twenty Miles Northwest of Aruba

If there was such a thing as the Platonic ideal of "ship-shape and Bristol fashion," the Sonya Class minesweeper would have been the Platonic ideal of its opposite.

The minesweeper didn't have a name. The hull number, and it possessed one, had long since fallen off the wooden hull in a drizzle of paint flecks. Only the grace of God— not that Cuban sailors were allowed to profess belief in God, of course—kept the water out. Certainly the quicky paint job they'd splashed on for the benefit of the CNN cameras wouldn't.

The engines . . . they were another story. There'd been no time to overhaul those, though Cuba, since the rise of the Castros, had made keeping ancient motors running something of an art. They strained, coughing great clouds of diesel to the heavens as the entire assembly of parts floating in loose formation made its maximum eight knots southward. It could possibly have managed eleven—the condition of the engines ruled out its specification speed of fourteen—but for the need to tow the Yevgenya Class. That boat was, if that were possible, in worse shape still.

On the bridge, gazing forward, stood the captain, a Castro by name but no relation to the ruling clan. *And what will happen to us if a storm comes up*, he thought, *only the God we're not supposed to believe in knows. He's not telling, but I'm pretty sure we drown. Hell, the only thing the navy has that even* looks *seaworthy is that replica of the* Granma *they haul out for parades.*

Still, if she'll only hold together for another forty hours, we'll be close enough to Aruba to defect. Not as good as defecting to the United States, of course, but a damned sight better than staying in Crown Prince Raul Castro's kingdom of the starving.

I wonder how many of the crew will willingly join me. About two thirds, I think. The rest, if they find out what I have in mind, will shoot me in the head and pitch my body over the side for the sharks. Even at that, I was lucky to convince higher command that this was such a suicide mission that only unmarried men should be taken.

The boat's chief maintenance officer—in a crew of a mere forty-three, he was, strictly speaking, the *only* maintenance officer—ahemed from behind. "Captain Castro, I've got the forward twin 30mm up. The rear 25mm is hopeless."

"No matter, we don't have much ammunition for it anyway," the boat's master replied. "The sonar?"

The maintenance officer's head rocked from side to side. "Won't be worth a shit for at least another day, sir. Maybe two. Assuming I can get it working at all."

"All right," the captain said. "We have that much time, anyway."

South of Cheddi Jagan Airport, Guyana

None of the Sukhois landed at the airport. The strip could take them well enough, but ordnance, fuel, and the ground crews were all back around Caracas. Still, in a fairly continuous stream, the distinctive aircraft each made at least one pass, after dropping their ordnance on the gringos' heads. This was done at Ortiz's order, despite the possibility of being lazed to destruction, in order to buck up the morale of the men and women frantically digging in, in a long arc running from Lana, Guyana, on the Essequibo, east-southeast toward Saint Cuthberts. Most of the paratrooper brigade's strength didn't stretch so far, however, being concentrated on the two roads that ran south from the airport, paralleling each other.

Every now and again a Tucano would fly overhead, dipping its wings in turn. There wasn't much fuel at the airport for them, nor was there much ordnance to carry, but what they could do, their pilots were determined to do.

A Sukhoi streaked above, causing Arrivillaga to wince at the sonic boom—it flew quite low—even as he muttered, "Don't like the flyboys, never did, but the gringos would have been on us already if not for them."

"What was that, Mao?" Larralde asked, heaving a

shovelful of dirt from the fighting position they took turns excavating.

"Just that we're lucky," the sergeant major replied. "And that the gringos should have been on us by now." *And, though I won't say it, that we're box of rocks stupid for not considering the possibility they might be and digging in starting as soon as we took this place. But, then, we already knew we were stupid or we'd not have made a career of the army, right?*

Larralde tossed another shovelful out of the hole. "Dumb as dirt of us not to start doing this about an hour after we arrived." He didn't quite understand the odd look his senior noncommissioned officer gave him in reply.

Mao saw a column of troops, maybe forty of them, bearing saws, picks, and shovels, marching down the asphalt road the eastern side of which it was Larralde's company's job to defend. Four of them were rolling barrels ahead of them. Another led a donkey pulling a small, light cart.

"Engineers are here, sir. Up out of the hole and let me dig, while you, for a refreshing change, go do an officer's job."

Larralde stabbed the shovel blade down into the dirt and left it there, the long wooden handle quivering. Putting a hand on each side of the narrow slit, he pushed up even as he kicked his legs up. A push with one arm rolled him over, a bit dirtier than he'd been but with his body out of the hole, at least. Standing, he brushed dirt from his hands and walked to greet his sapper support.

"Hey," Arrivillaga called, reaching down and picking up Larralde's helmet and load carrying equipment, "at least try to *look* the part, will you?" He tossed the helmet and the assembly toward his commander.

"I'll try," Larralde smiled, slipping his arms and shoulders into the webbing and placing the helmet onto his head.

"Thing is, sir," the engineer lieutenant said, as Larralde showed him on the ground what he wanted done, "I've got nothing. No mines, no wire—no engineer stakes even if I had wire, no vehicles, no dozers, no bucket loaders, no backhoes. *Nada.* I can't do what you want."

Larralde sounded disgusted, not with the engineer but with life, as he asked, "Well, what the hell *can* you do?"

"I can cut you some logs so your people can put up some half decent overhead cover," the engineer replied. "I can build you a—very limited, be it noted—number of wood and dirt obstacles. I've got my platoon sergeant and a small party out ripping up cattle fences for wire. You can have some of that, when it shows up, strung from tree to tree. We can do an abatis to block the road itself. I've got a little bit of explosive to spare, and we've got commo wire, clothespins, plastic spoons, and a few batteries, so I can make you a *few* booby traps in lieu of the mines I don't have. I can show your people how to put in antipersonnel stakes, 'pungi stakes,' the gringos call them. I can maybe make you a fougasse or two, and we've got some Russian MON command detonated directional mines."

"Why don't we have any lay and forget mines?" Larralde asked.

"Shit!" the engineer spat. "We were supposed to, sir— antitank mines, at least, since the previous government was stupid enough to sign onto the Ottawa Treaty. They were coming in by ship through Georgetown. The ship was about an hour's sailing out when that one got sunk in the harbor. They redirected it to New Amsterdam, where it sits, so I am told, sir, waiting for someone to unload it. The wire is there, too. Can't imagine how they'll get it to us even if they unload it, since the road between New Amsterdam and Georgetown is infested with guerillas, half the bridges are down, and the coastal railroad was cut three days ago.

"Might not have made any difference, though, even if it had managed to land at Georgetown; the Marines are much too busy seeing their own gear is unloaded to worry about ours. Motherfuckers."

Larralde tsked, "*Such* language." Sitting, he waved the lieutenant down next to him and pulled out a pen and notebook. Opening it, he began to make a sketch of the area. "Okay," he said, pointing his pen at the lieutenant, "first priority to the abatis . . ."

The first priority of work, so Arrivillaga had told the company, was security. Carlos Villareal figured survival was approximately as important, to the extent that the two didn't overlap. Thus, Lily lay down behind her rifle, facing south, while he dug furiously, stopping only to chop at the ubiquitous roots that barred their path to China.

It wasn't that Lily was unwilling to dig. Indeed, they'd tried switching on and off, off and on, already. The problem was that she just *couldn't* dig as fast in alternating stints as he could, unaided. It was a humiliating experience for her, but, as Carlos had told her, "Your sensitivities are not nearly as important as both of us surviving to go home.

So, as the sergeant major would say, 'shut up and soldier.'"
He'd smiled as he'd said it, trying to take out some of the
sting. It hadn't really worked; Vargas was still deeply
humiliated.

At least she didn't cry, Carlos thought. *I swear I couldn't
stand it if she had.*

★CHAPTER FORTY-SIX★

War is the unfolding of miscalculations.
—Barbara Tuchman, *The Guns of August*

Awartun Island, Guyana

"Pull off to the right," Snyder ordered through his intercom. The APC's wheels duly turned, causing the vehicle to crunch through the cheap, flimsy barrier and move on onto the island that was much of the bridge's support.

Snyder flicked the switch on the side of his helmet to radio. "Half perimeter on the far side, left to right, second, scouts, third. First platoon, you'll be staying here to guard the bridge. First Platoon and the Duckhunters"—Air Defense Artillery—"report to me." He waited then until one of the Russian-built air defense guns, a ZSU-23/4, pulled up in front of him. An elderly sergeant popped out of the hatch and dismounted with more agility than one would have expected.

"Yes, sir?" the sergeant, Master Sergeant Maldonado, asked. He sketched the flimsiest of salutes as he did.

"How do you defend this from an air attack?" Snyder asked.

Maldonado shrugged. "Mostly I spoil their aim. Defense is . . . difficult and improbable."

"Okay, fine; how do you set up to spoil their aim?"

The sergeant pointed to some very high ground to the northeast, Makeri Mountain, a good portion of which had recently been forested. "All the MANPADS"—MAN Portable Air Defense Systems, shoulder-fired antiaircraft missiles—"up there, along with one gun. The other gun right here, in case they try slipping in at just above water level."

"Do it." Snyder's first platoon leader trotted over. His salute was considerable more formal than Maldonado's had been. "You," the company commander said, pointing at First's platoon leader, "are working for him," the finger shifted to Maldonado. "Neither of you let this fucking bridge go down, whatever it takes."

"I can only promise to try," Maldonado replied.

"I'll put it this way," Snyder said, "if Reilly gets here and the bridge is down he'll probably shoot both of us."

"Okay, sir, I'll try *really* hard."

Mahdia Airport, Guyana

No matter how hard you try, Reilly mentally cursed, in war everything's twice as hard and takes twice as long as it should. Course, that's understandable when someone is trying to bomb the living shit out of you.

The planes hadn't been over in a while, maybe half an

hour. Half his command wasn't here anymore, either. He'd begun slipping them out by ones and twos from under the aerially induced inferno a couple of hours previously. They'd reform en route. Some of them weren't here, though, because they were dead or badly wounded.

About time for me to leave, too, he thought, but five or ten minutes to see to my hurt men won't be the end of the world.

Five minutes he could spare for his wounded, but there was no sense in wasting time. He trotted in the direction of the field aid station, the cast on his arm making the trot exceedingly awkward. It was open air, of course; there hadn't been time to set up tents. McCaverty rushed from litter to litter, doing a bit here and a little there to keep the men alive until they could be evacuated to the better facilities back at Camp Fulton. Some of the litters the doctor bypassed. These were the ones bearing men he couldn't save, or had already lost.

Corporal Tatiana Manduleanu was there, too, and while her medical skills were no more than those any field medic could boast of, her presence among all those wounded and, some of them, dying men was nearly as effective as the doctor's and in some cases, perhaps, more so. An image in profile—*magnificent profile,* Reilly thought—a soft hand stroking a bloody cheek, a squeeze of a shoulder, a deliberate low bend to give a one-eyed man a vision of heavenly cleavage: *She knows what she's doing, giving the boys a reminder that there's a reason to fight to stay alive.*

Not that she was just there for moral support. No,

she gave that almost unconsciously, even as she busied herself and Brewer with preparing the wounded for evacuation.

"Incredible, isn't she?" asked a familiar voice from behind. Reilly didn't turn. Not only did he recognize Joshua's voice, but he'd already more than half expected him to be here among the lame.

"Yeah, she is, Sergeant Major," Reilly agreed. "Maybe she's good at her regular job, I wouldn't know. But hookers are a dime a dozen; a field medic who can give the boys reason to live? That's a lot more rare and a lot more valuable."

And I know you would never argue that *point, old man.*

Reilly turned then, to see Joshua lofting and catching a blackish rock, one handed. "What's that?" he asked.

"Just something I picked up where the engineers did some insubordinate blasting to clear a way for the hovercraft."

"Interesting looking rock," Reilly observed. "You might want to have someone look at it. My man, Schiebel, collects rocks."

"Maybe," Joshua shrugged. "One of these days. For now, let's go check on the men."

Nodding, Reilly replied, "Just enough for an appearance, Sergeant Major. I've got to be on the road to Awartun Island Bridge in five minutes."

Even as Reilly spoke the words, another brace of Sukhois roared by overhead. No one doubted, at this point, where they were going.

Awartun Island, Guyana

"Six, this is One, over." One was the ZSU-23/4 sitting higher up on Makari Mountain.

"Six," Master Sergeant Maldonado replied. His track was about a hundred and fifty meters southeast of the bridge.

"I was tracking one on radar—slow mover; Tucano I think. It ducked down into the Essequibo before it came in range. Bet they're going to try to sneak up the river course."

"Roger, out," the platoon leader replied. He immediately ordered his gunner to orient the turret to the northwest, then put his field glasses to his eyes to scan in that direction himself.

The gun's turret spun then stopped. Banking left, a Tucano swept around the bend in the Essequibo, then leveled out.

"I've got him," announced the gunner.

"Fire!" All four barrels began to spit out 23mm shells at a combined rate of nearly three thousand, five hundred shells per minute. The forty rounds were gone in just over a second.

Maldonado roared with laughter as the camouflage-painted Tucano, caught in the fire of the four automatic cannon, simply disintegrated in a great flash. Bits and pieces of it fell into the river and splashed like a hailstorm of the gods.

"Teach you to fuck with the Duckhunters, motherfucker," the sergeant muttered.

A missile streaked off from the western slope of Makari Mountain. Maldonado heard the warhead itself explode, but if it did any damage to the next attacking plane—*Sukhoi, I think. Jet anyway*, he thought—it was tolerably hard to see.

The ZSU up on Makari opened up—one ear-splitting burst, then a second and a third—even as Maldonado had his own spun over to let the radar track. In a second, the four guns in front of him began belching long tongues of flame. The results were unspectacular, but the Sukhoi did abort its run. Maldonado thought he saw a thin stream of smoke trailing behind it as it veered off, climbing.

Neither he nor number one saw the next attacking aircraft. From somewhere northeast of Makari Mountain, a Sukhoi, which must have been going very low and then suddenly pulled up, released its bombs and lobbed them over the crest. Maldonado caught an uncertain glimpse of a couple of ovoids flying through the air and thought, *Shit*.

The bombs hit within a couple of seconds of each other. One landed in the river, several hundred meters away. The other?

"Oh, fuck!" Maldonado ducked down, pulling the hatch behind him. Even through the armor of the ZSU, the concussion was felt, internal organs rippling and the entire twenty-one ton assembly shuddering with the blast.

After giving debris and shrapnel time to fall to Earth, the master sergeant popped the hatch again and tentatively raised his head. With a sinking heart he ordered his driver to pull the vehicle closer to the bridge. Water and dirt, mixed in with chunks of steel and concrete, were *still* falling as they crested the low summit of Awartun Island.

"Well, shit," Maldonado cursed, looking at the massive gap recently torn in the bridge, "we did our best."

With a seriously sinking heart, the air defense platoon leader switched his radio to battalion command to give Reilly the bad news.

Intersection, Lethem Highway and Mahdia Road, Guyana

"He's taking the news rather well, don't you think?" asked Reilly's driver, Sergeant Schiebel, of the track commander, Sergeant Duke.

Duke looked at the remains of the battalion commander's helmet, clutched tightly in his left hand, as Reilly continued to beat the thing to scrap against the side of the APC. "Only because he's stuck using his left hand," Duke commented. "Otherwise, he'd have destroyed the helmet entirely by now and be working on something bigger and tougher."

"Possibly," Schiebel half-conceded, "but you must admit he's matured over the years. He didn't tell the air defense people he was going to line them up and shoot every tenth man personally. In the old days . . ."

"True," Duke agreed. "The question is, now what?"

Scowling, Reilly tossed away the remains of his helmet. From one pocket he pulled out a floppy jungle hat, which he placed on his head. "Order me another helmet," he said. "And get the commander of the engineers here. Ten minutes ago."

"I've got serious reservations we can rebuild that

bridge in anything like good time, sir," Trim said. "That's code for no fucking way, not this year. They tell me there's a fifty meter gap now, and what's standing is none too solid. And if I mass my engineers there the Venezuelan Air Force is going to make short work of them."

Reilly shook his head. "No, I know that," he agreed. "I don't want you to actually rebuild it. I want you to make it *look* like you're trying to actually rebuild it. Cut logs in the jungle and pile them up neatly as if they're going to be pilings. Start looting every boat for twenty miles in either direction and assemble them there as if you're trying to set up a pontoon bridge. Give the Venezuelans interesting things to think about and shoot at."

Pulling out his map, Reilly laid it on the ground and squatted down over it. Trim did likewise. "What can you tell me about this?" Reilly asked, a twig in his fingers pointing at Paku Rapids.

Trim considered. "If there's a river with no rapids to the other side of it, sir, it's likely that the rapids themselves are fairly shallow."

With a nod of his head, Reilly said, "That's what I thought.

"Okay, in the interim, while you're using maybe one platoon to look like they're repairing the bridge at Awartun Island, I want you to send the other to Kurupukari and improve that well enough to get trucks across at some point in the near future. Then I want you to send your bridge platoon—you have enough pontoons—"

"Three sets, sir, M4T6's," Trim replied. Apologetically, he added, "They're obsolete so Gordon got them cheap. Still, they're not *that* obsolete and that's enough for about four hundred and twenty-five feet of bridge."

"That should be fine. You have enough to build me a bridge to the east side of Paku Rapids, where there are no rapids."

"Suggestion, sir?" Trim offered.

"Shoot."

"I can build the bridge on the west bank, under the cover of the trees. We can build it completely, then swing it out and anchor it down."

"How long?" Reilly asked.

Trim looked over the map, scowling. "Better than a day. If I had ribbon bridge, it would take something like twenty minutes to an hour to *build* it. Pontoons are a lot slower. And, sir, it could be days or even weeks to get the vehicles carrying the pieces in." He looked down at the map again and clucked, disapprovingly, "Yes, if I can't get them close to Paku Rapids, then it could be a week, even two weeks.

"I'm also going to have to build some kind of abutments and corduroy on both sides or your tanks will turn them into bottomless morasses in nothing flat. That will take a little more time."

"Fine. Go. Get to work. If you need a few hundred people to fetch and carry, let me know."

Holding Base Snake (2nd Bn, and MI-17's), Twenty-two Miles South of Jonestown, Guyana

"Stand down!" Hampson called out. "Stand down; we're on hold again."

With curses, the men—special forces types, aviators, ground crew, and service support—began draping the nets over the helicopters and propping them up with poles and spreaders.

"Now what?" von Ahlenfeld asked.

Hampson shrugged. "Orders from regiment. Seems First Battalion is mostly held up south and west of the Essequibo. They don't know when they'll be able to cross in full force and attack toward Georgetown. Hence—"

"Hence we don't have an event that will more likely than not pin Chavez to his palace?"

"Correct, sir."

Lava shook his head with disgust, then sighed. "These things happen. Got to take 'em philosophically." He considered for a moment, then added, "Backbrief rehearsals, repetition twenty-nine, main tent, fourteen hundred hours."

Hampson nodded, sharply. "I'll see to it, sir."

The Drunken Bastard,
Eighty Miles Northwest of Aruba, Caribbean Sea

Only red light lit the *Bastard*'s interior. Outside, all was darkness barring only the thinnest sliver of the moon. The weather was calm enough, with just enough wave to the sea to give the patrol boat a gentle rocking motion.

Chin was leaning over his radar operator's shoulder, watching the screen intently, as was the radar man.

"Are you certain it's them?" the captain asked.

The operator shook his head, tapping lightly on a blip

on the screen with one finger. "No way to be certain, Skipper. But they match the distance the Cubans were likely to have been able to travel. Their course is almost right, though why they're heading for Aruba rather than Maracaibo, I can't guess at."

"What's their range?"

"Twelve miles, sir. We can be on their asses in fifteen minutes."

Chin called for his executive officer. "All hands," he said, "assume battle stations quietly. Loosen up the camouflage up front, over the 40mm, and in the rear, covering the Oerlikon, but don't jettison it."

"Sir?"

"We're going to intercept and pass by them close enough to positively identify them as the Cuban minesweepers. If they are, we pass them a few miles, then cut the camo loose and come up from behind. If not, we secure everything again and resume hunting. But—and this is important, XO—we can only blow our cover once, so it better be when we're damned sure of our target."

"Roger, Skipper. I'll see to it."

"Oh, and XO?"

"Sir?"

"See to it that the 40mm loads are mixed HE and armor piercing. There's a citadel in the *Sonya* Class that's proof against explosion. Let's see how it keeps out the water when we turn it into a colander."

★ CHAPTER FORTY-SEVEN ★

The water is deep, I cannot swim over,
And neither have I wings to fly.
Build me a . . .
—Traditional, *The Water is Wide*

The Drunken Bastard,
Eighty-nine Miles Northwest of Aruba, Caribbean Sea

A heavy duty, long-range night vision scope was mounted to the port side of the bridge. Chin looked through it long enough to get a really good mental image of the boats passing him, heading generally south. Then he turned away from the scope, blinked several times, and turned his attention to the opened up copy of *Janes* laid out on a flat surface in front of him.

"That's them," he whispered to his exec, tapping the heavy volume. "Ahead steady. Pass the word. Cut away the camouflage in eight minutes."

"Aye, aye, sir," the XO agreed, then climbed up on the starboard side and began to walk carefully forward.

Absently, Chin's hand began to caress the throttle. *Soon, my precious, soon.*

Buz, the crocodile, missed his adoring crowds of flies, singing his praises. This far out at sea, though, the only place they'd had to rest had been his scaly back, and when he'd had to dive to find a meal, they hadn't been able to stay with him. Now they were all gone and he was quite lonely.

For that matter, finding a meal had not been easy for most of the journey and he was also quite hungry, hungry enough to risk going near the big stinking thing he saw chugging through the water at a speed even he found contemptible.

Sonya-Class Minesweeper, Eighty-seven Miles Northwest of Aruba

Captain Castro paid little mind to the luxury yacht heading north and passing to his port side. He couldn't even hear its engines over the nagging cough that was all to indicate his own were even working.

What the yacht represented, however, was prominent in his mind. *Big boat . . . probably some rich man's toy. Good food. First class booze, rather than rotgut. Probably a few girls for company. And engines that can be relied on. Maybe even a TV to keep up with the news. Oh, God in Whom I am not supposed to believe, why could I not have been born in Miami?*

No matter; soon we'll dock in Aruba and I'll claim

sanctuary. The Dutch won't want me, of course, but the gringos will let me and my men in. Funny, that; that the country whose leaders most love the Castros—barring only Venezuela—is still the country with policies in place to damage them. Funny world, and evidence that not only is there a God, but He has a warped sense of humor.

Well, let me get to America and grow rich, and You and I can have a good laugh together and . . . what the . . .

The Drunken Bastard, Eighty-eight Miles Northwest of Aruba

Chin wore a headset that connected him with both guns, plus the engine room. With his own hands at the wheel, the boat made a leisurely one hundred-and-eighty degree turn. As it turned, sections and pieces of Styrofoam, canvas, and lumber were cast over the side and stern. Now was she revealed in all her warlike glory, with a 40mm gun fully manned and trained ahead on her foredeck, and another 20mm gun with a crewman firmly ensconced in the half moon shoulder mounts, with another two ready to feed the gun's ravenous appetite.

"I love this shit," Chin said aloud, in English rather than his native Mandarin. Gently his hand pushed the throttle forward, causing the *Bastard*'s nose to rise, even as the acceleration pushed her crew skipper to sternward.

When he judged the distance to be right, Chin queried, "40mm?"

"Manned and ready, Skipper."

"Oerlikon?"

"Same, Skipper."

"Forward gun, your target is the larger vessel. Oerlikon, I want you to do for the smaller, the one in tow."

"Aye, Skipper . . . Aye, aye."

Chin shifted the wheel slightly to clockwise. The *Bastard*, like the dainty, graceful lady she was, veered slightly to starboard. Chin moved the throttle forward, though not enough to cause his boat to begin to plane to any unsettling degree.

You know, Chin thought, *I don't think they know we're here. Tough shit on them.*

"Fire!"

Sonya-Class Minesweeper, Eighty-six Miles Northwest of Aruba

" . . . fuck!?" Castro shouted aloud, as the first round passed through his ship with the snap of breaking the sound barrier and the punch of shredding metal. That shell was followed by another, which exploded on his wooden hull, sending pieces of old, half rotten wood flying upward and outward. Another shell hit without exploding. He felt it through his feet as it smashed its way through armor and hull. Only then did he hear the first report of the gun that had launched it, in time with a fourth shell that sent still more of his hull into air and sea.

Castro's finger sought the button for the battle stations alarm. Overhead a speaker squawked and died with an electronic hiss. Hearing that death-hiss, he had the perfectly understandable, if pointless, thought, *God, I* hate *communism.*

No matter about the alarm, the blasts of the shells and the screams of crewmen caught by the smashing AP bolts and the fragments thrown by those were as good as any alarm. Men, some of them screaming and all frightened nearly out of their wits, most of them in their underwear, began emerging onto the deck and trying to sort themselves out.

The next set of shells came in, still striking amidships. *God knows what's keeping the engines running.*

"Get on the fucking 30mm!" Castro shouted from the bridge. There was a sudden strobe, which caused him to turn to the stern. There, he saw, a steady stream of tracers was making a colander out of the Yevgenya Class his own boat was towing. In the flickering of the tracers, he thought he saw some of the smaller boat's still smaller crew abandoning ship over the sides.

"Cut loose the tow!" Castro ordered. He saw his engineer take a couple of men in tow himself and head to the stern. *We've got to get rid of that thing or it will act like an anchor. And we're slow enough as it is.*

Forward, several of the crew began climbing into the small turret that housed the twin thirties. Unfortunately, just as the turret began to traverse in the direction of their assailant, the next volley from the enemy—*Jesus, Mary, and Joseph; who knew we even* had *enemies in this?*—struck on and around it. A ghastly scream, as from several throats, arose from the turret's open hatch. Then a sharp glow emerged from that hatch, followed by a blinding flash as one or more rounds of the boat's own ammunition went off. The screaming became considerably louder and, given that it was from burns now, worse.

Defenseless, Castro thought. *We're defenseless.* The thought was punctuated by another four rounds, striking mostly around the water line. The engines ceased their cough and simply died.

"Shit . . . Abandon ship," Captain Castro called. *How the hell do I let them know they can stop shooting now? I don't have a clue about their radio frequency. Maybe . . .*

"Abandon ship!"

The lights on the bridge were dimming now, fast, what with the engine no longer even pretending to feed power to the weak and old batteries. In the last few moments of light, Castro reached for a small case that held a flare pistol and a few rounds. As he was trying to load one, another several hits were scored on his command. He fumbled the shell and, cursing, reached for another. He slammed it in and stepped outside the bridge, aiming the flare pistol straight up. *Maybe if I let them see . . .*

Oh, please, work . . . unlike every other goddamned thing in the Cuban workers' paradise. PLEASE?

He pulled the trigger. The recoil very nearly broke his hand. But, *thank God*, the flare emerged and sailed upward, then broke into a bright, hanging light. Two more rounds struck the minesweeper, which began to take on a noticeable list to starboard. In a way, this was to the good, as the angle of the deck helped the crew get a lifeboat over the side, and then another.

Buz, perhaps no genius in objective terms but pretty damned bright for a crocodile, took one look at the flare, remembered a previous encounter—no pleasant memory, *that*—and decided that he wasn't hungry enough, after all, to hope to scrounge a meal from the big thing on top of the water.

Nor even to get close to it. My mom didn't raise no fools. For that matter, mostly she didn't raise us at all. In any case, I'm outa here, folks.

The Drunken Bastard

"Cease fire," Chin ordered, once he'd seen through the Very light that his opponent—*not much of one, maybe, but maybe not his fault, either*—had given up the unequal fight even before it began.

"Gunners and assistants, keep your guns trained on the major targets until they sink. The rest of you, small arms and prepare to receive visitors."

Paku Rapids, Essequibo River, Guyana

Trim recognized the voice of one of his platoon leaders over the roar of jets, above, the more distant explosions coming from Awartun Island, and the almost continuous buzz of chainsaws, half prepping trees to be felled to clear a path from the road to the new bridge. From somewhere to the east a heavy-duty compressor added to the din. Still further away, the rapids themselves added their own note to the symphony.

"Hump it, you motherfuckers!" cursed Master Sergeant Mike Sayer.

As he watched, a gang of Reilly's sweating grunts—*or*

they might be tankers—manhandled a deflated but damnably heavy pontoon from the back of a truck onto half a dozen stout poles laid on the ground. The baker's dozen men then took positions, five on each of two ropes attached to the float and another two at the rear with the sergeant in charge calling cadence from out front. On command, the ten began to haul on the ropes, slowly nudging the thing forward. As soon as the rearmost pole—or perhaps log would be a better description, emerged from the rear, the two men left there picked it up, straining and grunting, and trotted it to the front, laying it down again across the direction of travel.

"Good as any of Her Majesty's Sappers," commented Babcock-Moore, from behind. Trim flinched, startled. He hadn't, what with the jets and the bombing, heard his top NCO's approach.

"The bridge?" the engineer company commander asked.

"About as well as can be expected," Vic answered, with a shrug. He elaborated, "We've got about half the required span built under the overhang of the trees, other side of the island. "And the false bridge?" Moore asked, in his superior Received Pronunciation.

Since it didn't matter in the slightest if that bridge ever got repaired, assuming this one worked, Trim answered the question Moore was reluctant to ask. "Ten dead or wounded, of ours. Another half dozen of Reilly's. Those aircraft are murder."

"Another ten? Shit! Much more of this and we won't have a company, sir."

"The sooner this bridge is done and Reilly out of our

hair, the sooner we can abandon that demonstration," Trim replied.

Moore nodded, fatalistically. "Yes, sir. I know, sir. The men know, too, sir. But there's only so much a body can stand. Sir."

Awartun Island, Guyana

An ambulance siren picked up where the scream of the jets had left off. Corporal Manduleanu rode in back, comforting the wounded, as her driver screeched and swayed up the shattered remnants of the road.

If I can order men to stand this, Reilly thought, rising from out of a slit trench as the latest Venezuelan air raid roared off into the distance, *I can bloody well stand it with them. Be better if I thought this was going to work, but I'm beginning to doubt.*

He saw Tatiana in the back of the cross-marked Rover, holding a clear bag over her head with one hand while hanging on for dear life with the other.

You know, he thought, *if I were not married and she not a hooker . . . well, a man could do worse. Note to self: word with the sergeant major; consider concubinage or something.*

Even as Reilly watched, a crew of mixed infantry and sappers crept out of several holes and assembled at the log they'd been forced to abandon when the Sukhois had shown up. They'd been working together for several days by now; they didn't even need a command to bend as one, grasp as one, and lift the log onto their shoulders as one.

As one, too, they trotted off in the direction of the ruined bridge where this useless log would join a hundred of its mates, in a pile that grew faster than the engineers could make a show of bracing one to another. That was why the engineers' casualties were so much worse than his own; they had a much longer run to shelter from the shards of the old bridge.

A different Land Rover rumbled up from out of the smoke from the last attack. Stauer emerged, pointing to show his driver, Hosein, where he wanted the vehicle hidden. Then, as the Rover rolled off, he began a quick trot to Reilly.

"I don't think you can do this," Stauer said, as he plopped down beside his subordinate commander.

Reilly bit back the usual, automatic retort when someone told him he couldn't do something: *My ass!* Instead, he said, "I'm beginning to grow up, you know, boss, and this reverse child psychology bullshit works less and less well all the time."

Stauer laughed aloud, despite the circumstances. "Okay, so you're finally growing up. Let me try a different tack. Can you do this?"

Reilly sighed. Life was easier when "My ass!" was an acceptable answer. Truth be told . . . he decided to tell the truth. "I don't know. What happens if I can't?"

"We lose," Stauer answered, simply enough. "Eventually they figure out that Georgetown's not mined, figure out how to clear the mines in their own waters, and send enough here to crush us."

"Yeah. Thought so." One-armed—the other still in cast and sling—Reilly crawled fully out of the slit trench and began to walk southward.

"Where are you going?" Stauer asked.

"To the real bridge," Reilly shouted back, over one shoulder, "to put a little fire under some engineers' butts."

"Go then . . . and Lana sends her love, says not to worry about her or the baby, and *don't* get your ass killed."

I'll try.

"And where's your fucking helmet?" Stauer called.

"Lost it," Reilly answered, stomping off in search of his vehicle. It was true, too, in a way, but not in the way he intended Stauer to take it.

★CHAPTER FORTY-EIGHT★

The essential act of war is destruction, not necessarily
of human lives, but of the products of human labor.
—George Orwell, *1984*

The Drunken Bastard, Oranjestad, Aruba

The patrol boat rocked in the harbor, waiting for the
authorities to come take them into internment. The
authorities seemed in no particular hurry to do that.

Of the fifty-three men in the combined crews of the
Sonya and Yevgenya-Class minesweepers, Chin had been
able to recover thirty-seven, including Captain Castro. Of
the rest, who knew? Maybe they'd been killed by fire, or
succumbed to wounds after abandoning ship. Maybe they
were still floating out on the Caribbean somewhere. But
thirty-seven he'd found—no mean achievement, given the
light conditions—and thirty-six lay or sat on the forward
deck under armed guard. The thirty-seventh, the Cuban
captain, sat in the charthouse being interrogated. It wasn't
much of an interrogation; Castro was willing to spill

everything he knew. Among other things he knew were that, no, there'd be no more minesweepers from Cuba to help Hugo Chávez, no, he hadn't managed to get a radio signal out so there was little likelihood of the Venezuelan Navy or Air Force coming to look for them, and no, he didn't want to go back to Cuba. Both men conversed in English.

"I can understand that," Chin said, "neither I nor my crew want to go back to China, either."

"Fled the communists, did you, then?" the Cuban skipper had asked.

Chin laughed. "Oh, Captain Castro, we didn't flee the communists; we *were* the communists. But communism fled us. China's nothing more than industrial feudalism now, with all the best positions held by the children of high party cadres. I'm still a communist. I always will be. But, whatever the revolution brought to China, communism was not it."

"Sounds like Cuba," Castro commiserated, "except maybe that we still put on enough pretense to ensure poverty."

"Eh," Chin shrugged, "the American embargo hasn't helped you any, either."

"That, alone, doesn't account for it," the Cuban replied. "We trade freely with everyone else in the world, but we make nothing anybody wants. All we had, once upon a time, was something the Russians wanted, a dagger at America's breast. It wasn't much to trade, once the Russians lost the strength to push that dagger."

"I must admit," Chin said, "it was rather short-sighted of the Castros . . . the other Castros . . . to make an enemy so close and so powerful, when their friends were so far away."

"Not just an enemy," Castro said, "a vindictive enemy, and one not particularly constrained by principle when they feel threatened. Even so, though, whatever may be said, communism was a failure there, a total, complete, and utter failure.

"By the way, what's going to happen to us?"

Chin thought about that and admitted he didn't know. "You might be interned, as we're supposed to be. You might be returned to Cuba—"

"Good God, not *that!*"

"Well . . . it's a possibility."

"I can't go back to that hellhole!"

"Does your crew feel the same way?"

"Not all of them, I think," Castro replied. "Most, though."

"Hmmm . . . there *might* be a way to prevent it," Chin said. "C'mon, let's go up on deck. You'll need to translate."

"And so," Captain Castro translated for to his crew, "there is one way for us to avoid being sent home. Everyone who wants to enlist for the mercenary company of which this boat is a part, please stand and raise your right hands . . . ."

"Not bad, Skipper," Chin's exec said to him. "We go out with a crew of fifteen, and come back with a crew of forty-seven. And the five who didn't want to join us . . . well, they're Aruba's problem, now.

"Speaking of which," the XO pointed his chin at a

small boat approaching from portside, "here come the authorities now."

"All the codes destroyed?" Chin asked.

"Yes, sir. And the hard drives boiled in salt water for good measure, before we dumped them."

"Any last messages on the e-mail dump?"

"Just that Sergeant Ryan is going in, sir. Tomorrow night. And that Second Battalion is still standing by."

"Wish we could have been there for that," Chin sighed. "For either of those."

Punto Fijo, Venezuela

The target was the largest refinery in the world, though it was split between three locations and had sundry subsidiary facilities, notably Ryan's target, the enormous tank farm at Carirubana, north of Punta Fijo.

Navigation, even across the fifty miles of open water between the northeast Colombian coast and the Peninsula de Paraguana, was easy. Not only were there permanently burning flares atop the refinery from wastage of some of the refinery's byproducts, but the Venezuelan Navy and Coast Guard had essentially ceded the local waters to anyone brave or foolhardy enough to chance the mines. In effect, the three rubber boats with Sergeant Ryan, each holding four men and a frightful quantity of explosives, plus four folding mopeds, each, had the Gulf of Venezuela to themselves.

At least I hope *it's to ourselves,* thought Bronto, crouching in the front of the boat, peering frantically down into the water, from side to side. *But there's a dinosaur that doesn't know it's supposed to be extinct somewhere down there. And he has my number.*

Bronto could care less about the mines; at least that would be quick and probably painless. *Becoming an entree, however, is right out.*

Ryan, night vision goggles on his head and one hand on the throttle of the boat's electric—hence supremely quiet, especially as compared to the roar of the industrial towns to the east—motor, snickered as he watched Bronto's head turn frantically from one side of the boat to the other, his fingers fiddling with his own NVG's focus ring.

Can't say as I blame him, though. That fucking croc was big.

Ryan checked his watch and then his GPS. He looked left to where one of the three boats was already veering off toward Amuay and its refinery complex. *And I didn't even hear them change speed. This is good.*

There were about a hundred distinct subtargets in Ryan's major target, the Carirubuana tank farm, ranging from smaller tanks, almost not worth the bother, to five that were just outrageously huge. There were also a number of good sized tankers, five at last count, tied up to a floating wharf west of the tank farm, where they could be filled by pipeline. The tankers had been there, unmoving except for the up and down of the tides and the rocking of the waves, since the day of the mining, early in the war. Ryan didn't intend to do anything about them; getting the tanks would put a big enough dent in Venezuela's long-term economic prospects, all on its own.

Passing the docked tankers, Ryan reduced power and pulled the throttle *cum* steering handle toward himself, causing the inflatable boat to turn to starboard. There was enough artificial light around the tank farm, this close, that the NVG's became superfluous. He turned his off and pulled them from his face to hang around his neck.

As a practical matter, we couldn't possibly prep every tank for demo, Ryan thought, as the rubber boat coasted in toward the gravel and rock shoreline. *Besides there being about a hundred of them, they're lined up along about thirty miles of roads, in more than a square mile of area. So instead . . .*

As soon as the boat touched down, Bronto sprang out of it, almost as if he had a huge crocodile on his tail. The short, stout operative carried a silenced submachine gun in one hand and dragged a spike with a rope attached by the other. As soon as the rope grew taut, he laid the weapon down, turned and began to pull with all of his not inconsiderable strength, using the impetus and lift of the waves to haul the thing as far onto the shore as possible. The other three slid off the rubber gunwales and into the surf, then lent their own strength to the job of getting the heavily laden boat firmly ashore.

When Bronto judged that done, he used both arms to drive the spike through the gravel into the soil below. Then he picked up the submachine gun and returned at a trot to the boat. There Ryan, Rohrer, and Loser were already unloading the cargo, mostly mopeds and explosives, onto shore. They laid the cargo low, not piling it, on the off chance a guard might pass by. The explosives were already packed, four sets each, in some highly expendable civilian backpacks.

"Rohrer, Loser, head thataway," Ryan ordered, pointing to the east-northeast. "Bronto, you're with me."

As the first two puttered off, Ryan and Bronto unfolded their mopeds. Hoisting heavy packs onto their backs, they mounted and then began the jaunt to the south. Ryan in the lead, they passed up and over a ramp that surmounted the pipeline leading to the floating wharf, then turned generally east, passing between two linear cuts filled with greenish water. Sixty meters past those, they came to a small section of four tanks, two of them LNG tanks. A large pool, black as midnight and polluted as sin, stank just to the east. Ryan raised a fist to call a halt.

Both dismounted. While Bronto took one knee, facing toward the center of the complex, Ryan trotted to the nearest of the LNG tanks. He had to climb over a low berm, intended to control fire, to get close to it. Once there, he dumped his pack and removed a roughly twenty-five-pound shaped charge. Unfolding the thing's integral wire legs, he aimed it center of mass at the tank, but low, then flicked a switch to arm it, and another to set it for radio detonation. A small LED shone red, indicated the charge was now armed and dangerous. A green LED, the one for the radio-controlled detonator, flashed green. From the pack, Ryan pulled out a white phosphorous grenade. He pulled the grenade out of its protective cylinder just enough to remove the safety clip. Then he partially pushed it back in, grasped and yanked out the ring. He set the grenade, still in the tube, right in front of the shaped charge.

Holding the pack by one hand and one strap, he pattered over to the next tank and repeated the process, then did the same for the next two, these being oil or gasoline tanks. The smell said, "gasoline."

This is going to be better than the best Fourth of July . . . ever.

That task done, and his pack now empty, Ryan left the pack and hoofed back to the mopeds and Bronto. "Let's go."

The mopeds carried them around another midnight-black, stinking pool, to the next set of targets, some sixteen tanks, two very small, three large, and eleven of medium size. They were only interested in the three largest, plus the centermost of the mediums.

They stopped by the centermost medium and ditched the mopeds. This time—in part because, unburdened, he could, and in part because the target area was much more open than the first one—Ryan accompanied the heavily laden Bronto.

When Bronto was done, and without another word, both men remounted their mopeds and returned to the shore by the boat to pick up eight more charges.

"What the fu—!" Bronto exclaimed, as he tripped over the reclining form of a man, fast asleep inside one of the berms that surrounded a particularly large tank. There was a shotgun next to the sleeper, something he apparently forgot as he bolted upward to a sitting position. As the man sat up, Bronto continued his fall to the ground, landing with an *oof* and a thump.

"*Quien es?*" the roused guard asked. "Julio, is that you?"

"No, it isn't Julio," Ryan whispered, as he aimed his own submachine gun at the shadowy form still half on the ground. "Sorry about this."

The only sound made was the chattering of the weapon's bolt, the tinkle of spent casings hitting the gravel, and the surprised grunt of an unoffending security guard as five 9mm rounds tore his life away.

Ryan consulted his watch, once again. *Quarter to four. Almost time for us to be getting out of here.* He made a series of quick radio calls, first to Fails, then to each of the two teams that were aimed at one of the refinery complexes.

"Almost done here," Fails answered. "Had to kill two security guards," said the leader of the team at Amuay. "Otherwise, ready to go." "Already loading up to head to sea," said the last group.

"Sergeant Ryan," Bronto asked, returning from setting his final charge, that aimed at one of the two huge LNG tanks nearest the southern edge of the complex, "why didn't they guard this shit better? This was almost too easy."

"Because they're fundamentally unserious about war, Bronto," the team leader replied. "Most people in the world are. And because they're not serious, they don't—didn't anyway—give it serious thought.

"Let's go."

A mile or a bit more west of the arms that defined the opening of the harbor, three rubber boats, all close together, rocked with the gentle waves. To the east, both within the harbor and stretching north and south from it, the coastline was still brightly lit by the lights of the civilian communities that served the refineries. The boats, now without their burden of explosive charges, rode higher than they had.

"There are going to be a lot of widows and orphans in those towns in a few minutes," observed Rohrer. "There are still crews manning the refineries."

"Yeah," Ryan sadly agreed. *But fewer than you think.* "Nothing much to be done about it. When you make war, you have to assume war's going to be made on you in return." He keyed his microphone and said, "Team Amuay, detonate your target."

"Roger."

Ryan and his boat's crew glanced slightly northward, to where the beacon fire above the refinery burned in the night. They saw a single bright flash, and then the beacon went out. Four seconds, plus a little, later, the sound of the explosion reached them. A few seconds after that, a fireball formed and began to rise above the refinery. It was too far away to hear any screams from the workers who were, without a doubt, being burned alive in the inferno. The waters around the boats lit up with the flames from that inferno, reflected from the bottom side of the dark cloud forming above the wreck of the refinery.

"Fire the other refinery," Ryan ordered.

"Roger."

The flash came quickly, and the sound of the blast reached them, this time, before the fireball could form. This one was closer, close enough that they just might have been able to hear the screaming, intermixed with the roar of burning oil.

"Our turn," the team leader said to nobody in particular. He set the detonation control board on his lap, and turned a key. *Now* the armed charges were ready to receive their commands, as he was ready to send them. He flicked a switch. Another great flash told of several charges, probably four, assuming everything worked, going off as one. The tank farm was the farthest target, about two miles away. The flames leapt upward long before the sound of the blast reached them. Another switch was thrown, then another, and another. Each set still more Hells alight. He hesitated over the last switch; that was the one that was set to fire off two very large LNG tanks, which were also unfortunately close to Creolandia, the urbanization to the south of the tank farm.

"Nothing to be done about it," he said, softly, as he flicked the final firing switch.

Carirubana Tank Farm, Punto Fijo, Venezuela

Fire and smoke were everywhere. In the guard shack there was panic. The sound of sirens filled the air, as firefighting equipment rushed to the scene of the disaster.

So far, the blasts hadn't done all that much damage. The shaped charges, as planned, had burned their way into the tanks, causing some to split at the seams and gush oil in all directions, while others merely began to leak rapidly until the gushing fluid hit upon a piece of burning white phosphorous. Still, the flames were mostly contained inside the protective berms that surrounded each tank.

Then the two shaped charges by the largest LNG tanks

went off, along with another two aimed at, in one case, a gasoline tank, and in the other, a simple oil tank. The LNG tanks' charges had been set to hit center of mass, rather than at the base. Their jet streams punched right through the exterior wall, the several feet of insulation, and then the interior tank. At the same time, the explosions pulverized the cardboard cylinders holding the grenades. In one case, this also shattered the grenade body, released the white phosphorous. In the other, the grenade didn't shatter, but was thrown out to release its spoon and detonate normally, the shards of white phosphorous forming a flaming flower, brilliant even against the backdrop of burning oil.

LNG, with considerable energy release merely from conversion from liquid to a gaseous state, jetted out of the holes thus formed and began to spread. In milliseconds, the first gas touched the white phosphorous and began to burn. The flames quickly sped back to set the gas alight as it exited the holes formed. This, too, increased the heat inside the tanks. And with the heat, so increased the pressure. Quite quickly. When the first tank exploded, and all that gas went off, it simply leveled the town of Creolandia, killing more people than would be accurately counted for weeks. Indeed, the heat was so great, and the radius of that heat so large, that the town was destroyed, and its people incinerated, even the bones, along with every piece of firefighting equipment, and their crews, that had reached the scene. Moreover, the blast was sufficient to knock over, to completely collapse and crush, dozens more tanks, which then spilled their oil and gasoline onto the ground in a series of floods. That, too, burned.

It was Hell. It was war.

From where he sat in the back of the rubber boat, Ryan watched the spreading flames. He felt . . . indescribable. Part of him was filled with satisfaction at a job well and truly done. The other part . . .

I'm a murderer. I was always a killer . . . but this feels different than any other killing. How many people were there? Could I have done it differently? I confess, I don't know how.

Sighing, he started the ultra silent electric motor and spun the boat about, until the brightly burning and roaring flames were to his back. "Let's go get ourselves interned, guys."

★CHAPTER FORTY-NINE★

Always look on the bright side of life . . .
—Monty Python, *Life of Brian*

Miraflores Palace, Caracas, Venezuela

Hugo Chavez wept, openly and without shame, his shoulders heaving in great sobs. Even his military staff, quite despite the fact that most of them loathed him, felt sorry for him. The crowds, once buoyant and then grown sullen hostile, that had swarmed the area of the palace were dissipated as the news of the disaster sank in. Venezuela was ruined.

"Make peace, Mr. President," said Nicholas, the foreign minister. "It's all that's left. We don't know how many more tricks the enemy has to play on us; we only know that he doesn't seem to run out of them."

"No!" Chavez shrieked, through his unfeigned tears. "After everything they've done to us? No!"

It wasn't like we didn't start it, thought Quintero, the general. *That said, I'm inclined to agree with you, Chavez, you piece of peasant shit. Nobody should be allowed to do this to us and get away with it. Five thousand dead? Six thousand? Ten thousand? We may never know.*

That said, even if not said, we're getting nowhere . . .

"Make peace, Mr. President," Nicholas repeated. "We're stymied at *Ciudad* Guayana. The mercenaries— not even mercenaries, simple Guyanan troops under mercenary leadership—toss back every assault. Our troops in Guyana are starving. Soon, we'll be starving here, too.

"Basically, Hugo, we're fucked.

"And it's not as if I didn't warn you."

"The Cuban minesweepers aren't coming, either, Mr. President," Admiral Fernandez added. "The only way we're getting rid of those mines is if we make peace and the enemy *tells* us how many went where."

"What . . . what happened to the minesweepers?" Chavez asked, looking up and using one hand to wipe away the tears coursing down his ruddy face.

"Ambushed at sea, sir," Fernandez replied. "Most of their crews signed on with the mercenaries. We wouldn't even know what happened except that some of them, true to their country, refused to sign on. They're all interned by the Dutch on Aruba, though supposedly the faithful Cuban sailors will be released soon."

"And, no, Hugo," Nicholas said, "before you ask, the Dutch are not going to turn them over to us, no more than Columbia is going to turn over the planes that dropped the mines or the special forces team that destroyed Punto Fijo and the refineries. Before it became obvious we were losing the war, they might have . . . the Dutch, I mean, not the Colombians. Now? They're just not afraid of us anymore. And Trinidad and Tobago told me to bend over and kiss my own ass, adding that I was a Spanish pirate, to boot."

"There's one other thing," General Quintero said. He nodded in the direction of the blue-uniformed Air Force. "Right now, the Air Force is doing a good job of making sure that the mercenaries in Guyana stay on the west side of the Essequibo River. Eventually, though, the gringos are going to get across. Maybe by night. Maybe by some ford we don't know about and they haven't found yet. But get across they will. And then they'll hit our starving troops. Starving troops, Mr. President, are unlikely to put up much of a fight."

"I thought I gave orders for them to live off the land," Chavez said.

"Yes, Mr. President, you did. That's not as easy as it sounds."

South of Cheddi Jagan Airport, Guyana

"Dinner," announced Sergeant Major Arrivillaga, leading a scraggly looking burro by a rope, "is served. Or will be, once this thing is butchered and cooked." A dozen chickens, necks already wrung, were draped across the burro's bony back, as was a double sack of yucca.

Larralde glanced over the animal, distantly hoping it was too dumb to understand its fate. "What did it cost us?" he asked.

Mao sighed. "In money? Nothing. The farmer wouldn't sell, too worried about the day when *his* family would have had to eat the donkey. I had to take it. And the chickens. And the yucca. There weren't any eggs. Besides the yucca there were no fruits or vegetables near to hand, either. And flour was right out."

Larralde sighed. "Needs must."

"Yeah," Mao agreed. "But you know what? That farmer, who was probably fairly neutral to begin with, is going to be joining the guerillas soon. He'll have to, because that's going to be the only way for him to feed his wife and kids, and he'll want to, because he's got a good reason to hate us now."

"So why didn't you just save us the future trouble and kill him?" Larralde asked mildly.

"Because I'm a soldier, not a barbarian. And maybe, just maybe, if they can lift the siege—well, what other word is there for it?—in good time, we might be able to feed those people soon enough that he won't have to turn guerrilla. Maybe.

"I also ran into some transportation troops, waiting around pulling their puds while their truck sat idle for lack of gas. They said the Marines are eating high off the hog in Georgetown, out of our stores, because, since there's no way to transport it to us, they might as well."

"We'd have done the same in their circumstances. Besides, I've heard that Georgetown is seething at the rationing. Some of that food is probably going to feed the civilians."

"Drop in the bucket, that," Mao snorted. He grinned then. "Gotta confess, it's a satisfying notion that, if the people in Georgetown rise up and *win*, they'll get all the revenge on the Marines I'd ever dream of."

"Too true," Larralde agreed, likewise grinning at the thought. "On the other hand," he added, more soberly, "if we lose control of Georgetown, then there's no way we'll ever get resupplied."

"Point," Arrivillaga conceded. "Well . . . win a few, lose a few."

"Speaking of losing," Larralde said, "the troops are getting pretty convinced we're going to lose here, and stinking."

Not that this was any news to Arrivillaga—he kept his hand on the company's pulse a lot more closely than Larralde did—but he asked anyway, "Who did we lose?"

"Three people. Two deserters in the night, Gollarza and Flores. Their platoon leader thought they were off in the bushes, fucking, and so didn't report it until a couple of hours after you left. And Ponce shot himself in the foot, about an hour ago."

Mao scowled, *that*, even more than the desertion, was a bad sign. Very formally he asked, "Have I the major's permission to handle this?"

A little sadly, Larralde nodded.

"Field rules?"

Again, Larralde nodded agreement.

"Compan-eee," Mao shouted, loud enough to be heard over artillery fire, "formation . . . on me . . . and bring me that son of a bitch, Ponce."

Mao took one look at the medics, sympathetically carrying Ponce on a stretcher, and let out a scream of outrage. Storming over, he slapped one medic, punched the other, and then reached down and spilled the self-wounded man to the ground. Rifle in one hand, he bent over and grabbed a shrieking Private Ponce by the juncture of his shoulder harness. Then he dragged him, screaming still more with each jolt across the broken ground, and dumped him in the middle of the clearing where the company, minus minimal security, was forming in a C shape. There he let go of Ponce's harness, then gave the man a kidney kick.

"Bastard!

"Fall in," Mao ordered, hate and rage dripping from each syllable. "Parade . . . rest."

"Last night," Arrivillaga announced, "we had two deserters. If I can catch them they'll hang from the shortest tree I can find sufficient to lift their feet no more than half a millimeter off the ground. This motherfucker, however"—he gave Ponce another kick, for emphasis, raising another scream—"decided to shoot himself to get evacuated back. I don't have time or leisure to hang the son of a bitch at the moment, so this will have to do."

Without another word, Mao shouldered his rifle, aimed and fired, spattering Ponce's head like an overripe melon. The private barely had time to register shock before he was already food for the ants.

"And *that's* the penalty for a self-inflicted wound. Now where's Ponce's squad leader? Ah, there . . . good. You, you personally, bury the piece of shit. The rest of you, dismissed."

Lily Vargas alternated between throwing up and crying on Carlos' shoulder. "He . . . he . . . he . . . *murdered* him. Just like that . . . he *murdered* Ponce . . . he . . ."

"Shhhh, Lily," Carlos said. "It wasn't murder. It was an execution."

"There was no trial," she hissed. "No judge. No court. No *law!*"

"An execution," Carlos insisted. "There was no time for much else. Laws of war." *And I can recall an occasion when you were not so insistent on a trial for some criminals, dear.*

Again, she threw up—not that there was much for her to toss, given the short rations—and then fell into more sobbing.

"I . . . I *hate* this," she blubbered.

I'm not far behind you there, love, he thought, stroking her hair for whatever comfort it might give. *Maybe we should both take the route Eva and her boyfriend did, and just get the hell out of here.*

"Happier now?" Larralde asked, a couple of hours later, passing Arrivillaga a scrounged wooden bowl of donkey and yucca stew.

Mao's eyes narrowed as he took the proffer. "What are you talking about, sir? That was disgusting. That it was also necessary doesn't make it less disgusting."

"No, not much less."

Mao set the stew down; he didn't feel very hungry anymore. "I warned you, sir, before we ever started this, that there was going to be a price for the half-assed training we gave these boys and girls."

"Yeah, I know. Nothing to be done about it then, nothing to help with it now."

"Even so, Hugo fucked us. We should have had *years*

to get ready for this. We should have had minesweepers, and units already at full strength without taking street sweepings in at the last minute. We should have had professionals, properly trained and led, not this . . . this . . . rabble."

"You go to war with the army you have," Larralde answered. "It's just the way it is."

"Bullshit, sir; you plan your war and then make the army you need to fight it."

Larralde shook his head. "Hugo told me, back when I convinced him to interfere and alter the plan, that there wasn't time; he had to fight it, now, or there'd never be another chance."

"Still bullshit," Mao retorted. "And you can tell my cousin I said so. Hugo, too, for that matter. Moreover, you can—"

Whatever Mao was about to say was lost, as a gun, a very large gun, fired from somewhere to the south, its shell screeching past the company line to explode in the trees to the north.

★ CHAPTER FIFTY ★

Force and fraud are in war the two cardinal virtues.
—Thomas Hobbes, *Leviathan*

Paku Rapids, Essequibo River, Guyana

Like everything else in war, building the bridge, smoothing a path from the west bank of the Essequibo, through the rapids, prepping to drop some hundreds of trees to make a way suitable for heavy vehicles between the bridge and the highway, and corduroying the bridge's entrance and exit had taken twice as long as it should have, and been twice as hard. It had also cost the lives of three men, two drowned while working in the jungle's pitch black nights, and a third crushed by a falling tree. Considerably more had fallen by the ruined bridge to the north, as they strove to make the appearance of repairs.

Two men stood in the early evening gloom, by the east bank of the island that split the river, overlooking the gently undulating pontoon bridge that lay parallel to the bank. One of these was in full combat gear, with helmet.

The other wore the same, except that his helmet was missing, replaced by a floppy jungle hat. Both were soaked to about chest level.

Reilly took the floppy hat from his head, clutching it tightly in one hand. "I'd feel better about this if you were a good Catholic," he said. "But, still, you're a man of God. Do your thing, Chaplain."

Chaplain Wilson removed his helmet, passing it to Reilly. From his left cargo pocket he pulled a sodden tippet, a thin scarf, which he draped across the back of his neck, letting the long ends hang toward the ground at about knee level. Then, raising both arms Heavenward, he began to pray, "Lord, God of Hosts, Heavenly Father, bless this bridge . . ."

And the Holy Hand Grenade of Antioch, Reilly mentally, and irreverently, added.

To the west, as if to punctuate, began a series of explosions, joined by the sound of falling trees. The engineers were clearing the way.

A placid jaguar, high in a tree overlooking the river, watched the proceedings without any real comprehension. Even the explosion far off to the west didn't unsettle the beast. After all, it had been hearing similar sounds from the same direction for quite some time without any ill effects.

The gasoline motors of two small engineer boats sputtered to life. Under their coxswains' control, they pushed the boats away from the bank, taking the slack from the connecting coils that linked boats and bridge. On the opposite bank, a grunting crew of engineers, sweating in the sodden jungle's heat, likewise strained, pulling taut the ropes that led to the bridge's exit end.

Once the pontooned span was into the current, the river took over. Now it was the boats' task to control the rate at which the bridge swung outward. Their motors roared furiously with the strain, trying but not quite succeeding at their current power in holding the thing steady against the current. The bridge's swing picked up speed.

Now the crews on the ropes leading to the far side came into their own. Under the lashing tongues of their sergeants, they first pulled the ropes tight, then bent their own lines to bring the stout cables first against and then halfway around still stouter trees. Tree trunks smoked, as did thick leather gloves, but slowly the rate of swing dropped.

Then, inch by inch, with the engineer boats pulling steadily, the bridge was allowed to rotate down to where the prepared embankments awaited it. There, too, awaited still another crew of engineers, this one with strong steel cables to bind it fast to the trees to either side. Even as these leapt to, a further crew made the bridge fast to the near bank.

Sergeant John Wagner, tank commander of Charlie Three-three, kept his left hand on the pintle-mounted machine gun to his front. With the other he absent-mindedly stroked the ears of a placid basset hound, Three-three's mascot, that rode between the loader's hatch and Wagner's own. In action, the hound was trained to get down into the turret's bustle. For now though, riding atop the thing, having its luxurious ears stroked, was very nearly the basset's idea of short-legged, long-eared, doggie Heaven.

Wagner's tank emerged from the jungle and pivoted onto the rapidly crumbling black-surfaced road. An MP with flashlights directed the tank to follow the road to the north. This, Three-three did, until it met upon yet another flashlight-equipped MP, whose signals directed it back into the jungle, but to the opposite side. Another tank, Charlie Three-one, Wagner was sure, preceded his own into the jungle.

Just before the hard right turn, Wagner flipped his night vision goggles down over his eyes. He almost didn't need them; the smell of recently detonated explosives was strong enough practically to mark the trail on its own. And the exhaust from Three-one filled in for whatever the explosive's fumes didn't cover.

Once off the road, the tank plunged down into a depression—it was too broad to call it a ditch—that lined the side. Wagner braced for the impact, and absorbed it. The basset ignored it.

With a roar of the engine and a shuddering lurch, Three-three then climbed up again out of that depression. Once past it, Wagner saw a trail marked on both sides with chemlights. *They must be infrared*, Wagner thought, *or I'd have seen them without the goggles.* Lightsticks, mounted higher up, marked trees that had to be avoided.

The way was twisted, winding, and jolting. That the engineers had, arguably, traced out the best path for the battalion and cleared it to the best of their abilities didn't mean that it was a *good* path.

After a kidney-jarring drive that took well over an hour, Wagner halted his tank a couple of hundred meters from the rapids. He had to; Charlie Three-one was stopped, blocking the way. After a wait of perhaps ten minutes, Three-one rattled off. Wagner ordered his own forward to take the same holding position. There the tank waited, stationary but with its motor running, awaiting its ground guide. Even stationary, the churning engine caused it to vibrate like some live thing. To the dog, that was all gravy.

Wagner became aware of a shadow, a short-seeming shape, just to one side of the tank. "Charlie Three-three?" the shape shouted over the engine's roar.

"That's us," Wagner shouted back, both hands cupping his mouth.

Hey, where's my petting? the basset fumed. *I've got my rights, you know. Who do you think brings the luck to keep this monster moving, huh?*

Two cone-topped flashlights lit up in red. "Sergeant Sayer here; Bridge Platoon. Follow me!"

At the riverbank Sayer crossed his flashlights, bringing the tank to a stop. A good distance away a line of lights— white, red, white; one rising above the other—shone. The guide climbed aboard and shuffled across the steel deck to stand beside Wagner, who removed his helmet.

Pointing to the far bank—at least Wagner thought it was the far bank—the ground guide asked, "See those lights?"

"Roger."

"You're on your own from here to the island. Keep those lights lined up and you'll be fine. It's an island.

Another guide will meet you there and guide you to and across the bridge. Got it?"

"Got it."

"Okay, lemme unass and then go. Oh, and have your driver button up or he'll drown and flood your tank. This will piss off everyone who's supposed to be coming behind you. And then Colonel Reilly will shoot you."

The path down, Wagner was surprised to discover, was also corduroyed. Nothing else would feel quite the same as the tank lumbered—*pun not intended*—down it. The gun was hyperelevated, to keep it out of the water. Indeed, once the tank reached its tipping point and bounced down, the 105mm barrel remained parallel to the river's surface, until the tank leveled out on the rocks. After that point it aimed mostly at the sky. It served, as it turned out, as a pretty fair aiming marker for the three lights rising from the island ahead.

"I hate this fucking shit, Sergeant," the driver grumbled. No tank driver enjoyed driving blind.

"Would you rather be breathing water, Corporal Glass?" Wagner asked conversationally.

The water, though the river here was not deep, surged over the tank's hull and around the turret. The dog eyed the flood nervously. Sure, it knew it could swim the river, but it wasn't nearly as confident of the ability of the humans to do so. *And without them, who the hell feeds me and scratches my ears?*

"Tell your driver to unbutton," Babcock-Moore told Wagner, at the western edge of the island. "From here on, he has to watch and listen to *me*; there's no space or time to risk delayed commands."

"Roger, Top," Wagner replied, then intercommed Glass to tell him.

"Thank *God*," Glass said, as he hoisted the heavy hatch from over his head, letting in blessedly fresh air for a change and, for a change, able to see for himself. "If I'd wanted to be on a sub I'd have signed up for the *Naughtius*."

The first set of pontoons, already bobbing from previous crossings, sank down better than a foot and then buoyed right back up. *This* was the first event of the evening to upset the pooch. *You guys can't be fucking serious,* it howled, "Ahhwhoooh . . . rooo." *This is a tank, a metal monster. It doesn't* belong *on a float bridge. I shoulda listened to the frigging mules and deserted when I had the chance.* "Ahhwhoooh."

They crossed at Babcock-Moore's speed, and he was walking slowly. Even so, each pontoon sank perilously as the leading edge of the treads pressed upon it. The passage took two minutes, or slightly less. It only *seemed* like hours.

Moore patted the tank's rump as it rumbled off, down the infrared-marked trail, to its company's assembly area.

Gonna be a looongngng night. Nah, be realistic. It's going to be two *long nights, because at this rate, we won't get the entire battalion, with its attachments, across before daylight.*

Linden, Guyana

Speed of passage, however, picked up once the tanks were across. Everything else was in a much lower weight class, with no chance of upsetting the bridge. By an hour before dawn, the bulk of First Battalion had closed on the small city of Lethem, with only a few stragglers still to show up.

"Snyder? Six," Reilly radioed, with the power turned all the way up. "Are your people in contact anywhere?" His turretless Eland was parked on the Mackenzie side of town, along Republic Avenue, a couple of hundred meters from the Demerara's east bank. Snyder's heavily reinforced command was strung out in an east-west line, about forty miles to the north.

"No, sir," the Bravo commander replied, "but I've got both roads under observation, north and northeast of Vryheid."

"Any change to their status?"

"They seem dug in pretty well, with overhead cover. Some obstacles. No mines to speak of. For recon, they don't seem to be pushing anyone out much more than a klick from their front line. Also, we got two deserters during the night, a man and a woman. I don't know how much of what they say to believe, but the sheer fact that they deserted says morale's probably not good up there."

"Yeah," Reilly said. "Or they could be fuck buddies who couldn't stand the idea of one or the other getting killed."

"That's possible, too, Six."

"So what do you think, the main road"—the Soesdyke-Linden Highway—"or the one that parallels it to the east?"

Snyder hesitated for a half a minute before replying, "That's a pretty big call for you to dump on me, boss."

"Yeah, but you can see what's there and I can't, at least until we get the UAVs in range and ready to go. So which road?"

"East," Snyder answered. "The defense status is about the same, but the river really constricts your space to maneuver to the west. The east's more open, mostly farmland and pasture."

"East it is," Reilly agreed. "Leave one platoon in the east to screen my advance. Make it the scouts . . ."

"It is the scouts," Snyder interrupted.

"Good. The rest of your company, plus Third Battalion's Elands, I want you to take into an attack to threaten the Linden Highway, Low Wood, and Lana. I'll tell you when to begin, but assemble your boys starting now. If you make progress, good, but mostly I want you to attract their attention, pin them in place, and raise enough noise that they don't hear the rest of us coming until we're nearly upon them. Or until we put on the music, whichever comes first."

"Wilco."

"They don't know we're across," George said, confidently, his eyes scanning the surrounding skies. "If they did, they'd be on us like flies on shit. Instead, they're still going after the wrecked bridge."

Reilly nodded. That was his estimation, as well. "They're going to know soon enough," he said. Then he asked, "Did the sappers tuck the bridge back in under the trees?"

"Yes," the battalion's top NCO answered, "just as soon at the last vehicle was across."

"All right, then . . . time to start to roll. Or rock and roll, if you prefer."

George took a look at the floppy hat on Reilly's head and started to take off his own helmet. "You really need to take—."

Holding up a restraining hand, Reilly stopped him cold. "No, Top; it's my own goddamned temper that cost me the old one. My fault, my problem, and until a new one shows up . . ."

George dropped the hands that had begun tugging at his helmet straps. "You're pig-headed, sir; anyone ever tell you that?"

"Vices of my virtues, Top; I've always been that way."

Even heavily upgraded into Jaguars, the T-55 was not remotely as quiet as an American Abrams. Still, there were degrees of noisy. The sound a T-55, or a load of them, produced at five miles an hour, with the engine practically idling, was a lot less than the cacophony they put out rolling at thirty. It also cut down substantially on the dust raised, though Reilly had three water trucks at the point of the column to spread enough moisture to keep the dust to a minimum, anyway.

"Battalion," Reilly ordered over the radio, "speed of march is slow . . . Roll."

As he gave the command, already the sound of firing—Snyder's merry pirates in action—came from the northwest.

★ CHAPTER FIFTY-ONE ★

Valour is still *value*. The first duty for a man
is still that of subduing Fear. We must get rid of Fear;
we cannot act at all till then.
—Thomas Carlyle,
On Heroes, Hero-Worship and the Heroic in History

Soesdyke-Linden Highway,
South of Cheddi Jagan Airport, Guyana

Mao flopped himself behind the berm fronting Larralde's command bunker and slithered in. A stream of machine gun bullets followed him, chipping wood from the trees and raising meter-high spouts of dirt and dust from the berm.

"They're not really trying, sir," Arrivillaga announced. "This is a fucking feint."

"Seems like they're trying to me," Larralde said.

"No . . . no. I got a good look. There's not a single tank out there, only some armored cars—those old French jobs, I think—with guns. I figure I saw half of them and that half came to no more than ten vehicles. That's a company, though maybe a big one, and it's holding an entire battalion in place. But a company, attacking a battalion, is not serious. It's playacting. And, somehow, I think the rest of their heavy battalion got across the Essequibo. Just a feeling, mind you, but I know of no contrary facts to dispute it."

"Okay," Larralde agreed, "they're acting. And maybe they did cross the river in the night." He dropped down to the bottom of the dugout, picked up a field telephone, and began to turn the crank to contact higher. He passed on Mao's observation, and was duly tut-tutted away by the battalion operations officer.

"Look," Larralde insisted, "just pass it on to brigade, will you?" Finally, in exasperation, he slammed the phone back on its cradle.

Hmmm . . . maybe I should have let Hugo relieve the lot of them.

"Battalion says not to worry about it."

"Best proof possible that we *should* be worrying about it," Arrivillaga countered.

"Yeah." Changing the subject to something he *could* do something about, he asked, "How are the troops holding up?"

Mao gave a wicked and cynical grin. "Scared shitless, frankly. If I were the brigade commander I'd put a line of MPs out, about a kilometer back, to shoot on sight anyone who runs."

"Casualties?"

Mao shook his head. "Not a one, which is another reason I think it's a feint."

"Hm . . . if it's a feint here, I wonder where it won't be."

"East," Arrivillaga answered. "The river's too constricting to the west. Not that we can do much about that; it's not even our *battalion*'s sector."

Road to Saint Cuthberts, Guyana

The scouts, now rejoined to the mass of the battalion, were about five kilometers forward, moving in a ragged line to the north, slowly. Reilly had his own APC parked a half a klick south of the intersection. Dismounted, standing by the side of the road, he gave each of his subordinate units their final orders as they came abreast of him.

First came the battery. "Over there, one klick," Reilly told Bunn, the battery commander. His good arm stretched to the northwest, showing the direction. "Priority of fires to the scouts, initially, then to me, personally."

After the battery came C Company's fifteen functioning tanks, plus a weapons platoon. Two more Jaguars were broken down along the road to the south with Dumisani and Viljoen's crew trying desperately to get them moving again.

"Turn your mortars over to the battalion mortar platoon and your AT guns to the sergeant major," Reilly ordered. "Up this road . . . form on line, center of mass four kilometers in, parallel to the road and north of it, oriented northwest. Assume we're going to change to 'armor, Alpha' as soon as we break them."

"Roger, sir," Captain Green answered. "I'll keep my first platoon on my left."

"Good. Go."

A Company arrived, three platoons of mechanized infantry with a section of Elands, another of mortars, and a brace of towed, 60mm antitank guns.

"You won't need those for now," Reilly said, pointing at the guns. "Turn them over to the sergeant major. Your mortars go to Master Sergeant Peters. For the rest, form up behind the tanks, south of the road, spread out to support them."

Alpha drove off in the wake of Charlie. Peters' six 120mm mortars came next. Peters spit tobacco juice over the side of his vehicle, then turned his attention to Reilly.

"Sergeant Peters, take control of those four mortars gaggling about. You all fall in behind the infantry. Don't set up until I tell you, which isn't going to be until you can range the airport. Then . . ." Reilly stopped speaking, listening for a moment to the chattering of massed machine guns, interspersed with a series of heavier blasts. Then he said, happily and with a broad smile, "I see the scout platoon has made contact."

Soesdyke-Linden Highway, South of Cheddi Jagan Airport, Guyana

"Ah, shit," Mao said, as more firing broke out to the east. He repeated it as soon as he heard and felt the heavier blasts of a mass of cannon, firing from somewhere farther south. "I told you, didn't I?" Scant seconds later, the shells from those cannon began falling somewhere on the sister battalion to the east. Again, Arrivillaga repeated, "Ah, shit."

Suddenly the rate of cannon fire doubled, as some new battery, farther to the east, opened up.

"Heavy mortars," observed Larralde. "No cannon can match that rate of fire. You were right, Top, this attack wasn't serious."

"So what the fuck do we do, sir? This is heavy tactical thinking. That's your job, not mine."

Larralde licked his lips and exhaled loudly. "You stay here. I'm taking First and Third Platoon and stretching them at right angle. You thin out Second to cover the entire front." The major chewed at his lip for just a moment before shouting, "Go!"

As Larralde crept out from the command bunker, keeping carefully low lest that not serious attack on his company turn dreadfully serious for him, he heard something approximating music:

"I AM IRONMAN!"

"Now *that*," Mao shouted after his commander, "that is *serious*."

Tank Charlie Three-three,
Southeast of Cheddi Jagan Airport, Guyana

The basset hound didn't need to be told to get down into the bustle rack. As soon as it heard the first rounds of machine gun fire, it padded over on its own.

Stupid humans, it thought. *Disturbing my sleep for no*

worthwhile reason. Even so, it knew its duties. The dog raised its muzzle and added its own voice—*Ahwooo*—to: "I AM IRONMAN."

Wagner watched it go, then reached down to flick the lever that let his seat fall. Long experience let him flick it enough to drop him to where only the top of his head and his eyes peered out over the cupola. With one hand he reached back to pull the hatch to an almost closed position, over and protecting his head.

The grunts, still in their APC's, were about two to three hundred meters behind the line of tanks. Their machine guns rattled, rounds passing between the tanks, beating down any return fire that might have hurt their *Panzerkameraden*. It wasn't quite sufficient to suppress all the return fire; the Venezuelans were sending back a pretty good volume of small arms.

Watching the bright dots of the tracers, Wagner's eyes scanned for a target worthy of his main gun, the 105. He found it in the form of a bunker. Again he flicked the seat's lever, falling down to where his eyes were parallel with the commander's gun sight. He twisted the sight until he had a good view of the bunker.

"Gunner . . . HE, delay . . . one o'clock . . . bunker, with heavy machine gun," Wagner ordered through the intercom.

The turret spun smoothly as it and the gun gave off a hydraulic whine.

"Target," the gunner announced in a fraction of the second. The main gun already had a round of high explosive loaded.

"Fire!"

The tank rocked with the recoil. Peering again through his sight, Wagner saw a cloud of evil black smoke and a collection of splintered logs where the bunker had been. Immediately, he popped up again and began scanning for a new target. This was made considerably harder by the fact that Peters' mortars were now in operation, tossing between them a hundred or more shells a minute at the Venezuelan lines. Angry orange flowers blossomed, then turned black. Even this far back one could hear the whine of malevolent bits of shell casing, coursing through the air.

Wagner couldn't see them, but was pretty sure that the grunts were now pouring out of their carriers like a horde of angry soldier ants in full "lunch-em" mode and forming up for an assault. He popped his seat almost all the way down, stood on it, and took over once again the heavy machine gun mounted in front of the commander's cupola. Grasping the spade grips, one in each hand, he pressed his chest to the gun and automatically began to press the firing butterfly with his thumbs. The gun gave off a steady *thunkthunkthunkthunk*ing as it vibrated in Wagner's hands and against his chest. The first burst was high, flying over a fighting position the sergeant thought not worth wasting a major round on. He shifted his aim lower and pressed the butterfly again.

The gun was badly out of sync with the music:

"PLANNING HIS VENGEANCE

"THAT HE SOON WILL UNFOLD."

Behind the line of infantry, spreading out between their carriers and taking the prone, Reilly used binoculars to scan the Venezuelan line. He wasn't looking for anything in particular, just some indicator that they were on the cusp of breaking. Cessation of return fire from the bunkers that the tanks were crushing into so much strawberry jam couldn't say much about that. Each hit only indicated some of the enemy were dead, not that any of them were broken in spirit. The lessening of return fire helped a bit, but that was accounted for, in part at least, by death or wounds.

And one of the bastards with an RPG, holding his fire like a clever lad, could be the end of one of my crews.

No, what Reilly needed was . . .

Private Emilia Suárez—Second Squad, Third Platoon, Company A, First Parachute Battalion—could feel the hot urine running down her legs. Even so, she kept on with her job of breaking open boxes of machine gun ammunition and passing the bandoleers to the assistant gunner. The gun's barrel was smoking already. Even in her terror, she hoped she wouldn't have to help change the red hot barrel.

Suárez felt something like huge fists, lancing through the air to strike bags of meal. Before her eyes, the assistant gunner's chest exploded in a shower of blood, bone fragments, and torn guts and lungs, while the gunner's head simply disintegrated and disappeared, causing a red torrent to spray straight upwards for an eternal moment.

Still clutching in her hands the bandoleer she'd been about to pass to the AG, Suárez rocketed out of the machine gun bunker, then stood and ran, screaming her lungs out like some mad thing.

And that's *what I was looking for*, Reilly exulted.

Sweeping his field glasses a little higher, he saw four or five more troops doing the bugout boogie to the rear. "Gotcha, ya fuckers."

He picked up a microphone. Keying it cut off the music, allowing him to speak directly through the loudspeakers. It also sent out the same message via radio. "First Battalion! Into the assault . . . Forward."

I always did like the way the Russians did some *things,* Reilly thought, as his grunts arose, screaming, the tanks and APC's lurched forward, firing, and Black Sabbath resumed its soul-sucking chorus:

"NOW HE HAS HIS REVENGE!"

"Snyder? Reilly. Increase the pressure on the fuckers to your front. Now!

"*Faugh A Ballagh*, motherfuckers!" Clear the way.

The driver, Glass, heard the orders as well as Wagner had. On the word, "Forward," he gave the tank full throttle, lunging at the enemy line. The acceleration pressed Glass back into his seat, even as it threw Wagner into the commander's hatch, temporarily ruining the latter's aim.

A single RPG round lanced out, striking the tank to Three-three's left, next to the driver, in the overhang under the gun mantlet. The hot jet from the warhead must have burned through and struck a ready shell, because the tank exploded in an instant, the turret blown high into the air, spinning. Fires erupted, shooting upward from the now vacant turret ring and the still occupied driver's hatch.

With a curse—those had been his friends in that tank!—Wagner swung his machine gun over, peppering the spot from which the RPG appeared to have been launched with heavy chunks of bronze-jacketed lead: *Thunkthunkthunkthunkthunkthunkthunk.*

Others joined their fire to his. It was apparently too much for the enemy soldier who had destroyed the tank. Wagner spotted a single man, running pell-mell to the rear. He fired and missed; fired and missed. On the third burst, after a quick adjustment of aim, followed by a long, ten-round stream, the Venezuelan antitank gunner's legs went one way, while his body, spinning head over blood-gushing stumps, went the other.

Wagner laughed madly with the satisfaction of revenge, then ceased fire, scanning to his front for a worthy target.

Every tank's cannon was firing high explosive as fast as the loaders could sling in rounds and the gunners could find a target. Even so, the amount of steel falling on the Venezuelan line lessened as the mortars lifted off and shifted their fires farther to the northwest. The general area of the defenders' line was draped with thick, black smoke.

Glass nosed the tank into the smoke, then farther into it. It was hard to see in any detail, but he made it a point to run over any bodies he spotted lying on the ground. He couldn't see the results, but could easily imagine them bursting like grapes as the tracks pressed out any semblance of life. Once he thought he heard a scream from one of the grapes.

The tank lurched over a fighting position, then bounced down as the logs that made that position's over-head cover gave way, snapping and collapsing themselves and the dirt they'd carried. Fifty meters on, the smoke began to thin, revealing a disorganized flock of uniformed Venezuelans fleeing, mostly weaponless, for their lives. Over the driver's head the tanks' coaxial machine gun began to chatter, sweeping rounds across the panicking enemy, chopping them down like scrub brush.

Reilly's voice, calm—or perhaps a bit jubilant—came over the battalion net. "Reconfig; armor, Alpha. Scouts, you're attached to Charlie. Charlie?"

"Scouts, roger."

"Here, sir; Charlie."

"Green, you head for the airport. Smash them. Alpha?"

"Company, rather *Team* Alpha, over."

"You're with me. We'll cut west and sweep. Peters, give Alpha and Charlie back their mortars. Sergeant Major, they've got tanks, light ones anyway, hereabouts, somewhere. There's going to be a gap opening up between Alpha and Charlie. Take battalion's AT platoon and Alpha's and Charlie's sections. Move the AT guns northwest and find a firing position to cover Alpha's open northern flank and Charlie's western. Also round up Peters and battalion mortars and get them into position to support both Charlie and Alpha."

"On the way."

"Battery?"

"Here, sir," Bunn answered.

"Out of action. Displace toward the airfield behind Charlie. Set up to fire to the north."

"Wilco."

Only once was Sergeant Wagner moved to pity. As the tanks rolled forward, cutting down and crushing everything in their path, they came up the wire-topped, chain link fence that surrounded the airport. Some of the Venezuelans had already climbed the fence, hopped to the ground, and were legging it trippingly through the airport's southeastern outbuildings, for the north and a spurious safety. More, though, were still trying to climb the chain link and get over the wire. His tank's coax wasn't the first to begin sweeping the fence. But he felt nothing until he saw that coaxial machine gun begin firing from the left, chopping right as the gunner traversed to butcher the men—and a few women, it seemed—trying desperately to stick thick boots in narrow, diamond openings. It didn't seem precisely *wrong* to shoot them down like dogs; after all, they hadn't tried to surrender. The butchery was still distasteful to the point of being pitiful.

When the last of the fugitives lay broken and bleeding amidst the linear heap of them at the base of the fence, the company commander called, "Through the fence. Just knock it down. Then on to the airport."

Wagner's platoon leader asked, "Prisoners?"

"No time, unless they go very far out of their way to indicate the desire to surrender. Very far."

"Roger."

Lying at the base of the fence, staring upward, Private Emilia Sanchez couldn't feel her legs, or anything below her abdomen. This was just was well; if she'd been able to feel them, she'd have felt only bare bone and meat and leaking blood, along with tortured, exposed nerve endings.

She could feel the ground vibrate, though, under her head and shoulders. She closed her eyes tightly and began to pray. She was calm now, panic and screaming over, as she waited for the end. It was on her third *Ave Maria* that the tank called "Charlie Three-three" crushed her skull and then her torso, mashing her bloody remains down into the dirt below while, above, a dog howled mournfully.

She felt that, but only for a moment.

★CHAPTER FIFTY-TWO★

In the fields the bodies burning
As the war machine keeps turning.
—Black Sabbath, "War Pigs"

Soesdyke-Linden Highway,
South of Cheddi Jagan Airport, Guyana

Mao was everywhere, encouraging, exhorting, and—
yes—threatening where required. Two of the gringos'
armored vehicles—not tanks, unfortunately, but nearly as
dangerous—flickered their souls to the wind, south of
Second Platoon. They stood eloquent witnesses to his skill
and fortitude, to say nothing of his willingness to shoot
down any soldier he found shirking his or even her duty.

He knew it was hopeless. If he'd believed differently,
the blasts, the constant chattering of machine gun fire,
and the balls of fire rising above the airfield to the north
disabused him of the notion.

Lying beside a machine gun, directing its fire onto
one of the armored vehicles that had pulled back out of
RPG range, Mao felt something, someone flop to the

earth beside him. He turned to see Larralde, pale and breathless. A stream of tracers tore the air above the major, indicating that someone had been tracking him for death.

"They're . . . held up," Larralde sputtered, " . . . about five hundred . . . meters north . . . east . . . of . . . the new line . . . waiting . . . shooting."

"Afraid to close, sir?" Arrivillaga asked.

Larralde shook his head. "Don't think so . . . waiting . . . for . . . the terror . . . to build."

"Fuck 'em; we're not surrendering and we're not bolting." The sergeant major's face was a study in granite determination.

Larralde, still out of breath, still gave a warm smile. *You're a better soldier than I'll* ever *be, Mao*. He turned and began crawling away to the east, back to the other two thirds of the company.

"Any word on air support?" Mao called out.

"Few hours," Larralde answered. "Supposedly brigade's tank company is moving to our support."

"About fucking time!"

That was when the mortars began to pummel them with *intent*. A blast came from behind Larralde, from precisely where he'd just spoken with his top NCO. Unthinking, ignoring the steady blasting, he lunged to his feet and raced back. Stopping and looking down, Larralde saw the ruin a shell had made of Mao Arrivillaga.

His face, once granite, was charred, and half torn off. Blood leaked from a dozen or more ragged holes. One arm was missing. With a grief-stricken cry, Larralde fell to his knees and began to weep over his fallen comrade.

Word passed quickly from man to man to woman to man: "The sergeant major's dead." Even then, they didn't begin to bolt until those terrifying armored vehicles began to assault.

Sergeant Major George lay between a pair of fairly new 60mm high velocity guns mounted on old 57mm gun carriages, concealed by some tall grass with more, recently plucked grass breaking up the outline of the gunner's shields. The other six guns, also in sections of two, formed a ragged line, with two guns amidst a small copse of trees to the north, two in the shadows of some warehouses, set to fire under the abandoned commercial trucks parked there, and a final pair just peeking over a drainage ditch, not far to George's south. The vehicles, Land Rovers, all, he'd sent back to hide among the mortars. The guns and their crews, fairly hidden in their hasty positions, waited.

"Stupid fucking quasi-wogs," George muttered. "Get your heads out of your asses and send in your tanks. Quit your dawdling; I'm a busy man and have other things to be doing than nursemaiding . . ."

"Tanks, Sergeant Major," one of the gun captains called out.

"How many? What kind? SALUTE report, you shithead!"

"I count ten, repeat ten, tanks, moving south from the airport. Probably the parachute brigade's tank company. Like right this second. AMX-13's."

"That's better." George reared partway up, resting on his elbows. The grass was thinner toward the top, and he could just barely make out the tops of the enemy light tanks. "Now, c'mon . . . don't be chickens about this . . .

get a little closer . . . yeah, that's the ticket . . . closer . . . closer . . . FIRE!"

Eight lances of flame leapt forth from the line of guns. Three torrents of fire, topped by leaping turrets, geysered up from the line of enemy tanks. It was both a feature and a flaw of the AMX-13 that anything up to ten rounds might be sitting exposed on the twin rotary drum racks for the autoloader. It gave the tanks an awesome short-term rate of fire, but could, and in this case did, prove disastrous if the turret was penetrated.

Two more AMX-13's simply stopped dead in their tracks as penetrators from the 60's found drivers or engines or transmissions. The remaining five turned and practically leaped off the road to shelter behind the embankment. They then began a race to the northeast.

"Chickenshits!" George sneered. "Just when it was starting to get fun."

Frowning, the sergeant major thought, *Okay, so that's not entirely fair. So anyone might break when they take fifty percent losses, from an enemy they didn't see, in a fraction of a second. But so what? Screw fair.*

Carlos Villareal dragged Lily by one arm. In the other she retained her rifle, as did he in his free hand. No one, least of all Carlos, knew who had given the word to bug out. One minute, they were holding their temporary line—terrified, yes, but still facing the enemy armor that seemed content to keep their distance and toss shells at them—while the next that armor was moving forward at a walking pace, firing, accompanied by a small horde of shrieking infantry and some godawful terrifying music.

That's when Carlos heard someone put out the shout to fall back.

Shells were falling everywhere. More than once, Carlos had to drag Lily to the ground as a shell storm passed over them. Running through the low, clinging smoke, the pair stumbled across Major Larralde and, both were sorry to see, what remained of Sergeant Major Arrivillaga.

"Sir, come on!" Carlos implored. "Everyone's falling back to make a stand at the river." That last was, at best, supposition on his part.

Larralde looked up and shook his head. "No . . . no. I'm going to stay here with Mao. You two go on." Everything was lost save honor. It was Larralde's intention to stay with his chief noncom until the gringos came and killed him.

Alpha and Bravo were busy chivvying the Venezuelans in the general direction of Low Wood, by the Essequibo. They didn't really need Reilly, at the moment. Neither did Charlie, currently pursuing the fleeing remnants northward to Georgetown and destruction.

He saw a lone Venezuelan man, left behind when the mass of the Venezuelans had retreated. The man rocked back and forth, in obvious grief.

Tapping Duke on the shoulder, he pointed in the direction of the Venezuelan. Duke began traversing his machine gun to kill the man, until Reilly put a restraining hand on his arm. Shrugging, Duke relaxed his grip on the gun and verbally directed Schiebel over.

Reilly dismounted from the side hatch, walked the few short steps, and sat down heavily next to the mourning

Venezuelan. The Venezuelan stiffened as soon as Reilly sat down.

Reilly's Spanish was at least fair. "Your man?" It was a stupid thing to ask but he couldn't think of much else.

"My sergeant major," Larralde answered, in English.

"What was his name?"

"Arrivillaga. Mao Stalin Arrivillaga. Yeah, we sometimes go in for creative names in Venezuela."

"You speak pretty good English," Reilly commented.

"So did he. We had to learn it to go to your Ranger School, back before Chavez took over the country."

"Good man, then, I take it."

Larralde nodded. "The best. Best goddamned NCO in the whole Venezuelan Army. " The major smiled then, in remembrance, and added, "Though if he'd ever claimed I said that I'd have denied it."

"I see. Wait a minute," Reilly said, then held a hand to one ear, thumb and pinky outstretched, to indicate he wanted a radio. One of the RTO's in the back of the vehicle popped out of the hatch and brought him one. He held the microphone just far enough from his ear that the Venezuelan could hear without straining too badly.

"Sergeant Major? Reilly. You busy?"

"Not since we brushed off their tanks, no, sir, not really."

"We've got one of ours here," Reilly said, "from the other side. An 'Oh, Ranger Buddy' deal."

"I see. And?"

"Earliest reasonable convenience; can you arrange a burial detail, with honors?"

Deliberately, George pressed the button on the radio before beginning to speak, just so Reilly could hear his exasperated sigh. "You're a fucking romantic, you know that, boss? Yeah . . . send me a ten digit. I'll arrange the detail. Though it won't be for a couple of hours. That work?"

Reilly glanced at the Venezuelan, who nodded.

"That works." He handed the mike back to the RTO and stood up. "What's your name?" he asked.

"Larralde, Miguel, sir. Major."

"Miguel," Reilly said, gently, "your side's lost here. The only question is how many of your men"—he glanced at an obviously female corpse and added—"and women, too, are going to survive. You can affect that number."

"By doing what?" Larralde asked, though in his heart he already knew.

"By telling them to surrender . . . 'whilst yet my soldiers are in my command.'"

Larralde broadcast over the loudspeakers on Reilly's APC, the vehicle skirting behind the line of armored vehicles pinning the Venezuelans against the river. The message was short. "Drop your weapons. Come in. Surrender. You won't be harmed."

It worked with most of them, who were, after all, barely trained and generally quite young. But it didn't work with everyone.

Behind an immensely large tree, one of the few of this size in the area to have survived the depredations of the loggers, Lily Vargas cradled Carlos Villarreal's head on her bloodied lap. Carlos was very dead, killed, uselessly and impersonally, by a mortar shell. As Larralde had before,

Lily rocked with her grief. There was no one with her, however, to offer any sort of comfort at all.

Lily heard it before she saw it. One of the strange, ad hoc-looking mercenary armored personnel carriers pulled up about two hundred meters away. She could only barely make out the outline through the brush. A couple of men dismounted. Within a few minutes she saw some smoke rising, and heard a peal of very social sounding laughter.

The laughter infuriated her. *My Carlos is dead and they tell jokes? Not for long.*

After stopping the APC, Schiebel dismounted and built a small fire to brew up some coffee. Duke stood still, manning the machine gun and scanning for danger. Two of the RTO's likewise hung over the sides, weapons facing out. There was firing in the distance, but not much of it. Under the POW major's calls, it seemed that the Venezuelans had lost their heart for the fighting.

Can't really blame them, Duke thought, as he watched a thin line of them walk south under an even thinner guard. *You go up against Reilly, you go up against the best.*

The prisoners seemed awfully young to Duke, who was well into middle age himself. Indeed, he was seven full years older than Reilly. Again he looked at the downtrodden line of demoralized prisoners. *Poor sorry bastards.*

He looked toward the fire as Reilly gave a hearty laugh. *This prisoner probably never heard of an Irish wake,* Duke thought. *But Reilly sure as shit has and he knows the reason for them: Get people to remember the best of their dead loved ones, and laugh, and, in the laughter, keep the good memories alive while letting the grief die.*

". . . so there we both are," Larralde said, "crossing some godforsaken stream that fed the Yellow River, on a rope, and the rope's underwater, stretched out like over-cooked spaghetti, and Mao and I have our fingertips on it, kicking for all we're worth to keep our noses just barely above the water."

Laughing, Reilly beat the ground with his left fist. "Been there . . . done that!" he chortled. Recovering, he asked Schiebel, "Hey, Schieb, we got a bottle to . . . um . . . fortify that coffee."

"It's on the PC, sir, in my pack." Schiebel knew his colonel pretty damned well by this time. "Bushmills."

"Good choice." Reilly stood and said, "Hey, Duke, rifle Schieb's belongings and retrieve the bottle he has, purely without authorization, mind you, secreted there."

Chuckling himself—*Yup, he's giving the boy the* full *Irish wake treatment; bloody damned nice of him. Then again, it's not like the battle isn't over here, either*—Duke let go of his machine gun and turned. He disappeared for a moment then emerged with a bottle, surprisingly unopened, clutched triumphantly in one hand. That's when they heard the shots, two of them, close together, and then a third, all from close in.

Lily gently lifted Carlos' head and wriggled out from under it. Just as gently, she laid it to the ground and bent to lightly kiss his cold, bloodied lips. "Revenge," she whispered to her lover's corpse.

Taking her rifle across the crooks of her arms, just as the sergeant major had shown her months before, she began to crawl from her sheltering tree, across the dirt and sparse grass that the trees hadn't quite eliminated. Her head she kept tilted down, with white barely showing through narrowed eyes.

Spotting a small patch of brush, growing where a gap in the trees let the sun through, Lily aimed for that, squirming like a snake but keeping her rifle's muzzle up above the dirt. Reaching the brush, she lifted her head to peer through it. She saw a man, standing beside the enemy armored vehicles, with his left arm raised. There were two others there, but low, plus three more actually inside the vehicle. *Not good targets.*

Quietly, the girl put her left hand on the pistol grip and pulled the rifle—slowly, slowly, *Don't let them see*—out of the crook of her left arm and up against her shoulder. The left hand automatically moved to grasp the wooden grip behind the muzzle, her left elbow finding a spot on the ground for steadiness.

Pressing her cheek against the stock, Lily took aim. Once satisfied, she stroked the trigger, once, twice, and then, after a moment's hesitation, when her target failed to fall, a third time.

Reilly felt the first blow, in the back, not far above his kidney. It staggered him but did not knock him over. The second hit on the right side, passing through his lung. That hit as the pain from the first shot raced up his nerves to his brain. His eyes widened in surprise and shock, his mouth opening slightly as if to say something.

His left arm reached out, though to Duke it seemed as if his commander was reaching for him, not for the bottle he held.

The third bullet passed through his jungle hat and through the bone of his skull, from behind and high, exiting several inches around from his right eye. The hat and a four inch piece of the skull shot upward and to the right. The shock wave liquified a substantial chunk of his brain, and irretrievably damaged most of the rest.

Reilly dropped like a sack of potatoes, dead before he hit the ground. With a horrified cry, Duke threw himself behind the KORD machine gun and began throwing heavy rounds at the source of the fire. Still, his return fire could only kill the assailant; nothing was going to bring his colonel back.

Then his eyes lit on Larralde, sitting, horror-struck, no great distance from Reilly's body.

★ CHAPTER FIFTY-THREE ★

Though all the bright dreamings we cherished
Went down in disaster and woe,
The spirit of old is still with us
That never would bend to the foe.
—William Rooney, "The Men of the West"

Field Hospital, Camp Fulton, Guyana

The word passed fast, but not before the sun had gone down. Lana looked over some paperwork, laid out across her desk, under a crank-powered light. A noise, the shuffling of several pairs of feet, caused her to look up. As soon as she saw Stauer, Joseph, McCaverty, and Coffee enter her tent, worse, saw their faces, Lana gulped. Her stomach heaved as her heart sank.

"No," she pleaded. "No, it can't be."

Stauer had thought he'd known what to say. Faced with the woman's horror and pain, whatever he'd been about to say was lost. After a long, silent moment, he managed to get out, "I'm sorry, Lana."

She screamed then, a long, inarticulate cry of pure

anguish. Coffee and Joseph rushed to her side, wrapping arms around her and trying to comfort her, or at least calm her a bit. Eventually, they succeeded in the latter.

Leaving McCaverty standing alone by the tent door, Stauer took the couple of steps forward and then went to one knee in front of her desk.

"His APC crew said it was quick, Lana. Sudden. He didn't feel much pain, if any. I don't know if that helps."

Tears running freely down her face she shook her head. No, that didn't help much.

"There's another problem," Stauer continued. "Except for C Company, which is out of the area, just south of Georgetown, First Battalion's fallen apart at the news. A lot of them knew him a lot longer than you did. They want revenge. The XO and Sergeant Major George are trying to get control of them, but the troops won't listen. The RSM is there and one of them took a shot at *him* when he tried to bring them back to discipline. They want to kill all the prisoners and build Seamus a pyramid of skulls. George thinks they've already shot some people, maybe more than a dozen, though he says he can't prove it. And they just won't listen to anybody."

Lana shrugged, and shook her head, uncomprehendingly.

"You're carrying his child. You're his *wife*. You're all they have left of him. They'll listen to *you*."

Another shrug.

Stauer stood up and took one of Lana's hands in both of his own. "I need you to go get control of First Battalion. Doc McCaverty here will fly you to the main airport; the Venezuelans aren't flying much at night anymore. George will meet you there. Get control of them and keep them from doing something that will blacken your husband's memory through the ages."

Cheddi Jagan Airport, Guyana

It was Joshua, rather than George, who met Lana at the airfield, by the southeastern tip of the major runway. He drove himself in a blacked-out Land Rover. Without a word, he helped Lana down from the aircraft and then assisted her to walk to the automobile. "George had to stay with the troops," Joshua explained. "Otherwise they'd have run riot."

"Take me to Seamus, first," she said.

"Yes, ma'am," Joshua agreed. If the delay cost a few Venezuelan lives, well . . . so what?

They drove south, Lana's hands clutched protectively over her swollen belly. She thought she spotted bodies littering both sides of the road, but couldn't be certain. Even if it hadn't been darker than sin, her eyes still overflowed with tears. She *was* certain when they passed five wrecked Venezuelan tanks, since Joshua, cursing, had to slow down and weave his way around them. Some of the tanks still smoldered, leaving the heavy smell of charred flesh in the air. That made the tears worse.

Through the trees, off in the distance, she thought she saw fires burning. Joshua turned off the main road onto a dirt trail and set his course for those fires. As he closed, she was able to make out that there were four of them. They looked evenly spaced as, indeed, they proved to be.

The troops clustered around the body split to leave a path. Joshua pulled up between the pyres and stopped. Reilly lay before them,

"He always hated cots in the field," Lana sniffled. "He just *hated* them."

"I know," Joshua said. "I told his headquarters crew that, just this once, he wouldn't mind."

Lana's head jerked a few times. No, just this once he wouldn't mind.

A woman knelt beside the temporary bier, gently stroking Reilly's pale cheek. Lana couldn't see her face, but even through the loose-fitting battledress the shape shouted, "Tatiana Manduleanu." Her first impulse—to scream, "Away from him, whore!"—was uncharitable. It made Lana feel deeply ashamed.

She walked forward, herself, and likewise knelt. Tatiana stopped her stroking, leaning back to rest against her upturned heels. "I didn't want him to be alone," she said to Lana, softly. "Without a woman nearby to mourn, I mean."

Even more ashamed now, Lana whispered, "Thank you."

"It was too late when I got here," Tatiana said, then added, "It was too late when I got the call. I'm sorry . . . so sorry." Rocking further back for balance, Corporal Manduleanu stood, straight up. Even so, she took the trouble to just stand, rather than to blossom. This wasn't the time or the place for charm. She turned away and, likewise sniffling, walked over to Joshua, placing her arms around him and pressing her face to his chest. After a moment's uncertain hesitation, and a shuddering sob, the RSM wrapped one arm around the girl, patting her sympathetically, if awkwardly.

Lana stared at the corpse for long minutes. Whatever expression had been on Reilly's face when he died, someone had taken the care to close his eyes and massage his features. He looked at peace. Lana suspected that that somebody had been Tatiana, though it was possible someone else had done the service. Someone, probably not Tatiana, had replaced the hat on his head, covering the spot where, so Dr. McCaverty had told her, he'd received the wound that had killed him.

A single shot, coming from somewhere to the north, reminded her of the official reason she was here. *Was that someone killing a prisoner, husband? I hope not. You were ruthless enough, but if someone surrendered in good faith, I can't quite see you killing him out of hand for any reason.*

Stauer wants me to put a stop to it. In my heart, I don't want to. I want that whole country plunged in the grief I feel.

But you wouldn't want that, either, would you? And so, this one last time, I'll do what you want.

For just a second, she laughed inwardly. *Not that I didn't do lot of things that you wanted. But that was just our business. And I enjoyed doing them, too, if you never guessed.*

How do I do this, Seamus? How do I take command of a battalion run amok? "Don't think about it. You already know what's right; just do it!" *I can hear you say that. And so I shall.*

She stood up, pausing only a moment to stroke her man's cheek, as Tatiana had.

"Sergeant Major George?"

"Here, ma'am."

"Where is it worst?"

He knew precisely what she meant. "Alpha Company, then Bravo. Charlie's camped out along the road to Georgetown and doesn't have many prisoners."

"Bring me to Alpha."

Camp Fulton, Guyana

"Colombian Intelligence confirms Chavez is at Miraflores Palace," Boxer said. "And this time, there's no fucking forty-eight hour delay while some flunky at that head-quarters confirms it and decides about the bureaucratic implications."

Stauer looked skeptical. "How do we know? They've failed us before."

"CNN, actually," Boxer said.

"Oh, well, that's *different*."

"No, really. He's scheduled to speak from Miraflores, tonight. The cameras and newsies are all there. More importantly, his favorite mistress is there. CNN caught her on camera."

"You sure enough about it for me to order Lava's boys in?"

"War's gotta end sometime," Boxer said. "We can invest Georgetown and New Amsterdam—at least, if First Batt will calm down under Lana's influence, we can—but we can't take them, not at any cost that's acceptable to us. And eventually they're going to figure out that the mouth of the Demerara's not mined. Once that happens, we won't even be able to starve them into surrender."

Stauer thought of Reilly and his new-made widow. "The cost's already been too high."

"So you see my point?"

"I suppose. What did you tell the Colombians we were planning?"

Boxer grinned, sheepishly. "I didn't tell them, exactly. I suggested we had cruise missile capability at sea. Since we've obviously been fucking with Chavez unmercifully by sea, they didn't seem to have any problem accepting that." Boxer shrugged. "And I figured, if Hugo's got a mole in Colombian intel—and he well might—it could hardly hurt if he'd found something that caused him to orient his air defenses north toward the Caribbean, right?"

Stauer raised an eyebrow. "Not until they try to egress."

"Well, I don't have any proof that they've done that, anyway."

Holding Base Snake (SF and MI-17's), Twenty-two Miles South of Jonestown, Guyana

In the gloom, the men shuffled on board silently, in two files per helicopter. As much as they'd griped and bitched about the forced delay, they were scared enough now. Oh, no, they weren't shit-your-pants, "no, Sarge, I ain't a gonna go" scared. But they knew it was going to be tough and they were reasonably sure a number, possibly approaching all of them, were not going to be coming back.

It was too dark by far for Von Ahlenfeld to judge their

mental state by their faces. Instead, he listened, watched their posture, and looked for any sign of hesitation in boarding.

Scared they might well be, he thought, *but they're still willing. No, that's not right; they're* eager, *eager for this shot at history, for the adventure, for the glory of the thing. They're just a little nervous about it. So . . . we can do this.* If *they don't catch us in the air.*

Lava had more strikers than he needed. Indeed, he was going to have to leave several dozen behind. What he lacked was helicopters, that lack arising partly from the limitations of those he did have and partly from the loss of one critical HIP back on the Camp Fulton airstrip, in the beginning.

Like most things in war, this one had boiled down to a logistic problem. The Hips, MI-17's or, as the Russkis called them, "MI-8MT's," could not carry enough fuel to get themselves quite to Caracas. Even with extra tanks, and flying the straightest route, they ranged about sixty miles short of the target. With the route they were going to take, nap of the earth, snug in against the mountains that stretched from Canaima National Park, Venezuela, westwards, they'd fall closer to two hundred miles short.

That route was necessary because there weren't any ground radar stations aimed that way that ranged, and anything airborne would have a sad time of it, sorting them out from all that junk on the ground. Even so, almost two hundred miles short of the target was still *short of the target.* It was failure, in other words.

Sadly, too, there weren't going to be any BP stations on the way for a quick fill-up.

They'd actually kicked around, early in their planning, the possibility of grabbing an airfield, midway, and refueling there. That, however, made their prospects for an interception-free flight drop from "problematic but possible" all the way down to "no fucking way."

So, if they were going to refuel on the way, they'd have to carry it with them. If they were going to carry it with them, by the utterly sound military axiom that, "if you need one, you *must* start with more than one," two of von Ahlenfeld's five precious helicopters had to go to carrying fuel and little but. The "but" consisted of six rocket pods, with a mere sixteen 55mm rockets each, and a like number of machine gun pods, between the two of them, all stowed internally for the nonce. Normally, the rockets weren't good for much but indicating that the firer considered the target rude and boorish. These, however, had the *Ugroza* upgrades, making them precision guided and quite accurate. The machine gun pods were of the Russian four-barreled, gas operated, GshG-type, which the troops insisted on calling miniguns, quite despite that the only thing the two systems had in common was multiple barrels.

Since it was entirely possible that they'd lose one of those two "gas trucks" en route, each had to carry enough fuel for everybody. That left only three for troop carriers, and nobody for dedicated troop carrier escort on the first leg. For that matter, the three troop carriers couldn't even bolt on a few rocket pods each because, at least initially, *they* had to carry extended range fuel tanks or the two "gas trucks" couldn't have carried enough fuel for them to make it to Caracas and onward to internment. Since they were going fuel heavy, the number of troops they could carry had to be kept down.

The troop carriers were loading twenty-four heavily armed and armored men each. With the limited rockets and machine gun pods, and one machine gun per bird, mounted sideways, manned by the Hips' engineers, that was going to be *it* for fire support.

Ah, for the heady days of AC-130's on demand, mused von Ahlenfeld, who had also spent quite a few years in the group formerly known as "Delta." *Hell, for aircraft carriers on demand. Dammit.*

Moreover, for the last phase of the operation, the egress, they already *knew* they were going to be one chopper down, and possibly three. A goodly chunk of their rehearsal time had been spent practicing dropping their gear and running like hell for anything smoking and air-moveable.

On the plus side, if both "gas trucks" made it to the refueling point, there'd at least be enough gas for both of them to make it to the target. For the men in the assault force, this was not a huge plus, given the small amount of firepower they would carry. For those in headquarters, back at Camp Fulton, it was no plus at all.

Camp Fulton, Guyana

"Boss," Gordon said, "I think you ought to cancel this and call the Second Battalion back. Or not 'back,' but to stay in place. They haven't lifted off yet."

Meredith, the comptroller, nodded his head in agreement and said, "Lahela, show them the figures."

Electricity in the camp had been spotty from the beginning of the war. She briefed them the old fashioned way, from butcher paper clipped to an easel. The story on the butcher paper was frightening.

"Sirs, almost half of our capital purchases are lost or interned. And most of our ammunition stocks are down to critical levels. Between aircraft destroyed or about to be destroyed or interned, about twenty-seven million dollars, assuming we can still find good, used. Ships . . . assuming we don't get back the *Walewska* or the *Bastard*, about as much."

"It's worse than that," Meredith said. "We can't get another *Drunken Bastard*; they don't exist outside of museums and some virtual wrecks in Virginia. We'd have to buy another Dvora Class, and that would cost more than the *Countess*. Plus the landing craft. Plus *Namu*, most likely. We're looking at having to replace more than thirty million dollars' worth of naval equipment. I won't even talk about training replacement crews for the men we've lost.

"Thank God we haven't lost the *Naughtius. That*, we'd have to have a replacement custom built for."

Victor, sitting with his head resting on folded fingers, said, "Buying another Dvora might not be that bad. Israel's replacing some of them, at least, with Shaldags. They might be willing to part with one of the replaced units at a fair price."

Meredith shrugged. "Even so . . . fair *is* expensive for one of those."

Victor's nod conceded the point. "Though I wonder," he said, "if Norway still has those Hauks for sale. I'll check into that before we do anything."

Lahela flipped a sheet of butcher paper. This one showed ground equipment and ammunition lost or expended. Stauer's face showed no emotion. Even so, he shuddered inwardly at every item's cost, from a 105mm shell to a new-minted Jaguar tank.

"Lahela," Meredith said, sending a finger signal to flip to the next sheet. When she had, he added, "Some of our worst costs are real property. We've got a quarter of a million square feet of building space ruined, mostly burned, and a like amount seriously damaged. Along with a shitpot of furniture, installation property, electronics. And we've already cut down the timber locally, that we could. Getting more, here, in the middle of nowhere, is going to hurt."

"Are you suggesting we make peace?" Boxer asked.

"It would save some money," Bridges said. *To say nothing of lives.*

"We haven't had word one from Chavez suggesting he's remotely interested in peace," Stauer said.

Boxer, sighing, added, "And we won't have. Killing however many thousands of civilians in and around Punto Fijo has made it impossible for him to even think about it. He'd never survive the domestic backlash. Even if he somehow manages to pull it off, win here, and parade us or, more likely, our heads through the streets of Caracas, he still might not survive. It's a certainty he won't survive a free election if he doesn't."

"And that's the crux of the problem," Stauer finished. "Chavez can't make peace. His successor or successors can. They might not, but at least they *can*. So he has to die. We can't even capture him or his successor will probably be forced to continue the war to free him. Lava and Second Battalion go forward." *Quite despite that many or most of them won't be coming back.*

"And pass to Baluyev to get his boat in between Caracas and the Netherlands Antilles for potential air-sea rescue."

★ CHAPTER FIFTY-FOUR ★

The seventh rule of the ethics of means
and ends is that generally success or failure is a
mighty determinant of ethics.
—Saul Alinsky, *Rules for Radicals*

Holding Base Snake (SF and MI-17's),
Twenty-two Miles South of Jonestown, Guyana

Von Ahlenfeld boarded last. Surmounting the ridged
ramp, shuffling forward between the knees of sardine-
packed strikers, he came to his seat, on the starboard
front of the aircraft. In the dim red light, he saw Hampson
seated opposite and slightly aftward. The sergeant major
raised one thumb in Lava's direction, then gave a true
shit-eating grin, the red light reflecting off of white
teeth.

Sergeant major's job, von Ahlenfeld thought. *Buck up
the old man when everything's about ready to go to shit.*

Glancing forward at the chief pilot and air mission
commander, Mike Cruz, Lava shot him a visual question.

Have they called this off yet? Cruz shook his head, slowly. *We're still a go.*

The Hip's engineer then handed von Ahlenfeld a helmet so that he could communicate directly with the pilots, via intercom, as well as with the other helicopters once the time came for that.

"I sent a query, Lee," Cruz said. "Stauer says we go."

Nodding, the battalion commander said, "Your mission is to fly us there, Mike. Let's do it before I get cold feet."

"History in the making," Cruz replied, flipping his NOD's down and turning back to his controls. His tone was pure, albeit feigned, cynicism. Like the rest, he was scared. Like the rest, he wouldn't have missed this for the world.

The helicopter, which had been vibrating, anyway, as it idled, began to *thrum* and shake as the pilot applied power and finessed his pedals and collective. The passengers felt themselves pushed down into the nylon troop seats as it lifted, nosed down, and began the long journey to the north and east. Behind it, the other four Hips likewise lifted, turned, and began beating the air. Once they'd gained a little altitude, the last four shifted positions from the rough circle in which they'd begun to a staggered trail left, behind Cruz and von Ahlenfeld.

A long nap of the earth flight may have been too much for a bunch of Venezuelan kids, recently plucked from the street and most of them never having flown before, especially when the aircraft, a C-130, wasn't really intended for NOE flight. For long-service, elite regulars, in good helicopters, in the hands of expert pilots, even the greater jinking as the birds did their very nonlevel best to skim tree tops wasn't enough to discomfort them. Indeed, between the sound, the heat, the cocoonlike frame embracing them, and the continuous vibration, most of the troops fell fast asleep, only awakening—or half awakening, rather—when the Hips took profound nosedives to keep with the roll of the ground.

Von Ahlenfeld didn't sleep. Instead, under the red lights overhead and from a handheld flashlight, he studied the diagram of the target area, looking for flaws in the plan. He closed his eyes for a moment and rested his head back against the fuselage of the Hip, running through the sequence of events in his mind.

Not that I can change anything at the moment, he thought. *But at least I can mentally prepare to give the orders to change things, if necessary. If I find anything. Which I probably won't . . . after sitting on my ass worrying about it for over a month.*

But I'd best keep looking. He opened his eyes again and stared down at the diagram. It was a struggle to keep them open, not because he was short sleep, but simply because the helicopter, in the hands of an expert, was a self-propelled lullaby.

Von Ahlenfeld felt someone tapping his arm. He looked up to see the Hip's engineer holding out a cup of coffee, the Styrofoam glowing faintly reddish under the lights. He took it, nodded gratefully, and then went back to his diagram and his mental rehearsals.

Cruz turned the control over to his copilot and rested

his arms and legs. *Capable, these Russki jobs* are. *Easy to fly, they are* not.

Resting his body or not, Cruz's head and eyes swiveled almost frantically, looking through his NOD's for the Venezuelan fighter that was surely going to make a complete hash of his evening.

Yeah, yeah; I know it's not likely one will be anywhere near here. Wrong line between their major bases and where the action is in Guyana. Maintenance load at those bases is probably getting overwhelming, too. And we're low enough that the monkeys could hitch a ride. Though they'd overload us if they did.

Cruz did see an airborne light, through a patch in the cloud cover. With the NOD's on, though, registering distance was impossible. He watched for a moment and then tried some calculations in his head. That was useless, as he'd really known it would be.

Probably not a fighter, though, not with nav lights lit up. Then again, we haven't shown any air to air capability so why shouldn't they fly with lights? Still . . . it feels like some civvie airliner.

Sucks having to rely on feelings.

Cruz spent a few more minutes stretching and curling his fingers, then took the stick, saying, "Pilot's bird."

At the slight shudder as control slipped from one pilot to the other, Hampson jolted from his half sleeping state to full alert. His fingers immediately sought his eyes, sweeping away the residue of sleep, even as his temporarily confused mind raced to place himself.

Okay . . . haven't disembarked once yet . . . so haven't

reached the refueling point. Okay . . . still have that and another long flight before I get killed. Not burning . . . this is good; we haven't crashed yet. Okay . . . old soldier's best advice; sleep when you can.

He closed his eyes once again and did his best to follow that advice.

Interim Objective Anaconda,
Aguaro-Guariquito National Park, Venezuela

They'd picked this spot to land, refuel, and shuffle the loads for a number of reasons, no single one of them dispositive. In the first place, the park was huge. In the second, it was in the middle of nowhere and drew few tourists. Third, and a side benefit of that, was that it was also far, far from the nearest cell phone tower, just in case there were some civilian tourists there. Moreover, fourth, there wasn't a single power line anywhere that mattered; power lines *terrified* helicopter crews. Fifth, there was only one good road in. Sixth, the ground was varied, and included jungle, mountain, flats, sand dunes, and damned near every other kind of terrain but arctic. Of those, the open flats were the points of greatest interest.

Cruz, in the lead, lifted his NOD's, then spent a few moments blinking away the purple haze those left on his eyes. He consulted the GPS/map display mounted in front of him. The display showed his current location, a short portion of the route, and the landing spot, just a few kilometers ahead.

"V formation," he ordered, in a very low power

transmission. The staggered trail left formation shifted, with the two "gas trucks" swinging up to roughly equidistant positions from the lead bird, forming a triangle. The other two troop carriers likewise shifted, but to spots farther outside of the fuel carriers. "Short final," he sent to von Ahlenfeld over the intercom. The latter began to pass the word.

The NOD's came down, Cruz scanning for the chosen interim landing zone. He found it and shifted heading very slightly. If he felt any fear at coming in to a near postage stamp surrounded by jungle, which postage stamp he'd never before set foot on or seen in person, he suppressed that fear ruthlessly.

The landing was tricky in more ways than one. Most helicopters hovered nicely and could do a true vertical takeoff. A heavily loaded Hip really needed a certain amount of run to lift over substantial vertical obstacles.

Like those fucking trees to the north.

He measured the trees by eye and chose a spot on the ground certain to allow him to lift over them.

The interim LZ was large enough, at roughly three hundred by five hundred meters, that getting all five helicopters in, in V formation, wasn't too tight a squeeze. There was enough grass on the ground to prevent the choppers from raising great clouds of dust. And it was flat enough, and smooth enough. Even so, Cruz let the engineer, half hanging out of the door, talk him down, a fraction of a meter at a time.

Engineer guidance or no, the landing was rough, with the helicopter bouncing fiercely on its landing struts. As soon as the bouncing stopped, Hampson and von Ahlenfeld were on their feet, shouting over the helicopter's roar, "Interim LZ! Interim LZ!"

It was a fair bet that, had they not reminded the troops, one of them—just awakened—would have either debarked firing, or run off into the jungle in search of a palace that wasn't there. As it was, with the reminder, and under tight control from the team leaders and team sergeant, the strikers unloaded smoothly, and smoothly moved to take up a perimeter. Still others, carefully cross-trained during the long wait at Holding Position Snake, moved to the fuel helicopters and began unreeling the hoses and leading them to the gas-hungry troop carriers.

While they were doing that, the five copilots and five engineers began stripping off the extended range fuel tanks. These, the helicopters had emptied first. Once those were out of the way, they began to bolt on rocket and machine gun pods, connecting the control wires, pulling safety pins from fuses, and ensuring each was armed and ready. One chopper, Cruz's, got precisely nothing in the way of armament. It was also refueled with considerable care, such that it had very little more than the bare minimum to get to the target.

The configuration in which they'd flown was not the one in which they were going to land. To ensure the men loaded in that latter configuration, Hampson located himself centrally, at the open base of the triangle formed by the five Hips. Though it would slow the reload considerably, all of the men would have to pass by him on their way to reembark. The actual reorganization was taking place on the perimeter. And, though it had been rehearsed dozens of times, it was typically less than ideal:

"Where the fuck is Johansson? Goddammit; he's supposed to be with Sicher's team . . . . Hey . . . Sarge? I thought Sicher's team was supposed to be at three o'clock. Get a Delta over here; Garcia stepped in a hole and broke his ankle . . . Remember? We don't have a Delta . . . Crap. Right; go borrow Detachment Four's . . . Hey, anybody got a set of spare batteries for my NOD's? . . . Tell me; please just tell me, you didn't leave the RPG rounds back on Bird Four. Oh, *no!* You shithead; we're not going back aboard Bird Four."

Situation normal, thought Hampson, listening from the center and watching the shade of one trooper legging it for the right rear helicopter. *Ah, what the hell? I'd be worried if things went more smoothly, anyway.*

Helicopters Two through Five were loaded, each with either ten or fourteen men. Von Ahlenfeld personally led twenty-two to Hampson, who reported and then joined the rear of the line. Single file that last load moved, snaking around the end of the tail boom to avoid the invisibly spinning tail rotor. For the second time since lifting off, von Ahlenfeld clumped across the raised ridges of the ramp. Briefly, he turned and took a look around. It was too dark to see much of anything, but dark enough to see that there were no flying tracers, no burning buildings, no muzzle flashes.

This may be the last peaceful scene I ever witness in this life. Oh, well.

★ ★ ★

It had made a certain amount of sense to fly in formation from Snake to Anaconda. At the very least, it had given all five helicopters some of the benefit of Cruz's massive piloting experience. It had made the landing, cross-loading, refueling and arming run more smoothly. And it had held out the possibility that, were one bird to go down, von Ahlenfeld would know about it, because he or someone else could see it, in time to adjust his plans accordingly.

Now, however, they were about to enter the more densely populated parts of Venezuela. Five helicopters, heading to Caracas, looked altogether too much like an attack in progress. They made more noise and attracted more attention. And, worst of all, while one helicopter's IFF, Identification Friend or Foe, might fail, the statistical probability of all five, flying together, failing approached the impossible. Given the increased probability of running across a Venezuelan fighter, once they entered that built-up zone, that was a recipe for trooper *flambé*.

Thus, while all five took off approximately together from Anaconda, as soon as they could they split off in five different directions, each to fly a predetermined course, to a series of preplanned checkpoints, at a given speed in order to arrive in the target area at a particular time.

All flew on radio silence now, which silence they would maintain until they reached their penultimate checkpoint.

Caracas, Venezuela

The holding positions formed an almost perfect semicircle around the southern side of the city. To the west, or slightly northwest, of *Nueva Esparta*, Bird Two, fourteen troops, one rocket pod, one machine gun pod, kept position in a small valley, west of the highway. Counterclockwise from there, Bird Four, an ex gas truck, with ten soldiers, two rocket pods and two machine gun pods, slowly circled Ruiz Pineda. Centered south of the town, Cruz's Helicopter One, twenty-four soldiers, no pods, circled over a bend in the road a couple of miles south of Fort Tiuna. Northeast of that was Number Three, fourteen men, one of each kind of pod, moved in an oval between Cerro Verde and El Pauji. Hip Five, ten troops, four pods, hugged the mountains northeast of Los Chorros.

The positions, at seven miles from the target, were carefully calculated to ensure that nobody was likely to hear more than one helicopter over the sounds of the city, nor would anyone in the city see more than one, hence nobody was likely to suspect an attack or report on those suspicions. Someone on the mountains to the north could see, were they looking, as could someone in one of the skyscrapers that towered above the muck.

But how likely is it, Cruz mused, *that someone on the mountains will scan one hundred and eighty degrees and know what he's seeing? And how likely that any given one of those high rise offices will be occupied at this hour of the morning? Hell, if they're up and in those places at all it's probably because they're fucking somebody they shouldn't be fucking. And besides, if they haven't reported us yet, or don't in the next thirty seconds, they're too late.*

Von Ahlenfeld consulted his watch. *About time*. He

signaled for the radio to be set to high power. Then, switching from intercom to radio, he ordered, "Report."

"Two in position . . . Three; ready . . . Four, up . . . Five, let's do it."

"Gentlemen . . . good luck and godspeed. Now fucking *CHARGE!*"

Cruz half-dropped the ramp and gunned his engines. Hip Number One went from a couple of miles an hour to one hundred and fifty-six miles an hour in just a few seconds. Back in the cargo hold, the entire load of soldiers was forcibly bent at the waist, held in position only by their tightly cinched seatbelts. Once their inertia matched the speed of the helicopter, they straightened up again. Then they unbuckled as quickly as possible and lay down on the deck. Better to risk a broken bone or two than what was about to come through the cabin.

This is sooo *going to suck*, thought Rattus Hampson.

A veritable Charybdis of suckage, mused Lava, tugging off the headphones connected to the helicopter and pulling over his ears a different set with a boom mike to communicate with his ground troops by radio.

"You guys can't even begin to imagine how much this is going to suck!" shouted Cruz. Then he laughed, maniacally.

Fort Tiuna passed below in a blur. Over and past highways, cemeteries, monuments, and hospitals they flew. Cruz paid no attention to the folds of the ground now, except to stay enough above them not to crash. Speed was everything.

The Francisco Fajardo Highway passed below, then the marquee lights of the theater district. And then they were above Miraflores Palace. Cruz put on the figurative brakes, causing the cargo to scrunch forward, cursing.

A quick glance left told the pilot, *Good, no more than a few hundred people milling around Miraflores Park.*

Cruz looked down, confirming he was hovering directly over the palace's central, partially palm-treed courtyard. Then he almost completely cut power to the rotor before unbuckling himself and crouching as low as the cramped space of the cockpit would allow. Strobe flashes—rockets being launched by some of the other Hips—lit the cockpit from the outside.

★ CHAPTER FIFTY-FIVE ★

A man shall and must be valiant;
he must march forward, and quit himself like a man,
—trusting imperturbably in the appointment and *choice*
of the upper Powers; and, on the whole, not fear at all.
Now and always, the completeness of his victory over
Fear will determine how much of a man he is.
—Thomas Carlyle,
On Heroes, Hero-Worship and the Heroic in History

Miraflores Palace, Caracas, Venezuela

Marielena, the late Sergeant Major Arrivillaga's cousin, had a room at the palace. That was one of the major reasons Mao had mistakenly assumed she was one of Chavez's mistresses. True, she was only a secretary, but she was a *personal* secretary, and Chavez always wanted his personal secretary kept very close.

She'd drifted off to sleep worried sick about her favorite cousin and at least mildly concerned with his commanding officer, Larralde. She knew the mercenaries had crushed and routed the brigade of paratroopers—she was too close to the center of power not to know—but of personal word there'd been none. Certainly Hugo had been too proud to establish communications with the mercenaries and they, themselves, had shown no interest so far in communicating with Caracas. And the normal routes for such things, the Red Cross or the Swiss government, were still keeping to a hands off approach.

Somebody, though, the woman had thought before sleep took her *had better start talking to somebody or this thing will never end. We should never have started . . .*

Her dreams were fitful and disturbed, full of images and sounds either partially or wholly misunderstood. Thus, when the sounds of the helicopter over the palace, coupled with those of several more moving to spots around it, awakened her, she thought for a moment that she was still dreaming.

Cruz felt his stomach leap up as the chopper fell.

The tail rotor was the first thing to hit the tiled roof of the palace. It shattered, throwing its fragments for the most part into the southern wing. The tail boom then sheared, but stayed attached just long enough to push the nose somewhat downward. This caused the five blades of the main rotor to strike at the roofs of the other three sides of the palace and to begin chopping down the palm trees that graced the courtyard on those sides. With sounds partially composed of breaking tiles and chopping wood, but more of self-destructing transmission and shattering fiberglass, the rotor blades mostly disintegrated, sending deadly shards of ragged composite through everything in their lines of flight. More than a few ricocheted back, making jagged holes suddenly appear in the hull. From outside of the helicopter someone screamed with heartbreaking agony, a Venezuelan guard chopped in two by a piece of flying blade.

Descending at a speed that was, oh, way the hell out of anything the designers had had in mind, the landing struts collapsed. Before they did, one tire burst with a sound like a cannon shot. The helicopter began to roll to one side before the spinning rotor struck at the columns and then the ground, forcing it upright again. Still more chunks of deadly spinning debris flew through the air, to clang off walls and career back. The already perforated hull of the helicopter began to resemble a colander. Someone inside cried out with pain.

Cruz smelled spilled fuel. *Fuck it; I'd rather be chopped or shot than burned.* He half stood and shouted, "Getoffgetoffgetthefuckoff!"

Hampson was next up. From his prone position on the deck he leapt to his feet and charged down the ramp, rifle in both hands and muzzle forward. "Move it, people!" he shouted.

Through his NOD's Hampson saw a single guard, shaking in shock. He felt sorry for the man, even as he cut him down with a burst from the hip. The Venezuelan was tossed against the wall by the impacts. Before the dying guard slid to the floor, leaving a bloodstained section of wall behind him, the sergeant major was on one knee, aiming outward, rifle swinging first this way and then that, seeking a threat.

Behind the sergeant major a small flood of soldiers poured forth over the ramp, boots ringing on the metal.

Two of them dashed under arches held up by square columns. Their boots pattered across the tile and then they were into the palace and moving on to the southwestern corner, under a tower. This was to prevent both escape and reinforcement from outside. Two more teams of two did the same for the southeastern and northeastern corners. Out of Hampson's vision, a fourth pair emerged from the forward door, scurried past von Ahlenfeld, and made for the northwestern corner. Automatic rifle fire drummed the air as those forward teams killed anyone in their path. With the flash of grenades, windows shattered from shrapnel and concussion. This was the strikers making sure of their posts before taking them.

Hampson mentally counted the men off and, coming up one short, added that to the earlier scream and came up with, *One wounded inside.* He turned and bounded back inside the collanderized hull, emerging a few moments later dragging a wounded trooper by his combat harness.

You can make a Delta a sergeant major but he's still a Delta, Hampson thought, as he began cutting away cloth to get at a ragged wound.

Of the remaining nineteen men, including Hampson, the wounded man, and the three flight crew, a dozen, in three teams of four, followed hot on the heels of the men seizing the corners, barring those who had gone for the northwestern one. Once there, they stormed upward, then began cleaning out the upper floors of the building, in a counterclockwise fashion, with bullet, bayonet, and hand grenade. Shocked men screamed out in Spanish with their fear and pain. So did more than a few women:

maids, cooks, mistresses, secretaries, and a bureaucrat or two. A Spanish speaker with each team shouted out, repeatedly, "Assemble in the courtyard. Keep your hands open and above your heads. Armed persons will be killed on sight. Assemble in the courtyard . . ."

Cruz and his flight crew, supplemented by one Second Battalion man, took charge of the prisoners as they emerged from the palace, pale, fearful, and—often enough—weeping. Each was roughly and rudely searched before being flung face down to the dirt. There, deadly serious troopers pulled hands behind backs and flex-cuffed the wrists. Objections were slapped down and resistance met with tortured joints. The shots and explosions coming from the upper stories helped ensure cooperation even as they set the prisoners to more trembling and weeping.

Bolting upright, half awake, Marielena thought at first that the helicopter crash was part of her most recent dream. Only when she felt the blast of a grenade coming from some room down the corridor did she realize that, no, this was far too real to be any dream. Bit by bit, information fought its way through to her mind—the sounds of many helicopters, the shouted commands in English, the stream of tracers that seemed to pass by her bedroom window, unidentifiable explosions coming from outside the palace.

Oh, God, we've pissed off the United States and the gringos have come to spank us like naughty little boys and girls!

That thought was followed by a more frightening one. *Hugo! "Regime change." Imperialism. They've come to kill or capture Hugo! He, he above all, must be saved.*

Lack of loyalty was not one of the woman's failings, if, indeed, she had any. She jumped from the bed and took a robe from where it lay, folded over the back of a chair. Pulling it on, Marielena ran the few steps to her door and listened for a moment. The sounds of fighting—or perhaps of massacre—she heard did nothing but frighten her from opening the door. As they intensified, she thought, *The longer I wait, the harder it is.* She opened the door and stuck her head out.

To her left, someone shouted in Spanish, commands to move to the courtyard or be killed. Near the shouter, two men—*big* men; in Venezuelan terms, huge ones—kicked open a door. Another, leaning back against the wall, tossed something into the room thus opened. The door kickers flattened themselves against the wall to either side as a cloud of thick black smoke erupted on the wave of a blast. Then they went in, firing.

They won't shoot a woman, not if she's not doing something offensive. Be the woman they expect, girl; scream and run with your hair flying! Save Hugo.

It didn't require any great acting skill for Marielena. More than anything except to save the head of her country, she *wanted* to run, screaming, with her hair flying. She did; out the door and down the corridor towards Chavez's suite, the whole time shrieking like a madwoman, hands raised to the sky, with her hair and robe, both, trailing behind her.

Almost at the far end, a beefy arm reached out and yanked Marielena out of the main corridor and into a side one. She sucked in air to begin to scream. Then she saw who had pulled her off of her course.

"Mr. President," she said, as calmly as she could manage, which wasn't very, "the gringos are here and they've come to kill you! You must get to safety."

Where Marielena had had to awaken from a dream, Hugo Chavez had been fully awake and pacing his rooms when the helicopter had stopped overhead and begun its crashing descent. The president had been alone, having sent his mistress of the day to her own quarters lest his pacing disturb her rest.

Hearing the crash, Hugo's first thought had been, *Coup. Those bastard generals and admirals are trying to get rid of me. But . . . no . . . no, I know how a coup sounds and that's not it.*

He'd raced then for the ornate and gilded pistol he kept in the drawer of his nightstand. Tucking that in his belt, he knelt down and reached under the bed for the rifle he habitually kept there. He took care to jack the bolt as slowly and quietly as he could, consistent with feeding a round.

Standing, Chavez hesitated in indecision, trying to make some sense of the sounds that seemed to come from everywhere. *No, no coup. That would have come by ground, surrounded the palace openly, and presented an ultimatum.* He listened closely at a series of bangs, whooshes, and serious blasts coming from somewhere to the northwest. *And it wouldn't be preemptively rocketing the honor guard's barracks across the street, since the guard itself would hesitate until its commander figured out who was going to win out in the coup. If, indeed, they weren't at the heart of the thing.*

No, that's not fair. The Honor Guard is loyal, *even if no one else is.*

Unmistakably English commands rang from the courtyard. *So, the United States or the mercenaries based in Guyana that have been such a pain in the ass? No, probably not the United States; their government loves me the more I shit on them and the more I bash America in public. It's the mercenaries. And they're going to want me dead.*

So . . . run or fight and die? Hugo walked to the window that looked east. There, at the intersection of Urdeneta and Eighth, a Hip, the same model his own forces used, was disgorging a thin stream of troops. Those troops ran as if they were in heavy armor, something his own people rarely wore.

Most likely, the others I hear are doing the same, in between bouts of shooting up the town. The palace is surrounded and there is no practical escape above ground. Is there a place to hide? Yes . . . or at least maybe . . . down below . . . but can I get to it? If I can get to it, can I get to the tunnel that links with the metro station? If I can, is the exit inside or outside of the attackers' perimeter? Are they down there in the station? I've got to risk it; If I can get to the people and speak to them I can assemble a militia of a hundred thousand to drive the invaders off. Then, with some gringo bodies to display, I can pin the blame on the United States for everything, to include the fiasco in Guyana. I don't even have to make logical sense; everyone likes to blame the gringos. And then, maybe, just maybe, I might politically survive.

The palace was hardly a maze of secret passages. Yet,

given that Venezuela has seen its share of coup and counter-coup, it was the rare chief of state who hadn't taken some effort to make an escape possible. That's why there was a tunnel on the lowest level. Indeed, that tunnel had helped foil Chavez's own coup, back in 1992. It was also why it was possible to move from some rooms, at least, to others, without using the colonnade surrounding the courtyard. From his own quarters, Chavez went into a closet and emerged in the adjacent room.

I'm willing to bet that one was only put in so some president past could sneak a maid in for a quickie without her being seen. And probably maintained by most presidents past for similar reasons. Mentally, Hugo sneered. *I've got my failings, but at least I don't exploit the women of the poorer classes. Fuck them, yes, and why not, since I'm of the same class? But exploit them? No.*

From that trysting room, Chavez opened a door to a narrow service corridor. He listened for a moment, straining through the sounds of helicopters, muzzle blasts, grenades, and commands shouted in hateful English. *No . . . no one's in this corridor yet.* He walked along it until it bent inward, toward the courtyard. Here, the sounds of the gringos were strong. He waited, in indecision, until he heard a shrieking woman—*Marielena, I think*—fleeing down the colonnade. Wondering if it was the right thing to do, let alone the smart thing, Chavez snaked out an arm, grabbed her, and spun her into his temporary shelter.

"Mr. President . . ."

"Hey, where'd that woman go?" asked the grenadier who tossed the last grenade.

"What woman?" asked his team leader, Sergeant Emanuel Casavedes, nicknamed "Santa Ana" or "Auntie," for shorts.

"The one who ran off screaming from two doors down. She was there, and loud, and then she was gone, and quiet."

"Dunno. Was she armed?"

"Not that I saw."

"Then ignore her. Next room; standard entry."

The third member repeated his shout. "Assemble in the courtyard. Keep your hands open and above your heads. Armed persons will be killed on sight. Assemble in the courtyard . . ."

"Mierde," Chavez muttered under his breath, "the bastards are everywhere. There's no going forward until this section of the upper colonnade is free."

"What are we going to *do*, Mr. President?" Marielena asked, in a hush.

Hugo smiled, though the smile came hard under his very hard circumstances. He took the gilded pistol from his waistband and handed it to her. *"Miel,"* he whispered back, "under the circumstances, just call me 'Hugo.' Now back up and stay put unless and until I call for you. Shoot, but only if you're absolutely sure the target is a threat to us. Understand?"

She nodded and took the pistol as if frightened of it. Chavez folded her hand around it and carefully placed her trigger finger inside the guard. Then he pushed her gently backwards. He slid up to the very corner of the walls and took a knee. The president's rifle pointed for the moment at the ceiling.

The door down the corridor resounded with a double kick. Four or five seconds later came the blast, followed in a small fraction of a second by automatic fire.

That last grenade blast, coming from this side of the palace, was his signal. It was also a reminder of the reason he hadn't decided to wait until the gringos passed the small corridor in which he sheltered; before passing, they'd have donated a grenade and a stream of fire to it, too.

In a motion remarkably smooth for someone so heavy-set, Chavez shifted one foot forward, and leaned forward as well, while bringing the rifle down to horizontal. Even as the rifle was swinging down, as close to the corner as he could keep it, Chavez continued to lean forward. By the time the rifle reached horizontal, it was lined up as nicely as one could expect on the gringo shouting out in Spanish. Chavez fired, center of mass. At this range, he couldn't miss. Nor did he. The bullets struck where aimed; the gringo ceased his shouting and went down, arms and legs flying, to the floor.

Hugo then shifted his aim to the gringo nearest him, with his back pressed to the wall. He fired again and that gringo toppled over with his feet toward Chavez.

Chavez felt a hard punch on his right side. It forced him backwards, exposing more of his body to the first gringo he'd hit, now, unaccountably, sitting up with his rifle to his shoulder. Again he was punched, just as the first turned from a blow to a blood-gushing internal inferno. He flopped back to his rear end, rifle still held loosely in his arms. Again he was hit, though his solid construction kept him upright. Marielena screamed, though he heard it only distantly and distorted, as if through a waterfall.

Shit, Chavez thought, looking straight up, *all I wanted to do was to uplift my people. Was that so wrong, God?*

The next bullet smashed through the right side of Hugo Chavez's jaw, changed direction slightly, then passed through his brain, knocking a piece of his skull flying.

★CHAPTER FIFTY-SIX★

All who served the Revolution have plowed the sea.
—Simon Bolivar

Miraflores Palace, Caracas. Venzuela

"You all right, Auntie?" asked Casavedes' team mate. The other door kicker was out against the colonnade railing, his rifle aiming at the corridor from which the unidentified and now very dead assailant had sprung.

"To hell with me; check Rogers."

"I did," the door kicker answered sadly. "He's deader than chivalry."

Remorse swept over Casavedes. "Fuck; I didn't want to lose anybody."

"Shit . . ."

Whatever that door kicker had been about to say was lost as the other one opened fire on a pale shape emerging from the same little hallway. He didn't care if that shape had been womanly; fire had come from there and one of his teammates and friends was dead. Anyone else coming out was not going to get the chance to shoot. The woman was tossed back like a rag doll.

"Check 'em out," Auntie ordered, his chin pointing at the two bodies as he struggled to his feet against the pull of his arms, armor, and equipment. *I will never again bitch about the weight of the armor with inserts,* Casavedes swore to himself. *Never.*

The door kicker trotted to the bodies. He didn't recognize the woman, laying spread-eagled with her hair in a halo and her midsection a ghastly, bloody ruin. He did note she'd been very pretty and still had a pretty pistol clutched in one hand. The other was . . .

"Holy shit! Get on the horn, Auntie. Tell Lava the target is dead. Repeat, Chavez is dead."

Standing on the west side, von Ahlenfeld kept one eye on the firefight developing between his strikers who had landed at the palace helipad and the baseball diamond beyond it and the honor guards in and around the burning barracks to the northwest. He'd also been listening carefully and occasionally talking it up to encourage, guide and coordinate the troops. Then he heard the magic words, "Chavez is dead."

"Confirm that, Auntie," he'd demanded.

"I confirm, Lava. I'm looking at his face now. Nobody else in this country is quite that ugly, is likely to have a dead mistress quite that pretty, or is so recently and totally dead. For that matter, he had his driver's license in his pocket and that says, 'Hugo Rafael Chavez Frias.' And we're not talking about a little bit dead here, Lava; we're talking all the way dead. Open the dictionary to the word 'dead' and—"

"Can it, Auntie! I understand. Chavez is dead. Drag his body down here." Von Ahlenfeld consulted his watch. *Twelve minutes since we crashed in. Not bad, really.*

"Sergeant Major!" he shouted across the courtyard.

"Sir!"

"How many wounded have you got?"

"Two and one dead," Rattus Hampson replied.

"Account for everyone inside the palace. Collect a couple to help you with the wounded *and* the dead. It's time to torch the helicopter and leave."

Hampson's lip curled with distaste. He was a Christian man, not given to needless destruction. The burning Hip was very likely to lead to a burnt palace. *On the other hand, not my call whether it's needless or not.* "Roger, sir. Colonel Cruz?"

"Over here, Sergeant Major," Cruz called from the other side of the ruined Hip.

"Get your prisoners on their feet and send them running out the south entrance. Then I'll need your help and those of your team to move our wounded."

"Wilco," Cruz answered. To his own people he said, "You heard the sergeant major. Get 'em on their feet, point their faces to the south, and slap 'em along."

Miraflores Park Helipad, Caracas, Venezuela

I've been in worse spots, thought Major Hilton, commanding the two short teams stretched out west of the palace, facing the Honor Guard barracks across Urdaneta.

Hundreds of tongues of flame lanced out from the

building's windows, in every quadrant where flame hadn't taken hold. The lead launched on those eloquent tongues split the air, chipped wood and bark from the trees of the park, including the one behind which he sheltered, and occasionally found purchase in the flesh of Hilton's strikers. His one Delta and one ex-Navy corpsman worked on keeping those hit alive at the southern end of the park, west of Bicentennial Plaza. They also took turns at seeking out the wounded to drag back, which wasn't the safest job in the battalion.

I've been in worse spots . . . but I can't quite remember when or where.

The two Hips that had carried Hilton's men had arrived on station from the west just about as Cruz had put the brakes on his helicopter, over the palace. Number Two had come to a halt thirty feet over the northern corner of the baseball diamond, while Number Four had stopped over the Miraflores Park helipad. Both had swung their noses left and begun lashing the guard barracks with rocket fire, the rockets being guided by TV camera by the copilots in the Hips.

The *Ugroza* upgrades were a massive improvement on the old, unguided 55mm rockets. Even so, the windows of the guard barracks were not so large that more than one in three actually got into the building before detonating. Most of the street lights shattered from the concussion of warhead against exterior wall.

Number Two was the first to expend its single pod of sixteen. As soon as it had done so, it dropped down to the ball field, disgorging fourteen men who fanned out, six to the west along *Calle Puente la Union*, six to the north along *Avenida* Urdaneta, and two to set up an aid station west of Bicentennial Plaza. Those men discharged, Two pulled pitch, rising again over the trees to rake the barracks with machine gun fire from its single pod. Once that was seen to be in action, Number Four dropped to dismount Hilton and the nine other men with him. They, too, fanned out along Urdaneta, bringing the total of men facing the barracks to sixteen.

At that point Hips Two and Four ceased fire and pulled south, out of small arms range of the barracks, saving their ammunition for what was certain to be a difficult withdrawal.

The Honor Guard's initial reaction had been stunned silence, except where interrupted by the screams and cries of the wounded. They were not slouches, however, and had one company at all times on alert. These had poured like a flood toward the palace to secure their president. Caught in the crossfire of two machine guns facing the barracks, west of the palace, two marksmen firing from the northwest corner of the palace, another machine gun firing along from the intersection of Urdaneta and Eighth, and several rockets fired by Hips One and Three, that flood had evaporated, leaving, so far as Hilton could tell, fifty or sixty bodies littering the roadway. The *Pechenegs* could fire two-hundred-round bursts routinely and without overheating. If any of the guardsmen had made it across, it would have been a miracle.

Hilton, the guard commander's personal opponent, pictured in his mind what the guard commander was going through. *Half your troops are married and, barring your alert company, home with their wives, aren't they? And most of those are senior, no? Plus any of your officers that aren't married or living with a girl are elsewhere, at a BOQ, right? So you've got an inherent chain of command break, with not too senior privates taking charge of squads, corporals leading platoons, and sergeants trying to command companies, don't you? Your arms and ammunition are mostly locked up, and the Charge of Quarters or Staff Duty Officer is desperately trying to open the locks on the arms room doors, isn't he? And somebody who isn't even a supply clerk is hunting for the batteries for your night vision devices . . . or will be as soon as somebody notices they need batteries and aren't stored with them in.*

Or maybe you're the SDO, a junior lieutenant with no experience. No matter; first, you're going to try to get them armed, while you try to figure out what you're facing and what to do about us, while maybe desperately hoping someone senior shows up to take the burden off of you.

Still, you're an officer of Chavez's personal guard and you weren't hand-picked because you wouldn't try, or if your political loyalty was anything less than fanatical. And you're probably not stupid, even if inexperienced. So you're not going to try the unsupported mad rush across the avenue; you've seen how that worked out. And you're not going to try to come pouring out the doors, because you know that's exactly what my machine guns are focusing on now. You might try to come east, around the Palacio Blanco, but you've seen our helicopters there and won't want to get caught in the open of that parking lot.

I'm guessing you send your first company to report

"Ready to move" west, across the road past where we can see, with orders to outflank us. For the rest, those who take longer to get organized and armed, you've got to take the direct approach if you're to have a chance, you think, to save Hugo. And of those, some, some of the second tier to report "ready," you're going to send to man the windows to beat our fire down.

Which you can do, by the way, if Lava doesn't frigging hurry up and get Chavez.

JESUS! Hilton winced as a bullet from the barracks found a leg. *Oh . . . GOD, that hurts. Shit, shit, shit. Come on, Lee, kill the bastard and order the evacuation!*

Trying to keep as low to the ground and as much behind his covering tree as possible, Hilton let his rifle fall from his grip and bent at the waist to inspect the damage. He couldn't see anything much but his fingers touched no arterial spray.

Beats the alternative. Hilton's hand sought out the combat dressing attached to his harness and pulled it out. The plastic he ripped off with his teeth before unfolding and pressing the thing to his leg.

Unfortunately, at about that time, as he lifted himself slightly to get a little better angle, another bullet struck him on the shoulder where the ceramic plates didn't cover him. That bullet lost some energy burrowing through the fibers of his armor, but not enough that it couldn't penetrate the armor, his skin, smash into the bone of his shoulder, and then career off to pass above his heart, through his brachiocephalic artery, and then through his right lung.

The lung wound hardly mattered; Hilton was effectively dead already.

Located right by where the turn off from *Avenida Sucre*, North, led to Urdaneta, east, Searles, nicknamed "Opto," B Company's sergeant major, heard von Ahlenfeld give "mission accomplished" and the order to begin the evacuation. He waited several seconds for Hilton to acknowledge, then sent across the company net, "Hey, where's the fuck's the CO?"

Nobody had a clue.

Ah, shit. Searles jumped up and ran, rifle in hand, to the northeast in the general direction he had last seen Hilton heading. He stopped about halfway to the road and took a knee behind as stout a tree as was to be found in the area. *Let's see . . . the place where there's a gap where nobody is returning fire is . . . over there.* He leapt again to his feet much more nimbly than one might expect of a man of more than five decades and, with bullets dogging every step, ran forward.

He saw the still, twisted form on the ground in the green glow of his NOD's. Flopping down beside the body, Searles felt for breathing and then for a pulse. *Crap.*

"Lava, Opto. Hilton's dead."

"Shit," von Ahlenfeld answered. "We've got to get out of here. Can you evac the body? Can you do it while controlling the retrograde to the PZ?"

"Maybe. I'll try. Break, break. Bravo West, this is the sergeant major. The major's down. It's time to pull pitch. But it's gonna be *tricky* . . ."

As he spoke flames began rising from what looked to

be inside the palace. Hurriedly, Searles took a Russian clone of a Claymore mine and a VP-13 seismic fuse, then connected them and set them out pointing to the north. He didn't set the arming sequence and skedaddle until he saw the last of the men along Urdaneta had passed him. They, too, if they'd followed instructions, had left mines behind to discourage pursuit.

The southern entrance was suddenly lit orange yellow as the spilt fuel from the Hip caught fire, flames torching the shattered remnants of the palm tree and licking at the exposed wooden beams holding up the tile roof. In the glow, reflecting off white stucco, Chavez's cooling body had been laid out, spread-eagled, beside the doorway. Von Ahlenfeld's orders were that there was to be no doubt in Venezuelan minds that their president was dead. His rifle was not in evidence, leaving the bloody corpse looking strangely and pathetically helpless.

Von Ahlenfeld glanced down at the body and whispered: "'Old man, you fought well, but you lost in the end.'"

Hampson, with a body draped across his shoulders, slapped von Ahlenfeld's back and said, "Last man's out, sir. Cruz's party is controlling the evacuation."

Lava nodded and said, "Then let's get the fuck out of here."

Bicentennial Plaza, Caracas, Venezuela

Cruz watched as men dropped their armor at Konstantin's feet as they entered the plaza area. There was maybe enough fuel to make it to internment. There certainly wasn't an excess.

"Cruz, Number Five. They're pouring out of the barracks. I'm engaging."

"Roger," he answered.

"This is Four, ditto."

"Roger."

To his north and northeast, Cruz heard the double booms of rockets burning off their fuel in just over a second and then slamming into the ground to explode. A fair volume of screaming came right on the heels of that. From the east came the sail-ripping sound of a machine gun pod, joining the fray.

Out on the plaza, itself, Cruz's erstwhile engineer stood with arms outstretched and cone-topped lights gripped in his hands. Number Two guided in on the lights, came to a halt and began to settle to the ground. As soon as it was down, and well before it ceased bouncing, the former copilot began hustling, pushing, and generally moving people aboard. Some of those people were hobbling, others were being carried. It seemed that no one wasn't either wounded or dead or helping carry someone who was.

As soon as the copilot counted twenty-seven men and bodies aboard, he stopped the procession and ordered the helicopter off. It lifted in a choking swirl of dust then swung around to the south and west to cover the withdrawal as Four came in to load. After that, it would turn approximately east and go far enough to leave some doubt in Venezuelan minds as to its ultimate direction before switching to northwest and a course for the Netherlands Antilles.

"Three, you're up next," Cruz ordered.

"Roger. Twenty seconds."

"Faster if . . ." Cruz stopped speaking, shocked by a fiery explosion blossoming out to the northeast, briefly lighting the plaza with its flames.

"Five, Cruz? Five? Five?" *Goddammit!*

"Hurry up, Three!"

Seeing the aerial explosion, Hampson mentally checked off, *Well, that's three of eighty-seven we won't have to worry about loading. I wonder what that's going to do to the load plan. Nothing good, I'm sure.*

★CHAPTER FIFTY-SEVEN★

The time will come, when thou shalt lift thine eyes
To watch a long-drawn battle in the skies.
—Thomas Gray, "Luna Habitabilis" (1737)

At Sea, Ninety-seven Kilometers Northwest of Caracas, Venezuela

Praporschik Baluyev still hadn't ordered the really amazingly large quantity of explosives the Bertram yacht carried to be dumped over the side.

Maybe I should have, he thought, scanning the green-tinged skies to the southeast, *but it's easier to dump it at the last minute, if we ever must, than to try to shit it out of our asses if we need it but have already dumped it.*

The boat was pointed generally toward the Netherlands Antilles, with Kravchenko at the wheel. Litvinov sat beside Baluyev, in the other of the two fishing chairs, likewise scanning the horizon. Timur and Lada were down below, in the radio room. In theory they were listening on Second Battalion's push, but in practice still trying to work out their problems. At this range, Second Battalion didn't have much to say, anyway.

Or maybe they already have, Baluyev mused, *and are very quietly screwing. Very quietly.* He pulled his eye from the scope and thought, *Nah, there is no solution to their problems. Not given Tim's nature and hers. He can't understand why she won't settle down with him. She can't understand why it matters to him, what difference another dick or fifty makes. Poor bastards.*

Baluyev couldn't see a blessed thing, of course. No more could Litvinov. The curvature of the Earth blocked the Venezuelan coast at this range, while ships had been giving that coast a wide berth ever since the mines had gone in.

"One good thing," Litvinov said.

"What's that?"

"With nothing on the horizon, the Hips should stand out in the thermals once they pop over."

"True enough."

Bicentennial Plaza, Caracas, Venezuela

Three, once loaded, picked up and moved to a spot a bit to the east of Five's smoking wreckage. It had no rockets left, and little ammunition in its gun pod. What it had, it contributed to the general effort as Four broke off from its action to set down on the plaza. When that was gone, and it soon was, the Hip swung around to give its engineer, playing door gunner, a chance to use his machine gun. The other helicopter still in play had done the same.

Even with those two door guns, and reinforced with

the seismically fused Russian Claymore clones, the Honor Guard was across the road and creeping through the park and the ball field. The flash and boom of the cloned mines did a fair job of marking their progress.

Von Ahlenfeld, Konstantin, and Hampson—his wounded man having been tossed aboard Three—formed a tight little perimeter at the western edge of the plaza, while Cruz hustled the last lift aboard. Venezuelan tracers sparked green, passing mostly overhead.

In his radio's earpiece, von Ahlenfeld heard Cruz say, "The next bus won't be along for a couple of years, Lava. So if you guys don't want to be late for your next appointment . . ."

Von Ahlenfeld turned and, by the light of the now merrily flaming palace, saw Cruz standing on the ramp of the last Hip, beckoning them on.

"Let's get the fuck out of Dodge! Top, go!"

Hampson sprang to his feet and began churning across the plaza to the waiting Hip. Behind him went Konstantin. Von Ahlenfeld leapt up next, just in time to see Hampson caught in a burst of machine gun fire that cut his legs from under him and spun him head over heels, backwards.

Konstantin reached him first, going to one knee to examine the sergeant major as best he could under the flaring light.

"He's alive!" the Russian shouted to von Ahlenfeld. "But I don't know by how much."

Lava, judging the position of the machine gun that had cut down his sergeant major turned and donated a spray in that general direction. He sincerely doubted that he hit anything, but *Might ruin their aim for the next burst.*

"Can you carry him?"

Without answering, Konstantin pulled Hampson up into a fireman's carry. Then, staggering under the weight, the Russian made a slow trot for the Hip's ramp. There, Cruz met him and helped him onto the helicopter, before assisting in lowering Hampson to the deck.

Von Ahlenfeld crouched low and walked backwards, trusting that the tail rotor was too high to touch him. As he walked, he scanned, firing a burst at any movement he saw through the trees and looking especially keenly for the machine gun.

He never saw it. Fortunately, the door gunner in Two did. Following the door gun's tracers, von Ahlenfeld was gratified to see a three-man machine gun crew doing the "Spandau Ballet" atop *Avenida* Sucre.

"Get on the fucking helicopter, ya damned *idjit!*" Cruz shouted from the ramp. "We're taking off!"

Von Ahlenfeld turned and sprinted, launching himself from the ground to land belly first on the slowly lifting ramp. His fingers scrambled for purchase on the metal ridges, holding on for dear life until Cruz managed to grab his harness and drag him aboard.

"Everybody," von Ahlenfeld ordered, once he was sitting up in the cargo area, "fucking *split!*"

El Libertador Air Base (AKA Palo Negro Airport), Maracay, Venezuela

Operations on the base was in complete and utter confusion, as pilots on crew rest were ordered rousted out, planes set for ground attack missions in Guyana were disarmed and then rearmed with air to air munitions, some others were called back about a third of the way to Georgetown, and everyone worried about what the hell the reports of an attack on Caracas actually *meant*.

General Ortiz had no idea what was happening, except that someone had attacked Caracas, possibly focusing on Miraflores Palace. Even there, the reports were conflicting and there was no word from Hugo. He thought the attack had begun within the last ten minutes, but it was possible it had begun an hour ago and he had just gotten the word late.

I don't know if the United States attacked, if we're having a coup d'etat, *or if it's the mercenaries based in Guyana.*

What's the worst case? That's a no brainer; the worst case is that it's the gringos playing the "regime change" game and there are two carrier battle groups fifty miles north of here ready to shoot down anything I send up. My whole air force—even if it weren't the maintenance nightmare it's become since we invaded Guyana—couldn't take on one carrier.

Okay, what's the next worst case? A coup, a golpe de estado. That's next worst . . . maybe even worst . . . because I don't know who's behind it and I don't know how successful it's been or will be, and so I don't know which way to jump. At the very least, I don't want to happen what happened back in 1992, with air force fighting air force.

As for the mercenaries, is that even a possibility? I know . . . or at least intelligence tells me . . . that we smashed most of their air squadron on the ground. How could they be behind this?

On the other hand, how could they have been behind the mining of our ports, the destruction of our oil refining complex, the capture of one of our largest cities, or the smashing of our parachute brigade, an infantry brigade, and the support areas we set up for the invasion? And those we know they did. So it might have been the mercenaries.

Is there anything I can do that covers all possibilities? No. If I send up planes in pursuit of the raiders, and it turns out it was the gringos, I've lost those planes. If it turns out it was a coup, then I end up with air force fighting air force. If it was the mercenaries . . .

One of the officers on duty, a major, handed Ortiz a phone, saying, "It's the Army Chief of Staff."

Maybe he'll know something, Ortiz thought, picking up the phone and holding it to his ear.

"General Ortiz."

The voice on the other end sounded remarkably calm and satisfied. "Ortiz, Quintero. I am at Miraflores Palace, or what's left of it. Hugo's dead . . . Yes, there's no doubt he's dead; I've seen the body . . . Who did it? There's really no way to tell. They came in by helicopter, MI-17's. But gringo special forces use those, too, I'm told . . . No, we recovered no bodies; it was a very professional job . . . Yes, that smells like the gringos to me, too. And the survivors of the palace insist they were herded out like cattle before the place was torched. Given what they did at Punto Fijo, I doubt the mercenaries would be so considerate."

"So what now, General?" Ortiz asked.

"That depends a lot on where the air force stands," said Quintero. "Frankly, without Hugo, and with Hugo's palace guard having taken appalling casualties; with the failure in

Guyana—let's try not to fool ourselves; even now the mercenaries are investing Georgetown to starve the Marines into surrender—with the economic ruin caused by the war and by Bolivarism in general . . . I think it's time for a change. I also think we owe a debt to whoever did this, not that the burden doesn't rest quite lightly on my shoulders."

Ortiz went silent for the moment, thinking furiously. *Unanimity is critical in these things.* "What says the navy?"

Quintero laughed over the phone. "The navy says, 'Junta,' and the navy says, 'Peace.' So, for that matter, do I. The navy also says, and I join them in this wholeheartedly, 'Enough of this silly experiment in economic ruin through oil socialism.' Where does the air force stand?"

Hip Number Four, Fifty-one Kilometers Northwest of Caracas

Von Ahlenfeld felt ill from the severe, merciless bucking induced in the helicopter by Wing in Ground effect and as simple turbulence coming off the waves, cresting half a rotor's diameter below.

But at least we're still alive to be made ill, he thought. *Beats the crap out of the alternative.*

Bucking or not, it didn't feel to Lava as if the helicopter was moving all that quickly. He crawled forward, over the bodies of wounded and dead and between the shins of the wounded and exhausted, all the way to the engineer, still manning a door mounted machine gun.

"Why so slow?" Lava shouted to the engineer.

"Fuel ~~leak!~~" the engineer shouted back. He passed von Ahlenfeld a set of headphones to talk directly to the pilots.

"We took a hit, it seems," the pilot explained, much more calmly than a man should have been able to. Then again, the pilot, Artur Borsakov, a Russian, was ancient and had seen more crap flying a similar helicopter in Afghanistan than he generally cared to remember. "Fuel tank. What with all the shit flying around, I didn't notice it until we crested the mountains north of Caracas. We can still make it but we have to conserve power to conserve fuel to do it. That means flying low and slow."

"Any word on the others?" von Ahlenfeld asked.

"About ten and twenty kilometers ahead of us, near as I can tell," the Russian replied. "They're not losing fuel or having to fly so low and slow•so the gap is growing."

Anybody we get alive out of this is a victory, Lava thought. Getting me out, of course, is a greater victory.

Su-30, just crossing Venezuela's northern coast

Lieutenant Juan Rodriguez was, frankly, pissed. "We're a third of the way to Georgetown when they call. 'Oh, come back, Juan; we need help.' Right. 'Help.' We're carrying freakin' bombs, people, and two cannon pods with a grand total of three hundred rounds, and that are not zeroed to an aerial engagement, anyway. I've got no air-to-air missiles, and why should I have when neither Guyana nor the mercenaries have a single high performance fighter?

Our radar's gotten finicky because you haven't been able to maintain it. And I am by no means convinced that our ejection seats will work, either. But you 'need help.' Fine. I'll fucking try.

"And just what the fuck am I supposed to be looking for? 'Helicopters,' they say. That helps a lot; we have helicopters, too. 'Russian Hips,' they say. Oh, jeez, where was the last time I saw a Hip? Oh, I remember; it was on our own fucking base, carrying our own fucking troops. 'Use your IFF,' they say. Assholes! Half our birds' IFFs have stopped working! I'm not even sure they're still updating the codes.

"Moreover . . ."

"Juan, look left," said the weapons officer, Pedro Barrai, seated behind.

"What?! I was just getting warmed up! Whe . . . oh, there."

"It's a Hip, I think," Barrai said. "Out where *we* shouldn't have any Hips."

"It's a lot lower than I'm comfortable flying this pig," Rodriguez said, as he veered the aircraft to port. "And it's just fast enough to be a hard target, and too slow for us to match speed."

"You fly the plane, Juan. I get to shoot the guns. Them's the rules, remember?"

"Yeah. Shit. All right. Get ready. I'm going to try for a quartering shot from above. Hope to fuck I can pull out before we make a hole in the sea."

Barrai started to say, "You have my every—" He stopped himself, changing the message to, "Please don't."

Hip Number Four, Seventy-two Kilometers
Northwest of Caracas, Venezuela

"How's the fuel holding up?" von Ahlenfeld asked Borsakov, over the intercom.

"I still think we'll make it," the Russian replied, "but I passed on to the Spetznaz team in the boat to make way northwest, just in case I'm wrong."

Northwest or southeast? Lava wondered. *We've got wounded, more than that one itty bitty life raft will hold, and I'm not sure we can keep them afloat if we have to ditch. So ditching unnecessarily, while safer for the rest of us, would be very unsafe for the wounded. Hence, last option. Hence, good call, Borsakov. I think.*

"Roger," he said.

"How many wounded have we got back there?" Borsakov asked. "Wounded too badly to swim, I mean."

"Five and a couple of maybes," Lava answered.

"Shit. I was an All-Soviet Champion swimmer in my youth, but that was a fuck of a long time ago."

"Right . . . for all of us, everything was a fuck of a long time ago. We're buckling the wounded into life vests already."

"Yeah . . . good idea . . . even . . . Christ!"

As close to the cockpit as he was, von Ahlenfeld could see the fist-sized tracers flashing ahead before turning into explosions on the sea's rough surface. He was half-tossed to starboard as Borsakov pushed the Hip into a violent shift to port.

It was automatic, that port move, conditioned by

decades of training and experience. It was also just a bit too violent. The blades of the rotor skimmed the water, tossing the Hip into the beginnings of a sharp counterclockwise spin. Borsakov worked the foot pedals hard, recovering before he lost complete control of the aircraft. Even so, the transmission began to whine as if damaged from the shock, and the helicopter itself shuddered as if the blades were starting to shred.

"Oh, fuck!" Borsakov exclaimed. "We are not, repeat *not* going to make it to the Netherland's Antilles. Break, break . . . Baluyev? Borsakov."

"Baluyev here."

"Turn around. Don't spare the horses. We're dunking."

El Libertador Air Base (AKA Palo Negro Airport), Maracay, Venezuela

"All right," Ortiz agreed, "the air force is in." *It's either that, or we find ourselves very much on the outs.*

"What do you want me to do?"

"In the first place," Quintero said, "the navy wants its Marines back. Suspicious bastards seem to think that without a ground combat force they'll find themselves cut out of the political process."

And so they would be, though Ortiz.

"Okay, so?"

"So suspend combat operations. *All* combat operations. We need to make peace with Guyana, which is to say with the mercenaries. The fewer of them we kill, and the sooner we stop trying, the sooner and better that peace will be."

"All right." Ortiz held his hand over the receiver and ordered, "Cease offensive operations. Ground all planes," to the operations crew.

"Consider that done," he told Quintero.

Su-30, One Hundred and Nine Kilometers North-northeast of Caracas, Venezuela

"Did you hit it?" Rodriguez asked.

"Not a chance," answered Barrai. "Maybe got close."

Rodriguez snarled. "This thing turns like a hippopotamus in ballet slippers. I'll swing around for another . . ."

The radio crackled. "Victor Five One, this is base."

"Five One," Barrai replied.

"Your mission is aborted. Come on home."

"Roger." *How grand. This hot rodder will not now have a chance to drive me into the sea.* "Juan, orders. Head home. We're done."

Hip Number Four, Seventy-nine Kilometers Northwest of Caracas

"Colonel," Borsakov said via the intercom, "I can hold this thing steady for a few minutes. You've got to get the raft inflated and your people out, fast."

"What about your folks?" Lava asked.

"I'm sending my copilot and engineer out with you. For me, I'll ride the thing a couple of hundred meters off then ditch it."

"But—"

"Don't worry about me. All-Soviet Champion, remember? So what if it was fifty years ago? I'll be fine."

"Roger," Lava agreed.

"Good. The ramp's going down. Start unassing the helicopter, now. Break, break. Baluyev, turn around . . ."

I knew this was too fucking good to be true, thought von Ahlenfeld. "Konstantin, get our people off!"

Betram Sport Fisher, Eighty-one Kilometers Northwest of Caracas, Venezuela

Baluyev started, unaccountably, to laugh. The laughter grew, even over the muted roar of the boat's engine.

"What's so funny?" Litvinov asked.

"You can't hear it?"

"I can't hear shit but the motor."

"Wait a few minutes then," the praporschik advised. "You will."

Litvinov did as told, as the boat proceeded to the southeast. At first he couldn't quite believe his ears. As the boat progressed, he couldn't deny them. Somewhere, maybe a half mile away, a group of people, twenty or thirty of them, were singing:

"Always look on the bright side of life . . ."

Providence, Guyana

From somewhere to the north, the loudspeakers were

playing. The music could be heard, distantly and dimly, even this far back: " . . . This is the end . . . beautiful friend . . . This is the end . . . my only friend . . ."

Sunlight filtered through the trees and down on Lana's jungle-shrouded and camouflage-netted command post. And it *was* her command post. She had First Battalion now. She'd tried to turn it over to the XO, after cajoling and shaming the troops out of their proto-mutiny. That worthy had demurred, insisting, "When it came down to it, Lana, the boys wouldn't listen to me. They *would* listen to you. The one who should be in command is the one who *can* command, the one with the *mana*. Always." Stauer had ratified the XO's call, making a special effort to find her at First Battalion's command post, south of the town, and pin on her collar her husband's old rank.

Already fighting had broken out in the capital between Guyanans and the Marines, as the regiment sealed the place off and the Marines were forced to give up their internal security duties to defend the perimeter.

Lana was in the CP now, hot and bloated and miserable. She was sick, too, with the loss of her husband, and not a little upset that the most they'd been able to do for his body was pack it in ice, drive it around the companies to let the men get a last view, and then put it in a nylon body bag and into the regimental cemetery before it began to swell and stink.

Wiping away a sudden flood of tears, Lana vowed to herself that they'd give him a proper service as soon as they could, as soon as the war was finally over. Through the sniffles, she promised softly, "We'll exhume you and do a proper pyre, Seamus. You deserve that . . . the boys deserve that . . . oh, God, why . . ."

Schiebel popped his head into the CP, affecting not to notice Lana's sodden face. "We got a call from a forward outpost, Lana," he said. It was an Israeli thing, perhaps, but she preferred to be called by her given name, rank be damned. "They've got a white flag and a party of three, approaching our position."

Lana didn't have the rank or the position—*or the information and insight, for that matter*, she thought—for this one. The Venezuelans had been blindfolded and told to wait. Wait they had, for four hours while Stauer was rounded up.

"No," Stauer had insisted, to the Venezuelan Marine, de Castro. "No, I'm not letting you go, scot free. You want to eat, you surrender. You'll get repatriated when Venezuela pays for every goddamned twig and building wrecked and every round of ammunition expended to defeat your wanton aggression. You don't like that, fine. Stay where you are and die.

"On the other hand, my people, in *Ciudad* Guyana, get repatriated on chartered flights and your people don't interfere in the slightest."

De Castro, deeply ashamed, though only at the defeat, not at the aggression, replied, "I'll have to consult with higher authority."

"The junta that's replaced Chavez?" Stauer asked.

The Marine nodded, shallowly. "Yes, them."

"Inform them that weapons are cheap and replaceable; trained men quite expensive and hard to replace.

Especially when you're facing a probable civil war in your own country. And, by the way, we're keeping your arms. Don't try wrecking them if you ever want to see home."

De Castro sighed. He'd expected no better but his superiors and Caracas had insisted he try. "What about the civilians here who supported us?"

Stauer shook his head. "They stay, so they can be duly arrested, tried and shot for treason. Do this place a *world* of good, too. More important, it will make anyone who thinks about supporting you the *next* time you try this think twice, while denying you a cadre of people to use to keep fucking with Guyana. Live with it."

"*Vae victis,*" muttered de Castro.

★EPILOGUE★

I

Camp Street Jail, Georgetown, Guyana

The jail was a brightly colored, cheerful seeming—at least from the outside—razor wire encircled hell hole. This wasn't made any better by the frequent rattle of musketry—a new volley and a single following shot approximately every ten minutes for the last two days—that announced to the town that yet another collaborator or traitor has been stood against a wall and shot.

So much for abolishing the death penalty in 2010, thought Catherine Person, sitting on the bare floor of an unfurnished cell, awaiting her own call. She tried to be cheerful, amidst the dirt and squalor of the compound. Yet still every volley made her shudder. Sometimes, even, she wept, though as softly as she was able.

Two hours ago her boss from the embassy, Major

Pakhamov had come to her, bearing the news that, no, there was nothing he could do. And that, yes, he'd *tried*.

I believe him; I really do. No one's listening to reason around here. No one's . . .

The thought was cut off by footsteps, loud on the hard floor outside her cell. The steps stopped close by, followed by the sound of a bar door being squeaked open. She looked up to see three uniformed men, her countrymen, waiting with grim faces. One of them carried a short length of cheap rope.

"I didn't *do* anything," she insisted, as hopelessly as she'd insisted in front of the drum head court that had convicted her of treason and collaboration.

"You did enough," answered the senior of the prison guards, a sergeant. "You must come with us now. Can you walk, or must you be carried?"

She began to rise from the floor, trembling, suddenly weak, and unsteady. Two of the guards moved briskly to stand to either side of her, while the third, the sergeant, stepped behind her and pulled her hands back. Her wrists were forcibly crossed and then roughly bound.

At that, that final, irrefutable announcement that her life had come to an early end, Catherine's knees began to buckle. The flanking guards grasped her arms, holding her upright, if not exactly standing.

"Take her," the sergeant ordered.

As they reached the cell door, from farther inside the courtyard sounded yet another volley, followed by another single shot. Catherine's chin dropped to her chest as, again, tears began to flow. "I didn't *do* anything," she whispered.

Though, of course, she had.

║

Cemetery, Camp Fulton, Guyana

The regimental band played a slow, German dirge as the First Battalion marched in five blocks along the curving road that led to the cemetery. Behind the battalion, itself, also formed into their own ad hoc marching units, came some hundreds of other members of the regiment: mostly those who cared personally.

Few of the men, and none of the women, knew the words to the dirge. Only Nagy, Thor, and their few fellow Huns could sing along:

"Ich hatt' einen Kameraden

Einen bessern findst du nit . . ."

For the rest, they had to content themselves with humming along. In its own way, as loud as it was, arising from a thousand or more, that was more impressive than singing would have been. At the very least, the lack of articulation expressed the universal grief better.

The battalion, and friends, marched under the command of the XO. Lana . . . any of them would have carried her on their backs before letting her walk, even if she hadn't been in such an advanced stage of pregnancy. No, she didn't walk; she rode in an open topped Land Rover, driven by Dumisani and with Dani Viljoen seated in the back beside her.

All cried out for the time being, Lana wore mufti. Battle dress was insufficiently formal for the occasion and there'd been no time to get a maternity dress uniform made up. She rode just behind the band, itself fourth in the order of march, cocooned within the mournful music and the still more mournful humming.

He so loved his fucking Hun music, she thought. *Well, that and the Irish. Bastard; you promised to be careful.*

At that, the tears began to flow again. Viljoen put a beefy arm around her shuddering form, pulling her into his shoulder. With his other hand he stroked her face gently. "There, there . . ."

She nodded then, unaccountably, giggled for a moment. Viljoen thought she was giggling at her own emotions, her "weaknesses." It wasn't that.

I just realized; these two are the only real friends in the battalion I can have anymore. At least with them, no one's going to be able to accuse me of sleeping with the help.

Lana realized they were at the cemetery's gated entrance from the change in sound as the leading companies turned right to march slowly through the gate. She wiped her eyes quickly, then sat upright, at attention. It just wouldn't do to let them see her hunched over and sniveling. Viljoen, understanding, removed his arm and, likewise, sat up ramrod straight.

The cemetery glowed with a couple of hundred tiki torches Gordon had scrounged up from somewhere. The torches flickered in the night, half for light and half to keep off the mosquitoes. In Lana's view, the first company, Alpha, passed through a gap left in the torches, then peeled off to the right from the straight line of march to follow the curving circle they defined. The others did likewise, until her own vehicle reached the gap. Behind her, the trailing companies swung left, toward the five 105's the artillery battery had donated to the cause.

Dumi drove straight, to where Stauer, the staff, Chaplain Wilson, the RSM, and Sergeant Major George waited. Behind them a great pyramidal pyre of wood stood, atop it a crude wooden casket holding the nylon bag that held the remains of her husband. No one but those few people had been allowed to have anything to do with exhuming Reilly's body, or placing it in the casket or the casket on the pyre. It had been in the ground for some time, now, and stank. Badly. By plan, not fortune, it was downwind of where Dumi stopped the vehicle.

Viljoen dismounted and raced around to get Lana's door and help her step down. As her foot touched ground Stauer called the staff to "Present . . . Arms." He had them order arms as soon as Lana nodded. He then walked over and helped Viljoen guide Lana to a folding chair, set up under a stretched-out tarp. Dumi drove off as soon as she was seated, while Viljoen and Stauer stood, flanking Lana.

At Stauer's nod, Chaplain Wilson stood forth. Looking first at Lana, Wilson swept his gaze over the half circle of military mourners. "It is said," he began, "that no one is truly gone from us until we have forgotten them in our hearts. In this case, that will never happen . . ."

Even without the sequential booming of the guns, no one who wasn't standing next to her really noticed Lana's heartbroken sobbing. There was barely a man there who hadn't joined her. If there were one or two, Taps got to them.

With the final bugle call dying slowly in the night, Stauer bent down. "Lana," he said, "I can light the—"

She shook her head. "No . . . no, I'll . . . do it. But if you and Dani could help me stand?"

As they were helping her to her feet, Gordon stepped forward, bearing a torch in his right hand. She took it from him, a little uncertainly. The uncertainty disappeared as he stepped back and extended his left hand, which held a lighter. He held the lighter to the torch, flicked it, and held the flame to the combustible material wrapped around the stalk of the thing until it sprang to life on its own. Then, Stauer bearing her up on one side and Viljoen on the other, she walked forward to the pyre. As she came closer, she could smell that the wood had been liberally doused with some kind of fuel, gasoline or kerosene, most likely. She threw the torch onto the pyre, about midway up. It sat there a moment, flickering alone in the semi dark. Then, suddenly, the fuel caught, causing flame to race from the single torch outward to all sides. Before she had taken even half a step back, the single flame had grown to a pillar of fire, lighting the night even while casting long shadows on the ground, where men, women, and guns stood. As Stauer, Vilgoen, and Lana's shadows slid across the green-covered earth, the band struck up the old French march, "*La Victoire est à Nous.*"

They waited until the fire had pretty much burned itself out. Others, not Lana, would sift through the ashes for Reilly's bones and recognizable ashes to place them in a container much smaller, though altogether nicer, than the crude casket. That would then be buried in the spot that had once held his body.

While waiting for the fire to die, Stauer had searched

the ranks for his wife, Phillie. Catching her eye, he motioned her over with a nod of his head. "Why don't you stay with her, tonight?" he'd suggested in a whisper. "She really shouldn't be alone."

"I don't know," Phillie answered, doubtfully. "We've always been pretty good friends but she knows I never much liked *him*."

"That won't matter now," her husband assured her. "Really."

"You'll be okay with the kids?"

"Well, duh."

The troops marched behind now, with the band trailing and playing something somewhat more upbeat; "Sacred War." Only the Russians knew that one.

Viljoen sat up front, in the Land Rover, next to Dumisani. This was fine by him as, gay or not, he really wasn't all that good at the whole ever-so-caring-and-sensitive thing. He did care, but showing it? That came harder. *Let Phillie take care of all that.*

For her part, Phillie just held the weeping Lana in her arms, trying—if not generally succeeding—in comforting her. Suddenly, she felt Lana's body stiffen. The next second Lana sat bolt upright, eyes saucer-wide.

"Not home," she said.

"What?" Phillie asked.

"Not"—shudder—"home"—shudder—"hospital"—shudder . . . "I'm having the fucking baby."

Phillie blanched. "Oh, Christ. I'm not that kind of nurse. Ummm . . . shit . . . ummm . . . Dumi, stop the car! Stopitstopitstopit."

Phillie stood upright in the Land Rover, faced to the rear, and shouted out, "Send Doc Joseph here. Stat. I mean fast. I mean . . . Dddooocccc!"

Within a minute or so, Joseph arrived at the side of the Land Rover. Unceremoniously, Viljoen stood, reached over the side of the vehicle, hauled the medico in bodily and placed him in the back. Dumi slammed on the gas, racing toward the hospital, which was still in tents in an arc to the north.

Sergeant Major George watched the vehicle speed off for all of perhaps five seconds. Then, putting two and two together—or perhaps subtracting one from two—shouted, "Battalion . . . double time . . . .march! Follow that . . . ah, fuggit; you know what to do."

Airfield, Camp Fulton, Guyana

Maybe I didn't much like Reilly, Stauer thought, watching an Antonov taxi onto the newly cleared airfield, delivering Ryan's team back from Colombia. The other one, also now released by Colombia from its internment, would be along later in the day, carrying, if the Venezuelans were to be believed, the first increment of their reparations, some 7 tons of gold bullion. *Maybe I didn't like the son of a bitch, but I miss him.*

And I don't know what I'm going to do without him. Lana's got the devotion of First Battalion, and to keep them happy we're going to have to leave her in command there. I wonder, though, does she have his kind of finesse and drive? Time will tell, I suppose. No matter, there's nothing much to be done about it; they will have her or they'll have nobody. Fucking anarchists!

Tough on First's old XO, too. Not his fault that Reilly's mana descended on Lana rather than him. Still, he cheered up considerably when I told him we were raising two, maybe three, more infantry battalions and he could have one of them.

Lots of expansion coming, and Venezuela's going to pay for all of it and then some. The bastards.

Stauer heard behind him the distinctive cough of a Land Rover whose days are numbered. By the time he'd turned away from the airfield, RSM Joshua was dismounting from an ambulance driven by Corporal Manduleanu. *Hmmm . . . going to overcome his professional scruples, I wonder.*

"Curb your filthy thoughts, sir," Joshua called out. "I needed a ride and the corporal volunteered to give me one . . ." For a moment, the RSM looked uncharacteristically confused. "Wait, that didn't come out quite right."

Stauer's teeth flashed. "Oh, I'm *sure.*"

Joshua's eyes narrowed. "If you think, sir . . ."

Stauer waved it off. He pointed with his chin, half changing the subject with, "Has she decided what she wants to do, now that the emergency's over."

"Nah. Confused as ever."

She's not the only one.

"How's Lana?" Stauer asked.

A beaming Joshua answered, "She and the baby are fine. This despite the fact that nearly a thousand drunken louts are camped out around the maternity tent, serenading, if that's quite the term, mother and child. Yes, before you ask, of *course* with the band. And your chief medic is drunker than the rest. Seems he never delivered a baby before. For that matter, so's your wife, and for the same reason.

"Oh, and you know how Lana's never quite had a nickname?"

"Sure."

Joshua's smile grew quite broad. "By popular acclaim, she is now, officially, 'Mother Superior.'"

"She's not even Catholic," Stauer objected.

"I know," the RSM chuckled. "That's make it all the better."

"She's gonna hate it."

"Makes it better still."

Stauer cocked his head, smiling beatifically. *"Yeah."*

***

A brief note on the geography of Guyana, as presented:

Folks, it's wrong. Oh, sure, mostly it's right, but I'm sure it's wrong, at least here and there. I just can't tell you where. I used Google maps, some I dug out of the Brandt guidebook for Guyana, the ITMB map of Guyana and the Guianas, and a whole bunch of others. None of them entirely agree. Sometimes I was able to resolve discrepancies by finding photos of the places in question; other times, not. It's not the number one tourist destination of the western world, so not that many photographs are posted. Live with it. Who knows; in a few years maybe the roads and bridges will be done and might even match *one* of my maps.

***

★ACKNOWLEDGEMENTS★

Yolanda, who puts up with me, Toni Weisskopf, John Ringo, Dr. Scott Joseph, Dr. Rob Hampson, Ken Uecker, Neil Frandsen, Michael Gilson, Tim Arthur, Charlie Prael, Chris French, Ori Pomerantz, Leo Ross, Arun, Ron Friedman, Tom Wallis, Tim Lindell, John Raines, Victoria Heather Gold, the Kriegsmarine contingent of the Bar (you know who you are), Buz Ozburn, David Burkhead, Alen Ostanek, and Mike Sayer.

And the cover artist, the great Kurt Miller.

If I missed anybody, chalk it up to premature senility.